Eagle and Empire

Praise for *Eagle and Empire*

"The final volume of Smale's Clash of Eagles trilogy is relentless, with characters and readers hardly getting a breath before the next threat comes crashing down. . . . Smale's hard-hitting and satisfying conclusion will be a must for his readers, as the trilogy will be for any fan of alternate history." —*Publishers Weekly* (starred review)

"The pace . . . is breathless and the action relentless. . . . A satisfying culmination to the adventures of a Roman warrior in the New World." —*Kirkus Reviews*

Praise for *Eagle in Exile*

"[*Eagle in Exile*] has the pace and scope of a Michener or Uris epic. . . . Smale's action scenes slash across page after page, intense and bloody. . . . Grab your dagger and sword, for the battle continues."
        —*Kirkus Reviews* (starred review)

"The highlight of *Eagle in Exile* is the world Smale built. It's familiar, yet foreign. . . . The depth of knowledge and detail here is usually reserved for more straight-laced historical fiction books—like Bernard Cornwell's *Saxon Stories*—but by infusing those same principles with elements of speculative fiction, Smale winds up carving out something unique for readers." —*Tech Times*

"There is a lot of action, as well as twists and turns. . . . The thing I enjoyed the most in this story was the growth and expansion." —*SFRevu*

Praise for *Clash of Eagles*

"*Clash of Eagles* is that rarest and best of alternative histories: the one you BELIEVE, the one that makes sense. Smale has a storyteller's flair for character, and presents an ensemble cast with a depth of detail that George R. R. Martin would approve of. *Clash of Eagles* is a triple threat: It works as a novel, as historical speculation, and as cultural extrapolation. But its real value is singular: It's a ripping good yarn, and one that will keep you reading long past your bedtime."
        —MYKE COLE, award-winning
        author of *Shadow Ops: Control Point*

EAGLE AND EMPIRE

BOOK THREE OF THE CLASH OF EAGLES TRILOGY

ALAN SMALE

DEL REY • NEW YORK

2017 Del Rey Mass Market Edition

Copyright © 2017 by Alan Smale
Map copyright © 2015, 2017 by Simon M. Sullivan

Published in the United States by Del Rey, an imprint of Random House, a division of Penguin Random House LLC, New York.

DEL REY and the HOUSE colophon are registered trademarks of Penguin Random House LLC.

Originally published in hardcover in the United States by Del Rey, an imprint of Random House, a division of Penguin Random House LLC, in 2017.

ISBN 978-1-101-88532-1
Ebook ISBN 978-0-8041-7727-6

Printed in the United States of America

randomhousebooks.com

9 8 7 6 5 4 3 2 1

Del Rey mass market edition: November 2017

For friends old and new, who help me to fly

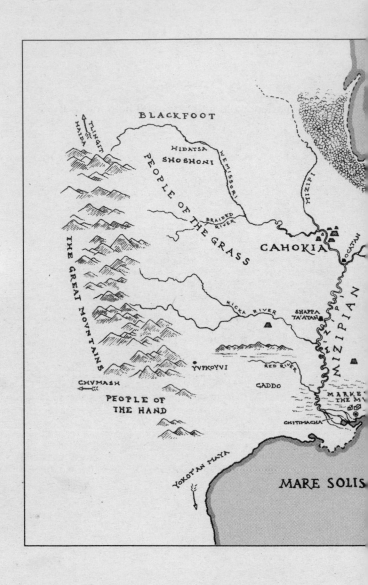

BLACKFOOT

HAIDA
TLINGIT

HIDATSA
SHOSHONI

PEOPLE OF THE GRASS

WEMISSORI

BRAIDED RIVER

CAHOKIA

MIZIPI

OCATAN

THE GREAT MOUNTAINS

KICKA RIVER

SHAPPA TA'ATAN

MIZIPI

MIZIPIAN

YVPKOYVI

RED RIVER

CHVMASH

GADDO

MARKE THE M

PEOPLE OF THE HAND

CHITIMACHA

YOKOT'AN MAYA

MARE SOLIS

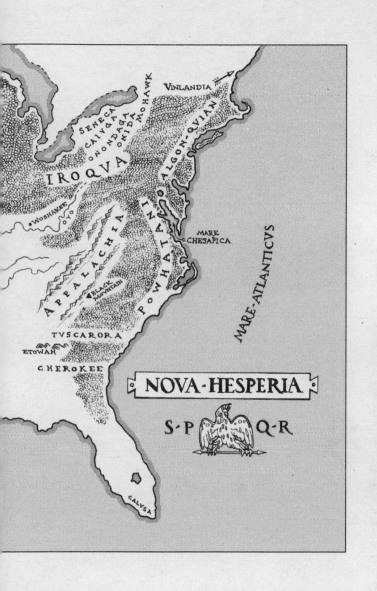

Contents

PART 1

CAHOKIA ROMANUS

CHAPTER 1

YEAR EIGHT, PLANTING MOON

As Marcellinus stepped out of the Southgate of the fortress of the Third Parthica, the elite horsemen of the Chernye Klobuki were wheeling around into a full charge in the torn-up grasslands just beyond. He glanced back at Enopay, but the boy was thanking the bemused sentries in perfect Latin and hadn't yet seen the exercising Rus cavalry. To distract him, Marcellinus said, "So, your opinion of our meeting with Decinius Sabinus?"

Enopay followed him out and switched back to speaking Cahokian. "It went well. With Roman help it will be much easier to prepare the fields and plant the corn. Being willing to work for what you eat, if even a few of your precious legionaries dirty their hands with Cahokian soil, will earn you huge—oh, merda, here they come again . . ." Abandoning his dignity, Enopay jumped behind Marcellinus. Back at the gate the sentries snorted with laughter.

The Chernye squadron was charging the fortress in a tight formation, a solid line forty horsemen wide. They wore mail shirts that were slit up the sides for easy riding, over tunics of varied color and fit. Most of the soldiers in the first rank carried long spears, some held over their heads ready to strike downward and others couched; successive waves carried bows, curved sabers, or whips. Some of their helmets were tall and fluted and others were bronzed and curved, but those warriors of the most terrifying aspect wore helmets with full steel visors that mimicked human faces.

The first rank swept by Marcellinus and Enopay, wheeling so close that the clods of earth kicked up by their horses' hooves spattered the wooden stockade. The horses, Marcellinus knew, were a purpose-bred cross between the spirited Arabs of the Near East and the steppe ponies the Mongols rode. Their manes flowed freely, and their nostrils were bloodshot; it was not unknown for Chernye horses to kick and bite the mounts of their enemies.

The second line of horsemen was on them in moments, some playfully waving their sabers. The thunder of their passing was deafening. Marcellinus stood firm, nodding in approval despite the violence of the assault on his senses, but by that point Enopay had retreated completely and was back inside the fortress gate.

The anarchy of the Chernye's appearance was deceptive. Marcellinus had first encountered them when serving as a centurion in Kievan Rus half a lifetime ago. Turkic steppe peoples by background, mercenaries by trade, they were among the best horsemen in the Roman world. Bringing them as auxiliaries to fight the Mongols was truly fighting fire with fire, and it was a pity they had only a few hundred of the elite warriors. The Romans had brought two wings of cavalry from southern Rus, the Third and Fourth Polovtsians, nomadic horsemen almost as ferocious as the Mongols but without their conquering spirit. The Polovtsians were excellent, but the Chernye were better.

"That is the last of them?" Enopay called anxiously.

The Chernye slowed to a trot, smoothly reorganizing their ranks into a single long, straight line for their next exercise. They made that look easy. Marcellinus knew it wasn't. "Yes. The coast is clear."

Enopay stepped out of the fortress again. "It is not that I fear the four-legs, you understand. Merely that if they should happen to make an error . . ."

"Of course," said Marcellinus, whose own heart was still racing. "A little prudence is quite understandable."

They turned and walked toward the riverbank. To their right the muddy brown ribbon of the Mizipi curved away to the south, half a mile wide. To their left stood the great fortress of the Legio III Parthica. Placed well back from the riverbank just south of the old city of Cahokia-across-the-water, the Roman fortress was enormous: a full quarter mile square with ramparts that loomed twenty feet above them. As always, the castra was a hive of activity. Now that the din of the cavalry had faded, from the other side of the tall wooden stockade they could hear the almost constant sounds of running or marching feet and the barked orders of centurions.

The imago of the Imperator fluttered over the fortress at half staff, as Hadrianus was not currently within. He and his Praetorian Guard were two days' ride to the west, deep in the prairie on an extended training exercise with the heavy armored Roman cavalry of the Ala I Gallorum et Pannoniorum Cataphractaria. Already a seasoned general when he ascended to the Imperial purple, Hadrianus liked to lead his forces from the front. And after two years in Nova Hesperia he obviously chafed for action; Marcellinus sometimes thought the Imperator might be exultant to see the massed horsemen of the Mongol Horde thundering over the Plains toward him.

As Marcellinus and Enopay approached their birch-bark canoe on the riverbank, the boy turned to him. "When the Romans go on into the west, you will go with them?"

"Perhaps I should," Marcellinus said. "Someone needs to keep them out of trouble."

"And I can come with you?"

Marcellinus raised his eyebrows. "You?"

"Yes, of course, me," Enopay said. "Always you go away, and always you leave me behind. You go to the Iroqua. You go to Shappa Ta'atan. Then you sail all the way to the Market of the Mud in a dragon ship *I* helped you rebuild, and after that you take it up the Wemissori to the buffalo hunt, and you come back, and then you run off to Ocatan! All that time I sit here counting and writing down numbers in my book. Gaius Marcellinus sees all the land, and Enopay, who was born in it, sees nothing."

Even now Enopay's hand rested possessively on the satchel he always carried over his shoulder. Three chiefs of Cahokia had relied on Enopay's record keeping, and when it came to bushels of corn or war bands of Wolf Warriors, even Decinius Sabinus regularly double-checked his quartermasters' and adjutants' figures against Enopay's. It was part of the reason Enopay and Marcellinus had come to see Sabinus today.

"We were banished," Marcellinus reminded him drily. "I was hardly voyaging to entertain myself."

"Nonetheless, I think that next time I will stow away under your decking planks. And . . . Eyanosa?"

Marcellinus sighed inwardly. He knew what was coming next. "Yes, Enopay?"

"I want to know why the Romans of Hadrianus are really here, and what it is that none of you will tell us." The boy fixed him with a penetrating stare. Marcellinus ignored the question; this was about the twelfth time Enopay had expressed his suspicions, and as there was nothing Marcellinus could say, he preferred to remain silent.

"So alert, the soldiers of Sabinus and Agrippa are," Enopay said. "So busy training. The Imperator so keen to lead his expeditions into the Grass and keep his troops battle-ready. He sends quinqueremes and long-ships and canoes to map the Mizipi tributaries out of the west, and places fortresses at the river confluences, and eagerly awaits the accounts of his scouts when they return from their moonslong trips across the Plains. And yet still you will not speak of it to me, which means you cannot. But one day someone will let something slip . . ."

Marcellinus was surprised that it had not happened

already. The officers and men of two full legions of Roma knew they had come to Nova Hesperia to fight Chinggis Khan and his Mongol army. Somehow, over the last ten months not a one of them had revealed this to the mound builders. Marcellinus was quite sure that if his own 33rd Hesperian Legion were still in existence and camped here by the Mizipi, they would have leaked the information by suppertime.

From far away they heard the faint throb of a single rhythmic drum. Enopay's ears perked up immediately. "Ah, good! Let us hurry."

Grateful for the distraction, Marcellinus followed Enopay along the southern wall of the castra toward the riverbank. The drums grew louder astonishingly quickly, now joined by the chirping of a martial flute.

"From upriver, then!" Enopay grinned and broke into a run. Marcellinus preserved a dignified walk.

Having just met with Decinius Sabinus in his legionary Praetorium, Marcellinus was wearing his full Roman dress uniform, and he needed to preserve dignitas in front of the officers and sentries who patrolled the wooden ramparts above him. Marcellinus possessed no authority over the troops of the Third, but had earned their grudging respect over the last year. He was not about to jeopardize that by scampering to see a ship.

Arriving next to Enopay on the riverbank, Marcellinus looked north up the Mizipi.

The quinquereme was barreling downriver in the center of the current. This was Maius, the Planting Moon, and the river was still in full spate with ice-cold meltwater.

"Now *that*," Enopay said with satisfaction, "is a really *big* canoe."

The quinquereme was two hundred feet long and twenty feet across at the beam. Its top deck stood fifteen feet clear of the water level, and its golden curving prow reared another twenty feet above that. The warship had its fighting towers erected at both bow and stern, with a dozen marines standing to attention atop each one. Despite the strength of the current, the quinquereme's oarsmen were getting little relief; the three ranks of oars dipped in perfect time with the sharp notes of the flute, slicing through the eddying water like a single machine. In a concession to the sweating soldiers at the rowing benches, the louvers were open to send a breeze into the enclosed hull.

Thousands of miles from its home harbor the warship somehow still looked brand-new. Its red bulwarks and upper decks gleamed, and the green paint at its waterline was clean and almost aglow. The large eye painted on its bow for good luck glinted with malevolence.

Along its top deck the sailors and marines stood straight-backed, in good order. When unregarded the men might stand easy, but while passing Nova Hesperia's major city the Legio VI Ferrata spared no effort to put on a good show.

"Don't do that."

Enopay was saluting the galley, a full-arm Roman salute, and after a moment of hesitation some of the sailors saluted him back.

"Why not?" Enopay said. "It shows them respect. Massages their pride."

Marcellinus shook his head. Even after a full year he still felt a chill at the sight of one of Roma's most powerful warships under weigh. He would never forget how seven of these giant galleys had assaulted Ocatan the previous spring, powering up the mighty river to crash onto its banks, their legionaries and auxiliary cavalry spilling out to storm the Mizipian town and take it with contemptuous ease. Ocatan was rebuilt now, a proud Mizipian city once more, with the Roman presence withdrawn to a fortress and harbor area thirty miles farther up the Oyo, but the dead could never be brought back to life.

The quinquereme was quickly past them. It had two steering oars that were controlled by a single helmsman using a transverse tiller, and that helmsman was having to fight to keep the ship in a steady line and not be pushed out of the current on the shallow bend. The wake from the quinquereme's passing splashed up against the muddy bank.

Enopay's eyes gleamed. "Perhaps I will not go west with you after all. Perhaps I will stow away on a quinquereme and go south."

Enopay feared horses and would sooner die than fly a Thunderbird. But when it came to warships the boy was in love. Marcellinus lifted one end of their canoe and pushed it toward the water. He held it steady for Enopay to get in, then shoved off and stepped in with a single movement. Grabbing a paddle, he dug in before the Mizipi current could push the canoe too heavily to the south.

"I am sad you do not trust me, Eyanosa," Enopay said, still following the Roman galley with his eyes as it disappeared into the distance. "I would very much like to think that one day we will be true friends again."

"Enopay, we will always be friends. Help me paddle."

All of a sudden Marcellinus wanted to get back into Cahokia and away from this river that was dominated so casually by the Roman warship. Even from here he could see the broad profile of the Great Mound rising above the other mounds of the city, the very tops of the giant poles that made up the Circle of the Cedars, and the smoke rising from thousands of huts spread over the five square miles where the ordinary people of Cahokia went about their daily business of grinding corn, drying meat, making pots, and scraping skins. High above the Great Mound he saw the swoop of tiny specks that could only be Catanwakuwa. To the mound's left a Sky Lantern hung in the air.

Marcellinus did not hate Roma, far from it, but the Imperium was too harsh, too brutal a thing to share the city with. Like Enopay, Marcellinus wanted the legions to move on into the west.

He doubted it would happen soon.

Enopay was watching him soberly, having picked up on his change of mood. "Hurit?"

"And Anapetu," Marcellinus said shortly. Despite his bedazzlement the boy did, at least, recall the grim connection between the Roman quinqueremes and the slaughter at Ocatan.

Enopay nodded and pulled hard, helping to straighten their course, and Marcellinus synchronized with him with the ease of long familiarity, and then all hell broke loose with a suddenness that almost made him drop the paddle. "Futete! What on earth?"

Great wafts of black sooty fug were rising from the Mound of the Smoke. God only knew what noxious weeds they had to burn to create such a signal. And now from the Master Mound came the din of rocks beating against tall sheets of copper.

At almost the same moment came the braying of Roman trumpets from far south of the city.

Such alarums could only mean the city was under attack from an enemy without . . . or within.

Marcellinus and Enopay glanced at each other in horror and then, as one, dug their paddles deep into the muddy waters and bent their backs, lifting the nose of the canoe out of the water in their rush.

Even as they landed on the east bank, Mahkah raced out of the city on a piebald steed, leaning forward into the gallop. He had taken to riding as if he had been doing it all his life. Marcellinus half expected to see Hanska by his side. She was also an instinctive rider, and the two of them drilled other members of the First Cahokian together.

The Mizipi bank was boggy, and Mahkah could not bring his mount all the way to its edge. He slid off the horse and stood beside it, patting its neck to calm it. Marcellinus hurried forward. "What? What is happening?"

"Fight. Big fight."

"Another?" Enopay looked accusingly at Marcellinus.

"What is it this time?"

"A boy of the Chipmunk clan caught stealing in the barracks of the 27th. They flogged him. Our warriors protested. Their soldiers turned on ours. Then?" Mahkah threw up his hands, and his horse reared. "Battle. Many dead already. You must go, Hotah. Take my steed to the Great Plaza, then another south."

As the Roman seized the reins, the stallion backed up, eyes wide and rolling. Marcellinus looked dubious. "He won't throw me?"

Mahkah grinned. "Maybe."

Marcellinus stepped into the stirrup and swung himself into the saddle. The horse sidestepped but quickly stilled as Marcellinus took control. "Enopay, come on. Mahkah, lift him up behind me."

The boy's eyes widened. "Me? No. I will get there when I get there."

"Maybe you can help."

"Not if my skull is broken!"

"Go!" Mahkah slapped the horse's rump, and as he lurched forward, Marcellinus grabbed the reins tightly and leaned in. Mahkah's legs were longer and the stirrups hung low; this would be a dodgy ride.

As he galloped through western Cahokia dogs barked at him, and more than one Wolf Warrior instinctively grabbed a spear or a club. Even now, mounted Romans in armor were a rare sight in the streets of the Great City. Especially with the alarums still sounding, a Roman at full gallop could only be seen as a threat. But Marcellinus was well known, and Cahokians scattered to let him pass.

Hanska awaited him in the Great Plaza astride her black Barbary, with a second horse beside her, a tan Thracian. Ciqala, the young son of Takoda and Kangee, stood close by, gaping.

Marcellinus slid off Mahkah's horse, which was already blown and panting, and pulled himself aboard the second mount. "Bad?"

"Fuck the 27th," Hanska said tersely. Spurring her horse, she took off southward like an arrow.

"Hanska . . ." Marcellinus swore again and looked around him. "You!" he shouted, and Ciqala took a step back, wide-eyed.

"Run to the longhouses. Find Sintikala and Chenoa and say to them: 'Mud!' "

The boy narrowed his eyes. He obviously had inherited his mother's distrust of the Roman. "Mud?"

"Bring mud! Tell them now!" Marcellinus dug in his heels, and the Thracian leaped forward.

Galloping after Hanska, Marcellinus passed Cahokian warriors running south with weapons in hand. Their destination was obvious. Marcellinus could hear the clang of steel even over the thunder of his horse's hooves. As he passed the Mound of the Women and the castra of the 27th Augustan hove into view, he saw Cahokians and Romans in bitter armed combat spilling out past its earthen embankment. It was less a battle than a brawl, gladius against ax, pugio against short spear, fists and rocks against similar weapons.

The fortress of the 27th was nowhere near as impressive as that of the Third. Agrippa's men had commandeered the site of the old Cahokian castra, which had been built soon after the sack of Cahokia, when a Mizipian army was preparing to march on the Haudenosaunee. The Romans had built up the existing earthworks and topped the earthen ramparts with wooden crenellations and walkways. The towers that loomed over the gates and corners of the fortress had none of the stout permanence of those of Sabinus's legion. It would take an earthquake to dislodge the fortifications of the Third. It might take just this battle to compromise the castra of the 27th Augustan.

Viewing the scene through a soldier's eyes, Marcellinus had to admit his Cahokians were doing a fine job of bottling up the forces of Roma. Agrippa's cohorts had obviously tried to pull the gates closed and failed; the gates now lay in the mud, splintered and wrecked. A phalanx of First Cahokian warriors twenty men wide and five deep now blocked the entranceway instead, pushing and shoving against the legionaries within. Their front line was protected by the Roman scuta shields they had acquired long before from the 33rd, and those in the second and fourth ranks of the phalanx were holding more of the broad shields over their heads in an admirable testudo.

In fact, few missiles were being launched down upon them because the wooden battlements were burning, alight with Cahokian liquid flame. Farther along the embankment a few legionary archers leaned over the crenellations to loose arrows obliquely into the Cahokian force, but they themselves were the targets of a group of Cahokian bowmen fifty feet back from the walls.

In between the archers and the castra walls a melee raged. A few hundred legionaries of the 27th Augustan fought in untidy hand-to-hand combat with a roughly equivalent number of Cahokians. Some Romans were in full armor, but others fought in their simple off-duty tunics. Similarly, the locals were a mix of Wolf Warriors, First Cahokian, and ordinary townsfolk. Some had Cahokian wooden or mat armor covering their chests and backs, others wore Roman helmets or breastplates, and still more had no armor at all, but they all howled with anger and fought like demons. It was sheer bloody mayhem, and the fact that scores of men were not already lying dead on the ground was a comment on both the evenness of the battle and its disorganization.

Marcellinus saw many warriors he recognized, but few of his lieutenants. Akecheta was away on the Wemissori River, captaining the *Concordia* on a trip to the Blackfoot territory, and Mahkah was somewhere behind him, presumably still running in from the Great City. Hanska had arrived ahead of Marcellinus and was off her horse and shoving herself into the roughest part of the scrap. Whether she was trying to break up the fight or crack some Roman heads together was not immediately apparent. Marcellinus did not see Tahtay or any of the elders of Cahokia, and for that matter he saw no Roman tribunes.

Marcellinus swore in several languages. This had gone to Hades in a handbasket much too quickly. He could not allow this battle to rage on. It must be quenched by whatever means necessary.

Gritting his teeth, Marcellinus slid off his horse and strode into the mess of soldiers and warriors. He seized two men wrestling over a gladius, shoved one back, and kicked the other, hardly caring which was which. "Stop!" Walking between them, he came upon two more men trading blows with sword and ax. "Break it up!"

Ah, there was Wahchintonka, similarly marching into the fray as though he were made of steel. Although his voice was lost in the furor, the seasoned war lieutenant was clearly bellowing, commanding Cahokians back, dragging combatants apart wherever he could. A few Roman centurions were doing likewise, yelling orders and trying to pull men back from the brawl. Again came the bray of trumpets as the cornicens signaled the legionaries to disengage. The men took little notice.

Marcellinus exhaled long and hard and strode deeper into the chaos, grabbing, pushing, shoving. Echoes of running the Iroqua gauntlet came suddenly back into his mind: the deafening hubbub, the whirl of limbs around him, the spitting.

Now as then, he held his head high and pushed on. Around him were braves he knew, or at least recognized, from the plazas and markets and fields. He could well die today at the hands of a man or woman he had known for half a dozen years.

In between Roman helmets Marcellinus caught a glimpse of Matoshka, of all people, also shouting and trying to order Cahokians back. The half-crippled elder was not so foolish as to place himself within reach of a Roman gladius, but when this hoary old bear shouted at a Cahokian, that brave took heed.

Matoshka and Wahchintonka were trying to stop

Cahokians fighting with Romans, while Marcellinus's First Cahokian assaulted the enemy's gate. The irony was acute.

A dozen Cahokians had backed an equal number of Roman soldiers up against the wall of their own fortress. Marcellinus knew he could never get there in time, and he did not. Cahokian blades slid up under Roman steel, dug deep into Roman bodies. The legionaries crashed onto their knees. Cahokian pugios sawed away at Roman scalps.

Guided by a sixth sense, Marcellinus glanced up at the skies.

Two Thunderbirds roared low over his head, the new lighter seven-person birds developed over the winter by Chenoa of the Wakinyan clan. The Thunderbirds disgorged their loads at the same time. Two wet black streams cascaded down over the mob. Mud; the Thunderbirds were strafing the combatants with the thick Mizipi mud they used for training. Ciqala must have taken Marcellinus's message after all. Chenoa herself piloted the lead Wakinyan, her body stocky and strong, her movements decisive.

The mud had spared Marcellinus but doused the combatants at the center of the fighting, Romans and Hesperians alike. Men slipped and went down. Some took advantage of the distraction to cut throats and slide spears into other men's guts, but the ferocious energy of the battle was wavering.

"Centurion! And Wahchintonka! To me!"

The Roman of the 27th thus hailed glowered at Marcellinus, gladius in one hand and vine stick of office in the other, held up before him like a shield. Marcellinus reached out his weaponless right hand and in Latin said, "We must join to stop the fighting. Come."

Wahchintonka was still a dozen feet away, out of earshot and only half looking at him, wary of the muddy legionaries to his right and left. To him Marcellinus waved three broad gestures in the Hesperian hand-talk: *Warrior! Halt! Come!*

If they didn't get it yet, they weren't going to. Marcellinus shoulder-barged a Cahokian, knocking him down, and shoved the man's Roman assailant back, jabbing his finger at the man's face in stern command. Nonetheless, the legionary raised his club.

"Stand down, soldier," snapped the centurion to his right, and Wahchintonka grabbed another Cahokian's belt to yank him away from the legionary. "Back off!" Marcellinus shouted in two languages. "Fall back! Fall back!"

He hurried on. In front of him two more men traded blows, but the Cahokian was quicker, and the Roman's feet appeared to give way beneath him. Another slash from the Cahokian and the Roman private was down and drowning in his own blood. Marcellinus's head threatened to start aching again, as it often did in times of bloodshed and stress. He clouted the Cahokian over the head, empty-handed. "Get away! Away!"

It was Dustu, whom Marcellinus had known since he was a boy, now as much a man as Tahtay was; indeed, he was one of Tahtay's most trusted lieutenants. Roman blood glistened on his gladius and was spattered along his forearm. His eyes were bright with battle fury as he raised his sword.

Marcellinus stood firm. "Fall back, Dustu. I have spoken."

At last the young man's mouth dropped open in recognition. He took an involuntary step back. Marcellinus nodded as if Dustu were in full retreat and moved on to the next man.

With dazzling speed Sintikala zoomed low over them, a long white streamer fluttering behind her Hawk. Behind her flew her daughter, Kimimela, and the Hawk clan deputy, Demothi, both of them also trailing flags of parley. Shocked, startled, soldiers on both sides threw themselves back away from the craft. But just ten feet away three Cahokians died almost at once, a woman and two men clad in only the shirts they had been wear-

ing to sow crops in the fields, hacked down by two legionaries, their armor parade-ground bright.

Marcellinus's head pounded, and at the same time an
ax blade clanged off his chest plate from a random, flailing backswing. Marcellinus slapped the Cahokian
down, an openhanded blow. The brave's opponent, a
Roman in the chain mail hauberk of a cavalryman,
leaped forward to take advantage of the situation, and
Marcellinus lunged and kicked him. Cahokian and cavalryman both snarled, and for a moment Marcellinus
thought they might team up against him in their fury.

"Step back, soldier! Break it up, now." Mollifying
words in both Latin and Cahokian, conciliatory in tone
but shouted at full volume. "We're all-done here. This
helps nobody. Stop!"

Chenoa's Thunderbird came around again. Another
torrent of mud rained down upon them.

Gradually, they made headway and the brawl subsided. Men disengaged, stepped back. Few Romans
would assault one of their own, and Marcellinus now
cut through the crowd like a blade. Most Cahokians
now retreated rather than cross him, and once their own
battle had paused, they moved to hold back the others.

A third Wakinyan, one of the original monsters with a
full twelve-man crew, lumbered through the air toward
the castra from the northwest. In the melee zone the
Cahokians were beating a hasty retreat while their
Roman opponents regrouped by the walls, at last forming an impromptu squad line.

Now Marcellinus was only thirty feet from the gateway of the Augustan castra, where the Cahokian squad
still wrestled with the Romans within. "First Cahokian!
To me! Retreat in good order!"

Some already were reversing carefully, and Marcellinus saw Hanska at the far end of their line berating the
men, ordering them back, while still holding out her gladius toward the mass of armored Romans that threatened them from the gateway. Marcellinus took the near
end of the line, and between them they got the First

Cahokian backed up en masse, one pace, two, then more, while still holding the line, awkwardly retreating as a unit without letting their guard down.

The risk now came from the Romans; the enraged legionaries bottled up within the camp might swarm out and fall upon the withdrawing Cahokians. Marcellinus caught sight of the cornicen on the battlements, watching the events outside the walls of the fortress with troubled eyes. "Trumpeter! Signal the retreat again! Do it now!"

The cornicen eyed Marcellinus but did nothing. Then the centurion to Marcellinus's right barked out in a strong bellow that would have done credit to Pollius Scapax: "Damn you, trumpeter, sound the stand-down or you'll have my boot up your ass!" and the soldier raised the cornu to his lips immediately.

The group of muddy Romans was retreating along the outside wall toward the gate. On the battlements the flames from the Cahokian liquid fire were burning out. Wahchintonka had arrived back by Marcellinus's side, looking around warily. The First Cahokian had retreated twenty feet from the gate, still in close order.

"Hold." Marcellinus stepped forward, Romans on his right and Cahokians on his left, and called to the guards: "Stand down. Stay inside. Throw away no more lives today."

The guards' leader was a tribune, Marcellinus suddenly realized: an older man, wiry and tight-eyed. He looked at Marcellinus with incomprehension and made a hand signal Marcellinus didn't understand. The legionaries began to surge forward.

"Heed him." The centurion to Marcellinus's right stepped up shoulder to shoulder with him. A second centurion joined them, and Marcellinus recognized him as the primus pilus of the 27th. Just last year, far to the east of here during a Wakinyan bombing assault, Marcellinus had come to warn this man about the dangers of the Cahokian liquid flame.

Marcellinus now stood with several bloody and mud-stained centurions of the 27th who saw no reason to add to the death toll of the day. Wahchintonka and Hanska stood to his left, and Matoshka beyond them. All knew that the rule of law had to be reestablished. All stared at the soldiers of Roma arrayed in the gateway and behind them in the Cardo.

Marcellinus raised his chin and addressed the tribune. "Where the hell is Praetor Agrippa? Have him brought here at once."

The tribune scowled but evidently decided not to take the responsibility for a massacre. "Stand down!" he called. "To barracks, the Fourth Cohort! Sentries, barrier the gate. And someone send for the chief medicus and the other bone boys."

The giant Wakinyan banked above them. Men cringed, but the great bird released no flame or even mud, merely swung around in the air and made its way north again.

Once again the cornicen sounded the stand-down, and then the call to barracks. The Roman centurions and the remaining legionaries stepped past them and into the camp. The First Cahokian broke ranks and stalked away. Their eyes still brimmed with hatred and bloodlust, but Marcellinus, Wahchintonka, Hanska, and the Roman officers were now in control. The battle was over.

CHAPTER 2

YEAR EIGHT, PLANTING MOON

Bareheaded, his helmet thrust under his arm, Marcellinus strode through Cahokia. Some stared as he passed. Others ignored him as if he were beneath contempt or frowned as if they could not decide what to think.

Perhaps they couldn't. In Cahokia, Marcellinus's position was as ambiguous as it had ever been. Over the last seven years his actions had led to the deaths of hundreds of Cahokians, perhaps even thousands, but had also saved countless others. Enopay had said it best: "They love you for steel or the Big Warm House, or they hate you for bringing change and confusion. They hate you for bringing war with the Iroqua or love you for bringing peace with them. Blame you for the murder of Great Sun Man or worship you for bringing Tahtay to rule in his place. Fear you anew for being Roman. Cling to you as the only reason Roma has not already razed our city to the ground." The boy had shrugged. "Everyone has an opinion about you. You are a hard man to ignore."

These days it seemed that Marcellinus was in an uneasy truce with everybody, fully trusted by no one. But in front of him now was one woman with whom he had never made peace. As he approached Nahimana's hut, Kangee stood in its doorway, staring at him with a mixture of astonishment and loathing.

Kangee had spit on him once, on one of his earliest

nights in Cahokia. Instructed by Nahimana to bring Marcellinus a blanket, she had shown her disdain by spitting on Cahokia's enemy as he lay defeated at the foot of a cedar pole.

Now he stopped a few feet away from her. "Takoda is safe?"

"Gaius." The warrior Takoda stepped up out of his hut, easing past his wife. Nahimana hobbled out close behind him.

"I feared perhaps you were in the fight."

Takoda eyed him calmly. "Do I appear such a fool as that?"

"Well . . ." Nahimana cackled.

Takoda gave her a brief look of irritation. "If we are to fight the Romans, we will choose the time. Today?" He shook his head. "Today was a poor time."

"I agree," Marcellinus said.

"Then we will have to pick a very good time." Nahimana was serious now, her eyes narrowed. "Those are hard men, bad men, in the Roman Twenty-Seven. They are not Gaius's Romans, who we could burn and bury with little loss to ourselves."

Now it was Marcellinus's turn to glare. "Never say that to my face!" Nahimana shrank back from him, perhaps the first time she had ever done so, and instantly he felt ashamed.

Takoda spoke again. "As for me, I mourn for our dead. And I rage that Roma treats us thus."

For Takoda to stand so calmly while speaking of rage sent a shiver down Marcellinus's spine. He inclined his head, his own flash of temper calming. "I understand, Takoda. I will speak to the Imperator on his return."

"He will speak to the Imperator." Kangee's voice was icy, laden with the scorn that rimmed her eyes.

For a moment Marcellinus thought she would spit again. He was still staring at her in frustration when a voice behind him broke the brittle silence. "Hotah. Come."

Only Tahtay and Mahkah called him Hotah. Marcellinus turned, and both of them stood there, with Chenoa by their side. The three of them stared at him with a seriousness almost as acidic as Kangee's.

"Come," Tahtay repeated.

"Where to?"

Tahtay eyed him coldly. "You will not question me, Hotah. When I tell you to come, you will come."

Marcellinus bit off a retort. His nerves were frayed, but this was hardly the time to get into an argument with Cahokia's war chief. "Yes, sir."

Marcellinus had rarely been invited into the fortress of Legio XXVII Augusta Martia Victrix, and he wasn't invited today. He bulled his way in past soldiers leery of disobeying a man who once had worn the white crest of a Praetor, even one with no legion to command.

He and Chenoa strode up the Cardo in Tahtay's wake in the late afternoon, the streets around them uncannily clear. The cohorts of the 27th Augustan were confined to barracks while tempers cooled, wounds were patched up, and centurions reimposed discipline on their men. For once there were no sounds of marching feet in the streets of the fort, no shouted orders or babble of camaraderie. They heard only the hammering of the Roman carpenters as they repaired the broken gates.

Marcellinus wished Kimimela were with them. Tahtay was in a fury, and at such times only Kimimela could make him breathe and think clearly.

He glanced at the warrior woman at his side. When the ancient Ojinjintka had passed away in her sleep the previous winter, the chiefdom of the Thunderbird clan had passed smoothly to her sister's daughter, Chenoa, who had been doing most of the work of organizing the clan anyway during her aunt's infirmity. Chenoa was a strong no-nonsense woman as robust as Ojinjintka had been frail, and she had stamped her authority on her clan immediately. She and Sintikala had put their heads together and then come to Marcellinus, and by springtime the Great Mound had two new launching rails, one dedicated to Wakinyan and the other to the smaller Cat-anwakuwa and Eagle craft, in addition to the original dual-use steel launching rail that Marcellinus had engineered for them five years earlier. Now all of Cahokia's different types of aerial craft could be hurled into the air at once and almost continuously.

After a brief commotion at the Praetorium door, Tahtay and Chenoa swept inside. Passing through to the inner sanctum, flanked by guards, Tahtay came to a halt practically nose to nose with Agrippa. "How dare you! You and your vile men! We should slay every one of you!"

Marcellinus took a step closer, fearing that Tahtay might physically attack the Praetor. Agrippa stood his ground and gazed calmly at the war chief. "Good afternoon, Tahtay of Cahokia. How might I be of assistance?"

"How? You can keep your filthy Roman hands off my people!"

"Believe me, I try my hardest never to touch even one of you. I do, however, express my apologies for today's escalation."

"What?" Exasperated, Tahtay spun on his heel and snapped at Marcellinus. "Hotah, what?"

"Escalation: increasing use of force." Marcellinus looked balefully at Agrippa. "Matters getting out of hand."

"Thank you." Tahtay turned back to Agrippa. "Well, if this happens again, the next *escalation* will be your castra burning down around your ears from our liquid fire. Where is the Imperator?"

"Out in the Grass," said Agrippa. "Which is where we'll drive your redskins after we destroy your stinking town if you don't keep your young thieves out of our barracks."

Tahtay threw up his hands. "Now I am responsible for every boy in Cahokia?"

Chenoa stepped forward. "Lucius Agrippa, Gaius

Wanageeska, Tahtay, sirs. I beg, sit and talk. We can send for pipe. Must be calm here between us."

Marcellinus raised his eyebrows. Chenoa's Latin was improving rapidly.

Agrippa grunted. "At least one of you savages talks sense."

"Huh," Tahtay said. "I will not smoke a pipe with this man."

Tahtay barely smoked tabaco at all, even in the sweat lodge. He claimed it hurt his chest and made him too short of breath to run well. But that was beside the point.

Agrippa considered for a moment and then raised his hands for calm. "Come now, war chief. You are responsible for every Cahokian, just as I am responsible for each soldier under my command. And I lost men today, just as you did, over a stupid incident that should never have occurred. I take the breakdown of discipline in my legion very seriously, and I assure you the contubernium ultimately responsible will be punished."

"Punished how?" Tahtay demanded. "Made to clean latrines? Slapped on the backs of their delicate hands?"

"You do not choose how my men are punished," Agrippa said. "Any more than my legionaries should have chosen how your thieving boy was punished. I am surprised we do not agree on this."

Tahtay opened his mouth and closed it again.

"So let us sit down with wine and water like grownups and discuss how we may avoid such events in the future."

"Just like we did last time?" Tahtay jeered.

Agrippa's eyes narrowed; he was clearly losing patience. Marcellinus stepped in and rapped his knuckles on the table. "War chief, heed Chenoa. Sit. Let us talk."

Tahtay hardly spared him a glance. "Eighty-five Cahokians dead and many more with broken heads and arms? I shall not sit. I shall not drink. I shall speak to Hadrianus of this. Send for me immediately when he returns."

"Certainly, Your Excellency," Agrippa said sardonically.

Tahtay blinked, unfamiliar with the word but recognizing the mockery in Agrippa's tone. He leaned closer to the Praetor, once again almost nose to nose with the man. "And Lucius Agrippa? This castra must be gone by the next full moon, and your men with it, moved across the Great River to its western shore as you swore. Until then, if any man of the 27th enters Cahokia or lays a hand on one of my Cahokians, we will tie him to a frame and cut into his skin and keep him alive for a very long time. I have spoken."

Tahtay turned and stamped out of the room. Looking worried, Chenoa bowed and hurried after him.

"Well," Agrippa said lightly. "Your young Fire Heart put me in my place and no mistake. Some wine, Gaius Marcellinus?"

Marcellinus stared him down. "Perhaps later. For now, speaking of fire, I must go and ensure the flames of Cahokian rebellion are out."

Agrippa nodded. "Make sure you do. Keep your redskins in check. Make no mistake; your precious barbarian tribe is scarcely a hairbreadth away from wholesale slaughter. And I am not the only man who thinks so."

Marcellinus steamed internally at the Praetor's language but managed to nod curtly.

"Oh, and Gaius Marcellinus? I was told you attempted to give orders to my men today. Centurions? Cornicens? Rankers? A tribune, even? *My* men."

"To restore the peace and save lives, Roman as well as Cahokian, I may have made some suggestions. I saw no one else in authority."

Agrippa shook his head. "Every centurion in my legion outranks you, Gaius Marcellinus. You're barely a step above the natives, and some of us think even that is debatable."

Marcellinus did not blink. "A good job, then, that I was in the middle of a riot and not an authorized military action. If you had *ordered* such a thing, I would naturally never have attempted to contain it."

"Of course I did not order it. Do you think me mad?"

"Not for a moment."

"Not for a moment, *sir*." Agrippa studied him. "We clapped you in irons once before, Gaius Marcellinus. We could certainly put you in them again."

Marcellinus inclined his head a fraction of an inch. "You could try. Sir."

Agrippa shook his head again. He poured himself some wine and regarded Marcellinus contemplatively. "You're an odd bird, Gaius. The spare Praetor, the man nobody wants. Barking his orders to men he does not command."

"Serving Roma and the Imperator," Marcellinus said doggedly. "Preventing a massacre. Because Roma is not at war with Cahokia. Roma has a bigger enemy."

"Do not lecture me, Gaius Marcellinus."

"No, sir. May I withdraw?"

"Please do. And Gaius Marcellinus? Don't think you can run off now and recruit Decinius Sabinus to gang up on me. That trick has run its course."

"I understand, sir," said Marcellinus, thin-lipped, and left.

"Aha," said Aelfric, arriving alongside Marcellinus as he walked into Cahokia that evening. "I'm quite sure I know where *you're* going." To add insult to injury, the Briton winked at him.

"I'm quite sure you don't." He looked his erstwhile tribune up and down. "And you? Cahokian dress? Decinius Sabinus knows you fraternize with barbarians?"

"Information gathering," Aelfric said. "Soothing the population with my relaxing presence. You think I'd do something this dodgy without my commanding officer's nod?"

Marcellinus snorted.

"Makes for good relations with the nefarious natives," Aelfric said. "At least *one* of Hadrianus's Praetors has a keen head on his shoulders." He looked sideways at Marcellinus. "I told him about me and Chumanee straight away, the first meeting we had."

Marcellinus nodded. "Sabinus wants to wield our influence. Use our connections. You with Chumanee and the Wolf Warriors. Me with Tahtay, Sintikala, and the Ravens."

"I see you've had that conversation, too."

The sun was setting behind the trees. "Does Tahtay know? By the treaty you're supposed to be out of town by nightfall."

"By the treaty, five thousand Romans aren't supposed to be parked a short walk from the Great Mound."

Marcellinus refused to be sidetracked. "Does Tahtay know or doesn't he?"

"I don't have your access to Tahtay. But Taianita knows."

"Well, *that* will help." Marcellinus glanced around them.

Aelfric was studying him in some amusement. "You don't know, do you?"

Marcellinus sighed and stopped walking. "All right. What don't I know this time?"

"Of course, you being a big pal of Tahtay's, I assumed you'd have picked up that he and Taianita . . . ?"

"You're kidding." Marcellinus stared at him. "Lovers?"

"Couldn't speak to that, but certainly close companions. Jesus, where have you *been* this winter? Hibernating?"

"Building throwing engines. Designing grain mills. Making launching rails. Teaching the First Cahokian to ride horses." Marcellinus looked around again, but nobody who spoke Latin was anywhere near. "Stopping the Sixth Ferrata and the Ocatani from killing one another while we rebuilt Ocatan. Stopping the 27th Augustan and the Cahokians from killing one another here. Usually, anyway. Eating interminable dinners with the Imperator and his Praetors. Spending interminable nights in the sweat lodge smoking with the elders. Exhorting Matoshka and the Wolf Warriors not to slit Roman throats in the night."

"Well, yes, of course. But apart from that."

"Apart from that?" Marcellinus warmed to his theme. "Bickering with the quartermasters and Enopay about grain shares. Coaxing Roman blacksmiths and Cahokian steelworkers to work together. Bribing legion engineers to build irrigation canals so we can grow even more corn to feed everyone. Negotiating with the Raven clan about Roman use of Sky Lanterns. Helping Chenoa with wire and other bits and pieces for the new Wakinyan Sevens." He grimaced. "Persuading Sintikala and the Hawks to scout far and wide without telling them why. Stopping Enopay from stowing away on a quinquereme and disappearing altogether. Trying to persuade my daughter to talk to me. Teaching Cahokians Latin—"

"Still no luck there?"

"Kimimela? None whatsoever."

The Briton looked at his face. "So you're not going to them now, Kimimela and . . . ?"

"No," Marcellinus said dolefully. "Off to dinner with Pahin and the Ravens."

After he had returned from the rebuilding of Ocatan, Marcellinus had slept in the fortress of Legio III Parthica for most of the winter, trying to build trust with Hadrianus and Decinius Sabinus. After the Midwinter Feast, once everyone was another year older and both leaders were in a good mood, he had negotiated with Hadrianus and Tahtay to spend three nights a week in Cahokia.

As was her right, Chenoa had claimed the large house on the mound adjacent to Sintikala's that once had belonged to Howahkan and then to Marcellinus. When in Cahokia, Marcellinus now stayed in a brand-new hut southeast of the Great Plaza built for him by his new Raven clan chief, Pahin, on a low mound near hers. To his embarrassment he had been welcomed into the new

Raven chief's family and was expected to eat with them most of the nights he spent in Cahokia.

Pahin was an earnest but rather bland woman who had inherited the chiefdom of one of Cahokia's principal clans against anyone's expectations, her own included. Everyone had assumed that the chiefdom would ultimately pass to Anapetu's daughter, Nashota, and not for many more years, since Anapetu had been in the prime of her middle age when she had died at Ocatan. But Nashota had also died on that terrible day, along with Anapetu's sisters, leaving her second cousin Pahin as the closest relative capable of assuming the chiefdom.

Pahin was pleasant enough, but she was not really Marcellinus's kind of person. And dining with Pahin's family just made him miss Anapetu all the more.

Sintikala he saw often enough, but mostly on business connected with the Hawk clan or in meetings with Tahtay. To Marcellinus's great sorrow, Kimimela's continuing animosity toward him was sufficient to keep him from eating dinner with them or relaxing with them in any social setting.

"Sorry." The Briton clapped him on the arm. "Well, I go this way, I'm afraid."

Forcing a grin, Marcellinus said, "Give my love to Chumanee."

"That, I will certainly do." Aelfric turned and walked into the neighborhood of the stone knappers. Marcellinus watched him on his way for a few moments, but the men and women Aelfric passed looked up and nodded at him companionably. He even stopped to exchange a few words here and there, or clasp arms in the Roman style with some of the men.

Aside from the First Cahokian, there were few in the Great City who would greet Marcellinus with such familiarity. He continued on his way, glancing up at the Mound of the Sun as he passed.

Tahtay and Taianita? Marcellinus was glad enough that Tahtay had company, having taken the death of Hurit so badly the previous year, but there were a hun-

dred girls he might have chosen rather than the translator from Shappa Ta'atan.

Ah, well. The young made their own choices. As for
Marcellinus, he was doomed to another evening of politeness with Pahin, diplomacy with the Sky Lantern
crews, and the grudging respect of their leader, Chogan.

Marcellinus ducked down into his hut to prepare for
dinner with his clan chief, but its stark emptiness drove
him out in moments.

The heavy cavalry of the Ala I Gallorum et Pannoniorum Cataphractaria walked back out of the west in a
long winding column, eight horses abreast and a hundred horsemen deep. The troopers and their horses all
looked exhausted, and well they might. All the men
wore their heavy scale armor and carried their long two-
handed contus lances, and the horses were no less en-
cumbered: leather chamfrons studded with steel
protected their heads, and barding with metal scales
shielded their necks and flanks. This was not easy equipment to wear at the height of a Hesperian summer.

Hadrianus, riding out in the lead with his master of
horse and his adjutant on either side, also wore armor of
stout plate but appeared as energetic and cheerful as if
he'd mounted his horse just moments before. That good
cheer faltered when he caught sight of his reception
committee of Tahtay, Chenoa, Wahchintonka, Marcellinus, and Decinius Sabinus.

The First Gallorum Cataphractaria broke into double
file and casual order as they threaded through the Westgate into the fortress of the Third Parthica. Many of the
tired horsemen did at least manage to raise their heads
or arms in brief salute to the crest of the blue bull that
hung over the gate. Marcellinus had no doubt that most
of them would be asleep in their barracks as soon as
they'd unsaddled and brushed down their horses.

Tahtay watched the spectacle of the cataphracts with
dour interest and waited for the Imperator to be ready.

Dismounting, Hadrianus took the initiative right

away. "I am profoundly sorry, Tahtay. Agrippa has identified the contubernium that began this. They were too violent with the Cahokian boy, and we will make an example of them. But you know, your people overreacted, too."

Tahtay nodded, not surprised. They all knew that the Imperator kept in close touch with Cahokia when he was away, using both mounted dispatch riders and Hawk messengers. "I heard it was your tame Cherokee who first objected to the mistreatment of the boy. Your own scouts, Hesperians from the eastern shores. My Cahokians jumped in to protect *them*."

"I heard it differently." The Imperator patted his horse and allowed it to be led away by his adjutant. Behind them, the imago was being raised slowly to its full height.

Tahtay frowned. "Nonetheless, the 27th is too close. Its castra has been far too close *all winter*. Cahokia still hates Roma for what it did to Ocatan and for being here at all. And in their turn, the troops of the 27th hate Cahokia for slaying the Wanageeska's legion. I have told you this many times, and still Agrippa's legion occupies a castra a mile south of my Great Plaza."

"Yes, yes," Hadrianus said impatiently.

Decinius Sabinus cleared his throat. "We have discussed this before, Tahtay. Roma must control both sides of the river. We must have easy access to our supply train and good communications with our garrison at Mare Chesapica. We must be able to address threats from the east and south should any emerge."

"Threats?" Tahtay shook his head.

Hadrianus stretched his legs and back. "Marcellinus?"

Reluctantly, Marcellinus nodded. "Roma must patrol. We must be able to send parties to Ocatan and beyond without having to continuously ferry cohorts back and forth across the Mizipi."

"Roma cannot have just a depot on one side of the

river and ten thousand men on the other," Sabinus added. "It is a matter of simple logistics."

"Then have them make camp farther away," Tahtay said.

"A day's march south," Chenoa added. "Not a step closer."

Hadrianus glanced at Sabinus and Marcellinus. "We will discuss it again. But . . ." He shrugged.

"And the four-legs?" Chenoa prompted.

Tahtay nodded. "She speaks of your stinking mules. Your horses I can tolerate, but the mules?" He made a sour face.

"They are fewer now," the Imperator pointed out. "We moved the bulk of the mules down to our fortress on the Oyo, near Ocatan. You requested this of me, Tahtay, and I did as you asked. And the more corn we receive from you and the more buffalo we can hunt, the smaller our supply train needs to be."

Sabinus nodded. "As trust grows between our peoples, perhaps we will be willing to consider further concessions."

Tahtay's eyebrows were already raised. "You speak of growing trust in a week when our peoples have been spear to spear in open war?"

"A brawl is not a war," Marcellinus said.

There was a long silence. Tahtay still stared at Hadrianus. "I believe you have heard me, Caesar."

"I have heard you, Tahtay of Cahokia. And I believe we should talk more, you and I, when we have buried our dead and the air between us is cooler. I mean this. I would welcome a closer understanding between us."

Tahtay nodded brusquely and turned away, with the other Cahokians at his heels. Sabinus tutted at the informality of the Cahokian contingent. Tahtay's behavior bordered on criminal disrespect when viewed from a Roman perspective, but Hadrianus no longer seemed to notice.

"May we talk with you more?" Sabinus inquired.

The Imperator either raised his eyes to heaven or

checked the position of the sun. It was not clear which. "If you will allow me a few moments to find myself a tunic that does not reek, and some meat . . ."

"Tahtay is right, of course, Caesar," said Marcellinus, and Sabinus shot him a reproachful look.

Hadrianus, now freshly bathed, wearing a tunic and cloak, and lying on a couch in his Praetorium, put his hand over his eyes to mimic fatigue. "If you say so, Gaius Marcellinus. But it's really all moot, is it not? The dead are still dead."

Sabinus cleared his throat again, an irritating habit that served as a prelude to whatever he was about to say. "If you will permit . . . ? We should like to broach an issue connected to our . . . more distant enemies."

The Imperator inclined his head.

"We have a proposal, Gaius Marcellinus and myself."

"Gaius Marcellinus," Hadrianus said sardonically. "Why do I feel no surprise? Very well, Decinius Sabinus. Speak your mind."

"Our experiences in Asia have made us well aware of the pace at which the Mongols can advance. Their lightning raids into our territories, their sudden appearance outside the walls of cities from Hangzhou to Samarkand and beyond."

The Imperator waved his hand to speed Sabinus along. Of the three of them, Hadrianus was surely the most keenly aware of the threat posed by the Mongol Khan. Sabinus nodded. "Here above all, we cannot afford surprises. Once over the western mountains, a Mongol strike force might then cross the Plains and be at our doorsteps in as little as twenty days."

"That would be a considerable feat," the Imperator objected. "We cannot think that they would know the terrain between the mountains and the Mizipi with sufficient accuracy to aim an arrow at our hearts in such a way."

"With local help they may," Marcellinus said. "Hesperian trails are too faint for Roman eyes to easily see but are well traveled by their traders. And despite our growing Roman presence on the Plains, a small Mongol force might slip between our troops and evade detection until dangerously close."

The Imperator stood and padded across the room on bare feet to pour himself more wine and water, though more water than wine, as was his custom. Marcellinus could almost see his sharp mind working, the wheels turning like linked cogs in a grain mill.

Sabinus took a deep breath. "Gaius and I propose a line of forts across the Grass and other arrays of forts up each of the major rivers, as far as they can go and be reasonably maintained. And, Caesar, we need to establish these lines as a matter of urgency."

Hadrianus glanced at Marcellinus, then back to the Praetor of the Third. "Forts? Nova Hesperia is a *large* land, gentlemen."

"Signal stations, rather. Smaller and much farther apart than the forts along our borders in Europa." Marcellinus stood and held out his arm. "Consider my body as the Mizipi, Caesar, with Cahokia around here." He pointed to his heart. "The Wemissori flows in from the west along my right arm, and is thoroughly patrolled. The Braided River flows into the Wemissori, perhaps here at my elbow. To the north of the Wemissori, here above my arm, between the Blackfoot and the Hidatsa and our own ships on patrol, we need fear no surprise. Down here at my waist the Kicka River flows into the Mizipi just below Shappa Ta'atan, and farther down the Mizipi the Red River comes in at perhaps the height of my knee. Thus, since Roma controls the Mizipi, it is this expanse to the west between my knee and shoulder that concerns us. This represents a north-south distance of some six or seven hundred miles. Now extend this westward." He drew a vertical line in the air an arm's length to his right. "A line of signal stations in the middle of the Grass, five hundred miles from the Mizipi and seven hundred miles long. At a separation of twenty miles, we would need just thirty-five stations."

"Any station that detects a Mongol incursion ignites a signal fire," said Sabinus. "The signal travels along the line to the nearest river, and then along the river to the Mizipi. Thus, whenever the Mongols approach, we learn about it promptly in Cahokia."

"Wood is sparse in many areas on the Plains," Marcellinus said. "The establishment of such signal stations will draw attention from the People of the Grass, the Pawnee and others. And while they have not yet been aggressive toward our legions, a permanent presence is a much different undertaking than the passage of our scouts or the temporary exercising of our horsemen."

Sabinus nodded. "We might even request—purchase—their assistance in building and staffing the signal stations."

"Perhaps." Marcellinus was dubious on this point. The People of the Grass might well agree to such a thing, but the chances of them treating the duty with the seriousness the Romans would expect seemed slim. "If so, with Romans and Hesperians billeted in smaller units, it could facilitate a better understanding between Roma and the native population. An understanding that will help us when it comes to war with the Khan."

"Or the redskins may just kill the legionaries in their sleep," said Hadrianus.

Marcellinus nodded calmly. "Or vice versa, of course. But I prefer to think positively."

"Very well." The Imperator drained his beaker of wine. "Bold but striking. Let us consider this further."

Sabinus glanced at Marcellinus. "I believe we would be best served by assigning the leading role to the 27th Augustan."

Amused, the Imperator turned to him. "The 27th make better guards, perhaps? Due to their excessive alertness and aggression?"

"The 27th needs something to do," Marcellinus said bluntly. "Something other than making trouble with Roma's allies."

Hadrianus's eyes narrowed. "You would say this to Agrippa's face?"

"Of course. I have said far worse. Praetor Sabinus here runs a tight ship. The Third works well with Cahokia, with the Cherokee, with the People of the Grass. But Agrippa's contempt for the Hesperians has propagated down through his chain of command. This threatens the peace in Cahokia and constitutes an unacceptable distraction from what Roma is here to achieve."

The Imperator was eyeing him glacially. Marcellinus had overstepped his bounds again, speaking too forcefully. But this time he chose not to lower his gaze. "I therefore concur with Praetor Sabinus that establishing a Line of Hadrianus across the grasslands would be an excellent task for the 27th Augusta Martia Victrix."

The Imperator looked from one man to the other with dark amusement. "I detect a certain similarity of tone between you. Whose idea was this originally, gentlemen?"

"The full scheme was arrived at jointly. The original idea, I believe, was Marcellinus's."

Marcellinus shook his head. "Praetor Sabinus made the original suggestion. I helped flesh it out with some pertinent details."

"Gaius Marcellinus is too modest," Sabinus said.

Marcellinus bowed his head. If it was anybody's idea, it was Sintikala's. It was she who had seeded the concept of a long line of signal stations into Marcellinus's mind many winters earlier, when it was Roma's arrival and advance that had formed the overriding threat.

"I know more of the Mongols. Marcellinus knows more of Nova Hesperia. It took both of us."

The Imperator stalked back and forth across the floor of the Praetorium deep in thought, tapping the rim of the beaker against his lip. Marcellinus and Sabinus sat calmly, not meeting each other's eyes.

Eventually, the master of the Roman world stopped, picked up the jug of wine, and came to serve his guests.

"A Line of Hadrianus." The Imperator grinned. "Something of a historical precedent, I feel."

"Indeed, Caesar."

"Very well, gentlemen. With the mustering of whatever redskin support is feasible and safe, we will deploy the 27th Augustan into the Grass. Decinius Sabinus, I trust you will not feel slighted if I assign the initial planning and logistics for this adventure to Gaius Marcellinus. We two, and Agrippa, will obviously supervise this at a high level."

"On the contrary," said Sabinus. "Not unlike the 27th, Marcellinus clearly needs something to do. It would be a splendid use of his . . . talents."

Marcellinus nodded wryly. He should have seen that coming. Under Imperator Hadrianus, no good deed went unpunished.

And the logistics for this would certainly be a substantial effort. Perhaps he should pay another call on Kanuna and Enopay. The Imperator was not the only man who could delegate.

CHAPTER 3

YEAR EIGHT, HEAT MOON

Of course, the secret of the Mongol presence in Nova Hesperia could not keep forever. In the Roman month of Julius, known locally as the Heat Moon, when the humidity had built to an almost unbearable degree and the mosquitoes were at their height and the *Concordia* got back from its latest trip up the Wemissori, the dam broke. It was as if the gigantic continent had suddenly become too small to contain all the warring nations within it.

Two new waterwheels had been installed in Cahokia Creek in the springtime. On hearing of the project over dinner one evening, Decinius Sabinus had offered to lend the city some Roman carpenters and engineers to speed the work along—an efficient flour milling operation was in everyone's interest—but Tahtay and Marcellinus had declined out of pride. The millstones and runner stones, the wooden gearing, and the millhouses that kept the enterprise safe from storms were entirely products of Cahokian craftsmanship, as overseen by Marcellinus, and they were inordinately proud of them.

Marcellinus's brickworks and steelworks had been largely staffed by men and boys. Likewise, when he had refurbished the *Concordia* in the Longhouse of the Ship his craftsmen had been predominantly male. The mills were a very different matter. In Cahokia, women ground the corn, women had very strong opinions about how the flour mills should work, and once the mills were operational, they were run entirely by women and girls.

So it was that when the *Concordia* returned, Marcellinus was helping to fine-tune the third and largest waterwheel with several dozen Cahokian women, with not a single other man in sight. It had to be said that he was enjoying the change of pace and picking up some interesting Cahokian vocabulary to boot, as the women were unblushingly specific on many topics Marcellinus previously had given little thought to. Nahimana was there, hobbling in some pain from her hip but nonetheless bossing the other women around with a proficiency and profanity that any centurion would envy.

Even Kangee was on the team, in a brief truce with Marcellinus that might not extend as far as a smile but at least allowed a measure of neutral conversation. And it was Kangee who first looked up and said, "Big canoe."

Marcellinus wiped the sweat from his face. Sure enough, the *Concordia* was nosing its way up the creek, with Akecheta at the helm and eight rather fierce-looking Blackfoot warriors standing at the prow, staring out with expressions of almost religious awe.

Marcellinus turned to try to see it through their eyes. After all these years he had grown so used to Cahokia's Great Mound that he had stopped seeing it for what it was: a monumental earthwork, an incredible engineering feat. A hundred feet tall, a thousand feet across at the base, it contained millions of cubic feet of earth and must have taken countless years of dedicated effort to construct. The three giant launch rails that ran parallel up its northern slope also might inspire awe. For that matter, the Longhouse of the Thunderbirds at the foot of the mound and the Longhouse of the Wings at its crown were probably the largest buildings the Blackfoot had ever seen. And beyond all that was the steelworks, puffing gouts of heavy smoke into the skies that drifted away over the bluffs. It was a shame the Raven clan and its Roman apprentices did not also have a Sky Lantern or two floating above the scene to complete the effect.

As the *Concordia* pulled in at the Longhouse of the Ship, Napayshni stepped out with the rope to moor the drekar. He still limped from the wound he had received fighting the Panther clan of the Shappa Ta'atani years before. The rowers shipped their oars and stood to stretch their weary arms and shoulders.

A lone brave was racing down the rearward slope of the Great Mound. From his fleetness of foot and his red sash, Marcellinus knew it was Tahtay. As soon as they caught sight of him, the Blackfoot warriors whooped and vaulted out of the longship to sprint toward him. They moved astonishingly fast despite the cloying humidity of high summer.

Now Marcellinus could see two Blackfoot elders sitting more sedately in the stern, and alongside them the stooped figure of the headman of the Hidatsa, the chieftain who two years earlier had permitted them to go on the Plains buffalo hunt that had led them to Tahtay. The headman's price for this assistance had been to see the Great City before he died, and Cahokia paid its debts. Beside him stood Sooleawa, the buffalo caller of the Hidatsa, in her elk-skin dress and hair band of buffalo hide, her loose black hair blowing freely in the Hidatsa style.

Now they stepped ashore, moving their heads back and forth almost comically. They resembled nothing so much as Roman farmers from the sticks stepping into the marbled Forum for the first time.

Tahtay and the Blackfoot warriors met halfway between the foot of the mound and Cahokia Creek, and an involuntary dance of glee broke out. Marcellinus smiled. Tahtay had grown so serious since the Romans had arrived. Even with Taianita and Dustu often by his side, he had so few friends that it was a joy to see him with his Fire Heart brothers.

However, when Tahtay summoned Marcellinus just after the evening meal, his face was stony enough to grind corn. Marcellinus walked into the war chief's house on the flat top of the Mound of the Sun to find Tahtay sitting with Enopay, Taianita, Dustu, and the Blackfoot warriors and elders around a mess of bowls of corn, fish bones, hazelnut cakes, and tea. The Blackfoot warriors studied Marcellinus intently, their elders ignored him, Taianita lolled back frowning, and Enopay wouldn't meet his eye at all.

Marcellinus was wearing a Cahokian tunic. Tahtay shook his head. "Dress in your Roman clothes. We go to Hadrianus."

"Now, Tahtay? Why?"

Tahtay stared at him with dead eyes. "There is trouble in the west. Fetch your Roman tunic and cloak and come back."

Marcellinus drew himself up and saluted. "Yes, sir."

Something was very wrong. The Blackfoot had brought news, and it was not good.

Romans ate later in the evening than Cahokians did, and the Imperator and Praetors dined even later than their men, and so Marcellinus and the others arrived at the Praetorium building of the Third Parthica to find Hadrianus still at table. Tahtay requested entry courteously enough, his face now more sad than angry.

They were just three: Tahtay, Taianita, and Marcellinus. A fourth, a Blackfoot friend of Tahtay's, had helped paddle the canoe the half mile across the Mizipi, but he had stayed with the boat. None of the Hesperians had spoken to Marcellinus during the journey, and he felt very much at a disadvantage as they were ushered into the Imperial presence by a Praetorian in full armor. He was surprised that Tahtay had brought only Taianita and discomfited that the war chief had not included Sintikala, Chenoa, or Kanuna, Cahokians with far more gravitas.

Hadrianus looked just as surprised to see them. Decinius Sabinus was there, along with two tribunes Marcellinus did not know. He breathed a quiet sigh of relief that Agrippa apparently was dining in his own castra. Whatever was going on, it would surely be easier to resolve without the Praetor of the 27th in attendance.

"Tahtay and Taianita, welcome," said the Imperator. "An unexpected pleasure. And Gaius Marcellinus."

"Caesar." Marcellinus bowed.

Decinius Sabinus got to his feet and bowed to Taianita, who smiled back at him. Marcellinus blinked. Both men knew her?

Hadrianus waved at the table behind him. "You will take wine?"

"I will," Tahtay said to Marcellinus's surprise, and moved to the table to pour. Equally unexpectedly, Taianita strolled over to the Imperator's couch and perched on the end of it. Neither Hadrianus, Sabinus, nor his two tribunes reacted to this overfamiliarity, and with a moment of shock Marcellinus realized that Tahtay and Taianita were now more frequent visitors to the Imperator's table than he might have supposed.

Tahtay brought wine and water to Marcellinus, handed a beaker to Taianita, then turned to the Imperator. "And so, Hadrianus, my friend, once again you have lied to me."

The Imperator's face was slightly red. It was not the drink but the blazing Hesperian sun of high summer. His sunburn and quizzical smile made him look a little comical. "Never before have I met a man who owned as little trust as you, Tahtay of Cahokia."

Tahtay gave a short sharp laugh. "Trust? You say so? Futete!"

"Certainly." Hadrianus raised his cup in toast. "As best I recall, I have not broken a promise to you this entire moon."

"Huh." Tahtay sipped his wine and for a moment seemed lost in thought. Then he nodded and spoke. "I am much saddened, Caesar. Truly, my heart grieves. Despite all the pain and violence between our peoples, over recent months I had begun to have hope. I had thought perhaps we were finally coming to an understanding, you and I. That this might not all end in bloodshed and ruin between your Romans and my people. But that is not so, is it?"

Sabinus looked wary. Hadrianus's smile faded. "Tahtay, you will need to stop speaking in riddles if you expect me to answer."

"There are many more Romans than you have told us of," Tahtay said. "Many, many more. You have tried to delude me into believing your army will one day march away into the Grass, but they have shown few signs of doing so. And today I know why. It is because other Roman legions have already arrived, far to the west past the Great Mountains. They have slain thousands upon thousands of Hesperians and enslaved the rest. The rivers are running with blood, Caesar. The land itself is weeping."

Tahtay stood upright, his face calm and his body controlled, but Marcellinus knew he must be surging with strong emotions to be using such words.

Hadrianus and his Praetor and tribunes sat so still that they might have been carved in stone. Tahtay nodded. "From your eyes I see that I am right."

Now the Imperator leaned forward, his expression intent. "Where are they, these new armies you speak of? How do you know of them?"

"I am a *savage*," Tahtay said brutally. "I am a *barbarian*. I am a *redskin*. So you call me, and perhaps I am. But I am not a fool, Caesar. Far from it. I can see that you have long known of this, and that confirmation is all I needed." He drained his beaker and tossed it aside, and it clattered across the floor. "I must go and summon the clan chiefs and elders and decide what must be done. Because if Roma has already taken the west, you have lied to me from the very start. You have no need to leave Cahokia. Ever. And that, Cahokia cannot tolerate."

"Wait, Tahtay." Hadrianus swung his legs off the couch. "I beg of you: tell me what you know. I am in earnest. Please answer me."

Tahtay's brow furrowed. He said nothing.

"You may tell him, Gaius Marcellinus."

Marcellinus looked carefully at his Imperator. "You release me from the oath I swore to you before Roma and Cahokia buried the ax?"

"Yes, yes, Marcellinus; you may speak candidly to Tahtay about the threat we face. Perhaps he will believe it more readily from you."

Still Marcellinus hesitated. "We should call a council of the elders. All should—"

Tahtay spun and fixed him with a glare. "*Merda*, Hotah! Tell me *now*!"

"They are not Romans," Marcellinus said. "The armies that have landed on Hesperia's western shores are Roma's implacable enemy, and will soon become enemies of Cahokia as they sweep across the land, destroying all in their path."

Tahtay eyed him unblinking. Marcellinus went on. "They are called Mongols, and they are utterly ruthless. They come from a continent we call Asia, far across the ocean to the west. In Asia the Mongols have already defeated many nations—great kingdoms, territories of mighty chiefs, in all as broad in extent as the land from the Mizipi to the Atlanticus."

Decinius Sabinus nodded, but everyone else in the room still stood or sat as if frozen. Marcellinus continued. "Caesar and his armies have fought long wars with the Mongols in Asia, trying to hold their forces in check and prevent them from sweeping over Europa and sacking its cities. Tahtay, I swear the truth of this to you. The Mongols are great warriors. They fight on horses, the same four-legs the Romans use. Their war chief, Chinggis Khan, is here to command his armies in person, just as Caesar commands the armies of Roma. And if the Mongols have already taken the whole western coast of Hesperia, and if the Blackfoot know of them now, it cannot be long before they break out beyond the Great Mountains and come flooding across the prairie to attack us here."

"*Merda . . .*" Taianita frowned, shook her head, and gestured to Marcellinus: *Speak true?*

Marcellinus held her gaze and hand-talked back: *I speak true. Wanageeska swears.*

Tahtay's eyes were wide. "Hotah, you, too, have fought these Mongols?"

"No." Marcellinus had faced the armies of Kara Khitai, steppe warriors of a similar vein to the Mongols, and he had partnered with the Chernye Klobuki and Polovtsians of southern Rus. He was familiar with the horsemen of Asia but had never seen the armies of the Great Khan in battle. "But about the Mongols you may believe these men of Roma and what they say."

"Asia is a *huge* land," Decinius Sabinus said. "Marcellinus may be too cautious on this score. The sum of the Mongol homelands, added to their conquests of the Jin and Song Empires, may well be larger in extent than *all* of Nova Hesperia. And when the Mongols swept over the Asian lands before we beat them back, they must have slain twenty million people. That is twenty thousand-thousand." He looked at Hadrianus. "More, you think?"

The Imperator shrugged. "Who's to say? Millions upon millions of the Song alone."

"Why? Why?" Tahtay shook his head. "It makes no sense. What would such men want? We do not know them. Why would they attack us?"

"Because that is what the Mongols do, Tahtay. They conquer."

"It is true." Marcellinus nodded. "War chief, we must hold a council. The Imperator and his Praetors, and myself, and you and your elders and clan chiefs. We must prepare for the Mongols. All of us together, as one."

Tahtay looked at Hadrianus, then at Sabinus. Marcellinus hoped that the war chief wasn't entering one of his funks. Again Marcellinus wished Kimimcla were there; she could push him out of such states with a well-chosen word, often an insult. But Kimimela was across the river in Cahokia, and Taianita appeared lost in thought.

Now she raised her head. "Caesar. Speak. If this true, why you not tell us from very start?"

Hadrianus gestured to Marcellinus, who said, "The Imperator and his Praetors believed it would weaken their negotiating position with you and . . . complicate matters."

"*All* my Praetors," Hadrianus said. "As I recall, Gaius Marcellinus, you were in full agreement."

Taianita turned to stare at Marcellinus.

"It's true," Marcellinus said. "I agreed, and at the Imperator's bidding I swore an oath not to tell Cahokia of the Mongols. An oath he has now relieved me of."

Tahtay was gazing past Marcellinus at the wall behind him, but the look of scorn on Taianita's face cut Marcellinus like a pugio blade.

"Worse than you?" Tahtay said at last. "The Mongols are worse than Romans? Worse than the Iroqua at their most terrible? Is that even possible?"

Sabinus smiled tightly. "Oh, yes, war chief. Did we not make peace with you, for all our flaws? Are we not talking now? The Mongols would make no such peace. The Mongols do not negotiate. They ride to war on their four-legs in the tens of thousands and cut down everyone in their path. If the Mongols had come to Cahokia in our place, they would have slaughtered or enslaved every person in your city. There would have been no discussion, no embassies or parleys or last-minute treaty mongering. I have seen them with my own eyes, and I give you my word: the Mongol Khan and his Horde are the most vicious and ruthless enemy I have ever faced."

"Roma is kindness itself by comparison," Hadrianus said sardonically.

"Huh." Finally, Tahtay met the Imperator's eye. After a long moment, he turned to Marcellinus. "These are all true words, Wanageeska? On your honor, on your oath?"

"Yes," Marcellinus said. "I swear by all the people I love, all—"

"You would swear on your daughter's life?"

Again the room went very quiet. The Imperator raised his eyebrows. Sabinus looked back and forth between Marcellinus and Tahtay. Taianita, her eyes large, now looked at the floor.

Marcellinus tried to keep his expression neutral. "Yes, I so swear."

Tahtay studied him intently, then nodded.

Hadrianus rose and went to fetch the pitcher of wine himself. "And now, Tahtay, please tell me more of what you have heard from the western reaches of Nova Hesperia."

"Death," Tahtay said. "Cruel men in armor who ride horses and trample the people. They have killed countless Hesperians, laid waste to entire villages and towns, slain whole tribes. Others they have chained and forced to mine gold from the rivers and mountains."

Sabinus nodded. "Merciless. Just as I said."

"In what numbers? How many Mongols and where?"

Tahtay shrugged. "Was Enopay there to count? No. We do not know how many. More than enough to smash the tribes all up and down the western seacoast. They are *everywhere*, Caesar. They are in the north, where the winters are cold and the peoples carve and paint tall poles in bright colors. They are in the south, where it is always warm and the people fish and eat clams and live in plenty. I knew little of these peoples until they were destroyed, but now a number have fled across the mountains. They came up a river and over the mountains and down the other side into the valley where the Wemissori begins, and there they met the Shoshoni."

"Shoshoni?" said Sabinus.

Tahtay grinned tautly. "The Shoshoni are the enemies of my other people, the Blackfoot. And then these Mongols pursued the western peoples over the mountains and fought a battle with the Shoshoni, who broke and came to the Blackfoot. They brought one thing, and you will want to see that thing, I think. Send word to the

Blackfoot who waits at our canoe, and he will bring it here to you."

The Imperator pointed at one of his Praetorians. "Make all haste to the Mizipi bank and bring the Blackfoot who waits at the canoe."

"And show him all due respect," Marcellinus added.

The Praetorian saluted and hurried from the room with a jangle of steel armor.

The Blackfoot unwrapped the bundle he had brought into the Imperial presence. Under the fabric was a long, slim tube of iron. Taianita frowned at it. "Is what?"

Tahtay was watching their eyes. "You have seen this before."

As no one else seemed inclined to say anything, Marcellinus took the tube. He put his nose to the end and sniffed. "Yes, this is just like mine."

"*Yours?*" said Tahtay.

"I did not make it. It is Mongol. I found it at the Market of the Mud."

"What does it do, Wanageeska?" Taianita asked.

"It shoots fire," Sabinus said. He pointed to one end. "Here sits a package of Jin salt, a black powder somewhat like your liquid flame. When ignited, it sends fire through the tube, blazing hot, and so it is known as a fire lance." He studied the tube professionally. "This one has a very smooth bore. Well engineered."

"The Mongols are coming," Hadrianus said, eyes flashing. "And when they do, they will bring many of these."

Taianita regarded him. "You are excited? War and death excite you?"

"Yes," said the Imperator. "After all this time? Yes. After all the planning and journeying and endless logistics of legionary travel, war with a worthy foe is at hand. For my money, it cannot come soon enough." He rubbed his hands together. "Well, then. Gentlemen, Taianita? I believe we must talk strategy."

"If so . . ." Tahtay took a deep breath and boldly met

the Imperator's eye. "If so, Caesar, we must know all you know of Mongols. And there must be no more tricks. No more lies. You must swear that now, to my eyes. You understand?"

The room was silent. The Praetorians dropped their hands to their sword hilts as Tahtay approached the Imperator. Sabinus looked concerned.

Marcellinus forced himself to breathe. This was a dangerous moment. One did not simply confront an Imperator and demand honesty.

Yet of all who stood in the Praetorium, Hadrianus seemed the least perturbed. "Must I cut my flesh, Tahtay of Cahokia? Would you believe me then?" Without waiting for an answer, he gestured. The nearest Praetorian drew his pugio and handed it to his Imperator, hilt first. With no hesitation, the most powerful man in the world raised his left arm, allowing the sleeve to drop away and leave his skin bare.

His eyes met Tahtay's. "And then, will you be as free with the truth as I and do all in your power to bring the Hesperian tribes to fight alongside Roma against these demons? Will you ally with me against them? If so, I will willingly swear an oath in blood, and share my blade with you."

Tahtay looked at Marcellinus, and a moment later so did Taianita.

Marcellinus swallowed, his mouth suddenly dry. Now this had become his responsibility?

But of course it had to be.

Hadrianus was about as trustworthy as any Imperator. Blunt, ruthless, and perfectly capable of manipulating the situation to his advantage.

And although Marcellinus liked and admired Tahtay, the war chief had lied to him just as much as Hadrianus had.

But war with the Mongol Khan had made strange bedfellows in Asia and would do so here as well. Marcellinus no longer had any doubts where the true enemy lay in Nova Hesperia: it lay to their west, in Chinggis's ruthless army. All the differences between Cahokia and Roma were as nothing compared with the atrocities committed by Chinggis and his men. They had left a trail of death, tens of millions of corpses, behind them in Asia. Such a thing must not be allowed to happen in Nova Hesperia.

From personal experience, Marcellinus also knew that an oath sworn in blood weighed upon a man's soul like no other.

"You should swear," he said. "Tahtay, Caesar, both of you. In good faith and in blood. And I will swear to help you both."

"I should not ask the other chiefs?" Tahtay asked Taianita in Cahokian.

Taianita looked again at Marcellinus and read his eyes. To Tahtay she said: "No, Fire Heart. The Wanageeska has spoken. We must do what is right, and we must do it now."

Nodding, Tahtay stepped forward and accepted the pugio from the Imperator.

The blade cut deep. Roman and Cahokian blood flowed once more and mingled.

CHAPTER 4

YEAR EIGHT, HEAT MOON

Despite Tahtay's promise when he had taken over as war chief of Cahokia, he had not completely done away with the Longhouse of the Sun on the top plateau of the Great Mound of Cahokia. He had dismantled it and left it in pieces for the rest of the year, but in the winter that followed he had rebuilt a much smaller version on the first plateau.

The new longhouse had no sheets of burnished copper to make it shine by day and no perpetual flame to light it at night, and Tahtay did not live there as his father had. The new longhouse was less than half the size of the Longhouse of the Wings at the Great Mound's crest and was used solely for meetings of the elders and clan chiefs.

And it was this new Longhouse of the Sun that they stood in today, as the Imperator and Praetors of Roma and the paramount chief of Cahokia held their council of war.

It was the first time Hadrianus had been invited there. The Great Mound was sacred space, and the Romans had not brought weapons or armor. To get there the Imperator had ridden through the streets of Cahokia with Marcellinus and Tahtay on one side and Sabinus and Agrippa on the other. Hadrianus wore a white linen tunic with a pair of vertical purple stripes leading from his shoulders to its lower hem, and over this a fine sagum cloak despite the heat. Sabinus and Marcellinus wore simple Roman tunics and sandals. Sintikala wore a leather flying tunic and a band in her hair decorated with hawk feathers, with her leather falcon mask hooked over her belt. Tahtay, in a buckskin tunic and his red sash of the Fire Hearts, was the best-dressed person in the meeting.

This was not, after all, a full council of the ranking Cahokians. The elders were prone to ramble, and the clan chiefs would need a great deal of background information before they could fully comprehend the topic of conversation. Today's council of war would include only Cahokians who were used to the Romans and were now at least partway knowledgeable about the crisis that faced them: Tahtay, Sintikala, Kanuna, Matoshka, Chenoa, Akecheta, and Mahkah. And Taianita, Kimimela, and Enopay, who were supposedly present only to help translate. On the Roman side, in addition to Sabinus and Agrippa, the Imperator had brought the First Tribune of the 27th, Mettius Fronto. Marcellinus had met Fronto infrequently but was impressed by his resolve; to Marcellinus's eye, Fronto's calmness and experience served as a useful counterweight to Agrippa's impetuosity. Finally, there was Aelfric, included by virtue of his familiarity with both Roma and Cahokia.

Now Sintikala walked to the front of the room, a long roll of deerskin in her arms. A rough easel stood there, Roman-made. She raised the deerskin, attached it carefully to the top of the easel, and released it. As it unrolled, even the Imperator gasped.

"Gods," Sabinus said quietly, and glanced reproachfully at Marcellinus as if accusing him of keeping secrets.

All stood spellbound. Made of deerskin cured and scraped thin and etched with tattooing ink, Sintikala's map showed the broad swath of Hesperia from the eastern coasts to the great mountain chain in the west and from north of the Wemissori clear down to the gulf of the Mare Solis. Shappa Ta'atan, Etowah, and other large Mizipian towns were marked, as were the lakes of the Iroqua and—added since Marcellinus had last seen it—the paths of several rivers that led into the Mizipi. Indicated with the crude sketch of a birdman were various mountains and ridges Sintikala could use to land her Hawk and take off again.

Sintikala stepped aside and said nothing. Her knowledge of Latin was growing day by day, but it was not sufficient for an occasion like this. She stood mute, regarding the Romans assembled before her.

Even without speaking, her presence dominated the room. Sintikala was slender and shorter than most of the men present, but muscular and fit. Everyone there, Roman and Cahokian, well knew her prowess in the air and her competence in commanding her clan. Her face was severe but was made striking by her high cheekbones and clear brown eyes. She was fiercely attractive, but daunting. During these moments as she gazed around the longhouse, even the Imperator said nothing.

Reluctantly, Kimimela stood and went to her mother's side. "Here is Hesperia," she said in fluent Latin. "Here, the bay of the Powhatani that you call Mare Chesapica. Up here, the Great Lakes of the Iroqua, Huron, and Ojibwa peoples. Cahokia is here, and this is the Great River of the Mizipi, leading down to the Market of the Mud. Here is Ocatan; here, Shappa Ta'atan."

Kimimela glanced at her mother, whose expression was guarded. Marcellinus knew Sintikala had mixed feelings about sharing her precious map with Roma. But Tahtay had insisted, and Tahtay was the only person who could command Sintikala to do anything.

"Here is the Wemissori River," Kimimela continued. "Hereabouts, this area, is where the Blackfoot roam and hunt the buffalo. This area and below is all grass. Until the line of the Great Mountains here in the west."

Tahtay stepped forward. "As best the Hawk chief or any of the rest of us know, the mountains run all the way south. Which is good, because they must have held back the Mongols until now. Without the barrier of the mountains, your Mongols might have been here already."

Sabinus nodded. "That matches the intelligence—the news—our scouts have brought us. The mountains are only four or five weeks distant, on horseback and riding at a fast scout's pace. We have come across Mongol outriders on the eastern slopes, but they are few. Chinggis's challenge will be to find a mountain pass clear enough to bring across several tumens of cavalry, and perhaps trebuchets and carts of weaponry besides."

"Trebuchets are throwing engines," Marcellinus explained. "Lighter than our onagers. They cast smaller missiles but are deadly for all that. The Mongols can strike quickly on horses, but for a long trek like this they will bring a baggage train with carts. Their armies must travel much more slowly than their scouts."

"Tell me about the people who live here." Hadrianus pointed to the bottom left of Sintikala's map. Here there were no markings at all; Sintikala could not fly that far.

"The People of the Hand," Marcellinus said. He held up his right hand with the fingers splayed. "So named because of the marks they etch on the rocks." He looked at Kanuna and the others to see if anyone else wanted to speak, but apparently he was on his own. "I have heard stories of cruelty about them from Son of the Sun of Shappa Ta'atan, although his words may not be reliable. In the past, his people were at war with the People of the Hand."

"Why?"

Marcellinus did not know, and neither did Kanuna or any of the other Cahokians. Tahtay leaned forward. "Why do they interest you, Caesar?"

The Imperator smiled tightly. "Were I the Mongol Khan, faced with a line of treacherous mountains, it might occur to me to travel around them rather than across them."

"We do not know how far they extend."

"They end well short of the coast, according to the

scouts of Calidius Verus," said Sabinus. "And also . . ." He waited, looking at Hadrianus for approval.

"Yes, yes, tell them."

"From the Market, we are hearing intelligence that the People of the Sun, those other peoples from south of the Mare Solis, have thrown in their lot with the Mongols. They have moved from being foes of Roma to being allies of Roma's enemies."

This was a tough linguistic nut for most of the Cahokians to crack, and there was a pause while Marcellinus and Enopay clarified. Sabinus waited patiently and then added, "If the Mongols were also able to recruit the People of the Hand, we would face a broad coalition from the west, southwest, and south. Thus, the Imperator needs to know whether the People of the Hand may be valuable allies, fearsome opponents, or merely irrelevant to the overall venture."

Several Cahokians looked irritated. Sabinus was not a man who used language simply. This time Marcellinus left it to Enopay to translate.

"The Mongols *do* make treaties, then," Taianita said suddenly, and everyone turned to look at her. "Today you speak of a Mongol treaty with the People of the Sun. But before you have told us that Mongols do not negotiate."

Agrippa looked pained. "Nor do they. Mongols do not make treaties. They serve ultimatums: 'Fight alongside us or die.' The People of the Sun already hated Roma, thanks to the bumbling of Calidius Verus. And the Sunners are a bloody people, in love with the brutal sacrifice of living humans. They would take little persuasion to join against a mutual enemy."

Taianita looked obstinate. "And are the People of the Hand also your enemy?"

The Imperator shook his head, bemused. "That is exactly what I am attempting to find out, Taianita."

"Speak more," Tahtay said. "Tell us of the Mongols, and why Cahokians should consider them *our* enemy."

"I have fought the Mongols myself," Lucius Agrippa

said. "So let me try to be clearer about this. Your Wana-geeska, our rogue Praetor, went to address the Haude-nosaunee. From them he managed to wring out a truce, a cease-fire from the Mourning War that your tribes had been fighting for . . . a thousand moons." Marcellinus stifled a smile. Agrippa might not be well versed in Hes-perian methods of reckoning time, but at least he was making a valiant effort. "You, Tahtay, spoke with Cae-sar on the battlefield, and the two of you managed to reach an agreement that halted the bloody war between our peoples that would otherwise have occurred on that day."

Agrippa's face betrayed no indication that he himself had strongly advocated for that battle. He continued: "No such conversations could take place between Roma and the Mongol Khan or between your people and his. The Mongols accept only immediate surrender. When cities resist, everyone in them is slaughtered. If they sur-render without a fight, their lives may be spared as long as they serve the Mongols absolutely. The Mongols are merciless if their subject populations do not bend the knee."

"We are far from the Great Mountains," Tahtay ob-jected. "Farther still from the western shores. None in Cahokia have been so far, not even Sintikala of the Hawk clan. And never before have we had news from so far away. The distance itself—"

"The distance is no barrier," Agrippa said. "The Plains, the big grass: they are no barrier. Mongols con-duct campaigns over huge distances." Kimimela and Enopay started to translate again, and Agrippa simpli-fied. "In Asia, Mongols have made war across distances much greater than the length of the Mizipi River, much farther than from Cahokia to the Chesapica or from Cahokia to the Great Mountains. And your plains are perfect terrain for the Mongols, just like their home-lands. From the spring through the late summer there is plenty of grass for their four-legs. Even in winter, the Mongols fight. Frozen rivers provide smooth paths for their armies, and their four-legs can dig through the snow for the remaining grass beneath. Only the mud of early spring and late autumn can hold them."

Hadrianus nodded. "I am no shaman, but I will make a prediction for you, Tahtay, and your wise men and women of Cahokia. I predict that when the Mongols come, they will drive ahead of them Hesperians from the west, perhaps also captives from the People of the Grass, the prisoners of their wars. The Mongol Khan often allows ragged, damaged survivors to escape from their battles so that their tales will spread terror ahead of his army. Hopelessness. Despair. The myth—the story—that the Mongols are invincible, in the hope that the cities ahead of them will surrender without a fight. And that's not even the half of it. Deception, intimidation, cruelty, confusion. The Mongols are masters of them all."

Tahtay's eyes were narrowed. Marcellinus could guess why: the Romans themselves played a pretty good game in spreading despair ahead of their armies. The survivors of the Sixth Ferrata's storming of Ocatan had poured into Cahokia a few days after the battle. Marcellinus could only wish with his deepest heart that his brave young friend Hurit and his wise Raven clan chief Anapetu had lived to be among them.

"Why?" Sintikala asked, once Kimimela had caught up with the translation. It was the first word the Hawk chief had spoken since entering the Longhouse of the Sun.

"Why what?" Agrippa eyed her warily.

She switched to Cahokian, which Kimimela translated even as her mother spoke the words. " 'Why does the Mongol Khan do this? Why does he want more and more? How can he hold the lands he has taken if he keeps moving forward? What does he want?' "

"Wealth and power," said the Imperator. "The Mongols have learned to love war and the booty it brings. Wealth beyond the dreams of warriors of the steppe.

And so, to ensure the loyalty of his generals and his men, the Khan must continue to fight."

"Chinggis sits always on a knife edge." Sabinus spoke now. "He needs more war and more plunder, or his own people will take him out of his tent one night, break his back, and leave him for the buzzards."

The Imperator inclined his head. "And that aside, the Mongol Khan wishes to defeat *me*. For I have stood in his way all across central Asia, and prevented him from ravaging Europa as he did Asia, stealing riches that do not belong to him."

There was a long and acid pause while the translators caught up, and then Tahtay nodded. "And so it is your fault that the Mongol Khan is here. You brought this evil man to our land."

Sabinus shook his head. "Chinggis Khan came to Hesperia even before Caesar's later legions. Caesar sent his armies here to fight the Mongol Khan once they learned he was here."

Tahtay turned to Marcellinus. "But not before *your* legion came here."

"No." Marcellinus met Tahtay's eye. "My legion came first, the Mongol Khan's army afterward. In all likelihood the Khan decided to come to Nova Hesperia in response to the news that my legion had come here. But let us be clear. Chinggis Khan wants the world. Not just this land. The world."

"And so does the Imperator," said Tahtay.

Marcellinus paused, wondering if he was about to get into trouble, and then pressed on regardless. "Yes. So does the Imperator. This is a battle for the world, and the battle will be fought here."

Sabinus looked sharply at Marcellinus. Hadrianus and Agrippa stood calmly. Tahtay put his hand up to his head. Kimimela watched him, alert to his moods.

Into the silence came Enopay's young voice, cracking a little as he said, "Caesar, how many legions do the Mongols have?"

Hadrianus looked thoughtfully at Enopay, then nodded to Decinius Sabinus, who answered. "Mongols number their forces differently. By the Mongol numbering, one hundred warriors make up a jaghun. Ten jaghuns make a mingghan. Ten mingghans make a tumen. According to our spies in the faraway lands of Jin and Song, where the Khan's big canoes sailed from, the Mongols shipped over at least four tumens to Nova Hesperia."

"Forty thousand men and women," Enopay said in Cahokian, and whistled.

"Womans, no," Sabinus said in Cahokian. "Mongol war parties, like Roman war parties, only mans." In Latin he continued: "They will surely have brought others, men and women who are not warriors. Slaves to look after the horses. Chinggis Khan's son Chagatai is also here, and Chagatai's wife, Yesulun Khatun, travels with them. Mongol queens often serve as administrators—as paramount chiefs—while their husbands lead their armies in battle. We suspect that Yesulun will rule in western Nova Hesperia with at least one tumen of warriors while Chinggis Khan and Chagatai bring the rest of their armies to do battle with Roma."

Agrippa nodded. "Their whole army is mounted. Every warrior of the Khan owns many horses, between four and six. And so they can trade mounts, and if they leave their baggage trains behind them, they can ride as fast as the lightning that comes with the thunder."

"And you?" Enopay said. "The Roman army, how many warriors in all?"

Sabinus looked at the Imperator.

"Oh, come on," Enopay said. "Always you are so careful. Why? When you want our help? I could guess many numbers, but let us hear them from you, our trusted allies."

Kanuna shook his head, left far behind. "Enopay?"

Enopay held up his hand and in Cahokian said: "I will translate in a moment. Let me hear the Roman chief's answer."

If Sabinus was startled that a boy of maybe twelve

winters had taken control of a high-level council of war, he did not show it. "We have two legions here, each of about forty-eight hundred legionaries plus about five hundred specialized cavalry. Add to that four alae, specialized cavalry wings containing, in our case, seven hundred and sixty-eight troopers apiece. And four cohortes equitatae, combined infantry and cavalry, each with six centuries of troops and four turmae of horsemen."

Enopay stared at him. "And so, some sixteen thousand men, close to five thousand of whom are mounted. Plus, of course, all the soldiers and marines of the Sixth Ferrata, whom you did not include in your reckoning."

A silence fell in the room. The Cahokians glanced from face to face, trying to understand what had just happened. Decinius Sabinus smiled and nodded in honest admiration. Lucius Agrippa looked peevishly at Marcellinus as if Enopay's perspicacity were all Marcellinus's fault. Then Hadrianus opened his mouth to speak but was interrupted by Tahtay, who stepped right to the heart of the matter. "Caesar, you are outnumbered. Can you defeat the Mongols?"

"Yes, Tahtay," the Imperator said. "With your help and the help of Cahokia, with its wings and liquid flame: with those, I believe we can destroy the Mongol Khan once and for all, and send him to hell. And then your land will forever be safe from them."

"And will it then also be safe from *you*?" Taianita asked.

Everyone stared at her in disbelief. Enopay winced. Tahtay did not react at all, did not so much as glance Taianita's way, but from the tightening around his eyes Marcellinus knew he was not pleased with the directness of her question.

"Oh, I'm sure we will come to a suitable agreement," the Imperator said. "After all, we are already friends and blood brothers. Personally, I will want to get back home to Europa just as soon as possible. But not while the Mongol Khan threatens Nova Hesperia. Right now he is my first concern, and he should be yours as well."

"Praetor, a word."

Just about to head down the cedar steps to the Great Plaza, Marcellinus looked around. "Decinius Sabinus?"

The two men walked along the mound edge, farther from listening ears. Sabinus glanced around casually. "Listen, Gaius. If we're drawing your people into this conflagration, it's important that you realize what we're dealing with."

Sabinus's tone held a trace of condescension. Marcellinus bristled a little. "I may not have battled the Khan myself, but it is clear enough what we face."

"Is it? Very well. But let me remind you anyway. Chinggis Khan began as a common herdsman and made himself the warlord and effective ruler of his entire country before he was thirty years of age. And then he conquered the Jin and the Song. The Song alone number perhaps sixty million people. The Song had ships and engineers and extensive military skills of their own, and now the Mongols own those, too.

"Gaius, the Mongols only *saw* the ocean for the first time in 1213 A.D. Now they've crossed the Jin Seas and the great ocean beyond it and are ready to fight us on a whole new continent. They're expert at campaigning on a variety of terrains: grass, desert, farmland, jungles, and now rivers and seas. We underestimate the Mongols at our peril."

Marcellinus shrugged. "They had substantial assistance. As you just said, the Song already knew the oceans."

"Yes, the Mongols learn from the peoples they conquer. No doubt they have brought with them a substantial number of engineers from the Jin and Song. They began as a primitive people, but they now have the Jin salt and the best armaments of a civilization that predates even Roma. They have throwing engines, thunder crash bombs, fire lances. They learn *fast*, the Mongols.

Much faster than Roma, which tends to be . . . staid. Set in its ways."

"Roma knows what works." Marcellinus studied Sabinus more closely. "Quintus, you do not think we can win."

Sabinus checked around them again for eavesdroppers. "Just between you and me? A private conversation between friends?"

All of a sudden Marcellinus's mouth was dry. Of all the Romans he had met in Nova Hesperia, he respected Sabinus the most. "A private conversation, my word on it. Let us be candid."

Sabinus nodded. "Candidly, then: no, I fear we may not prevail. It has been a tough call in Asia these past ten years . . ."

Now Sabinus met his eye. "I have faced the armies of the Mongol Khan, and they are utterly ruthless. In that briefing we pulled our punches so as not to terrify your Cahokian friends and rob them of what courage they have. But I have seen the aftermath of Mongol massacres of entire cities, the bones of the dead piled up in greasy mounds. I've seen the ragged, half-human remains of their slaves, driven ahead of them into battle as human shields. I would scarcely believe such atrocities if I had not seen them with my own eyes."

"Holy Jove," Marcellinus said.

The Praetor of the Third took a deep breath. "Agrippa may rant and rave and call your Cahokian friends barbarians, but you and I know better. We Romans, we are a people with principles, we are an Imperium of honor . . . but Gaius, your Hesperians are babes in the garden, innocents in the Eden of the Christ-Risen. They have no idea of the horror that faces them across the Grass. This will be a war unlike anything they have ever seen or could imagine. I fear for them. I fear for us all."

Marcellinus's face was hot. "Hesperia may yet surprise you, Decinius Sabinus."

Sabinus half smiled. "I hope so. We will need all the surprises we can get."

Marcellinus straightened. "Trust them, Quintus. Trust the Hesperians. We are in their land, and they know it better than we. They are smart and inventive, and although they are no Mongols, they surely have a ruthlessness that is all their own. Roma has legionary muscle, but the Hesperians have the understanding without which we will perish."

Sabinus studied him. "Understanding? Much good may *understanding* do us . . . Gaius, I will support you where I can, but I must be honest: sometimes I have no idea whether you are a sage or a babbling lunatic."

"Neither do I, Decinius Sabinus," Marcellinus said. "Neither do I."

Sabinus left him then, hurrying down the steps of the Master Mound to catch up with the Roman contingent, which awaited him by their horses outside the palisade gate.

Marcellinus stood alone and watched them ride out to the west, his thoughts grim. If Sabinus, the man who commanded arguably the most proficient and deadly of the Imperator's three experienced and battle-hardened legions—if Sabinus was already half beaten, it did not bode well for the coming war.

As Marcellinus stepped down into his hut, a shadowy form got to his feet from where he had been sitting at the end of Marcellinus's bed.

Startled within the confined space of the hut, Marcellinus could barely resist punching the man. "Merda, Norseman . . . One day I am going to cut your head off first and recognize your face only afterward."

Even if Marcellinus had not seen the Norseman, he certainly would have smelled him. It was clear that Isleifur Bjarnason had not seen a bath, or even a stream, for many days.

"Probably," said Isleifur Bjarnason. "But listen, Praetor, for I bring grave news. The Mongols of the Great Khan are *here*, in Nova Hesperia. The Mongols! And with five horses for every warrior . . . They have conquered the lands west of the Great Mountains, and even now their scouts swarm the mountaintops like goats looking for an easy pass to bring their armies through—"

Isleifur stopped abruptly and peered at Marcellinus. "You already knew?"

Marcellinus had not seen Isleifur Bjarnason for over a year; the Norseman had melted away into the woods long before the confrontation between Cahokia and the Third and 27th on the banks of the Oyo and had not been heard of since. Apparently he had traveled far and wide in the meantime.

Marcellinus smiled without humor. "For once, Norseman, your intelligence has arrived too late."

CHAPTER 5

YEAR EIGHT, THUNDER MOON

"Ah, Gaius Marcellinus, run to ground at last."

Enopay's mouth dropped open as the Imperator Hadrianus stepped down into Marcellinus's hut. On this day Hadrianus wore full uniform and armor, with his helmet tucked under his arm. His Imperial presence filled the room and stole all the air.

"Caesar." Belatedly Marcellinus rose to his feet and saluted. "I . . . did not expect—"

"Well, of course you didn't." Hadrianus surveyed his rude surroundings with some disdain: the low bed, and the bench and table where Marcellinus to this day schooled young Cahokians in reading and writing. His eyes lingered on the golden lares sitting on Marcellinus's small shrine to his household gods. He inspected the hearth, peered up through the crude chimney hole at the skies beyond. "And these are the barbarian accommodations that you favor over the barracks of the Third Parthica?"

"Yes, Caesar."

"Well, well. And have you given much thought to your future, I wonder?"

"My future, Caesar?"

Hadrianus looked at Enopay, who stammered, "I . . . I should leave, Caesar?"

"Stay, stay." The Imperator gestured at the pot of

goldenrod tea sitting over the embers of the fire. "If I may?"

"Of course, Caesar . . . Enopay, find the Imperator a cup."

The master of the world now investigated the bench with care, perhaps looking for splinters, and then sat. "So, your future, Gaius Marcellinus?"

"I sometimes believe I have an excess of good fortune in merely surviving to see each new dawn," Marcellinus said cautiously.

"Indeed you do. Until now, you have been useful enough to be kept alive. What use do you plan to be to me going forward?"

Marcellinus shook his head, baffled. "I will help complete the Line of Hadrianus. I will work with Tahtay and the Cahokian auxiliaries to prepare them for the coming war. And I will do my best to prevent Agrippa from upending our treaty with Cahokia into a bloody disaster."

"Such small ambitions." The Imperator looked at Enopay, who was still fumbling to find a clean beaker. "What do you think, boy? What sensible use can I make of this renegade?"

Enopay's eyes were wide, and his face flushed. "Already the Wanageeska has brought you great allies. He has prevented war between your people and ours, made sure your legións are fed. The First Cahokian—"

Hadrianus shrugged negligently. "I suppose he has brought me one nation. But I have it in mind that he should bring me another."

"Holy Jove," Marcellinus said. "Caesar, no, I beg of you. I must stay here."

Hadrianus smiled thinly. "You have not even heard my proposal."

"He does not need to." At last Enopay handed a beaker of tea to the Imperator. "We were both there yesterday, when you were looking at the map of Hesperia. You plan to send Gaius Marcellinus to the southwest in an attempt to ally with the People of the Hand."

Hadrianus took a sip. "Who better?"

Marcellinus opened his mouth and closed it again.

"I do hope you were not about to suggest Calidius Verus, even in jest. Since it seems he has antagonized the Yokot'an Maya, it would be naive to expect him to do any better with the People of the Hand. And it seems we know little of the Hand and what we might expect from them. The task requires a commander of some subtlety, along with an abundance of local knowledge. You would disagree?"

"No," Marcellinus said. "But I do not know all your tribunes, nor do I know which could be spared from their other duties—"

"None of them," the Imperator said.

Marcellinus snapped his fingers as an inspiration struck. "Centurion Manius Ifer of the Sixth Ferrata. He has been in country for years and seems to have gained extensive experience at leading mixed Roman and Hesperian expeditionary units—"

Hadrianus was already shaking his head. "You studied the map as carefully as I, Gaius Marcellinus. We are as close to the People of the Hand here as they are at the Market of the Mud. There is even a redskin trail that goes there, across the Plains and along a river. Long, undoubtedly tedious, but straightforward enough. Easy country and fresh water until you get to the Great Mountains, and then you follow them down."

"But that must be a thousand miles," Marcellinus objected.

Enopay was considering it. "Over a thousand either way. But to send an expedition of the Sixth, we would first need to send word two months down the Mizipi to their fortress on the gulf coast beyond the Market of the Mud. Then Verus's men would have to travel around the bay and up, through the full heat of the desert . . ." He trailed off at Marcellinus's expression. "I will stop speaking now."

"Thank you, Enopay."

The Imperator looked amused. "And if that were not enough, Verus has his hands full. His fleet patrols the whole of the Hesperian Nile, from the rapids two hundred miles north of here clear down to the Mare Solis. Not to mention his role in helping extend our signal stations along the Wemissori and the three other major tributaries out of the west that drain into the Mizipi. He is, in fact, at our harbor on the Oyo right now, putting the finishing touches to those logistics. So, Marcellinus, a joint force of Romans and Hesperians: that is your recommendation?"

"Yes, of course." Marcellinus took a deep breath. "But Caesar, I cannot go."

"You defy your Imperator?"

"I am needed here. Am I not?"

"You flatter yourself, Gaius Marcellinus. I do believe that by pooling our considerable talents and calling upon Tahtay's, Praetor Sabinus and I may be able to handle Cahokia in your absence."

"With Agrippa always a hairbreadth from unleashing his legionaries upon Cahokia?"

"You think me incapable of reining in Lucius Agrippa?"

Marcellinus backtracked quickly. "By no means, Caesar. I merely mean that you cannot be everywhere. Often you are out in the Grass—"

"What if the Mongols arrive here while we are away?" Enopay said.

Marcellinus turned on him. "*We?*"

"It seems unlikely. Our scouts would have warned us. But yes, you'd better not dally." Hadrianus walked to the door and looked down at the step as if irritated that he had to clamber up it to escape the house.

"Caesar, I implore you—"

Unexpectedly, Hadrianus cut him off with a Hesperian hand-talk gesture: *Be silent.* He turned. "Oh, and one other thing. That odd moment when Tahtay made you swear upon your daughter's life. He spoke, naturally, of Vestilia?"

Lying to the Imperator could be a death sentence. Marcellinus had never told a bald-faced lie to an Imperator of Roma in his life, and today would be a poor day to start. "No, Caesar."

A half smile played on Hadrianus's lips. "You sly old fox. You have a Cahokian daughter?"

"I do, Caesar. Although I would prefer that you not ask me where she might be found."

The Imperator made a great show of considering it. "*Perhaps* such a thing might be agreed to. But we need not discuss it further, Gaius Marcellinus, and it need not become common knowledge in the legions as long as you grant me the service for which I have asked. Which is not such a bad thing as all that. After all, I propose to give you responsibility, an opportunity to command honest Romans again after all these years relegated to keeping Hesperians in order. And I know how you hanker to travel. This task should be right up your alley. Which Cahokians would do for the task, d'you suppose?"

After a dazed moment, Marcellinus's mind began working again. He looked apologetically at Enopay. "Kanuna, if he could be persuaded to make such a long trip. He is the most flexible and . . . statesmanlike of the older Cahokians. Mahkah, and some of the other young warriors who are already accustomed to working with Romans and have traveled far in the past. Of course, we will also need translators who speak the languages of the Caddo and the Hand."

The Imperator pushed the doorskin aside. Beyond it Marcellinus saw four Praetorian guards standing watch, looking hot and uncomfortable. Their armor gleamed in the sun. "I concur with your plan. Select your Cahokians. I will have a warship sent from our Oyo harbor to ferry you along the Wemissori; it should arrive in a week or so. You will travel with four turmae of the Ala II Hispanorum Aravacorum under the command of the senior decurion Sextus Bassus. Bassus is a fine horseman and runs a tight expedition."

"Yes, Caesar."

Hadrianus gave him a long, appraising stare. "Gaius

Marcellinus, despite your fond opinion of yourself you have very few uses to me, and men with so many flaws do not customarily survive long in my favor. You wish to ensure your future with Roma? Go and earn it. You pride yourself on forging alliances? Go and forge another."

"Yes, Caesar."

The Imperator stepped out of the house. The doorskin fell back into place behind him.

"Shit." Marcellinus sat down on his bench with a thud. All of a sudden he vividly recalled the scorching sun, the blistering heat of Arabia. And now he had to travel deep into another desert on what was probably a fool's errand and ridiculously dangerous besides. Once again he had to make a huge journey at what might be exactly the wrong time.

And if that were not bad enough, Hadrianus knew he had a Cahokian daughter. "Futete. Damn it." Stricken, he looked at Enopay.

The boy leaned in so close that even an eavesdropper just outside the hut would not be able to hear. "Do not fear, Eyanosa. Most Cahokians do not even know you consider Kimi your daughter. And those who do? No Cahokian would give her away." Enopay stepped up to the door and peered out. Quietly, over his shoulder, he said: "And if Hadrianus does look, it will be for a girl much younger than fifteen winters. As long as you do what he asks, I do not believe he will bother. And all that about you having no other uses? He is just . . . Gaius?"

Enopay had turned to find Marcellinus with one hand on his golden lares and the other on a piece of old curled-up birch bark that lay on the shrine beside them. A piece of bark on which was written, in a rounded scrawl of charcoal, *Kimi thank Gaius*.

It was time to hide that piece of bark. Very carefully. For the time being, Marcellinus tucked it into the straw in his mattress. "Perhaps you are right."

Enopay nodded. "Of course I am right. Come. Let us go and talk to my grandfather."

Marcellinus followed him to the door. "Very well. But one thing I am absolutely sure of, Enopay, is that *you* will not be joining us on this crazy trip."

Mahkah and Hanska jumped at the chance to accompany him on the expedition into the southwest, and much to his surprise, so did the elderly Kanuna. Although they all stoutly claimed loyalty to Marcellinus as their primary reason, he was aware that the long shadows cast by the Roman fortresses over the city of Cahokia provided an even more powerful motivation. In addition, Kanuna had spent years of his youth traveling, and this probably would be his last chance to see somewhere new. Besides, for one who felt the cold as acutely as the elder did, traveling south for the winter must have had its appeal.

Marcellinus suspected that if he had issued a call for volunteers, a large fraction of the First Cahokian would have signed up, but there were good reasons to limit the number of Hesperians on the expedition. The Roman cavalry had trained together for years and were well accustomed to spending long days in the saddle. The Cahokians were learning fast, but few showed the natural riding aptitude of Mahkah and Hanska.

It would be bad enough just having to deal with Kanuna and Enopay, both of whom were horse-averse by inclination but suddenly well motivated to become expert riders. For to everyone's astonishment, not only did Kanuna and Hanska support Enopay's desire to come along on the journey, so did the expedition lead, Sextus Bassus, whom Enopay had somehow managed to impress with his bookkeeping skills. Kanuna claimed he had taken his first trip to faraway Etowah when he was little older than his grandson, and Hanska was always sympathetic to outsiders. And so Marcellinus gave it up, and Enopay got his place on the expedition after all.

* * *

She came to him out of the skies from the east, circling to gain height from the heat of the steelworks, looping up over the Great Mound and passing close by a Sky Lantern before swooping gracefully around him in a wide circle. From the top of the Mound of the Roman, Marcellinus watched and marveled at her skill in the air.

She glided down behind him, passing so closely over his hut that she almost grazed it with her knees, then kicked her legs free and pushed up the nose of her Catanwakuwa. Spilling air and alighting onto her feet, she needed only a few steps to bring herself and her craft to a complete halt.

"Very nice," Marcellinus said. "You're learning in . . . leaps and bounds." Meant as a compliment, it came out sounding patronizing. "You got my message, then?"

"Would I be here if I had not?" Kimimela said. He stepped forward to help her with the straps, but she had already lifted the Hawk from her shoulders, and all Marcellinus could find to do was steady it as she lowered it to the ground.

"Kimi, you once told me that I must tell you in person if I planned to leave Cahokia. Well, I am leaving now. Within the week."

That halted her. She looked up at him, the hurt in her eyes warring with her habitual disdain. "So soon? For how long?"

"Hadrianus is sending me to seek an alliance with the People of the Hand."

"Of the Hand? Shit . . ."

He tried a smile. "Bad word, Kimi."

She snorted. "Really? Anyone would think you were my father."

That silenced him. Kimimela dropped her gaze. "You will be gone many months. What will happen here while you are away?"

"Nothing bad, I hope."

"Agrippa may use your absence as an opportunity to break the treaty. Even more than he has already. I expect he can't wait to get you out of the way. This was his idea?"

"No. Agrippa is being kept busy completing the line of signal stations out in the Grass." Marcellinus steeled himself. "Kimimela, it is not a good idea for me to keep secrets from Roma, but they still do not know that you . . . were once my daughter. I would like to keep them unaware of it."

"So you are telling me that I cannot come with you."

It had not occurred to him that she might consider it. "You would want to? It might be . . ." *Dangerous?* He almost laughed. Was anywhere safe anymore?

"Oh, I cannot go." Kimimela pursed her lips. "My place now is with the Hawks and with my mother. And she cannot leave Cahokia either. But it would be nice if you had thought to ask me."

"I am taking some of the First Cahokian. Mahkah. Hanska and Mikasi. Kanuna and Enopay. Some guides and interpreters Verus will provide. And four turmae of Sabinus's cavalry."

She raised her eyebrows. "Four what?"

"Four groups of thirty-two troopers. A hundred twenty-eight men and their horses."

Her expression was sour. "And so you will lead Romans again."

"The turmae come with their own commander. Sextus Bassus."

"But you will command Bassus, of course." She looked at him with deep pain. "You are one person to Roma and another person to Cahokia. And you always have been."

"I have never lied to you, Kimimela."

"Except when it suited you." She looked away, but at least she did not run from him.

He began to feel irritated. "I could not always tell you all I knew. But neither could you. You knew of Tahtay's plan to bring the Army of Ten Thousand to the Roman fortresses last year. Did you tell me? You helped design the equipment that winched the Wakinyan into the air from level ground, along with Tahtay and Sintikala. Did any of you tell me about that? No, of course not."

"*That* was different," she said. "We served Cahokia. You always do what's best for *you*."

His exasperation grew. "Easiest for me would be to serve Roma hook, line, and sinker. Am I doing that?"

She looked at him coolly. "Aren't you?"

"I'm trying to do what's best for everyone. Somehow. And . . . Holy Juno, Kimi . . . if I die on this trip, I don't want harsh words like these to be the last we speak to each other. Not after all this. All right?"

Kimimela grimaced.

Marcellinus might never have the chance to say this again. "Kimimela, I love you. The day I became your father was the proudest . . ." He swallowed and began again. "You and Sintikala are the most important people in my life. I will do everything I can to keep you safe. Everything. I would die for you. And that is the truth."

Kimimela closed her eyes. When she opened them again, they were damp and glittering, her face forlorn. Marcellinus's heart almost broke in that moment. He reached out to her, but she held up her hand. "But what? Always with the Wanageeska there is a 'but.' A something-else."

The silence expanded between them. Kimimela stared into his eyes.

"Very well. *But* still I have to try to serve both Roma and Cahokia. Keep as many other people alive as possible—both Roman and Cahokian. And prepare to face the Mongol Khan. And so I must go to the southwest. The Imperator believes that he is coercing me to go, but in fact he is right, Kimi. I am the only man for the job. I *should* go."

Kimimela looked away across the plaza. Evening was coming, and the shadows were growing long.

"Kimimela? Please say something."

"I am bleeding," she said.

"What?" He scanned her briefly in alarm.

"Not . . ." She took another breath. "What I mean is,

my moon time has started. Several moons ago, in fact. I am not a girl anymore, Gaius. I am a woman."

Sintikala had not told him. Marcellinus inhaled deeply, blew it out, looked up at the graying sky. He felt awkward beyond measure and had no idea what to say. *Congratulations?*

"And so, as an adult, I need no father."

She was telling him it was over once and for all.

His heart was heavy. Perhaps it was just as well he was leaving Cahokia. "I understand."

"But," said Kimimela, and now her mouth quirked. "But nonetheless . . ."

She had said "nonetheless" in Latin. She was mocking him. The fading sunlight played about her face. Marcellinus waited, but she said nothing more. "Kimimela, what?"

"Despite that, when you leave Cahokia and trek all those weeks across the Grass to the deserts in the southwest . . . you *will* go as my father, Gaius."

Now it was she who reached out. Marcellinus grabbed her hands like a man drowning, before she could change her mind. Kimimela smiled at his haste and then tugged him closer. For one of the few times in their lives, father and daughter hugged. "Gods," Marcellinus said. "Thank you, Kimi. Thank you."

"And I love you," she said.

"All right," he said, startled, and she laughed.

Kimimela released him, and he stepped back.

"I love you, Gaius, Father," she said again very seriously. "Even though I am very often angry with you, I am angry with you *because* I love you."

"I love you, too, Kimimela."

Suddenly he could not bear the thought of leaving her. "Kimimela . . . could you not come with me?"

Kimimela hesitated. For a moment he thought maybe she was considering it after all and belatedly wondered what Sintikala would say about it.

"No," she said eventually. "Really I cannot. I *do* wish I could. I would like to travel by your side again. But for now my place is here. I must fly with my mother, and I must stand with Tahtay and tell him when to breathe, to stop him losing his temper and getting men killed. So go without me. But . . . do not forget me."

"I never will, Kimimela," Marcellinus said. "Never."

"We will have our time together one day," Kimimela said. "Won't we?"

"Yes, we will."

For a very long time she stood still, looking out over Cahokia from the top of the low Mound of the Roman. Then she said, "Because that is what I have wanted. And have never really had."

His vision blurred. He put his hands up to his face.

"Do not swear that we will," Kimimela said. "For that, you cannot swear."

Eyes closed, Marcellinus wondered how to answer her, but when he finally opened them again, she had gone, had run down the side of the mound, leaving her Hawk wing resting in the grass beside him.

In all the years Marcellinus had spent in Cahokia he had never been atop the Great Mound at night. He had stood there when the sun set, first when his life was in Great Sun Man's hands and later when Tahtay had taken over as paramount chief, but he had always left before dusk was over and full night had descended.

And this night was especially dark. It was the new moon, and heavy cloud blanketed the city in humidity, shrouding the starlight. The cedar steps up the mound were mostly level and even, but Marcellinus had still managed to trip over his own feet several times on his way to the mound's crest.

Once there, he stopped and turned. Despite the heat, Cahokia was studded with cooking fires. Their smoke, along with the aroma of roasting meat and corn, reached Marcellinus even at this height. Within and between the houses, often appearing to float back and forth through the streets and across the plazas, were the faint glows of lanterns in the hands of Cahokians going about their duties before turning in for the night.

Marcellinus looked left. Far away to the east were the bluffs, but he could not see them in the haze. Closer was the steady glow of the foundry in the steelworks and a much fainter glimmer of lamplight from the Big Warm House. In the summer months they let the furnaces idle, but the older Cahokians still went to the baths to soak their aching limbs in the hot air and cool water and complain about their grandchildren.

To his right the fires and lamps of western Cahokia extended as far as the river in cheerful disarray, all but disappearing into the murk. But beyond them the fortress of Legio III Parthica shone bright, its walls and streets defined by rows of brilliant military lanterns. By comparison with the scattered flames of Cahokia the castra looked oddly square and sharp, almost sinister.

And behind Marcellinus stood the Longhouse of the Wings, long and dark.

The sweat on his arms and brow had cooled, and his breathing had calmed. Marcellinus turned and approached the longhouse. Its tall door was ajar, and no light came from within. Hesitating only a moment, he walked inside.

Even to his night-adjusted eyes it seemed completely black within. He eased forward slowly, controlling his breathing, probing with each foot before putting his weight down to ensure that he would not trip over or bump into something he couldn't see. He felt rather than saw the dozens of Hawk wings swaying in the air above him, suspended from the rafters. He smelled tanned deerskin, leather, flax, new wood.

Ten short paces in, he stopped. Was she even here? "Sisika?"

"Hotah," said a male voice.

Marcellinus jumped. His hand instinctively slapped at his belt, but of course he had brought no weapon onto the sacred mound. Yet even as he moved, he knew the voice. "Tahtay?"

"Sintikala will come to you presently." The war chief was maybe twenty feet away to his left. Marcellinus turned to face him in the dark. "Why are you here, Tahtay? Is something wrong?"

Tahtay blew out a huge breath. "What a question to ask me in a Cahokia occupied by Roma, in the heart of a land swarming with armies that care nothing for my people and live only to destroy one another. A Cahokia where listening ears are everywhere, where anyone I have not known all my life—and even some I have— may be a spy, reporting my words to the Imperator. Where the Wanageeska, my friend and the friend of my father, serves me but also his Imperator; today he wears Cahokian clothes, yesterday and tomorrow Roman armor. Even in the sweat lodge I cannot speak freely. Only here in the center of Cahokia, where we are the only men on a great and sacred mound inside a tall palisade, while Wahchintonka, Dustu, and a few other trusted men guard the gates below."

The war chief sounded sorrowful and older than his years. They were alone here in the dark, and so Marcellinus steeled himself and said the words that sounded traitorous even to his own ears. "I'm sorry, Tahtay. If there had been any way to keep Roma from your city—"

"Perhaps we should have faced them in battle after all?"

"No. Not that."

Footfalls, as Tahtay paced back and forth. He obviously had better night vision than Marcellinus. Perhaps he had gotten it from the wolves. "On that desperate day when our army stood on the hillside ready for war, Cahokia had a fighting chance. But now your Romans will destroy us from within. Grind us down like the Mizipi grinds the riverbank, leaving nothing behind."

"Tahtay, the Romans need Cahokia. Its corn, its warriors, and its skills. Its flight and its liquid flame. Its knowledge of the land and the peoples that live here. And you are making them pay for what they receive."

"So that we will fight beside them against an impossible enemy."

"But Cahokia does not stand alone. Cahokia now leads a great Hesperian League: the Iroqua, the Powhatani, many of the other Algon-Quian peoples. And the Blackfoot."

"I am hardly the master of those tribes the way the Imperator rules Roma or the Khan commands the Mongol Horde. Even within Cahokia I have to persuade and cajole."

"Better to persuade by being right and lead from moral authority than force something wrong upon your people."

Tahtay laughed bitterly. "Moral authority, you say? Great Sun Man served Cahokia. He did not rule. I, too, serve the people."

"And that is why Great Sun Man was a great leader, and why you are his worthy successor."

Marcellinus wished they could have this discussion around a fire in the open air. He took a few cautious steps, swung his arms, hit nothing, and felt a little more free to move. "Tahtay, Cahokia forced the Romans to make their treaty by standing shoulder to shoulder with the other tribes of Nova Hesperia, and Cahokia can survive the coming war in the same way. By standing firm with the other Hesperian tribes you know now and more beside. I must leave soon for the People of the Hand. I go as a Roman, but if we succeed in allying with them, it will be because they, too, want to stand with their Hesperian brothers and sisters. Do you understand me?"

Tahtay had stopped pacing. "Perhaps."

"And that is why I am taking Kanuna. For he can speak for Cahokia in a way I cannot."

"I know. He and I have spoken of it in the smoke lodge."

Marcellinus stared into the darkness. "I will be gone many months, but while I am traveling, you must solidify our other alliances. You must meet with the Tadodaho of the Haudenosaunee. The Iroqua are strong and terrible fighters. They must stand with us, and us with them. You must maintain and build on your close ties with the Blackfoot. And more: reach south to the other mound-builder towns, reach into the Grass to the tribes that live there, the Hidatsa, the Shoshoni, the Pawnee. Perhaps even to the Cherokee if Roma does not already own them."

He could almost hear Tahtay's bitter smile. "All that?"

"You are not alone. Use the people you trust. Sintikala has the respect of the Iroqua. Wachiwi was once of the Oneida. Others have strong ties to the Algon-Quian or have brothers and sisters in the Grass. You do not need to go in every direction, all at once, by yourself. Have the chiefs of those other Mizipian tribes brought here or somewhere close by."

"And why would they agree?"

"Because otherwise they will be picked off one by one by the Mongols or by Roma. You are stronger when you all stand together. You know this."

"But if the Imperator . . . Ah." Tahtay started to pace again. "Of course, Roma will want us to make these alliances, too, so that we can help fight their war with the Khan."

"And you *will* have to help Roma fight its war. I do not pretend otherwise. This must be a true alliance with Roma. But once the war with the Mongols is won—"

"Huh. We—"

Marcellinus spoke over him remorselessly. "When the war is over, Hesperia must still be strong. Have I ever spoken to you of Tertius Gaudens?"

They had been speaking in Cahokian, and the sudden words in Latin seemed harsh and violent. Tahtay grunted. "No. Who is that?"

"It is a phrase, not a person. Tertius Gaudens, the Rejoicing Third. It is the military principle of letting two enemies fight each other so that a third can then defeat the weakened victor."

Tahtay blew out a long breath. "Hesperia can survive to be the Rejoicing Third?"

"Perhaps. But not at the expense of weakening Roma to the point where the Mongols . . . destroy them. For if the Romans are defeated by the Khan, then Cahokia—Hesperia—will fall, too."

He could almost hear Tahtay shaking his head. "It is so complicated. Sometimes I feel like I am falling off a tall rock. Tumbling down. But so slowly that it will take me a long time to hit the rocks at the bottom."

Marcellinus laughed. "You are not a buffalo, Tahtay. And I am not Sooleawa."

"No. Alas. Sooleawa is a strong and handsome woman." Tahtay paused. "You are taking Kanuna to the Hand to speak for Cahokia, and that is good. But you must also take Taianita."

That caught Marcellinus off guard. "Taianita?"

"Take her," Tahtay said.

Marcellinus could scarcely imagine it. "This is a Roman military expedition, Tahtay. It will be a long hard trip with many dangers."

"You cannot promise to keep her safe? In a group of your own Romans?" Although he could not see Tahtay, Marcellinus could almost imagine his eyes narrowing.

"It is not that," he said.

"You will pass through Caddo lands," Tahtay said. "She speaks Caddo and some words of other languages of the southern rivers and plains and deserts. And enough Latin to talk with the turmae."

"Calidius Verus will provide translators."

"Will you be able to trust them? You can trust her."

As Tahtay trusted her, Marcellinus suddenly realized. Taianita would be Tahtay's eyes and ears on this expedition. But still . . . "She is young. And as the only girl surrounded by over a hundred legionaries, she might find things difficult." Or *make* them difficult, he thought.

"You are taking Hanska, who is a woman. You are taking Enopay, who is also young. You have no excuse not to take Taianita. Hotah, I do not ask you for many things, but this? Please. It is important to me. I think it is the right thing to do. Will the Hand not have women chiefs as well as men? Is Taianita not persuasive? There are no Cahokian clan chiefs who can make the trip. She can help Kanuna, and she can help you."

Marcellinus sighed. "All right, Tahtay."

"Good." Now Marcellinus heard Tahtay scuffing at the ground with his moccasin. "And . . . Gaius? I am very sorry that I mentioned swearing on the life of your daughter. That was very foolish. Very foolish indeed. I was angry, and the wine was in my head, and for that moment I did not think. I needed you to swear on something, and . . . it came out. I am sometimes impetuous, too."

"Yes," Marcellinus said.

"But Roma is so very hard to trust, and sometimes you are Roma. I needed to know for sure." Tahtay's voice turned doleful. "I think I am wise, but I am not wise. Perhaps I will never be a good leader. I would not have risked Kimimela's life for anything. Is that what I have done? Is she in danger?"

"I hope not. Hadrianus promised not to seek her out as long as I led this expedition. And if he does, he will be looking for a girl much younger than Kimimela." Marcellinus took a deep breath. "But as you say, Roma is hard to trust."

A long silence fell. Was he still there? "Tahtay?"

"Hotah, I must ask yet another thing. Please do not die on this long trip to the southwest, because if you do . . . I fear for Cahokia. I fear for all the land."

The silence lengthened. "I'll be back, Tahtay. With the People of the Hand as allies, I hope. In the meantime . . . strengthen the League."

"I will do my best."

All of a sudden the air around Marcellinus felt different. The faintest of breezes touched his neck. Above him Hawks creaked and swayed as if the sky itself were roiling over his head.

This time he did not need to ask. Tahtay was gone. Marcellinus knew it. "Juno."

From above him and to the left there came a sudden double thumping sound so abrupt that it made him leap sideways away from it. Marcellinus banged into wooden shelving, and falcon masks and rolls of cordage bounced off his shoulders and arms. "Merda . . ."

After the thudding came the clatter of feet running to a standstill. For several long moments he heard nothing more. Then a faint rectangle of sky appeared above him, and a lithe figure dropped through it. He heard the slap of her feet as she landed on the rafters. Hawks trembled again. The rectangle of sky vanished as the trapdoor in the ceiling closed, and the longhouse was just as dark as it had been before.

She knew Marcellinus was there. He was sure of it. He had not known she flew by night—it seemed ridiculously dangerous—but she must have waited to land until she saw Tahtay depart.

Well, two could play at this night game. Marcellinus kept absolutely still and used all his concentration to try to sense where she was.

It was hopeless. He might have had bandages over his ears and eyes for all he could tell of her whereabouts.

The only credit he could take was that when her fingers grazed his arms, he did not lurch away in shock again.

He reached out blindly and found her. His fingertips coaxed her closer.

Softly, slowly, Sisika drifted into his arms.

Her hands slid up his arms to his shoulders and rested there. His fingers caressed the back of her flying tunic, coming to rest at her waist.

She lifted her right hand. Very gently, she touched his cheek. He could hear her breathing, smell the rich leather she wore and the intoxicating aroma of her skin. He had the feeling she was gazing into his eyes, but he could not see her face at all, not even the outline of her.

He leaned forward and down. His lips met the hard leather of her flying mask.

She giggled quietly. It was an oddly intimate sound that he had not heard from her before. Her hand slid behind his head, tugging him forward. He ducked lower and found the soft skin of her neck. He nuzzled her, kissed it, slid his lips down until they met the top of her tunic.

Lifting his hands from her waist, he felt for her mask, eased it up and away from her face, and found her lips with his fingers. She kissed them, an echo of the many times in the past he had kissed hers when she had placed them over his mouth to stop him from speaking. She squeezed his hand, kissed his fingers again, and for an instant he felt her tongue flicker across his knuckle, tasting him.

Once more he leaned forward. Their lips met. Her mouth opened. They melted into each other, gentle but purposeful. She pulled him in even closer, stroking his cheek. Her tongue felt like fire in his mouth, the taste and smell of her maddening him with their intensity. Yet he savored those long moments in the dark, their hands upon each other, close and warm, with wings over their heads and the solidity of the Great Mound of Cahokia beneath their feet.

He ran his hands down her sides again, over the supple leather. They both breathed more deeply now. Marcellinus swayed, for a moment unsure of his balance in the all-consuming dark, but she held him still. Her lips slipped away, and she laughed again, a young, delighted sound, as if she had no cares in the world and was thinking of nothing but him.

Now she kissed his shoulders and his chest. He caressed her bare arms. Her hand slid down his arm to his wrist, and their fingers twined.

Her lips found the scar on his arm where he had sworn an oath to her in blood years before, when they had faced imminent peril in Iroqua territory. She lingered there, exploring the scar with her tongue. It felt like a benediction, an affirmation, a rededication.

Marcellinus tilted his head back and felt the whisper of the air from the Hawks against his temples. For a moment there were no wars, no conflicted allegiances. Time stood still, and his life was very simple.

He found the ties that kept her tunic tight around her body and loosened them. His hands slid up under the leather, gliding across the warm skin beneath. He found scars and healed abrasions, the memories of bad landings and injuries sustained in fighting. With a shock that felt like lightning her hands were suddenly inside his tunic, too, rubbing up and across his stomach and chest and around to his back, tracing the shapes of his healed wounds, probing and kneading. As if they were medicus and healer as well as soldier and warrior, each of them traced the other's violent history, blessing it, forgiving it. Marcellinus was gasping now with the intensity of the sensations that coursed through him; Sisika was silent except for her steady deep breathing. He had the impression she was concentrating intently, memorizing every detail of him.

His hands continued on their journey of discovery. Just once, greatly daring, he ran his fingers around the curve of her breast. She sighed gently, leaning into the caress.

Then her arms went around him, and she gripped him tightly and stopped moving.

Still she had said nothing, but her meaning was clear. Reluctantly, Marcellinus slipped his hands out from beneath her tunic and rested them on her shoulders. Her forehead rested against his chest. He buried his face in her hair and breathed deeply.

As quietly as he could whisper the words and still be heard, he murmured: "I love you, Sisika."

Her lips moved against his chest and her fingers against the skin of his arm: the same words, mouthed and in the hand-talk. *I love you, Gaius*.

He felt light-headed, a little dizzy. "Never leave me."

I am always with you. Always.

Sintikala tilted her head back. "But I cannot be, Gaius."

He kissed her cheek, her neck. "I want to stay with you."

"But you are leaving Cahokia again. Your Imperator tells you to go."

"I must. For a while."

"To go where I cannot be with you." She released him, stepped away. Marcellinus felt bereft at the loss of her; it was all he could do not to lunge forward and seize her again. "I do not want to be *not there* for you, Gaius. In the wrong place." Her voice was heavy with sorrow.

She left the rest unsaid, but Marcellinus heard it anyway, the words she had spoken long ago after Great Sun Man had met his doom: *When my husband was killed, when he needed me most, I was not with him, I was not there. Today-now, once again I was in the wrong place. Not there. It is my life, to never be there. To fail. And then men die.*

She swallowed. "I cannot be there for you. You go alone."

"I will come back to you."

She said nothing. He could still hear her breathing, and so he knew she had not slipped away. "Sisika? Even while I am gone . . . I will always be with you, too. Because I love you more than my life. If you could see into my eyes . . ."

"I do not need to see your eyes, Gaius. Not tonight." She took his hand, placed it over her heart. "Just come back to me." Her voice was husky now. "Try hard."

"I will," he said.

"And I will fly. Always in the air. Always looking for you."

He thought it was over. Expected her to back away, perhaps to disappear from the longhouse as effortlessly as Tahtay, but she did not. She stood still for several long minutes while Marcellinus treasured her nearness and tried to commit every detail of the feel of her to his memory for the long months ahead.

But then she stepped forward again, her strong body thumping firmly into his. He grabbed her like a drowning man. Their arms went around each other, and their lips met once more.

Again, time and war went away.

CHAPTER 6

YEAR EIGHT, HUNTING MOON

It was as much as they could do to get Kanuna to step aboard the *Minerva*. It was not the quinquereme itself that the elder feared, although the warship seemed daunting even to Marcellinus. It was more the prospect of sharing it with more than a hundred horses and mules.

Enopay, of course, was clambering around the decks with the gleeful expression that another boy might wear on walking into a golden palace and being told its glittering contents were his to keep. Enopay had adored the *Concordia*, and that was merely a Norse dragon ship. The *Minerva* was much more substantial, and Enopay had gone aboard shortly after dawn, well before the rest of the Cahokians, having begged the indulgence of the ship's master. He had explored every nook and cranny and stepped off the galley only to help coax his grandfather up the gangplank.

"And so there are two hundred and seventy men who row," the boy said importantly. "In the lowest layer of the hull there are twenty-three men on each side, paddling backward with the lowest row of oars you see sticking out. There is then a middle layer of rowers and a top layer. On the middle layer sit fifty-six men on each side, two to an oar, for those oars are much larger. And the top is the same: fifty-six more men and twenty-eight more oars."

Kanuna looked down doubtfully, noting the separation among the three ranks of oars. "There can be very little room in there. It must be even worse than being up here."

"Much worse," Marcellinus said. "For down there all must row for hours at a time, and up here the air is fresh. Well," he said, glancing at the mules, "somewhat more fresh."

The quinquereme seemed overloaded. Four turmae of cavalrymen and their mounts took up a lot of deck space, and it was a high deck. "It will not tip over?" Kanuna said anxiously.

"Of course not," Enopay said with the scorn of the young.

"Probably not," Marcellinus amended. In fact, adding the expeditionary force to the oarsmen, the regular deck crew, and the marines of the Sixth Ferrata who would guard the vessel on its trip back east was stretching the *Minerva* to capacity. The ship's master would have to balance the boat carefully, and the masters of horse would have to take pains to ensure that the beasts stayed where they were put.

For the moment he had more immediate worries. Once loading was completed and the galley was under way, Marcellinus arrived on the poop deck of the *Minerva* to be greeted by none other than Calidius Verus, Praetor of the Sixth, the general who had led the storming and destruction of Ocatan.

If Marcellinus was irritated by Lucius Agrippa's insufferable attitude, that was nothing compared with his instant loathing for Praetor Calidius Verus. Portly and red-faced, Verus wore an air of being permanently nauseated by the "barbarians" around him. Marcellinus had difficulty remaining tactful even during the introductions. For his part, Verus made no reference to the lost 33rd Legion, Ocatan, or Marcellinus's long sojourn in Nova Hesperia but greeted him in a strangely familiar way as if they were old friends who had been out of each other's sight for only a short while.

Once the initial pleasantries were over, with Marcellinus wearing his forced smile like a rictus, Verus clasped his hands behind him and strode forward. "As instructed, I have two more guides and interpreters for you in addition to your own Taianita. I believe you are used to your word slaves coming in threes?"

Marcellinus did not respond. It would not have occurred to him in recent years to refer to Tahtay, Kimimela, and Enopay as word slaves.

Calidius Verus smiled thinly. "The first is an Iroqua youth who claims he once owed you his life."

Marcellinus's heart sank, his mouth dropping open at the same time. "*Pezi* is here?"

Verus nodded. "Truth be told, I begrudge his assignment to you. Young Pezi has been extremely helpful in our dealings with the Iroqua. He picked up his Latin wickedly fast, and his quick thinking a time or two has saved a great deal of bloodshed."

"If it was his blood at risk, then I am scarcely surprised."

Verus shrugged. "These redskins all place undue value on their own dirty hides. And Pezi is very candid about exposing the deceit of his people. Anyway, he speaks the jabber of the Handies, and so it appears I must yield him to you for the time being. Try not to damage him."

Marcellinus bit his tongue and moved on. "Who else?"

Verus pointed. "Her. The young pussycat standing by the rail with the stick up her rear end is the Chitimachan. It's the only name she'll answer to. No idea what her real name is and don't much care. Turns out she was stolen from the People of the Hand as a youngster and forcibly married into the Chitimachans, who run the Market of the Mud. Then, to add insult to injury, her trader husband used to take her with him back and forth to the southwest. So she's to be your guide."

There was certainly nothing wrong with the Chitimachan's hearing; as soon as Verus spoke her name, the young Hesperian on the deck below turned to gaze up at

Marcellinus, her expression dour. Nonetheless, she was attractive and slender, and Marcellinus was sure that the Chitimachan's time among Romans had not gone easily for her.

"Belongs to one of the oddest of these native pagan cults. Babbles in tongues at night when she sleeps, but don't be alarmed: she translates fast and fluently by day. Knows the trail and the lingos of many of the tribes along the shore of the Mare Solis. If matters go awry and you have to come back along the coast, she knows the territory like the back of her . . . Well."

The Chitimachan was still staring at Marcellinus, un-smiling and severe. Her gaze seemed to bore deep into him, and yet again in Nova Hesperia, Marcellinus had the disconcerting impression that the Chitimachan knew much more about him than he did about her.

He had expected to be guided by Norse or Roman scouts or perhaps a grizzled old Hesperian backwoods-man. To learn that their expedition was in the hands of a guide as young and daunting as the Chitimachan gave him pause.

Verus was regarding him, perhaps amused by his si-lence. "Thank you," Marcellinus said, stuck for some-thing to say.

"Gaius Marcellinus. Sir . . ." Verus suddenly looked somber. "By all accounts, you and I once had a friend in common. A friend who spoke of you so well that I al-most feel that we are comrades in arms and that some of the peculiarities of your past few years must be forgiven you. My apologies, but I wonder if I might prevail upon you to open a wound that might be somewhat painful."

The Praetor's patrician manners and circuitous way of speaking were already grating on Marcellinus. He was happy indeed that he would have to endure Calidius Verus for only a few hundred miles of river travel and not the trek across the Grass that would follow it. He forced himself to concentrate. "Sorry, what wound?"

"I speak of your First Tribune, back when you had the honor of commanding the 33rd Hesperian Legion."

Marcellinus blinked and raised his gaze to look back at the Great Mound, the Sky Lanterns above it, and the traces of the river bluffs visible beyond it to the east, now all falling behind them as the warship battled the Mizipi current upriver. "Ah. Corbulo. Of course."

Verus shuffled his feet. "Lucius Domitius Corbulo was a good man and an excellent officer. We served together in Germania, he and I, and a more courageous soldier or better dining companion I never had the pleasure of meeting."

"Corbulo had many fine qualities," Marcellinus said.

"We served together. Bloodied our gladii in many a battle and wenched together in many dark alleyways afterward." Verus stood shoulder to shoulder with Marcellinus now, gazing out over Cahokia but obviously seeing another time and place entirely. "We lost touch when he was sent east to Sindh. I had always planned to bring him on as my own First Tribune when the Sixth was redeployed to guard against the Mongol incursions, but you'd snapped him up for the Hesperian in the meantime, and who can blame you? I'm glad you had such a man by your side."

"Quite." Marcellinus swallowed.

"When I heard the 33rd had perished, my first thought was for Corbulo. Such a waste."

Did Calidius Verus have a tear in his eye? Marcellinus tactfully looked away. "A waste indeed."

"Gaius Marcellinus, if you would . . . How did my old friend meet his end? Did he die well?"

Corbulo had found Marcellinus wanting as a Praetor and had led an attempted mutiny against him before the battle with Cahokia. He might even have instigated an earlier attempt on Marcellinus's life in castra during the long trek across Nova Hesperia.

In turn, Marcellinus had slain him.

Would Verus want to hear that his good friend had perished at Marcellinus's hand? If Marcellinus revealed this bald truth, what might Verus do?

"Corbulo died fighting, as he would have wished. He

was always a fierce soldier and a cunning strategist. He . . . brooked no retreat."

Verus nodded. "You were close by when it happened?"

"I was, sir. It happened not far from here, just to the south of Cahokia. But I am afraid I can tell you no more."

Marcellinus stared stoically at the trees across the river, waiting for the inevitable next question. He felt Verus's long gaze upon him.

"Very well," Verus said eventually. "I thank you for your candor."

The Praetor patted Marcellinus on the arm, the fleeting touch of a comrade in sorrow, and walked away across the deck back to the helmsman. Marcellinus frowned out at the waters and glanced down at the ranks of oars beneath him, moving back and forth in perfect synchronization. And finally, unwillingly, he glanced back along the deck.

Maybe it was best to get all his unpleasant introductions over at once.

The Chitimachan was young and wiry and wore her hair in three braids. Perhaps twenty-five winters of age, she sat with her back straight and her hands clasped. Odd swirling tattoos lined her arms and shoulders, and she wore a fur tunic despite the moistness of the day. After all, where she had grown up it was even hotter. Marcellinus greeted her in Cahokian, and she responded in flawless Latin while examining him carefully from top to toe.

Her fellow translator had come back to join them and now bowed to Marcellinus in the Roman fashion. "Wanageeska. This is a pleasant surprise."

The youth was taller and broader in the shoulder and met his eye with a boldness rarely shown by the boy he used to be. "Surprise?" Marcellinus said. "You did not know you were assigned to me?"

"Guide a squadron of Roman horse to the People of

the Hand," Pezi said in Latin, and then reverted to Caho-kian. "That is all I was told. But I am happy to serve a man I already know to be brave and resourceful. Per-haps I may even return alive from the desert of the mad-men."

It was somewhat galling to discover that the friendlier of his new interpreters was a boy he despised. "Pezi, the last time I saw you, beneath an Iroqua stage, you sneered at me and threatened me."

Pezi nodded, not embarrassed. "You sent me to the Iroqua. Once among them, I had to serve them. They ordered me to interrogate you. How would I have fared if I had refused, if they had thought I was your spy?"

Calidius Verus was watching them from the rear deck. Marcellinus bit back a sharp retort. "I merely sent you with a message."

"And once I took that message, my debt to you was paid. You no longer owned me, Wanageeska. I owed you nothing. Is this not so?"

"It is so."

Marcellinus turned away, but Pezi stepped forward to stay by his side as he walked across the deck of the *Minerva*. "Nonetheless, I still give you my thanks and my loyalty. For without you, I would be dead."

"Think nothing of it," Marcellinus said shortly.

"Wanageeska . . . Gaius Marcellinus?"

Pezi's hand was on his arm. Marcellinus glowered at it icily until the youth removed it. "Gaius Marcellinus. I was Iroqua. And then I was Cahokian. And then Iroqua again, and now I serve Roma. You were Roman, Caho-kian, then Roman again. We are not different."

Marcellinus stared at him in disbelief. "You betrayed Cahokia to the Iroqua. You told them where high-ranking Cahokians lived so that Iroqua assassins could seek them out. We are very different, Pezi."

Pezi shook his head and grinned. The youth had ac-quired an astonishingly thick skin, for even in the face of Marcellinus's anger he continued: "And yet now we want the same thing, which is for Roma to succeed, for the Mongols to be defeated, for the land . . ." He looked around briefly to ensure they were not overheard. "For the land to be free. Now we are allies. Is *that* not so?"

Marcellinus was not taking kindly to being lectured by the word slave. "We have a job to do, Pezi. And we will do that job. For now? Leave me alone. This conversation is over."

Marcellinus certainly needed time to himself. Just as he had two years earlier when, sailing up the Wemissori in search of Tahtay, he could not escape the nagging fear that he was traveling in exactly the wrong direction at exactly the wrong time and leaving his Cahokian friends in the lurch. However, now as then, he had little choice. His mission was critical. It was even closely aligned with his previous desire to make a Hesperian League.

In the meantime he would be leading Roman soldiers again, men whom he didn't know and who were obviously leery of him, undertaking a long voyage by river and desert to a tribe of reputedly savage warriors whom even the Shappa Ta'atani thought bloodthirsty, while having to rely on Pezi and the Chitimachan.

Perhaps it was a good thing he had brought Taianita along after all. He glanced toward the prow of the galley, but she was not hard to spot. She sat inside a protective ring of people not wearing Roman garb: Mahkah, Hanska and Mikasi, Enopay and Kanuna, and Isleifur Bjarnason.

What had Marcellinus gotten his friends into now? He didn't know. Shaking his head and resolutely avoiding meeting the eye of Calidius Verus, he threaded his way between the horses of the Second Aravacorum to go sit next to Enopay.

CHAPTER 7

YEAR EIGHT, BEAVER MOON

If the Chitimachan and Isleifur Bjarnason had not assured him that a mighty range of mountains lay far ahead to the west, Marcellinus might have thought they were riding off the edge of the world. The relentlessness of the Plains and the almost complete absence of trees dazed his eyes and left his mind wandering. Never had he missed the bustle of Cahokia so painfully. He even missed the martial purposefulness and single-minded industry of the Roman fortresses. He would have given a lot to spend just five minutes a day surrounded by such cheerful turmoil instead of by taciturn cavalrymen and dour Cahokians.

He missed Sintikala and Kimimela, too, with a fierce desperation that he could not dwell on for long without feeling that his heart might break. His thoughts were tormented by those precious intimate moments with Sintikala in the dark. Again and again he returned to the memories of how she felt in his arms, against his lips, how she had stroked his chest and arms and cheek . . .

He was, he had to admit, a fool in love.

The Roman harbor at the confluence of the Wemissori and the unnamed minor tributary to its west was three weeks behind them now. After disembarking from the *Minerva*, the cavalry squadron had ridden alongside that river for just two days before branching out across a dry prairie wasteland that to Marcellinus looked trackless and featureless. The Chitimachan had ridden ahead of the company with the utmost confidence, sometimes changing direction subtly in response to cues and landmarks only she could see. Sextus Bassus had pursed his lips and looked ever more dubious, and Enopay had taken to inventorying the number of water skins the expeditionary force carried with an almost religious fervor.

By contrast, Isleifur Bjarnason was unflappable. He and the Chitimachan shared a campfire and sometimes rode together on the trail. They barely conversed at all as far as Marcellinus could see, yet they had established a strange understanding: perhaps the shared responsibility of scouts doomed to suffer the skepticism of others. Marcellinus took strength from Bjarnason's stoicism.

Meanwhile, Taianita was driving him to distraction. Intimidated by the clanking, armored mass of Roman cavalry that formed the bulk of their party, she had stuck to Marcellinus's side like glue when they started the passage across the prairie, constantly pestering him to teach her more and ever more Latin vocabulary. He had welcomed the diversion for the first few days. After that he would cheerfully have drowned her in a river if only they'd had one nearby. Eventually he had snapped at her unforgivably and she had gone to pester Pezi instead, who recovered quickly from his openmouthed shock at his good fortune and willingly helped her with her language studies.

"Do we really need all these soldiers?" Enopay asked.

Marcellinus grunted. "I hope not."

"I suppose we'll find out when we get there whether we have too many or too few."

"Yes. I suppose we will."

Since leaving the *Minerva* they had seen only a few isolated Hesperian homesteads; they were of the Pawnee tribe according to the Chitimachan, though neither she nor anyone else stopped to talk with them. Generally,

the Pawnee did not even snatch up weapons when the
Roman squadron came upon them but stood and stared
empty-handed in shock. Even after the turmae of the
Second Aravacorum were well past, Marcellinus might
look back and see the Pawnee still standing there gaping
at the soldiers and the four-legs. Obviously, the People
of the Grass had seen nothing quite like Roman cavalry
before.

He supposed that if some of them looked upon a horse
with recognition in their eyes, it would be worth stopping to interrogate them about how and when they had
seen one before and what manner of rider had been
astride it.

Despite the lack of any tangible threat, Sextus Bassus
took no chances. His auxiliaries rode every day in their
short-sleeved hauberks of chain mail armor. Each
trooper had his helmet ready to hand, hooked onto the
saddle in front of him, and either carried his flat oval
shield or slung it over his shoulder. Each man was armed
with a spatha sword and a hasta, a thrusting spear six
feet long made of ash wood and tipped with steel.

A different turma led every day, in strict rotation, and
the troopers in the leading turma were required to carry
their spears and shields at the ready at all times. Considering that they often could see for ten miles in every direction, that was probably overkill, but Marcellinus
could not fault the lead decurion for his caution: it
would obviously be inefficient to rearm and then disarm
for every blind hill or tree-lined depression they passed.

Besides, the discipline kept the men ready and made a
stirring sight for the few native Hesperians they did encounter. The horses were sleek Libyans and Hispanians,
light and well kept. The steel phalerae disks that decorated the horses' harness straps and bridles gleamed. Bassus even demanded that his men shave daily, something
Marcellinus had been lax about when his legionaries
had been on their long march. The Second Aravacorum
was making a powerful statement to the People of the
Grass, and Sextus Bassus was making one to his men as

well: we represent Roma, and we will be well turned out, we will not be shoddy. Only around the campfire in the evening did Bassus allow them to strip off their mail shirts and loll around in their tunics and cloaks.

Like his Cahokians, Marcellinus eschewed his armor, opting for comfort over preparedness for once. His mule could carry his mail shirt until he needed it. The cavalry helmets were of steel with bronzed cheek pieces, and Marcellinus found his uncomfortably warm; he would cram it onto his head at the last minute if a threat presented itself. Bassus never commented on Marcellinus's informality, and if the cavalrymen looked down on Marcellinus for it, they were wise enough not to let him know it.

Although the troopers were nominally under Marcellinus's command, he made little attempt to stamp his authority on the squadron; Bassus was a proud man, and he was doing a good job. Marcellinus had not held a Roman command position for more than eight years and was reluctant to do so now.

Alongside the Second Aravacorum rode Marcellinus's more motley crew: Mahkah, Hanska, Mikasi, Kanuna, and Enopay from Cahokia; Isleifur Bjarnason the Norse scout; and the guides and translators Taianita, the Chitimachan, and Pezi. Everyone in the party rode his or her own horse, though Enopay frequently preferred to share his grandfather's, holding on to Kanuna's waist. In addition to the horses they had brought thirty mules that trudged cheerfully after them carrying water, food, the light expedition tents, and extra armor and weapons. Enopay had been amazed and alarmed at how much baggage the Romans had piled onto the smaller four-legs—a burden of up to two hundred pounds per animal—but the mules seemed unfazed at the loads and, if anything, bore the heat of summer better than the horses did.

Once away from the Wemissori the expeditionary force had quickly fallen into a daily routine. Rising before dawn every morning and packing up camp with what seemed to the Hesperians to be almost indecent haste, they set off for three hours at a slow trot and then unloaded the four-legs and put them out for two hours to graze. Another three-hour drive was followed by a three-hour halt at noon and then a couple more hours of progress. By that time Romans and Hesperians alike had generally had enough of being on horseback and walked alongside their mounts for the few extra miles before finding a campsite and setting camp at dusk. It was a steady but efficient schedule that allowed them to cover twenty-five or even thirty miles a day without putting undue stress on the horses. Marcellinus found it less grueling than a forced infantry march, but his blisters were worse.

At last, after perhaps two hundred miles spent riding across dry prairie and nursing their dwindling water supply, they came across a thin muddy ribbon of water snaking its way through the grass. Greeted only by a contented grunt from the Chitimachan, they turned to follow it.

As if the river were a signal, the lands around them grew rockier and more arid, and the weather even hotter.

"Into Hades we go," said Marcellinus.

Isleifur grunted. "The Norse Hel is cold. This? This is balmy."

They had crossed the Grass to the Kicka River and would now follow that river upstream to the Great Mountains. They never could have made it so far by boat: barely thirty feet wide and often less than waist deep, the Kicka was not navigable for any vessel larger than a canoe or dugout. It contained no fish that Marcellinus could see, and he was at a loss to know how the locals they encountered survived. Unlike the brash Pawnee, these new people hid in their tipis as the Romans passed, terrified of the horses. The only person who spoke their language was the Chitimachan, and, ever severe, she did not deign to talk to them.

Marcellinus was forcibly reminded of his long-ago trek from the Mare Chesapica to Cahokia with the 33rd

Hesperian, when the small Iroqua villages would be deserted at their passing. It made him sad that once more he was leading a squadron of soldiers who terrified the people who lived here, whose land this had been from time immemorial. Bassus and the other Romans, of course, took it as their due.

By now they were a long way from anywhere. Once again Marcellinus felt isolated, an alien being in this landscape.

Hanska and Mikasi were sparring with spatha and shield, trying to grow more familiar with the cavalry weapons, having originally learned with the much shorter gladius. For some reason the legionaries were endlessly entertained by watching Hanska fight, though very few of them would risk sparring against her themselves.

Of course, Hanska was one of only three women in the party. The Chitimachan was arguably the most attractive, but she kept to herself, kept her back straight and her expression sullen, and rejected every overture of friendship except those from Pezi and Isleifur Bjarnason. Taianita at last had gotten over her nervousness at being surrounded by Roman cavalrymen. Now confident that she was safe among them, she became talkative and helpful, and even Marcellinus had to admit that her presence in the squadron had become an asset.

Mahkah chose not to assist the other members of the First Cahokian in providing a public spectacle. Mahkah was as cautious around Romans as he was with Iroqua; he thoroughly enjoyed riding his Roman horse but showed little inclination to fraternize with the men of the Second Aravacorum.

As for Pezi, he talked to the Romans at every opportunity, genuinely enthusiastic about soaking in as much Latin as possible.

Kanuna was permanently jittery. This night Marcellinus sought him out to find out why. Among all the elders of Cahokia, Kanuna and Ojinjintka were the two who had ranged farthest afield from the Great City in their younger days. Marcellinus had thought he might have been more at ease on the expedition.

"Then, I was not responsible for my grandson," Kanuna said soberly. "Back then I had few enough family at home to miss, and none were at risk from an enemy who makes a long camp in my own city and will not leave. And . . ."

Marcellinus raised an eyebrow. "There's more?"

"And at any moment an even worse enemy could rise up out of the Grass and charge down upon us."

Marcellinus smiled.

"You do not fear the Mongols?"

"By all accounts, Chinggis Khan faces a wall of mountains a thousand miles long. The likelihood of his breaching it and then arriving at the exact same patch of land we're camping on seems remote."

"Enopay says the Khan's army must be huge," Kanuna said. "With so many horses to browse the grass they will travel spread out over an immense area. And they, too, will not stray far from water. The Khan will travel along rivers where he can, just as we do. And the Kicka, for all its weakness, is one of the bigger rivers in the Grass."

Marcellinus shrugged. "I have been a soldier since I was younger than Tahtay. If I worried all the time about what might be over the next ridge, fretting over enemies I could not see, I'd have worried myself to death long ago. Besides, the Mongols send scouts ahead, just as the Romans do. We are unlikely to meet the entire Horde before we see outriders."

"We are not sending scouts now," Kanuna pointed out.

"That is because *we* are the scouts." Marcellinus grinned. "You have been comfortable in Cahokia far too long, my friend."

"Nonetheless, I would feel safer if we had Sintikala in the air above us, looking farther ahead than we can see from down here in the dirt."

Marcellinus felt a brief tug at his heart. "So would I."

Perhaps some of his yearning had leaked into his

voice, because Kanuna cocked an eye at him and changed the subject. "Even without the Mongols, I fear for Enopay. I did not think—and I mean no disrespect to you, my friend . . ." Kanuna looked mournful.

"What? You can speak plainly."

"I did not think to watch my grandson become Roman."

Marcellinus leaned back so that he could look past Kanuna into the main body of the camp. Enopay was wandering from fire to fire among the cavalrymen of the Fourth Turma, chatting to the men, asking questions, smiling. "You believe that is what Enopay is doing?"

Certainly Enopay was dazzled by the things of Roma, and certainly he was well accepted by the men of the Second Aravacorum. Enopay was good-natured and approachable, spoke excellent Latin, and had become something of a mascot for the soldiers. From the beginning they had made it their goal to make him comfortable on a horse. They made a fuss of him whenever they could, and Enopay knew enough Latin to insult them cheerfully for it. He was shrewd enough not to be bamboozled and mocked and sharp enough for them to admire him.

"Enopay adapts," Marcellinus said. "He survives. Look how he handled Avenaka."

Kanuna was still brooding. "And so he loses what makes him Cahokian."

"I do not think so. And if Cahokia and Roma are to continue to avoid war, maybe we need as many Enopays as we can find."

"Huh," said Kanuna. "For *that*, we would need more Wanageeskas."

"Perhaps Enopay will make them," Marcellinus said. "It certainly worked the first time. Him. Tahtay. Kimimela. Without their influence on me . . ."

But Kanuna's low mood was beginning to infect Marcellinus, too. Despite his confident words, every day Marcellinus worried about what might be happening back in Cahokia, what tricks Lucius Agrippa might be trying to dislodge the fragile peace. He worried that the Imperator might learn of his association with Kimimela and Sintikala. He worried that he should not have agreed to bring Kanuna, Enopay, and Taianita on such a grueling journey with such unknown dangers ahead.

And to be sure, when he had time to spare, he worried about the Mongol army.

But above all, he missed Sintikala with a deep and full heart.

In the coming weeks, as they followed the Kicka River upstream, the humidity, flat terrain, and long grasses of the prairies gave way to high plains with short grass and sagebrush and occasional high buttes. The river also changed, its wide, shallow banks becoming rocky, the waters flowing narrower and faster.

Mahkah saw the Great Mountain chain a full two days before Marcellinus did. For Marcellinus the hazy outline stayed tantalizingly out of reach even after most people claimed to see it clearly. Then he awoke one morning and was sure of it in the cool clear air of morning: a thin meandering line, scarcely above the horizon, not cloud, after all, but sharp peaks.

Two days after that they could see the mountains clearly, a sheer wall rising out of the Plains. Here was the formidable barrier, this the deadly palisade of rock that held back the Mongol tide. Isleifur and the Chitimachan insisted that even now the mountains were still a hundred miles away. Marcellinus balked at this estimate for a while—he had been nowhere else in the world except the Himalaya where mountains could be seen at such a distance, and the giants of the Himalaya were so tall that they were wreathed in cloud most seasons of the year—but the hard-nosed logic of his comrades persuaded him. And they were right. It took another five days of hard travel over increasingly arid terrain to get them closer to the gargantuan range.

Well east of the mountains, on rising ground of growing desert aridity, the Kicka River descended into a deep canyon. Guided by the Chitimachan, the expedition turned south, striking out across the high plains to converge gradually with the foothills of the Great Mountains where there were frequent streams of clear water. Although it was now nearing the end of November by the Roman reckoning and the Beaver Moon by the Cahokian, the daytime temperatures were rising again as they penetrated deeper into the southwest.

By Enopay's best guess—and by now even Sextus Bassus gave Enopay's estimates equal weight with his own—the expeditionary force was now a full eight hundred miles from the confluence where they had left the *Minerva* and thus eleven hundred miles from Cahokia.

"How much farther to the People of the Hand, Chitimachan?"

As usual, she stared at him as if he were a beetle before replying. "Not far. Two weeks, perhaps. Maybe less to the wide road."

This was new. "The wide road?"

"Perhaps ten nights," she said. "Although the Hand are all around us even now, and we do not see them. They will keep their distance, but we will see their marks on the rocks, feel their breath in our hair. They will send word ahead. They will be expecting us."

Bassus nodded. "Good." At Marcellinus's expression he grinned wryly. "Well, we wouldn't want to surprise them, would we?"

"Watch for snakes now," the guide added. "On the rocks. Very poisonous. If you hear a rattle, a clatter, like a gourd? Jump away. Keep your four-legs away from them, too; I see no reason why the snakes would not bite them as readily as us."

"Rattling snakes?" Shaking his head, Bassus spurred his horse, peeling off to take the message back to his men.

Marcellinus grunted. Snakes? Hidden warriors of the Hand? This wasn't getting any better. Not at all.

PART 2

THE PEOPLE OF THE HAND

Chapter 8

Year Nine, Crow Moon

As Marcellinus climbed the ladder up through the hatchway and back into the world, the bright desert sunlight stabbed his eyes, blinding him. An unseen hand grabbed his arm and guided him up onto terra firma.

His head pounded from the drums. He reeked of smoke. Yet he tried to keep his expression composed and beatific as if he had learned great things, been touched by the sublime.

He turned to help Kanuna, but the Cahokian elder had already ascended from the bowels of the earth to stand blinking by his side. The Chitimachan was clambering out behind him, stepping off the rude ladder and gingerly testing the ground beneath her feet as if surprised to find it there. The look of reverence on the translator's face, at least, was not faked; she had been so captivated by the underground ceremony that she had largely failed to translate for Marcellinus what was going on.

It had not mattered much. The mythology of the People of the Hand was as transparent to Marcellinus as the folklore of Red Horn and the Long-Nosed God back in Cahokia, which was to say, not at all. The intervals of flute playing he had, however, enjoyed. Despite his tin ear, Yupkoyvi flutes seemed more melodious than the Mizipian music he had been forced to endure in Cahokia, Ocatan, and Shappa Ta'atan.

Sweat already drenched him, and the sun on his sore neck burned like a blade. "This is our punishment for complaining about Cahokian winters," he murmured.

Equally aware of the hundreds of pairs of eyes fixed upon them, Kanuna nodded slowly as if Marcellinus had said a very profound thing. The Chitimachan prudently did not translate for their hosts.

Color surrounded them. Above flew the Macaw Warriors. Launching from the tops of the sandstone cliffs, the one-man craft resembled the Cahokian Hawks aside from the startling red of the parrot feathers that adorned them and made them glow impossibly brightly in the clear desert air. At any given time a half dozen Macaws might be swooping over their heads, buoyed by the hot air currents and the gentle breezes that blew along the mesa and provided lift.

Around the plaza's edge were cages for real macaws, birds with wings of bright scarlet and yellow and tails of blue. Marcellinus had seen a similar bird only once before, at the Market of the Mud. Beguiled by the creature's beauty, Kimimela had come close to losing a finger to its hooked and vicious beak. In Yupkoyvi the macaws were no tamer, but here they appeared to have a religious rather than a commercial significance.

In addition to the bright birds and the extensive use of their feathers, the people of the plaza were decorated with ornaments of turquoise and obsidian, with copper bells that jangled as they moved. Black and white pots provided an interesting but severe contrast.

The two Yupkoyvi shaman-chiefs who had preceded Marcellinus out of the underground kiva raised their arms in salutation, or praise, or something. Marcellinus bowed. The chieftain on the left, Cha'akmogwi, spoke, and the Chitimachan stood up a little straighter to translate. "'You have come to the center of the world, and you have not come in vain.'"

Marcellinus bowed again.

"'The spirits have spoken, and the shamans have relayed their words to us. We now speak them to you. The

People of the Hand were present at the making of this world, and we will be here when the world ends. Many foes have tried to wipe the People of the Hand from the world, but they have not succeeded. They will not succeed now. We are still here. We will always be here.' "

Marcellinus wished he had a hat to keep the sun off his forehead or, better still, that he was sheltering indoors in one of the cool rooms of the Yupkoyvi Great House with the other Romans. Cha'akmogwi was only telling Marcellinus what he already knew, repeating it for the benefit of the people in the plaza around them.

Now the other chief, his brother Chochokpi, spoke. " 'You seek our aid against the Thousand-Thousand Enemies, and we shall give it. Together we will have success in war. This, the spirits have foretold.' "

Marcellinus nodded sagely and endeavored to look gratified.

" 'The Thousand-Thousand Enemies will be scattered back into the seas from whence they came, there to waste away and drown and die.' "

The Thousand-Thousand Enemies were the Mongols. The Yupkoyvi had heard much of them from refugees and traders from the west, although they had not seen them with their own eyes. The Yupkoyvi themselves did not travel. Why should they? They lived at the center of the world, and the world came to them.

" 'We have sent out our signals. The roads shine out from Yupkoyvi to illuminate all the land. Our brothers of the west and north will heed the call, and all of the Yupkoyvi will come to stand shoulder to shoulder with you against the Thousand-Thousand Enemies.' "

"All of the Yupkoyvi," Kanuna muttered. "That's a relief."

Marcellinus elbowed him discreetly. The shaman-chief of the Hand was still speaking, and after a reproachful look the Chitimachan continued her litany. " 'And so we will summon our many-brothers from the mountains back here to the heart of the world to stand with the Kachada and his silver men and their many-brothers of the Great Mizipi River. If a mountain stands between us and our brothers, we will cut the mountain. If a river flows between us and our brothers, we will stop the river. We are the Yupkoyvi.'"

Chochokpi nodded and lowered his arms. Marcellinus, the Kachada, bowed again. By virtue of the ceremony he had just endured, he had apparently acquired yet another Hesperian name.

Off they went, the two chieftains of the Yupkoyvi. The crowd began to disperse, and Marcellinus at last relaxed his features and breathed out a long sigh of relief. He wondered if he would lose face if he disappeared into the Great House for a nap.

Smoke continued to gush from the hatchway to the underground kiva beside him. An unseen ventilation shaft drew in fresh air to feed the sagebrush that burned in the firebox, but the smoke could escape only the way the people did: up through the hatch. Down in the pit a stone slab deflected some of the direct heat, but it had still been stifling down there, surrounded by a hundred other people. It was a mercy that Marcellinus was not deterred by confined spaces.

They had spent the last three hours in this circular covered pit lit only by torches and the firebox in the central hearth. For most of it Marcellinus had sat on the masonry bench around its perimeter with sacred objects above him in wall niches. Occasionally he had stood or knelt as commanded. To either side of the firebox were square depressions covered by wooden boards that had served as foot drums. Behind the fire was the sipapu, a small hole that marked the entrance to the spirit world below, to the watery realm through which the Yupkoyvi's ancient ancestors had first emerged to populate the world. That there was an identical hole in every kiva did not seem to daunt them—each sipapu was apparently *the* genuine, first and only sipapu—but Marcellinus had long ago given up on finding logic in superstition.

He stood now on top of the kiva roof, a circular area leveled with rock, dirt, and juniper bark, held up from beneath by four large pillars. At ground level the Great House of Yupkoyvi surrounded him, massive and solid.

The broad plaza formed the center of a giant D-shaped structure that spanned several acres. Behind and around him was a tall semicircle of buildings or, more accurately, a single massive curved building of some five hundred rooms tiered five stories high. Several hundred feet in front of him was the high straight wall that enclosed the plaza, with only a single gate leading in and out. Another wall, running north-south, divided the D of the plaza into two halves.

The walls were constructed of the same golden sandstone as the cliffs that bounded the canyon. Many of the walls were three feet thick, with cores of sandstone rubble and outer veneers of facing stone, skillfully crafted, with plaster over much of the stone.

It was an almost unbelievable structure to find in the middle of a desert, yet it was just the most imposing of a dozen Great Houses in the Yupkoyvi canyon.

Monumental architecture on a grand scale, yet mostly empty. Many thousands of people could have lived in the vast warren of interconnected rooms. Only a few hundred actually did. Most of the rooms were stuffed with old weapons or tools or filled with trash. Some of the odd T-shaped doorways were blocked. Many whole areas of the house were decaying and unsafe, their roofs crumbling and falling in. The Yupkoyvi had raised no objection to the Romans stabling their mounts in the many ground-floor rooms that were otherwise unused.

For a sacred center, it was strangely profane. The Great House was broken and old, and it was the only one in the canyon that was still occupied at all.

"Your man approaches," Kanuna said.

Sextus Bassus strode across the plaza toward them in tunic and sandals, somehow managing to look crisp despite the heat. Marcellinus stifled a sigh. Seizing the opportunity to escape, Kanuna ambled off to see Enopay, who was waiting in the shade.

"A success, then, was it?" Bassus did not look exactly

elated. He took a subtle step backward; even in the open air, the sweat and smoke that clung to Marcellinus's tunic were quite ripe.

"Success," Marcellinus said sardonically. "We are now allies of the world's first people, and at any moment thousands of mighty warriors of the Hand will converge upon Yupkoyvi to fight by our sides against the foe."

Bassus shook his head. "This is a wild-goose chase, sir. You know it. I know it. We should go on."

"The Imperator ordered us to make a treaty. That's what we'll do. Uh, could I prevail upon you . . . ?" Marcellinus gestured.

Bassus handed over his water skin readily enough, and Marcellinus tilted his head back to gulp water and slake his parched throat as his lead decurion continued. "The Hand? Mighty warriors? Been hearing that for as long as I've been in Nova Hesperia, but . . . these people?"

Marcellinus looked around him. He did not see any true warriors in the plaza of the Great House either, aside from the ones they'd brought with them.

"They're telling you what you want to hear," Bassus said. "All primitives do it. The Handies here and your Cahokian chums, too, for that matter."

It was hard to deny, at least about the people of the southwest. Marcellinus shrugged helplessly.

"I'm not even convinced these *are* the People of the Hand," Bassus grumbled. "This is a shaman outpost. The embers of a dead culture. A washed-up people talking grand talk. There's nothing for us here."

"All the roads led here," Marcellinus reminded him. Wide roads, too. Yupkoyvi was the hub of a wheel with many spokes: roads straight enough for a Roman to be proud of radiated out into the desert in all directions, the best roads any of them had seen in Nova Hesperia. They had ridden into the area on one. It was so consistently level that on the first evening several cavalrymen had gotten down on their hands and knees and dug into the road's edge with their mattocks to see how it was made.

"Here or away." Isleifur Bjarnason had appeared at Marcellinus's shoulder. "But this canyon is the heart of the Hand, all right. They have information. They know things, mark my words. They haven't told us all there is to tell."

Bassus barely spared him a glance. The Norseman had never impressed him. "Sentiment blinds you."

Marcellinus laughed. "Sentiment? Bjarnason? You don't know him very well."

"Certainly this must have been a great place once, but it's played out now. There's been no new building here for generations. These people are living on past glories because they don't know how to do anything else." Bassus gestured after the Yupkoyvi chieftains. "Chack and Chock want you to believe they're big warlords of the desert, but they haven't done shit to back that up the whole month we've been here. They're selling you a bill of goods, sir. I'm not buying it."

"This is still the center of the whole area," Isleifur said.

"A hundred years ago. That does us no good now."

"No, today. It's still the hub. Information flows in here, and information flows out again along the great roads. The old women know a lot about the surrounding towns, even out to the coasts in the west and south. They're getting all that information from somewhere."

Bassus snorted. "Old women? Probably inventing it."

"No," Bjarnason said.

"Well, either way, we should go on."

North of Yupkoyvi they'd encountered tribes that lived in houses built in alcoves in the cliff sides. The Romans had not even been able to approach those high fortresses, so perfect were their defensive positions; Marcellinus, Bassus, Kanuna, and the interpreters had climbed the ladders and steep rock stairs to speak with the elders. Those elders had sent them on here to the "center of the world where all roads meet." On the way

to Yupkoyvi they had passed other towns, of which Tyuonyi was the largest, with a ring-shaped building at its
center, scores more houses spread out around it, and
families also living in carved-out chambers in the hill-
sides beyond. But the people of Tyuonyi also had de-
ferred to the masters of Yupkoyvi here in the sandstone
canyon, and the Roman expeditionary force had moved
along here.

It was not exactly what they had expected.

To the south and west lived yet more peoples, tribes
that generations earlier might have lived in the canyon
of the Yupkoyvi but now had villages and towns of their
own, with new buildings and even more complex systems of canals and irrigation. But the lands of the Hoho-
kam were five hundred more miles through the stark,
sunbaked desert, half again as far as they'd already
come since leaving the *Minerva*.

"We're not going any farther. It's here or nowhere." It
was all Marcellinus could do not to end the sentence
with *I have spoken*.

"Yes, sir." Bassus saluted with an exaggerated formality that verged on insolence and marched off back to his
men.

"Always the verpa," said Isleifur.

"He's not wrong," Marcellinus said. "Whatever
homegrown empire the People of the Hand once had, I
don't think it's here anymore."

Macaws squawked. Frowning against the sun's glare,
Marcellinus felt frustration creeping into his voice. "But
within living memory the People of the Hand struck
across the desert into the grasslands. Son of the Sun
went to Shappa Ta'atan in the first place to help them
fight the People of the Hand."

"Can't have been this lot," Isleifur said. "Maybe some
of the Handies to the north who were hiding in the
mountains."

"Perhaps."

Bjarnason held his eye. "Empires rise and fall. Perhaps
even the Imperium won't last forever."

Marcellinus gave him a look, remembering a conversation long before in which Isleifur had argued that in different circumstances the Norse might have commanded an empire of their own. But such historical second-guessing was pointless. "Not now, Bjarnason. It's too hot."

They walked across the plaza to where Enopay stood with Kanuna. "So what do you think, Enopay?" Bjarnason said. "Is this still the center of a mighty empire? Are we on the verge of a breakthrough?"

Marcellinus took a proffered water skin from Kanuna. It might take two more to truly slake his thirst. "Juno, Isleifur. You're relentless."

"If this was truly where the center of their Great House Empire used to be," Enopay said, "then it must have gone for a walk down one of its own wide roads one day and forgotten to come back."

"They have storehouses full of weapons here. Thousands upon thousands."

"But not the men to wield them. In this House there are maybe five hundreds of people. The men of the Hand who fought with these weapons are long gone, Eyanosa. North, south, east . . . who knows? Spread out, lost, gone. And we should be gone, too."

"One week more," Marcellinus said. "They only formally agreed to ally with us today. Let's at least give them the chance to show us what they've got. They say they've summoned their brothers from the west to come and tell us what we need to know of the Thousand . . . of the Mongols. Haida warriors who have fled all the way from the north, others from the Chumash farther south. Even if we only glean a bit more information and no warriors, it might still be worth it."

Enopay was shaking his head. "You believe them?"

"We can't afford not to," Marcellinus said wearily. "If they have information, we need it. If the Yupkoyvi somehow really can reach thousands of warriors of the Hand in the cliffs to the north willing to stand with us, we need them. This alliance is why we're here. If we leave now, we leave with nothing."

Enopay wiped sweat off his neck and looked around. "This place is even more rotten with shamans than Cahokia was under Avenaka. They make me nervous."

"Me, too," Kanuna said.

"What did you learn?"

Marcellinus looked up, chewed, swallowed, sighed. Pezi and Taianita were approaching him. Evidently he would not even be allowed to eat lunch in peace.

Not that it was worth much. Cactus fruits, a few nuts, juniper berries. A hard chunk of saltbush bread made from the low shrubs in the area. A tea of juniper sprigs. They had long ago finished the Cahokian tea they had brought with them.

"I learned that Yupkoyvi ceremonies go on forever."

Taianita's nose wrinkled. "You smell terrible. Like you've been on fire for two days."

"Sounds about right. Bread?"

Taianita almost shuddered as she shook her head. She was looking thinner, he noticed. So was Pezi. She lowered her voice. "Can we leave soon?"

"Another week. The warriors they're promising are probably a mirage. But Isleifur thinks we still might get some useful information."

Pezi looked across to where Bjarnason was sitting cross-legged, laboriously trying to talk with an old woman who was making pots. Marcellinus smiled, remembering Kimimela's joke that Bjarnason "liked his women wrinkly." In reality the astute Norseman knew all too well that it was the older women of any nation or tribe who held most of the history and wisdom of their communities in their heads and were often more willing to share it than the men. Pezi said: "He should get the Chitimachan to help him. And send the Romans far away."

Marcellinus just grunted.

"Maybe we could leave Isleifur behind to talk to his women and he could catch up to us later."

Taianita poked him. "What Pezi means is that it is as much as we can do to keep the horses grazed and watered here, and it's only going to get hotter."

"I know that," Marcellinus said patiently.

"No," said Pezi. "What Pezi means is that Bassus and his men are jeopardizing all this."

Under Bassus's discipline, the Roman cavalrymen had been polite and well behaved throughout their stay in Yupkoyvi. "Explain."

"They don't know how to talk to people like the Yupkoyvi. Even Bassus makes them nervous. While the Romans are around, they'll never tell all they know. We should have come alone."

If they'd come alone, the People of the Hand to the north might have killed them all. Marcellinus just shook his head.

Taianita reached for one of the cactus fruits Marcellinus wasn't eating. Pezi persisted. "Can we send them off somewhere? Bassus and his turmae. Perhaps make them go and build something? Another reservoir for water? That would build goodwill, and get him out from underfoot so you can talk again with Cha'akmogwi and Chochokpi without Bassus always frowning in the background."

Marcellinus raised his eyebrows. It wasn't a bad idea, one he wouldn't have been surprised to hear from Enopay. Perhaps Pezi had some redeeming value after all . . .

That was unfair. Pezi had value, and so did the other word slaves. At last Marcellinus had seen the virtue in bringing so many translators, because several different languages were spoken just within Yupkoyvi. The People of the Hand were actually many peoples. The translators were almost permanently busy, especially Pezi. Marcellinus had never seen the boy working so hard. His interest in languages was genuine.

Pezi mostly dealt with the elders, chiefs, and shamans. Because of her gender, the Chitimachan was relegated largely to dealing with issues of food and accommodations, which irked both her and Marcellinus, but it was valuable work that had to be done. Taianita was only slowly learning the language of the Hand and mostly helped oil the Cahokians' interactions with the Romans.

Taianita nodded. "Talk to them for the League rather than for Roma."

Marcellinus looked to the left and right, but none of Bassus's men were near. "Ever since we got here, Kanuna and I have been talking to them of the League."

"But all they see is Roma."

Maybe they were right. Both of them annoying as hell but . . . right.

"Very well. I'll talk to Bassus. We'll send them out tomorrow, and perhaps then you, me, Pezi, Isleifur, and Kanuna will give this another try—"

A hundred feet above their heads a Macaw Warrior squawked and rocked his wing back and forth. Taianita frowned at the discordant noise and glanced up into the blue.

Two more Macaw Warriors now squawked and straightened. Both turned to fly southeast, wings rocking. Other Macaws had whirled their craft around, those high up curving back toward the mesa top behind the Great House while those nearer the ground dipped to land in the sacred enclosure in the left plaza.

"Futete," Marcellinus said.

Isleifur's pot-making friend had frozen, her eyes glazing in shock and fear. Now she muttered a few words, gathered her wares, and ran. Isleifur leaped to his feet and headed for a ladder up to the second floor of the Great House. "Enemies!" he called over his shoulder to Marcellinus. "She says enemies come!"

Marcellinus jumped up and followed him up ladder after ladder until they were running together across the roof of the semicircular tenements. The People of the Hand were scattering, some running toward the gates to the city, others scooping up their children and possessions and disappearing into the buildings.

For an emergency, it was uncannily quiet. Marcellinus

heard no horns, no din of rocks being smashed against copper sheets, just the incongruous tinkling of the copper bells at the women's waists as they ran. The squawk of a Macaw was apparently the only alarm needed in a community of the Hand, and that alone was enough to galvanize everyone into action.

"There."

Bjarnason didn't need to point. Marcellinus had already seen the rhythmic flash of reflected sunlight off obsidian from the peak of the towering butte that stood sentry over the canyon's mouth several miles away, as well as the tall cloud of dust in the desert beyond it.

"To horse!" Sextus Bassus appeared below them, his voice booming across the plaza. "Second Aravacorum: ready horses, armor up, mount up, on the double!"

Marcellinus was scanning the canyon. "Sound the horn! Bring everyone back in!"

Bassus nodded and relayed the command. His cornicen gave three blasts of his horn at a volume that had some of the Hand leaping in shock. The trumpeter looked briefly pleased with himself, then sounded the alert again.

"The Fourth are to the west," Isleifur said. "Not too far. See them? Plenty of time."

The troopers of the four turmae took it in turns to exercise and forage for their horses. Grass had become increasingly difficult to find; there was precious little browsing for the four-legs anywhere near the Great House, and they generally had to go most of the way to the adjacent canyon. As for water, there were seeps and springs in the box canyons, many equipped with catch basins, and a dune dam and small reservoir a couple of miles south. Marcellinus saw three ten-man squads of cavalrymen in the distance, heading briskly back toward the Great House, their pack mules trotting gamely in their wake. "Good."

The dust cloud beyond the mouth of the canyon was already closer. It was moving faster than a man could run. Not the warriors of the Hand they'd been hoping for, then. Sweat prickled his skin, and he felt a moment of dizziness. "Mongols, here?"

"Must be," Isleifur said.

Marcellinus almost spit in frustration. "And we only find out *now*? When they're within ten miles?"

"Either the Handies' famous signal stations along their Great Roads are all crap or the Mongols sent outriders ahead to take them out and stop them from raising the alarm. The signal butte would be harder, though; the only way to the top is steep, hidden, well guarded—"

Marcellinus cut him off with a gesture. It didn't matter. What mattered was finding out as soon as possible how large a force they faced, and for that they needed to understand the signal flashes from the butte.

"Stay here. Watch their approach." Marcellinus ran for the ladders and slid down them, back to the floor of the plaza.

"Chochokpi *says* ten thousand men, spread over all across the plain." Pezi was shaking his head. "But Gaius, he has no idea; he is afraid and guessing. You can see it in his eyes."

"The sentries on the butte?"

Pezi looked wry. "All their signals say is *Many*. Perhaps they cannot see through all the dust the Mongol horses are kicking up."

"What do the Hawks . . . I mean the Macaws, what do they say?"

"They cannot yet see far enough either."

Bassus strode toward them, his steel plate armor gleaming in the sun. Beyond him his cavalrymen of the Second Aravacorum mostly had their horses saddled and barded and were in various stages of donning chain mail, boots, and helmets. Two other decurions walked among them, snapping out orders and pointing out girth straps and harnesses that were loose or crooked. The final decurion was with the troopers hurrying back across the canyon floor.

Bassus arrived and saluted. "Well, this is a pretty pass, sir."

Marcellinus grinned with confidence he did not feel. At a time like this, military bravado had to take over. "Certainly is, Decurion."

"No point in trying to get away," Bassus said. "Western end of the canyon's too tough for the horses to negotiate. The Mongols would catch us before we could haul ourselves out. And that would be undignified."

Marcellinus nodded. At a canter, the Mongols might be at the Great House in half an hour. The Romans simply would not have enough of a head start. "Plus, we'd be abandoning the Yupkoyvi."

Bassus snorted. "I don't give a good crap about the Handies. They couldn't warn us better than this? Fuck 'em. If you can get them to stand up for themselves and fight with us, well and good. If not, let them rot."

"I'll see what I can do."

Bassus broke into a run, heading back to his men. The Chitimachan had come to Marcellinus's side. Across the plaza Hanska, Mikasi, and Mahkah had appeared and were talking urgently to Kanuna. The Cahokians tended to sleep through the hottest part of the day. This must have been a rude awakening.

Chochokpi was still talking animatedly to Pezi, waving his arms and shaking his head. Pezi studied him. "He knew the Mongols would come."

"He just said that?"

"Of course not. He claims he is shocked, cannot understand it, does not know how this could have happened. But it's not true." Pezi looked at Marcellinus. "Gaius, I once was a liar and a coward. I can see those things clearly enough in others."

"Pezi speaks true," the Chitimachan said stolidly. "We are betrayed."

"But the People of the Hand are still at risk themselves. Aren't they?"

"Are they?"

Marcellinus nodded grimly. "We'll see. Pezi, tell Chock

to get all his warriors out and lined up, best at the front, ready to fight. Where the hell did Cha'akmogwi go?"

"Let's find out." Pezi strode forward, the Chitimachan by his side.

Cha'akmogwi glared at them and spoke. Pezi pointed at him and translated almost as fast as Chack spoke. "'Yes. Of course we knew.'"

Marcellinus jumped at a sudden sharp sound, his gladius already halfway out of its sheath. The Chitimachan had slapped the Yupkoyvi chieftain. Chack looked startled, then a sneer appeared on his face and he spoke derisively. Pezi pointed again and translated. "'You want your woman to kill me now? Then kill me and have two men less to help you defend against the Mongols.'"

Cha'akmogwi spoke. Pezi translated. "'We knew the Thousand-Thousand came. Last time they passed us by, far from here. Now? Word of you must have brought them.'" He turned. "Chack blames us for bringing the Thousand-Thousand Enemies down upon Yupkoyvi."

The Chitimachan continued the translation. "'But we are few, and you are strong. You must stand with us, protect the Great House. We allied with you for this, no?'"

As Chochokpi added some words, the Chitimachan said, "'This is the alliance you sought: we People of the Hand along with your men of steel and your beasts.'"

The fourth turmae of the Aravacorum cantered in through the gates of Yupkoyvi. Their decurion looked frazzled, and it was his young deputy who gave the orders to the other men to dismount and run for their armor and horse barding.

Marcellinus stepped forward and put his hands up to his mouth to form a trumpet. "Isleifur! How long?"

From the top of the Great House the Norseman turned and waved his arms in hand-talk. *Ten minutes.*

"Shit," said Marcellinus.

Bassus jogged back to them. "So what's it to be? Face

the Mongols outside or fortify and let the bastards siege us?"

The Great House of Yupkoyvi sat against the western wall of a long canyon that ran northwest to southeast. The Mongols were coming in from the southeast. As Bassus had noted already, the northwestern end was negotiable by horses, but only slowly and carefully. The staircases out of the canyon up to the massifs behind them were a hard and dizzying climb; if they tried that, the Mongols would pick them off one by one with arrows and make a sport of it.

Marcellinus looked along the walls of Yupkoyvi. The Great House was no fortress. The walls were thick but only eight feet high and flat-topped with no battlements or crenellations, and there was no time to build any. Nonetheless, they had over a hundred Romans and five hundred of the Yupkoyvi.

"The Mongols are horse archers," he said. "But if we can resist their arrows, hold them back . . . we're short of men, not weapons. There must be a year's worth of arrows in this dump."

Bassus pursed his lips. "The Mongols sieged and broke many a Jin and Song city."

"But that takes engineers and a big army. This may be a small contingent."

"Or a large contingent," Bassus said. "That dust cloud . . ."

"Four or five horses for every man," Marcellinus reminded him. "If it's a small group, they might not be able to break us. And if it's large, they'll have hell's own job getting enough browse for the horses and water for the men while they siege us." He shook his head. They didn't know enough yet. "So let's try to fortify but be ready to charge out if we decide we can take them."

"Fair enough."

Marcellinus turned to Pezi and the Chitimachan. "All right. Tell Chochokpi and Cha'ak . . . Cha'akmogwi to get all the Yupkoyvi who can fight, give them spears and shields, and get them up on the walls. Those who can't fight, get them to bring arrows out of the stores. As many as possible." He looked up at the cliff. "How many Macaw Warriors can they deploy at once? Get them ready to fly. And we'll need—merda, what the hell?"

Smoke gushed from the window of one of the tenements behind them against the mountain on the fourth level. Another window spilled black smoke on the other side of the complex. On the high roof of the fifth level men were attacking the roofline with pickaxes. "Pezi, ask Chochokpi what on earth—"

But Pezi was already snapping at Chochokpi, gesticulating, spitting out words, even as Chochokpi snarled back at him. Now Pezi turned. "They are killing Yupkoyvi. Their sacred house must not fall intact into the hands of the barbarians. This is the Center of the World. The Mongols shall not have it."

"And so they're doing the Mongols' work for them before they even arrive?"

Pezi shook his head. "Bassus was right. These people are mad. Stark, staring mad."

"This is fucking hopeless," said Bassus. "I *told* you. Half of them want us to protect 'em while the other half burn their own fucking town."

Marcellinus nodded. "Let's get on with this."

Bassus strode out into the center of the courtyard and began shouting orders. "Close the gates! Line the walls, tether the horses, prepare weapons!"

Marcellinus scanned the rooflines. The Great House covered two acres. The walls were high and thick, but the structure covered quite an area. Yet the site had no central tower or citadel that could be defended any more easily. They could not consolidate into a smaller area. They defended the whole house or nothing.

It was a tall order, and still the Yupkoyvi were arguing with his translator.

Marcellinus turned, grabbed Chochokpi by the throat, and rammed him back against the plaza wall. Chochokpi yelped, and his brother, Cha'akmogwi, drew a knife and stepped forward. "Stop him," Marcellinus said, and Pezi jerked up his stick and thrust it into Cha'akmogwi's chest. "Stay put."

"Tell him to get the Macaws back in the air," Marcellinus said. "Now. First we need to know how big the Mongol army is. Then we need them to attack the Mongols from above. And tell him to get his people to stop burning and grab weapons. Get them down here to defend their Great House. He gives the orders *now*, and if I don't see fast results, I'll kill him myself."

"Yes." Pezi rattled out orders at the shaman-chiefs and released Cha'akmogwi. The priest of the Hand stepped forward and began to call out his own orders, watching Marcellinus out of the corner of his eye.

Bassus turned and signaled to Marcellinus. The four turmae of horsemen had completed armoring up and were readying their bows, hasta, shields. Waiting for orders. Good.

Marcellinus released Chochokpi, and the man scurried off. The decurion pointed and walked toward the gate. Marcellinus hurried to join him on the walls of Yupkoyvi.

CHAPTER 9

YEAR NINE, CROW MOON

The cloud of dust approached, its contents indistinct, and then all of a sudden the Mongol squadron rode out of it as it reached the harder ground close to Yupkoyvi.

It was Marcellinus's first view of a Mongol force of any kind. His first impression was that they looked dirty and were dressed in a bewildering variety of styles.

As in all barbarian armies, no two men looked the same. Some wore leather armor, others what looked like quilted hide coats that might afford quite a bit of protection against a blade or an arrow. Some sported chain mail in the Roman style, perhaps captured in battle with Roma on the other side of the world. A few rode bare-chested with only a small round shield for protection or what looked like a silken shirt with no armor at all.

The men looked compact and strong. Some already wore their helmets, which were trimmed with fur and had leather flaps. Those who didn't seemed to wear their hair in two braids, one at each side of the head, but with the scalp in between shaved bare. It gave them an oddly unsettling look.

Their famed Mongol warhorses were unimpressive at first sight: short and thick-necked with shaggy manes and distended bellies. Yet those horses were the secret of the Mongols' success, with their legendary speed across the steppes of central Asia and their agility and stamina in battle.

"Two hundreds," Enopay said.

"You're sure?"

"One hundred Mongol warriors makes up a jaghun. I see many more than one hundred men but surely fewer than three hundreds. If Mongol squadrons travel in centuries, I mean in jaghuns, two hundreds of men may be all we face here."

Marcellinus looked down at him. "All?"

"Before it looked like many more because of the spare horses kicking up dust. Two hundreds is far better than a thousand. But yes, enough to be a challenge."

"Damn it," Bassus said.

"What? What do you see?"

"Back corner, tall Mongol warrior with the bright yellow armor? Those are thick leather plates, not copper or gold . . . but that must be Jebei Noyon, one of the Khan's trusted generals. They call Jebei the Arrow because . . . well, the story isn't clear, but some say he shot Chinggis Khan with an arrow once, before his Tayichiud tribe was conquered and he threw in his lot with the Khan." Bassus looked at Marcellinus. "He's tough. But he only has a couple hundred men."

"Whereas we have . . . shit."

Behind them women and children were running out of the Great House with armfuls of spears and arrows, dumping them onto the ground in the center of the plaza, and running back in. The men of Yupkoyvi were picking up spears, thrusting them forward experimentally, muttering at one another. Not one of them was wearing armor.

"Sweet Cybele," Bassus said. "This isn't happening."

"No shields," Enopay said. "Oh, at least they've found some bows now to go with the arrows. Um. See those men on the other side of the plaza, sneaking down the ladders into the kiva?"

Bassus turned back to Marcellinus. "Fuck these jokers; we're wasting time. We can't fortify this shit without concerted Handie support. Which we're not getting. It'd be the most pathetic siege ever. So out we go."

Marcellinus gave in to the inevitable. "Agreed. We ride out and take our chances."

Bassus eyed him. "You're no cavalryman, Gaius Marcellinus. I command this action. Yes?"

Cavalry tactics were not infantry tactics. Marcellinus had fought alongside cavalry wings as a centurion in Galicia-Volhynia and even commanded a mixed cohort as a tribune against the Khwarezmian Sultanate, but those battles were long ago, and today's action would be a purely mounted affair. Sextus Bassus had trained for this all his life. "Absolutely. Your men, your command."

"Isleifur Bjarnason. You're still here?"

Bjarnason frowned as Marcellinus drew near. "Where else would I be?"

"Anywhere." Marcellinus put his mouth near the Norseman's ear. "Don't die here. Disappear."

"Run away?"

"Yes. Get clear, get word back to Cahokia of what happened here. If we all die today, the Imperator learns nothing and all of this was for naught."

Startled, Bjarnason glanced around at the Mongol force before them and the cliffs behind. "Escape how? Tunnel? I'm not a magician."

"Don't sell yourself short. Get going. Don't tell me how you plan to do it."

"That should be easy enough." The Norseman looked around again and shook his head. "I haven't a bloody clue."

"Get one." Marcellinus clapped the man on the shoulder and climbed back to rejoin Enopay atop the front wall.

If anyone could find a way to survive this day, it was the Norseman. But even for him it might be a tough call.

Beneath them, Bassus was caucusing with his decurions and their deputies. "We'll need to close quickly to negate their arrow storm. Dirty bastards only fight hand to hand when they have no choice. They'd rather sit back and let their arrows do the fighting. So we won't give 'em that luxury. Full charge, break through their line, then wheel and mop 'em up."

His officers nodded grimly. All knew it could not be so simple. Bassus looked irritated. "Buck up. With our spears we've got the longer reach in the charge. Our horses are bigger than the scruffy-shit ponies the Mongols ride. And our spathas are longer than their sabers. All advantages to Roma, gentlemen."

"Sir, yes, sir."

That was all true. And with their steel helmets and greaves, breastplates and chain mail, the Roman auxiliaries were better armored than the Mongols.

But the Mongols had speed and agility on their side and outnumbered them almost two to one.

Bassus clapped his hands to get the attention of all the men. "Squadron, listen up. First Turma leads the charge, dense wedge formation." He winked. "You'll need to ride hard to keep up with me. Death or glory, eh, boys? Second and Third Turmae follow us in echelon, left and right, flying wedge, but for Cybele's sake, adjust your position according to how the fucking Mongols react. And listen up! Follow your decurions! Not like the last time against the Iroqua, you bastards. That was a fiasco. You embarrassed your stupid selves. So pay attention while I say it again: *follow your fucking decurions.*"

He turned. "Fourth Turma, hold fast in reserve. Rest up to start. Then pile in wherever we need help or you see an opportunity to break 'em. Try to take out Jebei Noyon if you can. Mongols lose their fucking minds if you kill whoever's telling them what to do. Not like you, though, eh? If I fall, you'll *keep fighting.*"

Bassus turned back to the Third. "And Third Turma? God's sake, this time *thrust* and don't slash. You're not gladiators putting on a show. Kill 'em clean, kill 'em quick. I'll be watching you from the field or from hell. Questions?"

Predictably, there were none.

"Saddle up, then." Now Bassus looked up at Marcellinus. "Close the gates behind us, but be ready to let us back in after. Keep trying to marshal this Handie rabble to defend themselves just in case we don't crush the enemy for you right out of the gate."

Marcellinus nodded. "Good luck, Decurion. Give them ten kinds of shit."

Bassus smiled, his mouth a thin line. "Ten kinds it is. Rip apart any of the bastards we miss."

"Consider it done."

Decurion Sextus Bassus blew out a long breath and then inhaled again. "And thank the gods for some action at last. I was getting so fucking bored in this town."

"Weren't we all?" Marcellinus smiled wryly.

Bassus made a clicking noise, and his horse raised its head and walked toward him. The decurion stepped into the stirrup and swung himself into the saddle in a single movement. He nodded once at Marcellinus, looked around him at the Great House with an expression of withering disgust, and trotted off to take the head of his formation.

"He's dead," Enopay said hollowly. "And he . . . He knows we're all dead, too. Doesn't he, Eyanosa?"

Marcellinus looked down at the boy. Time for his own lesson in bravado. "Don't talk nonsense, Enopay. Grab yourself a sword, stand tall, and keep your eyes open. Stay by me. And remember: ten kinds of shit."

Enopay wiped the sweat out of his eyes and tried to calm his breathing. "Sir, yes, sir."

"We still have the air advantage," Marcellinus said. "The Yupkoyvi have dozens of Macaws. The Mongols won't be expecting that."

"We hope," Enopay said.

The cornicen sounded his horn, and the cavalry of the Second Aravacorum poured out of the main gates of the Great House of Yupkoyvi and onto the field of battle.

* * *

No amateurs at war, the Mongols had stopped to prepare. They were changing horses, climbing onto fresh mounts, dropping their packs to the ground, and tying the bridles of their spare horses together so that they could not roam far while their masters were in battle. Marcellinus saw no orders being given, could not tell which were their squadron commanders, could no longer see Jebei Noyon. The Mongol army was just a solid mass of cavalry that was only now forming up into ranks.

Outside the gates of Yupkoyvi the Roman cavalry had quickly fallen into formation. The First Turma formed a tight triangular formation with Sextus Bassus shouting profane orders from its apex. Behind them on either side spread the Second and Third Turmae. The cavalry advanced out into the battlefield at a brisk walk.

Per orders, the Fourth waited in reserve just outside the wall. Their decurion paced back and forth in front of them. Marcellinus knew that commanding reserves was sometimes harder than being in the first wave. To see your comrades already in the fray and be helpless, knowing you might be ordered into the thickest and most desperate part of the fighting at any moment . . . he had always hated it. And the decurion of the Fourth looked very nervous as well as very young.

The Mongols were already advancing in a long double line. Without doubt they'd begin the battle with a cloud of arrows, wave upon wave, designed to kill as many as possible and shatter their enemy's resolve.

Marcellinus doubted that ploy would work here. Bassus was a tough commander with enough resolve to spare for everyone.

Now the Mongol front line parted neatly, dividing into two halves with a space left between them. Through the space from behind came six Mongols at the gallop, riding shoulder to shoulder. Their synchronization alone was quite a feat on such rocky terrain. Among the Roman troops, only the Chernye Klobuki could possibly have ridden in such a steady formation at such a savage gallop.

Then something large reared up behind the six horse-men, and Marcellinus understood.

A dozen years earlier he would have thought it was a kite. Now he knew better. "Futete . . ."

CHAPTER 10

YEAR NINE, CROW MOON

The Mongol craft climbed into the sky at an almost uncanny angle. The cord that joined it to the galloping Mongol horsemen was too fine to see except where the sun glinted off it. The craft's wing was broad and predatory, with a span about equal to that of a Cahokian Eagle but with a raw and jagged sawtooth shape to its trailing edge quite different from any Mizipian aerial craft. The apex of the wing came to a sharp point, making it appear to skewer the air as it flew. The craft had a long tail, indeed a little like a kite except that this tail was rigid and curved. Both the wings and the tail were etched with red and orange paint, making them glow in the desert sun.

Marcellinus recognized the stylized shape. It was supposed to represent the firebird from Slavic and Asian folklore, similar to the phoenix of Greek myth. The symbol still had power as far east as the Mongol lands. But they surely had not learned the trick of flight back home. The Hesperians of the western coasts must have possessed flight after all, and the Mongols had taken it for their own, adapting the craft to their own favored shapes and aspects.

Three men hung beneath the Mongol Firebird in a line, one behind the other, so closely that they almost overlapped. Mahkah shaded his eyes with his hand and squinted. "The first man holds a bar of wood to steer. The second carries a bow and also cords that lead to . . . sacks under the wings. The third pulls taut four ropes that attach to the back of the wings. As he tugs them, it changes the curve of the wing. To help direct the bird?" Mahkah shook his head. "Sintikala would understand."

The details hardly mattered. "*Damn* them," Marcellinus said.

Roma's biggest advantage over the Mongols had just disappeared. The two sides might be much more evenly matched than the Imperator had hoped. However, the prospect of Marcellinus's expeditionary force surviving to take this news back to Hadrianus seemed slim.

A thousand feet up in the air, the Mongol Firebird finally loosed its cable; the lead pilot reached forward to unhook it manually. The six horsemen who had towed it aloft wheeled away to the right and left and slowed to a canter as they went to rejoin their fellows.

The Firebird soared over the walls of the Great House, still rising, picking up more lift from the heat of the sun on the desert sands as well as the breeze that blew against the cliff.

"Shit," Taianita said. "Cowards . . ."

As one, the Macaws that had whirled over their heads were retreating for the safety of the cliff tops. Like a raptor terrorizing smaller birds, fear of the Firebird had banished all the Macaws from the air in a single stroke. "Pezi! Tell Chochokpi to order the Macaws back aloft! A single Mongol bird cannot possibly threaten all of them!"

But Marcellinus did not wait for a response. Even while Pezi was bellowing the translation at the Yupkoyvi chief, the Roman ran to the ladder down to the plaza of the Great House.

From directly above came a bright flash and a resounding thunderclap, as if a storm had just appeared over them. Marcellinus's boot slipped off the rung of the ladder, and he swung sideways, banging his shoulder on the sunbaked clay of the wall. He felt Taianita grab at his foot and guide it back onto the ladder.

Hot shards rained down around them, clinking as they landed on the roof beside him. With a dazed realization, Marcellinus saw they were slivers of porcelain.

A Jin thunderclap bomb had exploded in the air above them. From his discussions with the other Praetors back in Cahokia, Marcellinus knew that the thunderclap bombs contained the explosive Jin salt and sharp fragments of potsherds, all wrapped in a shell of stiff paper. Those were the small black powder bombs: the much larger and heavier thunder crash bombs were encased in iron, probably too heavy to haul aloft.

Fluttering down around him now were scarlet feathers.

"The Mongol bird just *blew up* a Macaw Warrior," Taianita said. *"Blew up."*

The Firebird streaked over them. Another explosion came, this time from the top of the sandstone cliff, hurling two Macaws into the sky. The wings and their pilots toppled untidily down the cliff to the canyon floor.

"Holy Jove," Marcellinus said. "Holy fucking Jove . . ."

The two mounted squads approached each other across the rocky ground of the Yupkoyvi canyon.

The Mongols had broken into five lines, each of around forty horsemen, some well armored in steel and carrying lances, others the nimbler, more lightly equipped horse archers. All five ranks came forward at the trot.

As Mahkah again arrived at Marcellinus's side, a single arrow arced high over the army, squealing in the air. "Whistling arrow," Marcellinus said.

On the signal, the first rank of horse archers whipped their horses into a gallop, and suddenly arrows were flying.

The Mongols were shooting, their arrows coming thick and fast even as they galloped, and then the first rank peeled off from the charge, moving obliquely in

front of the Romans to flank them. The second rank
came on with long lances at the ready. And behind *them*,
the remaining horse archers were shooting more arrows
high in the air. The storm of death flew over the Mongols' charging cavalry and came raining down on the
men and horses of the Second Aravacorum.

Marcellinus had never seen Mongol archers in action
before. Their rate of fire seemed uncanny. It was almost
impossible to believe that only a hundred or so archers
could loose their arrows swiftly enough to create such a
dark, deadly storm over the Romans.

Mahkah snapped his fingers twice a second. "They
are firing fast. Each archer holds several arrows in his
fingers, looses the bowstring with his thumb to shoot,
immediately nocks another."

At a snarled command from Bassus that was clearly
audible back at the Great House walls, the Roman cavalrymen spurred their mounts into a canter. The natural
bouncing gait helped make them harder targets and
closed the distance to the Mongols more speedily.

Another wave of arrows hurtled across the rapidly de-
creasing gap between the two armies, and then a third.
Romans were going down now, tumbling back off their
horses as their chain mail was pierced by the deadly
arrow swarm. Other arrows glanced off the barding on
the horse's breasts and heads.

Marcellinus could no longer hear the commands, but
at a separation of two hundred paces Bassus's First
Turma broke into a full gallop. The Second and Third
matched them, holding formation.

The two sides converged. Enopay swore under his
breath by Marcellinus's side, half covering his eyes and
half squinting to see better through the brightness and
dust of the afternoon. Mahkah stood still as a stone,
unblinking.

Lines of horses at a charge did not physically collide,
of course. No horse would consent to be charged straight
at a wall of men or a wall of other horses. The two lines
passed through each other, the soldiers of both sides fir-

ing arrows, throwing spears, aiming lances, swinging swords.

The Mongols' greater numbers prevailed, and their hooked lances did much greater damage than did the lighter hasta and spathas of the Romans. The Third Turma in particular had taken a beating in that first clash. Most of its troopers were down, unhorsed, struggling to their feet while their steeds bounded away from them.

The First and Second Turmae regrouped. The Romans were pausing to recover their breath. The Mongol light archers and their mounts apparently had no need to breathe, because they had already re-formed a line and were charging again. The archers leaned forward to brace themselves, almost standing in the stirrups as they sent another cloud of arrows into the Roman cavalry.

Above, the Mongol Firebird had turned. The light breeze was not in its favor and it seemed heavier than the three-pilot Cahokian Eagles, but it was making good headway back across the battlefield. The middle pilot was releasing more bombs, and they were falling away from the bird, one, two, three . . . Two ignited in midair, smoke bombs that gushed noxious black fumes and came to earth between the battle and the walls of Yup-koyvi. The third was a black powder bomb, yet another thunderclap, that exploded above Bassus and his men and showered them with lethally sharp shards of porcelain.

The effect was immediate. Legionaries jerked and flailed in their saddles, some tumbling off; their horses also reacted instantly as the shrapnel drove into them. Bassus's horse bucked, throwing him forward over its head and down onto the ground. Astonishingly, the decurion managed to roll and come up onto his feet, shaking his head as if dazed but still holding his sword. Others, less fortunate, lay still and crumpled on the ground.

Even through the smoke that now wreathed the battlefield it was clear that the three Roman turmae were broken. Most of the men were down, maybe half of the Second Turma on the left still mounted but struggling to control their horses, cut off from the others.

"Romans, to me!" Bassus roared. "To me! Form two lines, back to back! *Move*, you slack bastards!"

Outside the gate below Marcellinus the troopers of the Fourth milled, its decurion still standing by his horse. From ground level he could not see all that Marcellinus could from his greater height. Either that or the man had just lost his nerve. His men seemed to be arguing with him.

Out on the plain most of Bassus's cavalrymen were off their mounts, struggling to join up. Unmanned horses milled, some neighing in alarm and looking for a way to escape the field of battle, others wounded, staggering, dropping onto their haunches with plaintive and almost human screeches of pain. To Bassus's credit, the Roman lines were forming quickly: perhaps fifty men in chain mail with swords and spathas, some limping, cramming themselves together into two close-order lines, back to back.

A defensive infantry formation worked well enough against horsemen if their ranks were protected by scuta, the long shields borne by legionaries. With the smaller ovals carried by the Roman troopers, it was a desperate measure.

The Mongols would not charge, Marcellinus was sure. They would merely back up and loose wave after wave of arrows into the mass of men. Mongol arrows could pierce armor if shot squarely and at close range. It would only be a matter of time.

But this did not appear to be the Mongol plan. The light horse archers circled, but half a dozen warriors were dismounting, men in heavier armor who bore not simple lances of wood and steel but long tubes of iron.

"Fuck it," Marcellinus said. Bassus's foul mouth was contagious. "Fire lances. Enopay, stay right here. Mahkah, you're with me."

"Eyanosa, don't!" Enopay's terrified voice followed

him as he jumped down off the wall and ran for his horse. "Please, Gaius, no, no!"

Marcellinus forced himself to ignore the boy's cries. "Pezi, Chitimachan: close the gates behind us and tell Chack and Chock that if they don't defend the Great House, I'll come back and tear them apart with my bare hands."

Marcellinus swung himself up into the saddle. Just inside the gate, Taianita stood ready with spears. As he approached, she raised one to him. Marcellinus snatched it and tucked it into the leather scabbard behind the saddle. "Another, quick." Taking the second, he held it under his arm uncertainly in the couched position, but it did not feel right; it was more of a javelin than a lance. He took it into his hand again, remembering Bassus's posture as he had ridden out.

Marcellinus had always been a commander of infantry. A horse had carried him to battle on countless occasions, but he had always dismounted to fight. He would need to learn fast today.

Mahkah rode up and took a spear from Taianita. Hanska and Mikasi were not far behind him. The People of the Hand were still milling hopelessly around the plaza, there were no Macaws in the air, and Chack and Chock had disappeared again.

Nothing he could do about that. The hell with them. Marcellinus dug in his heels, and they rode through the gate together, out of the Great House and onto the battlefield.

"Ala Aravacorum!" Marcellinus shouted. "Fourth Turma, form up, three ranks!"

They surged toward him as soon as he burst out of the gate. Gods knew where their decurion had gone, for Marcellinus no longer saw him among them.

They were not forming ranks, but that was all right. Rattled by the Mongols' seemingly effortless defeat of the first three turmae, many were terrified out of their wits. It was enough that they were grouping up behind Marcellinus and the Cahokians, enough that they were still hearing orders and had not been panicked into fleeing and earning Mongol arrows in their backs.

"To Marcellinus!" The troopers of the Second Turma who had become detached from their fellows galloped around in a wide arc to join the Fourth.

Marcellinus's horse was cantering so jerkily beneath him that it was hard to spit the words out. "Spears up! If no spears, spatha! Weapons at the ready!"

Smoke wafted across them. Marcellinus could not tell how many men were still with him. His horse's head was bobbing, eyes wide, even as Marcellinus dug his heels into the animal's flanks. A horse took its confidence from its rider and the other horses it could see. As the troopers were on the verge of panic, the horses they rode were right on the edge of spooking, too. If Marcellinus's horse refused, bucked, or—even worse—bolted, their day was done and that would be that, and Marcellinus himself might be lying on the ground with a broken back, defenseless against a Mongol spear or blade.

But the horse he rode was young. Perhaps it had never yet failed a charge and so had no memory of failure.

Marcellinus and the remains of the Second Aravacorum squadron bore down upon the field of battle at speed. The Mongol horse archers were swinging around to counter them but would not form a line in time. Arrows began to fly. Disregarding them, Marcellinus headed straight for Bassus and his men, who had now achieved a messy two-line formation in the face of the approaching fire lancers.

Marcellinus thrust his first javelin down at one of the warriors on foot holding a fire lance, and even as it lodged in the man's chest, Marcellinus twisted his second javelin free from the leather cup behind him and raised it over his head.

The Mongol warrior staggered back three paces but did not fall. He touched the slow match to the Jin salt packet on his fire lance, and the lance ignited with a roar. Dazzling flame shot out of the iron tube, a deadly tongue of fire ten feet long.

Marcellinus's horse leaped away from the bright flame. As he grabbed at his reins, the spear slid out of his hand and clattered to the ground.

The fire lance swung around and flared directly at him. He felt the searing pain of flame across his chest and shoulder, saw bright sparks. Then his steed reared, and all at once Marcellinus was in the air.

He crashed down to earth. All the breath was knocked from his body. All around him were boots and hooves. He instinctively tried to swing his spear around before realizing that he no longer held it. Shaking his head to clear it, Marcellinus dragged in an agonizing breath and drew his spatha.

He saw flame and swung at it. His spatha rang against the metal tube of the Mongol fire lance. Marcellinus shoved himself up onto his knees and swung again.

Thrust, don't slash: good advice from Bassus to his Third Turma, and it became Marcellinus's instinct now. The tip of his spatha went up into the Mongol's unprotected armpit and through his shoulder. The man screamed. Marcellinus jerked the spatha out and away with difficulty and jabbed it forward again into the man's groin.

The fire lance fell, still gushing flame. When it bounced on the ground, one of Bassus's dismounted horsemen snatched it up with great presence of mind and jammed its bright jet of fire into the face of one of the Mongol cavalry horses.

An arrow went through Marcellinus's shoulder, fired at almost point-blank range. Marcellinus roared as the pain exploded in his shoulder, but he had no time to deal with it; he had to move. He almost made it up onto his feet before a Mongol boot thudded into his chest and a swinging saber knocked the spatha out of his hand.

He was under attack by two Mongol horsemen at once, and he had no weapon. He tried to grab at the nearer of the two to pull him from his horse, but a leather gauntlet slammed into his face with fearsome force. Once again Marcellinus felt as if he were flying, blue sky dazzling him.

The back of his head impacted the steel of Roman chain mail. Hands slid under his arms and hauled him up. Marcellinus found himself standing with a Roman cavalryman on each side, surrounded by Mongols on horseback and on foot. His fight was over.

Marcellinus and the men around him were captured. Other legionaries fought on, but the fire lances had done their damage. The Roman line was irredeemably breached, carved into small groups of three or four men, and the mounted Mongol warriors rode between them, slashing at the troopers and knocking them to the ground. One group of Romans had rallied and managed to pull three Mongols from their horses and stab them as they lay on the ground, but as soon as the Mongols saw that happen, they drew bows and shot a barrage of arrows at the helpless troopers from just a few yards away.

The fire lance closest to Marcellinus sputtered and went out, its black powder exhausted. Farther away two lances still spit their deadly fire. It blazed hotter and fiercer than any flame Marcellinus had seen before and was incredibly focused.

The men who wielded the lances seemed fascinated by them. Perhaps this was the first time these particular warriors had used their terrible weapons on human prey. Their faces were subtly different from those of the Mongols: they were Jin, men of the land that had birthed the dark powder, experts in its use. And now Marcellinus saw one of the men walk over to a fallen and injured Roman and apply the flame directly to the man's head and shoulders, bathing him in its full blast. The Roman screamed and thrashed, but only for a moment. Soon shock and pain drove him into insensibility and death. As this lance, too, ran out of powder, the Jin leaned over to study the devastation he had wrought on the Roman's flesh, his face showing only curiosity, as a shaman might look at an animal's entrails to augur the future.

Right now Marcellinus could see the future, too. He could surely predict the calamitous destruction that would come about when such weapons were turned on Cahokia and the legions of Roma.

On the edge of the melee, Mahkah broke away. With a last slash at the Mongol warrior he was battling with, he wheeled his horse and spurred it into a gallop. One of the warriors sheathed his sword, snatched up his bow from the saddle holster, and nocked an arrow.

Hanska had been knocked off her horse but was still on her feet, slashing with the sword in her right hand, the hasta spear in her left held ready to thrust. Two mounted Mongols were circling her, looking for their chance to take her down. Now she hefted the hasta overarm and cast it at the Mongol who was taking aim at the fleeing Mahkah.

She was almost fast enough. The spear lodged in the Mongol's thigh just as he loosed his arrow. He shouted in pain and spasmed, but even as the bow flew out of his grasp, the arrow was speeding on its way. It hit Mahkah in the left side of his back. Mahkah jerked and threw up his arms in an uncanny echo of the Mongol warrior's reaction to Hanska's spear, then slumped forward over his horse's neck. A second Mongol now shot at Mahkah, but Marcellinus could not see if his arrow struck the young brave. Mahkah's piebald steed kept going, still at the gallop, across the canyon.

Two other Roman cavalrymen also had broken out and were attempting to flee westward, bent low over their mounts. One of them was the hapless decurion of the Fourth Turma. Mongols pursued them, aiming bows and using their legs to raise themselves half out of their saddles. They shot, nocked more arrows, shot again. The decurion tumbled leftward off his horse's back to be dragged across the desert floor by his stirrups until his horse slowed. The second Roman died in the saddle, his horse turning to look almost comically at the inert rider on its back. The Mongols cantered after the decurion to finish him off, sabers and clubs at the ready.

Mahkah's mount had slowed to a trot but was well out of range of Mongol arrows. His body bounced up and down on its back, his arms now hanging on each side of the horse's neck. Fully engaged rounding up the Roman survivors, the Mongols declined to pursue him.

He was probably dead anyway. "Shit," said Marcellinus.

The first pain in his side grew suddenly even worse. His eyes closed in agony. In the very next moment the Roman cavalryman holding his right arm slapped him right in the same place. Marcellinus yelled in rage and thrashed to try to free himself.

"Christ, man, keep still," the cavalryman said. "You're on fire."

It was true. Marcellinus had taken the blast of the fire lance to his chest. His armor had saved him from the worst of it, but the tunic under his arm had been burned sheer away, and at its edges it was now in flames.

With great effort of will and against all his instincts, Marcellinus forced himself to go limp. The men let him fall and threw sand and gravel on him until they quenched the flames.

He lay there panting, inhaling the reek of his own scorched flesh. For a moment logical thought fled, and all he could think was that he would never see a Cahokian hearth fire again.

Never see Sintikala again.

"Fuck," he said, and at the same moment the cavalrymen standing over him groaned.

Glancing left, he saw the gates of Yupkoyvi creaking open even as he heard Enopay's voice cracking as he shouted, "No! Close them, idiots, close them!"

Cha'akmogwi and Chochokpi chose not to take their orders from a Cahokian boy. Yupkoyvi was surrendering without a fight, and it was only now that Marcellinus realized that since the Firebird had launched, he had not seen a single Macaw Warrior in flight.

Mongols on horseback moved around the battlefield. Where they found a Roman trooper down and wounded, they speared him from the saddle, driving down into the man's throat with all their weight until he was dead, robbing the wounded of life without even troubling to dismount. Other Mongols walked amid the devastation. As they came to each dead Roman, they knelt quickly, sliced the right ear from the corpse, tossed it into a rough hemp bag, and moved on to the next. Trophies of war or merely proof of their victory?

Mikasi grunted. "Hotah? Here."

Marcellinus turned his head. Sextus Bassus was down. His helmet was off, and he had a bad cut up his cheek and across his forehead. His right arm was terribly burned and blistered, and he was holding it straight, not moving it; the remains of his tunic stuck to the wound, and a sickening smell of cooked meat wafted on the air. Worse, his breathing was noisy and belabored, his breastplate cracked across, a huge gash in the chain mail beneath.

"Shit. Get his armor off."

Blood bubbled at the corners of Bassus's mouth. Mikasi looked sorrowful. "Hotah, Bassus is already dead."

"Do it."

Mikasi unbuckled the remains of the decurion's breastplate and drew it aside gingerly. "There is a hole."

There was indeed a deep and messy hole in Bassus's chest. As he tried to breathe, blood and bubbles spilled from it. "I see it. Help me get the chain mail away from it. Don't rock him, don't touch the hole. Bassus? Can you hear me?"

The decurion narrowed his eyes and panted. Blood frothed from his chest again.

"It is bad," Mikasi said. "Bassus now breathes through his ribs, not his mouth."

Marcellinus looked back at the wide-eyed cavalrymen lying behind him and tapped the boot of the closest with his fist to get his attention. "Soldier, rip the sleeve off your tunic. Give it to me. Quickly now."

The trooper did so. Very carefully, wrestling all the while with his own pain, Marcellinus lay the sleeve over the sucking wound and held it in place. More blood spilled from Bassus's mouth, but his anguished expression eased and his eyes met Marcellinus's. In moments, however, his discomfort seemed to increase and his eyes lost focus again. Marcellinus eased his pressure on the wound and felt a little air escape.

Marcellinus was no medicus, but he knew what his eyes were telling him. "Mikasi, Hanska: take over here. Let the air out from his chest but not in. Release the pressure every few moments. And clean that blood away from his mouth. D'you see?"

"Yes." Mikasi took over.

"Noyon," said one of the cavalrymen.

The Mongol general was approaching on foot, walking his dappled horse between the bodies of the slain. He was almost a head taller than the other Mongols, a lean, strong-looking man in his forties. His armor of yellow leather hung easily on him as if he had been born to it. He stared at Marcellinus and his captives with a cold and malevolent gaze, as if he would like nothing better than to rend them limb from limb with his own hands and leave their bodies to decay in the dust of the desert. He looked like a man without a soul, a murderous machine.

Daunted, Marcellinus looked at Jebei's horse instead, which was much less imposing. Small by the standard of the Libyans and Hispanians favored by the Romans, the general's mount was stocky, its mane tangled, its tail long and unkept. The Mongol horses were ugly beasts, but they were certainly hardy.

The general arrived. He stared at Marcellinus, who met his eye again. Jebei Noyon's gaze then lowered to take in the burn in Marcellinus's side, the hole where the arrow had passed through his shoulder, and then down at his right leg. It was only during these moments of inspection that Marcellinus realized that indeed, at some point in the battle he had received a bloody slash in his calf in almost the same place he had been injured in the fight on the Great Mound the day Great Sun Man had died. The pain of the leg wound had been masked by the agony of his burn.

Jebei turned his attention to Bassus, recognizing him as a Roman officer by the red plume on his helmet, and looked at the blood that was still spreading around his chest wound. Giving the other huddled Roman troopers a cursory glance, the Mongol general then looked carefully at Mikasi and Hanska. Hanska he examined from braids to boots with an intensity that would have seemed perverse if it were not so cold. It was clear that he had rarely, if ever, come across a woman warrior.

It was a little uncanny to be studied as if they were animals or already dead meat. Marcellinus felt chilled. Even in the battle's aftermath he could see the implacable ruthlessness of the Mongols. In those moments he understood their terrible reputation for ferocity. To Jebei Noyon, Marcellinus and the others were less than human.

Looking past the general, Marcellinus saw that meanwhile the Mongol warriors had ridden in through the gates of Yupkoyvi unopposed. The sounds of screams came from within. If the Yupkoyvi shaman-chiefs had hoped to preserve their people by opening the gates without further resistance, they were sadly mistaken. The Mongols lived by a different code. The People of the Hand had merely facilitated their own massacre.

Marcellinus swallowed with difficulty. What of Enopay? What of Taianita, the Chitimachan? Lying on the ground two hundred yards away, he could see nothing of them.

Marcellinus said: "We will need to carry my decurion to the Great House. Other men have wounds to be treated."

The Mongol general stared at him again with that cold, dispassionate interest.

"Come on, man, the battle is over. Help us."

Jebei raised his boot and drove it into Marcellinus's shoulder, just above the arrow wound. Marcellinus bellowed and fell back, eyes streaming with pain.

Hanska glared. "Or just kill us all and get it over with. Add our corpses to your pile and our ears to your bag of souvenirs. Why not? Bastard."

Jebei shook his head. He spoke in a guttural language the like of which Marcellinus had never heard before.

With dazed disbelief, Marcellinus saw Pezi and Taianita walking out of the gates of Yupkoyvi, accompanied by one of the Mongol horse archers. They drew up, and even more to his surprise, Pezi bowed deeply to Jebei Noyon, to Marcellinus, and to the almost unconscious form of Sextus Bassus. "Wanageeska."

"Pezi." The dizzy feeling of unreality swept Marcellinus again. He felt as if he might float away. He resisted the urge to laugh manically. "What now? Have you switched sides again?"

Pezi frowned and shook his head. "I think you have lost much blood." He made a rather imperious gesture to Taianita, ordering her forward, and Taianita knelt by Bassus to examine his wound.

"I told them Taianita is a great healer and knows much."

Marcellinus struggled to keep his face expressionless. Taianita was no Chumanee. She had some limited experience with battle wounds but knew little even of herbs, let alone of an injury as severe as Bassus's. "Be careful with your lies, Pezi."

"My lies may yet save our skins," Pezi said. "You should bow and honor me even as I honor you, so that these filthy men see that we are both important and do not add our ears to their bag."

"Sit up, Gaius." Taianita tugged at Marcellinus's arm, her young eyes lined with concern. "Sit *up*." Without waiting, she started to ease tatters of his tunic from the burned gash in his torso.

"Obey her, Wanageeska. Let her see," said Pezi, and Marcellinus relented. Perhaps if he could just breathe more easily his mind would not float away and he might make better sense of what was going on here. However, when he sat up, he immediately felt dizzy, as if his body no longer belonged to him.

Pezi bowed deeply again and addressed the Mongol general, first in the language of the Hand and then in Iroqua and a third language. Shaking his head he turned to Taianita, who tried a few words in Caddo.

The general stood impassive. He did not understand.

"Merda." Pezi looked back at the gates. "We need the other man. The demon."

Demon? Were not the Mongols all demons? Despite the tension of the moment, Marcellinus laughed with a slight edge of hysteria. He could not help it. None of this made sense. Was he delirious?

Perhaps the Mongol general saw Marcellinus's laughter as disrespect. He stepped forward, his eyes murderous, and once again raised his boot.

Pezi boldly moved between Marcellinus and the general with his eyes lowered, raised his arms, and in the hand-talk of the Plains gestured, *Back, stop, please, we talk, we beg, we beg.*

Jebei Noyon halted, and his hands danced in a few quick hand-talk gestures of his own. *Show respect. Kneel or die.*

"Gaius? Straight face, no laugh, and kneel if you want to live."

Taianita pushed at him roughly. Marcellinus struggled onto his knees, gasping at the pain. Pezi pushed his head down, almost into the ground. Marcellinus frowned at the dirt and pebbles beneath him, leaning against Taianita and trying to breathe.

Hand-talk? Was it so obvious that they had almost missed it and nearly died as a result? Perhaps there was no reason why they should have guessed a Mongol would know it, even a Mongol who had been in Nova Hesperia for several years.

"Ah, I see the demon," Pezi said.

"Demon?" Marcellinus said into the ground.

They let him up, and again he was racked with so much dizziness that he thought he might retch. He closed his eyes, opened them, and saw he was bleeding again. "Pezi, what are you talking about?"

"A warrior chief from the northwest, allied with the Mongols." Pezi was looking back toward Yupkoyvi. His movements were calm and assured, but knowing Pezi as he did, Marcellinus could see the deep fear in his eyes that he was trying to hide. "There he is. He is Tlin-Kit."

An extraordinary figure was walking toward them from the direction of the Great House. Covering his head was a wooden helmet with a full face mask on which was carved the face of a demon. The mask had bright copper eyebrows and was decorated with what might be real human hair. He wore armor of thick animal hide, fastened with wooden toggles and decorated with small metal disks. As the man approached, they saw that the disks were all of a uniform size, with square holes in the center. "Jin coins," muttered one of the legionaries.

Marcellinus would have thought Tlin-Kit a shaman if not for the thick wooden club with a wicked bone hook he carried in his right hand and the two severed Yupkoyvi heads that hung by their hair from his left. The heads knocked together obscenely, dripping blood. "Holy Jove."

The same legionary spit. "Fucking barbarian."

"Easy, trooper," Marcellinus said.

The warrior pushed his helmet up as he approached, which had the bizarre effect of making him appear to have two faces stacked one above the other. He said something guttural.

Pezi bowed deeply yet again. "Tlin-Kit."

Marcellinus had to admit that Pezi's courage had grown. Anyone who could face fearsome warriors like

Jebei Noyon and Tlin-Kit and calmly speak words in several different languages deserved Marcellinus's respect.

Tlin-Kit spared Pezi only a glance, then surveyed the prisoners. He spoke again, and Marcellinus recognized it as rough and strongly accented Algon-Quian.

Pezi responded in the same language, bowing and gesturing. Jebei Noyon and Tlin-Kit talked in Mongol, and then the warrior from the northwest spoke to Pezi again.

Pezi drew himself up and spoke in Latin. "Here is Jebei Noyon, one of the foremost generals of the Mongol Khan. Jebei wants to know which of you two rules here. But I fear that he might keep that chief alive and kill the other. So I say to him: both of you, you and Bassus. He asks again, which? I say both."

"Futete." Bassus was sweating and breathing hard, his voice a faint wheeze. "Save Gaius. Let the bastard kill me. I'm done for anyway."

"Be strong, Decurion," Marcellinus said. "Mongols respect strength above all else."

"Shit," said Mikasi, and looked at Hanska. If only the chiefs would be kept alive, the Cahokians were dead, too.

Jebei Noyon spoke again in his difficult flat speech, and the warrior Tlin-Kit again translated into his accented Algon-Quian, augmented with the hand-talk.

Pezi stared. He wiped sweat from his forehead and said nothing.

"'You will not eat,'" Taianita said mechanically as she translated, her brow furrowed. "'You will drink no more water than the drops that will keep you alive. Your wounds can weep blood into the rocks of this desert. You are not worth mercy. You . . .'" Her voice trailed off.

Marcellinus might have spoken, but it was too hard, and he did not want to risk antagonizing this Mongol general any further.

Pezi and Taianita were doing their best. For now, his life was in their hands.

"No, no," said Pezi, and then repeated it in hand-talk, *No, no, I beg*. He fell onto his knees and began to speak quickly in Algon-Quian.

Jebei Noyon nodded to the Mongol warrior by his side. The warrior reached down and slapped Pezi across the mouth.

Pezi recovered, sat up again, talked some more. Jebei Noyon said three words. They sounded dismissive. Tlin-Kit laughed cruelly and spit a short phrase in Algon-Quian. Then Jebei turned and walked away, his horse on one side and Tlin-Kit on the other. Pezi watched them go. Three Mongol warriors stayed, standing over them.

Marcellinus couldn't bear it anymore. "Begging for your life, Pezi?"

Pezi wiped the blood from his mouth. "Begging for yours."

"What? What did you tell them?"

"That you are important. That you have the ear of the Imperator of Roma."

Marcellinus's thoughts were coming slowly, as if swimming through mud, and for a sick moment all he could think of were the ears being hacked off by the Mongol horsemen. "What?"

Pezi clapped his hands abruptly in front of Marcellinus's face, making him reel back in shock. "Wanageeska, wake up! I tell them that the Imperator of Roma is here in Hesperia, which they clearly know already, and that *you* know him. That you are valuable and should be kept alive."

"Pezi, Mongols do not take hostages, and Hadrianus would not pay a bent sesterce to get me back."

Pezi looked exasperated. "Stop arguing and thank me. For Jebei's last words were to tell me that you Roman leaders and all the Cahokians, and perhaps the Romans that still survive, he will now spare and take to the Mongol Khan."

Marcellinus's heart lurched. "To the Khan? *Chinggis* Khan?"

"Of course. The Khan is far from here." Pezi glanced

at the retreating figure of Jebei Noyon. "The Arrow serves his chief. You may have information about Roma and Cahokia that his chief needs. So it is the Khan himself who will decree who lives and who dies."

"They'll torture us for information?"

"Mongols do not torture," Bassus muttered with difficulty.

"Perhaps they do now."

"Well. All I know is that we must now go to the plaza of the Great House." Pezi looked apologetic. "I am sorry, Wanageeska. We may not walk, may not even stand. We must crawl there."

"Crawl?"

One of the Mongols stepped forward and poked at Marcellinus's back with his saber.

"We must crawl before the Mongols." Pezi lowered himself onto his belly. "Crawl like the worms they say we are. I am sorry."

"What about him?" Hanska pointed to Bassus, outraged. "How does *he* crawl? Fuck this shit . . ."

She put her hands to the ground as if to stand. Two Mongol warriors shoved at her, one kicking her ankles.

"Hanska, Hanska!" Mikasi was already down, shaking his head at her in warning. "Do not anger them. Please. Join me down here."

"We will help Bassus between us," Pezi said. "Hanska, if you are dead, you can help no one. Please?"

"Futete." Hanska dropped onto the ground by Bassus's side. "All right. Let's go."

It was an hour before they arrived at the gates of Yupkoyvi, easing the lead decurion along the ground between them with agonizing slowness.

Appearing gradually before them as they entered the plaza was a mound of corpses.

The Mongols were sweeping the Great House from end to end, marching through each level in groups of twenty. Many dozens of the Hand had tried to hide in the rooms, kivas, and storage pits of Yupkoyvi. Now they were being dragged out into the open air, there to be slain swiftly by a sword blade to the throat and their amputated ears added to the Mongols' grisly collection. It was a systematic, heartless slaughter.

In addition, the Thousand-Thousand were stockpiling food, turquoise, obsidian, copper, furs, feathers, anything that might be of use or value. They seemed to take no pleasure or sorrow in their work. They were merely men following orders with a calm and chilling efficiency.

And there was Enopay on his hands and knees, too, his eyes red, his arms bloodied. "Fuck you, Mongol warrior! Fuck you!" Again he tried to rise; again the Mongol standing over him shoved him back down into the dirt with his boot.

The Mongols were slaying the women and children of Yupkoyvi with as little compunction as the men. Enopay was still alive only because he was Cahokian, and at any moment the hard-bitten Mongol looming over him could decide he was too noisy to be worth the trouble. "Enopay, stay down! I'm coming!"

"Gaius!" Enopay dropped to the plaza floor, put his palm up to his forehead, and stared wide-eyed. He obviously had not expected to see Marcellinus alive again. "Merda, merda . . ."

"Where is Kanuna?"

"Over there. I was trying to go to him. They struck him very hard."

Yes, Kanuna was sprawled out on the ground some hundred feet away, his face covered in blood and his arms and legs untidy, like a broken doll.

"Kanuna!" Heedless of the danger, Taianita pushed herself up and made as if to hurry across the plaza to the stricken elder.

A Mongol grabbed her by the hair and yanked her back. Taianita resisted, trying to kick him, but the Mongol warrior swung his elbow into her jaw. She fell over Marcellinus's legs and went down hard, unconscious. The Mongol bestrode her, studying her, his saber in his hand and his eyes cold.

From the ground Pezi started talking quickly in Algon-Quian, although this Mongol could not possibly have understood. Pezi ducked his head, bowing repeatedly. The warrior kicked him, looking disgusted, but left Tai-anita where she lay.

Enopay covered his face. "No, no, no, no . . ."

Marcellinus crawled to the boy as quickly as he was humanly able, tearing whatever skin was left off his forearms and knees and leaving a trail of blood across the plaza. "Enopay, hush, be still." He wrapped his arms around the boy, and Hanska and Mikasi crawled to them and held them both, in the dirt under the baking sun, as the Mongol soldier loomed over them with his deadly spear in his hand and the massacre of the Yup-koyvi continued around them.

CHAPTER 11

YEAR NINE, GRASS MOON

They rode out of Yupkoyvi the next morning. At the head of his jaghuns rode Jebei Noyon, the Arrow, sitting tall and proud. Once more he wore his resplendent yellow leather armor, and beside him a Mongol standard-bearer carried his spirit banner, a pole with a long fringe of jet black horsehair hanging from a circle of steel.

Between the two jaghuns rode the prisoners, lashed to the saddles of captured Roman mules. With Marcellinus were Sextus Bassus, Hanska, Mikasi, Enopay, Kanuna, Pezi, Taianita, and the Chitimachan, and behind them the two chiefs of Yupkoyvi, Cha'akmogwi and Chochokpi. Taianita had regained consciousness but was still groggy, nauseous, and sullen. The Mongols had killed the remaining rank-and-file Roman soldiers the previous nightfall after all, and so these were the last survivors of the massacre in the valley of the Great Houses, the only men and women who remained.

Marcellinus was sure they were living on borrowed time. They had little of use they could tell the Great Khan, nothing to barter for their lives. They would be curiosities, exhibits to show off Jebei Noyon's cleverness, along with the nauseating sacks of ears of the dead that enumerated the magnitude of his slaughter and were now being carried on either side of a Mongol pack-horse, blood seeping through the hides.

Behind the second jaghun came the other spoils of war: the fifty or so Roman horses that had survived the battle intact and the remainder of their mules, bearing the spears, turquoise, furs, feathers, and food of the People of the Hand.

As ordered, Isleifur Bjarnason had vanished. At any moment during the ravaging of Yupkoyvi, Marcellinus had expected to see the Norseman's bleeding body tossed out of one of the T-shaped doorways, since he probably would have fought to the death to resist capture. It did not happen. Unless his corpse already lay hidden in one of the Mongols' piles of bodies, Bjarnason had evaporated into the air, as he had on many other occasions.

As the day wore on, some of the Mongol warriors galloped ahead in pairs or in fours. They were scouts and skirmishers, moving quietly into the lands ahead, hunting for possible threats and potential victims. In midafternoon the jaghuns came upon a small native village by a river, three lodges that had each contained a family. The inhabitants now lay freshly slain with their bodies piled carelessly on the ground and flies buzzing around them. The Mongol outriders took no chances.

From the desert plains of the Hand they traveled north day after day, then up into the foothills of the Great Mountains, where the air was cooler and there were many streams. Jebei Noyon was as good as his word. The prisoners were allowed no food and drank only water. Toward the end of a week's traveling, when they were all so weak that they could barely stand once they were cut loose from the mules, the Arrow allowed them each a handful of dry corn and a strand of some tough and salty dried meat that could only be horseflesh. Taianita would not eat hers and gave it to Bassus.

Remarkably, the First Decurion had not died. Jebei Noyon had assigned a warrior to ride with him and dress his wound. Bassus got food when the rest of them did not. But as Bassus strengthened, Kanuna weakened.

Asleep on his mule much of the time, too weak to talk, he seemed to have lost all interest in living.

As for Marcellinus, he lived in a permanent daze. Without food and sufficient water he was still short of blood and quickly grew gaunt. His muscles dwindled. His burn wound and the gashes in his leg and shoulder still leaked from time to time, but eventually dried up.

He felt like a husk of a man, and the rest of their company was not much better. He did not know how much longer they could survive this.

Since their captors told them nothing, it was the Firebirds that flew overhead that gave the captives notice that at last they were approaching the camp of the Mongol Khan.

They were back on the high plains, traveling north with the tall crags of the Great Mountains to their left. The sun rose over the desert and set in early afternoon behind the massive peaks. It was little wonder this mighty mountain chain had been such an obstacle to the Khan. Yet somewhere still to the north of them there must be a break or at least a high pass negotiable by tens of thousands of warriors and their horses and carts, and the Mongol Khan had obviously found it.

The Firebirds, three of them, were flying up and down the line of the mountains. The wind was from the east, blowing up against the crags, and the three-man Mongol flying craft rode the surges and currents in the air, accustoming themselves to the ridge lift. Their pilots were by no means Cahokian in their skills; their flying was unsteady, their turns clumsy. More than once Marcellinus held his breath in the hope that the pilots would overcorrect and crash into the rocks or stall their craft and drop out of the air to crumple in a bone-smashed mess on the dry plains. It must have happened many times while the Mongols learned their flying skills, but Marcellinus never witnessed such a disaster.

The Firebirds must have relayed word to the Khan of their approach, because soon another jaghun came cantering south to meet them. For the first time Marcellinus saw joy and humanity on Mongol faces as warriors greeted one another and friends joked. Congratulations were obviously being exchanged. Men bragged of their conquests, traded news, shared fresh askutasquash and fruits, and slabs of buffalo meat for roasting over their fires that night. They brought an alcoholic beverage, too, that Pezi learned was called airag. Apparently the Mongols made it by fermenting the milk from their mares. It sounded awful and smelled worse, and drinking it made the Mongols roar with laughter and sing tunelessly for hours around their campfires.

There was no airag for the warriors who guarded the prisoners. Those warriors were resentful of missing the party and took out their frustration by poking the captives with their spears, especially Taianita, Hanska, and the Chitimachan. It was only the prisoners' calculated lack of reaction—assisted by their starvation diet of the last three weeks—that made the guards desist.

"Wanageeska? Tlin-Kit."

Marcellinus, who had been drowsing, came fully awake. The chief from the northwest, Tlin-Kit, stood before them. He wore a nondescript tunic and a wide-brimmed cedar bark hat in place of his armor and battle mask and was not holding his hooked club. If not for his size and distinctive tattoos, Marcellinus might not have recognized him.

The chief threw down a bag, which turned out to contain greasy strands of dried meat. As their Mongol guards did not object, Marcellinus quickly passed pieces of the jerky along the line of prisoners.

"Good evening, sir, and we thank you," said Pezi, and repeated the sentiment in Algon-Quian. Tlin-Kit ignored him. He looked at Taianita, who lay curled up asleep, and then said something to the Chitimachan in his bastardized Algon-Quian.

She looked surprised and answered in the same language.

"Be careful," Pezi said sotto voce.

The Chitimachan did not reply. She was busy holding the chief's gaze.

Tlin-Kit said something to the Mongol guards. They looked doubtful. Tlin-kit gestured across to a few rocks across the clearing. The guards shook their heads. Tlin-kit held up his arm, and the Chitimachan nodded.

"Chitimachan, what?" Marcellinus said.

One of the Mongol guards shrugged and stood to tie a cord around Tlin-Kit's wrist. The Chitimachan held up her arm, and they looped the other end of the cord around her wrists.

This did not look good. Marcellinus struggled futilely against his own bonds.

"Be calm," Pezi said. "He wants to talk only. Learn things from her."

"A likely story," Marcellinus said.

"The Mongol Khan will not be pleased if his captive is destroyed. She will be all right."

The Chitimachan walked off with the chief without speaking. To Marcellinus's surprise they indeed only went across the clearing to the rocks, where they sat and talked.

An hour later Tlin-Kit brought the Chitimachan back. The Mongol guards tied her back into the group of captives.

"Well?" Marcellinus demanded.

"He is lonely," the Chitimachan said. She leaned forward to take some dried meat from the hide in front of them. Her face wrinkled in disgust as she chewed, but she was right. They all needed strength no matter how distasteful the only food they were offered was. Marcellinus reached out for another morsel himself and then prodded her with his foot. "Come on, Chitimachan. What did he say to you?"

She sighed and stared up at the sky. "Mostly he wanted to boast to someone who will listen. The Mongols are all drunk and crazy, and he does not like their airag. He grew bored. He has not talked to a woman for many weeks.

"He tells me he is a great chief of his people. He comes from very far north, on the coast of the great ocean in the west. Tlin-Kit is the name of his people, not of himself." Her lips pursed briefly in the closest thing that the Chitimachan got to a smile. "Just as mine is. And it is pronounced more 'Tlingit,' the way he says it with his own mouth. There are islands offshore where he lives, and great animals in the sea that his people hunt from mighty canoes and with flying craft that they call Sea Eagles. It is these Sea Eagles that the Mongols have based their flying craft on, although he says they have changed the shape so much that they are now repellent to him. He himself, the Tlingit chief, is a mighty flier and has killed many of these great sea animals from flight, but the Mongols will not let him fly on a Firebird, for he is too important to risk."

Marcellinus nodded in resignation. Truly, Great Sun Man had been mistaken about the prevalence of flying craft across Nova Hesperia.

"The Tlingit chief was among the first to befriend the Cold Men—his name for the Mongols—when first they arrived along the coast several winters ago. The Cold Men told him they came from mighty lands to the west, yet crossed the great ocean by staying close to the land in the north. The distance is not so great there, perhaps.

"The chief understood their power. He allied his warriors with the Cold Men, and they helped him defeat his people's ancient inland enemies. He says that for a hundred-hundred winters they had fought a Mourning War against the weak fools from inland, but now those tribes are destroyed, their men, women, and children all dead. And so the chief has won his Mourning War, and his people have pronounced him a god for it."

Her expression was sour. Marcellinus understood that of all in the Hesperian party, the Chitimachan might have the most to say about who were the true gods and who were not.

"Another strong tribe from the northwest, the Haida, tried to fight the Mongol Khan. They were defeated and now serve the Khan as slaves and dig gold for the Mongols.

"Having defeated their ancient enemies, the Tlingit have now joined with the Cold Men for more plunder. The mighty chief enjoyed helping the Cold Men enslave the soft, babyish tribes to the south of his homeland. He likes war. He likes killing. The Cold Men make him even stronger."

The Chitimachan stopped talking and regarded them. Kanuna was shaking his head slowly; Enopay was doing the same, apparently unaware that he was unconsciously aping his grandfather.

"How many of the Tlingit have joined with the Cold Men?" Marcellinus asked.

The Chitimachan's tone took on a tinge of irony. "Mighty warriors without number, of whom he is the mightiest." She shrugged. "More than ten hundred, I think. Less than a hundred hundred."

Marcellinus rubbed his eyes. The peoples of Nova Hesperia were aligning themselves with the invading outlanders, either with Roma or with its mortal enemy.

The Chitimachan bit into another piece of dried meat, chewed, swallowed. "One more thing. The Cold Men you see? This is only one-third of them. The Mongol Khan has two other armies. One is farther north at the Braided River, preparing for war, and it is led by the Khan's son. The other is split into two parts. One part guards the ships and slaves on the western shore of the land; the other part is to the south of us here and headed toward the dawn."

"Eastward?"

"Yes." The Chitimachan's eyes were bleak. "They go to strike the Market of the Mud, my home, and do battle with the Romans of the south. He told me this with great gloating and satisfaction, the Tlingit did, because he wanted to look into my eyes and drink my pain as I

suffered. I mocked him and did not give him the pleasure, and I think he liked that, too: my contempt and my
strength. But I suffer now."

"I'm sorry," Marcellinus said.

She looked puzzled. Marcellinus clarified. "Sorry that
savage men from faraway lands have come into your
land to kill and destroy."

"It is only now that you are sorry, Roman? Now that
you are at their mercy?" She shook her head.

Marcellinus fell silent. He had other questions, but the
Chitimachan's face had closed against him, and he felt
that he must ask no more.

She sat stiff and upright. Her face was a wall. Whatever suffering the Chitimachan was feeling was buried
deep within her, yet somehow Marcellinus felt that inside she was screaming.

Further indignities awaited. The next morning the prisoners were kicked awake by their captors, and pilloried.

Marcellinus was first. As he knelt in the dust, his
hands tied behind his back, Jebei Noyon himself strode
over, carrying a thick wooden board four feet across
with a hole in the center and a rough iron hinge. Opening it, he slipped it around Marcellinus's neck, locked it
closed, and released it.

Helpless under its weight, Marcellinus tumbled forward. The board's edge hit the ground, wrenching his
neck, and with his hands tied behind him there was
nothing he could do about it. The pillory must have
weighed fifteen pounds. Tears sprung to his eyes, water
he did not even know was left in his body.

Jebei Noyon nodded, stood, and gestured: *Up*.

Marcellinus tried. The effort of rising to his feet with
the pressure of that thing on his neck, and without his
hands to help, was beyond him. Gritting his teeth, he
tried again and then blinked up at Jebei Noyon. "I
can't."

The Tayichiud general turned away and signaled. His
men brought forward other identical mobile pillories,

one each for Bassus, Hanska, Mikasi, Pezi, Cha'akmogwi, and Chochokpi, and fastened them on.

Marcellinus was completely powerless. He was immobilized, forced to hold his body up to reduce the pain in his neck, unable to move except in a way that would cause him even greater suffering. Even if his hands were free, he would not be able to feed himself or give himself water for as long as he was locked in this thing.

Enopay, Taianita, and the Chitimachan were spared from the pillories but not from the hobbles. Those came next, the same hobbles that the Mongols used to prevent their horses from straying too far at night. Once hobbled, the captives were roped together at the waist to form a line. Then the Mongols came and cut the bonds around their wrists.

Now able to support the weight of the board with his hands, Marcellinus rocked himself upright and stood. He could not see his body or the ground beneath him. The others stood, too, and as best they were able, they began to walk. The hobbles allowed them just a few inches' freedom of movement. It was enough to shuffle forward well enough, but Marcellinus could already tell that today's march would be slow, painful, and humiliating.

Yet he saw no mockery or sadistic joy in the eyes of Jebei Noyon or the other Mongols and Jin who surrounded them, merely satisfaction in a job well done.

The Mongols sent them out ahead on the trail. They pointed, and one of them gestured *Walk*, and the prisoners began to get the measure of their restraints.

The Tlingit chief from the northwest walked up to them just before they left the camp and said something to Pezi in quick Algon-Quian, then strode off again without waiting to see if he was understood. "Bastard," Pezi said in Latin.

"Well, Pezi? What?"

"It was a warning. We must walk fast and not stop. If we sit or lie down, they will shoot arrows into us."

"Merda," Taianita muttered.

They walked out of the Mongol night camp as best they could, in a straight line into the desert. Marcellinus was in the lead position of the group. Pezi was behind him, then came Hanska, with the others strung out behind her. Bassus, the most injured and least able to make a walk like this, brought up the rear, with Taianita just in front of him.

Marcellinus heard whimpering. He would rather not know who it was. He half turned, which was the best he could do, and peered back. Despite the Tlingit chieftain's warning, nobody appeared to be aiming a bow at them. "Listen up, everyone, just for a moment. This will be hell, but Jove only knows what they'll do to us if we don't keep going. Everyone keep a tight hold of the rope in front of you, and behind as well, if you can. If someone stumbles, try to hold them so they don't fall too heavily. Pezi, watch the ground in front of me and warn me if I'm about to trip or step in a hole or tread on a rattling snake. Everyone else, do the same for the person in front of you. Look ahead, warn them of obstacles or dangers. Bassus, shout out if you need to pause, and we'll do our best. Taianita, watch Bassus; tell me immediately if he looks woozy."

"Don't worry about me," Bassus muttered. "I won't slow you down."

Marcellinus nodded, bumping his chin on rough wood. "I'll try to keep the pace steady. All right? On."

They went on. Many of them stumbled, Marcellinus most of all, but amazingly, nobody fell. Minutes stretched into hours. The pain in Marcellinus's neck and calf muscles became almost unbearable, but he had little choice but to keep moving.

He touched his tongue to his parched lips. He could not help thinking that if the Mongols left them out here like this, they would die of thirst within the day.

That gruesome thought, he kept to himself.

The first of the Mongol jaghuns overtook them at noon, bearing down on them at an alarming canter. Most of the warriors rode past, including Jebei Noyon and the Tlingit. Twenty warriors, two arbans' worth, stopped and dismounted with bad grace to give the captives water and a little food. Marcellinus and the others were allowed to sit and rest for two hours while the Mongols' horses grazed.

Exhausted, they spoke little. Marcellinus could feel blood trickling down his chest and saw that every neck was chafed and bleeding among those wearing the heavy pillories. No one wasted any breath complaining.

Then the second jaghun trotted up, and Marcellinus and his small group of unfortunates were helped to their feet to continue their terrible walk.

In the afternoon Bassus fell five times, pulling Taianita and Mikasi down with him. Each time Marcellinus stopped the group until one of the implacable Mongol warriors arrived to gesture them to rise again. Taianita helped Bassus as best she could, ducking under the board around his neck to put her arm around his waist and support him, and they all walked on as slowly as they dared.

Fortunately, they did not have much farther to go. Escorted by the final jaghun, the prisoners arrived at the Khan's camp around midafternoon.

After the rigors, indignities, and starvation of the journey north, Marcellinus was almost relieved.

The camp of the Mongol Khan was amazingly colorful. This was no makeshift overnight halt like the camps of Jebei Noyon's scouting party. This was a small town.

The camp was circular and composed largely of a haphazard array of thousands of the one-man goatskin tents the Mongols had used on the trail. However, distributed among them was a series of surprisingly substantial structures twenty feet across and circular with a conical roof, midway between tents and buildings. Some were plain and utilitarian, covered in felt and skins or rough brown linen, but toward the center there were several much larger versions.

From behind them Bassus grunted, speaking for the first time in hours. "Yurts. They're all over the Asian steppes."

"They have Hesperian slaves," Pezi said flatly, and so they did: men and women wearing the tattoos and tunics of the land who moved around on their knees or hobbled, cooking, carrying, and doing the other work of the camp while the Mongol warriors talked and drank and sharpened their sabers.

As the line of Cahokian, Roman, and Yupkoyvi prisoners shuffled into the camp, few gave them any more than a cursory glance. Just another bunch of captives at the mercy of the Horde.

Farther into the camp the yurts were decorated in yellow, red, and green, boldly repeating patterns in diamond and lozenge shapes. Nor were the camp's inhabitants restricted in their clothing to the mostly functional browns and other drab colors of their war armor; many wore shirts and trousers in bright colors and patterns. Among them walked men and women—apparently the only women here who were not slaves—wearing robes of a startling light blue who, from their stately demeanor and the variety of amulets and other decorations on their clothing, Marcellinus took to be shamans. Everywhere he heard rough laughter, saw eating and drinking and merriment, saw discipline put aside at the end of a long day's work. All in all, the camp had a carnival atmosphere quite at odds with the grim nature of the Khan's ruthless subjugation of western Nova Hesperia.

Even amid the desperation of their predicament and the harshness of the journey, Marcellinus hit a new low point. Hesperia did not deserve this. It deserved neither the Imperator Hadrianus and his steel legions storming in from across the Mare Atlanticus to trample villages and smash down cities, murdering its men and using its women, nor the Mongol Khan and his mounted Horde assaulting the land from the opposite ocean to murder, destroy, despoil, enslave. What was happening on the Hesperian continent was a tragedy of the highest order.

If Marcellinus had had his freedom, he would right now have willingly renewed his pledge to do all in his power to help the bands, tribes, and nations of Hesperia against these giant, befouling monstrosities. He would have vowed it until his dying breath.

Unfortunately, his dying breath might not be long in coming.

They were halted, given water and a handful of corn each, and made to wait. When Pezi tried to ask questions, he was quieted, and Marcellinus's gestured requests that they be allowed to sit received frowns and curt refusals.

On a signal that Marcellinus didn't see they were moved on again, ushered into the nucleus of the camp. Here sat the largest and gaudiest of the yurts, with a wooden platform in front of it resting on a pile of carpets. Arranged symmetrically around the central yurt were four others covered in black cloth, with tents around them. Sitting or walking in this area were hundreds of warriors in predominantly black shirts and breeches. Even the horses that stood nearby and futilely attempted to graze on the stripped ground were black.

These men were strong, clear-eyed, and serious. None drank airag. None looked like men who enjoyed a tale around the campfire. Their slaves were all subdued, all kneeling, tethered by ropes to stakes driven deep into the ground. The Mongols who escorted Marcellinus and the others kept their backs straight and their eyes downcast, on their best submissive behavior. The warriors in black were the Khan's personal Keshik guard, and even the regular Mongol warriors were daunted by them.

The small procession of prisoners was halted. Once again, Marcellinus realized, he was going to be hauled into the presence of a great leader as a captive, with no chance to prepare himself and little hope of survival. He shook his head, dizzy again.

And at that moment, with no fanfare or warning at

all, Chinggis Khan stepped out of his yurt and walked into the mass of his personal guard, ignoring Marcellinus and the other prisoners completely.

The Mongol Khan, the terror of the eastern and now the western world, wore a simple blue robe with golden trim, a leather belt studded with silver, and heavy leather boots decorated with embroidered patterns in silver and gold. He was heavyset, broad-shouldered, and muscular. As with all Mongol warriors, the top of his head was shaved, but he wore small pigtails at the back of his head and over his brow. His hair was graying and his face was lined, but to a much lesser extent than many other men Marcellinus knew of sixty or more winters. He stood solid and firm, with not a hint of weakness.

He reappeared from greeting his guards, smiled as he spoke to Jebei Noyon, nodded with respect to the Tlingit chieftain. Even without being able to understand the Khan's words, Marcellinus unwillingly recognized a charisma in Chinggis that was lacking in the Imperator Hadrianus. It was, in fact, a higher degree of charisma than Marcellinus had seen in any other leader, be he Rus prince, Arabian sultan, or previous Roman Imperator. Chinggis Khan was a man who led a large and vicious army, who was responsible for the slaughter of millions and untold suffering among the survivors of his depredations, yet there was a measure of humanity and humor in his eyes that was missing from Jebei Noyon's.

Chinggis Khan was no mere killing machine. He was a leader, used to binding men to his side and bringing them along with him by the sheer strength of his will, the clarity of his vision, the certainty of his purpose.

Beside him was a man who could only be the Khan's other general, Subodei Badahur. Subodei looked ten years younger than the Khan and wore a long beard, but his most distinctive feature was a bandage that passed diagonally across his face to cover his right eye. He appeared stolid and competent. Behind them came a third man, shorter and less muscular than the Mongols, with the more pronounced facial features of a Jin. He wore a pale red silken shirt, and unlike the Mongols he had a full head of hair to go along with his pigtails.

These three men now approached Marcellinus and the other captives.

Chinggis Khan studied Marcellinus without speaking, taking in every detail of his face, clothing, and wounds, even down to his tattered boots. Marcellinus stared back until he was done.

The Khan moved along to Pezi. He gave each of the other prisoners the same searching study, and then he spoke. His voice was higher-toned than Marcellinus had instinctively expected. Thanks to Great Sun Man, Avenaka, Son of the Sun, and then the Imperator, Marcellinus had grown accustomed to his supreme leaders having rich baritone voices. Out of the corner of his eye he noted Pezi's lips moving, following the syllables and rhythm of the Khan's words even though he could have understood nothing of what the man was saying.

The Jin stepped forward and in flawless Latin said, "Chinggis Khan, the Gur-Khan, the Chosen-by-God, mighty ruler of the world, welcomes you to his camp. Who leads among you? Let him speak now."

Marcellinus could not stop the look of surprise that crossed his face at the fluency of the Jin's speech. He coughed; the water he had drunk just minutes ago seemed to have been immediately absorbed into his body, leaving his mouth just as dry as it had been before. Keenly aware of the probable death sentences that hung over them all, he said, "Mighty Khan, many of us lead, and others among us may have great value to you. I am Gaius Publius Marcellinus, once Praetor of the 33rd Hesperian Legion. I introduce to you Sextus Bassus, a ranking officer of the Third Parthian Legion and the leader of this expedition. I introduce to you Cha'akmogwi and Chochokpi, leaders of the Yupkoyvi, central city of the People of the Hand."

He waited while the Jin translated. The Khan spoke again, pointing to his men. "Subodei Badahur. Liu Po-Lin."

Smoothly, Po-Lin continued. "The Great Khan introduces you to the mighty general and terror of his enemies, Subodei Badahur. I myself am Liu Po-Lin; I am Jin and played some small role in the Mighty Khan's conquest of our mutual enemy, the Song Empire. Awaiting us are the fearless general Jebei Noyon and our honored vassal, the chief of the Tlingit tribe far to the north in our new territory, whom you have already met. You will come and sit?"

Warriors in black were removing the pillory boards from the necks of the prisoners and freeing them from the ropes and hobbles. Marcellinus rubbed the raw and cracked skin around his neck, and his hands came away bloody. A hobbled slave woman shuffled up to him with a bowl of water. Resisting the urge to snatch it from her and drain it in a series of gulps, Marcellinus rinsed the worst of the blood and grime from his face and neck. At the other end of the line of prisoners, Bassus was doing likewise. Nobody moved to free Cha'akmogwi and Chochokpi; it seemed that as rulers of none but the dead, their participation was not required.

"Would you bring a companion or word slave with you, one whom you trust?" the Jin asked politely.

Marcellinus looked down the line but, gallingly, knew he must choose the one with the most Latin, the one who was the fastest learner. "Pezi, here beside me, knows many tongues and is my leading speaker of words."

As Pezi was freed and washed, an even greater feeling of incredulity swept through Marcellinus. The youth who once had betrayed Cahokia and taunted Marcellinus in Iroqua captivity was now to be his right-hand man in a meeting with Roma's greatest enemy. Suddenly, he found himself unable to even look at the Iroqua boy.

The Khan and Subodei turned and walked back to the platform outside the large, lavishly decorated yurt. Marcellinus got to his feet, trying to work the knots out of his neck. Sextus Bassus limped up to them, and Pezi took his arm. "I can manage," Bassus said curtly.

The tunic and patch around Bassus's chest wound

looked dry. Better, in fact, than the gash in Marcellinus's leg, which he could now see for the first time that day. It was encrusted with blood, the skin around it white and strained.

Nothing he could do about that now. "Gentlemen, shall we proceed?" he murmured.

"Lead on," Bassus said, matching his ironical tone, and escorted by Liu Po-Lin and two Keshik warriors in black, they walked unsteadily across the gravel desert floor to take tea with the despotic and bloody conqueror of half of Asia.

They sat cross-legged on rugs, the Great Khan flanked by Subodei and Liu Po-Lin on one side and Jebei Noyon and the Tlingit chieftain on the other. Marcellinus faced them with Bassus to his left and Pezi to his right.

The tea was terrible, a strong black brew with a yellow, oily substance floating in it. It burned Marcellinus's lips and tongue, but he needed the liquid and considered it tactful to show honor to his hosts. The yellow mess was a kind of butter, half rancid, and as the whole mixture smelled like damp horse, he was in little doubt about what he was drinking. Mongols favored mares and geldings for their mounts, unlike the Romans, who largely rode stallions. Clearly the mares provided nutrition as well as transport.

The Khan waited for them to drink and wipe their mouths. Now he spoke. Liu Po-Lin translated. "'Tell me, great Roman leaders, does your Imperator truly believe he can defeat me in the battle for this land?'"

Marcellinus smiled and tried to mimic Po-Lin's style of speech. "Mighty Khan, Roma and the many peoples of Nova Hesperia who have allied with her will prove to be a formidable opponent to you on the fields of war. This I promise."

"'I regret that Roma will fail.'"

"I regret that the war must take place at all."

"'If Roma leaves this continent, which your Imperator has so arrogantly cursed with a Roman name, no war need occur.'"

"Roma does not plan to abandon this continent to your tender mercies. And the eastern nations of Nova Hesperia, too, are united against you. Roma will fight you. Hesperia will fight you. Attack the combined forces of Roma and Hesperia, great Khan, and *you* will fail."

This last statement earned Marcellinus sharp looks from both Jebei Noyon and Subodei Badahur. Chinggis Khan merely smiled.

A Keshik warrior refilled their cups with tea. Distracted earlier, Marcellinus now noted that his cup was porcelain, presumably originating from the Jin or Song Empire. He waited for the Khan to drink again and then sipped the hot brew. He needed all the strength he could get, regardless of how revolting the beverage was.

"'We have no need of you,'" Liu Po-Lin said. "'From my scouts and spies, I know the numbers of legionaries of Roma that face me. I know of their native allies of the Mizipi and the lakes. I know all things.'"

Marcellinus tried to keep his face straight, his wits about him. If the Khan truly wanted nothing from him, he would be dead already. Marcellinus was no diplomat and hardly the man who should be in this delicate position. But Sextus Bassus sat silent, his expression surly, and clearly would be no help in this conversation.

Marcellinus cleared his throat. "I congratulate Chinggis Khan on his skill with military intelligence. He will therefore also be aware that the many legions that face him across the Plains are strong, determined, remorseless, and dedicated to his utter destruction."

The Khan smiled. "'Three legions only and a few extra horsemen. But tell me of your companions now.'"

Marcellinus saw no reason not to tell him and every reason to elevate the importance of his companions in the Khan's eyes. "Sextus Bassus is a decurion of the Third Legion and master of our expedition. Pezi here is Iroqua and knows many languages. Kanuna is an elder of Cahokia, and Enopay is his grandson, wise beyond his years. Hanska and Mikasi are warrior chiefs of Cahokia and also have the ear of its paramount chieftain, Tahtay. My apologies for my terseness. My throat is dry."

Marcellinus was running out of words, even in Latin. He wished he'd been able to sleep for the last several nights. He took another gulp of the burning salty tea and decided some embellishment might be in order. "Of the others, Taianita and the Chitimachan are great speakers of words, like Pezi, and much respected from Shappa Ta'atan to the Market of the Mud. Chack . . . Cha'akmogwi and Chochokpi you know to be leaders of the People of the Hand." He had a moment of panic. Had he forgotten anyone?

"As for Praetor Gaius Publius Marcellinus, he is a great general of Roma," Pezi continued in Latin. "Victor of countless battles in Europa, he has lived in Cahokia for many winters. He is a close friend to Cahokia's chiefs and elders and is a confidant of the Imperator of Roma. That is the total of our company."

Marcellinus dipped his head, wondering if Pezi had just signed his death warrant. He felt himself begin to sweat.

Liu Po-Lin finished his translation. The Great Khan nodded respectfully, sipped his tea, and appeared lost in thought.

While Marcellinus waited, he noticed for the first time the bloody sacks of ears tossed carelessly on the ground at the side of the platform. His gorge rose, and he swallowed with difficulty.

The Mongol Khan looked left, out to where the other prisoners still stood, seeming to inspect them all again from afar.

Finally he spoke, and Liu Po-Lin hurried to speak his chilling words. " 'Cha'akmogwi and Chochokpi are leaders of a destroyed race, and thus they are no leaders at all. They are useless relics of a dead culture and so will die with it.' "

Marcellinus struggled to breathe.

" 'The Cahokian warriors are likewise useless to me, and they will also die.' "

"No," said Marcellinus. "No, Mighty Khan, they will not."

Chinggis Khan's eyes slowly turned to gaze upon Marcellinus. All trace of humanity had left them, replaced with a cold, almost reptilian look. Liu Po-Lin blanched. Jebei Noyon smiled faintly. The Tlingit chief and Subodei Badahur watched with interest.

A Mongol sword blade appeared at Marcellinus's throat. A Keshik warrior had arrived so silently that he had not noticed the man's approach.

"Please," Liu Po-Lin said. "You will not disagree."

Marcellinus swallowed. Panic bubbled up within him. What to do?

The Khan continued his judgment. " 'Kanuna, as an elder of Cahokia, may live to tell Cahokia of what he has seen. He will speak of my glory and of our ruthlessness, and Cahokia will tremble. The boy, Enopay . . .' " The Khan looked at Marcellinus appraisingly. Marcellinus tried to match the coldness of the man's gaze, though he was seething inside. Chinggis continued: " 'The boy is less tall than a wagon wheel and is Kanuna's kin, and so I make no war upon him. In your weakness and frailty, you will need assistance on your journey home. So for that I will allow you to keep the boy.' "

"Home?" said Bassus, the first word he had spoken. He did not have a blade at his throat.

The Khan was again looking out across the camp. " 'The word slaves, Pezi, Taianita, and the Chitimachan, I will keep. They may be of use to me.' "

Pezi gave a strangled gasp.

" 'You four shall leave my camp. Kanuna and Enopay and you, the commanders Marcellinus and Bassus. You will live with your shame, knowing yourself bested and broken in battle by the forces of the Chosen by God. You will report to your Imperator how you have brought about the deaths and enslavement of those you so recklessly brought to war.' "

Marcellinus raised his hand and pushed the naked blade away from his neck. "No, Mighty Khan. Kill my warriors? Enslave my speakers of words? No. We shall all live and leave together or we will all die together."

Now it was Bassus's turn to give Marcellinus a look of cold consternation.

Chinggis Khan smiled slightly. Po-Lin shook his head in warning and continued. "'You four will take back to Roma and Cahokia the facts of Mongol strength and invincibility. Of how easily the cream of Roman cavalry was destroyed under the hoof and heel of the Mongol Khan.

"'You will take back the knowledge of how the People of the Hand are no more. Of how the Mongols killed the men, women, and children of Yupkoyvi, and the parrots and the goats, and even the rats and mice, and left no living thing behind.

"'You will take back this warning, of how Cahokia will become as Yupkoyvi, dead and without form. Cahokia and all the other cities and towns along the Mizipi, along the Oyo, among the Lakes. The peoples of the Mizipi and the Iroqua, all will be no more if they oppose me.

"'Any nations that do not immediately bend the knee will die. I, Chinggis Khan, will own this land. Tell Hadrianus I will crush him under my boots as I crush your friends now. Tell him that the Mizipi will run red with Roman blood from Cahokia to the sea. It will be blocked, dammed with the legs and the arms and the heads of dead Romans, dead Cahokians, dead Iroqua.

"'My Mongol army cannot be stopped. Roma will retreat or be destroyed. Cahokia and the other nations of this land will bow to us or be annihilated. This is the message that you will carry.'"

"No," said Marcellinus. "We—"

A Keshik warrior seized Marcellinus's hair from behind, pulling his head back. Sharp steel was again at his throat. Again Marcellinus tried to reach for the saber, but his arms were grabbed, his wrists forced behind his back. A few feet away Bassus roared in pain as he was similarly restrained.

"*I will not stay,*" Pezi said. He made no move, kept his eyes lowered in respect, but spoke firmly. "Mighty Khan, I cannot serve you. I am pledged with my life to serve Gaius Marcellinus. If I am taken from him, I will not drink and I will not eat, and I will slay myself at the first opportunity. Know this."

Marcellinus would have gaped at the boy in astonishment if he'd been capable of moving his head.

"Let me go, Mighty Khan. Free me and I will run to tell my people, the Iroqua, of your greatness. Of how they must kneel and lay down their weapons or perish. And the other speakers of words also: Taianita is from Shappa Ta'atan, and the Chitimachan is from the Market of the Mud. Let them go and they, too, will flee to those other cities of the Mizipi in fear and terror and similarly tell their people of your invincibility."

"And the other warriors and chiefs?" Po-Lin appeared to be speaking for himself now in dark amusement. "What of them?"

Pezi raised his eyes and met the Mongol Khan's gaze, bold and fearless, and smiled. "The Mighty Khan wants blood. Can I deny him blood, I who am worthless in his sight? Can I save everyone? No, I cannot."

Marcellinus struggled, but Keshik hands still held him secure. His head was bent so far back now that he could no longer even see Chinggis Khan, could see naught but the blue sky above him.

He was yanked up onto his feet. Bassus shouted out again in pain, and Pezi, too, was grabbed. The three of them were marched off the platform back to the line of prisoners, who were watching with alarm.

The Keshik warriors were moving the platform off the felt rugs and rolling half a dozen of them back.

The warriors came for Cha'akmogwi first. He allowed them to stand him up and walk him forward, then all of a sudden realized what was about to befall him and began to thrash in their arms.

One of the Keshik warriors struck him a heavy blow to the back of the head. He went limp and groggy, and they dragged him the rest of the way and laid him down upon the carpet.

They picked up Chochokpi, who was too weak to resist them. He turned his head and looked accusingly at Marcellinus.

"Wanageeska?" Mikasi muttered hoarsely. "What is happening? What will they . . . ?"

From the bleak look in Marcellinus's eyes, he guessed it. "Shit."

When they came for Mikasi, he and Hanska erupted into violent action in the same moment. Sitting calm, quiet, and unarmed they had seemed to pose little threat, but now they simultaneously leaped up and whirled.

Hanska slammed her elbow into one Keshik's face and grabbed the sword out of his hand. Mikasi had already felled another black-garbed warrior with his fists and was wrestling with a second for possession of his blade. At the same time he kicked out at a third Keshik, catching him in the crotch and sending him tumbling over Taianita. She kicked the warrior in the face as he passed, breaking his nose.

Hanska stabbed Mikasi's assailant in the gut and whirled to slash another Mongol across the throat as he ran at her. Back to back, turning, she and Mikasi fended off four Keshik warriors.

One of the two men holding Marcellinus let him go and jumped forward. Marcellinus struggled and snarled, but the other man still gripped his arms in a clench of steel. He was held firmly, incapable of movement, incapable of helping Hanska and Mikasi.

Two Keshiks lunged simultaneously at Mikasi. He countered one, but the second blade caught him just below the ribs on the left side. The first Keshik swung again, low, carving a huge gash in Mikasi's leg. As Mikasi crumpled forward, he snapped a single word: "Go!"

Hanska did. Breaking off from Mikasi, she knocked

her assailant's sword aside and sprinted straight for the Mongol Khan.

Chinggis sat unmoving, but Jebei Noyon leaped past him, saber in hand. Two Keshiks converged on Hanska from either side; she bowled over one of them with brute force, but the other slashed at her sword arm. She roared, kicked, kept moving.

Jebei Noyon was now the only man between her and the Khan, and he was unarmored, wearing only his flowing robe, but Hanska was panting now with the effort and he was fresh. Their swords met. He parried her, swung hard, pushed her back, and then the other Keshiks stormed her from behind, tripping her, kicking her to the ground.

Her sword now gone, Hanska gave her bloodcurdling battle shriek and even now crawled forward toward the Khan until the Keshiks roped her ankles and dragged her away, still thrashing.

Mikasi was down, blood pouring like a river from his thigh. It was a critical wound. He would bleed out in minutes. He must have known it, but he sat upright, his eyes only on Hanska.

Chinggis Khan nodded and pointed to the ground.

Dozens of Keshiks had come running now. Those who had failed the Khan, the six guards who had failed to stop Mikasi and Hanska, now prostrated themselves before him.

The Khan pointed at three of them with sharp jabs of his fingers. These three men stayed down. The rest kowtowed deeply, then backed away with heads still lowered, shame and humiliation etched on their faces.

Jebei Noyon handed his saber to Chinggis. The Khan stepped forward. Apparently he himself would serve as the executioner of the men who had failed him.

His expression still bleak and hard edged, the Khan swung the saber in a great arc, slicing the head from the shoulders of the first doomed Keshik with a single blow.

Marcellinus averted his eyes. He cared little for the

fates of the Khan's guards, but the ruthless expression
on Chinggis's face was chilling him to the bone.

Beside him, Hanska looked back at Mikasi. Her face
creased with deep sorrow. She held out one hand. Thirty
feet away, Mikasi reached out a hand to her in return
and smiled. Despite his wound he attempted to stand,
but a Keshik held him down.

His grisly retribution completed, the Khan spoke. The
Keshiks holding the rope tugged on it and dragged
Hanska back across the ground to Mikasi. He almost
fell on her, and they embraced.

Keshiks rolled the carpets back over the living but
prostrate bodies of Cha'akmogwi and Chochokpi and
set the wooden platform back over them. Theirs would
be a death by suffocation.

The Mongol Khan looked once more at the scene before him, his expression serene once more. He met Marcellinus's eye and nodded. Then he turned, mounted the
platform, and walked into his yurt.

All was quiet. Kanuna sat, his arms around Enopay.
The others sat alone in their misery. The Mongols stood
unmoving.

For several agonizing minutes they waited for Mikasi
to die. Finally his eyes closed. Hanska held him for a
moment longer and then rolled onto her back, staring at
the sky, her face bleak.

On orders from Jebei Noyon, the remaining prisoners
were collected, tied, and hobbled again. Hanska did not
resist when they roped her back into the chain of prisoners, met nobody's eye, and did not respond to Taianita
or Bassus when they placed their hands on her arms in a
futile attempt to comfort her.

Marcellinus was numb. He could not believe that he
was still alive, that Mikasi was dead, that the two
shaman-chiefs of Yupkoyvi were even now dying an
agonizing death by suffocation beneath layers of choking felt.

Could not believe that Hanska had fought through to
within a dozen feet of laying her hands on the Mongol

Khan. Or that she now stood so broken and desolate before him.

Jebei spoke one last order, and the Keshiks guided their prisoners forward. They shuffled away from the yurt of the Great Khan and, painfully slowly, out through the Mongol camp.

"The Khan admires valor, and your woman warrior has shown it in abundance. Was not Jebei Noyon spared after shooting an arrow into the neck of the Great Khan? Did he not then grow in the Khan's service to become one of his mightiest generals? And so the Khan spares Hanska. You may need her strength to help you get home, for your way will be hard indeed. The Chosen-by-God gifts her back to you."

Hanska did not react, did not even blink, merely sat still and broken. Her life seemed to have no importance to her.

"Pezi also spoke bravely and has bought the lives of Taianita and the Chitimachan. They, too, may leave with you." Liu Po-Lin gave a small bow. "I have made the humble suggestion to the Khan that without the help of the women you will not survive the journey, wounded and frail as you are. But Pezi himself will stay to serve the Khan." Liu Po-Lin smiled. "One never knows when an extra fluent speaker of Latin may be advantageous."

Pezi stared aghast. He did not struggle, did not speak. He merely looked at the Jin and the Great Khan and then at Marcellinus, his eyes pleading. At the moment of being praised for valor, he seemed to have lost his strength altogether.

The Khan spoke, and Liu Po-Lin now adopted the formal voice he used when he was translating directly. "'And so, Gaius Publius Marcellinus and Sextus Bassus, you will travel in shame and defeat along a mighty river, escorted by women, children, and a broken old man.'"

Liu Po-Lin began to bow, but the Khan continued to speak, his eyes glinting. "Oh, but there is more," said the Jin. "The Mongol Khan has instructed me to convey

to you his next move in wresting Nova Hesperia from
the Roman grasp. When first you met his general Jebei
Noyon, he was returning from a mission even farther
south than Yupkoyvi. In the southlands of Nova Hesperia the continent narrows to an . . . isthmus? Yes? . . . A
mere one hundred and fifty li across, perhaps fifty of
your Roman miles? There the great sea of the west and
the gulf are separated by only two days' march. And
there we have taken the small, deadly fighting ships
of the Mongol fleet. With the help of the People of the
Sun, we have . . . portaged? . . . them from the sea to
the gulf. On hides greased with oil, our ships can slide
across the land just as they cruise the seas." Liu Po-Lin
smiled self-deprecatingly. "A minor suggestion of my
own. The Khan's general, Subodei Badahur, will make
haste to join them, and under his command our fighting
ships will destroy your Roman navy. Your southern legion will be crushed, and the Hesperian Market of the
Mud and the southern Mizipi will fall to the Mongol
Khan. He tells you this with joy, for he knows you cannot travel faster than his ships. By the time you arrive
back at the Mizipi, your southern legion will be lost.

"The Chosen-by-God wishes you a speedy journey
back to the Mizipi, Praetor Gaius Marcellinus. May you
weep at what you find, and may your Imperator Hadrianus weep when he learns what has befallen both your
expedition and his great legion of the Sixth Ironclads.

"And so the Khan bids you farewell, Gaius Marcellinus, until we all meet again, and urges you to paddle
fast. Paddle fast."

CHAPTER 12

YEAR NINE, PLANTING MOON

The raft was ten feet by eight, rough logs lashed together with thongs made of hide. Barely enough space for the seven of them: Marcellinus, Hanska, Kanuna, Enopay, Bassus, Taianita, and the Chitimachan.

The river was scarcely big enough to support their journey. Around two-thirds of the time it was deep enough for the raft to float, and the few able-bodied among them could pole it along. At other times they had to manhandle the raft laboriously through shallows or past meager rapids, over rocks, around low waterfalls.

Day by day, Bassus was recovering. After the battle at Yupkoyvi, Marcellinus wouldn't have bet on Bassus even surviving the night. Yet the man whose life had appeared to be bubbling out of him as a result of his sucking chest wound was soon able to do some gentle carrying and foraging, although poling the raft taxed his muscles in a way he still could not manage.

Kanuna, in contrast, was wasting away. His physical wounds were not severe, but witnessing the Mongol slaughter at Yupkoyvi had clearly damaged his will to live. Despite Enopay's and Marcellinus's best efforts, Kanuna's health was failing almost as they watched.

As for Hanska, she spoke to nobody, said nothing. She followed instructions calmly, sat where she was told on the raft, helped carry it when ordered to, but otherwise did not respond. She did not forage, rarely paddled, and never poled. Taianita, who dressed her wounds, sometimes hugged the bereft warrior for hours on end. Hanska would tolerate this from Taianita, but if anyone else touched her, even with a light finger to the arm, she shook it off. After the first few days Marcellinus gave it up and let her grieve in her own way.

Marcellinus was weak and dizzy much of the time. The blistered burn wound in his side was unbearably tender to the touch and leaked unpleasant fluids. Liu Po-Lin had been right about one thing: they certainly would have died if not for Taianita and the Chitimachan helping to pole and carry the raft; foraging for roots, berries, and wild mushrooms; and snaring occasional small mammals that Marcellinus decided not to ask too many questions about.

"And so we are free," Enopay said quietly, lying on the bank and staring down into the river, his arm in the water up to his elbow.

"Free." Marcellinus looked around them at the desolate terrain. They were descending from the high plateau, but food was still desperately hard to come by. Every day was a struggle, and he had never been so aware of the murderous scale of the continent of Nova Hesperia, where even a scrawny river like this could wend its way through hundreds of miles of desolate territory. "Yes, we're free all right."

"Free to tell our peoples how the Mongol Khan will destroy them without mercy."

Now Marcellinus looked at Enopay. "Free to report that the Khan and his warriors deserve no quarter. Free to do whatever we must to rid Hesperia of them once and for all."

"I think we cannot," Enopay said. "I think we are lost. All-done. Alive for now . . . but dead."

"No, we—"

"Hush, now." Enopay's hand closed, but the fish he was seeking had slipped from his grasp. Frustrated, the boy pulled his arm from the cold river and rubbed the feeling back into it before easing it under the water's surface once more.

A small dam would work better, cutting off a portion of the river. Herd the fish into it and then capture them. They had done that two days before. Perhaps they would do it again tomorrow. Today Marcellinus didn't have the energy. "Enopay? We will destroy the Mongols. I swear it."

"Ha. Will you also swear that Mikasi will come back to life? That my grandfather will live long enough to see Cahokia again?"

Those questions, Marcellinus had no answer for. He tried again. "We have been freed to take the story of the Khan's brutality home. He hopes that the account of their ruthlessness in Yupkoyvi will destroy Roman morale, just as the stories of their relentless massacres of the northern Song caused the rest of that empire to crumble. But that will not happen."

"Ha."

"Enopay, say 'Ha' one more time and I'll push you into the river with your damned fish."

Enopay gave up and rolled onto his back, wiping the water from his hand. The look he gave Marcellinus was bleak. "Do not misunderstand me, Eyanosa. I have not given up. I will do all I can to help Roma. I will urge and encourage and beg and plead Cahokia to stand strong. But no. At the end of the day, we cannot prevail against such evil men."

Decinius Sabinus had told Marcellinus the same thing. The mere memory of standing on the first plateau of Cahokia's Great Mound brought a lump to his throat. He swallowed. "Enopay, this defeatism is exactly what the Mongol Khan wants. It is why we are still alive. It's the job he has given us: to spread hopelessness and fear. If we are demoralized, his battle is already won."

"You think I am defeated? No." Enopay stood. "You think you are the only one who can swear high and mighty oaths? Here is mine. I am Enopay of Cahokia, and I will fight the Mongols until I die."

Marcellinus's blood chilled. "Enopay . . ."

"My grandfather will pass away soon, and I will not have him anymore. Cahokia is changed forever. The Romans are here to fight and die beside us. I will work without rest to help the Romans until the Mongols cut out my guts or suffocate me under a carpet. I have spoken. And so you must teach me to fight."

"You're joking," Marcellinus said. "You?"

"Yes, me." The boy frowned. "You are about to say that my skills in counting and keeping track of people and things make me better suited to work behind the battle line than on it. But one day I might find myself on that line whether we like it or not."

Marcellinus did not reply. Enopay persisted. "In Yupkoyvi you told me to pick up a sword. Next time I would like to know better what to do with it."

"And had you been more of a threat to them, the Mongols might have killed you there." It was moot anyway. "Enopay, I don't have the strength to teach you. I can barely pole, let alone wave a gladius."

Enopay looked at him, pain in his eyes, then stood and stalked off without a word. Marcellinus let him go, and stayed alone with the babbling brook and his thoughts.

When they first had been placed aboard the raft, Marcellinus had suspected a trick. Jebei Noyon himself had stood nearby on the bank, his hands behind his back and his face unreadable. Ten of the Khan's trusted Keshik warriors had escorted them to the waterside, unlocked the wooden pillories from around their necks, and cut the hobbles that chained their ankles. On board the raft were a single long pole, an unstrung hunting bow of much more primitive design than the Mongol war bows, two dozen arrows, and two pugios, the weapons all tied to the boards of the raft with sinew so that they could not easily be snatched up and used.

Many of the Keshiks carried strung Mongol composite bows with quivers of arrows slung over their shoulders. Marcellinus had half expected this to be a cruel joke and figured that they would be slaughtered for sport as soon as they reached the center of the river, but it was not so. The erstwhile captives had been allowed to pole and paddle themselves clear. Jebei Noyon, the general in yellow, strode away without looking back. The Keshiks merely stood and watched them until they passed out of sight.

Soon the current had plucked the raft and swept them through a high-sided canyon. This had been one of the most dangerous moments. Still in shock, their minds slowed by grief and hunger, they had been late to react to the rocks that threatened to tear the raft apart. Marcellinus had had to shout desperate profanities at them while fending off rocks with his bare hands before Enopay and Taianita stirred themselves from their funk and helped him, the Chitimachan grabbed the pole and started ineffectually trying to steer, and Bassus, lying down, worked at the knots that held the knives and bow down. When they later passed a stand of pinyon juniper and pine, Marcellinus made them beach the raft while they cut light branches and wove them together to form crude paddles. He also gave them a stern talking to, trying to focus their minds on the ordeals ahead rather than those they had just endured. They hated him for several days afterward, but at least the voyage went a little more smoothly.

For the first few weeks the river continued its halting journey through narrow canyons interspersed with steppe grassland and short-grass prairie. In the distance they saw mesas and escarpments, none of which they recognized. Once a dust storm appeared around them as if by magic, filling their mouths with grit and peppering the surface of the raft as they floated on the river, lying prone. Then, all of a sudden, they were free of the canyonlands and into what seemed to be a vast expanse of prairie, with no tree or living creature in sight.

None of them knew the river they were floating down. None had been there before. Enopay had glumly labeled it the Stream of Piss, and the name had caught on. Between Enopay and the Chitimachan, their best guess was that they were traveling parallel to the Kicka River they had ridden alongside into the west but two or three hundred miles south of it.

Three hundred miles south of the Kicka meant they were as much as six hundred miles south of the Wemissori. They had a *long* way to go.

"I'm sorry," Marcellinus said.

Kanuna turned his head with difficulty. The elder looked twenty winters older than he had just a few short weeks ago: limbs weary, face lined, lips cracked. "For what?"

Taianita and the Chitimachan were poling. Enopay, on the far side of the raft, appeared to be asleep. Hanska sat staring downriver. Marcellinus handed Kanuna a water skin. "Drink. Even a little. I am sorry that I brought you on this journey and your grandson, too."

Perhaps that was a shrug. "It is the Mongols who should apologize, and they never will. You? Your valor . . ." Kanuna's face creased, and he gave a weak cough that nonetheless seemed to rattle around his rib cage.

"I beg of you," said Marcellinus. "Today of all days, say nothing of valor."

"Then I will say this. Take care of Enopay for me, Gaius. And . . . take care of Cahokia."

"To the best of my small ability," Marcellinus said, grimacing, "I will, Kanuna. You know I will. But I wish I could do it with you by my side."

Kanuna coughed again. "When I saw your warriors coming . . . the first time, when the 33rd Hesperian marched on Cahokia. All that steel . . . it was the most terrible thing I had ever seen. Yet that was nothing. Since then, I have seen so much worse. Too many terrible things, Wanageeska."

"I'm sorry," Marcellinus said again.

"Never did I think I would outlive Great Sun Man.

But now I find I am glad that he will be the first to meet me once this is over."

Marcellinus stole a quick glance at Enopay, but the boy was still fast asleep.

"Nor did I think that I would see the end of the Mourning War with the Iroqua. Nor that my most desperate enemy might become my closest friend."

Marcellinus gently squeezed the elder's shoulder. "You are one of the best men I have ever known, Kanuna."

"Ha. But as for those Mongols . . ." Kanuna shook his head almost imperceptibly.

"Don't speak of them now," Marcellinus said.

"Destroy them. Cleanse the land of their filth. And then send the Romans away from our city as well."

It seemed impossible, beyond any rational hope. Marcellinus grinned and tried to make light of it. "If those are your last requests, you old fox, you set a high bar."

"Bar? Perhaps." Kanuna twitched his head again, not smiling. "But above all, Wanageeska: Enopay."

There, Marcellinus certainly could agree. "Enopay. Yes, I will always look after Enopay. You have my word, Kanuna."

Kanuna died in his sleep that night. His body was gaunt and emaciated, but his face was strangely peaceful, as if he welcomed the release. Marcellinus awoke to find Enopay sitting by his grandfather's side, his face solemn.

"He is the lucky one," Enopay said.

"I'm sorry, Enopay. And I'm doubly sorry that I brought you here."

"What? If you had not brought me, I would not have been with him at the end." Enopay tugged some of his grandfather's gray hair from the back of his head—it took no more than a soft pull to free it—and tucked it into his tunic.

Marcellinus's eyes were dry. None of them had the luxury of tears. Even though he had plenty of water to drink these days, his tongue still kept sticking to the roof of his mouth, and it hurt to swallow.

In death, Kanuna's face looked calm and composed and somehow younger. He looked again like the man Marcellinus had met long before, had first smoked tabaco with in the sweat lodge with Great Sun Man and the others. The man Marcellinus had talked with long into the night about steel and wheelbarrows and the Big Warm House back in those long-ago days when Marcellinus had hoped he could benefit the Great City and its people, perhaps the whole of the land, with his Roman ideas. He shook his head.

Enopay watched his grief. "You will help me bury him, Eyanosa? You, me, and Hanska if I can rouse her. Just us. Those who knew him longest, who loved him the best."

"Of course, Enopay."

They could not get Hanska's help. She looked briefly aghast at being asked to join a burial party and put her hands over her eyes and sat as if carved in stone. They had to leave her and accept Taianita's help instead.

They buried Kanuna in a shallow grave with a small mound covering him. A deeper burial would have been better and more appropriate, but they simply did not have the strength.

"Teach me to fight."

Marcellinus looked up, but Enopay was not talking to him. Hanska was sitting on the riverbank, hugging her knees and staring out across the brown water. On the other side of the river in the middle distance was a Caddo encampment of two lodges with a dugout on the bank next to them. The inhabitants ignored Marcellinus's group of survivors, showing no signs of approaching them.

Taianita and the Chitimachan were off foraging in the opposite direction. Marcellinus was sitting by Bassus, neither of them speaking. Enopay had returned from his own foraging trip with a pile of berries and wild turnips. He was directly facing Hanska, who was ignoring him.

"Teach me to fight," Enopay said again. "Hanska? I

need to know how to fight. And the Wanageeska will not teach me." He poked her with his toe.

She stood and walked away to the water's edge.

"Hanska?" Enopay got up and trotted after her. But when he reached out a hand to touch her arm, she shoved him away so hard that he fell.

"Juno, Hanska . . ." Marcellinus struggled to his feet, but Enopay hand-talked *Be silent* and stood again. "Hanska, I know why you are being like this. But I need to learn how to defend myself or perhaps I will die, too." Enopay walked around Hanska, standing perilously between her and the water, and stared up at her. "Yes, I am small. Yes, of course I am ridiculous. I do not look like a warrior. All the more reason for me to learn how to become one."

At that, Hanska looked down at him thoughtfully.

"Hanska?"

She grabbed his shoulders. "Shut *up*, boy. Stop talking. Leave me alone."

She released him. Enopay swayed on the water's edge, a hurt expression on his face. Hanska shook her head, looking neither sad nor angry, and walked away.

Marcellinus sighed, summoned up all his strength, and followed her.

She walked half a mile and then sat on a rock. Her head was still shaved at the sides in the Cahokian warrior style, but her hair was loose in mourning. It somehow made her look ferocious rather than vulnerable.

Marcellinus sat down beside her. "We need your help, Hanska."

She ignored him, as usual.

"Hanska? I know you can hear me. It's time to stop." He took a deep breath, hating himself. "Or are you too weak to help us? Too feeble and broken?"

Finally she stirred. "Fuck off."

Well, at least she was talking to him. "I'm sorry, Hanska."

"*You're* sorry?"

Her fingers flexed, forming fists. Marcellinus remembered Sintikala saying that she had killed people, some of them her friends, in her grief at losing her husband.

Perhaps Hanska would kill him. Nonetheless, he had to do this. "We need you. You're our strongest warrior."

Hanska looked around them very slowly and carefully, as if taking in her surroundings for the first time. "I see nobody here to fight. When I do, you can count on me. As you always do. For now . . ." She gestured in hand-talk: *Go away. Fuck off.*

Marcellinus looked at her and thought of trying to say something else. She had, in fact, fought magnificently, but he could hardly talk to her of the moment when Mikasi had died.

Perhaps this was hopeless. He stood. "If you need anything, Hanska, ask."

"I need nothing."

Marcellinus left her to her grief. But the next night when they went ashore, Hanska disappeared into a small copse for a while and returned carrying several rocks and a few stout pieces of wood. The next day on the raft they were all maddened by the repetitious sound of her knapping flint and her occasional swearing as she threw one rock overboard and began anew with another, but by the middle of the second day she had constructed a hardy ax with a wooden haft and a stone blade. By the end of the third day she had made two more and had moved on to making short thrusting spears out of ash wood and bone.

Next, Hanska made two practice swords out of wood and began to spar with Enopay. Hanska was showing signs of life again.

They had lost some altitude now, having descended from the high plains several days before. Once again, the temperature was rising steadily as they headed toward high summer on the prairie. By now the river had grown sluggish and meandering, weaving back and forth across the terrain, bounded by red mudflats. The lethargy of the river was not enough to propel the raft forward; between them Marcellinus, the Chitimachan, and Taianita took it in turns to pole the boat while one or two of the others paddled. The tedium of the landscape was such that Marcellinus sometimes would look up after what seemed like hours of sliding the long wooden pole into the water and shoving it hard into the sand and mud beneath it, sometimes pushing the edge of the raft under the water in his efforts to propel it forward, only to find that the terrain around him looked almost exactly the same as when he had begun his shift.

Few people lived along that river. Very occasionally they would pass a homestead. They did not ask for help, expected none, and for their part the inhabitants gazed at them until they were past. They were deep in Caddo land now. Taianita spoke the language, but the natives of the region did not look friendly, and neither she, Marcellinus, nor any of the others felt safe approaching them.

Conversation was almost negligible during the day. It was only in the evening when the foraging parties went out and the others effected repairs to the raft and their clothes that any discussions took place. It was a dour, relentless journey through a largely unchanging and inhospitable countryside.

Marcellinus found himself gripped by an overwhelming sense of frustration. The urgency of their quest was unmistakable: this was a ruthless race against time. Far to the south, Mongols under Subodei Badahur were advancing east to join their fleet and battle the Sixth Ferrata. Far to the north, Roma and the Hesperian League were preparing to face the twin armies of the Mongol Khan and his son Chagatai. Far to the west, on the other side of the Great Mountains, a vast territory Marcellinus had never seen was groaning under the Mongol rule of Yesulun, its people enslaved to mine gold for the invaders.

Up the Wemissori in Hidatsa and Blackfoot territory the Romans were on their own similar hunt for gold. Without the slavery, or at least not yet.

And in the meantime, Cahokia was still oppressed by Roman occupation. What would be happening there now? Was the Imperator really keeping Agrippa in check, or had it all gone to hell? Was Sintikala safe? Kimimela?

The alliance hung by a thread. Even if the Mongols could be resisted, Roma was surely still a huge threat to Cahokia and to the whole of the Hesperian League.

Marcellinus had spearheaded the first invasion of Nova Hesperia. Now he was hurrying to take information about its second invaders back to an allied army ranged against them.

And, if possible, preserve their own lives. Because if Marcellinus and his crew ended up behind the Mongol invasion line, their stay of execution might prove to have been brief indeed.

Individual homesteads now gave way to small villages of several lodges, a few families huddled together on the riverbanks living off small cultivated garden areas, rabbits, and the occasional buffalo. The Hidatsa and Blackfoot much farther north did not eat fish, and there was little sign that the locals here did either. On the whole river trip, the only people Marcellinus saw trying to catch fish were Enopay and Bassus.

The raft was floating through Caddo territory in earnest now, and Marcellinus constantly worried that its inhabitants might seek other prey. From time to time a Caddo band of six or twelve warriors might stand on the riverbank and watch the raft go by, looking at Taianita and the Chitimachan with hungry eyes. At the attention Taianita lowered her gaze, perturbed, and Marcellinus had her sit rather than draw even more attention by poling the raft. By contrast, the Chitimachan stared at the men contemptuously, perhaps chilling them with the ice of her stare. Hanska did not exactly brandish her ax, but she certainly made sure it was visible. Marcellinus and Bassus did the same with the wood bow and the blades, and everyone aboard the raft stared out confidently as if ready for anything. No reason for the people on the shore to realize these were the only weapons they owned or how weak and injured they still were.

The Chitimachan stirred. "I have been here before."

Marcellinus looked at her, uncomprehending. Taianita, poling the raft and sweating, scanned the banks and shook her head. To Marcellinus and perhaps to her, the landscape was gently rolling grassland as far as the eye could see, the kind of terrain that so numbed Marcellinus's senses that after a while it was hard to drag a coherent thought through his brain.

In the distance was a black smudge that might have been a buffalo herd. Unexpectedly, his mouth watered. Hard now to imagine that after the great buffalo hunt with the Blackfoot on the Plains he had gorged on so much meat that he had never wanted to see it again.

Another desultory river had joined them from the left a little while before, almost as still and lifeless as the one they were on. None of them had remarked on it at the time. Now the Chitimachan sat up. "This is now the Kicka. Many weeks east of where we rode alongside it before, but still the Kicka. We were on a tributary of it all the time. Now we will travel on it to the Mizipi."

Marcellinus groaned, and Enopay plunged his head into his hands. This meant they still had hundreds of miles to go before they met the Mizipi. And the Kicka flowed due southeast for much of its length, and so they would be moving farther away from Cahokia all that time rather than toward it. The Kicka fed into the Mizipi halfway between Cahokia and the Market of the Mud, well south of Shappa Ta'atan. From there they would have to fight the Mizipi upriver all the way or trek along its banks on foot.

Taianita caught his eye and shook her head, and she was right. They were all perpetually hungry and exhausted. It was not the time to discuss the length of the journey still ahead of them.

Suddenly, Marcellinus realized the brighter side of this coin. "Signal stations."

"What?" said the Chitimachan.

"The Roman way stations on the Line of Hadrianus. Any time now, we should start coming across them."

And so they did, the very next day.

The Roman outpost was surprisingly substantial. It was a two-story structure ten feet across at the base set within a turf rampart, the whole surrounded by a V-shaped ditch six feet deep and eight feet across. The upper floor had a parapet around it. Marcellinus knew it for simple wattle and daub, sticks of willow or hazel covered in clay, but the thickness and evenness of the clay made it almost indistinguishable from stone.

Suspended above the second floor was a platform of wood held aloft by four stout timber uprights. Providing access to the platform was a ladder sheathed in a column of wooden planks for protection against arrows, and on its top was a large bowl that surely contained the contubernium's signal fire.

They stared at the signal station from midriver for several minutes before going ashore. Somehow the military solidity of the structure was daunting. That, and the apparent absence of life within it.

"This is what you built? These are all across the Grass?"

Marcellinus nodded. In truth such a watchtower would be quick to build for trained legionaries, but it looked alien here, deep in the wilds of Hesperia. "One every twenty or thirty miles along every river and in a line north as far as the Wemissori. They may not all look quite like this."

"Shit," said Enopay, and looked at Marcellinus in admiration as if he were personally responsible for building every one of them. The Chitimachan, in contrast, was stone-faced, no doubt perceiving the watchtower as an affront to her land.

"Shouldn't there be a sentry?" Enopay asked.

"Of course there should." A post station was not much good without vigilant sentries. "We built these to be staffed by at least eight men on constant watch." This one might have held twelve or sixteen. Agrippa, or his tribunes or engineers, might have been leery of trouble from the Caddo.

Marcellinus's hails were not answered, and however hard he stared, he wasn't going to be able to see through the walls. "Hanska, you're with me. The rest of you, stay on the raft. Be ready to cast off at a second's notice."

The warrior glanced at the fortlet without interest. "Nobody's there."

"We don't know that. What if a Caddo war party attacked the Romans and they're still in the area?"

"Then why would we go in?"

"To find out. Come."

He expected her to refuse or ignore him. Instead Hanska shrugged, picked up her ax and slung a second one over her shoulder, and followed him up the slope to the signal post.

On the ground floor they found a rough table and chairs, a few bowls, and eight sleeping pallets. On the second were four more sleeping pallets and a sack of grain. Nowhere did they see any signs of a fight.

Hanska stooped quickly to touch the floorboards and examine her fingertips. "Some grass stalks. No dust."

She did not need to say any more. There were no personal effects or cooking tins, and the place was clean. No sign of a slaughter and every indication of a recent evacuation.

"They withdrew," Marcellinus said. "Probably recalled. Which must mean that the Mongol assault on Roma has begun."

"On Roma?" Hanska swung her ax into the wall nearest her. Splinters flew.

He stepped back and corrected himself quickly. "On Hesperia. On all of us."

She pulled the ax out, shook her head at him, and climbed the ladder onto the platform. When Marcellinus joined her, she was poking the ashes of the signal fire with an unburned stick. "A week? Maybe more."

Marcellinus scanned the horizon. The post was well sited. The sentries on watch would have seen any Mongol incursion from the west a good fifteen miles away. He could not see the next signal stations in the line to the north or the south, but the view was clear to the horizon, and any fire would have been easily visible.

He looked down the line of the river, feeling bleak. Abandoned a week or more ago? If he'd believed in gods, he'd have sworn they were all against him.

Hanska prowled the top of the tower, glancing back at the raft that awaited them on the riverbank. She looked at her feet and then turned to face him. "I'm sorry, Gaius."

Marcellinus nodded. He could see her eyes, and so he did not need to ask. Hanska told him anyway. "For . . . leaving you for a while. Falling into my own head. Not helping. Being useless. And acting like a verpa."

"No apology needed."

"For all of it." She raised her eyes to gaze into the blue of the sky. "I let you down."

"No. Never. Hanska, I'm sorry about—"

She raised her hand in a sudden motion and cut him off.

Marcellinus wanted to tell her that he understood. He wanted to say *If I ever lost Sintikala* . . . But that was a thought too large for his mind to encompass, and perhaps Hanska already knew. He leaned on the parapet, looking out over the endless grasslands.

What was happening in Cahokia? He had no idea. They had been away almost a full year. Once again he felt almost unspeakably apprehensive about what might have happened there in the meantime.

Eventually, he turned.

She had fallen still, staring at the ashes of the signal

fire. Marcellinus stepped forward, worried that she might have relapsed back into a fugue state. "Hanska?"

She drew herself up. "What do you need, sir?"

"Help me get everyone to safety. Pole the raft. Be strong. Guard us." He paused. "And let me not be the only person telling people what to do next."

Hanska nodded. "Yes, sir."

"And then . . . help me kill Mongols."

She studied his determined expression and almost grinned. "Wanageeska kill Mongols? Then I'm right beside you, sir."

"Another year, another enemy," he said. "Let's get out of here."

Two days later they came across the next riverine signal station. It was identical to the first except for a pervasive sour smell of burned wood and ash that wafted over the river. This time Marcellinus, Hanska, and Taianita stealthily approached the signal tower, creeping through the underbrush that surrounded it with axes and spears at the ready. But the sentry post was undamaged, the small living quarters again abandoned quickly but with no signs of trouble.

The smell of old fire came from the tower. The signal fire had been lit and had burned for some time before being quenched.

Digging his fingers into the ashes, Marcellinus found them still damp below the surface. From this and from the prints of the Roman caligae sandals in the dust outside the outpost, Hanska estimated this station had been abandoned by its Roman contubernium just two or three days before.

The Kicka River wound on. Now the river valley threaded between high, flat ridges and isolated monadnocks topped with trees. By now they had thrown caution to the winds. Gone were the long nights ashore, resting up behind field fortifications against the Caddo threat. Gone was their fear of the wandering Caddo warrior bands along the riverbanks. They traveled as fast as they were able, poling the raft all day and as far into the night as they could manage and dozing fitfully when they could. Rain and wind no longer kept them ashore. They fished from the craft when they could and went ashore for meat or berries only when their hunger and weakness drove them to it.

The river had grown in width, depth, and reliability. Marcellinus, Taianita, and Enopay had lashed fallen tree trunks to the edges of the raft to serve as outriggers and keep it more stable. Time was critical now. They passed three more Roman signal stations, all deserted, and did not go ashore to investigate them.

The Kicka might be larger and wider than the Stream of Piss, but its current was just as wan and provided as little help to them. For all their efforts at poling and paddling, it might have been faster to travel by land, but Bassus was still not strong enough to walk for any length of time. The Chitimachan suggested splitting the party, sending the fittest of them to run ahead. Marcellinus would not hear of it. They were a small enough group as it was, and few of them able-bodied enough to fight should the Caddo attack. Hesperian tribes raided one another all the time to appropriate women of childbearing age. Taianita, the Chitimachan, and even Hanska were still of such an age, and dividing the party would leave them even more at risk. Their little group certainly had nothing else of value.

They had to make haste. Marcellinus's fear that they would be cut off from the Romans by the advancing Mongol army was foremost in all their minds. It could easily happen. Perhaps it already had: the evidence of the deserted signal towers was confirmation that the armies of Chinggis Khan were moving much faster than they were.

"Boat," the Chitimachan said suddenly in Cahokian and then again in Latin. "Cymba, navis . . . merda."

Hanska grabbed her ax. Bassus, dozing, came awake

all at once and grabbed a spear. Marcellinus, who was poling the raft, snatched the pole up out of the river and held it quarterstaff-style, river water dripping down his arms. He glanced quickly at both banks and then behind him. He feared a Caddo dugout, always feared an assault, but saw nothing.

"Far ahead . . . Gone. Around the next bend."

Bassus peered up at her. "Good God, woman, what type of boat?"

She eyed him balefully. "The type with a sail."

"Holy fucking Jove . . ." Marcellinus jammed the pole into the mud at the river bottom so hard that it stuck, jolting the raft. He pulled it free and pushed back at more of an angle.

Enopay picked up a paddle. "Taianita, match me."

On the other side of the raft Taianita dug in, and after a few moments Hanska and the Chitimachan joined them from opposite sides of the raft, scooping with their bare hands.

Despite their best efforts, the bend in front of them opened up agonizingly slowly.

Bassus sat up, wincing, and peered downriver. "Knarr."

"Shit, Eyanosa," said Enopay. "Be careful."

The raft was rocking dangerously. Marcellinus eased up and squinted. "A knarr? You're sure? Juno . . ."

Bassus's face cleared, and for a moment he looked five years younger. The Chitimachan bowed her head, not exactly smiling but at least presenting a look of some relief. Enopay beamed from ear to ear. Marcellinus blew out a long breath. Relief surged through him. Despite the ache in his muscles and the other, different, ache in his belly he felt strong again. Strong.

"Odd," Hanska said.

"What? What?"

"That we are now all so happy to see Romans."

The wide-beamed Norse cargo ship held the contubernia of Roman legionaries of the 27th Augustan from the signal stations they had already passed and a crew of fifteen Roman sailors, their Caddo and Cherokee guides, and a few heavily armed marines of the Legio VI Ferrata. They were a little startled to be hailed in Latin from astern by Marcellinus's decidedly grubby and unkempt crew, and Marcellinus was equally startled when the centurion in command of the boat walked to its stern and pulled off his helmet. "Manius Ifer?"

Ifer met Marcellinus's eye, then glanced quickly at the other men and women on the raft. His gaze stopped on Hanska, the only other person he could have recognized, then swiveled back to Marcellinus.

The flinty look in Ifer's eye showed that he remembered their last encounter all too well.

"Manius Ifer is who?" Enopay asked quietly.

"He tried to steal your longship when we were at the Market of the Mud. Many of his century died in the ensuing battle. I barely stopped Sintikala from killing him."

Enopay raised his eyebrows. "You may regret that."

"Let me, then." Bassus sat up and raised his voice. "Decurion Sextus Bassus of the Legio III Parthian. Survivors here of a Roman expedition to the People of the Hand. Permission to come aboard?"

The knarr was fifty feet long and fifteen feet wide. It was capable of carrying over twenty tons of cargo, and its hull seemed cavernous to Marcellinus. After piling into it, they left the dilapidated and much-repaired raft that had been their home for the last months floating at the water's edge. None of them looked back as the knarr sailed on.

Ifer scrutinized him. "Gaius Marcellinus. Perhaps I should tie you up. For old time's sake."

"Or perhaps you should help me get back to Cahokia so that I can tell our Imperator what I know of the Mongol Khan and his plan of attack."

The other Romans on the knarr looked at one another and shook their heads. Ifer looked somber. "Trust me, we're fully aware of the Khan's intentions."

"What has happened?"

"Defeat," Ifer said tersely. "Mongol ships, scores of them in the dawn, out of nowhere. An entire fleet of Mongol and Jin battle junks. Some longboats of the People of the Sun assisting, and other big painted Hesperian canoes as well, provided by their allies the Tlingit, made of solid wood, much stouter than the usual birch-bark crap. They launched a surprise assault on the fortress of the Sixth in the great gulf. Blasted the fortress walls with bombs of Jin salt and sank two quinqueremes. The rest fled."

"Fled? Our warships?"

Ifer nodded, his eyes guarded. "Afraid so. Verus's orders. Save the fleet. So the Mongols sailed on, laid waste to the Market of the Mud, and kept going. The bastards are somewhere ahead of us now."

"Ahead?" Enopay said. "Upriver of us on the Mizipi already? Futete . . ." Ifer looked at him with the usual surprise Romans showed at finding a Hesperian speaking such fluent Latin.

"We know how the Mongols managed that," Marcellinus said. "Portage. Down in the land of the Yokot'an Maya, Nova Hesperia narrows to an isthmus fifty miles across. There, the slaves of the People of the Sun hauled the Mongol battle junks across deerskins coated with oil."

"We suspected something of the kind."

"You were there when the Mongol fleet attacked?"

"My century was off on operations, west of the Market of the Mud. The Sixth picked us up when they came through." Ifer shook his head grimly. "The Cherokee scouted ahead while we gathered everyone in, evacuating the troops from the signal stations. The river is blockaded north of us, at . . . Shappa Ta'atan? You know of it? I have not been so far north."

The Khan had split the Roman forces in two. "Of course. We're cut off from Cahokia?"

"Aye, until we run the blockade. Smash through, reunite with the Third and 27th."

"If you do," Enopay said.

Ifer frowned at the boy. "What did you say?"

"Does the Imperator know?"

The centurion shook his head with frustration. "Of course he doesn't know, boy. How could he? The Mongols are *ahead* of us, between us and Cahokia. Weren't you listening?"

"You should send runners." Enopay turned to Marcellinus. "Divide and divide and conquer and conquer. The Khan hopes to put wedges between the Roman forces in the south *and* in the north. If the Mongols destroy the rest of our fleet, they can not only split the Sixth from the other two legions but strand the Third and most of the 27th on the wrong side of the Mizipi. Cut them off from the Chesapica completely. We need to warn Hadrianus."

"Shit," Marcellinus said.

"*Our* fleet?" Ifer said.

Enopay met his gaze. "Are we not allies?"

Ifer shrugged. "Anyway, we'll get through, and we'll get to Cahokia long before runners."

Ifer's helmsman broke into the conversation. "Next fort."

Sure enough, the next Roman signal station had just come into view around the bend ahead of them. A contubernium of legionaries stood on its top platform. One of them waved.

Ifer nodded at Marcellinus and Bassus and stood to go to the prow of the knarr. Bassus grunted. "This boat is going to get crowded."

Marcellinus noted that the legionaries of the Sixth were staring openly at Taianita and the Chitimachan, perhaps the first comely women they had seen for months. Taianita was staring steadfastly ahead, ignoring them all, but the Chitimachan looked as though she was very close to punching someone.

That might at least provide some light relief. The rest of the news was unspeakably grim.

Having the Roman forces divided was obviously intolerable. But to lose control of the Mizipi so quickly and completely? He had not fully considered the implications of that.

Evidently his feelings of relief had come too soon. *Much* too soon.

CHAPTER 13

YEAR NINE, THUNDER MOON

Three days later the Kicka River spit the knarr out into the Mizipi and into the middle of a Roman flotilla.

Below the convergence of the Kicka and the Mizipi was a quinquereme that was being led by a Norse drekar. Just passing out of sight around the bend upriver of them was a second quinquereme. In between were a trireme and another Norse dragon ship.

The knarr's rejoining the convoy was announced by a deafening blast of Roman horns. The warships ahead and behind acknowledged the signal with brief cornu blasts of their own.

The wind was westerly, and the knarr had lost weigh in turning north. It swung in behind one of the drekars, which threw it a line. Marcellinus and the Hesperians boarded the drekar while Ifer took Bassus to the nearest quinquereme—the *Clementia*—to see a naval medicus.

The quinquereme ahead of them was the *Fortuna*, which hung back and waited for them to catch up. The *Fortuna* was the newest and best maintained of the great Roman galleys of the Sixth Ferrata, and served as the flagship.

And there on the poop deck, highly visible in his white Praetor's crest, was Calidius Verus. "Large as life and twice as fat," the Chitimachan muttered. Marcellinus grimaced but could not find it in himself to scold her for her disrespect.

As the drekar approached, one of the sailors threw a rope ladder over the side. "Just you," said the ship's master from the deck, easily recognizable by his fringed cloak and mushroom-tipped staff. "The rest of 'em can stay where they are. We don't wish bad luck on the Praetor's flagship by bringing redskin women and children aboard. We'll find 'em berths on another ship later."

Marcellinus looked at the faces of his remaining crew: Enopay, Hanska, Taianita, and the Chitimachan. Even after getting on one another's nerves for months mostly spent on a painfully small raft, it was surprisingly difficult to be parted from them. "I'm sorry. I'll be back soon."

Hand over hand, he climbed the rope ladder. The top deck was disconcertingly high, but as soon as his head came level with the bulwark, two Roman sailors grabbed his arms to haul him aboard.

Verus looked him over. "Well, well. Gaius Publius Marcellinus. You appear to have fallen upon hard times."

Marcellinus was surely a dirty and disreputable sight. He saluted. "Indeed, sir."

"And what of the four turmae of the Second Aravacorum, in whose company I last saw you?"

"Lost outside Yupkoyvi, central city of the People of the Hand," Marcellinus said. "Defeated in battle by an expeditionary force of the Mongol Khan under the leadership of his general Jebei Noyon."

Verus looked startled. "They sought you out directly?"

"In a way. They were evidently making their return from the southern isthmus of Nova Hesperia after portaging their fleet when they got wind of us."

Marcellinus stared into the eyes of his fellow Praetor, his expression cold, quite ready to turn and climb back down the ladder to his friends rather than face criticism from this man. But Verus stepped forward and clapped

him on the arm, ushering him away from the listening
ears of the crew. "Regrettable, sir, quite regrettable. But
believe me, I am suddenly well acquainted with military
disaster. We do what we can for our men, sir, we do indeed, but no good commander should berate himself for
defeat provided that he has done his best."

Marcellinus, whose feelings on such matters were
rather different, maintained a studied silence. Unseen on
the decks below them, the oarsmen dug deep and the
Fortuna surged forward up the Mizipi. Marcellinus did
not glance back at the drekar for fear of seeing Enopay's
face, which was undoubtedly forlorn at being abandoned.

Calidius Verus was still speaking. "These Mongol bastards are unbelievably thorough. Coldhearted butchers.
Maniacs. Believe me, we only survived by abandoning
the fortress and retreating out into the Mare Solis."

Marcellinus nodded and made no comment.

"It was not the time or the place to engage," Verus
continued. "This is a brown-water navy with largely riverine expertise. The Rhine, the Euphrates; hardly at
their best on the high seas, with the tides and tows and
all. We had not trained for such an action, had never
expected one."

"Just so," Marcellinus said.

Verus looked grim. "The Mongols aim to kill the legions one by one. Yes? Bottle up the Legio VI Ferrata,
keep us separate from the main force, and then split the
men on the Line of Hadrianus off from Cahokia and the
Chesapica. That will not hold. This time we engage; this
time we go through. The Hesperian Nile is Roman now,
and *we* will control it. Not the redskins and definitely
not the slant-eyes."

Marcellinus looked at the Praetor in open disbelief.
"What?"

"We will hammer them. We must pass through their
blockade to rejoin our comrades in the north, but we
must also do as much damage to the Khan's bastards as
possible."

"Those are two different military objectives," Marcellinus said. "Which is our primary goal? To pass through or to defeat the Mongol fleet so that Roma regains control of the Mizipi?"

"They're one and the same." Verus inspected him. "And as for you, man, how on earth did you manage to escape from the Khan's clutches?"

"We did not escape," Marcellinus said. "We were released. The Khan slew the soldiers but spared the commanders, as he has done many times in the Asian theater. Freed us so that we could bring stories of his ruthless victories to the Imperator. He hopes to damage morale."

Verus looked back to the Norse dragon ship, which was falling astern. "Well, at least he's a gentleman in that regard. Yet I also see Cahokians among the ranks of the saved."

"Yes. Hanska's valor saved her. She impressed the Khan with her bravery and strength. And Pezi is lost to us, enslaved by the Khan, but his words helped save the other translators." Marcellinus paused, but honesty forced him to admit it. "Without Pezi, things may have gone even worse. Your faith in him was not misplaced."

The Praetor smiled. "I pride myself on being a good judge of character. I suspected you would find him satisfactory. For a barbarian, Pezi has some fine qualities. Trapped with the Khan's forces now? I regret that and wish him well."

"Indeed, sir. And as for you, in the gulf . . . Forgive me, but how many legionaries did you lose in that action?"

Verus shrugged. "Two thousand? We have been rather too busy to count. But come: to be frank, you seem in need of a drink, and by Jove, it's long past the time I usually start. The Mongols may have robbed me of my fortress and a few galleys, but I did ensure I salvaged my best Falernian wines. Please, come below to my cabin and let us talk further over a cup or two."

All of a sudden, Marcellinus could bear it no longer.

"Praetor Verus, I regret that there is another matter that I must first bring to your attention."

"About your expedition to the southwest?"

"No, sir. It concerns your old friend Lucius Domitius Corbulo. I find myself unable to keep you in the dark any longer."

Calidius Verus had become very still. "Pray continue, sir."

Marcellinus paused, but there was really nothing for it: the truth must be spoken.

"Corbulo mutinied against my command. It happened upon our arrival in Cahokia, before the battle in which the 33rd was defeated. And I believe he conspired to have me murdered before that by Magyar auxiliaries while we trekked westward from the Mare Chesapica. Certainly such auxiliaries were by his side when he attempted to slay me."

Verus said nothing but examined Marcellinus carefully, as if seeing him for the first time.

Marcellinus took a deep breath. "I regret to inform you that in the fight that broke out subsequent to his attempt to depose me from Praetorship of the 33rd, Lucius Domitius Corbulo died at my hands."

Verus took a step back. His hand dropped to the hilt of his gladius. "Are you mad, sir?"

"Never more sane," Marcellinus said steadily. "And I exhort you, sir, to leave your sword where it is. I am in no mood for . . . unpleasantness."

The moment expanded. Marcellinus became aware that the chatter of conversation from the soldiers on the top deck had become muted but did not take his eye off Praetor Verus. Marcellinus's only weapon was a pugio, and it was under his tunic. He would have no time to draw it if Verus attacked him; unless he could quickly disarm Verus with a kick to his wrist, his only sane course of action would be to run and leap bodily off the *Fortuna* into the Mizipi.

Calidius Verus leaned forward. "You are a traitor, a fratricide, and a redskin lover. If you did not have the trust of the Imperator, I would slay you here and now, sir. I would indeed."

Fratricide? Marcellinus let it lie. "I understand."

"You will leave my flagship immediately. We shall not speak again."

"Glad to, sir."

Marcellinus backed away slowly and went to talk to the master of the *Fortuna* to signal the dragon ship.

He was very sure he was not a traitor to Roma. But as for "redskin lover," Marcellinus would feel infinitely better once he was away from the loathsome Verus and back in the company of his friends.

The fleet proceeded north.

By the best estimates of Titus Otho, ship's master of the *Providentia*, Shappa Ta'atan was five days away at a normal rowing speed. However, they were not proceeding apace; the legionaries, sailors, and marines were preparing for battle, and a key part of those preparations was to ensure that the men were rested and ready. To break a blockade and fight a naval engagement, the oarsmen might need to row at top speed for extended intervals. Such an effort would require them to be in peak condition.

Marcellinus was not briefed on the plan of attack. He had not spoken to Verus since being dismissed from the *Fortuna*, and for all his politeness and apparent respect, Titus Otho chose not to share his orders with Marcellinus. The limit of Marcellinus's own preparation was to ensure that he and all his Hesperians were armed with the best weapons available and that Hanska was provided with twice as many as she could reasonably use.

The oarsmen and marines on board were fleet soldiers, not slaves or freedmen, and the sailors were specialists from the Roman navy. Marcellinus saw sailors on these ships from Sardinia, Pannonia, and Illyria-Dalmatia, distinctive as always in their thick wool tunics of iron gray, the seaman's color, with blue scarves, Phrygian caps, and cloth sash belts. Despite Verus's allegations that they were untrained, to Marcellinus they appeared quite competent.

"So how many Roman troops in all?"

Enopay was doing his best to wash the sweat off his face and arms, using a pail of muddy water he had just hauled up from the Mizipi at the end of a long rope. He would end up dirtier than he had started, albeit cooler. A gladius and small shield lay by his side. To the amusement of the legionaries on the top deck of the *Providentia,* he had just been sparring with Hanska, who was now leaning on the bulwark staring morosely upriver, having barely broken a sweat during their training.

Unlike the legionaries, Marcellinus did not mock Enopay and would never laugh at anyone trying to better himself. But he hoped beyond hope that Enopay would never face an enemy in close combat. The boy had little coordination, and a short reach. He moved quickly and had a ready store of dirty tricks absorbed from Taianita and Hanska, but any Mongol warrior would make short work of him.

Of course, there was no guarantee any of them would survive this. From the best guess of the sailors aboard the *Providentia* who had fought the Mongol fleet in the gulf, they faced a force of some thirty Mongol and Jin battle junks, with help from as many as twenty large wooden canoes of the northwestern Tlingit tribe and an unknown number of longboats of the Yokot'an Maya. Although smaller than the Roman quinqueremes, the Mongol junks would be swift and maneuverable and would surely carry full complements of black powder weapons.

"How many of us?" Enopay shook his arms, and water droplets scattered across the deck in front of him. "I have not seen into every Roman vessel. But with six quinqueremes each loaded with five hundred troops, two triremes, four dragon ships, and the men we have seen in the five knarrs, we probably have three and a half thousands." He rubbed his face and grimaced at the taste of the Mizipi water on his lips. "But we will be going upriver and will need all the speed we can muster. Most of our troops will be rowing like fuck, not fighting."

Marcellinus winced. "Enopay, just because you are surrounded by Romans does not mean you should curse like one."

"Sorry. Anyway, at most only fifteen hundreds of us will be free to fight."

"And the Mongol fleet?"

"Can I see around bends in the Mizipi? I cannot. But the men say the battle junks have crews of perhaps fifty apiece, and there may be thirty of them in all. If the long canoes of the Tlingit each have sixty men and there are twenty canoes and"—he shrugged—"say, eight longboats of the Sun, they will have a little over three thousands of men in total. Given that the Mongols have the advantage of the current, the battle may be very close."

"We should get you ashore beforehand," Marcellinus said. "You, the Chitimachan, Taianita."

"You would have us walk to Cahokia from here? If Roma breaks the blockade, we will get to Cahokia quicker with you than on foot. If not, we would still have an army between us and the Great City. And . . ." Enopay shook his head.

"What?"

"And if you are gone as well as my grandfather, perhaps I do not want to return to Cahokia anyway."

Marcellinus opened his mouth, closed it again.

"However much you might try, I do not think you can protect me from this war," Enopay said matter-of-factly. "Shall we eat again? We are both still very thin."

The last time Marcellinus had seen the Legio VI Ferrata surge into battle, he had been on the receiving end of it, surrounded by the unfortunate populace of Ocatan as it was assaulted by seven quinqueremes of the Ironclads. Now he stood aboard one of the same quinqueremes with a Roman helmet strapped to his head and a scutum bearing the thunderbolt insignia of the VI Ferrata on his left arm. Once again, though, he was flanked by Hesperians: around him were Hanska, Taianita, the Chitimachan, and Enopay, all clutching Roman weapons with varying degrees of confidence.

The Roman fleet was powering upriver in formation. Leading the pack were the *Fortuna* and the *Triumphus*, rowing side by side, separated by fifty yards. Both quinqueremes had onagers on their middecks primed and ready for action. Both also had their fighting towers erected fore and aft and a battery of scorpios lining their bulwarks. A scorpio was a one-man ballista, a torsion-sprung crossbow seven feet across mounted on a post five feet high, which fired stout bolts of iron and wood five feet long. Similar but slightly larger was the harpax, a ballista that shot a combination of a harpoon and a grappling iron on a cable, enabling the quinquereme to spear and reel in an enemy ship for boarding. Each quinquereme possessed two of the harpax ballistae, at bow and stern.

Following the lead quinqueremes were two dragon ships each a hundred feet long. After them came another pair of quinqueremes, the *Providentia*, on which Marcellinus and his friends now stood, and the *Fides*, both also bristling with legionaries at arms and with their fighting turrets set for battle. In their wake came the cargo vessel known as the *Annona*, the two triremes, four smaller drekars, and five knarrs.

Bringing up the rear were the older quinqueremes, *Minerva* and *Clementia*. The *Minerva* had been in splendid condition when it had taken Marcellinus and the others downriver the previous year but was now substantially damaged from the Mongol attack. The scorch marks on its bow and all down its port side made it appear that the ship had taken a vicious black eye. The *Clementia* was in better shape, with only minimal damage and a freshly painted bow, but was serving as the fleet's hospital ship. Every Roman naval vessel had a medicus or two aboard, but the *Clementia* held a dedicated sick bay to care for those seriously wounded in the earlier battle. The galley was thus short of fighting men, and might need additional defense if any could be spared.

"Sir?"

"Yes, Hanska?"

"Good luck."

He nodded. "And to you, warrior."

She cocked an eye at him. "Oh, and sir? Don't force me to jump in and save your life again. That would just be embarrassing for both of us."

Marcellinus grinned. "Noted. But should the opportunity arise, please feel free to save Enopay's."

"I'll do that, sir."

Across the fifty yards that separated him from the *Fides*, Marcellinus could see the centurion Manius Ifer standing next to the *Fides*'s master with his hands clasped behind his back in a pose of complete calm and confidence. Marcellinus had learned recently that Ifer had been promoted to tribune pro tem of the Tenth Cohort. The appointment did not surprise him.

Marcellinus could not see Calidius Verus in the *Fortuna* from this far behind, but he certainly hoped the Praetor owned a bearing as calm as Manius Ifer's. For now they were rounding the last bend in the river that separated them from Shappa Ta'atan. A deafening blast of horns from the *Fortuna* was taken up quickly by the *Triumphus*. From belowdecks on the *Providentia* they heard a smattering of cheers from the three ranks of oarsmen beneath their feet. The drums that set the time for the rowers, however, did not increase their tempo, and the hortator who commanded them was swearing at the crew to maintain their current rhythm. "Not yet, you sons of whores, not yet . . ."

The ranks of marines and legionaries on the top deck in front of Marcellinus stood stolid, saving their breath, waiting for the fray. But Marcellinus could sense their energy and determination building. As they propelled themselves upriver into the dragon's maw, anticipation was rising.

And there was the enemy fleet, stretched across the river ahead of them.

The Mizipi was two thousand feet across at Shappa Ta'atan, and at first glance the ships that faced them seemed to span its entire width.

Marcellinus knew that the junks of the Jin that the Mongols had commandeered were two-masted and close to a hundred feet long, but he somehow had expected them to be delicate, perhaps paper-thin like the Jin and Song fans he had seen for sale long ago in markets along the Silk Road. The junks had, after all, been portaged across fifty miles of dry land. Instead he saw substantial wooden vessels, not open-hulled like Viking longships but with raised covered decks fore and aft. Their sails were tall, square, and flat; they looked to be strengthened with bamboo slats and hung from sturdy masts. Each junk was crammed with Mongol warriors.

Similarly, Marcellinus had known that the oceangoing canoes of the northwestern tribes were larger than the birch-bark canoes of the Cahokians and Haudenosaunee, but he had not expected them to be seventy feet long and as stout-sided as any Norse longship, though nowhere near as broad in the beam. As yet he was too far distant to see details, but their hulls seemed to be brightly painted with sharp, blocky images and martial patterns.

Finally, he had not anticipated the swarm of regular Mizipian canoes. "Futete."

Staring forward with eyes wide, Enopay rather automatically said, "Just because you are surrounded by Romans does not mean you should swear like one." He added: "Do not ask me to count the ships. They weave around too fast."

Trumpets sounded, the flutes at the stern of each quinquereme shrilled, and the pace of the drumbeats quickened as Roma settled in for the charge. Across the quarter-mile divide that separated them from the enemy they could hear the Mongols' war drums, the giant naccara drums as big as a man. On the junks the din they made must have been thunderous.

"Fuck," Hanska said in reverence.

The Chitimachan's head turned left and right as if she were looking for a hole to hide in. Taianita glanced at Marcellinus and then looked away quickly. Marcellinus tried to iron out the worried frown on his face and tightened his grip on his gladius.

In the past his battle fever would have been mounting at such a moment, excitement preparing him for the fight to come. But today all he felt was a nagging concern, a regret for opportunities missed, words left unsaid to people he loved and cared for. He took a deep breath and tried to marshal his thoughts.

At the same moment there came a single short blast from a cornu and the bellowed voice of the lookout. "Bombs!"

Marcellinus's first instinct was to look down into the water. Had the Mongols laid mines? Could their black powder somehow be impervious to water; could they guess a fuse length with such accuracy? But no, the bombs were flying through the air, seeming to hang lazily in the skies as they reached the peaks of their long arcs.

Another call from the lookout. "Trebuchets!"

Marcellinus had been so intent on staring at the enemy fleet that he had failed to notice the activity on the Mizipi's banks. The Jin trebuchets the Mongols were using were not powered by twisted rope and sinew like the Roman onagers Marcellinus had built for Cahokia. Instead, they were powered by men and ropes. To launch a missile, a team of warriors pulled horizontally with a titanic coordinated jerking motion, and their effort was translated by a pulley and multiplied by the lever action of a long throwing arm set on a high frame. The throwing arm acted as a sling, whipping around to fling its projectiles out over the river.

The legs of the trebuchets were sunk into the ground for stability, and from the large branches and other remains of fallen trees that lay around them it was clear that they had been built in place.

We could improve on those, Marcellinus thought. *A counterweight would work much more effectively, and besides, they'll miss us by several boat lengths.* Then the first bomb hit the water ahead of them and exploded into a smoky, blinding fog.

The trebuchets were not throwing balls of stone or steel, but gas bombs with fuses of hemp.

"Lime!" came the cry from the legionaries up and down the quinquereme, and men covered their eyes and noses with their cloaks; others knelt and bowed their heads to limit the amount they breathed. Marcellinus and the others emulated them. At the same time they heard a slamming from beneath them as the louvers were closed to limit the amount of noxious gas getting through to the oarsmen.

Fortunately, the trebuchets on the land were having trouble getting the Roman ships' range. The helmsman changed course to give the first clouds a wide berth, but then more bombs came. One or two fizzled without releasing their gas, but most ignited to spread their contents across the water's surface. The freshening breeze was from the northwest and blew the clouds of gas right over the central section of the Roman fleet.

As the *Providentia* rowed through the cloud, the coughing and choking started as the lime smoke irritated the men's throats. Despite the cloak Marcellinus held in front of his face, the lime gas made his eyes burn.

Only those on deck were affected. The flutes had fallen silent now, but the hortatory calls could be heard loud and clear, the drums still beat, and the oarsmen rowed steadily. Eventually Marcellinus stood and looked around him. Eyes were streaming, men were still coughing uncontrollably, and a few of the unluckiest even had blisters forming on their faces and arms where the gas had been densest, but the trebuchets were now behind them.

Ahead, most Mongol battle junks were striking their

sails and turning to their oars. In battle they would have no time for the intricacies of steering under sail. The center of the Mongol formation bulged as the enemy fleet formed a triangular shape similar to a Roman cuneus, reaching out to strike. A handful of Tlingit canoes and Maya longboats scurried ahead of them, eager to engage the Roman forces.

Likewise, it was as if the *Fortuna* and the *Triumphus* were racing to be first into battle. The *Fortuna* was slightly in front, and it seemed that the flagship would plow into the enemy ships first, but then the two onagers on its main deck released their loads. Giant boulders flew, and the *Fortuna* rocked and yawed in reaction. The *Triumphus* leaped ahead.

Hanska was shaking her head. "Fucking Shappa Ta'atani. Fuck."

Marcellinus glanced at Taianita.

"*I* am not Shappan," Taianita spit in a low tone. "I am *not* Shappan."

The birch-bark canoes of the Shappa Ta'atani now vied with those of the Tlingit and Maya, surging out ahead of the battle junks in their determination to meet the enemy. It was clear to them all that the Shappa Ta'atani had changed sides once again and allied with the Mongols. "They already betrayed their own Mizipian people to fight with the Romans against Ocatan," he said. "What else would you expect of Son of the Sun?"

Taianita scowled. "Really? You ask *me* that?"

Marcellinus grinned tightly. "They think they've chosen the winning side. Time to prove them wrong."

The Roman fleet was approaching the blockade at alarming speed. The junks that had appeared to form a solid line across the Great River had resolved into a swarm of individual ships. There must be more than thirty junks, after all—Marcellinus thought perhaps three dozen—but if the Roman vessels could smash through them and keep going, perhaps the Sixth could carry the day without losing too many more men . . .

Roman horns sounded again, and the two warships at

the front of the Roman column separated. The two dragon ships immediately in their wake followed suit. "Ah." Marcellinus nodded.

"What?" said Taianita. "Why do they—"

"Carving a path. The galleys will punch through the Mongol line, and then any Mongol big canoes caught in between them will be trapped between the Roman lines."

"The Mongol ships are lighter." Enopay frowned, his forehead lined far beyond his years. "The quinqueremes are . . . clubs. Blunt clubs. They can break through the line, trap the junks in between, which can then be destroyed by the other Roman vessels that come behind. That is what Verus wants. It may not be so easy."

Marcellinus felt a perverse need to defend his Roman commanding officer. "Not easy but a good strategy nonetheless. And we will enfilade as we go."

Hanska hefted her club. "I hope it is not *too* easy."

"Never fear, Hanska. We will find you Mongols to kill."

Hanska nodded, her eyes bleak. For a moment her expression was as fixed as it had been during the dark days along the Kicka River. Enopay glanced up in concern and leaned against her. Absently, Hanska touched Enopay's shoulder with the hand that was not holding her club.

No cheers came from below now. The oarsmen were too busy putting their backs into their rowing. On the upper deck the centurions brought their men to order. The artillerymen at the bulwarks were checking their scorpios, cranking the crossbows back, putting bolts in place. In the longships and knarrs the crews took up their bows and spears. The gunwales of their boats were close to water level, making them prime targets for the Tlingit and Shappan canoes.

"Stay close to me," Marcellinus said to Enopay. "Unless I'm in a melee. Then stay away."

Enopay gave him a quick glance. His expression spoke volumes.

As the enemy fleets came within range, the swell of noise was immediate, the din of the scorpios firing their bolts into the sails, men, and hulls of the Mongol battle junks. No Mongol arrows yet reached the *Providentia*, but they would soon enough.

The *Fortuna* and the *Triumphus* thundered into the Mongol line. Each had aimed to ram a Mongol junk, and the *Fortuna* hit hers fair and square. Her beaklike ramming prow caught the junk astern and crunched through its hull. Even as the junk's poop deck rose and splintered, the Mongol warriors aboard it were loosing their arrows to rake the *Fortuna*'s decks.

The junk the *Triumphus* had aimed for managed to skim past its lethal ram at the last second. It swung wide to avoid getting tangled in the oars of the quinquereme, and then its striking arm crashed down. This was a hinged pole fifty feet long tipped with a heavy slab of iron the shape of a hammerhead, similar to the Roman corvus but much longer. The corvus was essentially a broad gangplank designed to slam into an enemy ship's deck and hold it close enough for legionaries to board across it, but Marcellinus could see that the Mongol striking arms had a different function: their goal was to hold the ships apart, keep the enemy at a distance so that they could be bombarded. In light of their advantage with the black powder bombs and their excellent bowmanship, the Mongols favored bombardment over boarding; that matched their tactics on land of not engaging in hand-to-hand fighting unless forced to.

The striking arm of a second Mongol junk thumped into the deck of the *Triumphus* on its starboard side. A moment later came the boom of an explosion as a thunder crash bomb ignited. The *Triumphus* swayed ponderously from the impact. A cloud of black smoke drifted upward, and an acrid smell tinged the air.

As the *Fortuna* and *Triumphus* slowed as a result of their impacts, the two dragon ships steered into the gap between them. The drekar to starboard rammed a Mongol junk and came to an almost immediate halt in the river, its stern rising clear of the water. With a roar, Roman soldiers stepped up onto the longship's gunwale and leaped onto the foredeck of the junk. Mongols hurried to defend against them, and steel rang against steel. As for the left drekar, two Tlingit canoes barely any shorter were pulling alongside, arrows flying, and behind them several eight-man canoes of the Shappa Ta'atani.

Enemy ships swarmed the *Providentia* now, junks coming in from each side at an angle, Tlingit canoes passing behind, ready to assault them from the stern. Aboard the nearest junk Marcellinus saw the spark of fire. A slow flame smoldered, ready to ignite a thunder crash bomb. "Shoot that man!" Marcellinus shouted. The nearest legionary artilleryman saw the threat and swung his scorpio around, his bolt already loaded and ready.

The Jin warrior died with a scream, impaled against the hull of his boat, and his thunder crash bomb rolled away into the scuppers of the battle junk. Its fuse sparked and hissed. "Down!" Marcellinus shouted, but the next moment the bomb went off, strafing the crews of both ships with hot metal and ceramic shards. The battle junk took the worst of it, and water immediately gushed in through its hull.

Alongside the *Providentia*, the *Fides* arrowed away at a diagonal. Its way was blocked by four junks. Trying to plow through them would be suicide, and her ship's master was aiming to breach the line where it was weaker. Unfortunately, three of the four junks the *Fides* had avoided now changed course to converge on the *Providentia*.

Marcellinus had a brief mental image of a horse being taken down and mauled to death by a pack of dogs. He stepped up beside his ship's master. "We can't let them divide us like this. We must get alongside Verus in the *Fortuna*. Fight one battle, not many. Can we—"

"Fuck off," Titus Otho said tersely. "I'm busy."

It was too late anyway. The dragon ships ahead of

them had been boarded, their crews in a melee with the almost naked but ferocious warriors of the Tlingit and Shappa Ta'atani. The *Providentia* could not thread the needle between the two drekars, and if they changed course too dramatically, they risked being rammed by their own ships coming up from behind, as the *Minerva* and the *Clementia* had split to flank the battle.

Besides, the *Providentia* had its own problems. In all, six battle junks were converging on Marcellinus's quinquereme. A bolt from the *Minerva*'s ballista slammed into the hull of the leading junk just below where the Mongol helmsman stood, splintering the wood. To the helmsman's credit, the wake of his junk barely wavered. In a few moments they would be within striking-arm range.

The master of the *Providentia* was indeed busy shouting orders to his own helmsman. Vibius Caecina, tribune of the Eighth and Ninth Cohorts, was standing amidships directing the ballistarii, the catapult crew.

This was hardly Marcellinus's theater of war, but he could not help himself. He strode forward along the port line of artillerymen at their scorpios. "Target any Mongol readying a bomb, target anyone with a flame or a fuse, and after them the helmsmen—"

The *Providentia* rocked as two Mongol striking arms came down simultaneously into its starboard deck, one close to the prow and one barely thirty feet from where Marcellinus stood.

"Cut it! Guard them!"

The Roman marines around him acted instantly, some leaping forward with axes to try to cut the nearer striking arm away while others provided covering fire with scorpio bolts, arrows, and spears, or sheltered their axmen behind tall shields.

"Thunder crash!" Enopay shouted, and hit the deck.

It came arcing through the air from the first of the junks to port. The bomb exploded well above the *Providentia*, its fuse too short, but again came that unearthly crackling explosion of black powder. Shards of hot metal strafed the legionaries in front of Marcellinus. The blast threw many men through the air to slam into the decks, broken and still.

"Shit, shit . . ." Marcellinus spun and checked his people. Enopay was uninjured, but Hanska was staring with vicious hatred at a deep laceration in her right forearm. "Hanska?"

She raised her gaze and stared at the Mongol junk just a few dozen feet away across the water with a baleful expression. She wasn't seriously hurt.

The Romans had hacked away the tip of the rearmost striking arm. The harpax fired with an astonishingly loud twang, followed by the sound of scraping cable. The harpoon buried itself in the hull of the battle junk just below its poop deck. Men hauled. The Mongols on the junk dropped their oars, grabbed weapons, and swarmed the deck, ready for combat.

At Titus Otho's shouted command the helmsman put the *Providentia* hard to starboard. It swung toward the closest junk. From behind, the *Minerva* came around them to tackle the line of junks on the *Providentia*'s port side.

The battle junk crunched up against the *Providentia*. "Let them come to us! Get ready! Formation! Prepare to be boarded!" Marcellinus shouted.

The quinqueremes' upper decks were a dozen feet above the waterline, the junks' only slightly less. The two bands of warriors met on almost equal terms. The Romans braced, and the Mongols poured aboard.

With a bloodcurdling scream of rage Hanska was off and running, straight into the midst of the Mongols, her ax held high.

"Enopay, back, hide." Marcellinus scanned the deck briefly: two junks to starboard disgorging Mongol warriors, another two at striking-arm length, with a shooting war going on between Romans behind shields and Mongols behind the bulwark of their ship. Three more farther away, being rowed in curved paths, looking for an opening. The legionaries on the fighting towers alter-

nately strafing the Mongols on the *Providentia*'s deck
and holding off the other battle junks. A dedicated couple of centuries guarded the *Providentia*'s single onager,
which was still firing regularly over their heads at the
junks attempting to close with the *Fides*.

From behind Marcellinus came two almost simultaneous explosions. One was from close by, and the *Providentia* juddered hard, and the second explosion came
from farther away, setting fire to the fighting tower on
the *Minerva*.

Marcellinus was trained for command but had no
troops at his disposal. For the moment he was just a
soldier, and he could delay no longer. He realized that
Enopay was still by his side. "Juno, Enopay! Find
Romans and hide behind them!" Drawing his gladius,
he sprinted toward the nearest fray, where Mongols and
Romans were fighting for control of the rear starboard
bulwark of the *Providentia*.

As he saw his first Mongol faces close up in this battle,
Marcellinus's anger finally took hold of him. The massacre of the unarmed Romans and People of the Hand at
Yupkoyvi, the brutality of the forced march across the
desert, the Khan's murder of Mikasi and enslavement of
Pezi: his fury at all of this suddenly erupted and propelled him. His gladius sank into a Mongol arm until it
crunched on the bone. He snatched it back and swung at
an unprotected neck, kicked a warrior overboard. Parried as a warrior with Jin features stabbed low at his
already injured calf and slashed the man viciously across
his stomach. Blood not his own splashed across Marcellinus's chest and arm, and he pushed forward to reach
Hanska's side.

Hanska fought like a woman possessed, shoving her
way into the mass of Mongol sailors to stab and slay.
She screamed as she did so, the raw sound visibly terrifying the men around her. Marcellinus stayed well to her
left—in her berserker rage she might not recognize him
until after she had disemboweled him—and ensured
that no Mongol could flank her.

On his other side Roman legionaries fought with him shoulder to shoulder. Mongols had the advantage at distance fighting, but in hand-to-hand combat Romans had the edge. In equal numbers, the Romans' discipline and better steel would prevail.

Whether their numbers were truly equal, Marcellinus could not tell. Fighting was taking place in concentrated knots all across the deck of the warship. Behind and around him came the occasional flare and explosion of black powder, and sometimes the deck shifted beneath his feet, but he fought on: hacking, slashing, slaying.

CHAPTER 14

YEAR NINE, THUNDER MOON

By the time they cleared the deck of the *Providentia* the air around the ships was rank with smoke. Marcellinus had never been on a battlefield so obscured, and wished the wind would pick up and blow it clear.

Toward the end he had become separated from Hanska. She had leaped into one of the Mongol junks to help the Romans slaughter the surviving Mongols and Jin. Marcellinus had run forward to take control of the Second Century of the Fourth Cohort, who were defending the ship's onager upon the death of their centurion. Caecina, who had formerly been standing there, had vanished completely. Now Marcellinus looked around him and realized that for the moment, the battle here was won.

"Wait!" He ran back to Titus Otho, who was still commanding from the poop deck. "Don't cut the junks loose until we commandeer their black powder or any bombs they may have aboard them."

About to curse him again, the ship's master now thought better of it. He swung to give the order, while at the same time shouting to the hortator to get the oarsmen benched and ready to row again as soon as possible.

Men leaped aboard the junks. Legionaries . . . and a Cahokian boy. "Enopay!"

Not every Mongol aboard the ship was dead; many were wounded, dazed, still moving. Enopay did not respond but disappeared down a stairway into the sinking rear of the vessel.

Marcellinus ran, jumped up, and leaped across to the Mongol ship, his momentum almost carrying him head over heels. Legionaries came up empty-handed from beneath the foredeck, with other men grabbing Mongol weapons or spitefully stabbing their downed foes. Enopay reappeared, staggering up the rear stairway out of the sinking stern of the junk under the weight of a round metal ball. "Thunder crash bomb."

"Juno, Enopay . . ."

"I may not fight well, but I can carry. Help me get this onto the *Providentia*."

They clambered back aboard the quinquereme and cut the junk free. Hanska and the Chitimachan were helping the legionaries throw Mongol corpses off the *Providentia*'s deck into the river. Enopay stowed the thunder crash bomb amidships. Marcellinus ran back to stand beside Titus Otho, peering forward through the smoke. "What of the *Fortuna* and *Triumphus*?"

"Braced together in the thick of it," Titus Otho said. "We go to them now."

"Where's the *Fides*?"

"With us."

Marcellinus scanned the deck. "And where the hell is Vibius Caecina?"

"The most useless tribune in the Ironclads? Dead, we can only hope." For the first time, the ship's master grinned at him.

It was a ridiculous breach of discipline, but Marcellinus didn't care. "Let's get this ship to where the real battle is."

"Yeah." Otho peered through the smoke. "Fuck all this housekeeping and deck swabbing. I'm already bored."

"Tell me about the other tribunes. If Verus has his hands full, who's next in command? Who's worth the candle?"

Otho grinned again. "Figuring out who you need to assassinate to take command?"

This was a little close to the bone. Otho's flippant irreverence was proving trying. Marcellinus bit his tongue. "Hardly."

"Well, remember me for some advancement when you do."

"Just tell me, Otho. And which ships they're on."

"Verus himself commands the First Cohort. His First Tribune is Aurelius Dizala." Titus Otho nodded. "That one, Dizala, he's all right. If you could get him on your side, you'd be golden. Pun intended. But you won't. He's Verus's man through and through. So he commands the Second and Third Cohorts, and he'll be on the *Triumphus*. Cohorts Four and Five are on the *Minerva*, under Statius Paulinus. He's competent enough but young. Overwhelms easily once the spears fly. Probably taking orders from his own centurions by now. Flavius Urbicus, Sixth and Seventh Cohorts, is on the *Clementia*. Good man. You already know about Caecina, who you'll find anywhere except actually commanding the Eighth and Ninth. And Ifer over there on the *Fides* is keeping the Tenth straight for the time being, and hopefully forever, since he actually has a brain in his head."

"Dizala, Paulinus, Urbicus. Caecina. Ifer." Marcellinus looked from one quinquereme to the next, settling the names in his mind.

"I wouldn't try too hard," said the ship's master. "Half of 'em will be in Elysium by sunset."

A few moments later they came out of the smoke and took stock of their next riverine battleground.

The dozen battle junks that swarmed around the *Fortuna* were better armored than those that had attacked the *Providentia*. One was larger than the rest, its wide curving prow decorated with a tiger's face. It also flew a complicated standard on its mast. This must be Subodei Badahur's flagship, within his own personal squadron.

They were trying a more innovative approach than

Marcellinus had seen so far. Better able to resist bombardment from the decks and battle towers of the *Fortuna*, these junks were using their striking arms as delivery devices for thunder crash bombs. A Mongol sailor in the rigging would load one of the large metal bombs onto the end of the striking arm and set the fuse. He would light the fuse and drop the arm when the battle junk was at its closest approach to the *Fortuna*, carrying the deadly black powder bomb straight down to the quinquereme's deck.

It was a bold tactic that was having mixed success. Three junks already lay dead in the water, having been blasted by their own bombs or otherwise immobilized by the Romans, but the *Fortuna* had two broad and smoking holes side by side at its port bow and was listing and taking on water. To starboard it had been joined by the *Triumphus*, and the two ships were braced together stem to stern by harpax cable, their hulls moored together to make a single fighting platform. The *Triumphus* was taking heavy fire on its own flank, though its onager and scorpios were currently keeping the Mongols at bay. More soldiers were spilling up from belowdecks on both ships, presumably the oarsmen.

The *Providentia* was still several hundred feet away when two junks under full sail changed course to make a concerted and apparently suicidal run at her. With the wind directly behind them, their attackers approached at an almost uncanny rate.

"Trying to strip our oars," Titus Otho said tersely. "Helmsman! To port!"

Agonizingly slowly the quinquereme yawed to port in an attempt to ram one of the attack junks, but the sailing ships were much more nimble. The leftward junk arrived first, sliding along the hull of the *Providentia* closely enough to slam into its leading oars and smash them to matchwood. At the same time, a Mongol sailor slung one of the lighter thunderclap bombs onto the *Providentia*'s top deck, where it duly exploded. The nearer Romans and Cherokee had hurled themselves aside even before the junk arrived; those farther away did their best to protect themselves behind their round naval shields. The enemy sailor who had thrown the bomb now flew backward straight off the top deck of his own ship to splash into the river behind, already dead with a Roman scorpio bolt clean through his chest.

Two dozen oars had broken by the time the junk's momentum failed it. The ship then faced a barrage of Roman missiles and erupted in a mass of splinters and chunks of wood. Warriors jumped overboard.

Marcellinus was already running for the bow, but the *Providentia*'s crew was well trained; injured legionaries were being pulled away from the burning hole the Mongol bomb had carved in the top deck while other men flung water from the barrels on deck to quench the burning. Unlike Cahokian liquid flame, it appeared that the incendiary black powder of the Jin and Mongols could be neutralized by water.

As Marcellinus passed it, the great ballista on the *Providentia*'s deck fired and sent a huge bolt into the stern of the Mongol vessel that menaced them on the starboard side. The ballista bolt practically split the helmsman of the junk in two, and the tiller behind him exploded in a flurry of shards and splinters of wood. Although Marcellinus had not heard the command, at the same time the starboard oarsmen had backwatered, guiding the now helmless enemy vessel into the *Providentia*'s hull.

The legionary manning the harpax ballista had not been idle, and as he pulled the other attacking Mongol vessel toward the *Providentia,* the Roman corvus fell, locking it into place. A good half century of the Sixth Ferrata was already in position and now began to board the Mongol ship. Marcellinus swerved in midrun and joined them. As he leaped from the bulwark of the quinquereme, the brown river flashed beneath him, providing him with the sudden realization that if he went overboard, his armor would carry him down to the mud at the river bottom in moments. Then his boots landed on the deck of the Mongol ship and he was driving a

Roman hasta spear through the chest of a Mongol warrior and swinging his gladius, and all rational thought left his mind once more in the flurry of combat.

They made short work of the remaining Mongols, but this time there was no chance to search the junk for black powder. Marcellinus barely made it back up onto the deck of the *Providentia* before the Romans cut the wrecked junk loose with its cargo of corpses.

Breathing heavily, Marcellinus threaded his way to the bow of the *Providentia* and took stock.

The *Fides* was still beside them, having fought off its own attackers. The hospital ship *Clementia* had gotten off lightly and was gamely following them. A pitched war of attrition was going on to the east between the Roman archers on the flotilla of assembled drekars and triremes and a mixed force of bowmen of the Yokot'an Maya and Shappa Ta'atani on the other, but that would have to wait. If the two largest galleys of the Roman fleet went down with all hands, the battle was lost. The *Providentia* had to get to the *Fortuna* and the *Triumphus*.

Increasingly, their river battle was beginning to look like a land war. The *Fortuna* and *Triumphus* were locked together, a floating island under attack from at least a dozen Mongol ships, many Tlingit canoes, and two longboats of the Yokot'an Maya. In short, the Roman forces were besieged within a field fortification of floating wood, and it was up to the forces at Marcellinus's disposal to raise the siege.

And by that point, Marcellinus had little doubt that it was up to him. Vibius Caecina had reappeared but was sitting by the *Providentia*'s onager with his hand over his mouth, giving no orders. Marcellinus briefly considered going to talk to the tribune, then discarded the idea. At no point in the battle had Caecina approached Titus Otho to give him a command or offer intelligence. Neither had he fought with the Roman vexillations that had resisted the Mongol junks. For a while he had stood with the centurion of the launch team, attempting to look useful, but his demeanor spoke "civilian" to Marcellinus. As often happened in the lesser legions, it was the noncommissioned officers, centurions and others of similar rank such as the ships' masters, who were directing this battle.

Well. As it now seemed that Otho was willing to work with Marcellinus, so much the better.

He glanced across at the *Fides* just in time to catch the eye of Manius Ifer. Ifer pointed to port of the *Fortuna* and then to starboard of the *Triumphus* and made broad gestures in hand-talk. *Query: dock each side?*

As the Romans' expert in covert expeditions, Ifer had spent more time than most in the field with Hesperians. Naturally he would know the hand-talk by now. Marcellinus cast his gaze again over the beleaguered Roman vessels ahead of them and the positions of their Mongol assailants and made a series of broad gestures back. Ifer raised his eyebrows in surprise but nodded quickly and turned to talk to the master of the *Fides*.

Marcellinus made his way back to Titus Otho on the poop deck of the *Providentia*. "Swing around to port and raise the rowing tempo. We're going to smack Subodei Badahur right between the eyes."

Titus Otho nodded. "About bloody time. *Long* past bloody time. How do you boys want to proceed?"

"Boys?" Himself and Ifer? No matter. "Titus Otho, I have an idea in mind that you might not like."

"Oh?" The ship's master raised his eyebrows. "Try me. I like a challenge."

The *Providentia* went in first at slow ramming speed, hitting the *Fortuna* amidships at a forty-five-degree angle. With its hull weakened by the repeated assaults from the thunder crash bombs, the *Providentia*'s ram cleaved straight through the side of the Roman flagship with a grating cacophony of steel against wood.

Naturally enough, Badahur must have assumed his own flagship would be the *Providentia*'s target and had backwatered to bring its bow around to face the Roman quinquereme. Caught unaware, this junk became the focus of a hail of ballista fire and arrows from the *Providentia* and beat a hasty retreat. Her oarsmen had to put in a heroic effort to overcome the current.

As for the Mongol forces on the deck of the *Fortuna*, they could scarcely believe their eyes. The remains of the First Cohort under Calidius Verus's command was bottled up at the ship's stern, arrayed in a rough defensive formation between the growing Mongol force and the poop deck. The artillerymen with their scorpios had fallen back to line the bulwark at the front edge of this deck. The spectacular arrival of the *Providentia* had forced Badahur's flagship junk and two other junks back from pulling alongside the *Fortuna* and assailing the First Cohort from two sides. Now the tables were turned, with the Mongol forces divided and under attack from the First on the *Fortuna* and the Ninth Cohort on the *Providentia*.

The *Providentia*'s corvus fell into an open area of the *Fortuna*'s deck, but it was largely superfluous; the ships were locked fast together, and Marcellinus's legionaries were already rushing aboard over the port and starboard gunwales at the ship's prow. At the same time the *Fides* arrived on the far side of the *Triumphus* and moored to it in more conventional style with harpax bolts to stem and stern, delivering a further five hundred men directly to the heart of the battle.

"Keep them off," Marcellinus said to the artillerymen at the scorpios, then ran forward to give the same message to the centurion in charge of the onager crew. "Keep the ships of Badahur away. That's your one job. Hold them at bay. Nobody boards us again. Understood?"

"Sir, yes, sir," said the centurion. Vibius Caecina gaped at him. Marcellinus nodded curtly, resisting his urge to stab the man, and kept moving.

He had lost sight of Hanska, Taianita, and Enopay, but the mopping-up operation on the stern deck of the *Fortuna* was going well. Two quinquereme decks away, the legionaries of the *Fides* were in ruthless hand-to-hand with Mongol warriors, and Marcellinus was sure they would prevail; more Romans were joining the battle all the time from belowdecks on the *Fides*.

Perhaps it was time to save lives rather than destroy them. He ran up to a centurion, by his insignia the fourth centurion of the Ninth Cohort. "Rescue party. Belowdecks on the *Fortuna*. Let's leave no one behind. Yes?"

The man nodded tersely and gave the orders. He and Marcellinus jumped aboard the deck of the *Fortuna* at the head of a force of some sixty legionaries.

The *Fortuna* was listing badly to port, but the support of the *Providentia* was preventing it from rolling any farther. The foredecks of Verus's flagship were now mostly clear, mainly as a result of the firing of ballista and scorpio bolts right over the heads of Marcellinus and the Fourth Century to keep Badahur's junks at bay. Now those junks changed course, rowing around the bow of the *Fortuna* to lend support to the increasingly beleaguered Mongol force aboard the *Triumphus* next door.

As Marcellinus took a deep breath and prepared to run down the steps into the lower decks of the *Fortuna*, Enopay appeared beside him, panting, the gladius in his hand wavering with the effort of holding it. "Enopay! Damn it, go back!"

Enopay glanced around and gasped, "More dangerous . . . back there than . . . with you."

"Then stay close." Marcellinus pounded down the steps behind the centurion.

Ramming the *Fortuna* had been a calculated risk. After all this time in battle the oarsmen from below *should* have left the rowing decks. The *Fortuna* itself was so badly damaged, the holes in its sides so gaping, that it would never be navigable again. As a wooden vessel it would not quite sink but would eventually lie awash, completely bilged and incapable of salvage. If anything, the buoyancies of the *Providentia* and *Trium-*

phus were now holding the *Fortuna* up and preventing it from slumping even deeper into the Mizipi. But if there were men still belowdecks, perhaps injured men whom Verus had chosen to keep out of the battle, Marcellinus did not want them on his conscience.

It was even more cramped on the rowing decks than Marcellinus had thought possible. On the third and highest of the decks there was almost no headroom; the oarsmen must have had a backbreaking shuffle to get to and from their rowing stations. At this level there were two men per oar on either side, and many of the oars were still lying higgledy-piggledy across the thwarts and making their passage difficult. The lighting was dim, the louvers not having been opened again after the gas assault, and Marcellinus saw nothing. "Enopay, for Juno's sake, don't run ahead."

"But I know where I'm going," Enopay said, and disappeared.

Marcellinus banged his head, swore, ran forward, and looked down. Enopay had darted down through a hatchway, taking broad steps down to the deck below. Behind Marcellinus the men of the Fourth were spreading out, searching, many of them now running down other stairwells.

The second deck was much like the third: cramped, airless, empty of oarsmen. Here the floors were awash in several inches of water, with more flowing in, and with a chill Marcellinus realized that he was standing below the level of the Mizipi outside the ship. "Damn it. Enopay, there's nobody here."

"Come on. If there's anyone, they'll be where the *Providentia* came through."

"First deck is underwater," said a laconic voice from behind them. "Anyone down there is done."

"Anyone still down there was an idiot," Enopay said. "Eyanosa, come."

The cramped space and the water underfoot were increasingly oppressive, the light level even lower, and

Marcellinus banged his head on something hard that jutted out of the hull in front of him. "Shit."

"Watch out for the *Providentia*," Enopay said at the same moment.

Sure enough, Marcellinus's probing hand in front of him had just slapped the wet outer hull of the warship he had ridden in on.

"We can get around it," Enopay said, and disappeared again.

From sixty feet away beneath the hatchway where they had entered the second deck, the centurion called. "No one. We're out of here. Come on, sir."

"Get clear," Marcellinus said. "We're going aft."

He splashed through water, following Enopay. They were now in the rear of the *Fortuna*, and he became aware of an increasing rumbling sound and an ominous creaking. The rumbling was the noise of men running and fighting two decks up. He preferred not to speculate about the creaking.

"Man down," Enopay said. "Help me."

"Alive? Roman?"

"Sailor. Breathing. Unconscious."

Enopay pulled ineffectually at the man. Marcellinus helped him. In the dim light he at first thought that the sailor was holding a club in his hand, but once he seized it, he realized it was a bottle.

Marcellinus threw it away from them. It broke against the inside of the hull, filling the air around them with the sickly smell of wine. "Damn Verus."

"What?"

"Nothing. Let's get this man out."

Enopay heaved and Marcellinus shoved, and they got the sailor up into the third deck. "One more."

"Can't." Enopay was panting. "Too heavy."

Marcellinus leaned down and sniffed the sailor's lips. There was no hint of wine on his breath, and anyway, he did not look the type: well groomed and attired, wet only from the flooding river water he had been slumped in when they had found him.

"He is not drunk," Marcellinus said. "You agree?"

"What, Eyanosa? Wait, he's awake."

Hardly that, but the man was stirring. He raised a shaky hand to his head, opened his eyes, and tried to focus.

Marcellinus knew what a strong blow to the head could be like. "We're friends," he said gently. "But the *Fortuna* is finished. You have to come with us. Hurry."

As they emerged on the poop deck of the *Fortuna*, behind Roman lines, the ship creaked again and rolled to the left, putting the deck at an even greater angle. Marcellinus had never been so happy to get out of a confined space.

Leaving the stunned sailor with Enopay, Marcellinus pushed past the guards on the steps and ran up to Calidius Verus's side. The Praetor goggled at him. "Where the hell did you come from?"

"Belowdecks," Marcellinus said tersely. "I rescued the man you sent to fetch your wine."

Verus eyed his expression and turned his face back to the battle before them. "I believe we have more important matters to attend to."

"We do indeed." Marcellinus stalked forward, still breathing deeply, and looked between the scorpio men at the scene beyond.

The cohorts of the Sixth Ironclads were conducting a textbook military operation on the joined decks of the *Fortuna* and *Triumphus*. Uneven terrain, to be sure, but the ranked soldiers were in a triple formation, three grouped lines with shields guarding the first rank, bowmen behind, and men armed with a mix of hasta and pila. On both ships they were advancing in lockstep despite the bulwark and the slight gap between the decks that separated them. The Mongol line was being irrevocably pushed back. Unfortunately for the enemy, behind them were the legionaries from the *Providentia*. The Mongols faced a battle on two fronts, fighting unhorsed.

Calidius Verus was hurrying forward into the thick of the action now, flanked by his adjutants and a century of his First Cohort, keen to take personal charge of the remaining effort. Good enough. Perhaps the outcome here was not in doubt. Off to the side of them Manius Ifer's men from the *Fides* were fighting on the decks of the *Triumphus*. Ifer himself was leading his men, his tribune's helmet clearly visible at the front right edge of his troops. This was one of the most dangerous areas of a Roman formation; centurions customarily took that position, and the death toll among them was high. Marcellinus hoped Ifer would survive the day.

Looking farther afield, he realized that the ships of Subodei Badahur had broken off their attack on the *Fortuna*'s flank under heavy assault from the Roman artillery and had hoisted sail. He could even see Badahur himself waving his arms to give orders, the bandage distinctive across his face.

Marcellinus's first thought, that the Khan's best general was fleeing the battlefield, was soon disproved. Badahur aimed to cut off the *Minerva* and prevent it from going to the aid of the Romans, Norse, and Hesperians aboard the tangled mess of dragon ships and knarrs, Tlingit and Shappan canoes, and Maya longships that were doing battle. Even now, that whole combat area was being carried downriver on the Mizipi current, away from the larger war being fought on the decks of the four linked quinqueremes.

"Gaius!" Taianita sprinted toward him, gladius in hand, and Marcellinus gasped. Her tunic was doused with blood and what looked like entrails. Blood gushed from her mouth and was smeared all across her face and down her bare legs.

"Merda. Taianita, are you hurt?"

She spit. "Lost some teeth. Killed some Mongols." She grinned at him hideously, and he realized that she was not quite sane, not quite the Taianita he knew anymore. "Where is Son of the Sun? Where the fuck is he?"

Marcellinus pointed at the drekar battle. "Perhaps over there."

"Let's go. Let's get the verpa. Where's Hanska? Shit, come *on*."

"Taianita—"

"Futete!" Taianita ran from him to the edge of the *Fortuna*'s deck and measured the distance.

With horror he realized that in her battle madness Taianita was considering swimming across to the battle for the longships. With a few steps he arrived back at her side and grabbed her arm. Glancing back quickly, he saw that Manius Ifer's men had broken the Mongol column. The invaders were in rout, and shortly the Romans and allies would be victorious on the flagship.

The *Minerva* and *Clementia*, caught in a stronger part of the Mizipi current during their long fight, also had won their battles. Their oars were beginning to move, but it would be a while longer before they could rejoin the rest of the galleys. They had been carried back so far that they were almost back in range of the Jin trebuchets, and Badahur's ships would reach them first. "Damn it."

Neither the *Fortuna* nor the *Triumphus* would ever be riverworthy again. Their damage was too great. Marcellinus had to get everyone off the stricken ships and then cut the *Providentia* free.

Taianita was trying to pull away from him. Now she punched him on the shoulder. "Juno, Taianita, wait just—"

"Use your eyes, verpa," she snapped. "They've won. The bastard Shappans have the longships!"

"Shit . . ."

It was true. Some of the warriors of Shappa Ta'atan were manning the oars of the two drekars while others threw Roman corpses overboard in full armor, where they disappeared quickly into the murky river. Alongside the dragon ships, warriors of the Yokot'an Maya and the Tlingit were returning to their own longboats and canoes.

Beyond, one of the triremes was bilged and half sunk, its top deck now resting almost at water level and listing to starboard. Bodies, blood, and jagged burned holes covered the deck. The second trireme was already moving unsteadily toward Shappa Ta'atan, twisting back and forth in the current. The Shappans had themselves a prize.

Then the trireme suddenly straightened, the rowers on both decks pulling together.

That was impossible. Hesperians learned fast, but not that fast.

The Shappa Ta'atani had Roman prisoners at the oars.

Well, *that* made all the difference.

The Mongols' allies aimed to take the trireme and the two dragon ships to berth at Shappa Ta'atan. The Roman prisoners would become slaves of the Mongols or die terribly at their hands.

"Futete," Marcellinus said yet again. "Taianita, go find Hanska. Otho! Ifer!"

But it was Vibius Caecina who came to him first. Pale, sick, and shaking, the tribune saluted him. "You're needed on the rear deck, sir. Our Praetor is down."

On the *Triumphus* and the *Fortuna* the remaining Mongols had been crushed. The decks were littered with corpses, and the scuppers ran with blood. Roman sailors were dragging the bodies to the side and dumping them ignominiously into the river.

But the victory had come at a terrible cost to the Sixth Ferrata. Calidius Verus was smashed and bloodied, his legs crumpled under him. He coughed, and blood welled over his lower lip and spilled onto his chest. The Praetor clearly had only minutes to live.

By Verus's side stood another tribune. Marcellinus eyed him uncertainly. "Gaius Marcellinus reporting."

Getting no response, Marcellinus leaned forward. "And you are, sir?"

The tribune blinked and focused on him. "Aurelius Dizala, First Tribune."

Marcellinus nodded. "Your orders, sir?"

"Orders?" Dizala looked around and shook his head. "Dear God, man, my Praetor is not even dead yet. A moment's peace if you would be so kind."

"Yes, sir." Marcellinus looked back at the trireme moving slowly across the river. "No. Sir, I'm afraid we don't have that luxury. This cannot wait."

Caecina took a step back. Dizala looked him up and down. "Gaius Marcellinus. It was your decision to ram your own flagship? You gave that order?"

"I did, sir."

"If that's how you treat your friends, God alone knows how you deal with your enemies." Dizala shook his head. "It was well done. Unorthodox but . . ."

"It was a close thing, sir."

Dizala looked down at Verus and up again at Marcellinus. "Very well. Report."

"The quinqueremes are secure. Most Mongol ships in flight. But two drekars and a trireme have been captured by the Shappa Ta'atani and are under way for the city. They have Roman prisoners."

Dizala looked very tired. "I would think the right course of action was apparent."

"It is, sir," Marcellinus said. "Let us finish this once and for all. Praetor Calidius Verus wanted the Sixth to retain control of the Hesperian Nile. Crush Shappa Ta'atan now, rescue our prisoners, and Roma will hold the Mizipi. But I cannot commit your troops without your orders."

"It seems to me you already have."

Marcellinus grinned. "That was expediency in battle."

Verus coughed, his hands flailing weakly. Dizala knelt and wiped the new blood from his commander's mouth. The Praetor's head was lolling, and he was obviously no longer aware of his surroundings.

Life was draining from Calidius Verus. Marcellinus would never berate him for his drunkenness or his failures of command or achieve any kind of peace over the matter of Corbulo. None of that mattered anymore.

Dizala passed his hand over his eyes. He glanced at Caecina and then away. "Candidly, Marcellinus, I'm not up to any more today. You've crossed swords with these barbarians before? Then yours is the crest. Give the orders. Deal with them. Caecina, the field is Marcellinus's. Give him your support."

Caecina nodded dumbly. Marcellinus saluted. "Yes, sir."

Legionaries ran. Under Marcellinus's and Ifer's commands the soldiers from the two dead ships divided themselves between the *Fides* and the *Providentia*. The injured were helped to one or another of the navigable quinqueremes. Scorpios, shields, rope, and other vital equipment were passed from the *Fortuna*'s deck to the *Providentia*. Undamaged oars were brought up from belowdecks to replace those of the *Providentia* that had been smashed in the battle.

Marcellinus looked around with grim satisfaction. Despite his harsh thoughts about the Sixth Ferrata, they were now working as one, everyone moving on the double, everyone knowing his job and rushing to get it done. Meanwhile, at the prow of the *Providentia* and belowdecks, sailors and legionaries worked to cut the quinquereme loose with axes, saws, and levers. Otho was up front with them, his shouting and cursing almost louder than the banging and hammering of his crew. Oarsmen were already seated at their stations in the aft of the quinquereme, ready to row once they were able. The hortator and the drummer stood ready to give them the pace.

The warship shook several times, and its prow lifted. Otho looked back at Marcellinus and gave him the high sign.

"Go," Marcellinus said. "Back up, slowly."

The hortator nodded. Marcellinus heard his brisk instruction to the crew, and the drum began to beat time. As the *Providentia* backwatered, the *Fortuna* slumped even lower, muddy water rippling across its top deck.

Side by side, the *Providentia* and the *Fides* rowed for
Shappa Ta'atan. The captured dragon ships were at the
shore now, their prize crews jumping off and joining the
rest of the Shappan army at the water's edge. The trireme was still offshore.

Enopay looked behind them and all around. "We're
going to Shappa Ta'atan? Just us?"

"Just us?" Marcellinus laughed. "You weren't at Ocatan, Enopay. Even tired, even outnumbered, the Sixth
will destroy them."

"If the Shappans were smart, they would hide behind
their great walls."

"Let them. We'll have those walls down in moments."
Marcellinus jerked a thumb behind him. On his prior
orders the onagers on both the *Providentia* and the
Fides were being loaded for action.

"Look." Hanska was pointing downriver.

The eight junks of Subodei Badahur had not engaged
the two quinqueremes in the rear of the fleet. Carrying
full sail, they had passed them by. Junks were heading to
the shore on each side of the river, presumably to pick
up the artillery crews manning the trebuchets, while the
rest held formation and sailed on. The Tlingit and the
Maya were leaving, too, rowing their brightly colored
canoes and longboats close to the riverbank, where the
Roman warships could not easily go, following Badahur.

"The Mongols have abandoned the Shappans,"
Enopay said in wonder.

Taianita stared at the walls of Shappa Ta'atan. "They
must be feeling really fucking stupid right about now."

Her venom daunted them all. Hanska regarded the
girl with some concern.

Enopay looked around him at the resolute Roman
crew. "This is going to be a bloodbath, isn't it?"

"Yes," Marcellinus said. "Yes, it is."

"No, it isn't," said the ship's master, Titus Otho.
"They're surrendering."

Sure enough, the Shappa Ta'atani warriors on the

bank were laying their weapons down on the ground and stepping back. Behind them the gates of the city were swinging open in capitulation, with men disappearing from the battlements to file out onto the riverbank, unarmed. The trireme's gangplank was now down, the Shappans walking calmly off the ship onto dry land while the freed Romans mustered on its top deck.

"*Damn* it," Marcellinus said.

Otho looked at him sideways. "We could still . . . ?"

Marcellinus shook his head, his heart heavy. Much as his blood still boiled, much as he would have loved to have his revenge on Son of the Sun, he could hardly order a legion to attack unarmed Hesperians.

Otho shrugged and gave the order, and the hortator slowed the drums.

"I know these people," Marcellinus said. "We'll land to accept the surrender. We'll need troops from the *Providentia* to secure the banks, confiscate the weapons. While we're doing that, hold the other ships offshore at the ready in case of treachery. Scorpios up, onagers and ballistas armed." He looked at the Mizipian city again and at the Shappans now kneeling on the bank and muttered under his breath. There would be no resistance.

"No!" Taianita's cry was so harsh that it sounded as if it were tearing the skin of her throat. She ran off the poop deck and slumped to the deck, head in her hands.

"Hanska?" Marcellinus said, but the warrior was already going to talk to the girl.

"Phew," Enopay said in heartfelt relief.

Marcellinus just kept shaking his head.

"I know you want to hurt them," the boy said. "You and Taianita. Kill them all. But they are Hesperian. They did not ask for this. And our men are tired. If the fighting is over for today, you must be glad."

Marcellinus was certainly weary. Exhausted, in fact. And of course he knew that if the full force of Roma came down upon Shappa Ta'atan, hundreds of innocent people would be killed and injured and suffer terribly in other ways. But for once, he could barely stand to be magnanimous in victory. "Please be quiet, Enopay," he said, and went forward to prepare an honor guard.

The Shappa Ta'atani council of elders and clan chiefs claimed that Son of the Sun had fled the city, although he might just as well have been hiding in the Shappan sacred area. They insisted that he had betrayed them as well as Roma and that if he attempted to return, they would bind him and deliver him to Marcellinus. They pledged renewed allegiance to Roma, although Marcellinus did not believe them for a moment.

Standard Roman military protocol would have been to take hostages, the oldest sons or daughters of leading chiefs and elders, to accompany them back to Cahokia as an assurance of continued allegiance in the future. Marcellinus rejected that approach. He was not about to take slaves in Roma's name. Leave such barbarism for the Mongols. Nor would he deprive anyone of their children.

Instead he demanded tribute, and in large quantities: corn and beans and sunflower oil, fish and ash cakes and whatever else they had. The Shappa Ta'atani soon opened their granaries to the galleys' quartermasters.

Marcellinus informed them that the Romans would be making castra on the far bank overnight and leaving the next morning but that a strict watch would be kept, and if any Shappan vessel so much as touched the water overnight, it would be destroyed and Shappa Ta'atan would be pounded to rubble the next morning. The Shappans promptly took every canoe, dugout, and coracle inside the gate. Marcellinus demanded that the Shappan homesteads on the eastern shore of the Mizipi be evacuated and remain empty overnight to ensure the security of the Roman legion, and three Shappan elders accompanied two Norse knarrs across the river to hurry the homesteaders in packing up and leaving.

The Shappans showed every sign of being a people

vanquished and compliant, yet Marcellinus was rock-solid in his conviction that even if the bulk of the Shappa Ta'atani this time remained allies of Roma and Cahokia, he had not seen the last of Son of the Sun.

By dusk, the Roman fleet was moored and its soldiers and sailors were eating. Guards had been set, and Marcellinus finally was able to sit down on the bank and stare at the remains of the sunset over Shappa Ta'atan. The tribunes wanted to speak with him, but they could wait. Enopay wanted to talk, but Marcellinus sent him away with Hanska and Taianita.

He needed a few moments to himself, and it was only now that it finally sank in that the day had been a success.

The Sixth Ferrata had taken losses, including its Praetor, but they had achieved their goals. They had broken the blockade and vanquished the Mongol fleet. The Hesperian Nile was Roman again, even if in reality they now lacked the ships and troops to police it.

That would have to be sufficient for today. But one day a reckoning between Marcellinus and the Shappan chief must surely come.

CHAPTER 15

YEAR NINE, HUNTING MOON

Three weeks later, shortly after the dark of the Hunting Moon, the remains of the Legio VI Ferrata passed the mouth of the Oyo River where it emptied into the Mizipi at Ocatan. Even now, the sight of the four quinqueremes and the accompanying vessels was enough to prompt the Ocatani at the riverbank to hurry back through the gates of their town and bar them. From where Marcellinus stood at the prow of the *Providentia* he could see Mizipians lining the newly rebuilt town ramparts to watch the Roman ships pass.

The oarsmen were not rowing at full speed, and the ships were not in an attack posture. The fighting towers had been dismantled and stowed, the onagers and scorpios were covered, and the legionaries stood easy on deck. The galleys were ragged, with burn and scorch marks along their hulls and blistered paint. The hulls of the *Fides* and *Minerva* and both the prow and the stern of the *Providentia* had taken significant damage that the Sixth had made only a minimal effort to repair. Marcellinus and the surviving tribunes had agreed that in the aftermath of their tribulations downriver, appearances could be neglected till the crew joined up with the rest of the Roman army at Cahokia and had a chance to recuperate.

With so many troops injured or exhausted it was hard

enough to row the massive galleys against the incessant Mizipi current and build a secure camp on the shore every night. Over the last months the Sixth Ferrata had suffered both a major defeat and a Pyrrhic victory; they had prevailed at the blockade but had lost their commander, two tribunes, and more centurions than Marcellinus could count. The quartermaster and Enopay agreed that in all the Sixth was approaching Cahokia with a mere 2,500 men out of the 4,800 with which it had begun the year. More than five hundred men were injured, and every day brought more deaths as men finally succumbed to their wounds.

Understandably, the mood aboard the ships was dour. Among the tribunes Aurelius Dizala was grimly competent and nominally in command but prone to black depressions at the death of his Praetor and the damage to his legion. Flavius Urbicus, tribune of the Sixth and Seventh Cohorts and a popular man, had died two days after the river battle of wounds sustained defending the hospital ship *Clementia*. The only other surviving tribunes were Vibius Caecina, young and disgraced, who avoided Marcellinus wherever possible; Statius Paulinus, hardworking but not really leadership material; and Manius Ifer, whom Marcellinus was coming to respect more and more each day for his gruff pragmatism and down-to-earth good sense.

None of the tribunes was really stepping into the role as acting commander, but coordinating the voyage to Cahokia was largely a matter for the ships' masters in any case. Titus Otho and the other senior centurions who served as ships' masters of the quinqueremes largely made the navigational decisions among themselves, and woe betide anyone who disagreed with them. As the local expert, Marcellinus liaised among them all and made suggestions that generally were accepted as orders, and the flotilla made as steady and efficient a progress up the river as anyone could have wanted.

Unfortunately, the primus pilus of the Sixth, First Centurion Appius Gallus, could scarcely conceal his disdain for and distrust of Marcellinus. Marcellinus could not guess which of his many transgressions might have triggered such a response and did not care. The rank and file respected Marcellinus for his impromptu seizing of command during the battle, and the tribunes all treated him as an equal for the time being; besides, once they were safely back in Cahokia, Marcellinus would never have to see Gallus again. Once the masters and tribunes had accepted that Marcellinus's was a voice to be listened to, Gallus had to take his orders just as everyone else did. Every primus pilus Marcellinus had known would honor the chain of command even if he believed every officer above him was a chicken or a buffoon, and Appius Gallus was no different.

The Sixth had a small military harbor five miles up the Oyo River, established when they had moved their operations after withdrawing from Ocatan, but it was not sufficient to berth four quinqueremes, a trireme, and the other associated vessels. Besides, the Sixth needed to report to the Imperator posthaste. Thus, the flotilla would proceed straight to Cahokia and fall on the mercy of the other legions for accommodation or assistance in building its own fortress.

If they were even capable of such exertion. Rarely in his life had Marcellinus seen a group of men so chronically dog-tired.

As was he. There was a limit to what any man could reasonably endure, and Marcellinus felt about as close to his as he had ever been.

The smoke of Cahokia hung in the air. The Great City was just around the next bend in the river. The mood of the men was lightening.

"I should like to apologize to you, sir," came a voice from behind him on the poop deck of the *Providentia*. Marcellinus turned, half expecting Sextus Bassus, but it was First Tribune Aurelius Dizala, in full uniform and standing to attention.

Marcellinus had not seen Dizala for days, had not

even known the tribune had come aboard the *Providentia*. "Good grief, Dizala, you outrank me. Congratulations on bringing your legion through hell."

Dizala grunted uncomfortably. "Other men will be the judge of that, sir. Their verdict may not be as gracious."

Marcellinus studied him. "At ease, then, Tribune. What can I do for you?"

Dizala stood easy and walked forward to stand next to him. "You know, sir, I've never been this far north in Nova Hesperia. I've heard good things about Cahokia."

Marcellinus had no idea whom Dizala might have heard them from, but he appreciated the effort. "It's a fine place." Perhaps that was a little too glib and the waste of a good opportunity besides. He tried again. "Some from Roma see only barbarians. But if you can open your eyes, you'll see a grandeur about the city, and a people of fine quality. Look hard and try to understand them, if for no other reason than that understanding them may help Roma win this war."

Dizala shuffled his feet. "I wanted to apologize to you for my behavior and actions during the battle. I would like to think them uncharacteristic." He turned to face Marcellinus. "I have never before lost a commanding officer. Not once. I shall not pretend that I liked Praetor Calidius Verus or agreed with all his decisions. But it was . . ." He faced forward again. "Battle can be an awful thing."

"It can," Marcellinus said. "And I do not accept your apology, for you have no need to make it."

"Be that as it may . . ." Dizala held out his hand. "I cannot predict how the Imperator Hadrianus will judge our actions over the past months, either yours or mine. But I declare that I shall speak highly of you to him, whatever comes of it."

Marcellinus clasped the tribune's arm. "As will I when recounting your actions, for whatever that may be worth to the Imperator."

"Very good, sir." Dizala stepped back and came to attention. "With your permission, I will instruct Otho and the men to ready the ship for berthing."

Marcellinus grinned. "Please proceed, Aurelius Dizala. And if you see Enopay, please send him forward to me. Oh, and if I might ask a favor?"

"Name it."

"When we arrive in Cahokia, Bassus will report to the Imperator on the expedition's behalf and you will report on behalf of the Sixth. Yes?"

"I suppose so. Along with yourself, I presume."

"That is the favor. I would prefer not to go straight to Hadrianus."

Dizala looked perturbed. "It may be unwise to delay."

"Indeed. But I have been away from home a long time, and there are people I must see just as soon as possible."

"People who outrank the Imperator?"

Marcellinus looked again at the smoke from the hearth fires rising above Cahokia and said nothing.

"Never mind," Dizala said. "Of course, I'll cover as best I can. You'll come soon?"

"Soon enough, First Tribune. You may depend on it. Please impress upon Hadrianus that I am not attempting to run off, evade his judgment, or anything of that nature. I merely have obligations elsewhere for a few hours. I hope he will understand."

"Run away?" Dizala grinned. "If that were your goal, you'd have done it long before now."

They came around the slow turn, and Marcellinus's heart lurched as the view of the great mounds of Cahokia opened up before them. Two Sky Lanterns floated in the air above the Master Mound, and at a much greater altitude a half dozen Catanwakuwa flitted back and forth, looping around a stately Wakinyan in some complicated aerial maneuver. His breath caught in his throat.

"Well, you're in luck, sir. Looks like Himself is not at home and you get a breather after all."

The imago of the Imperator was at half mast over the fortress of the Legio III Parthica. Hadrianus was not there. Out on exercise, perhaps. "It appears that at last my luck is changing."

"Perhaps," Dizala said. "Have a good homecoming, sir." The tribune saluted and went back to talk to Titus Otho.

Yet again, Marcellinus returned to Cahokia battered, bruised, and war-weary.

This time he walked in alone and almost unregarded in a Cahokian tunic and moccasins, with a cloth draped over his head against the sun. It was the middle of the day, and many people were sheltering in their huts from the heat. On the streets he saw no one he recognized, and nobody seemed to recognize him.

Somewhere behind him were Hanska and Enopay, the only other Cahokians left alive. In the last week of the journey they both had become increasingly taciturn; the closer they got to Cahokia, the more they felt the intense grief of losing Mikasi and Kanuna. For each, the return to Cahokia would be bittersweet. Marcellinus would have been by their sides if they had asked, but they seemed to take more solace in their shared bereavement.

The tall statuesque Hanska and the small but shrewd Enopay made an odd pair, but Marcellinus had grown accustomed to unlikely friendships over the last few years. They had their pain in common, and he was content to leave them to reconnect with Cahokia in their own time. As for Taianita and the Chitimachan, Marcellinus did not even know which quinquereme they were traveling on, and despite his increased respect for them would not have chosen either as a companion for his return to the Great City.

It was the first time he had been truly alone for months. All in all, it was an oddly contemplative walk. Hardly a hero's welcome and all the better for that. He made it all the way to the Great Plaza before meeting someone he knew, and even then he did not recognize her right away. "Chumanee?"

He was mortified for startling her when she backed away, wide-eyed. "Chumanee, is everything all right?"

"Wanageeska . . ." Already she was scanning his arms and legs, looking for damage. "You are not hurt?"

A legionary medicus aboard the *Clementia* had long since treated Marcellinus's burn injury and the arrow hole in his shoulder. The wound in his calf was the only one visible. That was healing now, and it was anyway on the site of a previous wound, and so even Chumanee had not noticed it right away.

For once Marcellinus had no need of her services. "I am well. And you?"

"But how?" Chumanee asked, apparently mystified. And then a movement caught their eyes, and they both turned to look up the Great Mound.

A slender figure was hurtling down the mound. A girl, running like the wind with her hair flaring out behind her.

"Kimimela," Chumanee said. Marcellinus squinted. Was it really? The girl seemed too tall, and different in other ways he could not quite place.

How old was Kimimela now, anyway? Sixteen winters?

Kimimela slipped and tumbled, rolled, and came springing back up onto her feet in what seemed like an impossible single motion. Kept running as if nothing had happened, down onto level ground. She disappeared briefly behind the palisade at the foot of the mound, then came sprinting out of the big gates toward them.

At the last moment Marcellinus had the presence of mind to brace and lean forward. Kimimela launched herself and flew into his arms. He staggered back under the impact, Chumanee stepping smartly aside to avoid them.

Kimimela's eyes were wide. Her hair hung loose. She kissed his cheek experimentally and then seemed to freeze in place. "Huh."

"Kimimela," he said, lowering her to the ground. She had grown while he was away, was over an inch taller.

"You're alive." She prodded him, shaking her head as if trying to will herself to believe it. "How, how . . . ?"

"You didn't think I'd—ow!" Quick as an eel, she had punched him on the arm. Hard. "Gods, Kimi, you have *muscles* now."

Kimimela shook her head, staring, and started to cry.

His mouth went dry as he realized the other thing that was different about her. "Your hair? You're in mourning?"

"Of course I am, you idiot . . ."

"Sintikala?" He looked from Kimimela to Chumanee and back again, and a chill surrounded his heart. "What has happened?"

"Sintikala lives," Chumanee said.

"My mother lives; of course she does."

"Who, then? Tahtay?"

"You *verpa*." Kimimela lashed out, hitting him again on the shoulder, perilously close to his jaw. "Gah! Merda!"

"You, Wanageeska," Chumanee said. "Kimi wears her hair in mourning for *you*. Mahkah came home several moons ago. His horse was so lame that the Romans wanted to put it out of its pain, but he would not let them. Still he cares for it, although it will never bear him again. He told us you were all dead, your expedition wiped out by Mongols in the desert by Yupkoyvi."

"Dead," Kimimela said, suddenly very still and serious. "But you are not."

Almost overwhelmed by the strength of her emotion, Marcellinus reached out. He wanted to wipe away the tears that still trickled down her cheeks, but that seemed an impertinence out here in the plaza. He clutched her arm instead, squeezed. "It must have seemed that way to Mahkah once he crossed the canyon, climbed one of the great stairways, and looked back."

"Two months later Isleifur Bjarnason came back with no horse but the same story—"

Kimimela suddenly looked up. Above them, a Catanwakuwa lurched sideways in the air and tumbled out of formation. Marcellinus flinched. A broken wing? The Hawk was diving in a steep bank, curving around. "Shit . . ."

It was coming too fast. Marcellinus dropped to one knee and pulled Kimimela down with him. Chumanee crouched on the girl's other side.

The Catanwakuwa shot just a few feet over their heads. It was Sintikala, her hair streaming out behind her.

She seemed barely in control of her Hawk. Once past, she flipped it into a near stall, spilling air, and arced around once more, grazing the top of the palisade around the Great Mound. She landed hard, bounced, and skidded, almost dragged over backward.

She turned.

From thirty feet away, suddenly stock-still, the masked Sintikala regarded him. Marcellinus could see her un-blinking eyes behind the mask. Kimimela had filled out while Marcellinus was away; conversely, the Hawk chief seemed gaunt.

Sintikala walked toward them, the huge span of her wing still resting across her shoulders. As she approached, she tugged off her mask and dropped it onto the sand of the Great Plaza. Her hair, too, hung loose in mourning.

Sintikala walked right up to him. She raised her hands and placed them one on each side of his face. Her palms stroked his cheekbones, and her fingertips pushed hard into the flesh behind his ears. She regarded him for five long breaths. Stared into his eyes and read them.

"Alive," she said.

He swallowed. "Yes. Barely. And at great cost. The others—"

She turned and grabbed him. He smelled sweat and leather. She pulled his head down to hers and kissed him. Her hands slipped down onto his shoulders and arms.

"Yes," she said, as if to herself. "Alive."

Then she turned and strode away around the right-hand side of the Great Mound, abandoning her wing on the plaza behind her.

"Great Jove," Marcellinus said inadequately.

"She mourned you," Kimimela said. "Without ever quite giving up hope. You must understand, when my father died—"

"I know. She was *not there*. Nor when . . ." Marcellinus stopped. Even now he could not mention Great Sun Man by name.

Kimimela nodded. "And when you died, she was *not there* either."

Sintikala turned the corner and was gone.

"But I did not die."

Kimimela reached out to touch him on the arm again. "That will take us a little longer to believe. Come."

"Where?"

"To follow my mother."

Kimimela walked with Marcellinus to the crest of the Mound of the Hawk Chief. The doorskin of Sintikala's house was closed. No smoke came from the roof.

Kimimela halted and threw her arms around him, hugging him until his breath almost stopped. "You must go in."

"She did not invite me."

"I believe she did."

Marcellinus wanted nothing more in the whole world, yet he hesitated. Kimimela poked him, and now there was a glint in her eye. "You are afraid?"

"Apprehensive. It is not the same."

"I will be at Chenoa's house." Kimi pointed to the next mound. "The one that used to be Howahkan's, then was yours. Don't forget about me, Gaius. I want to talk with you, too. Remember that you are my father."

"Kimi—"

She was staring at him with a fixed intensity. "And I am so very, very glad that you did not die."

He reached for her shoulder, touched her face. "I'm so

happy I got to see you again. There were times when
I . . ." He swallowed.

Kimimela gave him a little shove. "Not now. Go,
idiot. Go to my mother."

"It's me," he said. Hearing no response, he pulled the
doorskin aside anyway, stepped in, tugged it closed behind him.

Sintikala's hut had no windows, but light spilled in
through the smoke hole in the ceiling and filtered
through cracks in the walls. It was nowhere near as dark
as night in the Longhouse of the Wings, but after the
brightness of the Cahokian day he could see her only in
outline as she walked to him and put her arms around
him.

He wished he could see her eyes, but perhaps it was
just as well that he could not.

He put his hands tentatively on her shoulders, and
then slipped his arms around her. She still wore the
leather flying tunic, but it was loose on her, the front
untied. She buried her face in his chest and inhaled
deeply, and he felt her ribs and chest swell against him.

Those ribs were closer to the surface now. She truly
was gaunt. Yet when he stroked her shoulders and arms
and felt around her back, she was still as muscular as
ever, still a panther in a woman's skin, hard and strong.
"Sisika . . ."

Her fingers found his lips. He kissed them, and they
slipped inside his mouth, grazed his teeth. He tasted dirt
and leather and Sintikala.

Her other hand slipped up under his tunic. It roved
across his back and down his side, and he realized she
was searching him for new scars or wounds, checking
for damage. She leaned back, using both hands to explore his stomach and his chest, his shoulders. She found
the new wound in his side, which was still covered with
a Roman bandage, and probed it carefully. She lingered
over the new scar on his shoulder, now mostly healed,
then moved on, her fingertips grazing his nipples as they

went on their way. He shivered a little at her touch, at the intentness of her study, but leaned back against the wall and let her do it.

"Gaius Publius Marcellinus," she whispered.

"Sisika. Sintikala." He smiled his joy. "Mighty Hawk chief."

Her hands clasped his upper arms, her fingers sinking into the skin and muscle to grip him tightly. She kissed his chest. He nuzzled her loose hair, found her ear, bent to kiss her neck. She sighed, her breath hot on his skin.

He could be patient no longer. He pushed her tunic off her shoulders and shoved it back, and now it was he who explored, searching her, discovering her. His eyes were adjusting, and he could see her now.

She wore only a brief linen chemise under the tunic. With true Sintikala-like directness she put her hand up to the neck of the chemise and tore it away, dropping it onto the ground at their feet.

The feel of her, the smell of her, began to madden him. He realized he was being too rough, almost mauling her in his urgency, and forced himself to ease up.

Sintikala clearly felt no such restraint. If he had not known it for passion, he might have thought himself under attack. Her hands pummeled him, her fingertips scored his arms and back. Her fingernails were always short, bitten back; if they had been long, she would have drawn blood. She was panting, almost growling, and Marcellinus became aware that he was as well. He had wanted this for so long . . .

She shoved him back against the wall, and he felt the wooden staves flex behind him. For a moment he had a vision of the house falling down around them and their bodies being found joined in the wreckage, and he gave a low, almost crazed laugh at the thought of it.

Marcellinus pulled his tunic up over his head and threw it aside. And now he was naked, his moccasins kicked off and his breechcloth pulled away while he had been distracted with attacking her in his turn.

He ran his hands down her sides as her strong body

pushed up against his. He tried to urge her back; he could see her bed now, thirty feet away on the other side of the big room, but even as he made the attempt, he knew they would not take the time to cross even that short distance.

Her urgency was palpable. With a moan she kissed his chest, his stomach, went lower to his thighs, as far as the knee. He shouted out and pulled at her, almost frantic now in his passion, and she leaped up into his arms.

Marcellinus spun her around and shoved her back against the wall. Again the wood creaked, and a wing spar that had rested against the wall clattered to the floor.

She grabbed his head, forced it down to her chest, and as he kissed and tasted her, his hands roved lower.

"Now," she said, her voice husky. "Now . . ."

It was time. They both knew it. She gave a little hop, and he seized her hips, lifted her. As he entered her, she cried out, a low sound of passion, and her hands clawed at him, pulling him in deeper. His tongue slid into her mouth, and he rammed her back against the wall again and again, she moaning, he crying her names and other words, Roman curse words, Cahokian words of love.

He felt the sensations building within him, and then out of his desperate, feral emotions emerged a thought, crystal clear and perfect: this was Sisika, Sintikala, the woman he loved, and had loved and missed and craved and wanted for years upon years, nigh on a decade now, the woman he thought he could never, ever have. And here they were, desperate for each other, both buried deep in the other in their own ways.

Now accustomed to the dim light, his eyes met hers. He looked deep into her and saw in her, too, the raging tension of all those years of love and lust. Those eyes pushed him over the edge now, and a fierce primal joy swept through him and racked him. Her eyes widened, her head went back, and as she came she screamed out her joy, and they were one.

Marcellinus and Sintikala, spent, complete, slumped

against the wall. Even as the shock waves rippled away, he clamped her to him in an iron grip, not wanting the moment to end, never wanting to let her go. Her hands were in his hair, her hips against his, and once again she stared into his eyes as if it were her turn to fill him, pouring her love into him, her intensity, her need.

They gasped a while longer, all the breath knocked out of them. Marcellinus stroked her hair, wiped the slick sweat from her cheeks. Sisika did the same to him.

All of a sudden he realized it was very hot. They were bathed in each other's sweat, but he did not move away, could not. Let their sweat mingle as their blood once had. He would never leave her again.

"I love you," he said in Cahokian and then in Latin.

"Alive," she said throatily, and when she smiled, it melted his heart. "*Very* alive."

"Yes. Alive again, now that I'm with you."

She slid off him, still breathing deeply. "I must braid my hair. Now that I no longer mourn."

He reached up, twisted the long black strands around his fingers, tugged her head back. "Not yet," he said, and kissed her lips, her cheeks, her neck, her breasts. She grabbed his hair, too, pulled him against her even more firmly. Thrust her hips against him, bit his shoulder, and they lost themselves in each other again.

It was much later, having at last made it the several paces across the room to the bed, that they examined each other more thoroughly. Marcellinus lay still, temporarily exhausted, still sweating. Sintikala climbed over him, roving with eyes and fingers and lips in the light from the smoke hole, learning all the muscles and ridges and scars of his body, the areas rough and smooth. She was gentle now but thorough, and by the time she was done, Marcellinus felt that nobody had ever known him so well.

She stepped away then to fetch them water to drink and splash over themselves. Being separated from her for even those moments felt like torture, but gave him the chance to watch her as she walked around her hut lithe and naked. He reveled in every detail of how she moved, confident and sure and proud.

She came back toward him with the bowl of water and paused, aware of his eyes roving over her. She tilted a hip to one side, pretending a coquettishness that was not at all in her nature, and shook her head. He laughed and reached for her.

She was still wet from where she had wiped herself down with water and a cloth. Her skin gleamed in the scattered rays of the sunlight, and somehow from the color of those rays Marcellinus realized it was drawing toward evening. He had to make good use of the light.

He eased her down onto the bed. She lay there, breathing easily, sipping again at her cup of water, and he knelt over her and began.

His exploration of her might have been even more complete and obsessive than hers of him. He felt as if he were memorizing her, blazing every detail of her into his memory, packing her even more deeply into his soul, piece by piece, touch and smell and taste. Soon Sisika began to breathe more heavily under the intensity of his touch, but he persisted, if anything becoming even more gentle, drawing it out until she lay almost in a trance, her eyes staring straight up as she reached her crescendo.

Then she pushed herself upright and stared at him with eyes now hooded by the dusk. On hands and knees she crawled toward him, and he lay back and yielded himself up to her slow, gentle fingers and willing lips in return, as night fell over Cahokia.

Hand in hand, barefoot and clad only in tunics, they walked out to meet the dawn. The steelworks was quiet, and the view to the east was clear for once. A fine haze shimmered over the bluffs in the distance. Marcellinus saw the glow from a few cooking fires even this early.

They stood and watched the sunrise, saying nothing. Sisika leaned on his shoulder.

"I am tired of being a Roman," he said.

Her lips made a moue. "And yet you will always be one."

"Truly. But I am tired of fighting. Responsibility. Frayed nerves. Tired of . . ." He laughed. "Worrying day by day what soldiers will eat and where they'll sleep. Worrying about tomorrow."

"A pity you brought such a terrible war to us, then," she said lightly.

"The war would have come even had I never lived."

"I think it *may* have been a little worse without you," she said. "Although my legs might not be so sore this morning."

"Whose fault is that?" He nudged her affectionately.

She grinned and became serious again, all in the same moment. "Gaius, I never want to be apart from you again, but we must be. I never want to be *not there* for you, and yet . . . I cannot be everywhere."

"Then we must fight together," he said without thinking about it.

Sintikala looked dubious. "You will fly?"

"You above, me below."

She smiled, her hands wandering over his body again, right there out in the open. "You underneath. Yes."

"That is not what I meant. But yes, I must be a Roman for a while longer. And you and I must fight the Khan. Together. But . . ."

He looked at her very seriously now, wondering what that would be like. To fight, with the woman he loved also fighting in the battle close by. Sintikala had been airborne during the Battle for Cahokia, of course, and beside him when they had fought the Panther clan, but his feelings for her had multiplied so many times since and were so much more intense today. Would he even be able to think straight? Would he make good decisions?

Then again, how good were his decisions in the heat of combat at the best of times?

"And after that?" she asked quietly.

"After?" Marcellinus shook his head. The coming

war loomed so large in his thoughts that it was almost impossible to consider an "after."

"We must destroy the Mongols," Sintikala said. "And then Roma must leave. And we must be just Hesperia, once more."

It felt like an impossible dream.

Very quietly, almost whispering it on the morning breeze, Sintikala said: "When Hesperia is free, then Gaius is also free."

"Free." He tasted the word. "I have never been free, I think. Not ever, in my whole life."

"But now you have something to be free for." Her fingers entwined with his.

Marcellinus nodded slowly.

"Think about it," she said. "Not too much. Not so that it slows your sword arm. But think about it."

"I will," he said. He stared out at the Great Mound of Cahokia for a few minutes, seeing nothing, and then shook himself as if awakening from sleep a second time and searched for something more mundane to say. "I half expected to see Kimimela still here, waiting for us on the mound's edge."

"Kimimela is flying." She smiled at him sideways, sensing his change of mood. "We, too, were flying."

He grinned back at her. "Yes, indeed we were."

"She will come to us soon." Sintikala nodded upward.

Sure enough, to the southwest three Catanwakuwa and two Eagles were floating lazily about two thousand feet in the air. "Don't you ever let your clan sleep?"

"No. Whenever I am awake, they must be wakeful too."

"Then they must be *really* tired this morning."

"You are tired? You must be getting old."

"Which is odd," Marcellinus said, "because I feel a great deal younger than I did yesterday."

The five Cahokian aerial craft were doing an odd dance in the sky. "Mock attacks?"

"Mahkah and the scouts told us of the Mongol flying

craft. And so we must practice to bring them down. That and some other new things."

The five wings were coming nearer and lower, and now they split apart in different directions as if their exercise was over. Marcellinus watched the Catanwakuwa soaring, banking, and flying but could not tell which was Kimimela. "Her flying has improved."

"She is my daughter."

"One day she may be better than you." He glanced left, wondering how she would take that.

"Of course," Sintikala said readily.

Marcellinus had ignored the two Eagle craft, looking past them at the Hawks, but now one of them swooped down to race between Sintikala's mound and the Great Mound just a hundred feet away. It banked to come back around. "Ah, this." Sintikala's eyes twinkled.

"What?"

"Wait and see." She patted his chest. "Try not to let your heart stop."

The Eagle approached, but it was surely flying too fast to land. Marcellinus watched it agreeably enough . . . and then, as it buzzed the flat top of Sintikala's mound at a height of eight feet or so, one of the pilots fell off. "Futete!"

Kimimela landed lightly on the ground, rolled on her shoulder and back, and came up again. Still moving too quickly to stop herself, she did something in between a cartwheel and a forward somersault, jumped up a second time, and skidded to a halt.

Freed of Kimimela's weight, the Eagle craft lurched upward, almost stalling. The two remaining pilots heaved mightily at their control bars, and the Eagle dipped below the mound top and came up again, gliding more slowly now. It coasted over the palisade wall to land at the base of the Great Mound.

Still fifteen feet away, Kimimela pirouetted and then did a formal Roman bow, chuckling. Sintikala released Marcellinus briefly and clapped her hands.

"Holy Jove," Marcellinus said, his heart still in his mouth.

Kimimela ran over and threw her arms around them both. "Gooood morning, lovers!"

"I *never* want to see you do that again," Marcellinus said. "Seriously, Kimi. Never. You hear?"

"Wait till you see what *else*—"

"No, no, no," said Marcellinus. "Just *no*—"

Sintikala tripped him, kicking his right ankle from under him and shoving, and the three of them collapsed onto the grassy mound top in a pile in something between a hug and a wrestling match.

Eventually they rolled apart. "Family breakfast?" Kimimela inquired archly. "I'm sure you two are *really* hungry . . ."

Marcellinus poked her ribs before she could get out of range, and she squealed and kicked out at him. He parried with his forearm and rolled forward to grab her nose. Sintikala chopped at him to break his grasp. She flipped him over and knelt on his shoulders to pin him to the ground, and Kimimela shoved grass into his mouth.

Marcellinus laughed, half choking, and spit. He had never been as happy in his entire life as he was in that moment.

CHAPTER 16

YEAR NINE, HUNTING MOON

"And so Lucius Agrippa was wrong and Decinius Sabinus was right. You are apparently worth keeping alive after all. Despite the chaos that inevitably follows in your wake."

At a loss to know how to respond, Marcellinus settled for: "Thank you, Caesar."

The Imperator Hadrianus looked at him sideways. "There were, I am sure, several in the city who were similarly gratified to learn of your survival."

Marcellinus nodded noncommittally. "Perhaps, Caesar."

Hadrianus studied him. Marcellinus was in full-dress Roman uniform for the first time in many months, but perhaps his formal clothing could not disguise his greatly changed mood. Even a meeting with the Imperator of the known world could not dampen Marcellinus's immense feeling of relaxed satisfaction after his night with Sintikala.

Having seen the imago flying at the finial once again, Marcellinus had crossed the river to the fortress of the Third Parthica by midmorning, but the Imperator had kept him waiting for several more hours. Maybe turnabout was fair play, or maybe Hadrianus really had more pressing business than dealing with his rogue Praetor. It was now a little after midday, and Marcellinus was alone with the Imperator in the Principia building. Sabinus was drilling his men in the grasslands beyond.

Apparently Hadrianus was not dismayed by what he saw. "Bassus says that it was well done. That no man could have done more to try to save Roman lives at Yupkoyvi than you did."

"I only wish I had succeeded."

The Imperator raised his eyebrows and continued to pace. "Yet you worked your utmost to save them, careless of your own life."

"I believed we were all dead anyway, so why not sell our lives as dearly as possible?"

"Quite, quite. And in addition, Bassus claims that you are the only reason that any of you survived your meeting with the Khan. You seem to have the man quite besotted."

Now Marcellinus shook his head. "Decurion Sextus Bassus showed great courage in the face of a gruesome injury and a ruthless enemy. Pezi was invaluable and remained calm when another word slave might have frozen or fled. I feel his loss keenly. Hanska's valor impressed the Mongol Khan at a crucial moment, even if her husband had to die to make it so." He thought about it. "In fact, we few are alive because we all stood together. Roman, Cahokian, Iroqua, Chitimachan . . . I believe it serves as a good object lesson."

"And I need such a lesson?"

"I spoke generally, Caesar. A lesson for Lucius Agrippa, perhaps."

Hadrianus looked amused. "Remarkably candid, Gaius Marcellinus. And then the victory on the river, smashing the Mongol blockade and bloodying Badahur's nose, preserving the bulk of the Sixth Ferrata. The credit for that goes to Taianita, perhaps? Or Enopay?"

In fact, both had provided significant help in their way, but even in Marcellinus's mild euphoria he was still wise enough to know he was testing his Imperator's patience. He dipped his head deferentially.

"The officers of the Sixth are calling it your victory.

Marcellinus's Victory on the Mizipi. I'm encouraged to learn that presiding over crushing defeat is not all you're capable of."

"I suppose that all depends on how you define defeat," Marcellinus said.

"Insolence, Gaius Marcellinus?"

Marcellinus just shook his head and smiled. He was weary of minding his language around the Imperator, and after all this he hardly believed Hadrianus was looking for an excuse to execute him.

"I would perhaps think better of such a victory," Hadrianus said carefully, "if you had not taken the opportunity to award yourself a field promotion all the way back up to your former rank."

"Not so. I requested no promotion and was granted none by the officers of the Sixth Ferrata. Where possible, I took my direction from Calidius Verus or, once he fell, from First Tribune Aurelius Dizala." He paused. "However, when orders were unavailable, I acted on my own initiative."

"Any centurion could have given you orders, Gaius Marcellinus."

"Perhaps. But I saw a job that needed doing, and I did it."

"And you did it." Hadrianus nodded. "Well, then. Given Calidius Verus's ineptitude, perhaps it is just as well that you were there."

"Verus was not inept," Marcellinus said somberly. "He had . . . May I be candid and . . . ?"

The Imperator nodded, gestured. Marcellinus poured himself a splash of the Imperator's wine, diluted it with three times as much water, and examined it carefully. "Verus was not my kind of general. He was too prone to hasty decisions. Too far removed from his men." He looked at Hadrianus. "Too damned patrician."

The Imperator looked at him wide-eyed, pretending to be scandalized. "Can such a thing be possible?"

"It can." Marcellinus sipped the wine. "In the pinch, Verus made errors, and one of them killed him. But his plan to break through the blockade was sound. He led the charge. He died well, doing his duty to Roma and to his men." Marcellinus had not forgotten Verus's words about saving his choice Falernian wines from his fortress in the gulf, or that last bottle he had sent his adjutant, Furnius, down to fetch from the hold of the stricken *Fortuna* that had almost resulted in the man's death. But there was scant reason now to recount such sins. Quite deliberately, Marcellinus raised his beaker in a silent toast to the man, took another tiny sip, then put it down. "Calidius Verus died bravely, and we should remember him well. And now I should like to return to Cahokia."

The Imperator shook his head. "I believe you have had too much desert sun, Gaius Marcellinus, and have forgotten who gives the orders here."

This time, Marcellinus relented. "My apologies, Caesar. I confess I am still extremely weary from the journey. But, with your leave . . . Caesar, I should like to be discharged from the army of Roma. If you believe that I have played a useful role over the past year and a half, then I am glad of it. If you think I have not, then I will be of no further use to you in any case. By my accounting, and even excluding my years in exile, I have now served in the Roman armed forces for more than twenty-five years. I thus beg you to discharge me and let me retire to Cahokia as a private citizen."

The Imperator seemed amused. "That would be inconvenient, Gaius Marcellinus, since I have just decided to make your field appointment a permanent one."

"My appointment, Caesar?"

Hadrianus waved his hand casually as if it were a matter of trivial import. "The Ironclads are short of a Praetor. Luckily, I appear to have a spare one."

Marcellinus stared at him. "Preposterous."

The Imperator raised his eyebrows. "And now you go *too* far in your informality, sir."

Marcellinus bowed and struggled to recover. "My profound apologies, Caesar. For a deluded moment I had thought your intent was to appoint me as Praetor of the Sixth Ferrata, which would be . . ." He trailed off.

"I did honor you with a legion once before, Gaius Marcellinus, if you recall. Regretfully, you lost it."

Marcellinus nodded. "Exactly my point, sir."

"In your defense, it was not a very *good* legion."

Suddenly Marcellinus's face was hot, and he could not help himself. "With all due respect . . . you are quite wrong, Caesar. They were fine soldiers and a fine legion. And their loss will be on my head for the rest of my life."

Hadrianus held his eye and nodded. "Good man."

"Me?" In Marcellinus's sudden anger, it took him a few moments to realize the Imperator had yet again been testing him.

"Of course, of course. And so I now offer you the chance to redeem yourself. I offer you permanent command of the Legio VI Ferrata."

Marcellinus stared. Once again the earth had fallen away from beneath his feet.

"Well, man?"

"Perhaps you are jesting with me?" Marcellinus inquired cautiously. "After all, you must have a dozen competent tribunes you could elevate."

"Yes, but none are local experts . . . Are you always this argumentative? Ah, yes, I remember now: constantly."

"My apologies," Marcellinus said. "I have perhaps forgotten how to behave in civilized society."

"Surely, surely."

The Imperator poured himself more wine and water. He topped up Marcellinus's beaker and handed it to him.

Marcellinus stared at it. "Let me put that another way. I wonder if you have given sufficient consideration to the other tribunes of the Sixth and how they would feel about being passed over for advancement."

"Feel?" Hadrianus shook his head dismissively. "None

of them have what it takes to lead the Sixth, and if they don't know that yet, it's time they learned."

"Aurelius Dizala has served nobly. By all accounts he made a splendid First Tribune for Calidius Verus."

"Then he will make you a fine First Tribune, too," Hadrianus pointed out. "But as it happens it is the recommendation of Aurelius Dizala, in addition to the fine if occasionally grudging words spoken on your behalf by other tribunes and men of the Sixth, that confirms my belief that this is the correct course of action." The Imperator took a drink of his wine. "And so? Second chances come all too rarely, Gaius Marcellinus. Do you want to command the Sixth or don't you?"

All of a sudden the world shifted around Marcellinus as it dawned on him that he *did* want to. Very much indeed. "Holy Jove."

The thought came as such a shock that he mistrusted it. Pouring his wine into the refuse jug at the rear of the table, he instead filled the beaker with pure, clear water and drank it down slowly. Had he gone mad?

Before he said another word it seemed important to analyze where this sudden desire had its roots. "A moment to ponder your offer, Caesar, if you please?"

"By all means."

His many failures notwithstanding, Marcellinus had faith in his skills as a leader of men. Again and again he had proved himself a good general and tactician. Despite the dangers and the losses the Sixth had taken, and despite his exhaustion afterward, the river battle at Shappa Ta'atan had invigorated him. It had been his first significant military victory in a decade, and he felt the power of that.

In a way, perhaps an unworthy, perverse way, Marcellinus had missed military command. Ripped out of his former life by a slaughter, perhaps at last he could finally admit that he had missed leading men in battle in a noble cause.

Marcellinus wanted his revenge on the Khan. Not for his invasion of Nova Hesperia, but for his murder of the

Romans and the People of the Hand, of Mikasi, Cha'akmogwi, Chochokpi. Even for his enslavement of Pezi, a young man who had finally begun to show promise and whom Marcellinus had vowed would never be enslaved again.

And for that revenge he needed to lead, not just react. Up till now Marcellinus had merely stepped into the breach where necessary. He had taken command of the reserve cavalry at Yupkoyvi, for whatever use that had been, and had next stamped his authority on the river battle at Shappa Ta'atan. But that had all been reactive, contingent on the events happening around him.

Just the night before, Marcellinus had told Sintikala he was weary of war. That was still true. Marcellinus heartily wished war did not have to come. But if it did, he needed to be the man to wage it.

His lovemaking with Sintikala had been one new beginning. Perhaps it was time for another.

"Gaius Marcellinus, have you perhaps fallen asleep on your feet?"

"Truly, I had never thought to be a Praetor again. I wished to give the matter the respect it deserves."

"Just so," Hadrianus murmured.

By all the gods, Marcellinus wanted to direct some significant hurt onto the Mongol Khan, Jebei Noyon, Subodei Badahur, and the rest of the Horde. And he wanted to do it with some power and authority. If he had to wage war, he needed to do so as an equal to Sabinus and Agrippa. Marcellinus's understanding of this land and its people was greater than theirs, and his opinions should count for at least as much.

Winning this war would take the best of both Hesperia and Roma. Too often Marcellinus had seen auxiliaries squandered as spear fodder, sent in first to soften up the enemy at a terrible cost in casualties. That could not be allowed to happen here. And the slaughter they had witnessed at Yupkoyvi could not be allowed to happen in Cahokia, either.

And beyond that?

Even if the joint forces of Roma and the Hesperian League could overcome the immense Mongol threat, then one day there must be a reckoning between Roma and Hesperia if the land was ever to be free. And in that reckoning, the more influence Marcellinus could bring to bear on the situation, the better.

And a Praetor wielded much more influence than a common foot soldier.

Marcellinus had to accept this commission. Offered the white plumed helmet of a Praetor again, he really had no choice but to wear it. Duty called.

Marcellinus realized that Imperator Hadrianus had sat down on his couch to wait patiently. As he might wait for someone whose opinion mattered. That, too, had changed.

As he stared, the Imperator looked up. "And so?"

Marcellinus bowed. "Imperator Hadrianus, having thought it through at . . ." Perhaps some self-deprecating humor was called for. "At quite considerable length, I would like to accept the command of the Legio VI Ferrata. However, to be easy in my heart about it, I should like to make some requests of you."

"Aha." The Imperator grinned. "And so the haggling begins?"

"It's best we both be clear. We would not want unpleasant surprises later."

"Well, quite."

Marcellinus took a deep breath. "I will accept the Praetorship of the Sixth. I will train its cohorts for battle and command them to the best of my abilities in the coming war with the armies of the Mongol Khan." He began to pace, a restless energy filling his limbs. "Right now, they are broken and disheartened. They have lost their previous Praetor, and some among them may think less than highly of me, so it will require some hard work."

Hadrianus nodded.

"However, in addition to commanding the Sixth, I would also request to command the Hesperian forces in battle. While the Cahokians will resist the idea of being absorbed into a Roman legion, I should like us to proceed as if the Cahokian fighters are essentially auxiliary cohorts within the Sixth."

"Doubling the size of your command. A shrewd move, Gaius Marcellinus."

"More than doubling. At the current time the surviving Sixth numbers some two and a half thousand men; when the centuries that maintain the Oyo garrison rejoin us, perhaps three thousand. I am hoping for a considerably larger number of Hesperians once all the councils are concluded." He cocked an eye at the Imperator. "Most of whom I brought to the table in the first place, if you'll recall."

"Perhaps. Go on."

"I will accept your commission as Praetor. However, when the war is successfully won and the Mongol Horde sent to burn in Hades, I would request to be discharged from the Roman army here in Nova Hesperia rather than withdrawing to Europa with you and the rest of the legions."

The Imperator smiled faintly. "You assume our legions will withdraw from Nova Hesperia at the conclusion of this campaign?"

"I certainly assume our treaty with Cahokia will continue while Tahtay and the Great City continue to show good faith. And in fact, I would plan to appoint some of my adjutants from the ranks of our auxiliaries. Throughout my career I have seen the virtue of employing local talent as adjutants and would wish to continue that practice."

Hadrianus shrugged. "You need not trouble me with such minutiae."

"Good. Next, there is the issue of the Damnatio Memoriae on myself and the Fighting 33rd. Naturally, it would be untenable for a disgraced general to be given the command of another legion." Marcellinus stared at his Imperator. "And the 33rd should not have borne the disgrace in the first place. Thus the Damnatio must be lifted, Caesar."

"Must?" Hadrianus said with evident amusement.

Marcellinus held his gaze. "Must."

"Then consider it done, Gaius Marcellinus. But in return you must surely recall that elevation back to the Praetorship would require the rededication of your oath of allegiance to your Imperator? A personal oath, to me?"

"Of course. And I will pledge that oath. But prior to that, I have one final matter to bring to your attention." Marcellinus took a deep breath. "I have a family in Cahokia."

Hadrianus raised an eyebrow. "Not merely a daughter? A wife and children?"

Wife? "It is a little more tangled than that. But suffice it to say that I have loved ones in the city, and as a man of honor I cannot abandon them when I take up command of the Sixth. Local dalliances and even marriages are hardly unheard of in the Roman army, and so I trust this will not be an issue . . . but now I see that you know of it already, Caesar."

Hadrianus was grinning. "Again you underestimate me, Gaius Marcellinus. I have known for some time. And how will Sintikala and Kimimela react to your new responsibilities, do you suppose?"

Any relief Marcellinus might have felt was instantly quenched by his sudden fear. Hadrianus laughed uproariously at his expression. "Come, man, I am the Imperator of Roma. It is my job to know things. Your darlings are wholly unaware that I have known for months of their importance to you. I see no reason why this should need to change."

Marcellinus did his best to recover. "Hard to predict how they will react. I will do my best to explain it to them." Immediately he felt he was being patronizing.

"Well, it is hardly in my interests to jeopardize Roma's rapport with the chief of the Hawk clan. Face the wrath of Sintikala?" Hadrianus shook his head. "Too rich for my blood. But I must say, it is a splendid strategic move on your part."

Still disconcerted, Marcellinus tried to match his Imperator's jocularity. "Yes, sir; strategy was always the motive uppermost in my mind."

"Is there anything else, or have we reached the end of your list of demands?"

"I believe I have finished," Marcellinus said.

"Very good. Then let us be clear on one final point. Misjudging me can be a fatal mistake, Gaius. Try to never do it again."

Marcellinus nodded. That was undoubtedly a threat. Yet it was also the first time the Imperator had ever called him familiarly by his praenomen without formally adding his cognomen, as was the custom in patrician society. The combination made for a peculiar mixed message.

"I have never doubted it, Caesar," he said. "And so I shall do my very best."

"And so, Gaius, what will be your first orders to your new legion?"

Gratefully, Marcellinus stepped onto safer ground. "We must allow the Sixth to rest from their long journey, but they also need work to do. We broke the Mongol blockade but took substantial losses in doing so, and this shortly after a vicious setback to the legion down in the Mare Solis. At the moment they are reliant on the Third and 27th for accommodations. This must be a further blow to their pride. We must get them back on their feet.

"They must build a fortress of their own. The Cahokians can provide lumber and the other legions can contribute nails and other materials, but the Sixth must build it themselves, with no assistance. It must be situated on the west side of the Mizipi, perhaps south of the fortress of the Third Parthica where the river bends. There are no Cahokian homesteads in that area.

"Logistics aside, I'll need to stamp quick authority upon them. As you have pointed out, I have already acquired some capital among the tribunes. However, First Centurion Appius Gallus may be a problem if not dealt with promptly. One of my first duties will be to have a stern talk with him. After that, I'll meet with my centurions."

Marcellinus pondered. "We must proceed in the correct order. Give me leave to broach this with our allies? In the interests of keeping relations smooth, Tahtay and the elders and clan chiefs must be briefed first; they must not hear about this through rumor and supposition. So I will meet with the Cahokians and then the tribunes. Thirdly, I will meet with Gallus and my centurions. And then, as soon as is feasible, we will commence construction of our new legionary fortress. Ah." Another thought had struck him. "Sabinus and Agrippa?"

"What of them?"

"Perhaps they should be the first to know. Since . . ." Although the words were in his mind, he found he could not quite say *We will be working together as equals from now on*. Given his history with Agrippa, that might prove to be an interesting experience.

"Ah, Gaius, Gaius. They already know, of course."

"They do?"

"Would I take such a momentous step without consulting my generals? It is the reason you had to wait so long today for an audience."

"And they agreed?"

"They did. Both of them."

"That's astounding," Marcellinus said, too surprised to be anything other than honest.

"Isn't it, though? Anyway, the formalities can wait until later. In the meantime . . ." The Imperator saluted him. "Praetor Gaius Marcellinus of the Legio VI Ferrata: please go about your duties and report back here at dusk to dine with us."

Marcellinus hesitated. "I thank you for the invitation, but perhaps it might be more appropriate for me to dine with my tribunes on this first evening. I should plunge in. Establish a rapport. Breakfast with you tomorrow instead, perhaps?"

Hadrianus nodded. "By all means, Praetor. By all means."

Marcellinus came to attention and saluted. "Thank you, Caesar."

"You must be fucking kidding me," said Aelfric. "Have they all gone crackers? Have *you*?"

"Keep your voice down," Marcellinus said, guiding him toward the Southgate of the fortress of the Third Parthica. "But yes, perhaps they have. And as for me . . ."

Aelfric was shaking his head. "I thought we were doomed before. Now I *know* there's no hope for us against the Khan."

"I need tribunes," Marcellinus said bluntly.

"What?"

"The Sixth Ferrata has lost two. I'll be confirming Manius Ifer as permanent tribune of the Tenth Cohort, but that still leaves the Sixth and Seventh Cohorts swinging in the breeze."

Aelfric scoffed. "Join your lot? Trade a terrific crew like the Third Parthians for the worst legion on the entire continent? Surely you jest."

"Oh, they won't be the worst legion for long."

"What's in it for me?"

"You? You get a promotion."

"Maybe I'm happy where I am."

"Maybe you are."

They stepped out of the gate and walked to the bank of the Mizipi. Aelfric was still shaking his head. "The Sixth Ironclads . . . an honorable name and history and all, but if you'll permit me to speak freely, I've heard some dodgy things about their new commander, and that's a fact."

"I don't doubt it."

Aelfric considered. "I'll need back pay for all those years I spent in country."

"Absolutely not," Marcellinus said.

"I like having cavalry around me, though, and you don't have much. I've been wondering how I ever allowed myself to go infantry in the first place. All those years doing my own walking when I could've gotten an animal to do it for me. And I've grown very fond of my horse."

Marcellinus nodded sagely. "I'm sure you have. You are a Briton, after all."

"That's sheep," Aelfric said. "Horses are different."

"I'm still negotiating with the other Praetors about cavalry," Marcellinus admitted. "The Sixth has only a few dozen horsemen of its own. The big alae came across with the Third and 27th. As a start, Sabinus has asked Hadrianus's permission to assign me the Cohors Equitata IX Thracum Syriaca."

Aelfric looked concerned. "The Ninth Syrian are solid horsemen, but there aren't many of 'em. Since Sabinus also has the cataphracts of the First Gallorum and two alae of Polovtsians under his command, I'd think he could spare you a few more nags than that. I'll have a word with him. And, um, since we're talking about Sabinus . . . ?"

"Yes, he's reluctantly agreed to me stealing you for the Sixth. Oh, and I'm prepared to let you spend three nights a week in Cahokia, too, provided it doesn't interfere with your duties. I'm anxious for the Sixth to pursue closer ties with Cahokia."

"Well, I like the sound of that." Aelfric looked at him sideways. "That's what you're doing? You and Sintikala are overnighting it now?"

"That's none of your business."

"You are, then." Aelfric whistled and shook his head. "I'm amazed you're still alive, you old dog."

Marcellinus grinned. "A little more deference, Tribune, if you would be so kind."

The next day, the sounds of hammering and swearing could be heard clear across the Mizipi. The Sixth had started before dawn: marched in formation by their various tribunes out of the fortresses of III Parthica and XXVII Augusta Martia Victrix, they were hard at work digging trenches, building ramparts, hauling earth, and hammering together barracks and stable blocks. As the Ironclads were short on engineers, Marcellinus had borrowed some from Sabinus to help lay out the fortress site. That aside, the construction would be performed entirely by the Ironclads. Marcellinus had even sent work squads from the cohorts of Statius Paulinus north with drekars and knarrs to haul the wood that would be needed.

The tribunes of the Sixth Ferrata had welcomed Marcellinus with some relief. If the rank and file had any reservations about their new Praetor, they were shrewd enough to conceal it. If anything, they seemed grateful to have someone competent in command again, a clear line of authority, a new direction. As well as happy to be kept busy with activities that were normal and familiar and, for the most part, did not involve oars.

Primus Pilus Appius Gallus was another story.

From where he and Sintikala stood on the crest of the Great Mound, Marcellinus saw Taianita enter the Great Plaza garbed in leather armor and with a gladius hanging from her belt. He could not see her face from that distance, but her walk was unmistakable, and Cahokian women who fought with the gladius were rare enough. The boys from the Raven clan playing chunkey against their fellows from the Chipmunk clan paused respectfully to let her pass between them.

Sintikala turned her head to see where he was looking. "Taianita did well on the journey?"

"She did," Marcellinus admitted. "Thought quickly. Worked hard. She got a bit wild during the battle, though."

"Sometimes a little wildness helps."

"Perhaps." Marcellinus cast his gaze back in the other direction, toward the crest of the adjacent Mound of the

Sun, where Tahtay was sparring with gladius and spear with Kimimela and Enopay.

Marcellinus had originally trained Tahtay in the use of the gladius. But since then Tahtay had trained extensively on a variety of weapons with the Blackfoot and the Romans, and the result was a curious mix of unorthodox weapon handling and swift footwork that was neither Cahokian, Roman, nor Blackfoot but an odd combination of all of them. Tahtay was a match for anyone now, and Marcellinus was glad that the war chief had not challenged *him* to a sparring match.

Certainly Tahtay was more than enough for Kimimela and Enopay. Kimi was fast with a short spear and club but not as adept with a blade. Enopay hacked away gamely and was a dirty fighter but gave away his every move in advance through his body language. From this distance they could just hear the tone of Tahtay's voice as he shouted instructions at Enopay while easily parrying his blows and pushing him back.

But over and above the training, Marcellinus was happy that they were a tight team. They were his original band of translators, appointed by Great Sun Man, without whom Marcellinus would have been dead several times over by now. He was glad they were important to one another, too.

Now Sintikala looked west. "Is your fortress large enough?"

"Maybe," he said. "I can't decide."

Sintikala was joking with him. Out of both pride and practicality Marcellinus had insisted that the Sixth construct a fortress even bigger than that of the Third Parthica. The Ironclads would fill only half such a fortress, but the Cahokians needed to become used to living in castra side by side with Roma. When they marched out into the prairie to do battle with the Mongol Khan, they would have to build a night camp and occupy it together. Romans and Hesperians needed to view one another as brothers in arms.

Wood was cheap, and Marcellinus had a point to make.

"Whoa." On the Mound of the Sun, Enopay had grabbed a spear and swung it around in a ruthless and unexpected attack on Tahtay's legs. At the same time Kimimela whirled her club at his head, and it seemed that neither of them was pulling punches. Tahtay tripped over backward, and the sound of laughter radiated from the mound.

"I'm glad he laughs." In light of the leg wound that had threatened to cripple Tahtay for life, Marcellinus was relieved that he had taken Enopay's attack so well.

"Only with them. His mood is never so light with anyone else."

"He has a lot to think about."

Below them, Taianita was jogging up the cedar stairs of the Great Mound. Sintikala sighed, and her hand slipped out of Marcellinus's.

"So we do not fight the Khan this year?" Not at all out of breath, Taianita climbed the final steps and came to stand on Marcellinus's other side.

"No. By the scouts' accounts, his army is still divided. Chagatai's half has crossed the Great Mountains in the north and is camped on the Wemissori. Chinggis's army is camped on the Braided River. They train, they fatten their horses."

"Good," she said. "More time for *me* to train to fight them."

Over on the Mound of the Sun, Tahtay had jumped up again and taken his revenge. Enopay was sprawled flat on his back, and Tahtay was raining blows onto Kimimela, who was parrying and shrieking in a good-natured way. When Tahtay ran her right off the edge of the mound, she rolled backward and somersaulted to a halt fifteen feet below. Everyone was laughing. Enopay sat up and shouted what was presumably an insult, and Tahtay whirled around and cast his spear, which stuck into the ground safely several feet to the right of the boy.

"You are already strong," Marcellinus pointed out to

Taianita. "Capable. You wear war tattoos from three battles. If you could work with Kimimela on gladius, it would help her a great deal."

"Perhaps, if she asks me." Taianita turned to Marcellinus. "Somehow you are still allowed on our Sacred Mound even though you are again a big Roman Praetor?"

"Apparently," Marcellinus said.

"Tahtay is not angry with you?"

"Relieved. Tahtay immediately saw the advantage of me having influence over the Imperator and the plan for battle. He would rather the warriors of the Hesperian League work with me than with Hadrianus or Decinius Sabinus, let alone Agrippa."

Enopay had also welcomed the news. Kimimela had been a harder sell but had come around once Sintikala pointed out that since Marcellinus had to be a Roman, he would be much safer when surrounded by a mass of other Romans who were pledged to protect him.

It had, of course, been Sintikala's reaction that Marcellinus had been most concerned about. In an ideal world he would not have scheduled his first night of passion with Sintikala and his reappointment to a Roman generalship within the same few short hours. But Sintikala had taken the development with the same calm acceptance as Tahtay, and now it was Marcellinus who had whiplash.

Taianita seemed to come to a decision. "Good. Then let me help you, Gaius."

"Me? How?"

"Work with you. With the legion. Let me serve you, as your adj . . . ?"

"Adjutant."

"I can translate. Work with Roma and Cahokia. Fight the Khan. And Son of the Sun, if he ever shows his bastard face again. I will be there, at the front of the battle, with you."

Marcellinus could only imagine the reaction of his tribunes, let alone Appius Gallus, if he appointed an attractive Cahokian woman to his staff as well as a child. For earlier that day he had solicited Enopay to assist him with record keeping and logistics for the Sixth Ferrata, and the boy had accepted with alacrity. Sometimes Marcellinus suspected that Enopay might end up the most Roman of all of them.

He stalled. "Let me think about it. Consider how best it might be done."

Taianita saw through him right away. "No, then."

"It would be difficult," he admitted.

"Difficult?" She leaned forward, pugnacious now. "I want to help Cahokia. I want to help Roma. Against the Mongols. Do you not hear me?"

Sintikala was nodding slowly. Marcellinus tried not to look exasperated. "I hear you, Taianita, but—"

"I want to fight Mongols. What they did to Yupkoyvi . . . What happened to Kanuna, to Mikasi. What happened to Pezi. And what almost happened to us." Fierceness burned in Taianita's eyes. "Gaius, we must drive them from the land. I will do anything, everything to destroy them. As much as I can. If I do not, then I may as well have died a beaten word slave in Shappa Ta'atan—"

"Fly Wakinyan," Sintikala said suddenly.

Taianita turned to look at her. "What?"

"You are strong, smart, agile. Willing to learn. And light. Chenoa would welcome you."

Taianita looked at Sintikala and Marcellinus and then up into the sky. It was clear that the idea had never occurred to her, and she was not sure what to make of it. "Thunderbirds? Not Hawks, with you?"

"Wakinyan first. You cannot learn to be a Catanwakuwa pilot by the spring, when the war will come. Hawk flight is not learned so quickly, and you are starting older than most. If . . . if we are all here two years from now and you have done well in the Thunderbird clan, then you and I will talk of Catanwakuwa again. For now, Wakinyan. If you learn fast and show promise, perhaps Eagles. Yes?"

Taianita looked thoughtful. "Perhaps I do not have the courage."

"You do not lack courage." Sintikala jerked her thumb at Marcellinus. "And if he can do it, you certainly can."

"Thanks," Marcellinus said.

Taianita looked again into the empty sky, and then down at the Great Plaza as if imagining how it might look from many times as high. She shivered suddenly. "Thank you. Let me think. And you, Gaius, you will think too about other ways I can help? I can speak languages. Work hard. You know this."

"I will. And I do."

She stood, still looking almost suspiciously up into the sky. Once she was gone, Marcellinus said, "Phew. Thank you for that."

"For what? Taianita would be good under a Wakinyan. And perhaps she could burn hundreds of Mongol warriors all at once, and it would make her feel better."

Even now, Sintikala's matter-of-factness about human devastation sometimes chilled him. "Maybe so."

On the Mound of the Sun, Tahtay, Kimimela, and Enopay had finished their mock battles and were sitting in a close circle, talking intently. "And what are those three plotting now?"

"If I knew, would I tell you?"

"Weren't there supposed to be no secrets between us anymore?" he demanded.

Sintikala shrugged and grinned. Her hand crept into his again. "Come into the Longhouse of the Wings with me, then, and I will show you some more secrets."

He blinked. "Must I?"

Sintikala turned and looked into his eyes.

"Oh, yes," Marcellinus said. "I must."

CHAPTER 17

YEAR NINE, FALLING LEAF MOON

Two Wakinyan thundered side by side over the massed ranks of the Seventh, Eighth, and Ninth Cohorts at a height of some four hundred feet. They discharged nothing—no water or mud, let alone Hesperian liquid flame—but Aelfric's cavalry of the Seventh was on the verge of breaking, and the foot soldiers of the Ninth under Vibius Caecina had broken formation already, milling around hopelessly while their centurions bellowed at them, on the verge of apoplexy.

Marcellinus was seriously considering taking the Ninth Cohort away from the tribune Vibius Caecina and reassigning it to Manius Ifer. He had no doubt of Ifer's ability to manage the Ninth and Tenth at the same time. He had trouble imagining that Caecina would ever be able to manage just the Eighth without tripping over his own feet. However, he could not afford to make enemies in his new legion just yet and did not wish to be thought to be acting precipitously. And though inexperienced, Caecina was personally popular with his men.

Marcellinus and the Sixth Ferrata were forty miles to the west of Cahokia. Featureless prairie extended to the horizon. Although the land around them was quite flat, Marcellinus was suffering under the odd optical illusion that they were executing their maneuvers at the base of a huge bowl-like indentation. He had already spent far too much time in terrain like this and would obviously be spending many more weeks in the great Hesperian Plains before this was all over.

It was barely a week since the Legio VI Ferrata had finished constructing its fortress. Its streets still smelled almost unbearably of freshly cut wood, and the mud was not yet dry on the wattle and daub. The fortress included a rather extensive hospital block in addition to the regular barracks units, and a full third of the legion had stayed behind to rest up.

It was premature for the Sixth Legion to go into an exercise this complex alongside allies they were unfamiliar with, but as far as Marcellinus was concerned, that was the point. It was now late in the Falling Leaf Moon. Autumn was well advanced, and the rains and snows of winter could start at any time. Before that happened, Marcellinus needed to know what he was dealing with.

And put simply, what he was dealing with was an army that had been serving as a navy for so long that they had almost forgotten how to handle themselves on land, alongside three double-sized cohorts of auxiliaries, many of whom had rarely adopted Roman formations before.

Under the seasoned Akecheta, the First Cahokian Cohort was larger than before but as reliable as ever. The troops of the Second Cahokian, under Mahkah, were a mile away, still learning how to march in step and advance and retreat as a unit. Hanska's Third Cahokian Cohort had unexpectedly mastered these skills rather quickly, perhaps because Hanska's scorn when they failed was terrifying. The Third Cahokian had thus quickly graduated to mock fighting alongside Aelfric's Roman Sixth and Seventh Cohorts, Romans and Hesperians fighting side by side, with the First and Third Cohorts facing them across the plains.

Marcellinus's war games would not pit Roman cohorts against Hesperian. He needed one army, not two. Auxiliaries and legionaries were different, certainly, but they had to learn to fight together and protect one another. Any lingering animosities would have no place on the battlefield when they went to confront the Mongols. The two peoples had to learn to fight as one, and quickly.

At least, much more quickly than they were doing now. Marcellinus shook his head and sought out his First Centurion.

"Well, Appius Gallus. It appears that we have a lot of work to do. Shall we get to it?"

Gallus's face was guarded. "I suppose so."

Marcellinus eyed him coolly. "I did not hear your answer, First Centurion."

"Yes, sir. Let's get to it."

Gallus was hard-bitten, strong, and capable. He was a little older than Marcellinus's last primus pilus, Pollius Scapax, had been, and shorter and more barrel-chested, too; if Gallus physically resembled anyone, it was Akecheta. Marcellinus studied him and even went so far as to walk around the man, examining him, as if his First Centurion were on parade.

If nothing else, Appius Gallus's clothing and armor were impeccable. He was turned out perfectly.

Marcellinus arrived back in front of Gallus and was gratified to see that his primus pilus was looking disconcerted. "Are we going to have a problem, Centurion, you and I?"

"No, sir."

Eyeing him coldly, Marcellinus snapped out: "I did not hear your answer, Centurion."

"Sir! No, sir!"

"Perhaps it has escaped your notice, but I am now your commanding officer. Who am I?"

"My commanding officer, sir."

"Louder, Centurion. Who am I?"

"Praetor Gaius Publius Marcellinus, commander of the Legio VI Ferrata, sir!"

"That's right. But you have a problem with that."

"Sir! No, sir!"

"You believe the Imperator was wrong to give me this command, perhaps? You scorn his judgment?"

"Sir! No, sir!"

Marcellinus walked around him again, scrutinizing him even more carefully. Now Gallus looked truly alarmed. He stared straight forward at full attention, eyes staring unfocused into the middle distance.

"And who are *you*, Centurion?"

"First Centurion of the Sixth Ferrata, sir!"

"Your name?"

"Primus Pilus Appius Gallus, sir!"

"And is the Sixth a disgrace to Roma?"

"No, sir! No, sir!"

"And if they were, would that reflect upon you?"

A momentary silence. Gallus opened his mouth, obviously unclear how to respond.

"I still can't hear you, Centurion. Do you have a tongue?"

"Sir, yes, sir!"

"Do you have a brain?"

"Sir, yes, sir!"

"If the Legio VI Ferrata is a disgrace, does that reflect poorly upon you?"

"It does, sir!"

"Then we must ensure it is not a disgrace. We must work together to make it the best legion in Nova Hesperia. And from what I see today, this will be a hard uphill slog."

"Yes, sir!"

"That was not a question, Centurion."

Gallus caught himself on the verge of responding. He stayed mute.

Marcellinus nodded. "And so, if you have any personal issue with me, Centurion, you must make it known now. As Praetor, I command the First Cohort of the Sixth Ferrata in battle. Unless I am called away elsewhere, in which case *you* command the First. Which means we must trust each other. Am I correct?"

"Correct, sir!"

"If you have a problem, you must speak it aloud, and if not, you must shut up and do your job. Well?"

Gallus frowned and breathed deeply. "Permission to speak freely, sir?"

Marcellinus kept him waiting. Finally, he said: "Permission granted. But tread carefully, Appius Gallus. Especially if you intend to slander the good name of the 33rd Legion."

"Ain't your loss of the 33rd that concerns me. Having seen 'em, I don't doubt the Cahokians were a formidable foe. Relieved we didn't have to fight 'em by the Oyo last year, truth be told. We'd have thrashed 'em right enough, but we'd have lost men. It would have weakened us for the fray with Chinggis."

"Right," Marcellinus said.

"Those Thunderbirds? War from the air, out of the blue with no time to prepare for it, after marching halfway across Nova Hesperia? I'm not surprised the 33rd came off worse, and that's no disrespect."

Gallus surveyed him. "We heard tell of you in Asia, long back. I was serving with the Eighteenth Legion back then, battling the Sindhs in hill country for all we was worth. At one point we was in castra just twenty miles away from your boys. And there's talk of all the Praetors in the legions, you know. Who's solid in battle. Who's an ass who gets his men killed. Fewer of those nowadays, luckily."

Marcellinus nodded and waited. This was a longer response than he had expected of Gallus, but it behooved him to let the man speak.

"You had a reputation, sir. A good one. Not one of your flashy hotshots—no Lucius Agrippa, say—and all the better for that. Solid commander. Puts his men and his duty first. And that's why the Ironclads have taken to you, sir, despite the loss of the 33rd and the Damnatio that Caesar decreed." Gallus paused. "With all due respect to the Imperator, sir, that Damnatio wasn't popular. No soldier wants to think he could be eternally damned just for being on the wrong battlefield."

"Quite."

"The men feel you've been up against it good and

proper ever since you arrived here. And to those who haven't, I've gone out of my way to make it plain. So my feelings are my own and not shared with the men. In front of the men I'll support you all the way. No question."

"Then what, Appius Gallus?"

Gallus looked momentarily exasperated. "It's the going native, sir. Living with the redskins and all. Fighting their battles for 'em, and with Roman swords, Roman tactics." The centurion shook his head. "That doesn't sit right with me. Have me flogged for saying so if you must. But it just doesn't."

Marcellinus nodded. "Come the day you find yourself in such a position, Appius Gallus, by all means make your own decisions about what's best for Roma, yourself, and the people around you. I made mine. I'll live with them."

"Yes, sir. But there is also the . . . fraternization. Sir."

"Ah," said Marcellinus. "I am, of course, the first Roman soldier ever to take a local wife?"

A local wife. Even as he spoke, he was grateful Sintikala was not present to hear their rocky and complex relationship reduced to such an unfortunate phrase. Marcellinus was not sure he yet understood the full depth of what Sintikala meant to him, but he was certain that "wife" did not cover it.

"Sir, no, sir."

"Yes, I fraternize with . . . *redskins*, as you call them, Centurion," Marcellinus said slowly and deliberately. "And I will not pretend to you that I do it solely for Roma's benefit. I do it for my own interests. And, I like to think, in Cahokia's interests, too."

"Yes, sir."

"But our war is not with the Cahokians. It's with the Mongol Khan, and I am dedicated to his destruction. I will do everything in my power to eradicate the Mongol threat. Whatever must be done, I will do. Do I make myself clear?"

"You do indeed, sir." Appius Gallus bowed his head and stepped back.

"You are not yet dismissed," Marcellinus said.

"Sir, no, sir." Gallus stood to attention again. His expression was stalwart, but the lines by his eyes made it clear he would rather be fighting Mongols in a muddy ditch than standing where he stood right now.

Marcellinus paced back and forth, choosing his words with care. "First Centurion, I thank you for your candor. You'll think of me what you will, and I cannot alter that. But you and I have a legion to command and a war to win. Do we not?"

Gallus nodded. "We do, sir."

Marcellinus briefly remembered the last days of the 33rd. He did not think Gallus was the mutinying type, but the point had to be made. "Now it is my turn to be candid. I have spent long enough looking back over my shoulder. When we go to war with the Mongol Khan, I need to know that the Sixth is behind me to the last man. That I have their trust and that they can trust me. To the last man. You understand?"

"Sir, yes, sir."

"You will support me in the name of the Imperium and of the Imperator. You may not like me, but you will support me. We will not tolerate gossip in the camp. We will maintain military discipline."

"Yes, sir."

"Calidius Verus . . ." Marcellinus considered briefly if this was the wise course but then plowed ahead. "I regret speaking ill of the dead, but Verus ran a slack ship. Right now the Third Parthian and 27th Augustan could run rings around the Sixth Ferrata. This is not acceptable. Verus let matters slide. I shall not. The Legio VI Ferrata is more than twelve hundred years old. It has a fine name and a noble reputation. And so, by the time the Ironclads take the field against the Mongol Khan, we will be second to none. Am I understood?"

By then Appius Gallus was regarding him with frank

astonishment. "Yes, sir. You are very much understood, sir."

Marcellinus stepped forward, holding Gallus's gaze. "We are clear, then, Appius Gallus?"

"Perfectly clear, sir."

Marcellinus nodded curtly. "Very well, Centurion. Dismissed."

As the unfortunate Gallus marched away, Marcellinus could have sworn the centurion's neck was glowing bright red in shame and embarrassment.

Well, so much for that. Next on Marcellinus's list: his first meeting with his adjutants.

Marcellinus's choice of adjutants had turned out to be relatively straightforward. He needed six, and so he chose three Romans and three Cahokians.

Enopay had been Marcellinus's obvious first choice, as the only person who was equally fluent in Latin and Cahokian, a skilled record keeper, and already conversant with Roman military terminology. His second and third choices had turned out to be equally simple. Takoda and Napayshni could also read and write, having been students in Marcellinus's original finger-talk classes in the winter of his first arrival in Cahokia. Napayshni had sustained a severe thigh wound in their desperate battle with the Panther clan on the banks of the Mizipi five years before. He walked quickly enough, but with a pronounced limp, and he would never run again and sometimes had difficulties with his balance. Marcellinus was keen to let the serious young brave play a valuable role rather than having him languish in shame in Cahokia, and Napayshni had jumped at the opportunity.

As for Takoda, he had long ago recovered from the injuries he had sustained keeping Marcellinus alive in the battle for Cahokia against the Iroqua, but Marcellinus felt the young warrior and his family had suffered enough on his account. Takoda was Nahimana's son, Kangee's husband, and a father to three strapping boys, and although to this day Kangee was no friend to Marcellinus, he felt an obligation to keep the brave out of harm's way. Takoda was courageous enough in battle but had clearly welcomed the appointment.

His Roman adjutants had been assigned by Aurelius Dizala; the terrible trio of Aulus, Furnius, and Sollonius were experienced, smart, and more or less interchangeable. They had already gained a rudimentary grasp of Cahokian and Cherokee, and Marcellinus was happy to see that they immediately treated their Cahokian colleagues as equals, even the ones who looked young enough to be their sons.

In addition, Furnius was Verus's former adjutant, the man who had almost died belowdecks fetching wine and had been rescued by Marcellinus and Enopay. He had not forgotten it and in all likelihood would throw himself between Marcellinus and danger should the moment call for it.

One thing all six had in common was the tendency to coddle Marcellinus like hens, a tendency he often cheerfully told them he would need to beat out of them by the time they went into battle.

"Wake up," Kimimela said. "Father? Now."

He came awake all at once and looked around, confused. Beside him in the bed Sintikala stirred and squinted up at her daughter. "Everyone is all right?"

"Yes, but you will want to see this with your own eyes."

Moments later they were out of the hut and running together in the early-morning light: Kimimela, Marcellinus, Sintikala. A two-horse cart awaited them at the foot of the Mound of the Hawk, carrying Sextus Bassus, Taianita, and two of Marcellinus's adjutants, Enopay and Aulus.

"Bassus." Marcellinus hadn't seen the decurion for weeks. "You are well?"

"Well enough," Sextus Bassus said. "I may never breathe as deeply as once I did, but at least I do still breathe. And that's something."

"It's everything." Marcellinus looked at Taianita. Hugging herself against the chill in the air, she was smiling and excited. He had rarely seen such a gleam in her eyes. "What is happening?"

"Wait," she said.

"None of you are going to tell me?"

They climbed aboard. Bassus flicked the reins, and the cart set off, rumbling and bumping past the Great Mound. As they rode into the West Plaza, a woman turned to face them. It was the Chitimachan.

With her were several dozen warriors wearing feathers of scarlet and green. Beyond them a Macaw rested on the ground, its color almost blinding in the early sun.

"Holy gods," Marcellinus said.

Sextus Bassus nodded in satisfaction. "It appears our trip to the Hand bore fruit after all. We just did not know it until today."

Marcellinus eyed him, still bemused. Bassus added. "At a high cost, it is true."

"The highest . . . But these were certainly the people we were looking for." The warriors of the Hand looked strong, hard-bitten, and very serious. "Are there more?"

"Many," said the Chitimachan. "Hundreds. Perhaps even a thousand warriors and twenty or thirty Macaw pilots. They await on the west bank. The warriors you see are their envoys, here to ensure that they will be welcomed by the Kachada and his silver men. And as well received by their many-brothers, of course, since there has been bad blood between the mound builders and the Hand in the past."

"Well received?" Marcellinus felt almost dazed. "Indeed they are, a thousand times so. Perhaps you would do me the honor of introducing us."

"We would never have found them," Marcellinus said. "Not in a hundred years of looking. And, once found, we might never have persuaded them to join us."

"But Jebei Noyon did your job for you," Tahtay said, and even at the sound of the name Taianita shuddered.

"Unfortunately, yes."

They stood on the Mound of the Sun, watching half a dozen Macaw Warriors jumping from the top of the Master Mound with Sintikala, Demothi, and others of the Hawk clan. Next to the bright red feathers that adorned the Macaws, the brown, green, and yellow wings of Cahokia's Catanwakuwa looked unusually drab. Down in the Great Plaza scores of other warriors of the Hand mingled with the Wolf Warriors of Wahchintonka, doing their best to communicate with handtalk and gesture. Some were even sparring already, joking with one another.

Marcellinus continued. "The Mongols destroyed their ceremonial center. The most sacred place in their landscape. Massacred their people. We suspected all along that the true strength of the People of the Hand lay hidden in the mountains, in their cliff houses and caves and other places they could fortify.

"Once they stopped receiving news and trade from Yupkoyvi, they went to investigate. Some Yupkoyvi who lived across the canyon from the Great House survived, and of course the sentries on top of the sentinel rock at the end of the canyon, but those who saw the devastation best were the Macaw Warriors on the cliff above. They told their brothers and sisters of the mountains the story of the Mongols' terrible attack on Yupkoyvi. And now the People of the Hand want their revenge on the Mongols and will stand with us against them."

"And so our Hesperian League grows stronger," Tahtay said.

"Yet still not as strong as Roma," Enopay added, which earned him a sharp look from the war chief.

"There is more," Marcellinus said, more to distract them than because it really mattered. "More even than the Mongols destroying their sacred center. For the People of the Hand know that the Shappa Ta'atani have joined with the Mongols against us once again, and that has only increased their resolve to join us. Many among their warriors have faced the Shappa Ta'atani before in battle and thirst to take their revenge."

Tahtay shook his head. "Why? Their lands are so far apart."

"I have no idea." Marcellinus had not understood the feud between the Shappa Ta'atani and the People of the Hand when Son of the Sun had first told him of it, and he knew no more now. From Marcellinus's own experiences of the Mourning War between Cahokia and the Haudenosaunee, he knew how hard it was to learn the roots of any generational blood feud. The origins of this one were not his concern.

Kimimela stirred. "In fact, Shappa Ta'atan and the mountain strongholds of the People of the Hand are not much farther apart than Cahokia and the Great Lakes of the Haudenosaunee."

They all considered that for a moment. Eventually Tahtay shook his head. "Really?"

Kimimela sighed. Enopay nodded. "I am the one with the numbers, and Kimimela is the one with the map, and both of us have seen the numbers and maps of the Roman scouts that Hadrianus holds."

"So yes," Kimimela said. *"Really."*

"I wish their people had not needed to die so terribly in order to make them come here," Taianita said. "Their sacred center, the core of everything that was special to them, gone. Will we, too . . . ?"

Marcellinus put his hand on her shoulder, afraid she was going to ask that most terrible of questions: *Will we become like them?* Could the city of Cahokia, the center of the mound-builder culture, be destroyed in this war? And that was a question that Marcellinus was not willing to hear spoken aloud.

"We will defeat the Mongols," he said. "This is a great day. Tahtay, Taianita? Less of the long faces. More of the hope. Come down and meet our new friends. With a smile."

PART 3

THE GREAT PLAINS

CHAPTER 18

YEAR TEN, CROW MOON

The Second Cahokian galloped across the grass with Mahkah out in front and Gaius Marcellinus trying to stay alongside them without risking serious physical injury. He was sitting forward in the saddle as far as he dared, leaning into the movement, but such a gallop would always feel precarious to him, especially with snow still on the ground.

Then the Wakinyan roared over them. His horse's head jerked back, eyes wide, and for a terrifying moment Marcellinus thought his mount might lose its mind and bolt.

Now Hanska and the Third galloped in, converging from the right to form a single column. As the lines came together, Hanska kicked her horse forward, and she, too, began to pull away from him.

At this speed it was all Marcellinus could do to stay on his horse. It was galling to have to admit that Mahkah and Hanska were already better riders than he was.

Ahead, Mahkah's arm came up, and the two companies slowed to a canter and then a trot. As best he could, Marcellinus tried to line himself up with the Cahokian warriors on either side of him to form an organized rank.

He was panting almost as much as his horse. Shit.

Another Wakinyan came over and released Cahokian

liquid flame in a long thin stream two hundred feet in front of them.

In principle, the horses could take this in stride. The mounted companies had spent weeks trying to accustom them to incendiaries. If the cavalry all went to hell at the first whiff of black powder and the first spark of flame, the war was already lost.

In practice, the horses still spooked badly. Troopers split off to the right and left. Some horses bolted altogether, and others stopped dead. Horses bumped into other horses. To Marcellinus's relief his own steed took the flame rather calmly, perhaps because this time its view was proscribed by its blinders and by the two horses in front.

"Gods," Marcellinus said at last to the brave riding next to him when they got all their mounts under control and Mahkah signaled a return to the Mizipi, some four miles away. "This is . . . hard work."

The warrior might have answered, but he was too busy quivering and trying to wipe the sweat out of his eyes.

Enopay was right after all. These animals were a menace. Time to switch to something safer.

It had been another hard winter. The Mizipi had frozen again, all the way across, and the Polovtsian auxiliaries had exercised out on its icy surface with frost nails in their horses' shoes to prevent them from slipping. Most Roman cavalry alae would exercise carefully in snow but drew the line at ice. But the peoples of central Asia habitually treated rivers as roads in the winter months and, if anything, seemed more comfortable exercising when the temperatures were below freezing than they did in the heat and haze of the summer.

Marcellinus was perpetually cold, but the buffalo robe he had been gifted by the Hidatsa after the hunt helped. And often he was rushing from place to place with such vigor that he generated his own warmth.

For half of his time he was a Cahokian, living with

Sintikala and Kimimela on the Mound of the Hawk Chief, working with the Hesperian craftsmen who fabricated the flying machines, talking strategy with Tahtay and Enopay, or making love with Sintikala.

For the other half he was the Praetor of the Sixth Ironclads, sleeping in his Praetorium house at the center of a Roman fortress on the west bank of the Mizipi, his days full of exercises, supplies, issues of discipline, and a thousand other details. Marcellinus's two lives had converged in quite an astonishing way to somehow become the best parts of both.

For Marcellinus had grown weary of subterfuge. He no longer concealed his Cahokian relationships from Roma. Nor would he hide his growing camaraderie with his tribunes and men of the Sixth Ferrata from his Cahokian friends. Let everyone, Cahokian or Roman, judge him for who he was and what he did. And in that, it surely helped that Sintikala, Kimimela, and the other Hawk and Thunderbird pilots were themselves held in deep respect by the Romans for their almost supernatural abilities in the air.

Sintikala never came to the Fortress of the Thunderbolt, as the Cahokians called the castra of the Sixth because of the massive lightning insignia in gold and red over its eastern gate that was visible even on the far bank of the river. Tahtay visited occasionally. Enopay, of course, as Marcellinus's adjutant and connoisseur of all things Roman, was there constantly and perhaps spent even more time in the fortress than Marcellinus did. The boy now spoke Latin like a Roman and was on first-name terms with the quartermaster and chief medicus, the ship's masters of the quinqueremes, the weapons men and blacksmiths and sutlers. And when Enopay was not with the Sixth, he was likely to be visiting the Fortress of the Bull of the Legio III Parthica. More than once Marcellinus had walked into the Praetorium of Decinius Sabinus only to find Enopay in earnest discussion with the Praetor, his satchel open and his birchbark notes spread across the table. It was quite possible that the boy was greasing the wheels of Roman-Cahokian cooperation more effectively than anybody else.

Enopay was now maybe fourteen winters and at last was beginning to resemble a young man rather than an unsettlingly precocious boy. Kimimela was seventeen winters, smart and energetic. And Tahtay was twenty winters and was growing into the strong and capable war chief Cahokia needed.

As for Marcellinus, at the last Midwinter Feast he had turned fifty years old. His three "children" viewed this milestone with awe, as if he were suddenly an elder or perhaps merely a fragile thing that needed to be tended with care. Marcellinus took it in good humor. He was fit and determined, hearty and strong, and exactly where he needed to be.

And so Marcellinus went from Sintikala's bed to training Romans and Hesperians, often in the bitter cold and wind; to walking the fortress of the Sixth Ironclads; to working in Cahokia's foundries and new factories; to talking with Tahtay, Kimimela, and Enopay; to dining with the Imperator and the other Praetors. One day he might exercise with the Cahokian cohorts, the next with the cohorts of the Sixth Legion, and on yet other days with parts of both together.

Marcellinus was almost desperately happy. That desperation led to him living each day as if it were his last, attempting to cram as much toil and usefulness and self-awareness and passion into it as he possibly could. Marcellinus and Sintikala could not make up for lost time, and even now could scarcely make up for the time he spent with his legion or she with her clan. But they gave it their very best efforts.

Certainly they were under no illusions. Terrible times were ahead. The odds of their both surviving the coming months were slender indeed. That just made it all the more important to wring as much joy out of each day and night as was humanly possible.

*   *   *

Snow drifted across the East Plaza in the freshening breeze. Enopay was the last to arrive, and he was grumpy. "Everyone else hides inside. What is so important that we cannot do the same?"

"It's hard to get you all together at once."

With Marcellinus already were Aelfric, Tahtay, and Kimimela. "All?" said Aelfric.

"Well, at a time when *I* am not busy, too," Marcellinus amended. "Anyway. Do you remember this?"

"This" was the elastic material from the south. The Iroqua had used it at Woshakee long before, the Shappa Ta'atani had used it to propel their winged priestesses into the air from the Temple Mound, and Sintikala had acquired a roll of it at the Market of the Mud. At that time they had thought to use it to launch their Hawks, but the experiments they had conducted with Kimimela on the Wemissori had been disheartening. None of them had paid attention to the material for a long while.

Marcellinus turned to Aelfric. "Do you remember what you said about it at the time?"

"Make a belt?"

"And whip it off, snap a rock into someone's eye with it."

"And how well does that work? Come on, man. If you didn't already know, we wouldn't be freezing our feet off having this conversation."

"You're the best among us with a sling," Marcellinus said to Tahtay. "Wouldn't you say so?"

"Perhaps. Better than *you*, surely."

"*I* protected you with a sling well enough when Ifer's men tried to steal the *Concordia* at the market," said Kimimela, aggrieved.

Marcellinus had forgotten that. "Yes, of course. Sorry. So in that case, I challenge you both."

Tahtay and Kimimela looked at each other and then at him. "We accept," Kimimela said.

"You don't even know what I'm going to say," he protested.

"We don't need to ask," Tahtay said. "You're going to use that toy elastic stuff against Kimimela and me."

"Well, not *against*. Sharpshooting." They looked unsure. He simplified. "Target practice."

Tahtay, as it happened, had his sling in his pouch, although it was unlikely that he ever saw a rabbit in the streets of Cahokia. Marcellinus had brought several slings, some of which had traveled all the way down and back up the Mizipi with him, and Kimimela chose one. Meanwhile, Enopay ran off and came back with six pots from his great-aunt's fireplace. Marcellinus decided not to inquire whether he had asked permission to take them.

They lined the pots up on the grass about fifty feet away, and then Marcellinus produced his slingshot: a Y-shaped piece of steel, hastily made, with a length of the southern elastic material attached to the top spokes of the Y.

"What?" They studied the device suspiciously.

"The advantage is that you don't need to whirl it around your head like a sling. It's quicker. You draw it back, place the stone in it." He did it once and shot a pebble into the air. "Oops." They lost sight of it immediately in the swirling snowflakes, had no idea where it might have ended up. He ought to be more careful. "Anyway . . ."

They each took two of the small iron pellets he gave them. With his sling, Tahtay hit his pot the first time, sending it bouncing across the gravel of the Great Plaza. Kimimela missed, but not by much. Marcellinus drew back the elastic of his slingshot, aimed carefully . . . and also missed. "Getting the range," he said apologetically.

Tahtay laughed and slung his second missile. It smacked into his original pot, breaking it into two pieces. This time Kimimela also hit her target fair and square, sending it skidding.

Marcellinus's second lead pellet slammed into the pot he was aiming for and shattered it into fragments.

"Huh," Tahtay said. Kimimela looked at Marcellinus

in astonishment. Enopay tried unsuccessfully to cover a grin.

They walked over and stared at the scattered wreckage of the pot. "And you'll remember that I'm a terrible shot with a sling," Marcellinus said, just to rub it in a little harder. "This is easier to aim. And did I mention that you don't have to whirl it around your head?"

Tahtay cleared his throat. "I can . . . borrow this for a day?"

"Oh, I have four more," Marcellinus said. "One for each of you."

Marcellinus had learned long before how the Cahokians had launched their Wakinyan from the ground during their attacks on the Roman fortresses of the Third Parthica and 27th Augustan on the banks of the Oyo. Tahtay and Kimimela had devised a winch with a large drum that was based on the original wood-and-steel wheels and gears that Marcellinus and his Ocatani artisans had created, along with a low wheeled cart capable of taking the weight of a fully crewed and loaded Thunderbird craft. This method had been tested on the Great Plaza of Cahokia, which was about as flat and level as any forum or marketplace in the Imperium, and implemented in action on carefully selected, almost manicured stretches of land to the north, east, and south of the Roman fortresses. Yet Tahtay and his launch teams had wrecked one of the Thunderbirds that night when its launch cart hit a rock, shattering a wheel just before the Wakinyan left the ground. The accident had killed two pilots outright and injured four more.

In the coming war, the allies could not rely on finding runways out in the Grass with the length and evenness necessary to launch the great birds. A more reliable method was required. Initially Marcellinus and Chenoa experimented with the idea of launching Wakinyan by using teams of horses the way the Mongols had launched their Firebirds at Yupkoyvi, but their results were nowhere near as gratifying.

The Eagles were easier. With the Roman skill at constructing outsized siege engines, it was straightforward for the legion's engineers to build an onager capable of throwing an Eagle into the air. And having achieved that, Roma flexed its engineering muscle even further. It was Marcellinus and Manius Ifer between them who came up with the winning suggestion for how to reliably launch a Wakinyan in war: a freestanding wooden tower 150 feet tall supported by wooden buttresses and steel and hemp cables, that could be carried to the battlefield in sections and assembled swiftly by dedicated and trained crews; a steel launch rail, also transported in sections, that could be fastened into place at the required angle, its top jutting out past the tower's crest with its base at ground level; and a combination of a torsion mechanism and a heavy counterweight that dropped inside the tower to throw the Wakinyan aloft.

The results were spectacular enough to be dangerous. The first Wakinyan launched from such a tower—fortunately uncrewed, with bags and weights in the place of pilots—ripped apart under the strain and plummeted to earth in several pieces, its wings stripped off by the ruthless acceleration.

Chenoa, Sintikala, Marcellinus, and Ifer had to tune the mechanism, lighten the counterweight, and devise a system for unfurling and locking the outermost third of each Wakinyan wing once the bird was aloft to make the launch tower safe for human Thunderbird pilots. But once the design kinks were worked out, Marcellinus's legionaries of the Sixth Ferrata built five more Wakinyan launch towers within two weeks. And after that it was simplicity itself to construct scaled-down versions of the tower and rail to launch Hawk and Eagle craft with greater force and stability than the onager-powered launches. For the first time, Cahokia's aerial craft were truly transportable, at least with smart and well-trained centuries of soldiers to carry and construct the launch mechanisms.

Marcellinus was buoyed by the successes, his spirits

soaring almost as high as the Thunderbirds. When you combined the ingenuity, industry, and inventive powers of Roma and Nova Hesperia, who could stand against them?

High above the Great Mound, Kimimela sparred in the air with Sooleawa, their two Hawks looping around each other so closely that they looked almost connected. Marcellinus, standing atop one of the new Wakinyan launch towers, was struck with a rare case of vertigo; he could look neither down through the wooden struts to the East Plaza far below him nor up into the sky where his daughter appeared to be flirting with death. These days he rarely feared for Sintikala. Her skill in the air was so assured, so uncanny, that it seemed impossible she could ever falter. His daughter was less experienced and more rash. On the ground Kimimela was infinitely distractible, often trying to do several things at once and doing none of them properly, and it was hard for Marcellinus to imagine that she would not have similar moments in the air, where a moment's inattention could prove fatal.

The Hidatsa headman and Blackfoot elders had left for home after two months in Cahokia, but the younger Blackfoot warriors had stayed at Tahtay's invitation, and the Hidatsa buffalo caller at Sintikala's. Sooleawa had taken to the air like a duck to water, achieving proficiency in just a few months in a way that gave the lie to Sintikala's recent insistence that it would take Taianita two years to achieve the aerial competency required for war. Unlike Kimimela, Sooleawa was as totally focused in flight as she was in every other activity she pursued.

One of the smaller Wakinyan, with Taianita and Luyu among its seven-person crew, had just taken off from the tower on which Marcellinus was standing As it had streaked past him, just a couple of feet above his head, he had been watching the top of the rail. For some reason, in the final instants of contact the launching Thunderbirds were snagging and being jerked to the right, and

Marcellinus could see no particular reason for that. Except, of course, that the whole tower swayed and almost seemed to crack like a whip as the weight of the Thunderbird went by, a disconcerting sensation when you were perched so high above the plaza. Marcellinus shook his head.

Unexpectedly, Sintikala flew close by him on his right side. Startled, he grabbed the railing even though he was standing securely on the small platform. Sintikala's laughter trailed behind her as she looped upward to chase after Taianita's Wakinyan and pass it on the right.

Sooleawa and Kimimela now parted company, soaring out and away from each other. Their Hawk wings were yellow-green in color with similar feathers on the wing edges and the physical builds of the two young women were comparable, but it was still easy to tell them apart in the air. Sooleawa flew her wing in a distinctive style, altering direction more quickly but much less smoothly than Kimimela and the others. Marcellinus imagined such agility and unpredictability would be an asset in battle, especially if the Mongols fired arrows or trebuchet bolts in an attempt to knock the Hesperian Hawks out of the skies.

Although that possibility was something that he tried hard not to dwell on.

Sooleawa lost height rapidly, spiraling down around the launch tower in broad loops and then using the speed she had gained to streak out in a straight line over the grass toward the exercising First Gallorum Cataphractaria. Watching, Marcellinus thought she would probably make it all the way over the heavy horsemen, though barely above helmet height, before she landed on the far side of them.

She did not. Kicking her legs free, swinging vertically, she shoved the nose of her craft up in a stall even more dramatic than Sintikala would attempt, then somehow curled the nose of her Hawk around, spilled air and twisted, and landed on her feet.

She turned, walking quickly away from the cavalry

with her wing still on her shoulders so that she would not interrupt their exercises. She was not wearing a flying tunic like the others; in fact, it looked like the same shapeless elk-skin dress she had been wearing at the Hidatsa camp when Marcellinus had first met her.

Suddenly careless of the height, Marcellinus grabbed at the railing and leaned out to study the buffalo caller more closely. At that moment Sooleawa broke into a run, lifting her legs from the ground and coasting a few feet under the wing, then dropped and ran a little more, her dress flapping around her knees.

"I know how she does it," Marcellinus said aloud, and looked into the skies for the Wakinyan of Chenoa and Taianita, the Catanwakuwa of Sintikala. "Holy Juno . . ."

As fast as he dared, he clambered down the ladder to the ground. He had an experiment he needed to try.

Marcellinus caught up to them later, as the sun was lowering toward the horizon and sending gold and silver through the snow-streaked grass. Sintikala and Chenoa stared intently at each other and talked of craft and pilots while Demothi, Taianita, Sooleawa, Kimimela, Luyu, and four or five other Hawk and Thunderbird clan members strolled behind, gossiping in a much more relaxed way. He hurried to Sintikala's side. "I know how she did it."

Chenoa looked at him blankly, irritated at the interruption. Sintikala raised an eyebrow. "How who did what?"

"Sooleawa, at the buffalo jump. I know how she threw herself off the cliff and lived."

She grinned. "So long, it has taken you? Why do you think I was so eager to make a Hawk of her?"

"But it's more important than that. We can use it." Marcellinus pulled a square of cotton from his pocket. "What happens if your Hawk wing breaks?"

"I mend it."

"Breaks in the air, I mean. Up high."

Chenoa looked impatient. "It does not happen, Gaius Wanageeska. We build our wings well. We test them close to the ground and fly them with care."

"But in war you will be under fire from the Mongols." Marcellinus unwrapped the cotton. He had attached sinew to each corner and connected the threads to a small piece of wood. To the wood he had fastened a little stone, as the wood itself was not heavy enough. "How do leaves hit the ground? Hard, like ballista balls?"

Sintikala shook her head, bemused. "Gaius, Chenoa and I have important matters to discuss. Tomorrow your Praetors want us to take—"

Marcellinus scrunched up the cotton and threw the rock as hard as he could. It arced up, and then the cotton opened behind it, slowing it. Arrested in its trajectory through the air, the rock swung beneath the fabric and drifted down toward the grass.

"Sky Lantern, plus Hawk wing, makes falling leaf," he said. He couldn't think of a better way of explaining it.

Both women stopped. Chenoa blinked and frowned. Sintikala watched as the rock came to earth and the cotton square crumpled down onto it. "Hmm."

"Falling leaf," he said again. "Perhaps with you as the rock."

Sintikala turned. "Sooleawa? Come here, please. Now."

"It is sacred," Sooleawa said obstinately. "Sacred to the hunt. Sacred to the people. It is between me and the buffalo, and I shall not speak of it."

"All right." Marcellinus addressed Sintikala instead. "But that is how I think such a thing *might* be done. At the buffalo jump Sooleawa's clothing was not a wing and she did not fly, but its billowing helped keep her straight and arrest her fall just enough that she did not smash herself on the rocks below. Like one of the flying squirrels we see in the forests. And perhaps long enough for Blackfoot men beneath to hold out what, a big blanket?"

No one answered. Sooleawa's face was set as if in stone.

Marcellinus shook his head. "It doesn't matter." He would love to know for sure, but Sooleawa's face was a mask and Chenoa was scowling, and he knew he was treading on sensitive territory. He tried another angle. "When I fly in the Wakinyan, the air sometimes catches in my clothes and drags the wing back, unbalancing it. This is why you and Kimi wear the tighter tunics when you fly. When sailing ships come into the wind, they are slowed; they can even stop dead in the water and then be blown back. And when Sooleawa turns in the air so fast, it is because she is cupping the air in her clothing. It billows. She is used to that because she is skilled in leaping from high places. She has trained for that, and so she instinctively uses the same technique when she flies."

Marcellinus threw the rock into the air again, and again it floated back down to the ground. "The rock comes down slowly because of the air that catches in the cotton. It . . . buoys the cotton, I suppose. And so, Sintikala, if you carry a much larger square of cotton when you fly, if your wing is shot away, you *may* not die when you fall out of the sky."

There was a long silence. Nobody looked at him.

"Go now," Sintikala said eventually. "We will speak of this alone, we women of the land."

About to protest, Marcellinus saw the warning look in her eye. "All right," he muttered. He picked up his rock and cotton and walked away, leaving the Hesperians to talk.

Safely away from them, he threw it into the air once again with all the force he could muster. Once again, the air in the cotton slowed the rock in flight and it came drifting down to drop into the sand of the Great Plaza. It was a little jerky. Perhaps, like the Sky Lantern bags, it needed a small hole in the middle.

Marcellinus eyed it thoughtfully. If the buffalo caller needed to preserve the secrets of her hunting ritual, that was fine with him. The pull of the cotton against the air was the important thing. He could work with that.

Then he glanced at the sun. He was due back at his legionary headquarters at sundown to meet with his tribunes and primus pilus about the military maneuvers in the Grass the next day. And the fortress of the Sixth was four miles away, on the other side of the river. "Futete."

Marcellinus snatched up his toy Falling Leaf and broke into a run. He would certainly get his exercise today.

His life with his new legion was far from easy. Marcellinus had changed a great deal over the last ten years in Nova Hesperia. It was not that he had forgotten how to lead Romans; after most of a lifetime spent in military service, the old ways of speaking and acting, even his body language and demeanor, had come right back with little difficulty. But Marcellinus had learned a great deal about family and community during his time in Cahokia, and the martial environment of the Fortress of the Thunderbolt was no longer entirely to his taste.

His men of the Legio VI Ferrata respected and obeyed him. Even before the Mongol attack in the gulf, they had suffered hugely in Nova Hesperia. Half of the Sixth had been on this Hesperian campaign for seven years now, in a blazing hot and dank environment for most of each year. Hostile head-hunting tribes had surrounded them in the long peninsula where they first had landed, and the longboats of the People of the Sun had never been far away. But over and above their difficulties with the climate, tribes, and sheer duration of the campaign, Calidius Verus had been a capricious leader.

Manius Ifer, in contrast, was a skilled engineer and strategist, and although he had received some challenging missions, he had been treated well in camp and his men had been given sufficient time to recover between tours of duty.

Then, of course, had come the shock of the Mongol assault and their long voyage up the Mizipi against its terrible current, all the while knowing that they were cut off from the rest of the Roman presence in Nova Hesperia. The legionaries of the Sixth were exhausted, and grateful to Marcellinus for leading them out of hell.

But things were looking up. Their new Fortress of the Thunderbolt was solid, close to other legions, and close to a sizable city of local allies. The stormiest times in the Roman-Cahokian alliance had taken place long before the arrival of the Sixth. It was notable that the foot soldiers of the Ironclads were already more relaxed around the Cahokians than were the troops of Sabinus's and Agrippa's legions. This was, of course, encouraged by Marcellinus and reinforced by the joint exercises between the Sixth Ferrata and the First, Second, and Third Cahokian Cohorts.

Marcellinus's private feelings about the Sixth Ferrata remained mixed. During their perilous trip upriver Marcellinus had believed his time with the Sixth was temporary. He had thus been able to overlook or suppress his dire memories from Ocatan, where the quinqueremes of the Sixth had stormed its gates and laid waste to the city, slaying warriors and innocents alike and mistreating the survivors in the aftermath. Marcellinus would sometimes meet the eyes of a young legionary in the streets of his fortress and wonder how many Ocatani lives that soldier had taken. Might he even be one of the men who had beaten Marcellinus so grievously on the Ocatani Temple Mound?

It should have been no greater than the dissonance he had experienced and ultimately overcome when befriending Cahokians who had defeated and slaughtered his Romans of the 33rd. But his bonds with Hurit and Anapetu had been closer than his attachments to, say, Aelfric or Pollius Scapax, and his pain at their loss had been more visceral.

Truth be told, Marcellinus's heart now lived with his Hesperian friends rather than his Roman troops. Nonetheless he gave it his best shot, sometimes impassive to a fault and at other times wearing a smile on his lips that was not quite reflected in his eyes.

However, Marcellinus remained steadfast. He *did* want to lead the Sixth against the Mongols. He *did* want to wreak havoc among the hordes of the Mongol Khan while minimizing the carnage on the Roman and Cahokian side. War was his profession, and he would conduct it to the best of his ability. His comfort was not the issue. He had a job to do.

And it was quite a job. In addition to restoring confidence to the Legio VI Ferrata, Marcellinus had some new skills to learn. For most of his career he had served in legions composed mostly of infantry. Yet now he was preparing for warfare on the Great Plains of Nova Hesperia against an enemy army of mounted horsemen, as part of a force that included a substantial number of heavy and light cavalry units.

Marcellinus needed to know how to command cavalry, and he spent many evenings talking with Sabinus and Aelfric, with the tribunes who led the alae, and with the decurions of individual turmae. He devoted considerable time in the depths of that winter to soaking up horse lore, studying the history of great cavalry actions, and speaking with Hadrianus, Sabinus, and Agrippa about their prior experiences fighting the Mongol armies. Above all, Marcellinus endured a number of long days in the saddle, exercising with the troopers and learning to think like a leader of cavalry as well as infantry.

Taking into account the complexity of the coalition forces arrayed under the Imperator's command; the multitude of peoples and approaches, terrains, conditions, and logistic issues; and even the climate of Nova Hesperia, the fast-approaching war against the Mongol Khan without doubt would be the most challenging of Marcellinus's career.

"Are you all right?"

Marcellinus raised his head. Kimimela stood at the

foot of the Mound of the Chiefs, looking up at him. "Hello, Kimi. Yes."

She hesitated. "I was worried. You haven't even moved for so long. I will leave you to talk."

Marcellinus was alone on the mound but grateful that he did not need to explain why he was sitting there. "I have said all I needed to say."

"Did you hear anything in return?"

Kimimela was serious. Cahokians did not joke about communing with the dead, and Marcellinus would not make light of it either. "Great Sun Man has no words for me."

It was later than he had thought. Time had gotten away from him. He looked north across the Great Plaza at the Master Mound on its opposite side, then at the Mound of the Hawks next to him where the Cahokians buried their wise men and inventors. Kimimela was daughter to Sintikala, and Sintikala was daughter to the man who had served Cahokia as war chief before Great Sun Man. That man, too, was buried in the mound beneath him.

Marcellinus was almost literally sitting on Kimimela's grandfather. It was an odd notion. "Did you want to come up?"

"If you want to be alone a while longer, I will leave you. Will you come to my mother's house tonight, or do you go to Roma?"

"Roma," Marcellinus said with regret. "Come up, Kimi. Perhaps I can hear the wisdom of Great Sun Man and the ancients through you."

"I doubt it. But I will try to help."

Kimimela knelt and placed her forehead on the ground, paying her respects to the mound and the chiefs buried within, just as Marcellinus had before setting foot on the mound's sacred slope. She stood and turned away, murmuring some words under her breath, then slowly climbed the cedar steps. "I have not been here for a very long time."

"Nor have I." The last time Marcellinus had set foot

on this mound was to slay an Iroqua captive for Great
Sun Man in Tahtay's place. He had come to the mound's
base since then to pay his respects to Great Sun Man in
death, but this was the first time he had felt moved to sit
on its slopes.

Kimimela sat down by his side. "Tomorrow you leave
for Forward Camp."

Marcellinus nodded.

"Again you leave Cahokia."

"Yes. It is spring, and time for war."

"Always, now, it is time for war."

That was irrefutable, and Marcellinus made no comment.

"We will come along, too, in just a few more days."

She and Sintikala and the rest of the Hawks. Marcellinus would march with his Sixth Ferrata along the
banks of the Wemissori to the confluence where the
Braided River joined it. His cohorts would be guarding
a wagon train of fifty of the new Cahokian wagons. The
four-wheeled wagons were each capable of carrying
3,500-pounds of supplies, and the new Roman road
they would follow along the bank was even and mostly
level. The wagons were covered with tall canvas hoods,
pulled by mules, and steered by Cahokian and Iroqua
drivers. At Forward Camp they would arrive at a castra
twice the area of the fortresses by the Mizipi's banks but
much more rudimentary, surrounded by a Hesperian
camp within an earthen rampart and ditch. Pulled up to
the banks alongside Forward Camp would be longships
and quinqueremes. And reaching off to the south and
north would be the string of fortlets that made up the
Line of Hadrianus. Forward Camp was around four
hundred miles from Cahokia, and the march there
would take the Sixth a little over two weeks.

Most of the Hawk clan would follow aboard the
quinqueremes *Minerva* and *Fides*, its pilots helping to
row, taking shifts with the Roman oarsmen. The upper
decks of both ships would be covered with Hawk and
Thunderbird wings and the disassembled launch towers.

On the banks alongside would come another line of Cahokian covered wagons, carrying other equipment.

The plan had always been to face the Mongols far from Cahokia, on terrain of the Romans' choosing. Fighting with the Mizipi at their backs would be a significant tactical disadvantage, in addition to exposing the Great City and the Roman bases there to unacceptable risk. Much better to march forward and meet the Mongol Horde out in the Grass from a well-supplied advance position.

Kimimela appraised him. "Are you strong?"

"Certainly." Marcellinus trained regularly with his daughter. She would know already that he was muscled, healthy, still lightning quick with a sword.

"Yet you are worried."

He did not answer.

"I love you," Kimimela said unexpectedly. "And not just because you taught me and not just because you are husband to my mother. I love you for *you*. Sternly. Fiercely."

Marcellinus felt inadequate to respond. He put his right arm around her and pressed his left hand into the dirt of the mound by his side to grasp the grass, his knuckles white. She was so precious to him. He was risking so much. They all were.

"Thank you," he said.

She leaned into him. "I wish that we were not going to war."

He nodded. "I, too."

"I fear that perhaps you are thinking you are broken. That you cannot do this. But I think you can. With our help."

He was mute.

"Enopay told me a funny story," she said. "Enopay, who is in love-and-love with everything Roman, and who I sometimes think is even more Roman than you are."

Now Marcellinus grinned. "I've thought that, too.

Ships, soldiers, aqueducts, basilicas. Enopay wants all
the things he has not seen. One day he—"

Kimimela elbowed him gently to cut him off. "Enopay
told me that when a Roman Imperator or one of his Praetors is awarded a great military triumph in Urbs Roma,
as he leads his procession through the streets lined with
marble, a word slave stands behind him in his cart and
keeps telling him he is no god but a man, that he is weak
and puny and will one day die like every other man."

"He does not *lead* the procession . . ." Marcellinus
stopped. The details were not important. "So you have
come to stand behind me as you used to stand behind
Tahtay? To tell me to breathe and stop being an idiot or
you'll smack my head?"

"Something like that." Kimimela hesitated. "You will
laugh at this, Gaius. But sometimes I worry that you are
not yet a man."

He looked sideways at her.

"To Roma, you are. But here in Hesperia, perhaps you
are not yet a man in your soul."

Marcellinus wondered if he should tell her. She looked
up into his eyes. "Oh, I know my mother's blood flows
within you. And that your blood beats in her heart, too.
She told me. And I love it."

He should have guessed that she would know. "For
me, that was the moment when I became a little less
Roman."

"You seem no less Roman to the rest of us. Now more
than ever. And my mother's blood is strong, but perhaps
for this coming war you will need more than that."

Marcellinus knew about the rites of passage for young
Cahokian males. He did not intend to go through such
a thing himself. "You bled when you became a woman.
I think I have done enough bleeding since I arrived in
Cahokia for any man."

"I must tell you of the day I thought you had died,"
Kimimela said very seriously. "The day Mahkah rode
back into Cahokia almost dead himself on a horse that
could barely walk, and told us that your expedition had

been wiped out by Mongols who appeared suddenly in a place you could not possibly have expected them." She looked at him. "I will not tell you how my mother took the news. That is for her to tell if she has not already. But part of her died inside on that day, and I thought she might never speak again, to me or to anyone else. And so I put on my Hawk wing and told Demothi to shoot me up into the air at dusk. He understood, and did not try to stop me."

"You don't need to tell me this," he said, suddenly afraid.

"Yes, I do. When Demothi cast me up over the Great Mound, I almost did not spread my wings."

Marcellinus could not help but picture it: a ball of deerskin and frail wooden spars arcing over Cahokia, with Kimimela curled up inside it. Curving down toward the ground. He shivered. "But you did."

"I feared for the people beneath me if I came crashing down on them, and I decided to feel the air upon my skin one more time. I opened up the wing and saw the fires of the city far below me. I started to fly with the wind, toward the sunset. Toward the southwest where I knew you were. But now I flew blindly. I saw nothing. A long time seemed to pass."

The chill spread across Marcellinus's neck, temples, and forehead. Flying blind, until she crashed and died. He reached out, took her hand.

"I thought that if you were dead and Roma was here, then I would go to be with you in death. I was lost in the dark of the air, and then I opened my eyes one last time. I was still much higher than I had thought I would be, and alongside me an owl was flying. A real bird. I knew the owl was there for me, watching over me as we flew. And so I landed safely and began to walk home. I slept, woke, slept again, and then came back to Cahokia the next noon. I had flown far, and in the flying I had learned that I was a true Hawk after all and that it was time to live."

Kimimela had been on her spirit journey, just as

Tahtay had. In her own mind, it had made her fully an adult. She turned to him. "To you, my mother is Sintikala and also Sisika. To me, you are also many men in one man. You are the Wanageeska. Gaius. A Roman Praetor. And also my father."

"And yet one of those men is not a man in his soul?" Marcellinus said, still mildly rankled.

"I am Kimimela. I am a butterfly who flies like a hawk, whose spirit is the owl. Tahtay is of the Fox clan, and his spirit is the wolf, and he is also Mingan of the Blackfoot and a Fire Heart, and one day if he lives he will take the name of his father and become Great Sun Man of Cahokia. As for Enopay, he was born a man. He popped out of his mother's womb already an adult in a baby's body. That is why his birth was her death. Enopay does not need to find his path, because he knows it already. Perhaps he needs no spirit animal."

"A duck, perhaps, or a fish," Marcellinus said. "I have never known a boy who loves the water and ships as Enopay does."

Kimimela frowned. Perhaps this was a blasphemous or disrespectful thing for Marcellinus to suggest. He did not know. She was a shock to him, this earnest and thoughtful young woman. He was at the same time touched by her seriousness and emotion and disconcerted by her story and her sudden mysticism. Now Kimimela looked up into his eyes. "You are not just who you were born, Gaius. None of us is. You are who you become. You should know this, you above anyone, Praetor Wanageeska Gaius Hotah Marcellinus Eyanosa of the Raven clan and the Sixth."

"And so?" Marcellinus asked. Did he need yet another name? Another brush with death, this time with a meaningful animal nearby?

"Be open," Kimimela said. "Open to everything about the land. Perhaps you can never truly be one of us. Our rites and journeys may not be for you. But be open, just in case. Do not step back and become fully Roman again."

He thought about it. "No. That is not what I want, to become fully Roman again."

"And what do you want?"

"To have fewer names," he said slowly, and looked down at her. "To be your father. Sintikala's husband. And a friend to Tahtay and Enopay. In a Cahokia without Roma."

Now she grinned. "And that is what we all want, too. So do not be killed by Mongols, Gaius." It was an echo of what a much younger Kimimela had once begged him long before: *Do not be killed by Iroqua, Gaius.*

He saw Sintikala in her face and in her eyes. She had her mother's fierceness, stubbornness, and strength. Yet Kimimela was very much her own person, with a playfulness and wicked humor that Sintikala rarely achieved.

Marcellinus loved Sintikala with an intensity that dwarfed any battle ardor he had ever experienced. His love for Kimimela was gentler and more protective but just as intense. He would die for either one of them.

He had no doubt that Kimimela loved him just as strongly. After all, she had almost died for him. The thought still chilled him to his core, and to compensate he pretended to brush off her fear for him with humor. "Oh, very well. If you insist, I shall attempt to survive."

"Be sure you do."

"And when did you become so wise?"

Airily she said, "Oh, I was born wise. And strong. But I needed you and Sintikala to help me step into it and know it."

She moved away from him and touched the surface of the ground with the palms of both hands. From her sudden absorption, Marcellinus knew he should not disturb her.

Then she stood up and turned to him, her face serious again. "Gaius Marcellinus. I will always be with you. Sometimes in the air. Sometimes not. But always standing behind you, whispering: *Live.*"

He nodded. She rested one hand on his shoulder for a moment, then her lip turned upward in that Sintikala-like quick grin and she walked away, down the steps of the mound.

Well. His daughter was growing up.

He had been so close to death, so often. Never had he been in such danger of dying within the month.

Never had he wanted so much to live.

But he did not think the answer to that lay with the gods, whether Roman or Cahokian. He needed no Roman gods, no lares. Even more, he needed no vision quest in the Hesperian style. That was for the Cahokians, and regardless of what Kimimela might say, their culture was not truly his. Marcellinus needed no animal of the spirit to guide him unless it was the eagle, by which he again meant the Aquila of Roma just as surely as the eagles of Hesperia.

For Marcellinus it was enough to have family, true family at last, after all these years. Yet . . .

"I will try to live, Kimi." Marcellinus paused and thought and spoke aloud the words that were on his lips and in his heart despite all their inherent contradictions. "By the gods of your people and mine, I will try very hard indeed."

CHAPTER 19

YEAR TEN, PLANTING MOON

Forward Camp was a complete mess: organized chaos in a dozen different languages.

A few hundred miles to the west and north of Forward Camp the terrain creased up into bluffs and crags, gorges and canyons, but the landscape around the camp itself consisted of tallgrass prairies and gentle rolling hills with almost no trees: easy country to march or canter through with long sight lines from the hillcrests. In planning a war it was advisable to have as few topographical challenges as possible and be able to see your enemy approach from as far away as you could.

The Braided River meandered in from the west, a hundred feet across at its widest point and considerably narrower in most other places, dotted with islands and mudflats but barely deep enough to be navigable by anything larger than a canoe. The Wemissori ran almost north-south here; it was much wider, four or five hundred feet across, and flowed with much more purpose. The Braided River dribbled into it as if with reluctance.

Three years earlier, when Marcellinus had met the Hidatsa and ultimately found Tahtay living among the Blackfoot, he had been much farther up the Wemissori, through gorges and around a great curve until the river eventually had flowed out of the west. Such was the

Braided River's lack of drama that Marcellinus did not even recall seeing it join the Wemissori.

The Braided River was easy to bridge, and two wide Roman pontoon bridges now spanned it fifty feet apart. Crossing the bigger river was less straightforward and required boats, but in addition to the quinqueremes and drekars, the legions now had dozens of wide rafts available.

In addition the Romans had chained both rivers, a technique Marcellinus had heard of in Europa and Asia but had never before seen. Heavy iron chains reached from one riverbank to another, supported by floating log booms. Such chain-and-boom systems formed an impenetrable obstacle to any craft that tried to pass upriver or down and would prevent Mongol vessels from passing by or Mongol fire ships from being driven downstream into the Roman pontoon bridges. The chain booms could be opened to allow quinqueremes to pass, but the unfortunate Hesperian traders who also used the river as a thoroughfare had no choice but to unload their boats, carry them around on land, and reload them on the other side of the massive chains.

A substantial contingent of the 27th Legion—four cohorts—was camped on the eastern side of the Wemissori to defend its bank, guard the chain boom, and resist any flanking assault. The larger part of Forward Camp lay in the immense, mostly flat area between the two rivers, north of the Braided and west of the Wemissori. The square castra in the center of Forward Camp held the Third and the rest of the 27th. The broad sprawl that surrounded that nucleus held the Sixth Ferrata, the troopers of the cavalry alae and the cohortes equitatae, most of the three Cahokian cohorts, and many hundreds of horses. The plains upriver of Forward Camp on the west bank of the Wemissori hosted further hundreds of Cahokian and Iroqua warriors, and the land downriver of the convergence was home to what seemed like a thousand-thousand mules. Four-legs were constantly on the move; the grass around Forward Camp was already overgrazed and torn up, and keeping them fed required trips off into the Grass in all directions.

Looming over this giant camp was the first of the six Wakinyan launch towers, 150 feet tall, the wood and steel scaffolding of its buttresses extending a similar length to the right and left to stabilize it. Marcellinus's old joke notwithstanding, it really did look a little as if the Cahokians had brought their Master Mound with them in a crude and skeletal form. Two of the Wakinyan had been brought ashore and assembled inside a hastily built longhouse. The rest had been left safe aboard the *Fides* to ensure that they would not get damaged in the confusion.

Alongside the Wakinyan launcher stood three Hawk launchers and three Eagle launchers, railed up and ready to go, their arrangement adding to the odd similarity of Forward Camp to the Great Plaza at Cahokia. Around them, lying like immense fallen beasts, were the unassembled pieces of the remaining towers.

On the river side of the camp Pahin, Chogan, and the other Ravens had set up four steep wooden ramps to launch the Sky Lanterns. Today a single Lantern floated eight hundred feet above the camp, crewed with Cahokian and Roman lookouts. Here in the Grass, the army would keep a constant watch on the horizon.

The Imperator's Praetorium tent was at the exact center of the castra, and Sabinus and Agrippa had quarters on either side of it. Marcellinus, always the contrarian, slept on hard ground in the outer camp with his mixed Cahokian and Roman forces. Tahtay and his Blackfoot, the Wolf Warriors under Wahchintonka, the People of the Hand, and the Tadodaho and his Iroqua were billeted in various areas in the outer camp. As Marcellinus had anticipated, the Cahokian summons to the Shappa Ta'atani had been rebuffed, and no warriors had come north in the springtime to join them. All the rumors they heard suggested that the Shappans had returned to their alliance with the Mongols.

The central castra was as well organized as any Roman

encampment, but in the outer area Marcellinus quickly
became dependent on his adjutants and Unega's Cherokee guides to find his way around. Forward Camp had
been only lightly occupied during the winter months,
and most of the troops and warriors inhabiting it now
had been there only a couple of weeks or, in the Sixth's
case, four days. That meant that nobody knew where
anything or anybody else was, and people spent much of
their days either lost or falling over one another. Although even Enopay threw up his hands at the prospect
of attempting an accurate count amid all this activity
and confusion, it was conceivable that the Hesperians
now formed the majority of the allied forces.

Despite the large number of nations clustered together
in crowded conditions, there was little infighting among
the allies. They were kept too busy by their generals and
chiefs. Every day was a solid round of construction
work, army drills, and exercises out in the Grass. But
that might not last. A significant fraction of the League's
forces was still not convinced of the seriousness of the
Mongol incursion. Hardly any of the Cahokians or Iroqua had seen the depredations of the Mongols with their
own eyes. Because of the tales brought by his Blackfoot
brothers, Tahtay believed in the threat completely, and
most other Hesperians took the view that any enemy
that worried the Romans, Blackfoot, and People of the
Hand was worth taking seriously. However, a growing
minority suspected the Mongol threat was either dramatically exaggerated or nonexistent. The outer area of
Forward Camp was as volatile as Jin salt and might explode into violence at any moment.

Just as he had right at the beginning of his Hesperian
adventure, Marcellinus made it his duty to be anywhere
and everywhere. He walked the camp by day and by
night, sometimes with Tahtay, Enopay, Sintikala, or the
Tadodaho of the Haudenosaunee, sometimes with Sabinus, Aelfric, Dizala, Gallus, or his quartermaster and
adjutants, talking in quick Latin about logistics, supplies, injuries.

Military action was rarely a clean and well-organized affair. Cohorts and alae, and the corresponding units of enemy infantry and cavalry, were not merely pieces on a game board. War on this scale was messy and contingent, and once the battles began, the generals would be lucky if they could even keep track of what was going on right in front of them in their own theaters. But with luck, at least they could prevent their armies from destroying themselves before they took the field.

Slowly but surely, the great Mongol armies were approaching. On the basis of the intelligence brought by the Norse scouts and the Hesperian merchants, they had a month at most before the armies of the Khan came within range. And a month was not long at all where an army of this size was concerned.

"We must dig channels," Enopay said obstinately. "Canals for crap. Our soldiers spend too much time carrying merda around in reeking carts. And half the Iroqua won't use the latrines anyway."

Marcellinus increased his pace. If he could not leave his youngest adjutant behind, perhaps he could at least make the boy short of breath. "Juno, Enopay, I know all that."

Enopay did a hop and skip to keep up. "How can you be a Roman and not believe in being clean? Is Roma a sewer? The men say no. Then why must Forward Camp be one?"

Marcellinus had missed his chance to go on an early-morning mounted exercise with Hanska and the Third Cahokian because his quartermaster of the Sixth Ferrata had been haranguing him about corn shipments from Cahokia and his chief blacksmith had been complaining that the current batch of steel was too brittle to mend the wagon wheels that had bent on the journey here. Now he wanted to perform a surprise inspection of the Ninth Cohort's tent area and see if there was any truth to Manius Ifer's quiet reports of dealings in contraband tabaco among Caecina's men, but Enopay was pursuing him through the streets ranting about shit. He stopped and turned on the boy. "This is an army camp. We'll be here perhaps one more month, and then we'll either be rotting here in the dirt ourselves or marching home to the Mizipi."

"And in the meantime—"

"Look, Enopay, sewers don't sluice themselves. We'd need running water. Pumps and pipes. A whole system. Or your channels of shit would just clog solid and we'd have a network of merda spanning the entire camp."

Marcellinus strode on. The boy broke into a trot. "It can't be that hard."

"No, not once we've built the aqueduct," Marcellinus said testily.

"All right, but at least—"

From the Sky Lantern far above them a horn sounded, and Marcellinus came to an abrupt halt, almost skidding in the mud.

"What?" Enopay looked around. The nearby legionaries also had stopped, suddenly alert.

They were too far from the edge of the sprawling camp, and that edge was half a mile from the nearest hill. "Tower," said Marcellinus, and ran toward the Wakinyan launch gantry. Jumping up, he started to climb the ladder.

"Futete." Below him, Enopay stood wide-eyed. "What? What's happening?"

"Come on up, Enopay. I need your eyes."

The Praetor reapplied himself to the climb, pulling himself up the ladder hand over hand. Enopay would follow or he wouldn't, but Marcellinus couldn't wait. He felt a new vibration through the tower and glanced back. Taianita and Manius Ifer had appeared and were coming, too, one on each side of the ladder, racing up after him, and yes, Enopay was gingerly pulling himself up and trying not to look down.

Marcellinus stepped onto the platform just below the tower's peak. A few feet above his head was the steel launching rail. Marcellinus glanced at it out of habit. It looked solid, ready to go if they needed it.

He looked out over Forward Camp and the grasslands beyond. Behind him the Roman castra was orderly enough, on the standard grid pattern; in front of him the outer camp was a sprawling mass of humanity, its tents and lodges arrayed in halfhcarted lanes that gave way to impromptu stabling areas. The horsemen of his Cohors IX Thracum Syriaca were half mounted and almost ready to go out into the Grass to forage. Beyond, a muddle of Hesperians walked around them, and mules dotted the low hills.

From the height of a Sky Lantern Marcellinus could have seen farther, but even from here he saw enough: a line of maybe half a dozen horsemen on a hill in the middle distance. They were a couple of miles away, but even with Marcellinus's fuzzy eyesight, at such a distance their appearance and demeanor set them apart from Roman or Hesperian riders. The shape of their armor, the odd glimpses of color, the additional horses that each rider led behind him; none were typical of Roma or its allies.

Taianita arrived by his side, breathing hard. "Five of them," she said. "Each with three extra mounts."

"Light cavalry. Scouts." Manius Ifer paused on the ladder just below the platform to grab Enopay's wrist and haul him up. The boy clambered painfully onto the platform in a crouched, crabbed posture more reminiscent of a man fifty years older, fear knotting his limbs. He seized the wooden rail in front of him. "Mongols?"

"No, fur merchants," Taianita said sarcastically.

Well, they were wearing furs; of that Marcellinus was sure.

"Should we try to parley with them?"

"They're scouts, not envoys." Manius Ifer now stood on Enopay's far side. "Envoys would be advancing toward us with purpose. These are wary. Seeing where we are, and how many."

"We should kill them or chase them off. Why do we

not send out soldiers after them?" Taianita was breathing more heavily than the climb up the tower warranted. Marcellinus could hardly blame her. If not for Pezi's bravery and sacrifice, Taianita might have spent the last year as a prisoner of the Mongols. No surprise that the mere sight of their scouts provoked a strong emotion in her.

"We want them to know where we are," Marcellinus said. "In a land this huge, opposing armies need scouts to bring them together. How else would we find each other to fight?"

Taianita shook her head, baffled, but Marcellinus was in no mood to explain any further. "Just these men? Do you see others, farther out?"

"There." Ifer was pointing toward the river. "And there. Less than ten in each group." Marcellinus could see nothing but muddy water and green hills. How Ifer could pick out anything at that distance was a mystery to him.

The five scouts on the nearby hill had halted. Obviously their facial expressions could not be seen at that distance, but their calm immobility seemed threatening. "They want us to know they're watching."

"We should be watching *them*," Taianita said.

"And we are." Marcellinus controlled his impatience with difficulty. "We have fifteen scouting parties along the rivers and in the Grass." Dawn and dusk were the scouts' hours to approach an enemy with the least risk of riding straight into foraging or exercising units. Even now, far from here, a small row of Roma's Norse or Gallic scouts might be giving the encamped army of Chinggis Khan a similarly cold inspection. Other Roman scouts would be on their way back toward the legions after surveillance on previous days to provide updated information about the Mongol armies' strengths and distances.

"I still think sending their heads back to the Khan would be a worthy message," Enopay said. "They want to demoralize us? Let us kill every Mongol who walks away from their army. Let them be scared to step away from their fellows."

Such piecemeal harassment of enemy forces was the Hesperian way. Marcellinus knew that from bitter experience. He turned to Ifer. "Back in Asia, how far ahead of the main army did Mongol scouts typically patrol?"

"Anything from a hundred miles ahead to a thousand. Generally around two hundred. But here, who knows?"

"Could they be closer than we think? Making better time than our scouts are telling us? Even outpacing our scouts?"

"With a baggage train it'll be hard for them to do better than fifteen, twenty miles a day. Most of the tales of Mongol lightning strikes in Europa were based on misdirection or lies."

Marcellinus was unconvinced. "We need exercises in deployment, right away, with the whole army. Battle lines. Damn it."

Hadrianus had wanted such exercises to begin the previous week. His Praetors had demurred, Marcellinus included. The men were not prepared yet. The Hesperians especially needed much more training in their individual cohorts before coming together as an army.

Well, the sands of time were draining away. They would just have to be ready now.

The closest Mongol scouts began to move again, this time to the right. They would keep their distance but climb to the top of a different hill for another view of the encampment of the Imperium and the League.

Two more cornu blasts came, each with a distinct pattern, separated by a few seconds. Ifer nodded and moved to the ladder. The first signal had come from the Sky Lantern above them, broadcasting the information that the Mongol scout party was on the move. The second signal came from behind them in camp and was the call to senior officers. The Imperator was summoning his Praetors. The tribunes would also muster, ready to execute whatever orders came down from on high.

The rank and file were preparing, too. Below Marcellinus men were marshaling, the laggards now out of their tents, centurions and decurions barking out orders to hurry their troops. Everyone knew today would be a day of action. Not a battle, but the next best thing.

And drifting above it all, and if anything even more apparent at the height of the Wakinyan launch tower, came another strong waft of ordure.

Enopay was not wrong. Forward Camp reeked.

By moonlight, Marcellinus walked the streets of the inner castra with Decinius Sabinus and Lucius Agrippa, agreeing on details of men and assignments for the deployment exercise they planned for the morrow. Afterward he exited into the still tragically disorganized mess of the outer camp to meet with Tahtay, Akecheta, Mahkah, and Hanska about Hesperian support of the exercise. Returning at long last to his tent, he found Sintikala and Enopay discussing how to construct a makeshift Longhouse of the Wings closer to the launchers, and the most efficient way of transporting more Catanwakuwa from the quinqueremes to this longhouse. They needed to complete this as a matter of some urgency, as they were still unable to fly the Hawk patrols that would become essential as the enemy neared. However, as soon as Marcellinus appeared, Enopay strategically yawned and excused himself, at which point Sintikala challenged Marcellinus to a skirmish of a most energetic and pleasant nature that kept them engaged for some time. They fell asleep wrapped around each other, which complicated their abrupt awakening just a few hours later.

In the dark before the dawn, the sky lit up, and there was an earsplitting bang that seemed to come from mere inches away. Marcellinus's eyes snapped open.

Through the walls of the deerskin tent Marcellinus saw the remains of a bright flash. Almost at the same time came another explosion, the scatter of sparks, and a sharp smell that he recognized from his nightmares.

Jin salt, the black powder of far eastern Asia, had

come to Forward Camp. The Mongols were assaulting them with thunderclap bombs.

Sintikala awoke all at once and lashed out, thumping Marcellinus on the side of the head. They rolled, limbs entangled. "Shit!"

Shoving him away, Sintikala leaped up and lunged for the doorskin of the tent. Marcellinus was on his feet just moments later. A deep fear gripped him. Even after all this time the images of the Night of Knives, the treacherous Iroqua night assault on Cahokia, were still vivid in his memory. Sintikala's accidental clipping of his ear brought a pulse of pain reminiscent of the head injury he had sustained later that day. And over and above it all was his terror-filled realization that the Mongols were *here* attacking Forward Camp when they should have still been at least two hundred miles away . . .

And, not least, his fear for Sintikala, who had just run naked out of the tent they shared into what might already be a battlefield.

He burst out of the tent and looked up into a sky where it seemed that the stars were exploding, yet he saw no enemies in the streets, only befuddled legionaries stirring themselves. The explosions still rang in his ears, along with the babble of confused voices in many languages, but he heard no screams of pain or torment.

Another dazzling light flashed above him. He instinctively flinched away—might such a glare blind him?—but soon glanced back to see a blob of red, white, and purple light falling slowly through the air. To illuminate the camp so that the attackers could pick out targets?

Forward Camp could not withstand a siege. That was not its purpose. Its fence of wattle and daub was mostly to keep the horses in and the mules out. A ditch six feet deep surrounded that fence, and the prairie sod and earth thus excavated formed a low wall around the camp, but they had no palisade. If the Mongols attacked in force, their defenses would provide little protection.

Marcellinus ducked back into his tent. He grabbed

breechcloth and tunic, greaves and breastplate, and dressed for war as best he could.

Another, much larger explosion came. Now he heard screaming, and it was only about a hundred yards away.

Marcellinus's head pounded. He needed to protect it or his confidence would be gone, sapped by his fear of a disabling injury. He grabbed his Praetor's helmet, despite the white plume that would glow in the rocket's glare and make him a target, and shoved it onto his head. He snatched a gladius, and finally he was ready for whatever the night might bring. Out he went again.

The support struts for the Wakinyan launcher were aflame, the wood blazing merrily. As he watched, a second thunderclap bomb came in, lobbed by an unseen engine outside the camp, and exploded in a sudden bright sun just a few tens of feet away from the main tower of the launcher. Marcellinus registered fleeting impressions of a myriad of small flying objects radiating from the explosion in a sharp cloud and then the screams of agony from the men who were trying to fight the fire.

Two Roman trumpets sounded at once. Then one mercifully fell silent, allowing him to decode the message of the other.

Marcellinus broke into a run, calling for Mahkah, then changed his mind and his direction, swerving right. "Hanska! Third Cahokian! Up and to horse!"

Mahkah was prudent where his horse was concerned. He loved the fine four-legs, and his guilt at being responsible for the crippling of one might slow him down at this critical time. Hanska, though, viewed horses with little sentiment and was crazy enough for anything. And indeed she was up already, she and a good two dozen of her warriors, only half of them wearing even a tunic, let alone armor, but all on their feet and rushing to their mounts as the skies erupted around them.

Marcellinus ran up to her, panting. "Blinkers!"

"I'm not fucking stupid," Hanska snapped, and indeed she had already strapped the leather cups to her horse's head, the tack that attached to the cheek plates and prevented a horse from seeing to the rear or the side, allowing it to look only directly ahead. "Who do we kill?"

"They must have a trebuchet throwing thunderclap bombs, with Jin rockets to light their way."

Hanska stamped her foot. "Yes, of course . . . Gaius, how *many* of *what*?"

"I don't know. Maybe Mongol light cavalry?"

"Very fucking useful." Hanska leaped onto her horse. "Third! Come on!"

Marcellinus's warhorse was in a stall deep in the castra. Even if he'd had time, he didn't know where to find it. A trooper of his First Cohort always brought it to him when he needed it. "Futete," he said.

He saw no saddled horse that did not already have a Cahokian astride it. He did, however, hear the chink of Roman armor and see three ragged centuries of the Sixth jogging toward the Westgate. They clearly had donned their armor in a hurry, but at least they were carrying scuta and pila.

That would have to do. He was almost relieved. Damned if he felt confident enough to ride an unfamiliar horse by night anyway. Horses had better night vision than people but were also more likely to spook in the dark. They sometimes could not tell shadows from holes and might shy or bolt without warning. He was better off on foot.

Marcellinus ran to his infantry. He did not recognize the centurion leading the squad, just another short-haired, muscular soldier with clear skin. Without tattoos, Marcellinus now found Romans difficult to tell apart. The centurion recognized him, though, or at least his Praetor's plume, and snapped him a salute. Marcellinus fell in alongside the centurion at a steady jog as another batch of the Sixth ran to join them.

Where the hell was Sintikala? As if in answer, he heard the creaking twang of the launch equipment behind him as a Catanwakuwa shot over his head. He glimpsed it only for an instant before it was gone into the night.

Briefly Marcellinus hoped she had found something to wear, and then there was no time for any further distracting thoughts because the Westgate was in front of them, and they were about to charge out of the camp and into gods knew what . . .

Yet another rocket exploded in the sky, just in time for its light to alert Marcellinus to a hole in front of him. He hopped over it and kept running, through the open gate and out into the night.

The gate was not wide enough for infantry and cavalry to exit side by side. Hanska's Third held up and waited for the four centuries of the Ironclads to jog on through, and then rode out to flank them.

The lead centurion raised his hand, a dark shadow in the night. "Walk. Close up," he commanded, and his soldiers slowed. Marcellinus came to a walk, too. It was a wise order. If they were about to fight, by all means let the soldiers get their breath back. If they continued to jog into the darkness, all it would take was for one man to trip over an unseen tussock and ten others would tumble over him.

Peering ahead, Marcellinus saw only the shadows of the low hills. The glare of the rockets had unsettled his night vision. The legionaries beside him were just dark ghosts that smelled of leather, steel, and fear.

They continued to advance. Behind them in the camp they could hear orders being shouted and the jangle and chink of armor as men hurried to obey them. That noise might well be covering up any quieter sounds of an ambush ahead. If there were Mongol cavalry nearby, the Romans would be able to see their silhouettes against the sky, but warriors might be squatting stealthily in the darkness all around them and not be noticed.

" 'Ware fire lances," Marcellinus said quietly to the centurion.

"Aye," said the man, and raised his voice to spread the warning. "Beware skulking Mongols with fire lances!"

As he said the words, the night lit up once again, right

in front of them. Marcellinus heard not the crack of black powder but the *whomph* of something large catching fire. He dropped forward instinctively. The legionaries around him reacted, too, each man grounding the heel of his scutum and taking a knee behind it. Marcellinus, who carried no shield, held up his left arm in front of his face in a futile attempt to block out that insanely bright light. He drew his right hand back, ready to swing his gladius, ready for a Mongol warrior to appear before him at any moment . . .

Now he recognized the bright shape outlined in fire. Behind the low rise ahead of them a Mongol trebuchet was ablaze, the wooden frame and ropes all burning and distinct. Scores of men milled around the base of the trebuchet. Had that been an accident, or had the Mongols set fire to the thing themselves?

The horses of Hanska's Third Cahokian whinnied in fear, and some bucked. Above the crackle of the fire and the barked commands in Latin came the sound of Cahokian curses. Once again the night had turned to pandemonium. Marcellinus swore, too. Had they been crazy to leave the confines of the camp?

"Up, in close order!" cried the centurion, and the men of the Sixth rose to their feet, shields raised and overlapping. "Forward, on the double!" and they jogged after him.

Marcellinus stayed where he was. The enemy warriors he saw guarding the trebuchet's base were holding spears and clubs but seemed dazed and uncertain. Some were already down on the ground. Perhaps injured or incapacitated?

A cloud of thick smoke blew across him. Marcellinus coughed. Was this a trap? Yet behind his four centuries of the Sixth he could hear more legionaries pounding up, racing out of the camp and spreading right and left in support; there seemed little chance that Mongol reinforcements could overwhelm them.

Now came the clangor of steel weapons as battle was joined. The legionaries had arrived at the base of the merrily blazing siege engine and set upon its guards. Men shrieked in agony as they were cut down.

More legionaries ran past Marcellinus with swords and spears raised, eager to engage the foe. Yet again, Marcellinus's instincts were rebelling. Where were the Mongols' horses? It did not feel right.

This was the trouble with night actions. This was why the Roman military tried to avoid them whenever possible. Too confusing, too much chance of chaos.

Over the commotion of the butchery he heard a whistling sound, followed by an earsplitting explosion not fifty feet away. Against the bright afterimage of its flash Marcellinus saw bodies hurled into the air, and the roaring and screaming redoubled. The gladius had slipped from his hand in the shock, and as he futilely held up his arms to try to ward off whatever was happening, bright shards of pain erupted in the palms of his hand and along his forearms. At the same time pottery plinked off his shoulder greaves and helmet. "Holy fucking Jove . . ."

Another thunderclap bomb. Parchment or thin deerskin wrapped around a lethal combination of black powder and sharp potsherds. If the explosion didn't get his soldiers, the shrapnel would. "Damn it—"

A horse appeared from nowhere beside him. Marcellinus dropped to the ground and rolled, hoping that it wouldn't trample him, that the Mongol astride it was not armed with one of those deadly hooked spears he had seen at Yupkoyvi or, worse, a fire lance . . .

"Get up!" Hanska shouted. "Gaius, they're killing the prisoners!"

He found his gladius, jumped to his feet, looked up at her. "What? More bombs?"

She reached down a strong arm, grabbed his forearm. "Just one, from the other trebuchet. The Mongols are retreating. Roma is killing *us* instead!"

Marcellinus kicked upward futilely. Hanska hauled on his arm. Her horse sidestepped, whinnying in protest, but somehow Marcellinus clambered up onto the horse's rump behind her. Her words still made no sense to him. Other trebuchet? Prisoners? "What the hell?"

"Hold on." Hanska spurred her horse, cantering straight toward the Roman legionaries and the men on foot they were hacking to the ground in the baleful light from the burning trebuchet. Marcellinus hurriedly flung his arms around her to avoid being thrown off.

Over her shoulder he saw several dozen mounted Mongol warriors a few hundred yards away, galloping across the plains away from a skeletal shadow that had to be a second trebuchet.

And right in front of him, a massacre. Everything became clear in an instant.

"Stand down!" Marcellinus bellowed at the top of his voice. "Sixth Ironclads, stand down, fall back!"

As Hanska's horse loomed over the Romans, they turned and raised their swords against her. In the light of the flickering flames he saw panic in their eyes, the daze of combat. In their bloodlust, they might easily take Hanska and Marcellinus for Mongol barbarians and cut them down as readily as they were killing the others. "Stop!" he shouted again. "Soldiers, stand down! For the love of all the gods, stop killing!"

CHAPTER 20

YEAR TEN, PLANTING MOON

"It was a trap," Marcellinus said, and lifted the beaker of water to his lips. His throat was seared, both from the smoke and from his frantic screaming at his troops. Horrific images still loomed before his eyes, sickening him. "A double trap."

Too tired and battered to stand, he sat on a camp stool in the Imperium tent in the middle of Forward Camp. He had pulled out most of the slivers of pottery that had lacerated his hands, but he was still dripping blood onto the floor. In front of him stood the Imperator and Lucius Agrippa. To his left were Tahtay, Sintikala, and Enopay, all staring at him with the same shocked disbelief as the Romans. Hanska stood by his side, sweating and glowering. She had refused to leave him, apparently fearing that he might be killed by his own leaders.

Behind him the centurion of the Sixth, who had led the evening's action, stood rigidly at attention and stared at a fixed point in space somewhere over his Imperator's left shoulder. The centurion's face was plastered in mud, ash, and blood. Hanska's face was equally dirty. Marcellinus doubted that he looked any better himself.

"Obviously a trap," Hadrianus said. "But perhaps we could trouble you to be a little more specific."

Marcellinus took another drink of water and spoke again, swallowing almost convulsively every few words against the smarting in his throat. "A Mongol special unit. Creeping forward under cover of darkness. They set up a trebuchet behind a low rise and used it to bombard the camp. They struck the Thunderbird launcher. Other damage." They nodded impatiently. They all knew about the damage to the camp.

He took a little more water, and anger strengthened his voice. "I went out with several centuries of the Sixth Ferrata and horsemen of the Third Cahokian. The Mongols set fire to their trebuchet, left their slaves behind, and withdrew."

"Slaves?"

"Yes. The Mongol trebuchets use human power in a concerted effort to throw the missiles. Pulling on the ropes, all together, thirty or fifty at a time. The Mongols had brought Hesperian prisoners, mostly Shoshoni and Hidatsa. The prisoners launched the missiles. Then the Mongols abandoned them to be cut down by our legionaries." Again Marcellinus felt sick. "It didn't feel right. Even in the dark I half recognized the languages they were speaking. They sounded familiar and not like the Mongol tongue . . . Anyway, the Mongols had armed the prisoners and told them the Romans would slay them. Half of them believed it, fought us in their panic. The other half begged for mercy. The legionaries did not understand them. Dozens were dead before I could order the stand-down."

Tahtay briefly closed his eyes. "Again Romans killing Hesperians."

"Not deliberately. It was not the fault of the legionaries, Tahtay. You must see that."

Tahtay raised his arm in a slicing motion, the handtalk for *be silent*. "Of course I understand. I am not an idiot. But now I must explain to my warriors that Romans have once again cut down people of the land."

"And that should make them hate the Mongols more," said Enopay. "Not the Romans."

"Perhaps. It may not be that simple."

Only a score or so of the Mongols' prisoners had survived. They had been herded into camp, bleeding and wailing in shock, sorrow, and understandable anger. They were men who had been pushed to their wits' end on the Mongols' leash and then had been almost hacked to death by Roma.

Lucius Agrippa could contain himself no longer. "Yes, yes, but in the meantime, Chagatai's army is here."

"Maybe," Tahtay said.

Agrippa eyed him balefully. "There is no *maybe*, war chief. We have flown Sky Lanterns. Sintikala has flown her Hawk. We see their camp, not ten miles distant, and their campfires as they warm themselves against the dawn chill. Their dust still hangs in the air. Somehow their entire army has crept in, undetected."

Tahtay looked at Sintikala. "Speak."

Sintikala pursed her lips and spoke reluctantly. "Not so many."

"Not so many as what?" Agrippa demanded.

Sintikala frowned at his tone and for a moment did not reply. Then she answered in Cahokian, still eschewing speaking Latin in front of the Imperator, with Enopay deftly translating. " 'By night I saw them from the air. Hundreds of campfires, just ten miles from Forward Camp, which would mean that thousands of men had arrived by night. A whole army. You launched a Sky Lantern in the dawn, and your Roman sentries, pilots, they told you the same. But it is not so.' "

"A ruse," Marcellinus said.

" 'Which they worked to conceal.' " Enopay heard more from Sintikala, then nodded. " 'An advance group of perhaps three or four jaghuns, just a few hundred men, must have ridden in at night, dragging branches behind them to throw dust into the air. Each man lit a fire. By night the camp has the appearance of the full army, but it is not so. When I flew again at dawn, the ruse became clear.' "

"Yet more Mongol trickery." The Imperator turned to Agrippa. "Has it worked? How is the mood in camp?"

Agrippa looked frustrated. "Word has already spread

throughout the armies. Naturally we all believed an entire Mongol army had closed to within striking distance without our knowing they were there. The legions are shaken, and the redskins are all aquiver that we have killed Hesperians in cold blood."

Hadrianus nodded. "Steps?"

"We have closed the gate between the inner castra and the outer camp. I have told my centurions they are personally responsible for keeping their men calm. On pain of death."

"Our commanders and elders, too," Tahtay said. "Akecheta, Mahkah, Wahchintonka, Matoshka, Chenoa. The Tadodaho and other chiefs of the Iroqua, Blackfoot, Cherokee. All walk the camp, speaking softly for calm."

Marcellinus spoke. "I will have the Sixth Ironclads build the rest of the launchers, bring in the other Hawks and Eagles, and put the outer camp to rights. I already sent out two centuries to tear down the Mongol trebuchets and . . . clean up after the slaughter. Bring the bodies in for burial."

After a short, morbid silence, Hadrianus shook his head. "Damn these Mongol bastards to Hades."

Marcellinus considered. "To get here these jaghuns must have come sixty or eighty miles a day for several days. We should launch an attack on them right away, while they're still tired. Their warriors may sleep in the saddle, but when do their horses sleep? They will be fatigued; some may even be foundered. And we must show our troops and warriors that the Khan's troops are not invincible."

The Imperator was nodding. "Decinius Sabinus already musters the Third for deployment."

"Surely you just have to tell the army what is really happening," Enopay said. "And then we—"

"Gods' sakes, Gaius Marcellinus, shut your word slave up before I slit his annoying throat." The Imperator turned on his heel and strode out of the room.

Enopay stared after him, eyes wide. "What? What? I spoke the wrong words?"

"You spoke words," Agrippa said drily. "And that was quite enough." He nodded to Marcellinus and followed his Imperator out of the tent.

Sintikala put her hand on Enopay's shoulder to comfort him but turned to Marcellinus. "And so now we attack the Mongols?"

Marcellinus wanted nothing more than to sleep for a few hours. That obviously wasn't going to happen. He gulped water again, stood. "Us? That's up to the Imperator. Soon, Sabinus will march the Third Parthica. In the meantime we must ensure that the remaining launch towers are being constructed correctly. We do not have long. The rest of Chagatai's army will not be far behind."

By midmorning the Legio III Parthica had deployed from Forward Camp and marched due west. Heavily outnumbered, Chagatai's Mongols chose not to engage them in battle. As soon as the legion came within a quarter mile, the jaghuns withdrew slowly ahead of them. Praetor Decinius Sabinus halted his men, whereupon the Mongol horsemen also stopped and dismounted. Sabinus commanded his troops forward once more, and again the few hundred Mongol light cavalry led their horses away.

In the rear of the Third Legion its engineers set up a launching ramp, stoked a flame to inflate the bag, and sent a Sky Lantern aloft with a mixed crew of four legionaries and four members of the Raven clan. Tethered to a barbed pole driven deep into the ground, the Sky Lantern rose a thousand feet into the air, and its crew took stock of the land before them to ensure that they were not being led into an ambush or flanked by another Mongol force.

What happened next was as visible to the rest of the army waiting at Forward Camp as it was to the crew of the Sky Lantern. Marcellinus saw it, too, from his perch atop the third Thunderbird launch tower where he stood with Chenoa supervising the installation of the steel launching rail.

At first it was merely a smudge on the far horizon. Then the message was taken up, and just minutes later the signal tower ten miles south of Forward Camp showed its flame, the gouts of smoke it produced being artfully sculpted with a blanket to produce a series of small black clouds that drifted up into the blue skies.

The signal fires had been lit. At long last, the Line of Hadrianus had served its purpose. Its message was clear. The second and much larger army, that of Chinggis Khan, was also on its way and only a few days distant.

The Mongols had timed their approach to perfection, the twin punches of the armies of Chagatai and Chinggis artfully coordinated. Another wave of alarm spread through Forward Camp.

Chinggis Khan had seized the initiative before he had even crossed the horizon. The Roman coalition had already been forced onto the defensive. The allies had to recapture their morale and momentum, and soon, or the war would be already half lost.

Two days later Marcellinus stepped up to take his place as part of a Wakinyan crew at the ground end of one of the giant rails. Around him the others in his crew all prepared themselves for launch in their own way, some stretching, others frowning at the sky and muttering in prayer. Chenoa's eyes roved over the craft and the tower, searching for any signs of defect. Demothi walked back and forth underneath the Wakinyan Seven and touched each spar and rod, also obsessively checking for any weakness. Luyu and Taianita were already strapped under the craft, one on each side. Luyu had been one of the crew when the Thunderbirds of Tahtay had bombed the Roman fortresses on the Oyo, and so she wore a battle tattoo and a falcon mask. Taianita, less experienced, had no mask to hide her trepidation. She chewed her lip and stared at the ground. The two braves who completed the crew were not known to Marcellinus and said no word to him. They sang their preflight rituals, then gestured to him to step up so that they could lift him into position and strap him in place.

The first Mongol army had appeared over the horizon to the northwest the previous afternoon, a broad swath of armed horsemen advancing at a walk, grazing their mounts as they came. This was the army of Chagatai, second son of Chinggis Khan. It had crossed the Great Mountains to the north and proceeded along the Wemissori, destroying Shoshoni, Blackfoot, Hidatsa, and Mandan communities as it came. The advance strike force of Mongols responsible for the morale-sapping night attack had fallen back to join up with the main army.

Chagatai's army clearly felt under no pressure to hurry. Mongol control of the meadows ahead meant less grazing land for the Roman four-legs, requiring them to ferry the horses squadron by squadron back across the river to the prairies behind them. The Romans had already moved the mules far downriver to preserve the nearer grass for the horses.

The larger army, led by Chinggis himself, was only a little farther away. As the Romans had long known, the Mongol Khan had brought his forces across the lower reaches of the Great Mountains, crossing them via a southern pass, and was now advancing eastward along the Braided River.

The Norse scouts of the Third Parthica had penetrated close to the Mongol baggage train before being chased away. The Norsemen reported that the army of Chinggis Khan still maintained its appearance of being the most cheerful and colorful they had ever seen. Their enemies' spirits were high. The carts appeared to contain trebuchets broken down into transportable parts and cargoes of metal tubing that were presumably fire lances. The largest and widest of the carts carried the Khan's yurt, all in one piece, and that cart required twenty horses to pull it.

The Norsemen had kept shaking their heads as they

briefed the Praetors on what they had seen. The Mongol Horde was enough to daunt even a Viking.

At that point the scouts had completed their useful work. They would not be allowed so close to the enemy forces again. Chagatai's army now had squads of skirmishers riding out two miles ahead to clear the way and check for traps and ambushes and engage or drive away any Romans foolish enough to approach. Any Romans who tried to scout Chinggis's army from now on risked being cut off from Forward Camp.

Thus, to gain any further strategic information about the approaching armies, they would have to take to the air.

This would be Marcellinus's sixth flight aboard a Wakinyan Seven, but as Chenoa and Sintikala were even now continuing to experiment with the design, this craft bore only a superficial resemblance to those he had flown previously. This Seven had just over half the wingspan of one of the full twelve-man Thunderbirds and a much more swept-back wing shape, with the larger pilots carried toward the center. Demothi would be in the central lead position, and Chenoa would captain the craft from the outermost point of the left wing. To Demothi's left would be Marcellinus, Taianita, and then Chenoa; to his right, the other two male pilots and then Luyu. The girl was so slight that she carried the lion's share of the weaponry, mostly pots of liquid flame. Chenoa also carried some liquid flame and Demothi bore one of Marcellinus's new slingshots, but Marcellinus and the others were unarmed.

They carried no sacks of incendiary so that they would be lighter and more nimble in the air. This would be purely a reconnaissance flight. They planned to stay high, and to deter the possibility of an attack by a Mongol Firebird, their Wakinyan would be escorted by half a dozen Catanwakuwa piloted by Sintikala, Kimimela, and others of the Hawk clan.

As always for Marcellinus, the launch consisted of what seemed like a half hour of agonized waiting, not daring to breathe while expecting each moment to be his last, followed by a swift punch to his spine that would have done credit to a mule and then a vertiginous floating-dropping sensation as the Thunderbird found its place in the air. If anything, watching the launch tower streak past his eyes was even more terrifying than rocketing off the Great Mound of Cahokia. The wooden tower that felt so solid when he was standing on it now seemed flimsy, as if it might buckle beneath them or simply blow away and cease to exist in the instants it took the Thunderbird to streak up the oiled steel rail and into the sky.

The outer edges of the wings unfurled and locked, revealing the prone bodies of Chenoa and Luyu at the wingtips. Marcellinus heard an eerie keening sound over the hum of the wind in the cables of steel and sinew. Luyu was singing, of all things, in a tuneless girlish soprano.

Marcellinus loosened his death grip on the rod in front of him and tried to focus on the land beneath. Experience had taught him that if he clutched it too tightly, his surge of terror when the ground came into clear view made him flinch and jerk the craft to one side. But until today his flights had all been over Cahokia, with its recognizable mounds, huts, longhouses, granaries, and borrow pits. From this altitude the prairie appeared featureless. He could see the horizon, a few indistinct curves of the Braided River to his left, and a smudge that might be the distant Wemissori off the right wingtip, but beneath him he could not identify hills, valleys, or even a copse of trees. As a result, he had no idea how high he was.

Chenoa called out, laconic words of command that Marcellinus and the others instantly obeyed. The Seven banked to change its course by a few degrees.

Somewhere nearby were the Hawks of Sintikala, Kimimela, and the others, but Marcellinus could not see them. The sky was lined with high cloud, gray rather than blue, and he saw no other wings. Perhaps they were above him, blocked from his view by the taut wing of the Thunderbird. Luyu mercifully fell silent, her song at an end. No one spoke. Marcellinus felt isolated, adrift in a gray world, and after a few minutes began to suffer from the odd illusion that they were suspended stationary in space and might be trapped up there, unable to come down.

Then he realized that the ground below was no longer featureless. He made every effort not to wrench at his control bar in his shock.

They had already reached the Mongol army of Chagatai. The Thunderbird was flying over the leading edge of a sea of warriors.

The grass beneath him resembled nothing so much as a rug covered with ants. Chagatai's forces were not riding in blocks like Roman cavalry but were spread out in small groups sparsely enough that they appeared to stretch to the horizon on both sides. They were grazing their horses as they walked and staying far enough apart that a full-sized Thunderbird with a cargo of liquid flame would do little damage.

How the hell high was he? How could they have gained so much height? Was it a trick of the air?

"Down," Chenoa said calmly at just that moment. They inched the bars closer to their chests. The horizon tilted. The Thunderbird angled down toward the prairie. Now he could pick out the wagon train in the center of Chagatai's army.

A Hawk appeared less than fifty feet to his left. Beyond, another dropped into formation next to it. The Wakinyan was vibrating, its sinews thrumming in the air, and for a moment he could not tell who the Hawk pilots were.

"South?" Demothi was asking Chenoa. "Along?"

"Yes." The Thunderbird banked again. Rather than travel farther behind the Mongol line, they were going to ride along it. "And lower."

Chagatai himself would be somewhere below them, a warrior chief in his early forties, already a leader of great renown in his own right. Marcellinus wondered if the Mongol general could see the Thunderbird above him, if he was aware he was being surveilled.

As they dropped, Marcellinus made more sense of what he was seeing. The Mongol light cavalry were mostly dressed in leather, a gray-brown color that from altitude naturally merged into the green-gray of the prairie. But now they were flying over a block of Mongol heavy cavalry in darker leather and steel. Unlike the light horsemen, the heavies rode in ranks in a solid block. If the light cavalry seemed ephemeral from the air, the heavies looked substantial, square, steely, and ready for anything.

Marcellinus could not count them or even estimate their numbers. He doubted that anyone else aboard the Thunderbird could either.

"Canoes." Taianita pointed without moving her hand far from her wooden control bar. The Wakinyan Sevens were light enough that even stretching out an arm had a noticeable effect.

Marcellinus screwed up his eyes, but for him they were just dark blips on the Wemissori. "You're sure?"

"Of course. Large. Probably of wood rather than birch bark."

Tlingit, then, rather than the lightweight canoes of the lakes and eastern woodlands. They must have been portaged over the northern mountains, perhaps by Hesperian slave labor. The Tlingit were a coastal tribe and would prefer riverine travel to a long trek on land. Those vessels carried warriors and supplies.

"Enough," Chenoa said. "On."

Everyone but Marcellinus seemed to know immediately what "on" meant. The Thunderbird banked sharply left away from the river, heading southwest. Chenoa shared Sintikala's uncanny reading of the skies; in changing direction she somehow nursed the unseen air currents and coaxed their craft higher. He supposed it was a trick akin to that of mariners who could read the color of the seas, the patterns of the wave tops, the almost imperceptible surface currents, and even the birds in the skies and the clouds and stars above them to steer the best course. Perhaps if you flew all your life, if you practically lived in the air, this was the kind of virtuosity you could aspire to.

Was Marcellinus that good at anything? Had he gained any skill over his half century of life that was even remotely similar? Well, to a man or woman of peace his speed with a sword and his reading of his enemy's movements might appear similarly uncanny . . . at least, he might hope so.

Then his woolgathering was dispelled, because just a few miles from Chagatai's forces he saw the even larger army of Chagatai's father, Chinggis Khan, the scourge of Asia and the implacable, ruthless foe of Roma.

Marcellinus's first hope was that he was mistaken, that they were really looking down upon one of the gigantic buffalo herds that might take a full day to pass by raft or horse. But the beasts below did not have the ungainly gait of buffalo. These were warriors on horseback, each leading several other horses, and there were carts sprinkled among them, too, tall-wheeled wagons similar to those the Romans and Hesperians had constructed for overland travel. This was an army of countless thousands of cavalry on the move. They were not organized into rigid units or even an established marching order like Roman cavalry. The Mongols were spread across the plains like a disease.

He realized that there was, after all, a shape to the Mongol formation. They were flying over the leading edge of an immense curve. The forces of the Khan were arranged in a loose circle. Within that circle, a massive but meandering group of Mongol horsemen formed a vanguard. Marcellinus's Thunderbird had already flown over the front of the left wing of the Mongol army, and far in the distance he could see the right. Interspersed between the groups of horsemen were foot soldiers, perhaps their Hesperian allies.

Somewhere in the center of this group would be the Keshiks, the thousand-strong personal guard of Chinggis Khan. But they were still too far away to be seen.

His fellow Wakinyan pilots had fallen silent. The wind soughed gently in the sinews and spars of the craft. For several minutes they had flown straight, taking in the scale of the army beneath. Only now did Marcellinus realize with a shock how much easier it had become to distinguish individual horses and riders. They were only, what, a couple of thousand feet above the army?

"Enough," he said. "We should go back. Chenoa?"

In a low tone, Chenoa gave the orders. The Thunderbird made a series of gentle turns in the air as she rode the complex breezes to sustain their altitude, and they turned east to ride the waves of air back toward the Roman lines.

None of the other pilots seemed concerned that they might lose too much height and be forced to land close to the Mongol army. Just a little earlier Marcellinus had felt safe, insulated from danger by thousands of feet of altitude. Now he felt incredibly vulnerable. What if they suffered a piloting error, a shift in the tension of the thin skins that made up the wing or the sinews that kept it taut? What if the winds changed? Marcellinus wanted to be away from here, back on the ground, surrounded by the allied forces of Roma and Nova Hesperia.

And then the reason his instinct for danger had clicked in became apparent. With shocking speed, Sintikala's Hawk shot past them and curved upward, waggling her wings.

"Firebird," Taianita said calmly. "Two. Back left."

The frame of the Thunderbird jerked. Chenoa glanced at Marcellinus in irritation, although he was sure it had not been his fault; his hands were loose around the control bar. "Sorry," Luyu said.

Two Mongol Firebirds were arcing up behind them at a speed that seemed impossible, side by side, still gaining height. Marcellinus could not see the light hempen cables that pulled them skyward, but he could certainly see the horses on the ground that were towing them aloft: two groups of a dozen horsemen riding in a close four-by-three formation. A lane opened up in front of them as other horsemen and Hesperian warriors moved aside.

Chenoa snapped orders. Marcellinus obeyed instinctively as she tightened the angle of the Thunderbird against the air, pointing the nose slightly downward, and then felt another jolt of alarm. Chenoa was putting the Wakinyan Seven into a shallow dive to increase its speed, but surely that would diminish the amount of time the bird could stay in the air . . .

Kimimela flew by, far above them and to the right. Marcellinus was relieved to see that she was leaving the area, streaking east. Either the wind currents at her altitude were stronger or his daughter was somehow fueled by terror.

The Mongol Firebirds were already a thousand feet higher than their Wakinyan and still gaining altitude. The squad of horsemen towing them aloft was slowing. "Cables dropped," Demothi said, although Marcellinus could not see them falling back to earth.

Luyu's pots of Hesperian liquid flame and her bow and arrow would be of use only against targets on the ground. They were powerless to protect them from the Firebirds.

"Something else launching," Taianita said. Some remote part of Marcellinus's brain admired her calm even as he looked back. Two other squads of horsemen were advancing at speed, this time much larger than twelve cavalrymen each. The nearer squad was at a canter, the farther one overhauling them at a full gallop, and as the two groups met, the nearer squad dropped away, its horses blown.

"Handoff," said Demothi.

Was that possible? Could the two Mongol groups really have passed something between them?

Yes. A cable. And now they could see the aerial craft that cable was hauling up from the ground.

They were looking at a new type of winged vehicle, one they had never seen before, several times longer than the Firebirds.

The larger Thunderbirds of Cahokia were twelve men wide. This craft looked as if it were a dozen men *long*, as if four Firebirds had been attached in a row, equipped with larger wings, and thrown aloft. It rippled sinuously, writhing into the skies, and its provenance was clear in its coloration of red, gold, and green.

"Damn," Marcellinus said.

A flash came from high in the sky ahead of them, then another and a third. "And what's *that*?"

"Kimimela signals Roma," Taianita said. "Summoning help for us."

"Good." Because, gods knew, they needed it.

The Firebirds were above and behind them now. The new snakelike aerial craft was gaining speed and height so rapidly that it was overtaking the Mongol squad that hauled it aloft.

It was much closer now, and the way it undulated combined with Marcellinus's fear to make him nauseous. Its resemblance to the feathered serpent of Yokot'an Maya iconography was obvious. Its lead pilot was wearing a gray mask and a bright feathered headdress.

This new creation looked and breathed Maya. They were being attacked by a flying craft of the People of the Sun, a craft they had not even known existed.

"Options?" Marcellinus said.

Chenoa ignored him. She was peering to the left and right of them with a look of absorbed distraction.

"Fly away fast," Demothi said. "No other choice. Now hush, Wanageeska."

They were passing over the front line of Chinggis's army, but with yet another pulse of fear Marcellinus saw that several squads of skirmishers were trotting out ahead of it, following the Thunderbird's direction. Right now the Wakinyan was outpacing them, but for how long?

"Left, follow me," Chenoa said. Marcellinus and the others noted the position of her hands and smoothly followed her motions. The right wingtip tilted up sharply as they caught some invisible air current that only Chenoa could see. "Woo," said Luyu, whose stomach must have just dropped away from her. And then, "Oh . . ."

"Shit!" Marcellinus shouted.

A Mongol Firebird swooped by just thirty feet away. Arrows whistled past Marcellinus's face, and the Wakinyan lurched as something heavy thumped into the wing just above Demothi. He and Chenoa both jerked to shove the craft back onto its original bearing. The rest of the pilots held steady.

From the other side came the Hawk of Sintikala, streaking from left to right a hundred feet higher. She, too, was shooting arrows, although Marcellinus was too busy to see if any hit the Firebird.

They were now out in front of the army of Chinggis Khan, and once again Marcellinus could not tell how high above the ground they were. He would just have to trust Chenoa and Demothi.

The Feathered Serpent craft writhed, two hundred feet above them but dropping toward them at an alarming rate. Eight men flew it, tugging on cords rather than control bars but lying supine just as the crew of the Thunderbird lay beneath their own craft. Interspersed between those eight hung four other warriors, men whose sole job appeared to be to hurl missiles at the Wakinyan.

These missiles came thick and fast now: small rocks mostly, sent on their way by slings. At first they flew safely past the Thunderbird. Then, as the Serpent loomed closer and matched the Thunderbird's speed, the rocks bounced off the taut material of its wing, each sending a sickening quiver through the craft.

Then one of the missiles exploded with the crack of the Jin black powder that was becoming ever more familiar.

They have our range! Marcellinus wanted to shout to

his fellow pilots, but he would just be stating the obvious, and they all had their hands full.

From their right came another Firebird. For a few gut-clenching moments it looked as if it would deliberately smash into their Wakinyan, but at the last moment it looped away and dropped below them.

The Firebird had been trying to drive Sintikala away, but she was too nimble. Now she swooped up beneath the Serpent. She loosed an arrow, and it smacked squarely into the chest of the Serpent's lead pilot.

The warrior recoiled but did not scream or release his hold on the steering cords. The arrow had lodged in his armor but failed to pierce it. Nonetheless his violent motion sent the whole Serpent rippling to the right as his fellow pilots had to match his course or face disaster.

The Thunderbird wallowed in the air. Marcellinus risked a look back. They were well in front of the Mongol army, which had not changed its pace from a slow amble. He had no idea where the skirmishers were.

Beneath them another pot of Jin salt erupted into flame. Taianita screamed, a sound that she quickly cut off. Like Luyu she murmured, "Sorry," and shook her head.

The two Firebirds were losing height. Perhaps they were not as sleek as the Cahokian Hawks or their pilots were not as skilled, but apparently they could not use the unseen air currents to claw back altitude in the way Sintikala and Chenoa often did, and that even Kimimela sometimes could achieve.

"Here she comes," said Luyu, as if she had heard Marcellinus's thoughts.

Sure enough, Kimimela was approaching again from the east, just a few hundred feet above the ground. She could not remain airborne much longer. Why had she come back? What was she playing at? Marcellinus's stomach lurched.

Above them, Sintikala and the Feathered Serpent continued their deadly duel. Marcellinus could not easily see what was going on past the Thunderbird wing, but he was sure that Sintikala's agile harassment of the Maya craft was all that was saving the Thunderbird from being blown out of the air. The crewmen of the Serpent were still hurling their pots of black powder on what must be suicidally short fuses, but timing the explosions accurately enough to set fire to the Thunderbird would be difficult with Sintikala disrupting their aim.

An arrow came through the deerskin of the wing. Marcellinus barely saw the arrow itself, but he heard the *whoosh* of its passing, heard the cry of the man beside him, saw the bright tear that suddenly opened up in the wing. The rip lengthened. "Chenoa?"

"I see it," she said. "Prepare—"

An explosion came directly above them. Flame scattered across the deerskin wing.

"Dive, dive!" Chenoa shouted.

Marcellinus swung his head to look downward so quickly that he pulled a muscle in his neck. He could see small bushes below them now, a stream. The ground was still maybe five hundred feet below them, but the other pilots had pulled their control bars into their chests, and the Thunderbird was dropping out of the sky.

A stream of Roman invective poured from his mouth. He could not help it.

"Gods, shut *up*!" Taianita shouted.

"Feet," Demothi said laconically. "Gaius? *Feet*."

The wing was burning. The ground was coming up fast. Belatedly, Marcellinus kicked free of the retaining bar that his ankles had rested on and swung in his harness, his boots now pointing to the prairie grass beneath them. "Futete . . ."

He heard Kimimela scream from close by, and then Chenoa's voice cut through it: "Push. Now pull. *Push!*"

The nose of the Thunderbird came up. Burning splinters were falling onto Marcellinus's neck now.

"Legs *up-up-up*!" For the first time on this whole flight, Chenoa was screaming.

Marcellinus was almost too late in bending his knees up and away from the impact and forcing himself to relax and not brace. The craft was dangerously unbalanced now. The Thunderbird's nose flipped upward into the air, throwing them all forward, and the wing crumpled. Marcellinus swung up and found himself looking at sky, and then his feet slammed into the ground and the rest of the burning craft collapsed onto him.

The earth seemed to be moving under him, and he felt a strong desire to vomit. His fingers were fumbling at the straps even as he heard a snapping crack next to his head. Luyu and the male Wakinyan pilot whose name he didn't know were breaking him free from the wreckage of the Thunderbird. Marcellinus staggered forward on wobbly legs, brushing chunks of flaming wood from his neck and shoulders.

"Now *run*," Chenoa said.

He started running without even knowing why, following the others but quickly falling behind. Taianita glanced back, shook her head in frustration, and slowed to wait for him. "Mongols, Wanageeska! Come!"

Indeed. Still half a mile away but coming on at a fast trot were the Mongol skirmishers.

Jove . . . Suddenly, Marcellinus found himself capable of running much faster. The tallgrass of the prairie tugged at his boots, trying to trip him.

He glimpsed movement ahead of him and risked a glance up. A few hundred yards away a Cahokian Hawk landed untidily. Kimimela. *Damn it.*

A pot bounced on the ground to his left and exploded with a bright flash and a crack. He glanced up in time to see the ripple of the Feathered Serpent as it curved in the air above his head. *Shit.* He swerved left and then right to make himself a harder target, and arrows thwacked into the ground around him. They were shooting at *him* specifically, he realized; none of the others running through the prairie around him were coming under fire. Did the Mongols somehow know who he was? *Come on, gods. Give me a break here.*

He sucked air into his aching lungs, but it was quickly becoming hopeless. He looked up again just in time to see Sintikala shoot two arrows into the Serpent from above. The first missed, but the second passed right through the Serpent's feathered wing, and he heard a satisfying scream of pain as the arrow found its mark.

Too low, the Serpent was already swinging back toward the Mongol line. But the horses of the skirmishers were closer. *Shit and shit again.*

"More right! That way!" They had reached Kimimela, who was bouncing on the balls of her feet in frustration. "No, follow me." She set off at a fleet run but had to slow down immediately; even Chenoa and Luyu were panting now.

Sintikala flew over them, waggling her wings. On foot ahead of them, Kimimela adjusted her direction to follow the course her mother indicated. At long last, Marcellinus allowed himself to feel some hope.

For yes, here came the cavalry. Galloping directly toward them across the tall grass were the horsemen of the Chernye Klobuki, the elite light cavalry of the western Asian steppe. Their harnesses jangled and some of them still used their whips, but once they caught sight of the running fugitives, they slowed to a trot. The first turma passed them and took up position between them and the approaching Mongol cavalrymen. The second curved out to the left at a canter, either seeing an enemy in that direction or threatening to flank the skirmishers.

The third Chernye turma trotted up to them. Thank the gods, they had brought spare horses.

Sintikala landed next to them, unstrapped her wing in two quick urgent movements, and ran to join them. "You came back?" she demanded of Kimimela. "Stupid, stupid!"

"*You* landed!" Kimimela shot back. "Stupid?"

Sintikala looked exasperated. "*I* ran out of air."

"And I knew you'd stay and fight until you did. Was I going to leave you both out here? No!"

Wearily, Marcellinus pulled himself onto the nearest

horse. It eyed him balefully, as if wondering whether to bite him. "Ladies. Can't this wait?"

"I'm with you." Kimimela took his arm and pulled herself up behind him rather than take a horse of her own. She had been on horseback only a few times before and clearly did not relish it now, especially not with one of the spirited and dangerous Chernye mounts. Still shaking her head angrily, Sintikala also mounted a horse. With varying degrees of agility and assurance, the remaining Wakinyan crew members climbed aboard mounts.

The decurion snapped out orders. Behind them the first and second turmae of the Chernye Klobuki merged and began to charge, nocking arrows. Beyond them and just a few hundred yards distant, perhaps fifty Mongol horsemen approached in a broad line. Once they achieved a full gallop, the front of the column curved to the left. The Chernye warriors braced themselves half out of the saddle in caracole formation and began to loose arrows in an attempt to hold the Mongols back. Marcellinus took stock. "Cahokians, we have to move. Chenoa?"

Reluctantly, Chenoa stepped into a stirrup and dragged herself aboard a horse. The horse resisted her, tossing its head, but its master leaned forward to knock his whip against its ears in warning. Despite her unfamiliarity with the four-legs, Chenoa maintained her tone of command. "Wakinyan crew? With me. Ride."

"Let's go," Marcellinus said to the impatient Chernye decurion. The nomad cavalry pulled their whips from their boots and leaned forward in the saddle. The Cahokians' borrowed mounts high-stepped and snorted, ready for the race home. "Hold on very tightly," Marcellinus added quickly to his crew. "This ride may be even scarier than the last."

CHAPTER 21

YEAR TEN, PLANTING MOON

"So we shall not rule the air after all," Decinius Sabinus said moodily. "Do the gods curse us?"

"Hush," said Marcellinus, although the only other person within earshot was Enopay. "Treasonous talk is punishable by death."

Sabinus stared at him as if he had lost his mind. "I meant that as wry humor," Marcellinus said quickly. "Gods' sakes, Quintus . . . I withdraw it."

"Humor poorly placed, sir." Shaking his head, Sabinus walked to the door of his Praetorium tent and frowned out over the camp.

It was dawn the next day, and Sabinus had been so critically busy the previous evening that he was only now hearing about the Feathered Serpents for the first time.

"We know nothing yet," Enopay said. "Pretty snakes in the air? Can they carry anything beyond four archers apiece? Probably not. Our Thunderbirds can rain fire. Those Serpents sound awkward and ungainly; a single mistake by any pilot pulls them all aside. Our Thunderbirds are elegant. So their horses can pull their Firebirds into the sky? Surely our towers can throw our Hawks higher and faster."

Marcellinus studied Sabinus's face and half wished that Enopay had not accompanied him. "Quintus, we knew before now that we faced a formidable coalition. The Serpents change nothing."

"Yes, you're right, of course." Decinius Sabinus's face told a different story.

"Enopay, a moment?"

"What?"

"Leave us, please."

The boy looked hurt, and for an absurd moment Marcellinus thought he might refuse. He gestured in hand-talk: *Please. Sorry. Go.*

"Yes, Praetor." Enopay saluted Roman-style and walked down the steps into the mud of Forward Camp.

Marcellinus joined Sabinus in the doorway. "Come, man. Chin up. We can win this."

"Can we?"

"Yes. We can."

Sabinus sighed. "My men are tired and unsettled, Gaius. The Third has been in country for four years now. *Four bloody years*, and even if we pulled up stakes today, it would be next year before we made landfall in Europa. This is the single longest campaign of my life. And my legionaries, so far from home: no family, no women, poor food, and little roistering. Not even a damned baths worthy of the name. And for all that, no battle glory or plunder to make the game worth the candle."

"We're about to change all that," Marcellinus said. "Starting today."

"Are we? We have three legions, plus Cahokia, the Iroqua, the Hand. The Mongols have four tumens, plus the Tlingit, the Sunners, and probably your damned Shappans again, too. And they have Jin salt in bombs more effective than the Greek fire of Cahokia."

"And we have Roman discipline and precision against an army of nomads."

Sabinus broke away and paced, casting an eye across the castra to where his tribunes were marshaling the co-horts of the Third Parthica. "I know you're trying to buck me up, Gaius, and I appreciate it. But the Mongols are far from simple nomads now. They're strong. Versatile. Ruthlessly well organized. They're a modern army, and you know that as well as I." He shook his head. "This war may very well be the death of me, Gaius. It may well, indeed. I'm quite serious."

Marcellinus had only a few moments before Sabinus would have to go speak with his tribunes, his primus pilus, his quartermaster. A legion's first set-piece action in a new war always required close attention from its Praetor. And Marcellinus himself had to talk with Appius Gallus and Tahtay, because once the Third Parthica cleared the gates, the Sixth and the Hesperian cohorts would deploy next. "Quintus Decinius Sabinus, I know this land, and I also know the power of Roma and the strength of Cahokia and its Hesperian allies. I've seen the armies of Chinggis and Chagatai from the air, and they're certainly impressive. It's disheartening that they also have large wings as well as small. But Roma has stood for nearly two thousand years and has faced far sterner adversaries than this. So the Mongols are fierce and merciless. What of it?"

Sabinus did not look at him, but Marcellinus knew he was listening.

He wanted to say: *Quintus, more than once I have been a broken man, but today I am not. And that is all Cahokia's doing. Breathe in their strength and stand strong yourself.*

Instead, he said: "I swear to you, sir, on my honor both as a Praetor of Roma and as a prominent figure in the Hesperian League, that together we can beat the living shit out of those bastards."

At last Decinius Sabinus smiled. "Yes? You say so?" he said in Cahokian. "Then say it to my eyes."

Amused at his use of the native tongue, Marcellinus held the man's gaze without blinking. Also in Cahokian he said: "Yes, mighty chief. We will destroy the Mongols. We will scalp their warriors and make their women and children weep. And then we will dance and feast. I have spoken."

Sabinus drew himself up and switched back to Latin. "Very well, Gaius Marcellinus. Though if it's all the same, I'll leave the dancing to you."

"Send the Mongols to Hades, Decinius Sabinus." Marcellinus saluted.

Sabinus saluted back and set off toward his tribunes.

The two Mongol camps were a mere eight miles from Forward Camp and were separated from each other by about the same distance. As Chinggis and Chagatai showed no signs of combining their forces, this day's action would take place on two fronts.

Skirmishers from both sides had been out since well before dawn. Mongol horsemen had probed across the Plains toward Forward Camp. Squadrons of light cavalry from the Ala II Hispanorum Aravacorum had darted out in the opposite direction, sometimes colliding with the Mongols in brief and inconclusive clashes. Mahkah and his fleetest riders of the Second Cahokian had lunged forward to within a half mile of Chinggis's camp before being chased back by Firebirds and arrow fire, as close to counting coup as they were likely to get before the true battle began.

Now, Legio III Parthica advanced across the grass toward the army of Chinggis Khan in a broad line of cohorts, flanked by alae of light cavalry. The cavalry of the Ala I Gallorum et Pannoniorum Cataphractaria followed, wearing their scale armor and bearing their heavy contus lances. Sabinus was leading with his First Cohort and the other odd-numbered cohorts, keeping the evens in reserve. Legionaries tired quickly in battles against a mostly mounted army, and choosing the right moment to relieve the front lines with fresh troops was key.

Somewhere across the Wemissori River to the north were several cohorts of the Legio XXVII Augusta Martia Victrix, along with the Alae III and IV Polovtsia. For now they would guard the army's wider flanks; unless the Mongols executed an enveloping action, the 27th and the western steppe auxiliaries would not fight today. The Chernye had seen action the previous day, of course, holding off the outriders of the Khan so that Marcellinus and the others could escape, and the Polovtsians had also been in the field, pushing back Mongol skirmishers and scouts. In exchange, so as not to leave the fighting legions short of cavalry, the Second Aravacorum would control the area between the Third and Sixth Legions, safeguarding the flanks of each and preventing an enterprising Mongol strike force from moving between them.

By midmorning Praetor Gaius Marcellinus was leading the Sixth Ferrata from the camp, heading for the other Mongol army, that of Chagatai. Flanking the Sixth were his Cahokian cavalry: the Second Cahokian of Mahkah on his left wing and the Third Cahokian of Hanska on his right. To his left rear Tahtay led a combined force consisting of the First Cahokian and the so-called Hesperian Auxiliary of Wahchintonka, which was to say the Wolf Warriors and a heterogeneous group of Iroqua and Blackfoot. As Marcellinus rode across the Plains, he had to stifle the nervous tic of looking back over his shoulder. Ideally he would have wanted the First Cahokian with him, but in his first action leading the Sixth Ferrata he needed to stand firm with his legion.

Marcellinus knew he should have been proud to lead the Ironclads into battle. Sabinus's Legio III Parthica had been formed by Septimius Severus more than a thousand years earlier. The Legio VI Ferrata had an even more ancient pedigree. It had its roots in the Sixth Legion that Julius Caesar had taken to Egypt. Disbanded for a year and then rededicated in 44 B.C., it had been commanded by Marcus Antonius in Judea and in his Parthian War. (Ironically for Marcellinus, a century later it had been put under the charge of one Gnaeus Domitius Corbulo, a distant ancestor of the Corbulo who had mutinied against him outside Cahokia.) The Sixth Ironclads had continued to earn a sterling reputation over the ensuing centuries. It was only over the last hundred years that some of their luster had tarnished, and their seaborne thrashing at the hands of the Mongols in the Mare Solis was one of their worst defeats ever. Marcellinus was determined to return the legion to some of its former glory, and to acquit himself well in the coming battle, both for his sake and for theirs. Yet despite the prestige of leading the Sixth Ferrata, a large part of his soul wished that he was riding with Tahtay at the head of the First Cahokian instead.

Marcellinus had the winding ribbon of the Wemissori River to his right, several hundred yards beyond Hanska's cavalry. On the Wemissori's far bank the Fifth Cohort of Agrippa's 27th Legion marched in a triple line. Far beyond, the right flank of the Fifth would be covered by the Cohors IV Gallorum Equitata, the Fourth Gallorum, roaming far and wide to check for Mongol strike forces.

A quarter mile behind the Sixth Ferrata came Marcellinus's corps of engineers and members of the Raven clan, protected by his horsemen of his Cohors Equitata IX Thracum Syriaca, the Ninth Syrian. On fifteen heavy Cahokian wagons the engineers carried three Sky Lanterns and the ramps, portable furnace, fuel, and bellows to launch them, plus the stripped down components for five throwing engines. The throwing engines were to relaunch any Cahokian Hawk or Eagle that landed behind the battle line. The aerial craft would initially launch from the towers; several of them were being moved out from Forward Camp, but much more slowly, and would remain far to the rear of the armies. They had brought none of the more conventional ballistae and onagers, which would not be effective against horse troops.

From his current position, riding a hundred feet in front of the Sixth, Marcellinus saw the two Norsemen, Isleifur Bjarnason and—what was his name, Einar Steensen? Steffensen?—standing dismounted next to a standard they had thrust into the ground. To the best of their reckoning this was the midway point: the flag marked a spot four miles distant from Forward Camp and an equal distance from the camp of Chagatai. Here the Roman and Cahokian forces would stop and await battle.

They stood on a wide prairie with low, gently rolling hills. A stream lay to their rear, and the Wemissori to the north. If they advanced beyond this point, the Mongols would gain the advantage; the Romans would be too far away from their launchers and too extended to fall back to their camp quickly at need. They would go no farther. If the Mongols did not meet them here in battle, the Sixth would withdraw that afternoon.

One thing was sure: the Mongols were not near yet or Bjarnason and Steensen or Steffensen would be mounted and racing back across the grass toward him.

"Good enough," he said to Dizala. "We halt here."

"Aye." Dizala gestured to his trumpeter to spread the order down the line of the legion and beyond it to the cavalry. Piece by piece, the Sixth came to a halt. The adjutants came forward to be in position for any further orders.

Harking to the trumpet, Bjarnason got on his horse and rode back to Marcellinus's position. "Well, fancy meeting you lot here. Out for a stroll, are we?"

"Report," Marcellinus said tersely, in no mood for banter.

"Oh, the bastards are on the move. They're just taking their sweet time about it. Are you all right?"

"Of course."

Marcellinus would have appreciated a little more formality and military discipline. Perhaps he would get it from the other one. He peered out at the forward scout. "What the hell is his name, again?"

"Who, Einar Stenberg?"

"Yes. Thank you."

"He's a straight arrow. Trustworthy."

"I'm sure he is. How far are the Mongols?"

"Two miles, maybe."

"Maybe? Go forward and make a better estimate."

Bjarnason flinched at Marcellinus's tone. He saluted and trotted away.

Marcellinus fell silent. There was little else to do at the moment. The centurions had ordered their men to stand easy. Some were obsessively checking and rechecking weapons and kit; others were sipping water, gnawing on deer jerky or hazelnut cakes, or looking at the skies and discussing the weather. Some were even sitting down to play knucklebones.

"Shit," said Marcellinus.

"They'll be fine," Appius Gallus said, sensing criticism. "A little break in the tension is good for 'em. A breather after the march. Little rituals will settle 'em down. They'll be up on their toes again as soon as you say the word."

Marcellinus nodded curtly. He didn't doubt it. Hurry up and wait had been central to the military experience since Roma was nothing more than a scrappy village squabbling with the villages on the next hills.

It was his own nerves he was worried about. It was almost a decade since Marcellinus had led legionaries in battle. But he chose not to mention that.

The first Sky Lantern drifted skyward and was soon at its operating height of a thousand feet. The wind was from south of east, meaning the Lantern eased forward and seemed to lean in over the waiting legion. Marcellinus saw Chogan tossing fuel into the fire jar, while Romans with wide colored paddles signaled to their colleagues on the ground. Past the Sky Lantern and much higher, a Catanwakuwa sailed on the breeze.

The wind favored Roma. Was that enough to make the Mongols decline battle for the day?

He heard a familiar *whomph* sound, but from quite a distance. Far away a black powder bomb had gone off, its smoke drifting lazily into the air.

He glanced up at the Sky Lantern just in time to see Chogan's signal. Five miles away, battle had been joined between the forces of Decinius Sabinus and those of Chinggis Khan.

The war for Nova Hesperia had begun while Marcellinus, the Sixth, and his Cahokian cohorts sat . . . and waited.

"Shit," he said again.

"Eyes up," Aurelius Dizala said. "Here we go."

The Norse scout Stenberg was cantering back toward them, his gladius raised above his head. A few hundred yards behind him a long, dark line was emerging.

"About fucking time," Marcellinus said, and his adjutants laughed dutifully, Enopay's laugh pitched a little higher than the others. About to give the order to rouse the legion for action, Marcellinus saw it was unnecessary. All up and down the line of the Sixth Ironclads, centurions were bringing the men to their feet, mustering them for inspection. Marcellinus trusted that Mahkah and Hanska would be similarly bringing their horsemen to order and preparing for the onslaught.

The Mongols were coming. They would fight today after all.

Marcellinus felt a brief moment of dislocation. In battle with the Iroqua on Cahokian soil, he had fought with Mahkah and Hanska by his side, and Takoda, too. Now Mahkah and Hanska would command light Cahokian cavalry in the service of the Imperator, miles away from Marcellinus, and Takoda stood by with his other five adjutants, waiting to help with logistics.

Even farther away, Tahtay was standing at the head of the First Cahokian, ready to lead them into gods knew what.

Meanwhile, Marcellinus was surrounded by the cohorts of Roma. He would spend the coming hours commanding and fighting alongside men he'd known for less than a year.

For his first foray back into Roman military command, Marcellinus had chosen a standard triplex acies line. From left to right on the front line were the Fourth, Third, Second, and First Cohorts, with broad gaps left between them, putting the double-strength First Cohort under Appius Gallus in the front right position. Behind them the second line consisted of the Fifth, Sixth, and Seventh Cohorts, offset to form a checkered pattern. The third line consisted of the Tenth, Ninth, and Eighth. This wrapped line was essential to keep the cohorts together with the tribunes who led them. Without that, Statius Paulinus's cohorts would have been at opposite sides of the legionary formation.

The intervals between the front cohorts were key to the success of the formation. The gaps allowed more flexibility in advancing, permitted the cohorts in the second line to move forward and support or relieve the first, and provided channels down which his light infantry or cavalry could sally out into the fray. Any enemy foot soldiers or cavalry who ventured into the intervals would come under attack from three sides.

It was into one of those gaps in the formation that Einar Stenberg now rode, with Bjarnason not far behind. For the rest of the battle they would serve as couriers.

The chessboard arrangement of Marcellinus's cohorts was repeated within his individual units. The Mongols invariably opened offensives with an arrow cloud from their light cavalry, which was armed with their infamous composite bows. The Sixth would present a united front, returning fire with bows while defending themselves behind a wall of scuta. Once the missiles gave way to the shock attack of a full Mongol cavalry charge, the cohorts would have the flexibility and maneuverability necessary to deal with that, too.

After that, anything could happen.

The dark line before them was now recognizable as a broad swath of horsemen. "Well, then," said Praetor Gaius Marcellinus. "Better get to it."

Dizala nodded. "Good luck, sir."

"And to you, and may the gods smile on us." Marcellinus knew no gods, but other men did, and it was what a general was supposed to say at such moments.

Marcellinus studied his front line and nodded in satisfaction, making the gesture broad enough to be seen at a distance. He considered prebattle speeches an exercise in self-indulgence; anything he said would be inaudible beyond fifty feet away, and Romans did not have hand-talkers to spread the words onward as Hesperians did. Let each centurion fire up his men in his own way, undisturbed. Nonetheless the nearby centurions ordered pila raised in salute, and some of the men even gave Marcellinus a mild cheer. Marcellinus raised his fist in a return salute.

Marcellinus threaded his way through to the rear of his army. During the action he was supposed to remain behind the First Cohort with his band of adjutants, signalmen, and scouts. From there he would direct the legion to the best of his abilities and could be found by dispatch riders from the Imperator if they needed him.

Beyond the rear of the Sixth Ironclads he saw a line of several dozen carts bearing water, ready to replenish men and horses as necessary during the long afternoon. Behind them were the Sky Lantern ramps and throwing engines. Wearing his white-plumed Praetor's helmet and sitting astride his great gray Thessalian steed with its scale armor barding, Marcellinus was a very recognizable figure, and as he rode out, the leader of each crew raised his gladius high, the signal that his ramps or engines were ready for action. Behind would be the first in the long line of signalmen who would relay information back to Forward Camp and the crews that were launching Hawks and Thunderbirds.

All was as ready as it could be. In the meantime, the advancing Mongols had halved the separation between themselves and his front line. In mere minutes they would launch their attack . . .

Marcellinus blinked and looked again, and a murmur rippled through his cohorts. What he had initially taken for an unbroken line of cavalry was no such thing. Ahead of the cavalry marched a squad of, what, infantry? Did the Mongols plan to use their fire lances right off the bat?

He hoped so. A thrown pilum had a much greater range than a fire lance. No matter how well armored, its Mongol wielder would quickly be killed or at least knocked back. The smart time to use the fire lances was not against fresh troops but later in the battle, once the cohorts were disordered and weary.

No. The first line had a solid core of marching infantry at its center, Hesperian in all likelihood, preceded by a wide line of other foot soldiers—

"Damn Chagatai to hell," Marcellinus said.

Right now, he should dismount and allow his horse to be moved back by his adjutants. His helmet and extra height made him a ridiculously easy target. But he could not yet dispense with the mobility the Thessalian provided. Spurring it on, Marcellinus galloped back to the front line. After a moment of consternation his adjutants and trumpeter hurried after him.

The Mongols were driving prisoners before them. The men were not infantry but Hesperian captives. By their tattoos, scarifications and paint, clothing, and hair Marcellinus recognized Blackfoot, Hidatsa, Cherokee, and what could only be Shoshoni. Brutally forcing them forward were other Hesperians, allies of the Mongol Khan: a few Tlingit and Haida, but by far the most plentiful were . . . the Shappa Ta'atani.

Marcellinus cursed again. This was going to make for one hell of a complicated battlefield.

He turned and snapped a series of instructions to his trumpeter, who looked perplexed. Marcellinus didn't blame him. He had no idea whether there were clear cornu signals for the orders he had just given. He pointed to his Cahokian adjutants and gave them another set of orders. The adjutants ran.

Another thought struck him. He turned again to his unfortunate cornicen. "Lanceae, not pila, for the Shappans. You hear? Lanceae! Lanceae!"

The line of Hesperian prisoners was just three hundred feet away. The front ranks of Marcellinus's legion had figured it out; his legionaries were swaying left and right on the balls of their feet as soldiers did when they were exchanging words, talking grimly to one another.

For most of their time in Nova Hesperia the legionaries had lived in tents, barracks, and galleys. To most of them, all natives looked alike. And even if they didn't, their centurions might even now be deciding that the prisoners were already casualties of war and should be dispatched as quickly as possible to get at the real enemies behind them.

And once upon a time, Marcellinus would have made that same ruthless decision.

At last, his trumpeter gave the commands. The cornu blared a complicated sequence of notes, quickly taken up by the lead trumpeters for each cohort and spread to the far corners of the Sixth. Centurions looked right and left, irritated. Some shook their heads.

The Cahokian adjutants stepped forward now: Takoda, Napayshni, and Enopay, one at the front of each of the First, Second, and Third Cohorts. Marcellinus hated bringing Enopay to the battlefield, hated it more than anything he had yet done, but he had little choice. For all intents and purposes Enopay had to be considered a man now, even if he didn't look like one.

His three adjutants began to hand-talk in giant, emphasized motions, each saying the same thing.

More trumpet calls, and the cohorts walked forward to meet the attack. This, at least, was normal tactics. Advancing troops were more confident than troops at rest. Stepping up to meet your opponent was always preferable to standing waiting for him. Against enemies on foot a running charge was often best, but it used precious energy. Striding with determination was almost as good.

But now, following Marcellinus's order, the front line of his legion began to open. Shields that had overlapped to form a wall parted as the men behind them came into open order—grudgingly in many cases.

Arrows began to fly. The Mongol horse archers were now within bow range and were loosing arrows at a forty-five-degree angle to shower down upon the front rows of Roman troops. Marcellinus's soldiers hastily raised their scuta.

The Hesperian prisoners were running now, straight for the Roman front line, forced on by the Shappans and the Mongol horsemen.

The Mongols were almost within spear range. The front rank of the Sixth Ferrata stepped forward to hurl their weapons. With relief Marcellinus saw that his message had gotten through: Aurelius Dizala had given the order to cast the legion's lighter throwing javelins rather than the heavy pila. First, the lanceae had a longer range and would cause damage sooner in the Shappan ranks before they closed for a melee. Second, it saved the heavy pila for battle at close quarters against the Mongol horsemen.

Even so, to hurl the lanceae the legionaries had to shift their scuta and expose themselves to the rain of Mongol arrows. Some legionaries went down immediately, but the javelins were on their way, over the heads of the Hesperians on foot and into the Shappans and Mongol horsemen who followed them. The second rank stepped past the first, their own spears at the ready, but the Mongol front line was almost upon them.

Now the prisoners revolted. Some dropped to the ground to scurry forward on their hands and knees. Others turned on their Shappan tormenters. It became a messy brawl of Hesperians, becoming increasingly compressed as they were trapped between the lines of advancing Romans and Mongols.

The new front rank of Romans threw their spears and fell into close order, scuta overlapping. More spears flew from ranks farther back, over the heads of their brothers in arms. The Romans had the Mongols' range now, and as Marcellinus had expected, the Mongol horsemen broke away, wheeling around again to send more arrows into the Roman lines.

Marcellinus had ordered his front line eased at the critical moment to give at least some of the prisoners a chance to escape through his ranks. The hand-talking adjutants had sent the word to the prisoners, and the calmer among them had cooperated in their own salvation. In some places the plan had fallen short, and many Hesperians now lay dead in front of the Roman lines. But Marcellinus suspected that the Mongols had been banking on a much higher level of chaos, with countless corpses impeding the Roman advance. That had not happened. Lives had been saved.

Yet there was little respite. Behind the prisoners the Shappa Ta'atani, perhaps as many as two thousand of them, marched in tight formation directly toward the center of Marcellinus's line. They wore an odd mixture of Roman and Mongol helmets, Roman breastplates and greaves, and Mongol leather armor, but in terms of their discipline and the rigor of their ranked formation they might have given the First Cahokian a run for their money.

More shouted commands from Marcellinus, more cornu blasts and bellowing of centurions. The cohorts of the Sixth Ferrata once again stepped forward to hurl spears, and perhaps one man in four of the Shappan front line fell wounded.

Other Shappan braves stepped up to take their place. The warriors of Shappa Ta'atan formed a solid core of infantry. On either side came the wings of Mongol cavalry, again shooting wave upon wave of arrows into the cohorts of the Sixth Ferrata. Relatively few legionaries were going down, though. The Sixth was not nicknamed the Ironclads for nothing; they were heavily armored and quick to adopt a defensive posture, the men at the front kneeling with scuta aslant, those behind standing with shields held above their heads. The Mongols could not inflict high casualties on such a formation with arrow fire alone.

Well. Suffice it to say that this was already a completely different battle from the one that the Imperator and Praetors had envisaged just that morning.

Marcellinus could not see Son of the Sun. The Shappan chief must be within his army somewhere—Marcellinus couldn't imagine the clan chiefs and warriors of Shappa Ta'atan fighting for the Khan under any other commander—but Marcellinus could not spot him. Once he did, sparks would fly.

The first three ranks of the legion stepped forward, spears held overarm, ready to be thrust down into the Shappan ranks. They advanced in silence, and Marcellinus could see that this unnerved the Shappans. In response, they began to whoop and catcall and bang their axes, clubs, and swords against their shields. But Roma would not be cowed by that.

Scores of the Mongols' erstwhile prisoners had emerged from the back of the first line of cohorts. They were being gathered together by the optios and hustled back toward the water wagons to be held under guard in case of treachery. Marcellinus expected none. Few wore warrior tattoos, and they looked battered and beaten.

"Back, sir," said his adjutant, Furnius. "Come back now . . . Here they come!"

The Mongols were charging. They would attack on either side of their Shappa Ta'atani vassals, their left wing attacking the First Cohort and their right focused on routing Paulinus's Fourth.

It was Marcellinus's first view of a full Mongol charge. He hoped it would not be his last.

CHAPTER 22

YEAR TEN, PLANTING MOON

Marcellinus had barely regained his place back behind the First Cohort when the phalanx of the Shappa Ta'atani crashed into the center of his front line. Just before impact Dizala's cohorts raised a sudden ruckus, banging their spears against the iron rims of their shields. If the abrupt din threw fear into the warriors of Son of the Sun, it was not apparent from where Marcellinus stood.

Shields clashed, and steel rang against steel. Dizala's troops had stepped up, punching their shield bosses into the Shappan line and following with overhand spear thrusts. The legionaries behind surged forward to hold the line firm. The Shappans who did not go down immediately swung their axes and clubs, and each legionary tried to catch the impact on the steel rim of his scuta rather than the flat. Where they failed, Marcellinus heard splintering and screeches of pain where the axes cleaved the wood, but the line held, his soldiers still powering forward to split the Shappan ranks. The cohorts advanced six feet, then eight, and then the Shappan line stood firm. Their spears mostly lodged in Shappan bodies, the leading Romans drew gladii.

The leading line of Mongol horsemen was three hundred yards distant and approaching at a canter. Although Marcellinus could not see all the ranks of the cavalry that faced him, he knew from his Sky Lantern's signals that the Mongol force was moving forward in five lines, each separated by about two hundred yards. The first two lines were heavy cavalry, with more horse archers making up the ranks that followed.

Marcellinus knew what would happen next. Aelfric and the other tribunes would know, too. There was no preparing for it, no orders he could give that would help. They just had to wait.

Takoda trotted up to bring Marcellinus his shield, a large oval in the cavalry style. "Should I stay with you?" the brave asked quietly.

Cahokian company was not unwelcome. And at this time of all times, Marcellinus remembered a much younger Takoda coming to cut his bonds with a chert blade at dawn on his very first day in the Great City as he lay out in the open at the base of a red cedar pole, wounded and desolate and waiting for death. He and Takoda had been through a lot together in the intervening years. "If you would."

Takoda was a warrior, but also a gentle man who loved his family and his neighbors, who loved Cahokia and the Mizipi and all of the land. He did not deserve to be at the hub of a war between two invading foreign powers that eventually might decide the fate of the world.

Marcellinus looked again at the Mongol line. More than anything, he wanted them all wiped from the earth.

The Mongol heavy cavalry lumbered forward. And now they were at arrow range, and their stirrup-to-stirrup formation was parting to make channels for the light cavalry.

They poured through, sleek and merciless in their gray leather armor, standing in their stirrups, raising their bodies clear of their wooden saddles with those devastating composite bows in their hands.

"Testudo!" Marcellinus roared, and beside him Takoda jumped at his sudden shout, his horse backing up. But his First Cohort was doing it, the front rank dropping to one knee with shields angled, the ranks behind raising scuta to interlock them over their heads against the arrow shower.

The Mongol horsemen galloped through, a steady stream of light cavalry, and turned to form an oblique line. They were already loosing arrows in waves, their horses maintaining formation. It was amazing that so few warriors could pump out so many arrows so quickly, but now Marcellinus saw that the horse archers behind the heavy cavalry were also firing arrows up at forty-five degrees to rain down on the legionaries.

The First Cohort staggered back as the onslaught struck. At such close range, arrows from those Mongol composite bows might punch through chain mail or even a breastplate. Shields and helmets would protect the areas they covered, but they still left plenty of vulnerability.

Amid the arrows came the crackle and flash of black powder grenades. The Mongols were hurling pots of the Jin salt into the midranks of the First. Black smoke wafted up where they struck. Men fell, others moving forward to take their place. A few hundred yards away Marcellinus's left wing was suffering the same barrage.

The first wave of Mongol light cavalry curved away to the right. Behind them the heavies spurred their horses, spears at the ready.

Marcellinus assessed quickly. Shappan warriors forming a solid phalanx of infantry to assault the center of his line. Mongol archers loosing arrows and flinging pots of black powder. And the Mongol heavy cavalry thundering in to drive home the advantage.

This was a coordinated assault as sophisticated as any Marcellinus had seen in any of his former campaigns, and it was flawlessly executed. Sabinus was right. The Mongols had come a long way.

The Second and Third Cohorts were still deep in combat with the ranked warriors of Shappa Ta'atan. Right in front of Marcellinus his First Cohort was only now recovering. Forced into disarray by the intensity of the arrow attack, his men were not yet ready to engage. A few moments earlier he had seen the crest of Appius Gallus bobbing on the left corner of the First, perilously close to the melee but looking the other way, undoubtedly shouting orders at his front line. But now Marcellinus could not see his primus pilus at all.

Marcellinus urged his horse forward between the First and Second Cohorts. "Pila! Pila, damn you!"

The men reacted to him out of quick instinct. Their shields came down, and the heavy pila came up into position. As Marcellinus arrived just behind the front line, the second and third ranks dropped their pila between the men in front of them, grinding the spear butts into the dirt, their sharp tips pointing up at an angle to form a bristling hedge.

And just in time, because the Mongol heavy cavalry was upon them.

No horses—not even the ugly, wild, and aggressive Mongol ponies—would ride headlong into a mass of armed men. But the Mongol arrows and the daunting sight of the heavy cavalry bearing down on the line had had their effect; already the line was buckling as men stepped back. Marcellinus heard Gallus yelling and now saw the First Centurion several ranks back in his cohort, shoving men into position.

The Mongol heavies carried vicious hooked spears that were twelve feet long. Right behind the line of heavy cavalry were two more lines of light cavalry, firing arrows into the Roman line between the armored horses of their own heavies. Marcellinus found an instant to admire both their courage and their recklessness and also to curse the calm confidence with which Lucius Agrippa had assured him that the Mongols would not come to the melee until they had to, would keep their distance and rely on missile fire until their hands were forced . . . but the Khan's shock troops had come to the fore in the first minutes of battle.

And gods, it had almost worked. The First Cohort, supposedly the toughest and most experienced cohort of the Sixth Ironclads, had nearly collapsed in the face of their charge.

Horses galloped up from behind Marcellinus as his adjutants arrived to defend him. From his left he heard Aulus snarl, "Jupiter's sake, sir, get back!" More practically, Sollonius handed him a heavy pilum, at the same time inserting himself between his Praetor and the front line.

Right behind Sollonius was Takoda. So much for Marcellinus keeping the young brave out of harm's way . . .

The Mongol heavies waded into the front line of the Sixth Ferrata. Their long spears thrust past the sharp briar patch of Roman steel. But the First was rising to the occasion again at last, the men pushing forward to shove their scuta into the faces of the Mongol horses even as the Mongol warriors leaned over to smash clubs and axes into those shields. Legionaries stabbed their pila forward, knocking Mongols back and sometimes off their steeds. Close to Marcellinus two legionaries fell to their knees, slain almost simultaneously with arrows buried deep in their chests. The men behind them tried to bull their way forward, but their path was blocked by the bodies.

Not so far away half a dozen legionaries had broken formation to drag Mongol warriors from horseback. Two of the Romans fell, but the others thrust their gladii deep into the warriors' bodies, mindless of the horses' hooves rearing above their heads.

The second rank of Mongol heavy cavalry was forcing itself into the fray, cleaving the Roman line. Two Mongols came straight for Marcellinus. Spurring his horse forward, Marcellinus raised his pilum high and swung it down into the mailed chest of the nearer of them. It did not breach the man's armor. Beside him Sollonius slashed at the horse's face with his gladius, and it neighed and backed up. Aulus nocked an arrow and loosed it even as his horse reared. The arrow buried itself in the Mongol cavalryman's arm.

The second Mongol threw his spear. With no time to bring his shield around, Marcellinus instinctively shoved with his legs, standing in the saddle, and the heavy spear's tip slammed into his breastplate instead of his neck or face. But the spear's weight smashed him back, and he sprawled onto his horse's rump, in danger of being unseated.

He felt himself jerked upright. It was Takoda, yanking on his arm. Sollonius was trading sword blows with the first Mongol horseman, and Aulus had grabbed the reins of Marcellinus's horse to steady it. "Back!" Aulus was shouting, his face set, eyes furious. "Back, back, *now*!"

In front of him the front lines of the First wrestled with the Mongol heavies. Not thirty feet behind him the legionaries of his Second Cohort were still in combat with the warriors of Shappa Ta'atan. Arrows, stones, and the occasional black powder grenade tumbled down on the rearward ranks of his cohorts. A pall of smoke was building over them all as Marcellinus allowed himself to be steered back into the middle of his army by his adjutants.

"All right, damn it, give me my horse." Now safely behind the First, Marcellinus plucked the reins of his horse from Aulus's hands. Next to him the Seventh Cohort had arrayed into a battle line, facing right, with the Eighth hurrying to fall into position beside it. Smart, smart; the Mongol line of horsemen might curve around to flank them at any moment. At the far end of the line of the Sixth he saw Aelfric on foot, running with his gladius in his hand and his scutum high over his head, pulling some of his centuries in line with Ifer's Tenth. Something critical was happening over there on his left, but he would have to leave it to Ifer and Aelfric for now—

Above Marcellinus, the Sky Lantern exploded.

"Fuck!" Aulus shouted, profoundly rattled. "Fuck everything!"

"Easy, soldier," Marcellinus said, and looked up.

The cotton bag of the Sky Lantern was ablaze, hot red

flames licking up its side. A man fell from it, a legionary, windmilling in the air until he crashed to earth far behind the Ninth and mercifully beyond Marcellinus's sight. The other pilots clung to the frame except for one of the Ravens, who appeared to be standing on the wooden platform slashing with an ax. As Marcellinus watched, the fire jar dropped from the center of the frame, tumbling to earth to shatter into a thousand flaming pieces.

But nothing could lighten the Lantern enough to save it. It began to fall out of the air. Another man, a Cahokian this time, lost his grip and plummeted to the ground.

The Raven still standing was Chogan. Marcellinus saw him shake his head and then deliberately leap clear of the Sky Lantern in a graceful swan dive. Above him a square of cloth opened, jerking him in the air to sway beneath it.

It was the first use of a Falling Leaf from altitude. For obvious reasons, they had never tested it from a killing height with a human being before.

Still blazing, the remains of the Sky Lantern crumpled to earth. Chogan followed it down, his arms and legs thrashing as if he were trying to climb away from the ground as it came up to meet him. The cotton square of the Falling Leaf fluttered above him. It was arresting his speed, but would it be enough?

Marcellinus looked away, feeling sick. And in moving his head he now caught sight of a Feathered Serpent of the Yokot'an Maya rippling away, writhing northward back across the sky toward the Mongol line.

It was surely this Serpent that had dealt the death blow to the Sky Lantern. Hawks assailed it now. Two were flying back from the western edge of the battle line. Two more arced up from behind the Sixth Legion, newly launched. Arrows flew. Much quicker than the Serpent, the Hawks overhauled it and pumped arrows into it at almost point-blank range.

The Maya craft shivered in the air as the arrows hit.

Much more gently than the Lantern, it began to sink earthward. Two of its pilots hung limp in their straps, and without their help the rest of its crew could not possibly control it. Even now the Hawk pilots were still shooting arrows, taking their revenge. It would soon be over.

Marcellinus brought his attention back to earth. The Mongol heavies had disengaged from the Roman front line and were cantering back across the grass. Once they were out of the way, the Mongol horse archers again brought their terrible bows to bear, firing into his ranks.

Shit. Too much was happening at once. "We must change out the front line!" Marcellinus snapped to Sollonius, but Appius Gallus was already on it. The third and fourth lines were stepping forward with scuta raised to allow their fellows to rotate out. The next Mongol assault would face fresh legionaries. Those men who had already fought could rest.

Marcellinus would get no more signals from his doomed Sky Lantern, and it would take a while to launch another. "How do the Second and Third fare?" he asked Aulus.

"How the hell would I know?" said his adjutant.

Ignoring the insubordination—time might be of the essence—Marcellinus looked back along the ranks of his army. The cohorts of First Tribune Aurelius Dizala had given little ground in the face of the Shappan infantry assault. The Mongol heavies were wheeling and would soon be back in another terrifying attack.

He coughed as a wave of black smoke blew past. To Takoda, he said: "What's happening with Aelfric on the left? Find out."

"I will." Takoda spurred his horse and rode off.

Marcellinus had not consciously heard a trumpet signal for some time. Then again, he'd been busy. "Call for news," he told Aulus. "Learn what you can. Then come tell me. I'm going to the center front with Sollonius. And bad-mouth me one more time, soldier, and I'll leave you bleeding in the dirt."

Aulus was panting. Beneath his bluster, his adjutant was terrified. Now he gulped. "Sir, yes, sir. Sorry, sir."

"Better." Marcellinus nodded curtly, applied his heels to his horse's flanks, and galloped along the rear of the Second and Third, looking for Aurelius Dizala.

The Cahokian force under Tahtay and Wahchintonka had also come under heavy assault from the Mongol cavalry and had been pushed back. Now, thanks to defensive interference from the Ninth Syrian and a heroic and costly countercharge from Mahkah's Second Cahokian, they were advancing again to rejoin the Sixth. And nobody had heard anything from Hanska or her warriors since the battle had begun.

"Juno," Marcellinus said to Enopay, who had brought him this news and other dispatches as he and Sollonius stood dismounted at the rear of the Third Cohort. Battlefield confusion was growing. Marcellinus had tried to get to the front lines, where Dizala's cohorts were still grinding against the Shappa Ta'atani in the slog of the melee, but the press of soldiers was too great. Instead, he had diverted to give encouragement to the centurions of Statius Paulinus's Fourth Cohort, who had faced an onslaught from the Mongol cavalry of the same force and fury that the First had experienced, but at the cost of many more men. They had been pushed back fifty feet but had held there, largely because the Fifth was behind them and they couldn't retreat any farther. Bodies, Roman and Mongol, littered the battlefield in front of their line.

The Mongols had dropped back to mount fresh horses and regroup and were returning to formation, preparing to move in again. "You know what you face," Marcellinus had concluded to the Fourth. "Set more spears. Farther forward. Pull *their* spears, yank the verpa off their horses. But watch out for the barbs on those spears."

"Sir, yes, sir," said the centurions.

Marcellinus saluted them. "Give them hell. Make them bleed. Show these bastards how Roma can fight."

The men cheered him, which at least showed they still had animus, battle spirit. Marcellinus had nodded as if it were his due, as a commander must, and then had seen Enopay running nimbly through the Ninth Cohort. Enopay had waved the hand-talk for *news* just as soon as he had seen Marcellinus and was now giving him that news, for what it was worth.

"Also, they shot down our Sky Lantern."

"I saw that," Marcellinus said.

"Do we launch another?"

Marcellinus surely wanted to. Only a Sky Lantern could tell him what was going on farther away on the battlefield. "Did Chogan live?"

"Yes, but he is hurt. Broken leg, broken arm."

Marcellinus breathed a huge sigh of relief. "Good. All right. Ask Chogan and Sintikala, or whoever's in charge of Raven and Hawk at the moment, whether we can spare Hawks to stay close and protect the Sky Lanterns next time a Serpent or Firebird comes from the enemy—"

"Never mind." Enopay pointed. A new Sky Lantern was already rising over the rear of Marcellinus's army.

"Talk to the Hawks anyway," Marcellinus said. "And make sure we get every signal we can out of that Lantern before it gets blown out of the sky as well."

Enopay's eyes widened in alarm. "Yes, sir."

Had that sounded cold? Well, they were at war.

A roar came from behind him. From the Shappa Ta'atani. Marcellinus turned. "Jove. I hate complicated battles."

"I hate all of them," Enopay said fervently. "Oh, here's Napayshni."

Napayshni was running toward them as best he could, favoring his wounded leg. "Where the hell is your horse, Napayshni?"

"I sent it to Tahtay," Napayshni panted. "The First Cahokian has rejoined."

And indeed, here came Tahtay himself, cantering along the rear of the Sixth Cohort, sitting astride Napayshni's horse as stiffly as if he were carved from wood.

Cahokia's war chief was not a relaxed horseman, and Marcellinus sometimes marveled that he could persuade his steeds to move at all, since his discomfort and lack of confidence were so apparent to man and beast.

"Hotah." Tahtay saluted. "You still live, at least. And Enopay, too." His eyes looked haunted.

Marcellinus nodded impatiently. "Where is the First Cahokian?"

"A mile distant." Tahtay pointed.

"Hard or easy?"

"An easy mile now. The turmae of your Syrians chased the Mongols away from us. We wanted to come to hand to hand with them, but they stayed at bow distance." Tahtay spit. "Cowards."

Marcellinus shook his head. "The First is fresh? You have not fought yet today?"

"Bows and arrows only; I told you."

"How would you like to fight Shappa Ta'atani?"

If it were possible, Tahtay's face grew even grimmer. "Now?"

"Yes, of course now."

Marcellinus looked back at his front line. Aurelius Dizala and his centurions and optios had restored some order among his men but were still losing ground. Marcellinus glanced around. "Quickly, Tahtay. The Mongol heavies are about to charge again. I only have moments. Bring the First Cahokian and Wahchintonka's auxiliaries through to fight the Shappans. Yes?"

Tahtay looked forward and back, measuring distances. "So Mizipian kills Mizipian again?"

"Just as the Shappans killed Ocatani. Or have you forgotten?"

"I have forgotten nothing." The war chief looked down at Marcellinus, his eyes troubled, and for a moment Marcellinus thought his young friend was going to say something else or even refuse the order.

They did not have time for that. "Tahtay. Pull yourself together. Get moving."

"Mongols charging, sir," said Sollonius. "Lights flowing through the line of heavies as before. Praetor?"

Tahtay blanched at the sight of the Mongol line bearing down on them. "Merda . . . I'll bring the First." He kicked ineffectually at his horse's flanks and, when it did nothing, swore and jumped off it. "Keep your damned horse, Napayshni." He sprinted away.

"Here we go, shit," Sollonius said. "Arrows coming, shield up, shield *up*!" He lunged forward, raising his shield in front of Marcellinus. "Here we go again—"

"Breach!" Marcellinus shouted, and stepped back smartly. The rear of the Third Cohort was bulging out toward them. The last ranks were being pushed back, and now they began to break.

That meant that the front line was breaking, too.

"Fuck," Marcellinus said to Sollonius.

"Yes, sir," his adjutant replied automatically.

Marcellinus turned to Enopay. "Didn't I order you to go talk to the Hawks?"

"Uh, yes. Sorry. I was worried about Tahtay. He seems . . . not himself."

Marcellinus handed Enopay the reins of his horse. "Go. Take this back past the Ninth Cohort and *stay there*."

Enopay looked uncertainly up at the Thessalian. "Yes, sir."

"Sollonius, you're with me." Marcellinus strode toward the exploding rear of the Third Cohort.

Marcellinus was to learn later that the Shappa Ta'atani had literally taken a battering ram to the front of the Third Cohort. Having seen the rams used by the Sixth Ferrata in knocking down the gates of Ocatan, they had experimented with using the idea themselves.

And then they had brought liquid flame, presumably of their own manufacture, and placed a liberal quantity of it on the front of their ram.

They had slammed the front of the Roman line with a battering ram that had then burst into flame, searing the legionaries to either side of it. The shock had forced the Roman files apart. The Shappans had followed up with a credible impression of a Roman cuneus, the wedge or pig's-head formation that had broken many a mob of barbarians in Roma's past. And so, after a melee that had lasted nearly an hour with little advantage in ground and position, they had managed to shatter the Third Cohort.

At last, here came the First Cahokian. Tahtay led them, jogging easily out front. Akecheta was running at the front left corner of the cohort as a good centurion should, but was panting visibly. His men were equipped with Roman breastplates, Roman armor, Roman helmets. Most carried their gladii to stop them from banging against their legs in their sheaths as they ran. Others wore their swords at their waists and carried clubs, short spears, axes.

Marcellinus was not about to object. Let each Cahokian wield the weapon he felt most comfortable with.

"Form up!" he shouted to Tahtay and Akecheta even before they arrived. Akecheta began snapping out orders as Marcellinus turned to Furnius. "Have the Third Cohort prepare to break off and fall back in good order. I'm bringing the First Cahokian in to relieve them."

Furnius looked alarmed. "Bringing? No, sir. You stay back."

Ignoring that, Marcellinus continued. "Tell Dizala. But first make sure the First and Fourth Cohorts and everyone behind them continues to stand firm against the Mongol charge."

Marcellinus badly needed to be in three places at once. But that wasn't possible. For now, he would have to trust Appius Gallus and his tribunes. Ahead of him Aurelius Dizala had been in close affray for what? An hour?

Someone touched his arm. "Hotah?"

Soldiers were not supposed to lay hands on their commanding officers in the field. It was all Marcellinus could

do to stop himself from shaking off Tahtay's hand.
"What?"

Tahtay was looking past him with troubled eyes. Marcellinus glanced where the boy was staring, but it was
just a battle, and a battle they had to get into very soon
now—

Damn it.

For all Tahtay's newfound maturity, for all his keen
sense in council with the Imperator and the Praetors, for
all that he gave the impression of being a magnificent
leader . . . today was still only Tahtay's second large-
scale battle.

And in his first he had been beaten to the ground, his
leg smashed, almost crippled.

Tahtay's grip on Marcellinus's arm was strengthening,
and Marcellinus recognized the look in his war chief's
eyes. Tahtay was losing his nerve.

Futete. After all this?

He needed Kimimela here to stiffen Tahtay's spine.
Why hadn't he thought of that? It would have been ten
times better to have Kimimela whispering her strength
and determination into Tahtay's ear than to have her
careering dangerously around above them in the skies.

"We need to crush them, war chief," Marcellinus said
bluntly. "Twice now the Shappa Ta'atani have betrayed
Cahokia. They have murdered Ocatani. And before that
they would have murdered the First Cahokian on the
river had we given them the chance. Is it not so?"

"Of course," Tahtay said, but his response was auto-
matic. He was sweating hard, looking neither back at
his men nor up at Marcellinus but longingly to where
the Third Cohort was even now withdrawing in ranks
and streaming past the First Cahokian.

"Forward! Walk! Close order!" In the meantime,
Akecheta had gotten the First aligned in ranks. Dustu
was in the first line along with many other warriors
Marcellinus had fought alongside.

For more reasons than Marcellinus had time to count,
they needed to crush the Shappa Ta'atani. They were a

dangerous distraction, forcing his attention away from the Mongols. The Sixth Ironclads were fully taxed in resisting the Mongol attacks. He needed the Cahokians to take care of the Shappans.

"Tahtay? We have to smash them. Today-now. Head on. And you must lead the First. You are war chief of Cahokia."

"Yes."

What could Marcellinus say? *Don't be afraid?*

Marcellinus leaned in. "Tahtay, I am not Kimimela. But she is right here, behind us both, and she is telling you not to be an idiot or she'll smack your head. Now get your damned hand off my arm and lead your men into battle. Kill Shappa Ta'atani."

Tahtay took a step back, looked behind him.

Hating himself, Marcellinus grabbed the war chief by the shoulders and physically shook him. "Tahtay! Stand up and act like a man. Hurit is watching. And your father."

Tahtay turned slowly to stare at Marcellinus, his disbelief turning to shock and anger, and Marcellinus realized he had gone too far. "Tahtay, I—"

Tahtay lashed out, his fist swinging up in a ruthless uppercut. With his Roman helmet on, Marcellinus's chin and nose were the only unprotected areas of his face.

Marcellinus barely reacted quickly enough. Tahtay's fist struck his cheek rather than his chin, knocking him sideways.

Furnius swore, drew his gladius, leaped forward.

"Stop!" Marcellinus flung up his arms to shove his adjutant away. "Halt! Drop back."

Tahtay's eyes blazed. "Fuck you, Hotah. When we are done here, you are a dead man."

Marcellinus nodded. "As you say, war chief."

"You use my father against me? And Hurit? And next you will say Mahkah and Mikasi? Who else? Is there anyone you will not use to get what you want, to make me fight your Roman war?"

Marcellinus's mouth went dry. "Mahkah?"

"Yes, Mahkah, who with Hanska and Takoda saved us from the Iroqua. Who stood over us both and took wounds for us. Do not pretend you did not know."

"Tahtay." Marcellinus seized the war chief again. "What the hell happened to Mahkah?"

"Enopay did not tell you?"

"Tahtay . . ."

"We were assaulted by Mongols. The Ninth Syrian and the Second Cahokian came in to help us, with the Second trying to be stalwart and courageous, to keep up with your Romans. Mahkah coming in between the Mongols and me, Dustu, Akecheta, his other brothers. He fell, Hotah. He is dead, destroyed. Mahkah is dead. Are you happy now? You and your great war and your great Romans?"

"Tahtay." Dustu had seen what was going on and come striding back. "The Wanageeska is not your enemy. Come. Lead us. We need you."

Tahtay blinked and looked up at Marcellinus again. The weight did not drop from his shoulders as it did when Kimimela spoke, but his eyes had cleared just a little. Perhaps his anger had helped. "Later, Hotah. We will talk more."

Marcellinus nodded curtly. Tahtay stepped away.

Mahkah was dead?

Damn it.

But they were at war. Many more lives were at stake. Marcellinus had lost men before, and he would lose more today. For now he needed to harden his heart. Later there would be time to grieve.

In front of him, the melee had ceased. The Third Cohort were streaming past them in two groups. The Shappans had stepped away to breathe and form up again. They knew better than to spill into a gap between two columns of Romans, and they, too, must have welcomed the respite. Tired and wounded warriors limped back from the Shappan front line. Newer, fresher warriors came forward to take their places. Among them

Marcellinus recognized some of the clan chiefs he had feasted with on the Shappan Temple Mound during the Green Corn Festival. There were the chiefs of Beaver and Deer, and off to the side, bent forward and winded, was the young chief of the Snake clan.

Bodies lay in the area between the two armies. Romans were dragging their dead back, and after a pause the Shappans did likewise.

From his left and right he felt the shock and heard the furor as the Mongol heavies again slammed into the Roman front line. Again came the crackle of small explosions from Jin salt weapons. "Great Jove . . ."

He tried to put it out of his mind. One fight at a time.

And then the sound of mounted warfare retreated from his consciousness, for Son of the Sun had stepped forward into the gap between the two armies.

Suddenly Marcellinus felt a rage of a strength that startled him, coupled with a wave of fear.

The combination rocked him. For all his most formidable opponents—the Huron at the Battle for Cahokia, Avenaka on the Great Mound just after his murder of Great Sun Man, and Son of the Sun himself at their last face-to-face meeting on the banks of the Mizipi—Marcellinus had felt a wariness and a respect. This sudden fear was a new thing, and it shook him.

Had this land changed him? Had he gained family and community at the cost of his courage in battle?

If so, he might be about to lose all of it. And die with Tahtay's hatred uppermost in his mind.

If only Tahtay hadn't told him about Mahkah's death. Marcellinus would give anything not to have that appalling realization in his mind, distracting him from the here and now.

An explosion came from far to his left. Another grenade of that damned Jin salt. Legionaries howled in pain. White smoke wafted over the battle line, but it did not buckle. Good men. Brave men.

Son of the Sun was marshaling his front line, keeping a wary eye on the First Cahokian, where Akecheta and

Tahtay were doing the same thing. The Cahokian and Shappan forces stood a scant twenty yards apart. Warriors whooped, preparing themselves to fight. Some Shappans held bows, although once the fray began again, they'd get off just a single arrow before having to drop the weapon and bring up a club or an ax.

The two Hesperian armies looked well matched. Some Shappans wore the Roman breastplates and greaves that they had been given by the Sixth Ferrata to help them take Ocatan. Others wore the traditional Hesperian wooden or matting armor.

Not one wore a helmet. Perhaps the Shappans considered them unmanly. It was a choice they might regret. Also, none carried Roman shields or weapons, clearly preferring the clubs and axes of their heritage. The Shappans as a nation wore less war paint than did the Cahokians; instead their faces bore more tattoos and vicious-looking scarifications. Some looked horrific, like patched-up human beings from a nightmare.

By comparison, the First Cahokian was neat and orderly in its use of Roman weapons and helmets. But if anything, their uniformity made them look odd, un-Hesperian, almost effete compared with the Shappa Ta'atani.

Son of the Sun was a large man and heavyset, but today he appeared a giant. He wore wooden chest armor and over it the copper gorget of his office. In his right hand he held a mace, not of ceremonial chert but a longer, heavier, and more vicious battle weapon of hard wood with a large rounded rock set into its business end. His arms and legs were bare, showing off his hard musculature in addition to a daunting array of tattoos and scarifications. And as Marcellinus looked along the rallying ranks of the First Cahokian, Son of the Sun finally turned and caught sight of him.

The Shappan war chief's mouth cracked open into a broad, manic smile. He took a single step forward. Behind him, his men were lined up and ready.

With a new shock, Marcellinus saw that his gladius

hung from the chief's waist, Marcellinus's gladius with the ornate hilt from his campaign against the Khwar-ezmian Sultanate. The sword he had traded for Taianita on the riverbank outside Shappa Ta'atan.

Holding his gaze, Son of the Sun drew it now, pointed it at Marcellinus, and waggled it. With his other hand he beckoned.

The war chief's meaning was clear. It was an invitation to single combat.

Only a fraction of the First Cahokian had been with Marcellinus on the river. Akecheta had, of course, and now broke off from his haranguing of the First to look worriedly at Marcellinus. Tahtay was looking back and forth between them, perplexed, and Marcellinus remembered that Tahtay had never before seen the Shappan war chief.

Marcellinus assumed a look of imperious contempt and raised his arms to make the hand-talk in the same phrases the chief had used to him on the riverbank: *You want fight? Then we all fight.* Unable to resist, he followed this with an obscene gesture, and the First Cahokians who saw it broke out in that tense, aggressive laughter sometimes heard on fields of war. Out loud, Marcellinus shouted "First Cahokian! Let us slay the traitors of Shappa Ta'atan who murdered our brothers and sisters at Ocatan!"

The First Cahokian growled and braced. Tahtay nodded to Akecheta.

"Maintain the line! Walk forward! Pila! Kill Shappa Ta'atani!" Akecheta bellowed. His commands were in Latin, as were almost all battle commands to the First Cahokian, and quizzical expressions briefly crossed the faces of some of the Shappa Ta'atani.

Son of the Sun shrugged disdainfully, sheathed the gladius, and raised his mace. His voice boomed. "Kill Cahokians."

The Cahokian front line took one step forward and cast their pila. At the same moment the Shappa Ta'atani threw their own spears and charged forward after them.

The First Cahokian's discipline held. They stepped up to face the Shappan charge, as cool as any Romans, thrusting their scuta forward. Those with thrusting spears or swords swung them, jabbing down over the top of the scuta at their enemies. Many of the Shappans were quick enough to avoid the thrusts and bring their clubs and axes down on Cahokian shields. The lines engaged, howling profanities.

Despite his earlier moment of nerves Tahtay had thrown himself forward with the rest of the First. His sword met a Shappan tomahawk and smashed it away; the young man slashed downward almost immediately to cleave the wooden armor of his assailant.

But that was all that Marcellinus saw, because Son of the Sun was barreling toward him.

Marcellinus raised his shield and broke into a run. If he was standing still when Son of the Sun impacted him, he might be bowled over. Beside and behind him other Cahokians surged, with Furnius drawing a blade and throwing himself forward, too.

Marcellinus and Son of the Sun met at something like full running speed, Marcellinus ramming the boss of his shield into his opponent as hard as he could. At the same time Son of the Sun leaped, bringing down that gigantic stone mace.

Son of the Sun's stone club met the steel-lined rim of the shield, and the impact of his charge knocked Marcellinus backward. However, the momentum of the moving shield boss with Marcellinus's weight behind it had smashed Son of the Sun's arm back into his body and thrown him off balance as well. The Shappan war chief bounced away and crashed into one of his own warriors. He fell onto his right knee, not quite tumbling over entirely.

The back of Marcellinus's helmet banged against the breastplate of the man behind him as he fell. Flat on his back, he found himself glimpsing sky through a long fissure in his shield. Son of the Sun's blow had bent the steel rim and cracked the wood of the shield from top to bottom. He swung it anyway, just as Son of the Sun pushed himself up and brought the mace down again.

The shield exploded into a mess of wood and splinters. Marcellinus threw the remains aside and tried to roll away, but all around him were the legs of warriors. The two armies were fighting at close quarters, and he had almost no space to maneuver. Furnius was no longer beside him, and it was a mercy that Marcellinus had not already been kicked in the head.

It was fear as much as dexterity that brought Marcellinus onto his feet again: fear of Son of the Sun's speed, fear of being trampled in the scrimmage. Right beside him a Shappan and a Cahokian wrestled for possession of an ax, kicking and barging each other. Just six feet away Son of the Sun tried to swing, but two of his own warriors blundered into him, carrying him back.

The Shappan front line drove forward again. Shappan warriors lunged. With his sword in his hand but no shield, Marcellinus shoved against them. All around was the reek of sweat, leather, smoke, and blood.

It was almost absurd. Only a few feet separated Son of the Sun from Marcellinus, but neither could bring his weapons up to attack. Warriors of the First Cahokian were coming to defend and protect him. Furnius was yelling in Latin—"Let me through! Let me through!"—but the Cahokians could not have complied even if they had understood.

Similarly, Shappan warriors were attempting to get past Son of the Sun to attack Marcellinus. One brave almost succeeded in shoving through the throng, and Marcellinus recognized the chief of the Beaver clan, a man who had shown him no harm or disrespect in Shappa Ta'atan, one of the few clan chiefs there he had liked.

With a strange howl the whole front line surged again like a tidal wave, carrying them with it. Marcellinus snatched his gladius back before he punctured the Cahokian brave who was pressed against him on his right, and then the swell of battle thrust him toward Son of the

Sun again, jamming them up against each other without either managing to get in a good blow. Son of the Sun loomed over him, baring his teeth, and again Marcellinus felt that baffling terror.

Fear was the killer. Fear would slow his brain and his arm and leave him dead in the dirt. Where was his battle ardor, that berserker fury that had sustained him in hot war throughout his life?

His arms almost pinned, Marcellinus aimed a head butt. Son of the Sun, still grinning that insane battle grin, merely leaned away. And now the war chief thrust hard at the men who crowded him on either side, trying to free up space.

Very well. Marcellinus could not fight the tide, and he could not wrestle a thousand men. And if he did not face his fear, he might as well be dead already.

Marcellinus relaxed. Gravity, and the pressure of the bodies around him, dragged him down. The sky disappeared, and he saw only tunics and steel and heard the grunting of men shoving and punching each other as best they could.

He was on the ground, and all around him was a snake pit of legs, moccasins, and mud. He clutched his sword close, trying to guard his head and keep his presence of mind.

There. Son of the Sun's gladius, Marcellinus's old jeweled gladius that he knew so well, hung down to his left, only four men away from him.

He slashed at the legs between him and that gladius, careless of whether they belonged to friend or foe. A knee cracked into his helmet, momentarily dizzying him, and his anger began to build. He scrambled forward through the mud. In the process he shoved a brave over, and then another. The second landed on top of him in a crunch of pain and then rolled away. Marcellinus kept going, relentless and bloody-minded.

He was buffeted sideways. He took another kick to the helmet. "Fuck!" Too many of those and it would be all over. His first instinct was to hamstring the offender, but no, he might be a Cahokian, even someone Marcellinus knew.

Something else plinked against his helmet. It was his own gladius with the ornate hilt, still hanging from Son of the Sun's belt. The war chief was directly above him. With no further thought Marcellinus rolled onto his back and thrust upward with the sword he held in his hand. Blood cascaded down over his face.

The mace came thumping down into the mud by his head. Son of the Sun glared down at him from a sea of arms and heads and weapons with painfully bright streaks of white sky behind it, and mercifully Marcellinus kept his grip on his gladius as yet another warrior tripped over him.

Marcellinus stabbed upward into Son of the Sun's abdomen. Rolled and stabbed again as the mace almost took his head off. Twisted and slashed deep into Son of the Sun's thigh.

Son of the Sun crashed down almost on top of him. The mace was no longer in his hands, but he would not have been able to swing it in such a confined space anyway. Instead the Shappan chief had drawn the jeweled gladius. He thrust it forward, and its blade skated off Marcellinus's breastplate; Son of the Sun had been aiming for his guts but had had his blow knocked aside by the scrum of people above them.

Marcellinus's head rang yet again as he was hit from behind. Moments later he was kicked in the back, but his rage was now all directed forward, and his pugio had appeared in his hand without him having any memory of drawing it.

Son of the Sun thrust the gladius at Marcellinus's throat. Marcellinus was in danger of being killed by his own weapon.

Marcellinus had nowhere to retreat to. He had to grab at the sword blade and push it away with his bare hand. Its sharp edge scored a bloody line along his palm and across the bony edge of his wrist, and again he barely noticed the pain.

Marcellinus jabbed his pugio into Son of the Sun's face, and the war chief roared as it sliced into his nose. He rammed his knee into Marcellinus's gut. Marcellinus gasped, all the air driven out of him, but his fury made up for it. He twisted and thrust forward, and the point of his pugio slid into Son of the Sun's windpipe.

The war chief's eyes went wide. He gurgled and punched at Marcellinus, who ducked his head just in time. Son of the Sun's fist slammed into his helmet.

Marcellinus wrenched sideways with what remained of his strength, and the pugio came free. He leaned in and stared into his enemy's eyes for one second, two . . . and the hatred he saw there pulled his remaining reason from him, and he slashed again at the Shappan chief's throat like a man possessed.

Hands came down and grabbed at Marcellinus's shoulders. Furnius had found him. Marcellinus resisted. He wanted to be sure that Son of the Sun was dead. But he certainly was or would be in moments; he lolled back, his face suddenly vacant, and when one of his own Shappans tripped and toppled over the war chief, he did not react at all.

More hands came down. Friends or enemies? Aside from his bloody pugio the nearest weapon was his jeweled gladius, and thát was out of arm's reach. Marcellinus lunged for it anyway but could not get to it.

He didn't care. He didn't want it back now anyway. What good were jewels to him? What good the memories?

Instead, he grabbed the copper gorget from Son of the Sun's chest. He tore it free and thrust it into his sleeve. Only then did Marcellinus allow himself to be dragged up and away from the body of the treacherous chieftain.

CHAPTER 23

YEAR TEN, PLANTING MOON

Furnius pulled Marcellinus to his feet while Takoda took his other side, shield in hand, protecting him. Around them Cahokians and Shappa Ta'atani still hacked away at one another. Marcellinus allowed his adjutants to draw him back out of the combat zone, and as he did so, his eyes met those of the young Snake clan chief in the third row of the Shappan line, his expression unreadable. Did he know that Marcellinus had just slain his chief?

Furnius and Takoda hustled him back. Dustu had appeared, holding out a gladius in the rear guard, his eyes alert for danger. As soon as they were clear, he nodded to Marcellinus and ran back into the fight.

The breath had returned to Marcellinus's body, and with it harsh aches in his chest, sharp pain in his sliced-up hand, and the throb of bruising in his back and shoulders. It didn't matter. "Got the bastard," Marcellinus said.

"Back, back, back farther . . ." Furnius was shaken, almost babbling, and now Marcellinus saw the wounds to his adjutant's arms and shoulders, the blood pouring down his leg. For the first time he wondered how old Furnius was, whether he'd seen much action before. "Jupiter, sir, are you crazy? Back, back to your guards."

"Easy, soldier. None of that was your fault."

"Fine for you to say. The Imperator—"

Furnius's face creased, and he dropped to his knees and retched.

Yes, if Marcellinus had died, Hadrianus would have taken it out on his adjutants' hides. Marcellinus pulled down another deep breath, winced, and patted the man rather distantly on the shoulder.

He was standing between centuries of the Eighth and Ninth who were waiting in reserve to be sent in. Their shields rested against their legs, but all clutched their pila or gladii, their eyes wide and darting. Half were staring at him in open amazement.

Marcellinus raised himself up onto his toes, peering out over the continuing melee. What he saw made little sense to him. "What happened?"

"The hand came in," Takoda said.

"Whose hand?" Marcellinus shook his head and looked more closely.

While Marcellinus had been pursuing his vendetta in the middle of the line, the Shappans' right flank had collapsed. They were still engaged in hand-to-hand fighting, but it appeared that they also were battling an enemy beside and behind them. In the center of the line the tide was turning, and the First Cahokian had the other flank of the Shappa Ta'atani almost enveloped.

Then he looked up. Macaws were mobbing the Shappa Ta'atani, their red and green feathers dazzling in the air. At least ten Macaws, along with a single Eagle that looped back and forth over the Shappans just a couple of hundred feet up. Aboard it was Taianita, shooting arrow after arrow into the bodies of her former tormenters from the air while her two fellow pilots focused on steering the craft and not colliding with the much faster Macaws.

The Eagle was low enough that a stray Mongol arrow from the battlefield might easily reach it. Marcellinus grimaced, but this was hardly a day when he could criticize anyone else for recklessness.

Takoda peered at him. "Wanageeska? You understand? The People of the Hand, the warriors from the southwest. They came to fight the Shappa Ta'atani."

"How the hell . . . ?" The Hand were supposed to be on the right wing of the Third Legion, forming the strong link between the Third and the 27th. Miles away across the Grass.

But sure enough, he could see them now, the brutal warriors of the Hand carving a deep hole in the side of the Shappa Ta'atani phalanx. Half of them were fighting the Shappans while the other half guarded their own rear against the Mongols, and a dozen or more Macaws were spitting arrows into the whole mess.

Takoda waved his hand, a gesture meaning *All changed*. "And now they are here. You remember that they have warred with the Shappa Ta'atani before, no?"

Furnius stood, wiping his mouth, all business again. He frowned up at the leftmost of two Sky Lanterns, whose crew appeared to be signaling down.

Enopay arrived at a run, taking in Marcellinus's disheveled and bloody appearance. By the expression in the boy's eyes, Marcellinus must look terrible. "Report, Enopay."

"Futete, Eyanosa . . . What happened?"

"Gods, what do you think happened? I got in a fight."

"Do you need Chumanee?"

"Report, Enopay. Now."

Enopay shook his head in disbelief. "Uh, yes, sir."

Furnius broke in, reporting what the Sky Lanterns were telling him. "Shappans folding, and Mongol cavalry falling back."

"Falling back?" Marcellinus could surely use a higher vantage point right now. "Where's my horse?"

"You told me to take it away," Enopay said.

"It's probably at the back with your *guards*," Furnius added pointedly.

"Definitely falling back? Not just regrouping to attack again?"

He already knew the answer. From his left the remains of the Fourth Cohort were cheering. Others burst for-

ward into a run to fall on the left flank of the hapless
Shappa Ta'atani.

Taianita's Eagle shot over him, losing height. The
front line of the Ninth jumped back as it came to ground.
She landed on her feet, then crumpled; the two other
pilots both dropped to their knees under the full weight
of the craft. Legionaries jumped to lift the wing off their
shoulders.

Was Taianita injured? No, Marcellinus saw no blood.
She was just exhausted.

But she had been in the air right over the Shappan
army. He needed to know what she'd seen. He gestured
to two of his nearest foot soldiers. "Go help her. Bring
her here. Carry her if you need to. But be gentle with
her."

"The Shappans have broken," Furnius said.

Marcellinus heard a roar and turned. It was true. The
Shappa Ta'atani ranks had sheared and fractured, and
warriors were fleeing away across the battlefield with
the brightly feathered warriors of the Hand in hot pursuit, Macaws in the air as well as braves on the ground.
The First Cahokian left them to it, some sinking to their
knees, dog-tired, others cheering and hurling insults.

And the Mongol cavalry certainly had withdrawn. All
along the front of the Sixth Ferrata his legionaries were
standing down, his centurions wiping their brows, taking stock of who in their ranks was alive, who was dead.

"Taianita?"

His legionaries had brought her, one on each side, half
supporting and half carrying her. Her eyes were wild.
She looked gleeful and chagrined, an odd swirl of emotions, and by the way she clutched her stomach Marcellinus wondered if she was about to be sick like Furnius.
Over her shoulder he saw Napayshni riding toward
them between the lines of the cohorts.

"Killing them," Taianita said with something like awe.

"What?"

Her eyes burned, her glee unholy. "The Hand. And
then the Mongols."

Napayshni arrived. "The Mongols turned on the Shappa Ta'atani as they fled. Hacking them down from horseback." He looked shaken.

"The Shappans? They weren't attacking the Hand?"

"No; the Hand retreated when they saw the Mongols bearing down on them. They're safe behind our line again. But the Shappans . . . slaughtered."

Marcellinus wasn't surprised. "The Mongols despise cowardice. And failure."

"I killed a lot of them first," Taianita said viciously. "Arrows. Took them down. But I didn't see Son of the Sun." She kicked at a tussock of grass. "Didn't see him. Didn't."

Marcellinus pulled the copper gorget from his sleeve and held it out to her. "Taianita, I killed Son of the Sun. I sent him to hell."

She stared at him for a second, and then her mood immediately broke and she threw her arms around him, sobbing. Marcellinus looked down at her, simultaneously moved and baffled.

Enopay's eyes were troubled. "The Mongols kill their own allies now?"

"Allies they consider worthless. They kill their own warriors, too, if they believe them to be cowards or unworthy. Taianita, please . . . Let me go. I have to talk with my tribunes and hear any dispatches that may have come in. Go back and rest. We will talk later. Yes?" Taianita released him, still sniffling. "Enopay, take Taianita back to the Thunderbird clan. Make sure someone looks after her. Takoda, go with them and then bring my horse to me." All of a sudden he felt exhausted.

"I will do it. Come." Enopay took Taianita's hand. She stood calmly now, brushing at her eyes with the other hand as if trying to absorb everything that had happened. "Is it over, Eyanosa?" the boy asked. "The war?"

"The battle, maybe, for today at least. We should go and find out." Marcellinus looked to see which of his other adjutants was nearby. "Aulus? If the battle really is over, have the tribunes assign squads to carts to start collecting our dead. Roman *and* Cahokian, mind. No distinction. Have them all brought to Forward Camp."

Marcellinus paused, then added, "Don't just spread the order and leave. Supervise the operation. Get it done. I'm holding you personally responsible."

Aulus gulped. "Sir, yes, sir."

He looked so ashen that Marcellinus almost regretted the order. But this might be a long campaign, and earlier Aulus had shown insubordination at one of the least opportune moments. After today, his adjutant would not make that mistake again.

Once they were sure the Mongols had left the field, the Imperator sounded the retreat and the news was carried from one end of the line to the other by cornu.

Marcellinus's trumpeters sent out the general order to stand down, at which point most of his legion and all the Cahokians dropped their weapons and sat down where they were, some in ranks, others scattered across the plains. Appius Gallus raised his eyebrows, but Marcellinus waved away his objections.

Gods, this had been a long, hot day, and if anything it was getting hotter. Marcellinus, his Sixth Ferrata, and his First Cahokian were completely spent. They could only hope that the Mongols were similarly weary.

Now that the scouts could easily bring dispatches again, Marcellinus learned more.

Just a few miles away from Marcellinus's battlefield the Legio III Parthica had spent its afternoon embroiled in a similar action. Uncomplicated by an infantry assault by Hesperian warriors, they had suffered wave after wave of mounted Mongol assaults all afternoon with little respite. They had sustained significant casualties, largely from arrow attacks, and had wrought damage on perhaps an equivalent number of Mongol light cavalrymen, a painful battle of attrition with no conclusive result.

It turned out that the Mongol cavalry had cut down

many of the fleeing Shappans in passing as they galloped back, but not all. The rest, the Mongols had merely contemptuously abandoned to their fate.

The tattered remains of the Shappa Ta'atani had fled to the Wemissori but had found no relief there. The Tlingit war canoes had retreated upriver with the rest of the Mongol army. The hapless and leaderless Shappa Ta'atani instead found the cohorts of the 27th that had been stationed on the flanks, soldiers who had spent all day guarding against the risk of an enveloping strike attack that had never come. Deprived of action while their comrades had spent the day fighting, Agrippa's men lost no time in rounding up and annihilating the Shappa Ta'atani. None survived.

Tahtay set off back to camp with his warriors of the Hesperian League without consulting Marcellinus. Marcellinus was not surprised. He would do his best to make his peace with the war chief later.

And just as Marcellinus was beginning to get really worried, Hanska appeared with her Third Cahokian Cohort from an entirely unexpected direction. They had assisted the People of the Hand with the latter half of their hazardous journey across the battlefield and then ducked around the rear of the Sixth to join up with the remains of Mahkah's Second.

Hanska had done all of this on her own initiative, totally disobeying the orders Marcellinus had given her. Because one of her best friends, Mahkah, had fallen in battle that day, Marcellinus doubted he would ever discipline her for it.

The Mongols made no attempt to retrieve the bodies of their dead. They just fell back and left a battlefield strewn with corpses.

Certainly the Romans would not expend the energy to give their enemies an honorable burial, but the bodies were gruesome to behold and many already stank. The horses shied away from them, and some of the legionaries did, too. The centurions drew straws, and the men of the losing centuries made a second pass with mules to loop ropes around the heels of the Mongol corpses and drag them off the killing fields.

It took the legions and auxiliary cohorts of the Roman alliance more than three hours to march back to Forward Camp and filter back into their barracks and tents. After getting his soldiers and warriors settled, Marcellinus headed to the hospital area to ensure that the wounded were getting good care. Only after that did he go to meet with his Imperator and the other Praetors and chiefs.

"Fuck this shit." Aelfric stormed into Marcellinus's tent. "They're not ready, and we're just getting them killed."

Marcellinus thought of the fresh-faced boys in the cohorts of the Sixth whose bodies were also still being carried from the battlefield. "Everyone has a first battle."

"And for some, it's their last." Aelfric slumped into a chair. "Dear sweet Christ, I thought I was ready to come back to the legions. I'd had my little holiday out with the wild men and was ready to come home."

"Wild men?"

"Barbarians. Hesperians." He wilted a little under Marcellinus's frown. "Sorry. I guess I've grown unused to . . . casualties."

"Then you'd better get used to them again."

Aelfric stared. "Well. You certainly turned hard again fast." He leaned forward. "This was *Mahkah*."

"I know who it was!"

Marcellinus felt the loss of Mahkah like a physical ache. He had first met Mahkah as a callow and uncoordinated youth of sixteen winters on the river on the way to Woshakee. Since then Mahkah had stayed by Marcellinus's side in battle in Cahokia, all the way down the Mizipi and up the Wemissori, across the Plains to the buffalo jump, and back to Cahokia again. He had saved Marcellinus's life, perhaps more than once. Mahkah had grown into a fine warrior and a fine man. And by giving that warrior his own command and an almost impossi-

ble job to do, Marcellinus had gotten him killed on the
first day of the war.

"Christ. I'm sorry."

Marcellinus blinked and looked up. After snapping at
Aelfric he had put his head in his hands and sunk down
into his chair. Now Aelfric was looking down at him
with concern in his eyes. "Sorry, man."

"Believe me," Marcellinus said with some difficulty,
then cleared his throat and began again. "Aelfric, believe me when I tell you that Mahkah's death was the
last thing I wanted and one of the biggest weights on my
mind at this moment."

"Aye." Aelfric sat back.

"But we're at war. Eventually we'll drink beer and
toast the men we've lost. For now, we just need to figure
out tomorrow." He studied the Briton's face.

"Give them to me, man," Aelfric said. "Let me have
them."

"Who?"

"Mahkah's Second Cahokian. What's left of 'em, anyway. Who else is going to command them?"

"Hanska, of course." Over half of the Second had
died that day, and Hanska had already ridden across the
battlefield in support of the survivors.

"Don't be daft. Hanska's even madder than you, and
she'll get them killed even quicker than Mahkah did."

"Good luck telling her that." Marcellinus was very
tired, and he still had a lot to do tonight. "Aelfric, you
have two cohorts of the Sixth to lead. And then you say
you're unprepared for casualties. And now you say you
want to lead the Second. Well, which is it? Do I have a
tribune or don't I?"

Aelfric glowered at him.

Marcellinus stared back. "If you're not up for this
anymore . . . Aelfric, if you choose to desert, I won't
send out men to look for you."

"Desert?" Aelfric stood abruptly. "Who mentioned
desertion? I'm staying. I'll lead the cohorts. But lots of
cohorts have attached cavalry. Give me the Second and

I'll lead them, too. They *know* me. Jesus, I rode with Mahkah all the time. Give them to anyone else and they're on *your* conscience."

"They're on my conscience anyway, thank you very much. And they're Cahokian. They go to Hanska unless she or Tahtay says otherwise."

Aelfric passed his hand in front of his eyes, looked at the roof of the tent as if praying, and then said: "All right. If you say so."

"And we still have work to do." Marcellinus stood, picked up some buffalo jerky, and looked at it for a moment. He really should eat something. "Round up Dizala and Appius Gallus and get back here with them as soon as you can. We need to plan."

Another long, awful pause descended. Aelfric stared at him, his face unreadable.

"Well?" Marcellinus demanded. They were at war, and either Marcellinus was in charge of his tribune or he was not. If not, he would need to find another one. He found himself running through names in his mind.

But eventually Aelfric nodded. "Sir, yes, sir." He saluted and stepped out of the tent.

After his meeting with Dizala, Aelfric, and Gallus, Marcellinus walked the camp. He found his legionaries and warriors surprisingly busy. Despite their arduous day or perhaps because of it, their blood was up. They were soldiers, after all, and they had waited a long time for this.

In the Roman part of the camp, Marcellinus found a quiet satisfaction at their day's work, which he felt they deserved. Some were ready to avenge today's deaths among their friends and comrades. Others had savored the intoxication of killing and wanted to kill again. All, having come so far and finally arrived on the field of battle, shared the feeling of armies throughout history: *Let's get this over with.*

Many were at the rudimentary shrines the legions had brought into the field: the temples of Sol Invictus and

Cybele, the prayer rail of the Christ-Risen, the dark thatched hut where the followers of the Mithraic cult performed their ceremonies. A surprising number stood at the shrine to Jupiter Imperator or paid their respects to the Aquilae of the three legions.

Over in the Hesperian part of the camp the mood was more lively. The braves had fought lightly armored and were more used to running and walking long distances, and so they had retained more energy.

The First Cahokian was celebrating its victory over the Shappa Ta'atani. The Ocatani among them, or those of them who had Ocatani friends and relatives, felt that they had avenged their past defeat, somehow eliding the odd fact that they were surrounded by men of the Sixth Ironclads who had inflicted the major role in that defeat.

If the First Cahokian was happy, the Wolf Warriors, who had been deprived of a war against the Iroqua and then of a second war against Roma, were almost delirious with joy. Those who had taken Mongol or Shappan scalps paraded their trophies with pride. Those who had yet to score bragged of the bravery they would exhibit on the morrow. Where the Romans were swapping vile jokes and relaxing over games of knucklebones, the Cahokians were singing and drumming their songs to Red Horn, and once the brightly decorated People of the Hand showed up at the party, it seemed quite possible that war dances could break out at any moment.

Despite the many deaths they had suffered this day, no one seemed cowed. All were ready to fight again.

As Marcellinus walked around that night exchanging comments with his legionaries and warriors, slapping backs and arms, exchanging jokes and insults, he did not come across Tahtay, Kimimela, Enopay, or Taianita. He suspected they were hiding together somewhere and wondered what they were talking about. He did find Sintikala, who was engaged in technical discussions with Demothi, Chenoa, and Manius Ifer about how they might speed the deployment of the launching towers farther into the field. By the set of Sintikala's shoulders and her frown he could tell that her day had been taxing. After listening for a few minutes and offering some suggestions, none particularly profound, he faded away into the background to let the experts talk.

And as his friendship with Aelfric appeared strained and Isleifur Bjarnason was off drinking illicit Hesperian beer with the other Norse scouts—a fact Marcellinus decided not to notice—that left him alone again.

The day on the battlefield had been hot and muggy, and if anything it was even hotter now. Marcellinus decided that perhaps he could be forgiven for going back to his tent to lie down.

They expected to fight the Mongols again the very next day. But it was not to be. That night they experienced at first hand the volatility of weather conditions on the Great Plains of Nova Hesperia.

Although they had paid it little attention in the thick of battle, the heat and humidity had been building through the afternoon. The light breeze of the morning and noontime had dropped completely by midafternoon, and that had made their trek home a chore. The evening was sweltering and unpleasant, broken at midnight by an intense thunderstorm that for a few nightmare moments convinced half of Forward Camp that they were again under attack from Mongol black powder bombs. After what seemed like an hour of almost continuous lightning the storm settled down into a steady downpour that lasted most of the night.

The next day dawned clear and much cooler with a fresh blue sky overhead, but the ground underfoot was a morass. They would not fight today, and probably not the next day or even the day after that.

The rain had damped down the dust in the air and presumably helped wash the blood into the ground, but those were its only virtues. The tents of the men and the heavy canvas tarpaulins that had provided cover for the horses were soaked through where they had not blown away during the night. Some of the fences around the camp had subsided. One of the Wakinyan towers had been struck by lightning, sending a tremor of superstitious fear through some of the Hesperians, though not those of the Thunderbird and Hawk clans, who were more pragmatic about weather than their earthbound fellows.

The aggressive energy the men had built up the previous day suddenly found itself with no outlet. The atmosphere in the camp quickly turned dark and bloody. By noon, Forward Camp was simmering like a pressure cooker. Fights broke out. A squabble between some Onondaga and Wolf Warriors turned into a vicious running battle. To avoid inflaming the situation any further Marcellinus ordered his legionaries of the Sixth out of the way; Tahtay, Wahchintonka, and the Tadodaho waded in with the First and Third Cahokian Cohorts and some handpicked Oneida to break it up, but by the time it was over three hundred warriors were dead.

As the other two Praetors largely washed their hands of what happened outside the central castra area where their own men were billeted, this naturally became Marcellinus's problem. Enopay might have approved of his solution. In principle such battles between allies within camp were punishable with death, but at the moment good warriors were at a premium. Instead, Marcellinus chose to seize the opportunity to help fix a persistent problem. The ringleaders and their accomplices literally got to shovel shit for the rest of the week.

"Seems the Mongols have found an easy way to defeat us," Isleifur Bjarnason said gloomily. "Just stick us in a swamp."

Marcellinus looked around him for eavesdroppers. The Viking was not the most tactful man in the camp. "The Mongols are wading in the same swamp."

"D'you think they're doing us the favor of killing one another as well?"

"Without doubt," Marcellinus said. "We'll march over tomorrow and pick up a few keepsakes off their corpses, then it's off home to Cahokia."

"Tomorrow?" Bjarnason poked the toe of his boot into the mud. "Right."

Ironically, that day had seen no casualties in the field. At dawn Hadrianus had sent out his scouts and skirmishers, but few got their horses any faster than a walk, and most of the scouts dismounted and walked beside their mounts to reduce the chances of injury. They met parties of enemy skirmishers patrolling the same ground, but under such tricky conditions not even the Mongols wanted to fight. There was some posturing, some incomprehensible verbal mockery combined with insulting gestures, but nowhere did the two sides come to blows.

"At least the rain put paid to the infernal dust around here."

"Well, hooray," Bjarnason said. "No dust."

Marcellinus studied his scout for a moment.

"Uh, sorry, sir."

"No, I . . ." Marcellinus took a deep breath and looked around him. "I don't suppose you'd have any of that beer left and be willing to part with a cup or two?"

Bjarnason grinned. "Aelfric is safeguarding it. I mean . . . aye, I do believe some might be found."

Marcellinus looked at the skies. It was entirely possible that it might rain again this evening. "Then please lead on."

Isleifur's eyes twinkled. "That's an order, sir, is it?"

If Marcellinus had to sit through one more stilted dinner in Hadrianus's Praetorium tent, he might start picking fights himself. "Yes, Norseman. It is."

"And you'll tell the Imperator . . . ?"

"That I'm keeping the peace. And restoring morale. My own."

"And mine," Isleifur said. "Well, then. Off we go."

CHAPTER 24

YEAR TEN, FLOWER MOON

The delay was not all bad. The hiatus gave the wounded time to heal. Marcellinus led small groups of his infantry on limited but useful exercises. He tried to apologize to Tahtay, who curtly pushed the matter aside and refused to discuss it. Either the war chief was embarrassed at his failure of nerve or Kimimela and Enopay had helped smooth things over behind the scenes. They had not returned to their former friendship, though. Tahtay continued to be brusque with him, and their conversations did not stray beyond logistical issues.

While waiting for the mud to dry, both sides continued to send out patrols and skirmishing forces to guard against the twin possibilities of deception and surprise. Both kept the size of those patrols down to a few troopers. The opposing patrols largely passed one another in silence and did not engage. The Cahokian Hawks were permitted to approach almost to the edge of the Mongol camp before being chased away by Firebirds, and the Romans allowed the Mongol aerial craft almost the same latitude. There must be order in war, there must be scouting and careful surveillance, and the leaders of both sides understood that.

Chinggis Khan had a reputation for deception, cunning ambushes, and surprise assaults, but even with meticulous patrolling the Romans detected none. The continuing concern, of course, was that the Mongols would send a covert force to attack them from the rear. But with Sintikala's Hawks constantly in the air and additional surveillance from Eagles and Sky Lanterns, the chances of such a surprise succeeding were greatly reduced.

Instead, the Mongols devoted their energies to merging their camps. Both aerial and ground reconnaissance revealed that mingghans from Chagatai's camp were being steadily transferred to swell the ranks at Chinggis's. By nightfall on the third day Chagatai's campsite was abandoned, leaving only a large discolored scar on the prairie.

That night the Mongols held quite the celebration in their newly merged camp. The roar was audible at Forward Camp. Roma's rank and file had come to war without wine, but their enemies had clearly made the time to distill airag. From the din and the drumming, it appeared that the Mongols were quite happy with how their war against Roma was proceeding.

The Horde did not, however, let down its guard. Sintikala reported that a fourth of the Khan's army kept a steady and presumably sober guard, day and night. Just like the Romans, the Mongols were taking all due care to avoid surprise attacks.

"And so, gentlemen, we face battle again on the morrow. Your thoughts?"

They lay on couches in the Imperator's Praetorium tent, each propped up on his elbow in the Roman style: Hadrianus, who had just spoken, still nibbling on a leg of roasted duck; Decinius Sabinus, who lay as stiff as if he were made of wood but who had put away much more food and drink than Marcellinus might have expected; Lucius Agrippa, lolling more like an aesthete than a soldier in his tunic and sagum cloak; and finally Marcellinus and Tahtay, both visibly awkward and uncomfortable. Tahtay wore a Cahokian tunic but Roman military sandals, which fit his feet better and allowed him to run a great deal faster. His clothes and long hair emphasized his difference from the men around him.

"Kill them all," Agrippa said. "Let them come. Let them be bombed by liquid fire. Once we can persuade the Cahokians to risk their precious Thunderbirds, that is."

Decinius Sabinus reached for the bowl of askuta-squash, then changed his mind and plucked out another of what might have been honeyed stuffed dormice if they had been in Roma but here was presumably some kind of vole. Tahtay had reacted with subdued horror on first seeing the dish, and Marcellinus was happy to follow the war chief's lead and stick to more recognizable fare, but Sabinus seemed quite the connoisseur of the small rodents. It had to be said that the Imperator's chefs were doing their best with the limited resources available.

As Sabinus was obviously avoiding the question, Marcellinus grasped the nettle. "I for one do not think we should merely *let them come.*"

Agrippa shook his head. Admonished by Hadrianus on one too many occasions for picking fights with Marcellinus over military topics, he had become more circumspect with his disdain.

His mouth full, Hadrianus waved his beaker of wine at Marcellinus to continue.

Marcellinus bowed his head respectfully. "Many years ago the Iroqua defeated Cahokia in battle. They did so by being more energetic, inventive, and innovative than we anticipated."

Tahtay eyed him, stony-faced. Marcellinus glanced back at him in mute apology. "Here again we face a resourceful enemy. One who adjusts his tactics according to the needs of the day. An enemy that does not fear to try new things."

Marcellinus took a gulp of his water. "And so, if the Mongols are innovative, we must be more so. If they are cunning, we must outwit them. If the Mongols throw caution to the winds, then Roma must already be . . . sailing on those winds."

"A poet as well as a sage," said Agrippa.

Marcellinus grinned. "One tries." He turned serious again. "Caesar, we have already taken more losses on the battlefield than I am comfortable with. I am sure that you, too, are disconcerted by them."

Hadrianus inclined his head. "I regret the loss of every legionary under my command."

"Just so, just so." Marcellinus paused. He was picking up the Imperator's verbal tics. He should stop that lest he be accused of mockery. "Anyway. We have suffered losses because we expected the Khan that we met on the plains of Asia a decade ago. This is not that Khan. This is a Khan who has learned much from the Jin in the meantime and even more from the Tlingit and Haida of the northwest with their Fishing Eagle craft that he has turned into Firebirds. As a result he has flying machines, black powder bombs, fire lances, siege engines, rockets. He may have even more tricks up his sleeve. If you remain the same army he met in Asia, you risk even greater losses."

" 'We,' " Lucius Agrippa said pointedly.

Marcellinus had switched from "we" to "you" in midstream. He quickly conceded the point. "We, indeed."

"We came to Cahokia for Greek fire," the Imperator objected. "And for flight. And now we have them."

"And we will use those things, but the Mongol Khan will expect them. We must work harder to outsmart him. Much harder."

"And so you suggest what, exactly?" Agrippa demanded.

Marcellinus smiled, refusing to be rattled. "Then you agree that the Mongol Khan has learned from the best? And that we must do the same?"

He told them what he had in mind. Tahtay's eyes widened. Marcellinus's fellow Praetors frowned and bombarded him with questions and objections. Unable to lie almost supine under such interrogation, Marcellinus stood to answer them.

Hadrianus remained aloof from the discussion. He appeared lost in thought, ignoring the debate, but Marcellinus knew he was listening to every word.

Eventually Sabinus and Agrippa ran out of questions. Tahtay now sat upright with his knees up to his chest, a position that made him look less like an overburdened war chief and more like the spirited youth he used to be. His perpetual frown was gone, and his visage was clearer than it had been for many days.

Sabinus looked at him dourly. "One of us, at least, finds virtue in your plan."

"Of course," Tahtay said.

"Then you're as mad as he is."

"That's a matter of degree, I think." Marcellinus eased himself down.

"We cannot possibly place the Imperator at such risk," Sabinus said.

Hadrianus grunted and spoke for the first time in a while. "I think the Imperator might be the person best placed to make that call."

Sabinus shook his head, but when Hadrianus skewered him with a look, he said, "Yes, Caesar."

"Lucius Agrippa," the Imperator said, "in your early acquaintance with Gaius Marcellinus, you accused him of having few strategic skills."

Marcellinus remembered the moment vividly. He pursed his lips and did his best to mimic Agrippa's sneering tone that day. " 'Strong on tactics. Weak on strategy. Not a general of long-term vision.' Do you still hold this view?"

"I do," Agrippa said. "Although we might quibble about where strategy leaves off and tactics begin."

"A poet to the left of me, a philosopher to the right." Hadrianus grinned. "We will proceed as Gaius suggests, with a few significant changes."

Agrippa and Sabinus both swiveled to stare at him. "Just like that?"

"Yes, just like that." Hadrianus continued to speak, laying out his version of Marcellinus's original ideas.

Marcellinus found himself nodding almost continuously. The Imperator had a keen tactical brain himself, and he knew his legions and alae well. "Yes, Caesar. Much better, your view of things."

"My thanks, Gaius Marcellinus," said the ruler of the known world a little drily.

"I still protest," Sabinus said. "And I must have that known."

As well he might. On many previous occasions Marcellinus had aligned himself with Sabinus, and the two men had stood together. Today they did not, and the plan proposed by Marcellinus and his Imperator put the cream of Sabinus's forces at risk.

"So noted, Decinius Sabinus, but by all means, try to look a *little* cheerful."

"It is a plan with many merits," said Agrippa, who had visibly begun warming to the ideas once they started to come out of his Imperator's mouth rather than Marcellinus's.

Hadrianus drained his beaker and got to his feet. A new restless light shone in his eyes. At long last he appeared to be enjoying himself. "Well, well. You may be earning your keep at last, Gaius Marcellinus. Indeed, I am fast approaching the point where I will no longer regret staying your execution."

Marcellinus paused. Even now, his Imperator's sense of humor could be alarming. "Thank you, Caesar."

"Perhaps you should wait to see how this turns out before reaching such a bold conclusion," Sabinus said sourly.

Hadrianus raised his eyebrows and threw his cloak over his shoulders. "So cautious all of a sudden, gentlemen. It does not suit you."

The meeting broke up, and the Praetors and Tahtay dispersed to brief their various tribunes, adjutants, elders, and lieutenants. Marcellinus found himself walking along the Cardo with Sabinus, who glanced back and then said: "One thing we can be sure of. One way or the other, at least this accursed war will be quickly over."

"Strength, Decinius Sabinus," Marcellinus said.

Sabinus did not smile. "The Imperator has an impetuous streak. So does Agrippa. You play to them both."

"That does not make the plan a poor one."

"It places the Imperator at risk."

"The men need to know that Hadrianus is with them, taking the same risks, advancing as far from safety as they do. When he commits himself to the endeavor, so will they. And he will, of course, be surrounded by thousands of legionaries. He would be at worse risk here in camp if the Mongols were to flank us."

"But in addition, the plan also throws to the winds many of our key advantages."

"And in the process gains us other advantages that are even more critical. Including that of surprise."

"We shall see, sir." Sabinus gave him a curt nod as they parted company. "Indeed, we shall see."

Marcellinus continued on his way toward the Southgate out of the inner castra, still mulling things over. For all his confidence in the war council, there was still much to coordinate and even more that could go wrong.

And if Sabinus and Agrippa were so dubious about the plan, Marcellinus could hardly wait to hear how Sintikala, Chenoa, and Pahin would receive it. He might be in for a long night.

The armies of Roma and Cahokia took the field of battle very early the next morning. Rather than funnel out through the Westgate of Forward Camp as they had done before, they ripped apart the castra walls and dragged aside the fence around the wider encampment before dawn, then marched out across the earthworks and through the ditch. A full-strength legion marching six abreast created a column well over a mile long, and channeling men into such a column required laborious logistic control by the tribunes and centurions. Today they had no time for that.

The legions were led from the camp by Imperator Hadrianus III himself, riding his splendid Nisaean horse and surrounded by gleaming Praetorian Guards. Hadrianus would not ride into combat at their head, of course—it had been more than a thousand years since a Roman Imperator had put himself in extremis like that—but it was a fine thing for his men to see him taking the lead. The cheers reverberated through the camp, and Marcellinus hoped they would be heard far across the plains.

Marcellinus led the Legio VI Ferrata out of the camp immediately following the Praetorians. He felt a little absurd parading out on his high horse with his polished armor and gleaming white-crested helmet, but he was loudly cheered all the same. His adjutants Aulus and Furnius rode to his left, their chests puffed out farther than usual, and Takoda and Napayshni were to his right; Enopay and Sollonius would stay in the rear to begin with, to coordinate with the engineers and associated centuries that would follow in their wake.

Today the Sixth Ferrata would be an integrated force of Romans and Hesperians. Marcellinus was done with banishing his Cahokian friends to the wings of his legion. The First Cahokian marched out amid the Sixth Legion, between its Third and Fourth Cohorts, many of them carrying the same scutum shields with their golden lightning-bolt crest. Hanska and her combined Second and Third Cahokian rode out with the mounted Ninth Syrian Cohort. He was almost painfully aware that Sintikala and Kimimela were aboard two of the Hawks that circled overhead, but he restrained himself from peering up and kept his chin level and his gaze forward.

After the Sixth would come the engineers and legionaries in charge of the launch towers, half a dozen of which had been dismantled and loaded into mule-drawn wagons overnight. Next would come the Polovtsians and the other cavalry wings. Once clear of the camp the horsemen would ride past the infantry and fan out into a broad escort and advance guard. The Third and 27th

Legions would be taking the field at the same time, marching out of camp to the north and then swinging around to join them.

The foot soldiers of the Sixth Legion did not march in the triple lines they would assume in battle. Marcellinus's men walked in broad, loose columns, cohort by cohort and century by century. This was not a drill, and there was no need to maintain an onerous formation over a walk of many miles. Plenty of time to fall into ranks once combat was imminent.

As the three legions and associated cavalry proceeded into the Grass, the horsemen of the Praetorians guided them into place with the help of scouts and dispatch riders, standard-bearers and trumpeters. Marcellinus and the other Praetors and tribunes passed orders down through their ranks to the individual centuries to adjust their paths. Gradually the three legions moved into a line that extended across many miles of prairie. It might be impossible to keep this line straight across such a distance and over such varied terrain, but it was a credible effort nonetheless. This was Imperial Roma on the move, a well-oiled machine.

By the time they were two miles from Forward Camp, they had completed their reorganization, with the Third Parthica assuming the central position, flanked by the Ironclads on the left and the 27th on the right.

It was still early in the morning when they first saw arbans of Mongol skirmishers, light unarmored cavalry riding in groups of ten. As soon as the Mongol riders came in sight, squadrons of the Third Polovtsian cantered forward to push them back.

Roma had its own advance riders, of course. Norse scouts trotted ahead of the legions, along with a few turmae of the Fourth Gallorum, checking for ambushes and other traps and watching for the approach of the Mongol army.

After a while Marcellinus and his adjutants dismounted and walked to keep their horses fresh and stretch their own legs. Behind them in the ranks men chatted, gossiped, bragged; their centurions had little reason to keep them quiet when they were in such good spirits. It was this camaraderie that made men an army rather than a crowd, and the officers would have been foolish to damp it down. Come the fight, those bonds would be critical. A hundred yards to the right even Appius Gallus was, if not exactly smiling, at least engaged in a spirited and friendly conversation with the nearest foot soldiers.

Marcellinus was receiving intelligence and information from his scouts as they proceeded. Signals from above and written messages from the sides as the Hawks, scouts, and mounted dispatch riders moved back and forth across the face of the great army, relaying logistic details. From time to time Marcellinus ordered a roll call by trumpet signal, cohort by cohort, but it was largely make-work and pageantry; he could see most of them anyway, and their tribunes or First Centurions would signal him if they encountered any difficulties. Above him Hawks, Eagles, and Macaws were scouting forward as well and would provide plenty of notice of any encroaching Mongol forces larger than a couple of dozen skirmishers.

Despite riding in the vanguard of a mighty army of tens of thousands of soldiers or perhaps because of it, Marcellinus once again felt strangely alone. Alongside, behind, and even above him was almost every friend he possessed: Tahtay, Kimimela, and Enopay; Sintikala and Chenoa; Aelfric and Isleifur; Hanska and Taianita. None were within earshot at the moment.

He would have given a lot to have Kimimela riding beside him today. Perhaps he should have suggested that. She could easily have dropped back to one of the field launchers once the Mongols appeared. But it would have been an indulgence.

In the meantime, it was a beautiful day on the prairies, and as a result of the cooling effect of the rains it wasn't too sultry for a change. Marcellinus became absorbed by the clouds, the birds on the wing, the tussocks of grass and small bushes on the ground around him.

Toward the end of the second hour Marcellinus spied Isleifur Bjarnason and Einar Stenberg ahead of them. As before, they had marked the halfway point between the camps of the Imperator and the Mongol Khan. The legions passed that point and kept going. Marcellinus grinned and saluted them, and they fell in to ride behind him, Stenberg to his left and Bjarnason to his right.

By then the Imperator had dropped back to ride behind the Third, still surrounded by his Praetorians. During the coming battle Hadrianus's position would be the hub of information, but he would be free to move in a crisis as circumstances warranted.

Glancing back, Marcellinus saw congestion in the ranks. Two nearby rises in the terrain had forced several centuries closer together, and they were impeding one another. Men were swearing good-naturedly. Marcellinus left them to it. The centurions would sort it out.

Another small group of Mongol skirmishers from Chinggis's army cantered over the plains toward them, loosed arrows, then turned and galloped away. None of the arrows struck home, and a round of laughter and cheerful profanity chased the enemy horsemen back across the plains.

You never could tell with armies. Sometimes they were somber and bloody-minded before battle, and then the very next day the same legion could display a devil-may-care braggadocio. In this case the hiatus had done the men good: that and their current confident and somewhat audacious march into enemy territory.

Marcellinus hoped that confidence would translate into them fighting like demons in what? An hour? Less?

"Mongols," Aulus said suddenly. "Here we go."

His adjutant hardly needed to point. Marcellinus had been aware of the rising level of the naccara drums in the distance for some time, and ten minutes earlier Sintikala had begun to weave back and forth above him in a pattern that he had no difficulty interpreting. As they came over a small rise, the enemy was evident: a line of Mongol horsemen in the middle distance. They were so close to the giant, sprawling Mongol encampment that they could see its smoke and smell it on the winds, similar to the reek of Forward Camp but also, in many ways, very different. They were surely within range of the Mongol aerial craft, but as yet they saw none.

Now came a long trumpet blast from the central point of the Third Parthica far to the north, bringing the legions to order. Marcellinus nodded to his cornicen, who echoed the signal along the massed line of the Sixth Ferrata. Centurions bellowed, and their men began to move into position, standing taller even as they continued their advance.

The Ala II Hispanorum Aravacorum came forward, passing between the Sixth Ferrata and the Third Parthica. They wheeled left, riding in a double column to cover and protect the front line of the Sixth. To the right the Third Polovtsians were doing the same for the Third Parthica, providing security as the men maneuvered. And by all appearances it was as well that they had such cover, for the infantry was taking its time getting into position.

Three-quarters of a mile ahead the Mongol lines were beginning to form. The sun from over Marcellinus's left shoulder glistened off the steel lamellar armor worn by the warriors and horses of the heavies in a very different way than it did from the hide armor of the light horse archers.

To Marcellinus's eye it seemed that the Mongols were forming lines in considerable haste. By virtue of the Romans' rapid and early deployment into the field and by continuing their march to within sight of the Mongol camp, they had caught the Khan's army by surprise, forcing them to hurry their formations.

That had been, of course, precisely Marcellinus's intent when he had proposed this strategy.

This time it was the legions whose movements seemed

calm and almost casual as they ambled together into close order.

And thus the Sixth had not yet completed its transition into triplex acies when the Second Aravacorum charged the Mongols' right flank.

The heavy horsemen of the Ala I Gallorum et Pannoniorum Cataphractaria broke out and followed. The two Polovtsian cavalry wings surged out after them, and in their wake the smaller mounted units of the Fourth Gallorum, the Ninth Syrian, and the Second and Third Cahokian. All of a sudden the massed cavalry of all three legions was pouring through the ranks of the Roman infantry and across the plains toward the Mongol army. In their charge they closed into a rough echelon, which was about the best they could do; Roman squadrons in such numbers could not maintain the type of close formation that the Mongols could achieve.

None of the Roman cohorts were fully deployed when the combined alae thundered into the field. It looked like an impetuous action, even a mistake. It was not.

The right flank of Mongol armies—of all Asian steppe armies, in fact—was sacred. Traditionally, most major Mongol offensives came from the right. The Khan would often put his most trusted general in charge of the right wing. In attacking that wing Roma was going for the jugular straightaway, first thing.

Marcellinus and his Imperator were done with being passive defenders, inviting the waves of Mongol aggression to crash against the rock of their legions. No longer would they wait for the Mongol Horde to come to them. The best form of defense was attack, and today the forces of Roma and Hesperia would do all they could to wrong-foot their opponents. They would regain the initiative and, with luck, keep it for the rest of the war.

Marcellinus watched the Ala II Hispanorum Aravacorum ride into battle with something like wistfulness. Gods knew he was no horseman, but the assault of the combined alae was a magnificent sight to behold. Just for a moment he would have loved to be a part of that massive charge straight into the enemy.

And even now, the Mongols were still scurrying to get into position.

"Forward!" Marcellinus roared, raising his gladius high over his head and using his knees to start his horse walking again. Behind him, trumpets sounded and centurions relayed their orders. The Sixth Ferrata advanced, shields up and pila at the ready.

Once they were in motion, Marcellinus gave his second order, this time to Takoda, who twisted in the saddle to make wide gestures in the warrior sign language. Hesperians ran through the ranks and out in front of the steadily advancing legionaries; among them Marcellinus could pick out Cahokians, Blackfoot, Mohawk, Huron, Onondaga, Cherokee, and People of the Hand. None of those braves of the Hesperian League wore armor beyond the traditional wooden or reed mat chest protection, and none carried Roman weapons or shields, having left them at the rear of the formation. Today the Hesperians would fight with their own weapons. Some had bows slung over their shoulders, others carried light spears, but most were armed with long clubs, slings, or larger versions of Marcellinus's new slingshots. Ahead of them all sprinted Tahtay, with Dustu to his left and a Blackfoot warrior whose name Marcellinus had forgotten to his right. They darted like gazelles, jumping over grassy tussocks and rocks that might have tripped lesser men, and Marcellinus knew they could keep that up all day.

The first lines of Roman foot soldiers accelerated their pace in a forlorn attempt to keep up with the Hesperian League. Their centurions snapped at them, and they desisted. Legionaries were strong fighters and men of enviable stamina, but they could hardly run in armor for another mile and hope to fight a battle at the end of it. Their turn would come. But not yet.

By then the Second Aravacorum was almost upon the Mongols. They had quickly raised their initial trot to a canter and were coming up to full speed. Behind them, the cataphracts in their heavy armor were at the most ponderous of gallops, their twelve-foot contus lances couched under their arms, ready for impact.

Around the heavies spilled the two Polovtsian alae, loosing arrows at the Mongol line. For now, their lances were still holstered in the leather holders that hung from their saddles, although they would surely snatch them out soon. Behind came the cohortes equitatae. Moving considerably faster than the cataphracts and beginning to pass them but not as good at shooting arrows from the gallop, those cavalrymen had already drawn their long spatha swords.

The Roman cavalry plowed into the Mongol line. The heavies crashed through, unseating many a Mongol. The Polovtsians wheeled, continuing to shoot arrows from a distance, but the Second Aravacorum and the Ninth Syrian were already into the melee, hacking at the Mongol horsemen with a will.

Within moments the Mongol line was completely disrupted. Having barreled through, the Roman heavies were all set to smash into the second line next. Two hundred yards beyond that the Mongol heavy cavalry was coming together at last, shoulder to shoulder and stirrup to stirrup, preparing their countercharge.

Marcellinus relinquished his place at the head of the Sixth to Aurelius Dizala and rode to the right, still flanked by his adjutants. Reaching his First Cohort, he snapped a salute to Appius Gallus and peered north.

The infantry maneuvers appeared to be going as planned. The Third Parthica was hanging back, and beyond them the 27th Augustan was matching the Sixth in advancing smartly, their neatly arrayed shields a vivid swath of red. The huge Roman infantry line was bending, with the wings coming forward to form two horns out ahead of the Third.

The Mongol generals would realize that the Romans were attempting to envelop them and push them back against their own camp. No one, least of all Marcellinus or the Imperator, expected this gambit to succeed. The Mongols were agile and quick-thinking; they would counterattack, and soon, but at least the curved Roman formation would bring the enemy under fire more quickly and prevent them from executing the broad assaults that had formed the core of their strategy in the first battle.

Enopay was running forward from the rear of the Sixth. Marcellinus really should have expended the time to teach the boy to ride.

"Trebuchets," Enopay panted as he arrived. "Grouped together into three clumps and defended by simple wooden field fortifications. Far left, far right, center. If we keep moving forward, we'll be in range of them."

"Grouped? Tell Chenoa."

"Sintikala signaled me, so Chenoa already knows."

Marcellinus couldn't yet see the trebuchets. The terrain here was more creased than he would like, and his men were blocking his view. He snapped his fingers to hurry the boy up. "Come on, Enopay. Distance and direction?"

Enopay pointed. "The nearest cluster is a quarter mile."

The human-powered Jin trebuchets had a range of just a few hundred feet, less than half that of the Roman and Cahokian throwing engines, when firing the larger metal-encased thunder crash bombs. Much farther for the lighter thunderclap bombs that were wrapped in paper or deerskin. The trebuchets would provide a last-ditch defense of the Mongol camp.

"Chenoa will target them from the air?"

"Yes," Enopay said. "So don't get too close to them yet."

Marcellinus devoutly hoped the Mongol trebuchets weren't crewed by Hesperian prisoners, because Chenoa could not hesitate: she would bomb them with liquid flame as soon as she could safely get her Thunderbirds to them. Nothing Marcellinus could do about it this time. "And what do the scouts say?"

"That the Imperator is now up behind the Third, surrounded by his Praetorians. The Chernye Klobuki will remain in reserve with him for now. No canoes moving nearby on the rivers. No Mongol attempts at flanking us. Oh, and Subodei Badahur has been sighted in the central block of the Mongol army, and Jebei Noyon holds their left wing as before, which means that on this wing you face Chagatai again."

The Polovtsians had wheeled around and charged again into the Mongol lines, and now Marcellinus glimpsed Hanska's Third Cahokian Cohort similarly riding out from the mass of Mongols and arcing around to strike back into the line.

Ahead of her was the Second Aravacorum. He hoped Hanska would latch on to them and that they would all ride out together, as ordered. If they got cut off from the rest of the alae deep within the Mongol cavalry . . .

"She will be all right," Enopay said. "She is unkillable."

"She'd better be," Marcellinus said, switching to Cahokian. "When you're able, tell me where Kimimela and Sintikala are."

"Sir, yes, sir," Enopay responded in Latin.

Aulus called to him. "Signal from Aelfric. Permission to assault the leftmost battery of trebuchets with the Sixth Cohort?"

Yes, even Marcellinus could see the trebuchets now. "Tell him to wait for the air attack. Chenoa gets the first strike. Once the Thunderbirds pass, Aelfric can go ahead and mount his ground attack without further confirmation from me."

A trumpet blared. "Mongols charging," Enopay said.

Marcellinus nodded. "Aulus, halt the advance; hold the line here." The cornicen was within earshot, and so the signal came almost immediately; Enopay put his hand up to his ear to block the clamor.

Sure enough, they were coming full on, a column of Mongol light cavalry thundering toward Marcellinus's First Cohort and already nocking arrows to fire in caracole. It looked like the Romans' initial advantage was over.

"Come on, sir," Aulus said. Enopay, the only adjutant with no horse, was already running back to safety at the rear of the First. "Sir?"

A second cornu sounded, and Marcellinus's front line raised shields. Marcellinus and his adjutants made haste, riding back through the ranks to take their place behind the First Cohort. There they found Sollonius, who looked relieved to see Marcellinus following common sense for once.

Mongol arrows began to rain upon his line, but Marcellinus was watching the Roman cavalry. Having wrought their havoc, the Second Aravacorum was falling into a sleek column and riding back toward the left-hand end of the Sixth. The two Polovtsian alae were all mixed up together as usual, but once they got themselves sorted out, the Third Polovtsia would move to join Sabinus's legion while the Fourth hightailed it across the field to support Agrippa's 27th Augustan.

For a few dire moments Marcellinus saw nothing else and began to worry. Then the heavily armored horses of the Ala I Cataphractaria exploded out of the Mongol line in much more of an organized formation than he might have expected; on either side of them were the light horsemen of the Ninth Syrian and Hanska's Third, jumbled together almost as badly as the Polovtsians. And yes, there was Hanska herself, raised up out of the saddle and waving a bloody spatha over her head. Probably screeching her bloodcurdling battle scream and scaring the crap out of everyone around her.

"Told you," Enopay said.

"Yes, adjutant, thank you," Marcellinus said, and winked at him.

Ten minutes later they were in a pitched battle. Almost as soon as the allied cavalrymen cleared the Mongol line, the Horde was on the move, charging out in pursuit. Chagatai might have hoped to run down the stragglers, or perhaps thought that the withdrawing horsemen would disrupt the Roman line. Neither happened. The Roman and Cahokian cavalry were already well clear and cantered safely back through the gaps between the infantry cohorts of the Sixth Ferrata, which then closed up behind them. This left only moments for the Fifth through Seventh Cohorts to step forward into position and create an unbroken line of Roman steel, but all those drills out on the west bank of the Mizipi were paying off now.

Through his discussions with Gallus, Sabinus, and Agrippa, Marcellinus had become familiar with the Mongol names for their various formations. Their formation from the first day, with broad rows of horsemen attacking in waves, was known as the Lake Formation. Today he was enjoying the dubious honor of seeing two different formations attacking his legion at the same time. The first was Moving Bush, in which independent squads of light horse archers assaulted almost randomly from different directions, each pummeling a small section of his line with great ferocity and then breaking away. The second was the more deadly Chisel Formation, similar to the Roman cuneus: a narrow but deep squadron of fully armored heavy cavalry that came at full charge and slammed obliquely into the front of his First Cohort with such ferocity that Marcellinus half expected sparks to fly and the grass around them to catch fire. In principle, the Chisel allowed his men to attack the Mongol flanks. In practice, the heavy horsemen at a gallop were moving too fast for infantry to assail them effectively.

The nice theory was that horsemen could never break a determined infantry position. The truth of it was that the Mongols' horses were trained to be almost as dangerous as their warriors, and it would take a stout Roman cohort indeed to resist the combination of biting, kicking horses and the long hooked spears and sabers of their riders. In the face of such concerted and focused battering, the most that Marcellinus could hope was that his line would only bend, not break, and would reestablish itself promptly once the Mongol heavies were beaten back.

Tahtay and the others were, however, having much better success with the light cavalry. It turned out that an athletic Cahokian, Blackfoot, or Iroqua warrior with a long club was quite as nimble as a Mongol horse archer, if not as fast. A well-aimed blow with the club could cause substantial injury to a horse's legs or chest. An even better-aimed blow could knock the rider right out of the saddle to either sprawl painfully across his horse or tumble off onto the ground.

All this simultaneous activity had the odd consequence that at any given moment some sections of Marcellinus's line would be hooting and laughing and mocking fallen Mongols or leaping forward to spear to death enemies who had been knocked to the ground, even as other sections were locked together in furious combat with heavily armored adversaries and grimly fighting for their lives.

Meanwhile, Marcellinus was watching the skies.

At first he thought there were spots in his eyes, perhaps afterimages of the flashes of light from polished Roman helmets. He blinked and squinted. They were real.

A trumpet shrieked, and at the same time Sollonius said: "Thunderbirds, incoming. Bit low, though. Sir?"

Marcellinus grinned. "Look again, adjutant."

It was rare indeed that Marcellinus got to correct someone else on his long-distance vision.

Here they came, slow and stately: three Sky Lanterns in free flight, riding the wind at an altitude of about fifteen hundred feet.

"A Sky Lantern can carry a far heavier cargo than a Wakinyan," Marcellinus said.

"Liquid flame?" Enopay shook his head. "But they can't steer. Can't go back . . ."

"Once they drop their load, they'll rise in altitude. They'll go west with the wind, hopefully far beyond the battlefield. Once down, the crews will cross the Wemissori and find their way back. If we can, we'll send horses for them."

"Your idea? It sounds like you."

"Yes."

"Rather them than me," Sollonius said with fervor.

The clangor of sword against shield, spear against sword drew Marcellinus's attention back to his front line. He spurred his horse forward without responding but overheard Enopay's wry reply: "Probably safer up there in the skies than down here with the Praetor."

It took another ten minutes before the Sky Lanterns passed over their heads on their inexorable journey toward the Mongol line.

Sollonius nodded. "All right, this time I'm certain. Thunderbirds, incoming."

"And Sintikala is overhead," Enopay reported in Cahokian and sotto voce.

Marcellinus glanced up just once. Yes, the woman he loved was flying two thousand feet above his head.

Did she know he was there? Of course she did. Even if she couldn't see him.

A dogfight broke out above the Sixth shortly afterward. Firebirds formed the vanguard of a Mongol aerial blitz, followed by two of the writhing and disconcerting Feathered Serpents of the Maya.

One of the Serpents dropped a thunder crash bomb over the Sixth Ferrata. It exploded just as it hit the ground and tore an immense hole in the Fourth Cohort, flinging men through the air, screaming in pain.

Its second bomb exploded above the Eighth. Molten shrapnel rained down on Vibius Caecina's men, but the loss of life was much less, and it was the last bomb the Serpent managed to deliver. Six Eagles and Hawks converged on it from three directions with startling rapidity, perforating its wing with the broad-headed arrows devised by Sintikala that would maximize the rips in the canvas. Those arrows must have done serious damage, because rather than merely fluttering down to earth the Feathered Serpent folded and plummeted, barely missing the third rank of the Ninth as it smashed into the ground.

"Sintikala, overhead again," Enopay said.

Marcellinus grunted. "You don't say."

The second Serpent writhed leftward sharply, heading for the Third Legion. "Good. Let them go and bother Decinius Sabinus for a while."

To his right the tip of the latest Mongol Chisel had impacted his First Cohort front and center, and the enemy cavalry was carving a hole in his front line. Legionaries fell back, and centurions and optios snarled vile threats at their own men. Appius Gallus himself was running in on foot carrying a contus lance, which he thrust into the face of a Mongol heavy at the front of the line. Good man.

Marcellinus was looking for the Wakinyan, and now he saw them. They had looped to the south to avoid the aerial conflict with the Feathered Serpents and were returning to their course. They began to separate, fanning out in the sky, just as he, Sintikala, and Chenoa had planned the previous evening—

"Shit," Sollonius said. "Jupiter, fuck, sir: *take cover*!"

CHAPTER 25

YEAR TEN, FLOWER MOON

Marcellinus reacted immediately, kicking his leg up and over his wood and leather saddle. He half slid, half tumbled to the ground without even knowing where the threat was coming from.

Then came the loudest explosion that he had heard yet, and he was knocked off his feet and back against his horse.

The horse reared, whinnying. Marcellinus was on the ground with something heavy on top of him and his horse's hooves kicking clods of earth into the air just a few feet away. A dark shadow passed over him.

From next to his ear came a screech of pain that terminated in a choking cough. Broken porcelain rained down over them.

Marcellinus twisted and shoved, trying to free himself. "Enopay! Enopay!"

"Jupiterrr . . . !"

While the First's attention had been drawn away by the heavy cavalry attack, a Firebird had come in fast and low and thrown a thunderclap bomb. Seeing it coming, Sollonius had flung himself in front of his Praetor and had taken the brunt of the blast.

Sollonius's armor had protected his torso from the worst of it, but he was bleeding extensively from the back of his neck, arms, and legs, and the left side of his face was a mass of blood. He writhed on the ground in his agony in an unconscious parody of the Serpent that had flown by just moments before.

"Aulus! Get a medicus here!"

It was Enopay's voice. In relief, Marcellinus turned to see the boy already running away—unharmed—between the columns of legionaries. Aulus stood dazed, and Enopay had obviously decided it would be quicker to run for help himself than to wait for Aulus to signal for it.

Napayshni hurried to Marcellinus's side, guilt twisting his face. "I am sorry I was not beside you, Wanageeska . . ."

"I'm not." Marcellinus looked up, scanning the skies. Sintikala and Kimimela were high above them, turning to help escort the five Wakinyan that were about to overfly the Sixth.

"There, look," Napayshni said. "The Firebird has come down in the land of no men."

"No-man's-land," said Marcellinus, and indeed the three Firebird pilots were shucking their wing in the area between the two armies, trying to keep their heads low.

It didn't matter. A war party of six Iroqua loped toward them. The pilots turned to face the threat, and one tried to draw the bow he had slung over his shoulder, but the first three Iroqua were already slamming their clubs and axes into the Mongols' bodies while the other three covered them, ready to ward off any enemy horsemen that might be approaching. None were. The Firebird pilots were soon dead and scalped.

"I'm starting to like the Iroqua," Marcellinus said, and at Napayshni's pained expression he added quickly: "I was joking . . . but some are fierce fighters."

Sollonius had stopped crying out now but was curled into a ball hissing air through his teeth, still bleeding profusely. Chumanee was coming at a run with Enopay trotting behind her, weaving between Romans who looked startled to see a woman on the battlefield. Marcellinus nodded at her and almost threw himself on the ground again when he heard a detonation behind him.

It was the *whump* of Cahokian liquid fire. The left-most of the Sky Lanterns had just released a barrage onto the trebuchets. He saw the familiar red and white flames and the oily cloud rising up, heard the cries and screams of men doused in the agonizing incendiary.

A Thunderbird passed over him and almost immediately began to spray the Chisel column with liquid flame—a little too soon, as part of the Roman front line got spattered. Foul words howled in Latin turned to cheers as the Mongol heavies broke off their attack and scattered away.

For a few brief, miraculous moments, the Sixth Legion's front line was unassailed. "Forward!" Marcellinus shouted. "Cornicen, sound the advance! Take ground!"

Freed of the weight of much of its load of liquid fire, the first Sky Lantern rose dramatically in the air. By this time Marcellinus was actually learning something from his aerial reconnaissance crews: from an Eagle, Taianita was signaling down to Enopay, who quickly relayed the information.

The second Sky Lantern was overflying the Mongol camp, targeting the crude corral where the Mongols were keeping most of their remounts and the wagons that carried their black powder bombs. The third was conducting a literal scorched-earth policy and setting fire to what remained of the grass along the right side of the camp, bringing ruin to the two-mile-long stretch of open runway that the Mongol horsemen had been using to haul their Firebirds and Feathered Serpents aloft and managing to destroy several of the flying craft on the ground. Once their missions were over, the Sky Lanterns climbed higher into the sky and kept going into the west.

Right now, there were no Mongol craft in the air and the jaghuns responsible for launching them were scurrying to regroup. Marcellinus hoped they would not get the chance.

The assault of the Sky Lanterns had rendered the skies safe for the Thunderbirds, and the huge aerial craft were making the most of the opportunity. The first two Thunderbirds were spraying Mongol horsemen in the field with liquid flame, with variable results—the cavalry were too spread out, too mobile, and too well armored to suffer as badly from the liquid fire as infantry and civilians did, but the Wakinyan certainly put a crimp in the Mongols' maneuverability. The third Wakinyan diverted once its pilots saw the damage the trebuchets had sustained from the Sky Lantern attack and instead flew on over the Mongol camp, saturation bombing the central area where the Keshik tents surrounded the great yurt of the Mongol Khan and burning more of the supply wagons in the rear of the camp, along with the unfortunate oxen that had hauled the wagons across the continent.

Turning sharply right, those Wakinyan were able to fly over the Wemissori before having to land. The fourth and fifth Thunderbirds had disappeared off through the Jin salt smoke and haze to the right, presumably to menace the central grouping of trebuchets that threatened the Legio III Parthica.

Now Aelfric led his detachment of legionaries from the Sixth and Seventh Cohorts forward to assault the trebuchet towers that remained unburned and mop up the Mongols who manned them.

Once the Wakinyan were past, the Mongol light cavalry set about organizing itself in broad lines for another wave attack on the Sixth. It was clear that they lacked some of the vigor they had shown earlier in the war and that the aerial assaults were having an effect on the Mongols' morale. Capitalizing on that, Marcellinus sent the joint force of the Ninth Syrian and Hanska's Third Cahokian back into the field in a hit-and-run attack to break them up, then marched his legion forward another hundred feet.

"Damn this smoke," he said.

"Your other Roman battles had no smoke?" Takoda was guarding Marcellinus now, his eyes flickering nervously from the battle line to the skies, from behind him to in front of him and over to his right. Aulus and Furnius had moved to the back to prepare dispatches to send to the Imperator. Enopay had gone off to the area they were using as a hospital with Sollonius and Chumanee, and Napayshni was busy sending runners back and forth to the tribunes of the Sixth to receive their reports.

Of course, there was no reason Takoda should know about Roman battles. "These are my first battles where the enemy has the exploding black powder. Nor have any of my previous opponents thrown buckets of stinking pitch."

"Oh." Takoda's eyebrows shot up. "Then you are doing quite well."

"Thank you. Although it's mostly because of you."

That was true enough. The Sixth was taking casualties, but not at an unacceptable level. Its cohorts were standing firm and fighting with calm efficiency. But it was Cahokian ingenuity and bravery that had made all the difference. The valor of the Hawk and Thunderbird clans had mostly negated the threat from their enemies' Firebirds and Feathered Serpents as well as considerably disrupting their cavalry charges. The aerial attacks with the Cahokian liquid flame had disabled the Mongols' siege engines, strafed their camp and killed or stampeded many of their remounts, and helped prevent further Firebird launches.

And then there were the Hesperian foot soldiers. Rather than fight like Romans, the braves of the First Cahokian were fighting like Hesperians, joining the Blackfoot, Iroqua, and Wolf Warriors in running around in ruthless and agile war parties to sow death and confusion among Chagatai's light horse archers.

A sheet of fire leaped into the sky far to Marcellinus's right. He hoped that would be one of the remaining

Thunderbirds dropping its fiery load over the central grouping of Mongol trebuchets. Almost absently, Marcellinus noted that Aelfric's cohorts had moved back to join the rest of the Ironclads.

For a brief moment he allowed himself to hope that the worst of all this was over, that they were finally gaining the upper hand over the forces of the Mongol Khan.

A short cornu blast came from behind him: not a signal but someone trying to get his attention. Marcellinus turned to find five men riding up behind him: Aurelius Dizala, the adjutant Aulus, Isleifur Bjarnason, Einar Stenberg, and a signalman bearing a cornu. None looked elated at the successes of the Sixth. "Juno. What?"

"We're fucked," Aulus said, ever economical with information.

Exasperated, Marcellinus looked instead at Aurelius Dizala.

"The 27th has broken," Dizala said tersely. "Bjarnason?"

The Viking dismounted in a single swift movement. "They pushed forward too hard. Cohorts got split. Then the Mongols broke and fled toward the Wemissori, and the Fourth Polovtsian chased them, with three cohorts of the 27th Augustan in hot pursuit. It was a trick, of course. The Yokot'an Maya swept in to cut them off, then the Mongols turned on them. Circled them into a tight crush and dropped thunder crash bombs into them with Feathered Serpents. Drove the rest into the Wemissori, where the Tlingit were waiting in force in canoes to hack them to death in the water. Bloodbath."

"Futete. His other cohorts?"

"When I left, Agrippa had pulled them south to latch on to the Third Parthica."

A chill began at the base of Marcellinus's spine and wormed its way upward. "Leaving the right field wide open?"

Bjarnason nodded. "We're flanked. Many thousands of warriors under Jebei Noyon are pouring around our right side. Don't know yet whether they'll target the Third Parthica or come all the way around to hit us in the rear."

"Either way they can take out our launch towers and maybe cut us off from Forward Camp. Where's Hadrianus?"

Bjarnason shook his head and pointed to Einar Stenberg, who took up the tale. "Since the charge, Sabinus's Third Parthica has been fighting a steady battle of attrition against Badahur's forces. Slow and cautious."

"Shock me again," Aurelius Dizala muttered.

Takoda raised his hand and interrupted. "Our Mongols are moving out."

Marcellinus swung himself up into the saddle to see over the men in front of him. It was true. The heavy cavalry of Chagatai that had previously been assaulting the Sixth was regrouping in front of their burning camp, but some mingghans were already moving north. The horse archers had split into two. One group was cantering north with all due speed, and the remainder had lined up to form a wall to keep the heavies secure, their horses panting and ducking their heads in a futile attempt to find forage in the hacked-up mud beneath them. All attacks on the Roman line had ceased.

Scattered cheers were breaking out in his cohorts. They had no idea what was really happening. They weren't going to be so thrilled when they found out.

"They haven't suffered much from the air," Stenberg continued, still reporting on the Third Parthica. "Our Hawks held the Firebirds back, and we don't think they can launch the Serpents anymore. The center holds. But I couldn't see the Praetorians anywhere. They—and the Imperator—are either wrapped up deep inside the Third or falling back to castra."

Marcellinus had little doubt about which was the more likely. He scanned his cohorts, taking in positions, strengths, gaps in his lines. Some of his centurions had ordered their men to sit and rest while they could. In his left wing Hanska's Third were off their horses, also taking a breather. Tahtay's Hesperians were walking back and forth, breathing, calming down after the battle. He saw no Catanwakuwa in the air. Maybe they were back defending their launchers from the Mongols.

Dizala looked at Marcellinus. "Caesar will have no safety within the Third. We must get to him, quick as we can."

Marcellinus nodded. "Can your men lead? The First Cohort has borne the brunt for the past hour."

"Certainly."

For the march across to the Imperator's position Marcellinus needed his freshest men up front and the most battle-weary in the rear. But he couldn't leave the launch towers unprotected, not with the Mongols sweeping around the broken 27th. To Furnius he said: "Sound the signals. Second and Third Cohorts lead out to the north, battle formation." Aelfric's men had also seen more than their fair share of combat. The other cohorts had gotten off lightly in comparison. "Fourth and Fifth Cohorts to follow, under Paulinus. Ifer takes the Tenth and Caecina's Eighth and Ninth back to protect the launch towers if he can. Make it clear Ifer is the ranking officer for that action. The First Cohort joins with Aelfric's men to bring up the rear. Tahtay and the First Cahokian with us, if they can." He was getting tired. This was quite a day. "Is that everyone?"

"Everyone but the Cohors Equitata."

"Right. The Ninth Syrian and Hanska's Third guard our east flank to defend us in case the Mongols come in to attack. Send the signals. Dizala: go. I'll join you presently. And march the men slowly. They need to arrive ready to fight."

His First Tribune saluted and cantered away.

Marcellinus looked to the skies again, unsettled by Sintikala's absence. How long had it been since he'd seen a Cahokian aerial craft at all?

Well. Nothing he could do about it.

The sun was only just past the meridian. Even after all

this it was still only early afternoon. He blew out a long breath.

The Second Cohort was already leading off. Time to go.

"Takoda, go tell Appius Gallus that the First Cohort is his. Stay with them. I'll be moving up to join Dizala. Napayshni, you're with me. Norsemen: go to Tahtay and Wahchintonka. Make sure they understand what's going on. Send Tahtay to me if he's able."

"Where's Enopay?" Isleifur demanded.

"With the hospital crew." He was about to point, but damn it, the pieces of his legion had moved around so much that he couldn't tell anymore in which direction the wounded men had been taken. "I can't worry about that now."

"Can't worry about Enopay?"

Marcellinus passed a hand over his eyes. Holy Jove. "All right. After you've talked to Tahtay, go get me a report on casualties from the hospital crew. If you find Enopay, keep him with you. Make sure he doesn't do anything stupid. But go to Tahtay first—"

"Aye, got it." Without even waiting for Marcellinus to finish, Bjarnason rode off into the organized chaos that was the Sixth Ferrata.

As they marched north, the launch towers to their east went up in bright crackling explosions. The legions had just lost their launch capability for local air support. Ifer's cohorts obviously had not gotten there in time.

Even more smoke drifted toward them. Otherwise, the skies were still empty. Marcellinus had no idea where Sintikala might be, or Kimimela, Taianita, Sooleawa. But he had no time to dwell on that, because the Ironclads were marching straight into another hot war.

The flanking Mongol forces must have hit the Third Parthica from beside and behind just minutes before Marcellinus and Tahtay met up with Aurelius Dizala at the front of the Sixth's marching line. The rear cohorts of the Third had disintegrated, and by the looks of things its front line had already been carved into two parts by relentless Mongol attack.

Under pressure from three sides, Decinius Sabinus must have given the only orders he could. The Third Legion was forming up into defensive military squares, two cohorts to a square.

It was not an easy maneuver. Mongol horse archers swarmed around them, wheeling into the legionaries' exposed flanks and firing arrow after arrow. The Mongols had no reason to close for hand-to-hand combat here. With the Romans so disorganized, the havoc they could cause with a barrage of arrows at close range from horseback was quite enough. Soldiers were falling out of line to lie crumpled on the torn-up soil. Even as Marcellinus watched in horror, one cohort—Decinius's Ninth, based on the glimpse he got of their signifer—panicked and fell apart, dooming themselves to slaughter. The Tenth Cohort beat a hasty retreat to merge up with the Fifth and Fourth behind them. As far as Marcellinus could see, the other cohorts were maintaining cohesion.

Where was the Third's tough Polovtsian cavalry? Probably still on the far side of the legion at what previously had been the front line, battling the main army of Chinggis and Subodei Badahur. Sabinus could have had no warning that his cohorts were about to face a major attack from Jebei Noyon in the rear.

"Furnius: signal. Send in the Ninth Syrian to harry those horse archers."

Furnius glanced behind them. "What about the minghghans that took out the launch towers? They could still come for us."

"I know. But I don't see them. Perhaps Ifer's men are holding them off." Or those Mongol troopers might even now be galloping eastward to devastate Forward Camp. The camp was not defensible, of course; if attacked, its garrison would fall back to the river to protect the quinqueremes and the other matériel still aboard them. The warships were essentially floating forts and would cast off if they had to, making them almost unassailable from land. "Futete, Furnius, sound the damned signals."

"Sir, yes, sir . . . Shit."

"What *now*, soldier?"

Furnius pointed. "Fire lances."

CHAPTER 26

YEAR TEN, FLOWER MOON

It was the first time in the whole war that Marcellinus had seen a sizable contingent of Mongol and Jin infantry. Although technically they were cavalrymen who had dismounted.

They were not marching—Mongols had no infantry drills, no concept of advancing in step—but they were at least walking together side by side in open order in two broad ranks of at least two hundred men apiece. Each warrior wore heavy scale armor and carried a fire lance, with a second lance hanging over his shoulder by a leather strap. Behind them came two ranks of heavy cavalry with those heinous hooked spears, and following them were two lines of light horse archers with arrows nocked.

Their strategy was obvious. The fire lancers would break the Roman orbis formations, carving them into pieces with flame. The heavies would penetrate the ensuing breaches to slay the legionaries while the archers guarded their rear and shot past them into the mass of men beyond.

It would be bloody, fiery slaughter.

"Furnius, belay my previous orders. Signal Hanska and the Ninth Syrian to fall in behind me on the double."

"You will not lead the charge," Furnius said flatly. "Can't let you do it. Caesar's direct orders."

"I'm overriding them. My responsibility."

Furnius merely shook his head.

The hell with it. Marcellinus turned in the saddle, and of course Hanska was watching him from several hundred yards away, ready whenever he needed her. He made several large hand-talk gestures. Hanska nodded and nudged her horse forward, shouting orders to her men. Marcellinus glared at Furnius. "Order the Ninth Syrian to join us, if you would. Without them I'm even more likely to get myself killed. No?"

"Holy Jupiter . . ." Furnius shook his head in exasperation and practically sprinted to the cornicen's side.

"Where do you need us, Hotah?" Tahtay asked.

"Other side of me and Hanska and the other cavalry. We charge. You follow us in. Then the Second and Third Cohorts of the Ironclads." He cocked an eye at Dizala. "Right?"

Dizala nodded grimly. "Right, sir."

"All right, let's—"

Furnius pointed suddenly. "Monsters."

Marcellinus turned back to look across the battlefield and for a moment had no idea what he was looking at. Suddenly he feared he was hallucinating shades from out of his nightmares. But from Dizala's exclamation and Tahtay's curse in the Blackfoot tongue he knew he was not alone in seeing them, and in a few moments it became clearer: a mixed force of Tlingit and Maya warriors was running up beside the Jin fire lancers in their support.

The Tlingit wore fur tunics or thick double hides of caribou or elk to armor them, over hide trousers or leather leggings, and were shod in beaded moccasins. Some wore additional armor constructed of slats of cedar painted in bright patterns and bearing images of eagles and whales. They carried big wooden clubs with wicked-looking bone hooks, long double-bladed knives, bows, and a range of other Hesperian weapons. But it was their tall helmets that singled them out from other Hesperians: grotesque masks of carved wood with the

faces of demons and what looked like human hair and
teeth as ornamentation.

Marcellinus could easily pick out the Tlingit warrior
chief they had met in the southwest. He wore his demon
mask with the copper eyebrows and moose hide armor
fastened with toggles and bore a club studded with bone
hooks.

By contrast, the warriors of the Yokot'an Maya appeared gaudy and—perhaps deceptively—nowhere near
as deadly. Most wore breechcloths and feathers, some
only loincloths and stripes of red body paint. The better
equipped among them carried shields of deerskin
stretched over wooden frames painted with crude repre-
sentations of great wild cats or predatory birds. Their
hair was short at the sides but left long at the back and
braided with bright feathers, with the front shaved to
emphasize the regal slope of their foreheads. They carried clubs, spears, slings, bows.

The Maya chief was easy to identify. He wore the pelt
of a large spotted cat and a headdress adorned with long
feathers of blue, green, and gold, and sat astride a fine
Thessalian horse that must have been stolen from the
Romans in a previous battle. He carried a heavy club
spiked with obsidian, and his forehead, too, was slanted
in the same style as the masters of the Maya longboats
they had seen in the south. His ears, nose, and lips were
pierced with golden plugs, and just like the chief at the
Market of the Mud, he wore a necklace of heavy jade.

Marcellinus's first sight of the Yokot'an Maya at the
Market of the Mud had been startling, and his encounter with the Tlingit chief after the Battle of Yupkoyvi
had been even more unnerving, but at least he knew
what he was looking at today. For most of his Romans
and Cahokians, though, their appearance came as a terrible shock. The brutal depictions of human faces on the
Tlingit helmets, side by side with the exotic and fearsome visages of their old enemies, the Maya, stopped
the Sixth in their tracks.

The Ironclads had been in battle for several hours.

They had faced wave upon wave of Mongols, and many of their number had already fallen. To be confronted suddenly with a warrior force of unknown provenance was a major blow.

His soldiers of Roma and Cahokia were facing an odd alliance of the ruthless warrior tribes of the Hesperian coastal northwest and the bloodthirsty civilization of the far south, all in service to a tyrannical warlord from the steppes of eastern Asia.

If that wasn't a nightmare, nothing was.

"Great gods," Aurelius Dizala said, aghast, and then seemed to pull himself together. "Uh, full charge, sir?"

"Damned right," Marcellinus said. "Straight down their throats."

The time for caution was long past. With the bulk of Sabinus's Third Legion facing imminent destruction and the whereabouts of the Imperator unknown, a steady advance under shields was out of the question. They had to punch through the alliance of Jin and Mongol, Tlingit and Maya, to prevent further catastrophic losses among the Third Parthica.

Marcellinus looked down at Tahtay. Today he saw no hesitation on the young man's face, no uncertainty or fear. Still, he had to ask. "You're ready for this, Tahtay?"

Tahtay barely spared him a glance. "To face the men of fire? Yes. We will tear them apart."

Odd, what daunted his young friend and what didn't. Then again, in some ways Marcellinus was the same.

Of course, the Hesperians looked less alien to Tahtay than to the Romans. And Tahtay would much rather kill warriors from Asia than those from the land.

At his silence, Tahtay looked up at him. "For Yupkoyvi."

A place Tahtay had never been. But surely Taianita had told him every detail of the slaughter the Mongols had perpetrated. A massacre in which the fire lances had played a gruesome part.

Marcellinus nodded. "For Yupkoyvi. And Cahokia." For certainly neither of them wanted Jin fire lancers marching into the Great City. War chief and Praetor looked each other in the eye. Both nodded.

Tahtay hefted his long metal-studded club, of the type that already had proved so effective against the Khan's horsemen. Its solid clout would make it a good weapon against Mongol armored infantry, too, but Marcellinus was glad he did not have to run with anything so heavy. Especially toward an enemy who could shoot a ten-foot stream of flame.

He wanted to say *Be careful, Tahtay*. But those were not words one said to a warrior. "Listen for our signals. Be ready."

Tahtay nodded and sprinted back toward his warriors of Cahokia and the Blackfoot, hand-talking as best he could to Akecheta and Wahchintonka as he ran.

"Oh, no," Aurelius Dizala said. "Holy Son of God, why?"

Startled by his tribune's tone, Marcellinus looked first at the Mongol line, which was still advancing toward the orbis of the Third Parthica. For once they were not loosing arrows, not exposing the Roman infantry square to a withering arrow storm. Such a cloud would be less effective against a well-armored square. More likely they were playing a game of intimidation, allowing fear of the fire lancers to soak into the Roman front lines in the hope that dread of the black powder weapons would do half their work for them.

But now Marcellinus saw why Dizala was cursing.

"Oh, merda" was all he could manage in return.

Facing the Mongols was a solid wall of the tall, curved scuta emblazoned with the blue bull of III Parthica. Interspersed here and there were several shields bearing the device of the red lion, probably held by legionaries of the 27th who had gotten displaced from their units in the heat of battle. But now Marcellinus saw oval scorpion shields belonging to the Praetorian Guard, and the tall guardsmen with the distinctive blue plumes that held them.

Except that Praetorians had to be at least six feet tall

and one among them was not. Marcellinus had been scanning the line for Sabinus or one of his tribunes, when his eye was arrested by this anomalous figure.

It was Hadrianus, dressed in the uniform of an ordinary guardsman. He stood in the front line, coolly studying the approaching Jin fire lancers and passing orders right and left, pumping up his men. Despite his disguise, his aristocratic bearing was obvious. Surely even the Mongols must see that this was a man used to having his orders obeyed.

The Imperator had his faults, but lack of courage was not one of them.

"Futete. Marcellinus? Uh, sir?" Furnius had caught sight of his Imperator and was verging on panic.

"Easy, soldier. I see him. Stand up straight and stop babbling."

Furnius swallowed. "Sir, yes, sir."

"Let's get him out of there."

"Yes, sir."

Marcellinus was about to lead a charge against a unified force of Mongol cavalry, Jin fire lancers, and Maya and Tlingit infantry. Behind him his troops were fraying, and in front of him his Imperator was in a ridiculously vulnerable position. Matters were speedily going from desperate to downright awful.

And so he grinned a confident grin he certainly did not feel and sat up straighter in the saddle. "Then sound the horns, adjutant. Forward the Sixth Ferrata, and forward the First Cahokian!"

Even under deadly archer fire Sabinus's men had done a creditable job of lining up in their defensive infantry squares. Their weariness was obvious, but desperation spurred them on. Bodies lay bent and broken all around them.

A cohort consisted of six centuries, and so allowing for casualties, the two-cohort squares should contain about a thousand men each. That was consistent with the orbis Marcellinus saw before him now: a haphazard

square 120 feet on a side, each side consisting of legionaries standing in close order three deep. The front row
of men had taken a knee and held their scutum shields
directly in front of them and their spears out at an angle.
The second row also held outthrust spears, with the
third row close behind them, its soldiers each bearing
either a pilum or a bow. Each side of the square thus
made a wall that bristled with sharp points.

Under usual circumstances a well-formed infantry
square might provide an impenetrable barrier to cavalry,
turning the military action into a slow, debilitating
grind. That would not be the case here. The fire lances
would carve its front line into pieces, inflicting grievous
burn wounds on the infantry, allowing the mounted
heavy cavalrymen to penetrate the destroyed formation
and cut down the remaining foot soldiers of Roma.

The horses moved forward at a trot, with the soldiers
of the Sixth and the warriors of Cahokia gamely doing
their best to keep up. "Slow down!" Marcellinus called
back. "Save your breath for the fight!"

As they approached the square, Marcellinus saw
more. Centurions and optios passed their Imperator's
orders up and down the line and shoved foot soldiers
into position with their staffs to close up the order. Perhaps brutal, but essential when everyone's life was at
risk. Signiferi stood in the front line holding their standards high, generally round silvered disks of their centuries mounted on a pole, although some were the vexillum
flaglike standards of the special units. They wore small
round shields over their shoulders, but their most distinctive features were the animal skins they wore on
their heads: bear, lion, leopard. The signiferi were re-
monstrating with the tired legionaries, bucking them up
and stiffening their spines, but Marcellinus guessed they
also were trying to distract attention from Hadrianus.
No man wanted to die knowing the dishonor of not
having been able to protect his Imperator.

The leader of the Mongol jaghun raised a blue flag
over his head and snapped it to the left and right. In re-

sponse, the Mongol light horse archers peeled off the back line and charged the Sixth as a single column. They nocked arrows even as they galloped, and soon these arrows began to fly in earnest, the foremost archers loosing missiles into the Sixth and then curving away to come around again. They would form a steady stream of fire until stopped.

"Countercharge, countercharge!" Dizala shouted. Not waiting for the signal, he spurred his horse forward. Marcellinus followed, and the Ninth Syrian fell in behind them, storming into the fray.

Together, the Ninth Syrian and the Cahokians were achieving their objective, which was the disruption of the Mongol attack. Meanwhile, the infantry of the Ironclads had regained their fighting spirit and were charging into the colorful mass of gold and blue and green that made up the forces of the Yokot'an Maya and Tlingit.

The long line of Jin fire lancers was walking forward again with its protective rank of Mongol heavy cavalry close behind. Leather masks in front of their faces provided some protection from the fire they were about to unleash into the Third Parthica.

Thirty feet away from the Roman line the fire lancers halted. Centurions shouted, and some of the legionaries hurled javelins, but the Jin soldiers did not even trouble to protect themselves; the javelins bounced off their heavy armor without effect. In return the light horse archers now fired a wave of arrows into the Roman line.

The arrows must have served as a signal, for at that point each Jin foot soldier grounded his fire lance in front of him. From a pot, pouch, or box at his waist each man produced a short length of what looked like burning rope. They were fuses of the type that Decinius Sabinus had termed a "slow match," a cord impregnated with saltpeter that burned slowly and was an effective way of lighting a bomb or a lance on the battlefield. The Jin soldiers applied their slow matches to the large bulbs of black powder on their fire lances.

Two hundred fire lances ignited with a roar, shooting concentrated flame a distance of ten paces in front of them. The trails of smoke that arose from them soon entwined above them into an ominous cloud.

The lancers stepped forward as one, a line of fire projecting in front of them. From Yupkoyvi, Marcellinus knew their lances would burn for at least five minutes before sputtering.

With perfect clarity, Marcellinus saw the Imperator Hadrianus step forward from the Roman line with his shield up. Beside him stepped a signifer of the Third, and on his other side a Praetorian centurion. As the Imperator raised his gladius, there came a second roar, this time of focused Roman rage just as powerful as the tongues of Mongol flame.

The legionaries of the Third Parthica cast their pila, the iron-shanked spears flying forward in a cloud of steel of their own. And the Romans stormed forward after them.

Hadrianus would not wait in line to be burned. He evidently had no wish to see his orbis broken up around him, its ranks cleaved, his men slaughtered. He would meet attack with attack in an all-or-nothing surge out of the breach.

And running through the horses of Marcellinus's Sixth and streaking out ahead of them was Tahtay with his Blackfoot around him and Akecheta and the warriors of the First running behind him with spears and swords raised and nary a shield among them.

Tahtay's warriors were dancing amid the Mongol horses now, and Marcellinus could scarcely bear to watch. It became a deadly game of chicken, repeated a hundred times. A Mongol warrior would bear down on a Cahokian, shooting an arrow or wielding a saber. At the very last moment the Cahokian would leap aside and bring his long club around to strike at the horse or rider. When it worked, the braves might knock a horse archer clean out of the saddle. If the Mongol's foot caught in the stirrups, he might be dragged along by his horse; if not, he might fall to the earth, where other Cahokian warriors could converge on him and pummel him to death. When it failed, the brave would fall, his face, neck, or shoulder slashed by a saber, a spear or an arrow through his gut, or a shattered skull. The combination of fire and arrows could be deadly, but so could the combination of heavy clubs and sharp steel in Roman and Cahokian hands.

Marcellinus slid off his horse again. There was no way the poor beast could cope with the unholy mix of streaking fire, smoke, noise, and bright colors. For the remainder of this battle Marcellinus once again would fight on foot. In some desperation Furnius had rearmed him. In his hands now was a contus lance, a weapon more appropriate for a mounted warrior; a Cahokian ax was slung over his shoulder, and at his waist he wore his gladius.

This time, anger was not hard to come by. He was surrounded by warriors of his First Cahokian and legionaries of the Sixth. Tahtay was close by, fighting at great personal risk like a man possessed. Ahead of him were Romans in peril, among them the Imperator of Roma going blade to blade with the Mongol foe.

Marcellinus had fallen to a fire lancer outside Yupkoyvi. It would not happen here. He chose an enemy, raised his heavy contus, and charged forward.

The Jin lancer saw Marcellinus coming and turned his deadly torrent of flame toward him. Marcellinus swung his lance around quarterstaff-style; it was a clumsy move, but the heavy wood of the contus parried the barrel of the fire lance. Hot sparks raked Marcellinus's cheek, but he kept running forward, reversing his grip on his lance and thrusting it forward. It smashed into the Jin's face mask and propelled the man backward. The column of fire arced into the air, and around Marcellinus came Dustu, leaping at the Jin. With the dull crack of his club, the lancer was tumbling into the dirt, his skull cracked and his neck probably broken.

The fire lance hit the ground, still spewing flame. Marcellinus jumped over it and chose his next Jin target.

Men came to his side to fight. For a while it was Appius Gallus and three anonymous legionaries of the First. Then, as Marcellinus pulled his sword from the gut of a Mongol archer he had just dragged from his mount and stabbed, he found Dustu again to his left and Takoda to his right.

Takoda wasn't supposed to be fighting. Then again, neither was Marcellinus.

It was a surreal fight. Marcellinus had no breath to speak, neither to berate nor to command. He was sucking burning air into his lungs, and every time he closed with a fire lancer, it got worse. The men around him were coughing, their eyes streaming. It was not hard to imagine they were in Hades, buried deep in the underworld, there to fight forever.

The blur of combat continued. Fortunately, their foes were easy to pick out. Wearing bright feathers? A foe of the Yokot'an Maya: stab him with a gladius. A sinister helmet looming out of the smoke bearing a carved human face out of a nightmare? Cleave it with an ax.

A Jin bearing a fire lance? Most definitely a foe. And now, after several minutes spent battling with Tlingit and Maya, Marcellinus was back among them. Fortunately, the fire lances were two-handed weapons; once Marcellinus had driven back the Mongol horseman who was guarding him, the Jin could only swing his weapon and try to spray him with flame. Many times Marcellinus felt the hot breath of fire scorch his flesh or beat against his breastplate with a noise as if he were being hosed down with water. Each time, he sent the Jin to hell.

They got into a rhythm, now, he and Dustu and Takoda and four others of the First Cahokian who had joined them. Dustu and one of the other Cahokians would club at the Mongol cataphract in his heavy armor and try to take down either the horse or the man. Takoda and the rest would drive back any surrounding Mongols, isolating the fire lancer. Marcellinus would then assault the Jin if there was not already a legionary from the Third Parthica leaping in to do the job himself. All around them other teams of Romans and Cahokians were doing the same thing.

And then as Marcellinus leaped forward through the smoke, he came across Tahtay with his sash pinned and knew he could go no farther.

Tahtay was battling a fire lancer. His ten-foot sash was taut, one end attached to his waist, its other end hammered into the ground with a stake. As a Fire Heart of the Blackfoot, Tahtay could not retreat from the position he now held even if it meant his death.

Marcellinus did not need to ask why Tahtay had chosen that spot to make his stand. Hadrianus was fighting just twenty feet behind him, a gladius in one hand and his shield in the other. Because of the crush of battle they could get no closer to the Imperator than that, but Takoda and Dustu came in around Marcellinus and Tahtay, along with a battered-looking foot soldier of the Third with gladius and scutum and a Praetorian with so much blood on his face and so many burns across his body that it was a wonder he could still move, let alone fight, and the six of them waged a defensive action then and there against an onslaught of a dozen more Jin fire lancers and their Mongol escorts.

Marcellinus had lost the heavy lance long before. He had fought with the ax for a while, but now his gladius was in his hand, his last remaining weapon. Even in the fierce melee, with his mind a haze of battle fury, Marcellinus instinctively felt the moment when the battle turned.

The Jin were beginning to lose spirit. Most were on their second fire lances now, the first having coughed and died. They were backing up, away from the infantry square of the Third, and they kept stealing glances behind them as if they expected the Mongol heavies to desert them at any moment.

A prescient fear, because that was exactly what the

Mongol cavalry did. Marcellinus neither saw nor heard a signal, but with one accord the Mongol horsemen steered their mounts left and galloped away, leaving fifty fire lancers unsupported. Most fought on and were cut down; a dozen attempted to flee and were chased and gutted. The remainder dropped their lances and fell to their knees trying to surrender, but it was much too late for that, and they perished, too.

Marcellinus pulled his gladius from the neck of a Jin warrior and blinked, his eyes stinging from the smoke. Dustu and Takoda were now to his left, and Furnius had somehow appeared on his other side, wide-eyed and bloodied. They all turned this way and that, peering into the haze for enemies.

As clear thought returned, Marcellinus realized he no longer could see the Imperator and had become separated from Tahtay; he could not, in fact, even see the infantry square of the Third they had just been fighting tooth and nail to defend.

The sun struggled to pierce the pall of smoke above them, its golden orb so obscured that Marcellinus could look straight at it without discomfort. And so that direction must be south or slightly west of south, and they needed it behind them if they were to walk back into the area where the Roman orbis had stood.

He coughed as another wave of smoke rolled across the battlefield. Damn it. After surviving so many attacks, was it his fate to die from asphyxiation?

Never had Marcellinus been on a battlefield where the air was so full of explosions and smoke. He was in no doubt: what they were witnessing today was the future of warfare. And it was terrifying.

"That way," said Furnius. "Holy Cybele . . ."

Marcellinus's answer was forestalled by another thick, retching cough. He merely nodded, and they walked north.

The first man he saw was Akecheta with a bloody burn across his face, and then others coalesced from the hellscape around them. Here were the Cahokians, their clubs and axes bloody. Some already wore the distinctive Mongol scalps on their belts, others the feathered braids of the Maya, dripping gore onto their legs and onto the ground. Even in the thick of battle the Hesperians would have their trophies, though having seen their skill at scalping, Marcellinus knew that such trophy hunting had not slowed them down more than a few moments.

And here, now, were the remains of the Imperator's Praetorian Guard, scattered among the other more conventionally armored legionaries of the First and Second Cohorts of III Parthica. Praetorians, yes, obvious by their distinctive armor and plumes, battered and burned, sooty and sweat-stained, pale shadows of the splendid figures they had cut when Marcellinus had first seen them in the Oyo Valley all those years before. The smoke was clearing now that the fire lances were all out, rising to reveal a battlefield scene out of hell.

Recognizing Marcellinus, the Praetorians ushered him, Furnius, and the two Cahokians forward into a large square of smoky, sooty legionaries.

And there Marcellinus found his Imperator. Praetorians knelt on either side of him, and for a long and anguished moment Marcellinus thought Hadrianus was dead. Then the Imperator turned his head an inch at a time, torturously slowly, and looked at Marcellinus.

Marcellinus moved closer. Blood-darkened bandages swathed the Imperator's midsection. His face was as pale as parchment, and he had closed his eyes again, and although his breathing was irregular and unsteady Marcellinus did not think he had lost consciousness. "Hail, Caesar."

The Imperator almost grinned, though he looked as if it pained him. "Gaius. Hail."

"He should not speak," the Praetorian said to Marcellinus, and then leaned over Hadrianus. "You must not try to speak, Caesar." But Hadrianus's head lolled to one side, and now he was certainly out cold.

Above them, brightly colored flying craft appeared,

sending a wave of alarm across the square until they were identified as Macaw Warriors of the Hand rather than aerial warriors of the Yokot'an Maya. Marcellinus looked around him for a ranking tribune of the Third but saw only its primus pilus, weary and begrimed, exchanging notes with the Imperator's adjutants.

And now they heard the deep rumble of hooves. Horsemen were bearing down on them from the north.

Takoda's shoulders fell, and Dustu's chin dropped to his chest as if he had suddenly fallen asleep. Both men were dirty, smoky, and ragged, their arms straight down by their sides, weapons almost slipping from their fingers. Marcellinus could not imagine they could fight anymore today.

"Fuck," said Furnius, the only one of them who seemed to have retained the power of speech.

However, the Praetorians were not reacting with alarm, and listening to the sound, Marcellinus nodded with relief.

Moments later the Chernye Klobuki thundered in all around them, their leader's face the picture of concern and chagrin, and Marcellinus found that he could speak after all. "Merda. Decinius Sabinus."

Tied onto the horse behind the Chernye decurion was the limp body of a familiar figure, his white helmet still strapped to his head, his body a hacked-up mass of bloody wounds. Alongside rode Aelfric and a tribune of the Third, their faces grim.

Praetor Decinius Sabinus had fallen in battle, just as he had predicted he would.

As they cut Sabinus off the horse and laid him on the ground, the primus pilus of the Third came running, calling Sabinus's name and crying out curses to the gods. Aelfric and the other tribune dismounted more quietly, their heads lowered.

Suddenly, Marcellinus's remaining strength gave out. He collapsed to the ground beside Sabinus, not in grief, for he was too drained by the combat he had just been through to feel much of anything. It was more through some kind of fellow feeling that was based on the camaraderie they had shared over the last year. A fragmented, inchoate feeling that Decinius Sabinus might be dead, but at least he did not deserve to be alone.

Then he rubbed his eyes. The Imperator down, Sabinus down, and a Praetor, two tribunes, and a primus pilus all standing around in shock, saying nothing, doing nothing.

Marcellinus roughly shoved himself back up onto his feet. Time to get up to date on what was going on elsewhere on this terrible battlefield.

The central contingent of Mongol horsemen under the command of Subodei Badahur had fallen back in the face of repeated onslaughts from the cataphracts of the Ala I Gallorum et Pannoniorum. The damage done to the Khan's camp by Cahokia's Sky Lanterns and Thunderbirds earlier that day had dramatically reduced the number of remounts available to the Mongol cavalry, and they badly needed to consolidate. Meanwhile, Lucius Agrippa had managed to bring order back to his fragmented cohorts and, with the support of the Ala IV Polovtsia, had reestablished a line.

The army of Jebei Noyon was already past that line, of course, but now faced a stiff counterattack. Once again the People of the Hand were fighting their own war within a war, specifically targeting Jebei and his guards to exact revenge for the destruction of Yupkoyvi.

It appeared that the blood vendettas of Hesperian Mourning Wars could sometimes be useful after all.

They could not expect this respite to last for long. Jebei's forces still stood between them and Forward Camp, and the Mongol heavies might soon be back.

"Juno, Tahtay . . ."

The Cahokian war chief staggered toward him, sweaty and bloody. He bore weeping blisters from fire lance burns on both arms and had more bruises on his arms and legs than Marcellinus had ever seen before. He had a deep cut over his right eye, and a flap of skin hung loose on his shoulder.

Most terrifying of all, a long gash on his leg dripped blood. The new injury was perilously close to the wound Tahtay had suffered in the Battle of Cahokia that had crippled him for so long and risked finishing him as a warrior.

But Tahtay grinned. It was a ferocious grin, unhinged and unsettling. "I am fine."

"You pinned your sash," Marcellinus said.

"I did. And I unpinned it once we won."

"Tahtay . . ." Marcellinus gestured to where the Imperator lay surrounded by his Praetorians. "We may not be declaring victory. Not just yet."

"Merda." Tahtay's jaw dropped.

"Wanageeska?" It was Takoda. "There is something you need to see. Outside the square. Come quickly."

"Hanska." Marcellinus felt a huge rush of relief as his centurion slid off her horse. She still lived.

"Not her," Takoda said.

Hanska grinned and pointed. Marcellinus followed her finger and once again feared he might be seeing things.

Sintikala sprinted across the battlefield, running on light feet and keeping her head low, almost as if she were flying very close to the ground but never quite touching it. She wore no helmet or body armor, merely a tight flying tunic and boots, her legs ridiculously bare. Her falcon mask was pushed up on her forehead like a small echo of a Tlingit war mask, and as she constantly glanced up and around her, birdlike, he glimpsed the jagged Hawk paint around her eyes. Her ax was in her hand, but she held it low, close to the ground, to avoid drawing attention to it.

Yet she was hardly invisible. A Mongol horseman pulled his horse's head around and galloped forward to ride her down. She darted sideways and looped back to evade him with that same quick alertness she displayed in the air, always with that unerring feel for space and distance and that heart-stopping flair for being on the brink of disaster. She ran on. Another Mongol horseman saw her and then another, and each time she ducked under or away from the saber or spear of the horseman without striking back and kept moving, putting Roman cavalrymen between her and her assailants as soon as she could. She never stumbled or tripped or even seemed aware of the torn-up ground and tussocks of rough grass beneath her.

It was an uncanny dance, and in those moments Marcellinus loved her with a fierce ardor. It was a good job that he himself was not under attack from an enemy, for he was spellbound at her perilous looping journey across the field of war.

There was no point sending aid to her. Cavalry would merely alert more Mongol attackers to her presence, and besides, there wasn't time. She would be upon them in moments.

As she arrived and launched herself, he caught her and spun her around. Hanska stepped her horse forward to provide cover.

Sintikala kissed his lips and his cheeks, five hot quick kisses that set his soul on fire. He could hardly believe she was whole and in his embrace.

Unarmored, she had run to his side through the battlefield. He felt an irrational flash of anger at her for risking herself, then swallowed it. Now of all times, he could not snap at her.

"It's good to see you," he said.

Sintikala raised her eyebrows at the triteness of the expression and grinned quickly. Then she jumped up off the ground and into his arms again for a rib-cracking hug. It was probably only his breastplate that saved him from serious damage.

Even as she did it, Marcellinus realized she was looking over his shoulder into the east.

"Why the hell did you land?" he said.

"I was tired of being so far above you," she said. "I wanted to be *there*. Meaning here. With you."

He knew her better than that. "And?"

Sintikala caught sight of whatever she was looking for in the skies. She nodded in satisfaction. "And the Mongol Khan is less than half a mile from where we stand. We have only minutes to get there before the skies explode around him."

CHAPTER 27

YEAR TEN, FLOWER MOON

Once again, Roma sounded no trumpet blasts and gave no warnings. Merely a sudden break on the western side of the big military square, an inexplicable parting in an area where the square was not currently facing Mongol attack. Legionary infantry rolled away from the gap to widen it. And then, with a sound like thunder, the Chernye Klobuki roared out of that gap in a tight column eight horsemen wide, with Hanska's Third Cahokian riding as hard as they could among them. Their prize: the Mongol Khan.

Sabinus was dead. The Imperator was wounded, perhaps seriously. Agrippa was way across the battlefield, the legions split and scattered, their cohorts fighting a dozen different battles across this enormous killing field. And now that the Khan had moved forward, sensing victory, Marcellinus had only Sintikala, Aelfric, Hanska's Third . . . and the elite Chernye Klobuki. Excellent riders and fighters, perilously few of them, but they were all he had to support the plan that Sintikala had already put into action, a last-ditch plan to grab victory from defeat by means of one sharp, killing thrust into the Mongol forces.

They could win this, but only with speed and surprise. With recklessness and immediate action.

The Mongol horsemen in their path scattered. In some

cases their horses made the decision for them, scurrying out of the way. The small, fierce horses the Chernye rode were not so different from those of the Mongols. Like recognized like, and chose not to impede them.

Half a minute later six Thunderbirds raced over their heads, three on each side of them, at a height of about eight hundred feet. They continued on in a straight line, with perhaps two dozen Eagles and Hawks above, beside, and behind them.

This was the formation that Chenoa had called "two horns" in a discussion during the rains. It had been just one of a dozen possibilities for large-scale aerial maneuvers that she, Marcellinus, and Sintikala had discussed, and they had never expected to perform it from a launch so far away.

The nearby launch towers were all crumpled and burning. These Thunderbirds, launched from Forward Camp, were already close to the absolute limit of their range.

By this time the Mongols must have realized that the Cahokians were cautious in their use of Wakinyan. They did not like to place the sacred birds at risk. And so there was no way they could have anticipated that Cahokia would dispatch six Thunderbirds from so far away on a one-way mission over the remaining Mongol army. Chinggis had felt safe to come forward because he no longer feared an aerial assault.

As the Thunderbirds passed the vanguard of the galloping Chernye Klobuki, they began to release Cahokian liquid flame in two broad swaths over the enemy cavalry to either side of them. Mongol horsemen scattered or burned. Once again the shrieks of tormented men and horses and the smell of burning flesh wafted across the prairie.

The Wakinyan flew on, three on each side of the Chernye's headlong path, hazy but substantial shadows in the smoke. The great birds now banked slightly left; from their altitude their pilots could see the Keshiks surrounding the Mongol Khan and adjusted course to scorch the earth to either side of them.

The Mongols were reacting now. Drums were sounding, and mingghan units scurried to form up. But these Mongols were on tired horses, and the Chernye's were fresh.

From behind the Chernye, too, signals were sounding. The other cavalry alae could not know about the proximity of the Mongol Khan, but they saw Roma's elite horsemen spearheading what looked like a suicidal charge into the core of the Mongol army along a path carved for them by a small fleet of Cahokian aerial craft. Turmae of the Ala II Hispanorum Aravacorum, the legions' Cohortes Equitatae, and even some among the weary Polovtsians raced to follow the Chernye Klobuki into the attack.

In the middle of the Chernye pack, Marcellinus thought his body might get torn apart. It had taken him entirely too long to get his balance and relax into the forward seat required for a strong gallop, and the small of his back felt like it might crack and splinter. His legs burned. He was not the horseman that the Chernye were, and he had fallen back fifty yards into the throng of galloping horses. Sintikala still rode by his side, but she looked more scared than he had ever seen her. Sintikala ruled the air but was not a strong rider of horses and probably would have fallen even farther back if she had been left to her own skills. Her mount, however, had caught the thrill of the chase and was pounding along hell for leather. Where Aelfric was, Marcellinus hadn't the slightest idea. He had lost sight of the Briton almost immediately after they had broken out of the infantry square.

All of a sudden, Eagles were diving over his head and beginning to loose arrows and fling pots of liquid flame. Stray splashes of the incendiary skittered up Marcellinus's arm, lacerating his skin and raising large weals, but despite the searing pain, he did not release his grip on the reins.

The Chernye were spreading their formation outward as they galloped, and now the reason became obvious: they were storming into the Mongol Khan's Keshik bodyguard. Mongols in black tunics and red-trimmed armor were all around them, horses rearing, riders grabbing their reins, swinging spears and sabers. On seeing the Wakinyan overhead the Mongols had spread out to reduce the damage their liquid flame could cause, and the Chernye were now galloping through them. The smoke was still thick, the visibility no more than a couple hundred feet in any direction, and this had shielded their lightning approach.

Ahead of them the two lines of Thunderbirds were converging. The rightmost group of three Wakinyan was turning inward. The line of charging Chernye kinked to the left as well, guided to their target by the Thunderbirds' trajectories.

The great craft could not stay aloft much longer; they were only a few hundred feet from the ground, riding the last hints of the wind and the hot, fiery updrafts they were creating with their liquid flame. Marcellinus was galloping too hard to be able to focus on the pilots who hung beneath the great craft, but he was sure Chenoa would be leading them, shouting her orders from on high as they glided above the core of the Mongol army.

Without doubt the small, ungainly horses of the Asian steppe the Chernye rode had greater stamina than the Thessalians, Barbs, and Libyans of Marcellinus's experience. This was the same type of horse that had allowed the Mongols to pillage Asia and western Hesperia, a crucial element in their success. But after galloping two miles, even they were wearing out.

The Chernye column was slowing to a canter, the horses panting. Some were blown and had peeled off. Marcellinus's mount was foaming at the mouth in an alarming way, but its legs still seemed strong and it tossed its head, excited from the charge. Sintikala was lagging behind him, holding her reins in one hand and reaching back for a lance with the other.

The Keshiks had recovered from their surprise and were whipping their horses forward to match the speed of the Chernye. Still spurring his mount on, Marcellinus drew his spatha, mentally thanking Aelfric for reminding him just before they had set out that to fight effectively from horseback he would need the longer sword. His gladius would do him little good in the fight ahead, although it still hung at his waist. He was not as adept with the spatha and had to remember that it was primarily a slashing rather than a thrusting weapon. But since most of the Keshiks would be armed with lances and sabers anyway—

One came at him from the left, and Marcellinus swung at him. The Keshik swayed away from the blow and slashed with his saber. The blade clanged off Marcellinus's shoulder greaves, and then Sintikala's lance caught the Keshik under the arm and knocked him forward. Marcellinus brought down his sword, but the Keshik had somehow disappeared from beneath it. He had jerked his horse's head to the left, and the two combatants had separated with startling speed.

Marcellinus had never fought in a running cavalry battle before. His instincts and reactions were going to be all wrong. Perhaps Sintikala had the right idea with her lance after all.

But warriors on horseback were rushing up behind them, and he had no time to change weapons. Worse, his horse chose that moment to startle and buck, pitching Marcellinus painfully up out of the saddle. He fought to regain control, but the warriors were right on top of them. Twisting in his saddle, he raised his blade.

"Polovtsians!" Sintikala shouted, and with a blast of relief Marcellinus saw that it was true. The warriors of the Ala III Polovtsia had caught up to them and were threading between the tired horses of the Chernye, hacking and slashing at the Keshiks as they passed.

Marcellinus dragged the breath back into his body and tugged at his horse's head to trot alongside the Polovtsians. He noted another line of Roman cavalry dashing forward to his left, cutting another path through the left-hand side of the Keshiks. Beyond them was a terrifying wasteland of burning prairie, with men and fallen horses writhing on the ground.

He felt a light blow on his back and jerked up his spatha but quickly lowered it again. Instinctively he had pulled his horse's head to the right to steer away from the killing field, and in doing so he had careered into a turma of Polovtsians. One of them had knocked him on the back as a warning as he surged by. Marcellinus grinned—under the circumstances probably more of a grimace of embarrassment—and rode on.

As his horse picked up speed again, Marcellinus tried to visualize how all this would look from above them. Chenoa's Thunderbirds had carved two wide swaths of devastation with the Cahokian liquid flame and had taken out hundreds of Mongols in the process, many of them Keshik warriors. Marcellinus and the cavalry of the western Asian steppe were riding through the unburned strip of prairie in between, close to its leftmost edge. In the smoke and confusion he could not clearly see how wide this unburned section was, but based on the separation of the Wakinyan as they had flown over, it could be only a couple of hundred yards.

Perhaps less. Marcellinus had penetrated beyond the point where the Thunderbirds had begun to converge.

They must have ridden well past the Mongol camp now. That would be perhaps a mile behind them and to their left. Ahead would be open prairie. Perhaps the Wakinyan of Chenoa would even now be landing in that prairie. Marcellinus hoped they had passed far enough ahead of the Mongol army that they would not be caught and slaughtered. Or had they retained enough height to reach the Wemissori, as he and Chenoa had originally envisioned?

The column of Chernye and Polovtsian horsemen was now curving to the right, so—

Marcellinus no longer needed to guess. His cavalry was slowing, assailed by a Mongol charge from the rear right. Seeing Marcellinus and Sintikala, six riders of the Chernye Klobuki coalesced around them to protect them.

Aelfric arrived alongside him, panting so hard that he could not speak and giving Marcellinus a wild-eyed look. Marcellinus was amazed the Briton had found them amid this pandemonium. Glancing back, he saw Hanska and the Third closing in, too.

The reek of burning was strong around them. They were approaching the point where the Thunderbirds had converged. Many of the Mongol horses had balked at riding across the burning, smoldering grass, and Mongol warriors were running across it on foot to protect their Khan. Some carried fire lances, others sabers. All looked desperate.

But the Roman cavalry had spent long hours in their exercises to the west of the Mizipi accustoming their horses to the reek of the Cahokian liquid flame and the burning grass it created. They had the edge, and quickly moved in to contain the fire lancers before they could light their deadly weapons.

"Looking up. Guard me." Sintikala was staring into the sky, searching out her fellow Hawks and studying their flight patterns. Marcellinus and Aelfric fell in on either side to safeguard her.

"All right?" Marcellinus asked Hanska.

Hanska just shook her head and blew out a long breath. "Shit."

Sintikala pointed. "That way." She spurred her horse forward, and Marcellinus, Aelfric, and Hanska followed her into the mass of Roman and Mongol cavalrymen, carving their way into the middle of the battle.

Even to Marcellinus it was clear where the Mongol Khan must be. Eagles and Hawks whirled and dipped and soared, firing arrows, throwing pots of liquid flame. They would surely be centering their attacks on the Khan and his closest guards.

And high above them all a single Hawk circled, a white ribbon fluttering behind its wing. It was Kimimela of the Hawk clan, marking out the position of the Mongol Khan.

Almost a decade earlier her mother had marked Marcellinus's position on a Cahokian battlefield in exactly the same way. How far Marcellinus had come since then. How he yearned to have the two of them safe with him, far away from this terrible conflict . . .

Then Kimimela came under attack, a Mongol Firebird arcing up toward her.

Damn it. Marcellinus couldn't watch. Instead, he dragged his eyes down to the desperate fight before him.

He was staring into a mass of dueling cavalrymen. Mongols and Tlingit fought Romans, Polovtsians, and Cahokians, with heavy and light cavalry all mixed together. Men were locked in battle with sword and lance, ax and club, landing blows while their horses moved beneath them. In some cases the horses themselves were fighting, maddened by the fury and flame, snapping and kicking at one another.

There was Jebei Noyon himself, his yellow armor standing out, wielding a giant ax and dealing blow after blow onto the armor of three warriors of the Hand on horseback who were assaulting him, with four Keshiks whirling around, trying to get into the fray. Above Jebei his position, too, was marked by the red blur of looping Macaws.

All eyes would surely go to Jebei in such a situation. But just fifty feet away from the fearsome Tayichiud general Marcellinus caught sight of a small but discordant detail.

Mongol warriors were practically born into the saddle. The joke was that Mongol infants could ride before they could walk, although Marcellinus was by no means sure that it *was* a joke. Mongols certainly had an instinctive understanding of horses that matched Sintikala's instinct for the air, and she had flown strapped to her father's chest before *she* could walk. Her earliest memories were of being airborne.

And of all the Mongols, the Keshik were the elite. They were the quickest, the strongest, the sturdiest. They rode as if they were welded to the horse, the closest thing to the mythical centaur that Marcellinus had ever seen.

All but one.

Not a hundred feet from him, a slender warrior in black leather sat on a dun horse, fidgeting with a knife in his hands. He wore the same helmet as any other Mongol and his features were indistinct, but even from this distance it was clear that he did not have a full beard. The three men to his right, however, were broad-chested and strong, full-bearded.

Suddenly, Marcellinus realized that the warrior was not fidgeting at all. He was making subtle hand-talk gestures: *Chief. Left.*

Marcellinus's breath caught in his throat. "Sintikala. There."

Without the clue of Pezi's presence, Marcellinus might never have spotted the Mongol Khan. There was little enough variation in appearance and quality of armor between the Keshik warriors, nor did Marcellinus have the time to study faces. No banner or crest marked his position, and his black armor was the same as that of the two Keshiks who flanked him. His horse was pie-bald, which was something of a clue, as such horses had a special significance in Mongol culture, but it was not the only such horse in the field and was as shaggy-maned and poorly groomed a beast as any other.

Unlike Jebei Noyon, the Khan was remaining nondescript. He had done just as the Imperator had and removed all distinctive signs so that he would blend in with his men. But Marcellinus had seen Chinggis Khan before, and now he had no doubts at all.

And from the way Hanska surged forward, Marcellinus knew that she had recognized the Khan as well.

"Go to his left," Marcellinus shouted in Cahokian. "Don't spook him!"

Terse words, but Hanska understood. Fighting her way directly toward Chinggis would give away the fact that they had recognized him. Instead she raised her ax and shoved out leftward. Well and good, but in a fraction of a second Marcellinus realized they also had the opposite problem: Hanska was one of the most distinctive warriors in the Cahokian army, and the Khan would undoubtedly remember her, too.

But he could not call her back now. Rage had gripped her, and she was slicing a path through the warriors with berserker strength. The Khan had had Mikasi killed, and that was all Hanska was thinking about right now, if she was thinking at all.

Marcellinus called quick orders to the Third Cahokian, urging them forward as a screen between Hanska and the Khan. The six troopers of the Chernye who were shadowing Marcellinus pushed to the right, raising a ruckus, and Marcellinus slotted in behind them.

Despite this, the Khan saw them. He sat up in his saddle and looked straight across the battle line at Marcellinus and then at Sintikala, and finally his gaze locked on Hanska.

Chinggis Khan put his head to one side. He looked back at the liquid flame–blasted heath behind him and to the right, where Jebei Noyon fought like a man possessed against the warriors of the Hand. Now more of them arriving, drawn to Jebei like moths to a flame, the elegance of their feathered armor contrasting oddly with their clumsiness on horseback.

Hanska had fought her way forward so rapidly that she was in danger of getting detached from the rest of the Third. Marcellinus tried to bull his way up behind her but found his path blocked by a saber-wielding Keshik warrior on a dark steed with a mane so long that it dragged on the ground. Despite the horse's unlovely appearance, it moved quickly, rearing up and kicking. Marcellinus's horse hastily backed away, snorting, and bumped into Sintikala's.

A javelin appeared by Marcellinus's waist. Sintikala

was passing him a longer-reach weapon. He grabbed it with his left hand and raised it overarm, still clutching spatha and reins with his right, but the Cahokian troopers were pushing through and the Keshiks backed away, exchanging blows with the nearest of them. Two more Keshiks came into the attack, and it was probably half a minute before Marcellinus and the Cahokians could dispatch those warriors.

Marcellinus's javelin was stuck in the guts of the original Keshik, who had fallen to the ground, his horse chased away by Sintikala. He wrenched at it to try to get it out, but it was barbed and had stuck firmly in the man's ribs. "Leave it," Sintikala called. "I have more."

They cantered forward toward the Mongol Khan again. Hanska had halved the distance between herself and the Khan, but there she had gotten stalled, she and five of her men in harsh battle with an equal number of Keshiks.

As Marcellinus rode around them, he jammed the second of his spears into the neck of one of her assailants. It was a lucky blow. He had been aiming for the man's shoulder, but the erratic behavior of his horse had thrown off his aim.

Side by side, Marcellinus and Sintikala pushed forward, Cahokian horsemen around them. Time seemed to slow as they opened up space and closed the distance between them and the Khan. They were only twenty feet away now, and still the Khan was watching their desperate efforts with some amusement.

A Macaw arrowed down out of the sky and slammed into Jebei Noyon, knocking him clear off his horse and twenty feet across the ground. The Macaw, out of control, cartwheeled across the grass after him, its pilot being whipped around in her straps. The warriors of the Hand howled and once again swarmed the Mongol chieftain. Already badly wounded, he went under. At last, the Hand had achieved the vengeance they sought.

Meanwhile, undistracted by the drama and stolid in their loyalty to their Khan, the Keshik warriors on either side of Chinggis slid bows off their shoulders and nocked their arrows. Chinggis raised his arm in a Roman salute in obvious mockery and then, with an ironic half smile, waved good-bye to Marcellinus.

And then Pezi attacked the Mongol Khan.

CHAPTER 28

YEAR TEN, FLOWER MOON

With so much going on, Marcellinus had stopped paying attention to the boy. So had everyone else. Now the word slave shinned off his horse, ducked behind the horse of the Keshik separating him from the Khan, and leaped up at him.

Someone behind Chinggis must have shouted out a warning, because the Khan began to move even as the boy grabbed him by the belt and drove the knife up and under his armor. Chinggis's arm dealt Pezi a heavy blow. At the same time both of the Khan's bodyguards dropped their bows and drew steel, the first whipping his saber down so fast that it was a blur. Startled by the sudden activity, the Khan's horse bucked and kicked. The kick missed Pezi, but as the horse's hooves came down again, they scored the boy's legs. Pezi screamed.

The Khan twisted, peering down at himself. Blood from his wound had splashed down onto his horse's flanks.

"Split." Sintikala spurred her horse to the right. Marcellinus felt an instant of fear as she left his side.

Keshik warriors were converging on them. Marcellinus leaned forward, kicked at his increasingly reluctant horse, managed to dodge around two warriors who were heading for Hanska, and galloped into the suddenly appearing space, straight toward Chinggis Khan.

He reached behind him, and his questing hand found the third javelin in the quiver behind his saddle. He dragged it free.

Chinggis shouted an order, his high voice cutting through the din. The bodyguards to either side of the Khan recovered their composure and raised their bows once again.

A Mongol arrow drove through Marcellinus's breastplate and into his chest. The arrow did not knock him back and did not reach his heart, but as his horse kept up its gallop, the iron point grated against his rib, making him howl. He tried to raise his lance, and the pain came again, almost unbearable.

The Keshik guards moved forward. On the ground behind the Khan, Pezi shoved himself shakily upright. Blood poured from his chest and legs, but the knife was still in his hand, and this time he thrust it up under the barding of the Khan's horse, slashing the animal deeply in the thigh.

Even as Marcellinus saw that, he was suddenly flying, airborne with no idea why. The ground came up to meet him and smashed the wind from him.

His horse had thrown him and was cantering away, snorting and squealing. The spatha had disappeared from his right hand, but his left still clutched the javelin. He looked up in time to see Sintikala hurl herself bodily off her horse and crash into the second Keshik. The bodyguard was not as lucky as Marcellinus. He got caught in his stirrups and flailed, painfully falling sideways.

Marcellinus came up onto one knee, gasping, looking for enemies. Where had the Mongol Khan disappeared to?

Behind him. The Khan's horse had bucked again at the sudden stab to its thigh and had leaped past Marcellinus. Chinggis mostly had it under control, although it still tossed its head and rolled its eyes.

Marcellinus snapped the arrow that still jutted from his chest, threw it aside, and stood. Chinggis drew his saber. Six more Keshiks hurried forward, two on mounts and four on foot. Behind the Khan, Hanska's Third Cahokian had caught up to her, and Chernye Klobuki were pouring in to engage the Keshiks.

Two arrows plinked off Marcellinus's back. A third grazed his helmet. He had to move.

Hardly thinking anymore, trying to shove aside his fear and ignore the grating pain in his chest, Marcellinus ran forward with javelin raised.

The Khan's horse's ears went back. Chinggis slapped its flanks with his whip, then dropped the lash as the horse began to canter forward. The Khan raised his saber.

Sintikala had killed her Keshik and was fighting two more as the Chernye came in, firing arrows and slashing with their sabers. The field around them was a mass of mounted warriors battling hand to hand, with Marcellinus and Sintikala the only ones on foot and separated by two dozen yards.

As the Mongol Khan ran him down, slashing with the saber, Marcellinus hurled his javelin and threw himself aside. Trying to thrust at the Khan while still holding it would have been deadly dangerous; the impact would have knocked Marcellinus off his feet.

The javelin drove into the horse's leather barding just above the throat and hung there. The horse flinched and tossed its head back but looked to have suffered little injury.

A heavy pilum would have served Marcellinus well now, but his only remaining weapon was the gladius that hung from his belt. He drew it and waited for the Khan to swing his horse around into another charge.

It did not happen. The horse reared, still in pain from the wound Pezi had inflicted, and skittered in distress. The Khan swung his feet out of the stirrups, dropped to the ground in a single motion, and strode forward toward Marcellinus.

As he did, he sheathed his saber and drew a mace from the strap that had held it on his back.

The mace was a much longer and heavier weapon than a gladius. This was now a very one-sided fight.

Marcellinus eyed him warily. Chinggis Khan was shorter than Marcellinus, but his shoulders and arms bulged with muscle. Fifteen years Marcellinus's senior, the Khan still looked strong and hale, his graying hair the only sign of his age. Chinggis moved like a warrior, hefted the mace one-handed as if it were a toy, and eyed Marcellinus with predatory intent.

The Mongol Khan was a dangerous opponent, and again Marcellinus felt a quite uncharacteristic surge of fear.

"I am not kneeling at your feet now," he said to the Mongol Khan. "You should have killed me when I was."

The Khan could not have understood him but spit out a few words in a steady voice, his tone almost hypnotic. Ten feet from Marcellinus, he cut the air with a swing of the mace and raised it over his head again.

Marcellinus stepped forward. His gladius felt like a toothpick in his hand by comparison.

He needed the battle fury that gave him confidence, or the fight was already lost. He tried to recall the slaughter at Yupkoyvi, Enopay's fear, the callous burning of the Roman soldier by the Jin.

And then Hanska screamed. Marcellinus flicked a glance to his left. She was fighting, her ax coming down and swinging around again so fast that it almost eluded the eye, dueling with a Keshik in an attempt to get past him for her own chance at the Mongol Khan. Her scream was not of pain but of raw, relentless, berserker anger.

And on breathing in her rage, Marcellinus felt it, too.

War be damned. Roma be damned. Marcellinus owed it to Hanska to kill this man.

He leaped forward, suddenly careless of the disparity of weapons between himself and the Mongol Khan. The saber was a slashing weapon and the mace a swinging weapon, and they were what the Khan was used to, and so Marcellinus ended his leap by thrusting the gladius forward in a direct and unsubtle line straight at the Khan's face.

Unable to parry at that speed, the Khan stepped left to avoid the blade. His mace came around, as quick as Hanska's ax, and swooped toward Marcellinus's head. Such a blow would surely kill him. Marcellinus dodged it, jumping to his right to follow the Khan's direction. He was watching Chinggis's eyes, alert for any tell that might give away the Khan's next move.

Marcellinus whipped the gladius forward. Its blade struck the Khan's gauntlet and glanced off. It was Chinggis's right hand, the hand that held the mace, but that hand was uninjured and still in motion, swinging the heavy weapon. Marcellinus lunged with the gladius again and only at the last moment saw the rock in the Khan's left hand.

Pulling his strike, Marcellinus jumped back. The rock flew from the Khan's hand and struck Marcellinus's shoulder. If he had not retreated, it would have flown into his face.

As they separated, the Khan pulled his saber out of his belt with his left hand. Marcellinus sneered and pulled out his pugio. Both men glanced left and right, but they were unassailed. The melee still raged around them. Marcellinus could hear Hanska grunting as she traded blow after blow with her Keshik adversary, but for him and the Khan, their own duel was the only one that mattered.

Marcellinus moved left. The mace was still in Chinggis's right hand, and crowding the Khan a little would help reduce his advantage from having the longer weapon. From the way Chinggis held his saber Marcellinus could tell the man was not a truly ambidextrous fighter, but the risk was plain: if Marcellinus swung his gladius and the Khan parried with the saber, Marcellinus would have no time to protect himself from the blow from the mace that would follow.

He was still watching the Khan's eyes, and the Khan was watching his. The Khan was not gripped by battle ardor. He was cold and calculating, constantly measuring distances, gauging responses, evaluating threats.

Marcellinus's anger still burned. He feinted left; the Khan reacted immediately. He ducked left again and swung, but the Khan jumped and lifted his mace, and both men fell back. A failed blow by either man might be his last.

Behind the Khan, Hanska lost her footing and tumbled over backward. She shrieked and rolled, but the Keshik was upon her. And Marcellinus's rage became unbearable.

Time to take a leaf out of Hanska's book. Marcellinus bellowed, a sudden blast of sound, and saw a flicker of uncertainty in the Khan's eyes a moment before he leaped.

Marcellinus threw himself forward, gladius held high. The Khan slashed with the saber; Marcellinus twisted so that the blow bounced off his shoulder rather than cutting into his neck. Chinggis raised the mace to parry Marcellinus's sword, but instead of swinging it down, Marcellinus punched forward again, the pommel of the sword crunching into the Khan's nose.

Chinggis Khan shrieked. Landing almost on top of the Khan, Marcellinus stabbed his pugio into Chinggis's neck below the leather flaps of his helmet. Blood spurted. The mace clipped Marcellinus's head. It was the wooden shaft and not the heavy ball at its tip, but Marcellinus's head rang, and for a dangerous moment his vision swam.

The Khan dropped the mace and swung, his gauntlet slamming into Marcellinus's cheek.

Suddenly the gladius was gone from Marcellinus's hand. He whipped the pugio around again and missed. The Khan stepped back and switched the saber back into his right hand, his left clutching at his neck.

The saber came around. Marcellinus held up an armored forearm and kicked out at the Khan's knee. The saber glanced off his arm, and he kicked again.

The Khan went down. Marcellinus grabbed his helmet with an iron grip, and threw all his weight forward.

He looked up, and she was running toward him: Hanska of Cahokia, screaming, her ax high.

The Mongol Khan struggled. Marcellinus leaned on the man to hold him firm. Blood still poured from the conqueror's neck.

Hanska slowed to a walk and quietened. She seemed suddenly mesmerized by the Khan. She had probably dreamed of this moment for a long time.

The Khan saw her coming. He still struggled, but his blood was spilling over Marcellinus's hands, and he appeared to be weakening.

Marcellinus stole quick glances around him. Keshiks were on their knees, facing him. Cahokians and Romans stood over them, sweating. The furor of the battles taking place farther away had not abated, but close by, at least, everyone knew it was over. Out of the corner of his eye Marcellinus saw Pezi crawling forward, dragging himself toward them. Aelfric was to his left, panting, covered in mud.

"Now, Hanska," Marcellinus said. "He's yours."

Hanska nodded. "For Mikasi," she said, almost sadly.

She measured the distance, swung her heavy ax. It smashed into Chinggis Khan's face, sinking deep into his skull. The strength of the impact knocked Marcellinus backward into the mud, the dead Khan lying across his legs.

All around them the Keshiks moaned, almost a keening sound, at the death of their beloved leader. The Romans and Hesperians stood silent. Perhaps they couldn't believe their eyes. Pezi made a strange noise that might have been a cough or a short laugh, that he cut off quickly.

Hanska looked into the Khan's ruined face, then calmly pulled off his helmet and brought out her pugio to scalp him. Her face was a mask; if anything, she looked thoughtful rather than exultant. Perhaps she had never expected to see the Khan lying dead. Perhaps she had never expected to survive this battle.

As she carved into the Khan's hairline, the Keshiks ceased their keening and lowered their heads as if in prayer. One began to sob quietly. More blood poured onto Marcellinus's chest.

Hanska stood and fastened the conqueror's bloody scalp to her belt, then looked down to where Marcellinus sat, his muscles still quivering with the effort, shaken by the blows to his head, body, and arms.

She lifted the body of the Khan off him. "Up you come, sir." Marcellinus held out a hand, and Hanska hauled him to his feet.

Instead of letting go, she pulled him closer and stared into his eyes. There he saw deep gratitude, respect, and sorrow. He nodded, and Hanska squeezed his hand and released him without comment.

Around them the struggle had abated, at least in the immediate area. The wind had picked up, but patchy smoke still swirled around them. Those Mongol warriors who could see that their leader had fallen were backing away, trying to withdraw without showing their backs to the Chernye Klobuki and the Polovtsians, who would kill them as soon as they turned tail.

Other Keshiks, however, were moving in to converge upon Marcellinus.

Shit. Did he have to fight yet again? He didn't think he could. He was all-done.

Aelfric strolled to his side. "So, Praetor. That drink you offered me after I helped you kill Corbulo. Did I ever get it?"

"I don't think so. Sorry."

"Bloody typical. Yet here I am again."

"Here you are again."

Then they heard a single voice, wailing. Marcellinus turned around, almost irritated and still a little dazed, trying to figure out where it was coming from. One of the Keshik?

It was Pezi. Pezi was somehow standing, holding himself up by clutching the saddle of his horse, and he was weeping and wailing and crying out words in the Mongol tongue. Then he switched briefly to Cahokian and in the same wailing tone cried out: "Wanageeska! I am spreading the word that their Khan is dead. Put me on a horse! Do not leave me here!"

A dozen yards from Pezi a Keshik warrior smashed a Polovtsian cavalryman to the ground and jerked his horse's head around. Seeing and hearing Pezi, he spurred his horse forward, heading for the boy. But Sintikala was faster, cantering her horse to Pezi's side in his defense.

Again came Pezi's voice. "Let them leave, Wanageeska! Give the Keshiks the body of the Khan and let them leave! Trust me, Wanageeska! Do it!"

"Trust *him*?" said Aelfric.

Pezi, once a coward and a liar, had come through at exactly the right moment at tremendous risk to himself. Marcellinus could not have defeated the Khan without the word slave's courage. "Absolutely," he said, and raised his voice. "Do as he says! Back up! Let them leave!" He repeated it in Latin for the Chernye.

The Cahokians and Chernye Klobuki withdrew together, away from the Khan's body. The Keshiks walked past them to stand by their fallen leader.

Sintikala rode over to Marcellinus. How she had gotten her horse back, Marcellinus didn't know; he had no idea where his own had gone. She gestured for him to climb up behind her, and he gave it a try, but with the arrow wound to his chest and the bruising to his arms and back, there was no way. "I can't."

She looked alarmed. "Will you live?"

"Yes. If you don't make me get up there."

Sintikala blinked. Then she got off the horse and put her arms around him for just a moment. He could feel her heart pumping hard. She was breathing heavily, chest moving in and out. He wanted to hold her, but it was too painful. "I love you, Sintikala."

"I love you, Gaius. Let us do this. Hold on to me."

She put his foot into the stirrup and half pushed, half lifted him until he could get into the saddle, bracing himself on her shoulder.

"Let them leave!" Marcellinus shouted to the Chernye, to anyone who could hear him. Damn, even shouting was agony with that accursed arrowhead still lodged in his rib. "Let . . . Futete."

Sintikala raised her voice. "Let the Mongols depart to spread the word among their people that their Khan has fallen!"

"Exactly," Marcellinus said. "Thank you."

Taking the horse's reins, Sintikala walked him over to where Pezi still howled. "Shut up now," she said. "They're going."

Pezi peered up at Marcellinus. "You came for me. Thank you and thank you . . . If you had not, the Keshiks would have taken me. As the Khan's servant they would have killed me to serve him in the afterlife."

The Mongols were trying to lift Chinggis Khan's body onto his horse, but the horse was resisting their efforts. Eventually they gave it up and raised him onto their shoulders instead. Grouping up, they walked eastward. From a safe distance the Romans, Chernye, and Cahokians watched them go.

"Once again you owe the Wanageeska a life," Sintikala said.

Pezi's face cracked into a grin that quickly contorted with pain. "Or perhaps the Wanageeska now owes me one!"

A battle spread over such a large area, broken into so many distinct parts and amid such confusion, could not be ended all at once. It took trumpets and dispatch riders on the Roman side and drums, signal flags, and post riders on the Mongol side. It took a giant wailing Mongol horn sounding from far back from the battlefield. It took the defeat of another two hundred Mongols and Jin on foot bearing fire lances, with substantial deaths among the centuries of the Third Parthica that resisted them. Other jaghuns, seeking revenge, attempted to drive a Chisel Formation into groups of tired Romans, but the news of the Mongol Khan's death had spread among the legions, too, cheering them and stiffening their spines, and few of the vengeance attacks resulted in major Roman casualties. Other skirmishes and smaller actions continued until the end of the afternoon.

Marcellinus and Sintikala, the Third Cahokian, the Chernye Klobuki, and other remaining mounted regiments of Roma regrouped with the Third Parthica in the late afternoon. By then Pezi was draped unconscious on his Mongol horse, and Marcellinus yearned to be safely unconscious, too. For all his wounds, aches, and pains, he could have fallen asleep in the saddle.

But that luxury was not for him. Agrippa, the Praetorians, and several cohorts of the 27th had already left the field, clustered in a strong defensive formation around their wounded Imperator.

Agrippa had left the phased withdrawal of the rest of the army to its tribunes, but Marcellinus had no idea what orders the other Praetor might have given. He could leave nothing to chance. The remains of this bloody and smoky battlefield, strewn with the bodies of dead men and horses, now appeared to be his responsibility.

"Contact my tribunes," he said to his Roman adjutants and Norse scouts once he found them. "I need reports from every cohort as soon as you can. Sooner." He turned to Napayshni and Takoda. "You two: the same. Get reports and locations from Tahtay and Wahchintonka. And the Thunderbird clan. Does anyone know what happened to Chenoa's Wakinyan? Any signals? And if you see Chumanee, I need her right now. Don't send me a medicus. Send me Chumanee. Enopay, you're with me."

And later, to the tribunes of the Third: "Find the freshest cavalry. Collect your scouts. Break it to them that their day is not over. The Mongols might even now be sending jaghuns to flank us. I don't think so, but they might, and we don't have enough birds in the air to watch for them. Send scouts west, patrols and skirmishers south and north. Find trumpeters to go with them."

Marcellinus did not lead his troops back to Forward Camp. Once the Sixth had mopped up the fire lancers and chased away the last of the Mongol heavy infantry, Aurelius Dizala took command and retreated along with the survivors of the Third Parthica, conveying and safeguarding the Roman wounded as best they could. The Hesperian League—Tahtay, Akecheta, and the First Cahokian, along with the Wolf Warriors, the Iroqua, the Blackfoot, and the Hand—had chosen to return separately. Marcellinus wondered what they had talked about on their long walk home to Forward Camp.

Marcellinus and Sintikala finally withdrew from the battlefield, escorted by Aelfric's Sixth Cohort, Hanska's Third Cahokian, and the Ninth Syrian. On the way Kimimela found them, careering down to earth in front of them in an untidy and exhausted landing that snapped her right wing strut and made Sintikala shake her head disapprovingly even as Kimi ran to hug them both, half crying.

Once she composed herself, she gave her report from the flying clans.

It turned out that Chenoa's Wakinyan had made it to the Wemissori after all. Two of her Thunderbirds managed to fly across and land on the far side. Others came down on the near bank, but sufficiently distant from the closest Mongol mounted squadrons that they could cross the river in safety. One overly optimistic Wakinyan crew had tried to fly to the far bank but crash-landed midriver, and two pilots had drowned before they could be cut free from their craft.

Those drownings were the only casualties the Thunderbird clan had suffered in their whole day of war making. The Hawk clan was not so fortunate; Kimimela was brusque and imprecise about the numbers, but Marcellinus's best guess was that they had lost perhaps two dozen Catanwakuwa pilots. Some had been forced to land behind enemy lines and had been killed instantly, and others had been shot down in dogfights with the Firebirds and Feathered Serpents. Kimimela had barely survived her own aerial battle with the Firebird. Several well-aimed slingshot pellets had forced the Firebird to lose height, and its pilots had chosen to fly back behind the Mongol lines rather than continue to fight her.

Others had, however, been saved. Five Hawk pilots had suffered disabling attacks to their wings at altitude. Cutting themselves free, they had drifted to earth under their Falling Leaf canopies. Four had survived unscathed. A fifth had broken both ankles in the violence of her landing, but at least she was still alive.

Kimimela climbed up on Sintikala's horse behind her, and they cantered east to take control of the Hawk clan. After so long on the ground, Sintikala was keen to get back into the air before nightfall to see for herself where the Mongol forces were, find out whether any Hesperian forces were stranded, and see if she could determine where the Sky Lantern pilots had landed.

Once they left, Aelfric pulled in beside Marcellinus, and they led the last cohorts home.

"Whew." Aelfric whistled. "This'll be a tale to tell your grandkids."

Marcellinus shook his head. "Kimimela doesn't want children."

Aelfric grinned. "So she says now. Ah, well. In that case you'll just have to tell it to mine."

PART 4

CAHOKIA

CHAPTER 29

YEAR TEN, FLOWER MOON

"They will lay the Mongol Khan's body in a great cart," Pezi said. "They will carry him home in a long procession across the Grass back to the west, back to a ship, back to the Mongol land he comes from. And in that land there will be a kurultai."

Tahtay shook his head. "A what?"

"A council," Hadrianus said. "A powwow. To choose the Khan's successor. Which, given the hatred and jealousy that Jochi, Chagatai, and Ogodei have for one another, will be no easy task."

It was a meeting of the invalids. The Imperator lay flat on his couch, his stomach bound tightly in white linen. He was gray-faced and sallow, and his eyes were only half open. To Hadrianus's left stood his chief medicus, an elderly Greek with a lined face who fussed over him and whom he was constantly having to wave away.

Not ten feet from him, lying in a wooden cot that two legionaries had carried into the Imperial presence, was Pezi, sometime word slave of the Iroqua, Cahokia, Roma, and the Mongols. Both of Pezi's legs had been broken and were set and splinted with wood to keep them straight. Once again Marcellinus was in the presence of a brave young man who might never walk properly again.

Also crowded into the Praetorium tent behind the

Imperator were Lucius Agrippa and his First Tribune, Mettius Fronto, both looking battered and bruised; Aurelius Dizala from the Sixth; and the First Tribune of the Third Parthica, Antonius Caster. Standing with Marcellinus were Sintikala and Enopay.

"The Mongol Khan will be buried at the place of his birth." Pezi paused, trying to remember. "Khenti Aimag? The Onon River? A place of good medicine for the Mongols. Far-and-far."

Marcellinus nodded. Central Asia was indeed a very long way from here.

Taianita sat by Pezi's side, her face the picture of concern. Her past gratitude for Pezi's valor on her behalf was equaled by her care for him now that he had been recovered. She had stayed with him while he was unconscious and had helped the legionary medicus do his work on the boy. As Pezi spoke, he occasionally glanced sideways at her, as if startled that someone like Taianita could possibly care whether he lived or died.

By now everyone knew that Taianita was for Tahtay, and Tahtay for Taianita. But Taianita and Pezi shared an odd bond: both had been word slaves for harsh, sadistic masters, and Pezi had spoken up for Taianita and almost died for it.

And then Pezi had risked his life once again. Attacking the great Chinggis Khan with a puny knife on the battlefield was one of the bravest things Marcellinus had ever seen. Pezi was as far from being a warrior as it was possible to get, yet he had acted without hesitation at a crucial moment. What must he have endured in the Khan's service to provoke such a desperate gamble? Marcellinus had decided he would never ask.

Marcellinus was scarcely in any better condition than the Imperator or Pezi, beaten and banged up as always. When Chumanee had caught sight of him, she had merely nodded and gotten to work. She had carved the arrowhead out of his chest, thoroughly cleansed his wounds with her dark liquid, and painted them with her thick white salve before binding them up with Cahokian woven cloth.

For preferring Cahokian care to Roman, Lucius Agrippa had called Marcellinus a barbarian. Marcellinus, too exhausted to argue, had merely agreed.

Tahtay had somehow survived the battle without serious injury. The renewed gash in his leg had proved to be superficial, though his many bruises and blisters made him grimace. Now he stirred. "The Mongols have withdrawn. They spent last night in a camp thirty miles back. They have sent no flanking actions. Their army retreats undivided. Our scouts have spoken, Norse as well as Cahokian, and Sintikala and the Hawks confirm it."

"They are all-done," Pezi said.

"Perhaps we should continue to watch a little longer," Dizala said drily.

"And we will," said Tahtay. "For maybe they are just resting, as we are. Perhaps they plan to return to do battle with us again later."

Pezi frowned. "Do Mongol riders hurry west, ahead of the main army?"

Since Sintikala showed no sign of responding, Marcellinus said, "Yes. Our Hawks and scouts have seen three jaghuns of Keshik riders galloping west, each with many remounts. They're traveling fast." So fast that the disgruntled Bjarnason and Stenberg had not been able to keep up in their attempt to shadow the group. But Sintikala had seen them, and Demothi and the others continued to watch over them as they rode.

"Then I am right," Pezi said. "Chagatai will make haste to leave Nova Hesperia. He probably rides with that forward group. His armies will not be back."

The Imperator nodded weakly. "I agree. But explain it to them if you would."

Pezi took the beaker of water Taianita pushed into his hand, drank, and spoke. "Chinggis Khan is dead. His trusted Keshik bodyguards must take the news back to the Mongol heartland and the Khan's other sons as soon as they can. And so Chagatai must go with them, to bend the Keshiks to his will, and shape how the news is spoken and heard once they get home.

"At kurultai, the brothers and their armies will meet. There, Chagatai must present himself as the man who helped conquer the huge realm of western Nova Hesperia and whose wife still rules it on his behalf. In addition, he must proclaim himself the hero who dealt the Roman army a mortal blow. Chagatai must recount this as his triumph. He must steal victory from defeat. Otherwise he is merely the son who could not prevent his father from being slain.

"And so Chagatai gains no advantage by fighting on. If he and the Great Khan had conquered the whole of Nova Hesperia, his claim to be chosen as Chinggis's successor would be that much stronger. If he could take back gold and furs, that would help, too. But he cannot, and further glory and booty would take too long to acquire. He will leave."

Agrippa nodded crisply. "By Mongol standards there's little enough in Nova Hesperia to plunder. The gold is still in the ground, and there are no carpets or silks or fine glass, no rich nobles to fleece. If I were Chagatai, I'd certainly go home. Stake my claim to become the Great Khan and seek richer lands to prey on."

"Leaving his army to follow behind in the command of Subodei Badahur," Pezi added. "The army, bearing the body of the Khan."

The other Romans were nodding, but the Cahokians were lost and even Marcellinus had to ask. "Pezi, are you sure?"

The Iroqua word slave took another drink and rubbed his leg. "I spent much time learning the Mongol tongue and talking with their captains. Ingratiating myself helped ensure my survival, I think. So I constantly talked and listened."

Of that, at least, Marcellinus had no doubt.

"At the moment, the blame for the loss of so many men can be placed at the Khan's door," Fronto said thoughtfully. "And at Jebei Noyon's, since he's also usefully dead. Chagatai will claim the credit for rescuing as much as possible from a bad situation. Dealing a heavy blow to the legions and an injury to Roma's Imperator against heavy odds. And two other leading Praetors are dead. All respect due, Imperator; that might play well on the steppes."

Painfully slowly, Hadrianus sat up. "He'll need every advantage he can get. Jochi and Chagatai have always hated each other. Jochi is rash and showed his father too little respect. Chagatai is ruthless and unbending, hot-tempered. That is why Chinggis brought Chagatai here with him to Nova Hesperia, so that he would not go to war with his brother Jochi while the Great Khan's eyes were elsewhere."

Pezi thought for a moment. "The captains told me that because of this feud between the first two brothers, Chinggis wanted Ogodei as his successor. But Ogodei is now chief of the Jin and Song Empires, which are huge and grand. He has less interest in being paramount chief and conquering other lands. Many of the Mongol captains favor the fourth brother, Tolui, but he treads warily around Jochi and Chagatai. I think I have that right?"

"Yes." Agrippa turned to Marcellinus and the tribunes. "So far, so good. Everything Pezi says confirms our intelligence, but that is now several years old. Who knows what has happened in the Mongol lands in the meantime? Chagatai must be keen to find out."

"Chinggis wanted the Imperator of Roma dead, and all his generals." Pezi ducked his head, almost cringing, in an echo of his fawning, submissive behavior of the past. "Wanted this above all else, to prove that he was the strongest, the Chosen-by-Heaven, the ruler of the world. But Chagatai thinks only of power and plunder. Freed from his father, he will leave to fight other wars."

Marcellinus knew little enough of Mongol politics and personalities, but he certainly understood the logistics of Hesperian travel. "The timing would make sense. It's late in the Flower Moon now—almost the month of

Julius. If Chagatai and his Keshiks hurry, just a few strong men on fast horses with many remounts, they can get back over the Great Mountains before the snows come, then back to the western coast of the continent. Maybe even set sail, if they can. But if they delay, they'll have to either overwinter east of the mountains until the snows melt in spring or take a long detour south . . . through the lands of the People of the Hand."

Tahtay had been waiting to say something for some time, with gradually increasing agitation. Now he broke in. "But what if you are all wrong? You speak of what sort of man this Mongol is, or that Mongol, and how far it is to the edge of the land as if this were finished. But what if the Mongols turn and ride back to strike Cahokia?"

The Imperator gestured. "Gaius Marcellinus?"

"If they do, we will get there first," Marcellinus said. "Forward Camp is a little over four hundred miles from Cahokia. At the Mongols' best, if each of their warriors has several replacement mounts, they can travel eighty or ninety miles a day. That would take them a little over five days. But they cannot be at their best after two hard-fought battles. The men will be weary, and our Wakin-yan attacks destroyed a number of their remounts."

He nodded to Enopay, who cleared his throat importantly and continued. "But also there are rivers. If the army rides south, they must cross the Braided River and two other rivers before they get to Cahokia-across-the-water, and then cross the Mizipi to get to Cahokia itself. If they go north instead, they will cross the Wemissori and follow it, then cross the Mizipi north of Cahokia, and another river or two, and Cahokia Creek. For either route, all those rivers will add much time. The four-legs can swim, but then they are tired and must rest, and if the Mongols want to take their big weapons, the trebu-chets and fire lances and Firebirds, they will need a pon-toon bridge or lots of rafts. So, eight days, then? Ten? More?"

"And traveling down the Wemissori on the quinqueremes, with the current, if we hurry, we can be back at Cahokia in four," Marcellinus finished.

Tahtay looked doubtful. "Your big canoes cannot take all your Roman and my Hesperian warriors and all their horses. We have not lost so many that everyone would fit."

"The cavalry will come overland," Marcellinus said. "But our ships can ferry them across the rivers. The Mongols have only the Tlingit canoes, too small to help much with a large force of men and horses."

"And if the Mongols turn, we will know right away," Enopay added.

Sintikala inclined her head. Her Hawks were keeping the Mongols under constant scrutiny, and flying far and wide over the whole area of Cahokia down to Ocatan and beyond to protect against any surprises. In Asia and Europa the Mongols were renowned for their lightning attacks, but it was much harder for them to appear out of nowhere when they could be watched from above and their progress could be assessed.

"We will remain here at Forward Camp a few days longer, Tahtay," said the Imperator. "Regroup. Rest. Heal. Then, if the Mongols continue to retreat, we will start our own withdrawal." He smiled. "Well done, Pezi. Well done."

Pezi glowed. Taianita grinned.

Marcellinus and Enopay looked at each other quizzically. These were strange days indeed.

As they walked out of the tent together, back into the turmoil and havoc of Forward Camp, Tahtay wrinkled his nose. "This camp is a dirty hell. I would think it the most evil place imaginable if I had not seen war."

Marcellinus checked around them. The tribunes had made haste back to their cohorts, and Enopay had stayed behind to talk further with Pezi and Taianita. It was the first time he had been truly alone with Tahtay since before the battles, and gods knew they had been through hell in the meantime. Had Tahtay forgiven him yet? He racked his brains for a safe topic. "I still can't believe you pinned your sash for the Imperator of Roma."

"I had no choice. And Enopay would have done the same."

Marcellinus raised his eyebrows. "Enopay would crawl a thousand miles before he'd face a man with a sword in battle."

Tahtay walked beside him companionably enough. "And for Enopay that is the right choice, because we need him to think, not fight. But I meant that his words were in my head when I pinned my sash. It is what Enopay would have told me to do. If the Imperator had died, what then of Cahokia afterward? Could I trust Agrippa or even Sabinus? I do not think so."

At Marcellinus's silence, Tahtay looked sideways at him. "And if I had not, Hotah? What if instead of pinning my sash and fighting for your Imperator, the war chief of Cahokia had run away or stood aside and let Hadrianus and his men burn? What would his legionaries and tribunes say then? That was not possible. I had to show dignitas, and virtus, and animus."

Dignity, valor, and martial spirit. "You're right," Marcellinus admitted. "That's exactly what Enopay would say."

"And besides, I like Hadrianus. Of all the new Romans, he is the one I least want to see burned to a crisp or rotting in a hole in the ground."

Perhaps that was not so hard to understand. Marcellinus had long ago noted the strange kinship between the war chief and the Imperator. They shared the loneliness of command, the responsibility of knowing that all eyes were on them all the time. Marcellinus himself knew something about that.

"And he and I swore an oath in blood to stand together against the Mongol Khan. You do not remember, you who love oaths so much?"

Certainly Marcellinus remembered that. But to this day he did not believe that the swearing of such oaths meant as much to the Imperator as it did to him.

Tahtay nodded. "The Imperator has my blood in him now, as I have his. That will help him heal. And perhaps help him keep faith with us now that we have stood by his side in battle."

"I hope you are right," Marcellinus said. "I really do."

Tahtay stopped walking and poked a hole in the mud with his moccasin. "And when Roma leaves, you will go with them?"

"No," Marcellinus said, shocked, and then: "You believe Roma will leave?"

"Of course. They have won their war here. Why would they stay?"

Marcellinus could think of a dozen reasons, but right now Tahtay's first question was more important to him. "When I agreed to lead the Sixth Ferrata into battle against the Mongol Khan, it was on the condition that I would be discharged once the war was won. That I'd retire from the army, here in Nova . . . in Hesperia."

Now that he had said the words, Marcellinus could not remember whether Hadrianus had in fact explicitly agreed to this. He frowned.

"Ah. You arranged all that with the Imperator, then?"

Marcellinus looked up quickly. "With your permission, of course, war chief. Always, I would work for my grain, for Cahokia . . ."

It was the paramount chief's prerogative to say who could live in Cahokia and who could not. If Tahtay held too many grudges, Marcellinus could quickly become a man without a country. Again.

Tahtay stared at him long and hard, and then grinned wryly. "Of course. For if I said not, Kimimela would break my balls and my Hawk chief would never smile again for the rest of her life. Her smiles are rare enough even now. And then there is Nahimana, and Takoda, and Hanska." He met Marcellinus's eye. "But I had to ask, because you seem so . . . Roman again now. And also—I must admit it: sometimes I think Cahokia should be just for Cahokians, and Hesperia just for Hesperians."

After another uncomfortable silence, Marcellinus checked around himself again for eavesdroppers and said: "I agree. And I also agree that Roma must leave. Whether they wish it or not."

CHAPTER 30

YEAR TEN, HEAT MOON

It was their last evening on the Wemissori. The next day, the leading ships in the Roman fleet would arrive back in Cahokia.

The galleys did not sail the river by night. The risk of holing a ship on a submerged tree trunk or rock, running aground, or sticking firmly in the river mud was too great. Even if night travel had been safe, the vessels were so crowded with Romans and Hesperians and their weaponry and supplies that there was no room for everyone to lie down. Instead they moored along the bank at dusk, and the Roman cohorts threw up makeshift field fortifications in a line parallel to the shore: a shallow berm studded with sharpened stakes, with a deep ditch beyond it. The Hesperians politely asked whom the Romans were protecting themselves against—they were at peace with the Iroqua, Blackfoot, People of the Hand, and the other tribes that had departed from Forward Camp days before, presumably heading back to their homelands, and the Mongols were even farther away and still making haste westward—but old Roman habits died hard, and no tribune or centurion would allow his men to sleep unprotected.

It might have been better for Hadrianus to have remained in his stateroom on board the *Providentia*, but he would not hear of it: as Imperator, he slept among his men. And so his Praetorians had carried him ashore on his litter and installed him in his Praetorium tent, where he sat up and dined with Marcellinus, Agrippa, and the lead tribunes of his three war-battered legions, with his Greek medicus flickering around behind him like a fussy ghost.

After dinner Marcellinus went to stand outside the tent, looking out across the Wemissori past the great warships that loomed along the bank.

Cahokia was near, and Marcellinus was craving their first view of the Great City. Approaching from the north, they would first see the Circle of the Cedars poking up over the tree line and then the longhouses on top of the Master Mound, all wreathed in the smoke that rose from the hearth fires of the city.

He would be home, but Sintikala would not. The ships of the Roman fleet were spread out along the Wemissori. The *Providentia*, the *Clementia*, and the smaller ships of Roma and Cahokia had left first with the Imperator, the wounded, and as many other legionaries as they could take. Loading the *Minerva* and the *Fides* with the Hawk, Eagle, and Thunderbird craft had been a task left for last, as it was more careful work that could be achieved more readily once almost everyone else was out of the way. It might be two or three days before Marcellinus would see Sintikala and Kimimela again, and he was less than happy about that.

Not that he had much time at leisure. These were his last days as a Praetor, and his pride was driving him to do all he could to ensure that he was leaving the Sixth Ferrata—his last ever Roman command—in as organized a shape as possible . . .

He shook himself, dismissing such woolgathering. There was serious work to be done tonight. The imminent meeting between Tahtay and the Imperator would be critical for Cahokia, for Roma, and for Marcellinus himself.

Yet despite the risks that might lie ahead, Marcellinus

found that he was looking forward to it. He wanted all this to be over.

Soon he saw the war chief threading his way between the Roman campfires toward him. As Tahtay arrived in front of the Praetorium tent, neither of them said a word. They hardly needed to.

Tahtay nodded to Marcellinus. Marcellinus nodded back. Then the Imperator's Praetorians pulled the tent flaps aside, and the two of them walked into the presence of the Imperator.

"Ah, Tahtay." The Imperator raised a hand in greeting, then allowed it to fall back down beside him. Even at that easy movement, his medicus frowned. "Forgive me for not arising to greet you."

"You look better, Caesar," Tahtay said courteously.

"I . . ." The Imperator coughed, and his face creased in sudden pain. They waited patiently for him to recover. "I offer you wine, although I am afraid I am not permitted to join you just yet." He tilted his head, indicating the medicus, who sighed.

"Not tonight, sir," Tahtay said.

"Then sit, sit."

Marcellinus did so, but Tahtay remained standing. "Tomorrow we will be back in Cahokia," he said. "And so tonight we must speak of the future of the great alliance between Roma and the Hesperian League. We would not want any mistakes or misunderstandings at this late date, after our friendship has survived so much."

Tahtay's expression and tone were pleasant enough, but Marcellinus knew the war chief well enough to see the iron resolve that lay beneath them and the restless energy that churned within him.

"You and I, Caesar, we swore a blood oath," Tahtay continued. "We vowed to do everything in our power to help each other destroy the Mongols. That, we have done. That slate is clean. Our debt of war is paid. Is it not so?"

The Imperator stirred painfully, but his voice was as strong as ever. "It is so, Tahtay."

"And so, when we arrive in Cahokia, what then? What next?"

Hadrianus half smiled. "Then, of course, my army must be resupplied. You promised me corn, Tahtay, and my legions will require all the corn in your granaries. In a month or so you will harvest new corn from your fields to replace it, no? And we will also need beans, askutasquash, and whatever dried fish and meat you can spare for our journey."

"Your journey home, Caesar? Out of Cahokia, then, and back to your own land?"

"Yes," Hadrianus said. "Back to Roma."

"All the legions, Caesar?" Agrippa ventured.

The Imperator smiled. "You would prefer to stay, Lucius Agrippa? Perhaps as a general of a garrison in Cahokia, attempting to enforce the peace here with a limited number of cohorts? Or leading an expedition back up the Wemissori for gold?"

"No, Caesar," Agrippa said, taken aback. "Those would not be my preferred choices."

Hadrianus looked back at Tahtay. "I will be quite candid with you, Tahtay, for you have earned it. The Cahokians and their allies have served us well. We have too few legions to hold a territory of this size, and those legions are beyond weary." The Imperator's voice came stronger now. He seemed amused at the surprise on Tahtay's face. "It has been a long campaign, and these legions are needed elsewhere. Like Lucius, there are few among my Romans who would welcome an even more extended posting here in the bowels of Nova Hesperia." He glanced pointedly at Marcellinus before continuing.

"And so we will fall back: some of us to the south aboard our ships, others on horses and mules to the east. Now we are confident that the Mongols' retreat is permanent, I have already sent the Polovtsians ahead along Marcellinus's road back to Chesapica. The sturdiest of our infantry cohorts and the other cavalry will be on the march just as soon as they are resupplied at Cahokia. The rest of us will be on our way a day or so later, riding the Mizipi south. With vigorous rowing the fleet can be at the Market of the Mud in little more than a month and then out into the Mare Solis. Then up the coast and across the Atlanticus just as soon as weather permits."

"That is good news. And I wish you well on your journey, Caesar." Tahtay stood back and shot Marcellinus a relieved look, but Marcellinus's eyes were on Lucius Agrippa. The Praetor seemed altogether too calm, and the conversation between him and the Imperator felt staged. He waited.

Hadrianus nodded in thanks, and his eyes narrowed. "However . . ."

Here it came.

"By the terms of our original treaty, I promised you that Cahokia and Ocatan would be free and independent cities within Nova Hesperia. In return you promised me corn, guides, and gold. Corn and guides we have received in abundance. But I see no gold."

Tahtay stood, speechless.

The Imperator's tone became quiet, conciliatory. "Pinning your sash was brave and noble, Tahtay. We will not forget your loyalty and valor on Roma's behalf, and that is why we will honor our agreement in full. We will pause in Cahokia to load our corn and then be gone. But we must also have gold, and you must provide it if you wish to keep your lands free of Roma."

"But since then we have fought by your side. Helped you win a war we knew nothing about when we made our treaty. That counts for nothing?"

"It counts for a great deal. But if my legions had never come to Nova Hesperia, what then? Without us, Cahokia would have fallen to the Mongols. By now this entire land would be groaning under the Mongol heel. We fought so that you might be brought into the light as Roman subjects rather than toiling in the darkness as Mongol slaves. I am sure you will agree that allying with Roma was the better bargain. But now Roma must be paid for the blood it has spilled on your behalf, and that payment must be in gold.

"By the time of the Midsummer Feast next year, I am confident that your Blackfoot and Hidatsa friends can deliver enough gold to our garrison at the Chesapica to fill a drekar. If so, then I believe I will be able to satisfy my senators that there is no need for Roma to march into your lands once again."

Lucius Agrippa spoke again at last. "Naturally, we will require such a payment on an annual basis."

Tahtay's lip curled. "You speak now of *tribute*?"

The Imperator smiled. "Do we have an agreement, Tahtay of Cahokia?"

The war chief shook his head. "I know nothing about how to collect gold from rivers or pull it from the earth!"

"You are an ingenious people," Hadrianus said. "I am confident that you will learn quickly."

Marcellinus could see Tahtay's mind spinning. "But if I swear to this, Roma will leave Hesperia for good?"

"Our garrisons will remain at Vinlandia and Chesapica and perhaps also in the far south," said Agrippa. "Those outposts will be permanent. But Cahokia and all other Mizipian cities and towns will be left in peace."

"And if I do not swear?"

Agrippa smiled. "Then perhaps the Imperator might be forced to retract his generous offer."

"Just so," Hadrianus said. "Just so."

Tahtay looked dour, and was obviously only controlling himself with difficulty. "And if I have the corn brought to the banks of the Mizipi, you will truly go? Load your food and leave our lands as quickly as you can? *You* will swear this to *me*?"

"I cannot swear in blood this time, for I have little to spare," Hadrianus said. "But yes, Tahtay: the legions will leave, and this will all be over."

Tahtay studied the Imperator's face, then looked at Marcellinus, and finally nodded grimly. "Well, then. It appears I have little choice. Let me talk to my council, and see what can be done."

And with that, the war chief bowed and abruptly withdrew from the Imperial presence.

Marcellinus caught up with Tahtay before he had gone a hundred yards. He had been afraid his young friend would run in his attempt to get as far as possible from the Praetorium tent of Hadrianus, but the war chief was walking at a determined pace, threading his way between the Roman tents. "Tahtay, wait."

Tahtay kept moving. "I am sure that the Imperator has sent you after me to coax and cajole so that I will do what he wants. Is that not the service he demands from you?"

"Hadrianus did not send me."

"Then what?" The war chief glanced at him, then slowed, blowing out his anger in a long breath. "Kimimela is right. I am an idiot. I wanted to believe well of the Imperator. I believed he would show us as much honor as we have shown him. But I was wrong, and Sintikala and the others were right. After going through all this, we have won nothing."

By the Imperator's lights, he was being astonishingly generous. Marcellinus was sure that if it had been left to Agrippa, the Praetor would have driven a much harsher bargain. He drew Tahtay toward the muddy riverbank and away from the tents, so that they would not be overheard. "Tahtay, Roma will leave Cahokia. The Great City will no longer be subject to an army of occupation. The remaining cohorts will be on the coast of the Atlanticus, weeks away from mound-builder territory. Perhaps it is the best we could have hoped for."

"Chesapica is not so far," Tahtay said bitterly. "And what of our brothers of the Powhatani? Are they not also Hesperian? Are they not of the League?"

Just a few years earlier, a Cahokian paramount chief would have given scant thought to what happened in the territory of the Algon-Quian. "Yes, you are right. Chesapica is not so far."

"And I must command the Blackfoot and the Sho-

shoni and the Hidatsa of the Plains to mine gold for
Roma?" Tahtay raised his hands above his head in frustration. "How can I do that? How can I tell all my chiefs
this? I cannot. I will not."

"Better you than a man like Agrippa or Verus," Marcellinus pointed out.

Tahtay looked at him long and hard. For a moment
Marcellinus thought he would turn on his heel and
march away again, but the war chief seemed to calm
himself and regain his resolve. "Very well, then. And so,
now it is time for you to decide. Who are you today?
Who will you be?"

The blunt question caught him by surprise. "Me?"

"Yes, you. Are you Roman or Cahokian? My friend
or Roma's? Hotah or Praetor?"

Marcellinus felt brittle. "Always I have tried to be
both."

Tahtay was already shaking his head. "Yes, always
you try that, Gaius. Always you try."

At that, Marcellinus was silent.

Tahtay studied him. "Let me be clear, perhaps for the
last time. When I gathered my Army of Ten Thousand
against Roma, when we prepared to attack the Third
and 27th Legions, there were things we could not tell
you, neither I, nor Kimimela, nor Sintikala. And it was
the same with you and Roma: you knew of the Mongols
for many moons before you told Cahokia."

"We—"

Tahtay made a sharp gesture to cut him off. "And
now we are here, you and I, on the banks of the Wemissori. And once again I have made plans, Hotah. I was
not sure I would need them, whether to believe what
Sintikala and the others have been telling me all this
time, but after what I just heard? Now I am sure. I am
very sure.

"But after all you and I have been through, I find that
I do not want to keep you in the dark again. We have all
deceived one another enough these past two hands of
winters. If you and I are friends, if we ever were, then we

should have no secrets. And if you and Sintikala are really to be husband and wife, the two of you should never have secrets again either."

Tahtay put his head on one side, as he had occasionally when he was a boy. "And if we all cannot be honest, perhaps you belong with Roma after all. And so I need to know. Are you the big Praetor, Gaius Publius Marcellinus? Or are you Wanageeska of the Raven clan? Kimi says you can have all of these names, but that is not for her to say. I say you cannot, and I am what you made me: the paramount chief of Cahokia."

Marcellinus looked into his eyes. "And so it has come to that? I must declare myself, be one or the other?"

"Yes. For there is much I would tell you. Many suspicions and many plans. But I cannot tell the Praetor. I will only tell Hotah.

"So. Today-now, my friend. Here, before me and before the sky, you must choose."

CHAPTER 31

YEAR TEN, HEAT MOON

The next day, as the leading quinqueremes traveled in convoy down the Wemissori, a knarr dropped back to the *Clementia* to summon Marcellinus to the *Providentia*. He pulled himself up the rope ladder onto the flagship to find Lucius Agrippa on the poop deck next to the ship's master, Titus Otho, who was conferring with Mettius Fronto and the captain of the Imperator's Praetorian Guard.

Marcellinus stepped aside to wait patiently and watch the wooded banks of the Wemissori speed by as 270 cheerful oarsmen renewed their efforts and the helmsman steered the massive quinquereme back into the center of the current. Calidius Verus had been right about one thing, at least: as a brown-water navy, the Sixth Ferrata was superb.

Marcellinus spotted Vibius Caecina amidships but was saved from the obligation of conversing with his tribune when Praetor Agrippa finished his conversation and beckoned Marcellinus over. Fronto and the Praetorian went to starboard to continue their debate out of earshot.

Agrippa eyed him without enthusiasm. "Good Christ, how long is this day? Infernal river."

Marcellinus nodded. He had spent more than his fair share of tedious days on Hesperian waterways. "As long as five normal days, I'll wager. You're looking better."

"Just as well. Considering that I have to do your work as well as my own all the way down the blasted Mizipi."

So the Imperator did still plan to discharge Marcellinus from the army at Cahokia after all. "Well, that should keep you out of trouble."

"Oh, I won't be pining for your company, I assure you. But there are many among us, particularly in the 27th, who would much prefer to drag you back to Roma in chains to stand trial."

"Trial?" Immediately, Marcellinus wished he hadn't risen to the bait.

Agrippa stared past him, down the river. "For your loss of the 33rd, to begin with. After that? Insubordination at every turn. Loss of control of your Hesperian auxiliaries several times during the battle with the Khan, leading to heavy casualties in my legion, Sabinus's, and probably your own. An accounting is surely due for all this, but it appears that you will evade it." He turned his gaze on Marcellinus. "You realize, of course, that if the Imperator had died in battle, I would be in command here. And in that case, your story would be coming to a quick and bloody end."

"I suppose I might be grateful for that, at least," Marcellinus said. "Deaths at Hesperian hands can be slow and painful."

"Then we can only pray that the Hesperians tire of you." Agrippa shook his head. "In the meantime, Gaius Marcellinus, by all means enjoy your squalid little paradise among the barbarians . . . and your stinking redskin whore."

Marcellinus's hand twitched toward his gladius, but he restrained himself. Instead, and with some difficulty, he smiled. He would hardly rise to Agrippa's goading, not with a hundred witnesses spread out over the decks before him.

Instead, he looked astern. As he had expected, the Cahokian longship *Concordia* was approaching from the rear under full sail. "Enough banter, Lucius, my friend. Tahtay is coming to speak with the Imperator about the arrangements once we get to Cahokia. Will you send word to him belowdecks?"

Agrippa snorted. "There is nothing the Imperator needs to tell Tahtay that he has not already said. And we have a policy of not allowing redskins aboard his flagship."

Marcellinus gritted his teeth. "I am tiring of that word, Lucius Agrippa. And I am in earnest when I say that it is in your interests and everyone else's that Tahtay be allowed to speak to Hadrianus as soon as possible."

"The Imperator is not well. And he is hardly at the beck and call of your barbarian protégé." Agrippa noted the expression on Marcellinus's face and sighed in exasperation. "Certainly Hadrianus will speak again with Tahtay before we leave Cahokia for the south, but for now his damned Greek is adamant that he not be disturbed. You and I, between us, can certainly oversee the berthing and restocking. The Cahokians will be bringing the corn to the bank as agreed, no? The sooner we are loaded, the sooner we leave."

"As you wish, Lucius Agrippa." Marcellinus stood back to stand beside the ship's master, Titus Otho, who was stalwartly pretending to ignore their conversation, and to him said: "When we get to Cahokia and the Imperator asks, please remember that I did my best to persuade Agrippa to let Tahtay come aboard."

"Yes, sir," Otho said, and gave him a curious look.

The *Providentia* made a slow turn to starboard and entered the Mizipi, with the *Clementia* and the *Concordia* not far behind.

They saw the Hawks in the air as they rounded the final bend before Cahokia. By this time Marcellinus and Otho were sitting comfortably at the rear of the poop deck with their feet up, swapping war stories, and Agrippa had gone forward to talk again with Mettius Fronto.

They saw the Circle of the Cedars and the Master Mound in the distance, and then the Mounds of the

Flowers and the River came into view . . . and the very next moment Agrippa came running back to them, shouting orders down to the hortator: "Hold, hold!"

As well he might. A forest of palisade stakes lined the riverbank, jutting out at a forty-five-degree angle. Behind them was a more conventional palisade that extended down the bank for a mile or more and then turned inland. Bastions jutted out every two hundred feet, with firing platforms.

Braves lined the palisade. And on the riverine mounds, onagers were clearly visible.

The entire eastern shore of the Mizipi was barred against the Romans. Evidently there would be no sacks of Cahokian corn lying ashore for the taking.

Otho grinned at Marcellinus and said quietly, "Well, you weren't wrong. That's quite a sight."

Agrippa leaped back up onto the poop deck and turned to call across the decks. "Romans, to arms, on the double!"

Now Otho shook his head and stood. "Belay that. With respect, sir, I'll be giving the orders on this ship."

Agrippa glared venomously, then turned back to survey the Great City, the armaments, the Hawks in the air. "Treachery, Gaius Marcellinus? And clearly a long time in the making."

Marcellinus remained seated, stared at him, and said nothing.

"My Praetor assures me we face no immediate threat," Otho said. "Unless I see otherwise, that's good enough for me. So we'll be heading in to dock by the fortress of the Sixth, as planned. And there we'll off-load."

Agrippa stepped closer, looming over Marcellinus. "Well, man? Will we face attack?"

Marcellinus glanced at Cahokia's defenses. "To my eye, Praetor, it appears that we will be quite safe as long as we do not attempt to go ashore to the east."

Behind them the *Clementia* had also backwatered and was holding its position. The *Concordia* came on, pulling up alongside the *Providentia*.

"It is not Roma's river, Lucius Agrippa," Marcellinus said mildly. "It is Cahokia's river, and they exercise control over it."

Agrippa gave him a look that was equal parts hatred and triumph. "Do they now? And with your approval, perhaps even at your suggestion? I believe you may have gone too far at last, *Wanageeska*."

"You credit me with too much power." Marcellinus looked again at the heavily guarded shore and could not resist needling Agrippa just a little. "Tertius Gaudens, Praetor. I believe that we face odds we should not attempt to overcome. Even a general as *weak in strategy* as myself can see that."

"The Rejoicing Third?" Agrippa smiled grimly. "Any rejoicing by your barbarians might be premature. What do you want?"

"I?" Marcellinus said. "I do not speak for the League. Only Tahtay can do that. I suggest that you invite Tahtay aboard with all haste and inform the Imperator."

Otho pointed. "Eagle."

Indeed, a Cahokian three-person craft was making haste toward them from the direction of the Master Mound of Cahokia, trailing a white ribbon. Marcellinus looked up at it. "Ah. The Hawk chief approaches. And if you're extremely lucky, Lucius Agrippa, I will not tell her what you called her."

The *Concordia* kissed the side of the *Providentia*, and Tahtay came up the rope ladder hand over hand, with Enopay and Wahchintonka close behind him. Otho was steering the *Providentia* toward the fortress of the Sixth on the western bank, but Agrippa was adamant that they should not berth until the Imperator concurred. And then the Praetorians brought Hadrianus to the poop deck on a litter, manhandling it awkwardly up and through the rear hatch, with the Greek medicus wringing his hands in their wake.

The Eagle bearing Sintikala, Chenoa, and Kimimela came in to land on the deck of the flagship, the women running it to a halt and then allowing the marines to lift the wing off their shoulders. By then Agrippa's disquiet was clear to see. He had thought that Sintikala was several days' sailing behind them, up the Wemissori.

Apparently not.

"Tahtay," the Imperator said as soon as the war chief came within earshot. "What is the meaning of this?" He waved generally, his gesture taking in the Cahokians themselves as well as the extensive fortifications along the eastern riverbank.

Tahtay bowed. "Caesar. Welcome to Cahokia. Now you will appreciate why I wished to speak with you sooner."

Hadrianus snorted. "All this was not built in a day. You planned this deceit all along."

Sintikala and Chenoa came to stand by Tahtay, one on each side, with Enopay, Kimimela, and Wahchintonka behind them. Tahtay smiled and shook his head. "This, deceit? Indeed, work on the new stockade began as soon as our armies left Cahokia, but only out of prudence. What if the Khan's armies had bypassed ours and made a direct assault on Cahokia? A wise war chief does not leave his home city unguarded. Our inner palisade would not have been sufficient against a Mongol attack. We needed to guard our banks as well."

Now Tahtay's face hardened. "But now that prudence has paid for itself. How clear your eyes, Caesar, when you accuse me of deceit. I wonder at the medicine for lies that you must have within you that permits such treachery of your own."

The Imperator held his gaze, his expression bleak. "You are speaking in riddles again, Tahtay. Get to the point."

Tahtay stared. "As for myself, I am not a suspicious man. I am very trusting. When you tell me something, I accept that it is so. The first Roman I ever met was Gaius Marcellinus, and to him an oath is as sacred as it is to me. And so I wanted to believe that all Romans would be the same, and that you would honor our bond of friendship. But since then I have been talking to others less naive: to Pezi, who has a strong streak of deviousness and suspicion; and to Enopay, whose mind is sharp beyond his years; and to Sintikala and Chenoa, who until yesterday were aboard the *Fides* and the *Minerva* far to the north and west. And even then, I did not want to believe them." He paused. "Caesar, when you and I were negotiating by the Oyo long ago, you with your legions behind you and me with my Army of Ten Thousand at my back, certainly you wanted corn, and guides, and gold. But also you wanted the Cahokian liquid flame—the Greek fire as you call it among yourselves—and above all, above anything else, you wanted the Cahokian power of flight, our Hawks and our Thunderbirds. Did you not?"

Now the war chief began to pace. He continued to talk softly, but the Praetorian Guards who stood around the rails of the *Providentia* watched him carefully, their hands on their gladius hilts. "So let us consider the long road ahead of you, Caesar. You will sail back to Europa and then march on to Asia. There you will again face Mongol armies, this time led by the sons of Chinggis: Jochi, Chagatai, Ogodei, and the other one.

"But the Mongols are leaving Nova Hesperia with the Firebirds and Feathered Serpents that they acquired here.

"The forces of Roma only defeated the Mongols out in the Grass because of our flying craft, our Wakinyan and Catanwakuwa, our Eagles and Sky Lanterns. Back in Asia you will again face assault from the air, but you will not have our flying machines to conquer the threat.

"Or will you?"

The tribunes looked at one another. Agrippa and the Imperator looked only at Tahtay. Hadrianus wore a slight grin, Agrippa a scowl. Tahtay stopped pacing and looked carefully from face to face. "Many of your quinqueremes are here, ready to load food. But two days behind are the *Fides* and the *Minerva*, their decks laden with Hawks and Thunderbirds and the steel rails to launch them. The launching towers you left behind, but those would be easy to re-create. And the remaining Greek fire is aboard a drekar that follows a safe distance behind the *Fides*. Three ships worth more than gold to you, Caesar. Air power and incendiaries that would change the Imperium just as they changed Cahokia. And in time, with such fine examples, your Romans of big clever might learn to make more." Tahtay nodded. "I think that an Imperator who brought such a cargo home to Urbs Roma would be rich indeed, and his campaign judged an even greater success than one that merely defeated a Khan and earned the promise of future gold. Is it not so?"

"I would laugh," Hadrianus said, "if it would not hurt so much. Is there no perfidy you do not imagine me capable of? It must be taxing to bear such suspicions all of the day and all night, too."

"I?" Tahtay shook his head. "I would have trusted you to the ends of the earth, Caesar. And you would have robbed me, for in this I was a fool. Luckily, I have friends around me of greater wisdom."

Now Sintikala spoke, her voice strong. Enopay listened attentively, then stepped forward to translate. "'Caesar, you know that Cahokia will not give you wings and will not sell them to you for any price. They are Cahokia's, and they are sacred to us. So you seek to take them. Your first ships, here, will load all the Cahokian corn we provide and make ready to depart. And then the later ships, bearing our wings and our fire, they will speed past Cahokia without stopping, and your warships will hurry after them, and our longship and war canoes could never catch or defeat them.'" Sintikala frowned, leaned forward to study the Imperator's face, and finally spoke directly to him in Latin for the first time. "Is *that* not so? It is so. I see it in your eyes."

A long silence descended. Agrippa and the tribunes were waiting for the Imperator, and Hadrianus appeared to be lost in contemplation, smiling up at Sintikala.

To Marcellinus he said, "She really is a marvelous woman. Yet so hostile. How do you even bear it?"

"Please answer her question, Caesar," Marcellinus said.

"Answer? Steal your wings? It is a marvelous idea. I am surprised we never thought of it ourselves."

Sintikala barked out a word, and at its abruptness the Praetorian nearest her half drew his sword.

" 'Nonsense,' " Enopay said harshly in translation.

"Sheathe your blade," Agrippa muttered to the Praetorian. "I will tell you when it is time."

" 'Of course you thought of it,' " Sintikala said to Hadrianus through Enopay. " 'It is your plan. We know it for a fact. It is clear in a hundred ways, a hundred things you have done to set it in place, and the way your marines and sailors now behave on the *Fides*. They are ready for action, Imperator.' " Her anger was building, and for a heart-stopping moment Marcellinus thought she would lurch forward toward the Imperator. " 'What would you have done with me? With my daughter, my other pilots? Would you have stolen us away too in chains? Slit our throats? Or merely put us ashore? I wonder.' "

"Guard your tongue in the Imperator's presence!" Agrippa snapped. "Gaius, Tahtay: get her under control or get her off this ship."

Neither Marcellinus nor Tahtay moved. Hadrianus shook his head and raised his hand to quell Agrippa without once taking his gaze off the Hawk chief.

"Mother," Kimimela said very softly from behind her, and only then did Sintikala lower her eyes, glowering at the floor instead.

"Stolen you is my guess," Enopay said to her, but in Latin so that everyone would hear.

Tahtay tutted and bowed. "I apologize, Caesar. Sintikala is angry, and Enopay is upset, for he loves so much about Roma and hates to be so disappointed in you. As do I. My blood beats in your veins, and yours in mine. I pinned my sash for you in the Battle of the Grass, and there I saw you fight even more valiantly than the men around you. You have my utmost respect, and your treachery is regrettable. And to thwart it, we have taken certain steps."

"Steps?" Agrippa demanded.

"Three things," Tahtay said. "First: long ago, in the river battle at Shappa Ta'atan, Enopay recovered a thunder crash bomb from one of the Mongol battle junks. That bomb is hidden in one of your ships, with a long fuse. If our Hawks, Thunderbirds, and pilots are not off-loaded safely at Cahokia, that fuse will be lit, and the bomb will hole the ship. The hull should quickly fill, stranding the vessel."

Agrippa nodded grimly. "So you have already placed a bomb aboard the *Fides* or the *Minerva*. Hardly the act of a trusted ally."

Sintikala raised her eyes to stare at Agrippa.

The Imperator shook his head. "Please do not interrupt, Lucius Agrippa. Tahtay is busy providing us with information that may prove useful. Pray continue, war chief."

"The second thing? You see it before you. No corn and no landing on the Cahokian side of the river. If you were to attack us, you would face a hard fight, and even if you won, our corn is no longer in the granaries. We have hidden it until we are sure of you.

"And so you will not fight. You will not enter Cahokia. You will land only here on the western shore, unload your galleys, occupy your forts to rest if you must, and then when all is ready and all our people and flying craft are returned, you will leave."

"Will we?" Agrippa was grinning contemptuously at him. "Will we indeed?"

Hadrianus gave his Praetor a warning look. "And the third precaution, that you are bursting with eagerness to tell us about?"

"Enopay?" Tahtay gestured to Enopay: *Speak.*

"I love the Romans," Enopay said wistfully. "You are such a powerful people. Such industry! Such ideas! Your general, here, brought us bricks and warm houses and Roman iron and steel. And you, Caesar, you brought us the idea of blocking a river with iron—a whole river! With iron! Well. Such a thing would never have occurred to us."

Agrippa stopped grinning and stood very still. His tribune, Mettius Fronto, glanced at the Praetorians, then down at Hadrianus, and then back to Enopay.

Even in his weakness, the Imperator's voice had gained an edge. "What? Spit it out, boy."

Tahtay hand-talked to Enopay, *Respect. And more quick.*

"Sorry. I will make haste. While we were at war, our friends here at home were not idle. We adopted your idea, and our metalworkers have been busy, and the Mizipi is now blocked at Ocatan. Steel chains and giant log booms, just as you did at Forward Camp. And there is more. As part of our treaty you helped us rebuild Ocatan after your devastation of it. But since you last saw the gates and walls of Ocatan, they have been built ever stronger, ever higher, just like the ones you see here. I think that today a Roman army would not storm through them so easily. And there, too, we have set up throwing engines and launchers for Wakinyan and Eagles as well as Hawks, and the warriors of the Haudenosaunee are not on their way back to the Great Lakes after all but by now will have arrived there to join the Ocatani. Perhaps by now they have also buried bags of liquid flame outside the wall as traps for you, as I suggested. You will find out, I suppose, if you attempt to beach your warships at Ocatan and conquer the town in order to open the river."

Tahtay nodded. "And so, Caesar, even if you throw us off your ships and sail away without corn, you will not pass Ocatan. Ocatan is Cahokia's southern door. And you will not pass through that door until we permit it."

"You cocky little bastards," Agrippa said. "You filthy redskins think you're so clever. Let's see how clever you feel when we gut you and toss you into your own river."

The Imperator raised a hand. "Lucius! Control yourself! Be silent."

Agrippa could not. He turned on Marcellinus. "And you? I smell your influence behind all this. The stench is nauseating. Will you stand there pleading ignorance, as always?"

"By no means," Marcellinus said. "Tahtay told me of all this last night, and I believe Cahokia has acted wisely."

The Imperator raised his eyebrows. Marcellinus could not escape the feeling that even now Hadrianus was enjoying himself. "Gaius Marcellinus, faithless to Roma after all? Surely not."

The Praetorians braced as Agrippa's hand fell to his sword hilt. "So much for your oaths, you bastard. You'll lie as dead as the rest of them by sunset."

"I serve Roma, as I always have," Marcellinus said calmly. "I am with Tahtay in this because I believe it is in Roma's interests to honor its treaties and respect its allies." Now he fixed Agrippa with a strong stare. "Roma means something very different—and much more honorable—to me than it does to you, Lucius Agrippa. I will always fight for that honor. And so I would advise you to take your hand away from your gladius."

The tension on the deck mounted. Enopay stood frozen in place. Sintikala was still glaring at Hadrianus as if willing him to burst into flames.

The Praetorians looked at the tribunes and the Imperator, waiting for a signal.

Then Hadrianus smiled. "Lucius. Gaius. Gods' sakes, do I have to listen to you two squabble forever and a day?"

"Yes, sirs," said Tahtay. "I implore you, heed the Imperator. There is no need for any unpleasantness. Even now I believe we can all part friends.

"Cahokia will keep its word. When the final quinqueremes arrive, they will dock here and we will help you unload our people and our craft. Then we will give you the corn that we promised. We will assist you to leave with the haste you clearly desire. We will remove our thunder crash bomb from your vessel and unblock our river at Ocatan. We will grant you safe passage from Nova Hesperia as long as your various forces keep moving down the Mizipi and along the rough trail the Wanageeska and his legion cut ten winters ago, before he was the Wanageeska. We will not harass you. But you can be sure that we will be watching you."

Sintikala spoke. This time it was Kimimela who translated. "'Safe passage as long as you harm none of our Hesperian peoples, and go home back to Europa, and leave our lands in peace.'"

Tahtay walked back to stand shoulder to shoulder with Sintikala. For the first time, steel entered his tone. "And then? No more armies of Roma will come to Nova Hesperia. When you first arrived, the Algon-Quian resisted you, and then the Iroqua, and then Cahokia, one after another. Next time, the massed armies of the Hesperian League will face you. United and as one."

"You will be welcome as traders, in small groups and unarmed," Enopay said. "The mound builders of the Great River and the Haudenosaunee of the Lakes and the tribes of the Grass and the Hand, we all love to trade. Hesperia has gold and furs, and you want them. And you have many things Hesperians would like, as no one knows better than I. And that is how you will get your gold. Not as taxes or tribute, but in trade."

"But coming to Hesperia as soldiers?" Tahtay shook his head. "Never again, Hadrianus my friend, never again. We will never be your vassals. We will never be your province. There will be no governors, no garrisons, no Roman armies in our lands. Hesperia is not part of your Imperium, and it never will be."

The Imperator raised both hands, wincing a little from the effort. The Praetorians waited like coiled springs. The Greek medicus had retreated entirely, his back to the ship's rail. Agrippa eyed Marcellinus malevolently, his hand still on his gladius hilt.

But Marcellinus was watching Hadrianus as the Imperator brought his hands together. And clapped once, twice, three times.

"Good," he said. "Well done, Tahtay. Wise precautions and well thought out, but they will not be required. My legions will leave Nova Hesperia in peace, with corn but without Catanwakuwa, and take our chances against the new Khans back in the east. You did, however, once promise us Sky Lanterns. They are of Roman invention, are they not?"

"Indeed," Tahtay said. "And so not sacred to us. This can be our first trade, Caesar: we will give you one Sky Lantern for every Norse drekar you leave behind you."

Hadrianus nodded. "Agreed. We'll just have to try to build our own wings from scratch. Now we know the trick can be done."

Tahtay bowed courteously. "Of course, you are welcome to try."

"May your wings all fall from the sky," Sintikala said contemptuously in Cahokian. "You will never fly as we do. Never."

Needless to say, no one volunteered to translate that.

"I believe our business here is done," Tahtay said. "I apologize that it was so lengthy. I trust you will send the appropriate signals to the *Fides* and *Minerva* to command them to halt here. And by all means, land at your fortresses: I give you my word that they have not been touched since you left, and we have set no traps for you within them. The western bank of the Mizipi is yours for now, and I wish you good day, Caesar— Oh. One last thing."

The Imperator shook his head. "Gods, Tahtay, do you never tire?"

"It is a small thing and easy to grant. Your Praetor, Gaius Marcellinus. I believe you plan to discharge him from your army. We have found him an acceptable teacher of Latin and of Roman customs, and so we believe he may be of further use to us. On that basis, we are willing to retain him here as your ambassador."

Hadrianus's amusement was plain. "Ambassador, is it?"

"In fact, due to his experience with our peoples, Marcellinus is the only Roman ambassador acceptable to the Cahokian council and to the Hesperian League. We request that you consider this to ease any future . . . difficulties between our peoples."

"I will, of course, supervise the unloading and reloading of the Sixth before I relinquish command to Aurelius Dizala," Marcellinus said. "And I would talk further with you, Caesar, about the logistics of your withdrawal."

"Well, of course," the Imperator said. "We must get our money's worth from you, Gaius Marcellinus, must we not?"

It was midmorning four days later. On the far side of the Mizipi centurions paced back and forth, supervising the final stages of the loading of Cahokian flour and beans. From the deck, the ship's master of the *Fides* hurled invective down on them; apparently the foot soldiers of the Third were doing everything wrong. Marcellinus grinned.

As for Aelfric, he was standing atop the Mound of the Flowers with Chumanee. Marcellinus climbed uphill, his many wounds still complaining.

At the top, he turned. The last time he had stood up here, he had been overlooking captured Viking longships and a sea of attacking Iroqua. Today, his view was of warships of Roma, visible over a stout Cahokian defensive palisade manned by Wolf Warriors, Iroqua, and Blackfoot.

He shook his head and walked over to his friends. "You had to make me climb a mound just to say goodbye? That is, if you're really going."

"Aye, we're going all right," Aelfric said. "You just try to stop us. I'm off to Roma, an honorable discharge, and a plot of land back home. Back to good honest baths, decent food, and a bit of comfort. Best of all, away from *this* heathen wasteland." Chumanee jabbed him in the ribs and stuck out her tongue, and both laughed.

Marcellinus pretended confusion. "Decent food? So you're not going back to Britannia, then?"

"Like you've ever been," Aelfric scoffed. "But if you ever do find yourself back on the right side of the Atlanticus and on God's own island . . . you're always welcome, and for as long as you like. We'll have ourselves a little farm near the moors. Just go to Eboracum and ask around. I'll be famous there."

"The land of the Brigantes?" Marcellinus mock shivered. "Now there's a barbarian wasteland if ever there was one. I'd be afraid to set foot."

Aelfric nodded. "And rightly so. But I'll make sure no one kills and eats you."

"I never really thought you'd go, Aelfric. You hinted at it often enough. But I thought you were just taunting me to keep me hoping."

"Well, truly, I didn't make up my mind until this morning."

Chumanee was rolling her eyes, her Latin now fluent enough to follow their banter. Now she made the hand-talk for *enough* and bowed to Marcellinus. "Wanageeska? Thank you for keeping me alive."

Aelfric's eyebrows furrowed. "Pretty sure you've got that the wrong way around, Chumanee."

"No." She switched back to Cahokian. "Down the Mizipi, up the Mizipi, across the Grass, out of the Grass, everywhere we went, the Wanageeska watched out for me." Chumanee stepped forward to hug him.

"As best I could." Marcellinus grinned. "Good healers are hard to come by."

"But even more than that, I speak of my life in Cahokia and of"—she jerked her head sideways in mock derision—"*this* hairy warrior. I think perhaps I owe you all of this."

"I did nothing, of course?" Aelfric asked, mildly aggrieved. "Not a thing?"

She smiled sweetly. "You, I will always be thanking."

Marcellinus smiled back at them.

"Any messages?" Aelfric asked. "You know, if I should happen to bump into . . . anyone special, back home?"

Vestilia. Marcellinus's first daughter, his daughter by blood, so far away, who must now be twenty-six winters . . . twenty-six *years* of age. If she had inherited her mother's skills at social climbing, Vestilia might be quite prominent in Roman society by now. "I doubt Vestilia ever thinks of me."

But Marcellinus had changed a great deal over the last dozen years, and maybe Vestilia had, too. Who was to say? "Well, all right. If you do come across her, tell her that I still live. Tell her the truth, or as much of it as she wants to hear. And tell her I am happy and wish her well."

Chumanee was looking back and forth between them. "Wife?" she probed gently.

"Daughter," Marcellinus said.

Chumanee raised her eyebrows. "Oh! We should try to find her. I would like to meet her."

How would Vestilia or Julia react to this tall, slender barbarian woman married to a lowly Roman tribune, and a Briton at that? Somehow, Marcellinus had difficulty picturing such a meeting. "Only if you wish it. You will not miss Cahokia?"

Her eyes sparkled. "Always. But I will see the world!"

"Well," Aelfric amended, "a cold and windy part of it, anyway."

Longships and knarrs had been passing back and forth across the Mizipi all morning, between the west bank and the small gate in the Cahokian palisade on the eastern shore. The Norse vessels could carry several tons of cargo and were much less unwieldy than the quinqueremes for short journeys. Now, however, the stream of matériel seemed to be abating.

There was still a flurry of activity around the quinqueremes. The *Minerva* had finished loading men, and the *Fides* was almost done. Some of their oars were already set. Soldiers were still filing onto the *Providentia*, *Clementia*, and *Annona*, but it would not be long now.

"Almost time," Marcellinus said, and turned to his tribune. "Well, good-bye, Aelfric. I'm glad you lived."

The Briton reached out and grasped his arm, met his eye, nodded. "And I, you. You've made life interesting. And . . . I thank you, Gaius. For more than we have time to discuss."

Marcellinus nodded, smiled, and clapped the man on the back, and Chumanee stepped forward to throw her arms around them both.

Just after noon, the quinqueremes of Roma put out into the Mizipi. Drums beat, martial flutes sounded a cheery tune, and strong oars pulled the warships into the current. The Imperator's flagship, *Providentia*, took the lead, and the other ships fell in behind it: *Minerva*, *Fides*, *Clementia*, and the cargo vessel *Annona*. The Norse knarr, the trireme, and two of the drekars had left already to get a head start; the quinqueremes would easily catch up.

Cheering Cahokians lined the shores. Supposedly they were honoring Roma, but there was unquestionably a strong streak of simple joy at their departure.

Tahtay, Sintikala, and many of the elders stood atop the Mound of the Flowers alongside Marcellinus and Enopay. In the air above them Kimimela chased the buzzards as they spiraled in an updraft to gain height. Marcellinus almost wished he was up there, too, for the view.

"And just like that, they go."

Marcellinus rubbed his eyes. He felt like he might never get the smoke out of them. Weeks after the last battle, he still felt exhausted and punchy. "Yes, Enopay. Just like that."

Enopay looked wry. "It was so hard to get rid of the Romans for so long. All those years we wished they would go and knew they never would. And now they are running away so quickly that there are many men I never got to bid farewell."

The boy was in mourning, Marcellinus realized. Best not to say anything flippant. Yet it was hard: all Marcellinus felt was a light-headed relief. Though even now it was difficult not to keep checking behind him for enemies.

"And so now you are Roma's ambassador in Cahokia. I trust that your dealings with us will be firm but fair."

Marcellinus looked at him sideways.

"And that you will bring us aqueducts and basilicas and a forum."

"Well, of course," Marcellinus said. "There is nothing Cahokia needs more than a forum with marbled columns."

"No, there isn't," Enopay said wistfully. "Nothing at all."

EPILOGUE

YEAR ELEVEN, DANCING MOON

It was the day of the Midsummer Feast in Cahokia, almost a year later. For the last two weeks Youtin had been at the Circle of the Cedars every dawn and dusk, making his observations of the sun. The old shaman now walked slowly with sticks, and it was widely accepted that his young acolyte Kiche did much of the real work, but it was Youtin who took responsibility and who made the pronouncement that morning from the top of the Great Mound. Tahtay listened carefully, showing the old man deep respect and thus helping to heal the last fracture in Cahokian society. As soon as Youtin had finished, Tahtay repeated the announcement with greater volume and followed it by asking the women to commence the preparation of food in the huge jars. Today, Cahokia would feast.

The previous weeks had seen long discussions in the smoke lodge of the elders and even more extensive debate in a full council of clan chiefs. As a result, on the evening of the Midsummer Feast, Tahtay came to the crest of the Great Mound in the full regalia of a war chief of Cahokia: the feathered cloak, the kilt, and the ear spools of the Long-Nosed God. He lacked only the chert mace that went with the title of Great Sun Man, which would not be his for a little longer.

The ceremonial clothing of a Cahokian paramount

chief no longer looked outlandish to Marcellinus. On Tahtay this evening it looked just right, and well earned.

The Great Plaza was packed, and so were the streets beyond in all directions, out to the east and west and as far back as the Mound of the Women. Cahokia had never been so crowded. Tahtay made his speech not only to his own people, the residents of Cahokia and Ocatan, but also to extensive contingents from the Haudenosaunee, Blackfoot, Cherokee, Ojibwa, Huron, Powhatani, and People of the Hand. After the Midsummer Feast the sachems and headmen of the other tribes would stay another moon for a powwow, the first massed gathering of the Hesperian League in peacetime.

As Tahtay made clear during his long oration, Cahokia did not rule the other members of the League. He carefully claimed no precedence over the chiefs of the other tribes. When decisions of great import were needed, all would speak, all would listen, all would decide, and all would have to agree. The Hesperian League would largely follow the precedents set by the Haudenosaunee League.

However, Cahokia's preeminence was clear to everyone there. It was the biggest city and close to being centrally located in the great continent of Hesperia, the Mizipi and its tributaries made it the hub of the river network that provided the major Hesperian thoroughfares, and Cahokia had the best wings and pilots. If envoys came from Roma seeking trade, it would be Cahokia's leaders and Marcellinus whom they would negotiate with first. And so, if Cahokia was the first among equals, it was first by a considerable margin.

Sintikala stood by Tahtay's side on the crest of the Great Mound. Their eminence and association were also clear to all. At such moments the city bowed to them. Behind Tahtay stood his wife, Taianita, and his leading advisers, Enopay and Dustu, and behind them the array of other clan chiefs and elders, with Chenoa, Pahin, Matoshka, Howahkan, Wahchintonka, and Hanska among them. There, too, stood the Tadodaho of the

Haudenosaunee, a craggy elder of the Blackfoot, and the young, bronzed leader of the People of the Hand.

Marcellinus listened to the speech from the left edge of the Great Plaza. He stood next to Takoda, Nahimana, and their family, with his arms wrapped around Kimimela. The parts of the speech he could not hear, he read from the hand-talkers on the first plateau and out to the side on the Mound of the Sun, or just ignored. He still did not understand all the allusions to Red Horn and the other figures of Cahokian mythology.

He ought to do something about that. After all, his arms and back were now etched with Cahokian war tattoos. He owed his hosts the courtesy of trying to understand them.

Takoda's hair was streaked with early gray. His oldest child, a mere babe in arms when Marcellinus had first arrived, was a stout young man of twelve winters. His second child, nine winters old, Marcellinus still only knew as Ciqala, even though that just meant "baby" in Cahokian, and Ciqala had a baby brother of his own. And at long last Kangee appeared to be mellowing toward Marcellinus. Just a little. On good days.

Nahimana was even older and more acerbic than ever, but she had recovered completely from her stroke, and if her hip was no better than it had been when Marcellinus first arrived, at least it was no worse. It seemed entirely likely that she would outlive him.

So many Cahokians had not. Friends who had died in battles or in their catastrophic aftermath, who would remain in his thoughts and his heart forever. The beautiful, skillful, and cheeky Hurit. His wise and clever Raven clan chief, Anapetu. Too many braves, among them the courageous and funny Mahkah, Yahto, and Mikasi. His wise old friend Kanuna. And hundreds of other men and women he had known by sight or reputation who had fallen in the battles of Cahokia, Yupkoyvi, Shappa Ta'atan, and the Grass. Even longer ago, his comrades in arms from across the Atlanticus: Pollius Scapax, Thorkell Sigurdsson, even Corbulo. And Great Sun

Man, whose steady presence Marcellinus missed to this day.

So much war. So much blood.

The shadows lengthened, and the rays of the sun shone even more golden on the thatched roofs of Cahokia. The summer humidity had respectfully taken two steps back; by the standards of the bottomlands it was a dry evening, and tonight's feasting would be comfortable. Around the plaza's edges a host of women stood next to tall jars of food. Feeding this immense crowd would be impossible, but just as Enopay had advised Great Sun Man many years before, many people had contributed food of their own.

Over the smells of people, smoke, and cooking meat the most prevalent was that of the terrible mash beer the Cahokians favored, laced with fermented tree sap. Marcellinus, of course, had made his own arrangements. Brewing the kind of beer he liked could be done only in small batches, and if he had subverted the attention of the artisans in Cahokia's steelworks to ensure there would be enough tonight to slake their thirsts and those of his other close friends, that would be their secret.

Tahtay reached the end of his long speech. At just that moment, the sun set. The crowd roared so loudly that Marcellinus thought his ears might burst. Kimimela hugged him all the more.

Up on the crest of the Great Mound, Tahtay turned to his advisers and elders. The applause from the masses died down, replaced with a babble of conversation and a determined movement toward the vats of food.

"Tahtay did not mention the west," Kimimela said, her eyes serious.

Marcellinus grunted. "You expected him to?"

"Perhaps."

Predictably, Isleifur had faded into the trees rather than climb aboard a Roman quinquereme. He and the scouts of the Hand had been busy that winter and spring and had brought back their reports not long since. The Mongol army under Subodei Badahur had completed its

long trek back to the western coast and set sail back to
Asia with the body of their deceased Khan. But they had
left a sizable contingent of Mongol warriors to hold the
lands west of the Great Mountain range. The traders
and refugees out of the west confirmed that Yesulun
Khatun, Chagatai's wife, had indeed remained behind to
administer the region.

Hesperians from the tribes up and down the western
coast were still in forced servitude to the invaders. Even
now they were sluicing gold out of the rivers and breaking it out of the mountains to give to their Mongol over-
lords. The continent of Nova Hesperia was not yet free
from the Mongol curse, and sometime in the coming
weeks the Hesperian League would have to decide what
to do about that.

Marcellinus shook his head. "That's a topic for powwow. Tonight should be a happy occasion. Gods know
we've earned one."

"Well, in that case," Kimimela said, eyes twinkling,
"is it perhaps time for you to go back and see *your lady
wife*?"

Kimimela had used an expression in patrician Latin
that described her mother about as badly as any phrase
possibly could. Marcellinus grinned and pinched her.
"Gods, yes. I've certainly spent enough time enduring
your company."

Kimimela back-kicked him, which he leaned into and
blocked with his forearm, and they set off to thread
their way through the crowd to the blankets at the front
of the Great Plaza where Tahtay and his chiefs and
elders would eventually come down to sprawl and eat.
As they walked, Marcellinus nodded to men and women
he had fought alongside and flown with, smiled at the
members of the perennially young brickworks gang,
even bowed and stopped to exchange a few words with
an Onondaga warrior. Really, he knew a *lot* of people in
this city now.

"Great Juno. Everyone you know is in between us and
where we want to be." Kimimela slid between two fam-

ilies whose members were cheerfully shouting at one another, having already sampled the mash beer, and grumbled, "If we'd been up on the mound with Tahtay and the others, this would be much easier."

"I'm an outlander," Marcellinus reminded her. "A private citizen. Not appropriate for me to be up there."

She blew a cheerful raspberry. "Futete. Merda, that, and you know it."

"Bad words, Kimi . . ." He shoved her before she could poke him again.

A dragon ship had arrived back at Vinlandia just weeks beforehand with the news that the Imperator had survived his journey across the Atlanticus. The longship had also brought a parchment decree from the Senate confirming Marcellinus's elevation as ambassador to Nova Hesperia, a second decree confirming the annulment of the Damnatio Memoriae on the 33rd Hesperian Legion, and a handwritten letter from Hadrianus to Marcellinus.

As expected, the Imperator had arrived back in Roma to be greeted by jubilation at his great military victory. The Senate had rejoiced to hear how his legions had killed the Khan and smashed the Mongol army. Once all the arrangements were made, Hadrianus and Agrippa would enjoy a great triumph, parading through the streets of Roma. Several weeks of gladiatorial games would follow.

By adding Nova Hesperia to the Roman map as an ally and protected state, the Imperator had achieved part of his original ambition. The sun now set a good deal farther west on the Imperium than it had just a few years before. And if Hadrianus's influence over his new ally was looser than normal and communications with his ambassador were rather limited, that was surely just a function of Cahokia's immense distance from Urbs Roma.

It was true enough that Marcellinus went to the smoke lodge with the elders three times out of four. True enough that he could be included in any clan chief discussion that interested him. Doubly true that on Roma's inevitable return he would again step up to adopt a central role. But it was also true that these days Marcellinus wanted nothing more than to tinker in his workshops in the afternoons, chatter with his friends in the evenings, and enjoy his nights and mornings with Sintikala. If he ever felt in need of a little gratuitous terror, he could get himself launched under an Eagle craft with Kimimela and Sintikala with a Falling Leaf on his back for safety. There he would wobble around a thousand feet above the city and eventually fumble his way back down to earth again, sweating and exhilarated.

"Ooh, ooh," Kimimela said as they approached the blankets. "Wait, stop. Sinopa of the Blackfoot is here."

As she halted him, Marcellinus peered between the dozen or so people who still stood between them and the blankets. Despite what Kimimela had said earlier, Tahtay had only just that moment arrived, talking in a relaxed way to the Tadodaho. Sintikala, Chenoa, and Enopay were laughing together over something, which in itself was a sight rare enough to be disconcerting. Akecheta and Hanska had shown up and were looking around, even more awkward than Marcellinus in social settings; fortunately, they soon saw Isleifur Bjarnason, hand in hand with Sooleawa of the Hidatsa, and hurried over to talk to them.

With Sooleawa and Isleifur stood three young men of the Blackfoot tribe. Marcellinus nodded. "Sinopa is the exceptionally ugly young brave with the tattoos? Don't hit me again, Kimi, or I'll sneak off to the longhouse and cut all the sinews on your Hawk."

"What do I say to him?"

Marcellinus shook his head. " 'Hello'?"

"Oh, I've *met* him already . . . Help me?"

"Good grief."

"What?"

"Sorry, I got distracted. Look, Wachiwi is sitting with

Pezi and some Oneida braves. Laughing. And now I *know* the Hesperian League has a bright future."

Kimimela almost stamped her foot. "Wanageeska! Hear me! You must assist me in greeting Sinopa of the Blackfoot!"

"Kimimela, you will be chief of the Hawk clan one day. Do you tell me now that you lack courage?"

Sintikala had seen Marcellinus. Touching Chenoa on the arm in farewell, she hurried forward. Kimimela sighed. "I see that *once again* I must do everything myself."

"Perhaps not for long," Marcellinus said, and the next moment Sintikala had grabbed him in an embrace that squeezed all the air from his lungs but was still exhilarating. The traditional Cahokian prudishness about public displays of affection be damned: Marcellinus kissed her.

"And so I go," Kimimela said. "Quickly."

Marcellinus thought of hugging Enopay as well but instead honored him with a deep Roman bow, which the young man blinked at and then returned with exactly the correct Roman level of formality. "Ambassador Eyanosa."

"Enopay. You are well?"

Sintikala turned to talk to Sooleawa. Enopay's eyes followed Kimimela regretfully. "Where is she going?"

"Merely an errand of diplomacy to the Blackfoot." Kimimela had reached her target now, showing not a hint of hesitation, and by the look on Sinopa's face he was delighted to see her. "You all grow up so fast."

"Even me?" Enopay asked hopefully.

"You're right. Never mind." Marcellinus spotted Napayshni, who was waiting inconspicuously at the edge of the gathering, and beckoned him over. Eyes conspiratorial, Napayshni delivered him a pot of very good beer and withdrew.

Marcellinus drank deeply. "Ah, it's good to have adjutants."

"I, too, miss Roma," Enopay said.

Marcellinus looked at him sideways. "Ha."

"And you do not?"

He hesitated. After his flippancy with Kimimela he was inclined to duck the question with a jest and beckon for a second beer, but Enopay's expression was serious. "I do not miss the legions. I do not miss Lucius Agrippa overmuch. And I do not miss war. But I think maybe you speak of the city of Roma across the big water and not the Roman Imperium that wishes to own the world."

Enopay watched him with those alert eyes that missed nothing.

"I don't know, Enopay. I don't want to live in Roma, or anywhere other than right here in Cahokia. And so I would fear to even visit Roma, for if I did, I might never be able to get away to come back here again afterward." He turned to face Enopay so that the boy could see his eyes. "But sometimes I do miss the grandeur of the Forum. I miss the Seven Hills, and the baths, and, yes, the great aqueducts. I do wonder how Vestilia lives now. I miss Greeks and Aegyptians and Africans and some of the men I met in Galicia-Volhynia, Khwarezmia, and Sindh. And there's a Briton I wouldn't mind seeing again. So yes, I do think about it. And you?"

"I miss the great ships and the shine and gleam of it all. The . . . pageantry?" Enopay looked glum. "My life will be a poor thing if I never again see anything as grand as a quinquereme."

"You will. I am sure."

"And I miss the big talk. The Roman confidence. The idea that nothing is impossible."

"That confidence is a two-edged sword."

"Surely, but it is also invigorating." Enopay sat up straight. "All right now. Enough moping. To business."

"Business?"

"Serious talk of the future. Here is what will happen to us all. I have seen it in a dream, and so I know that it is true."

Marcellinus laughed. "Juno, Enopay. I don't believe you have ever suffered a prophetic dream."

"Well, not when I was asleep. But here is what I believe when I am awake."

Enopay took a long look around the bustle and feasting that surrounded them in the plaza, the smoke and food, all wrapped in the laughter of Hesperians in the dusk light. "Tahtay will be happy at last. He will be a strong leader to Cahokia and to the Hesperian League, as we always knew he would."

"Always?"

"In another year the elders and chiefs of Cahokia will grant him the title of Great Sun Man, and Tahtay will accept it. He will rule wisely, but only when he needs to. And Taianita will bear him many strong children. They will run so fast that nobody can catch them, and grow up to be warriors.

"Kimimela may love her young Blackfoot for a while, or perhaps someone else, but she will not marry. Instead she will become the chief of the Hawk clan, and sooner rather than later, because Sintikala will yield her position as chief long before she gets old. Sintikala will not become Ojinjintka, who led her clan until the bitter, creaky end. Sintikala has much else to enjoy. Ah, good; I see from your eyes that you and she have discussed this."

Marcellinus grinned and said nothing. Enopay continued. "As chief of the Hawk clan, Kimimela will stand by Tahtay's side, just as Sintikala stood by Great Sun Man's side and now stands by Tahtay's, and Kimimela and Tahtay will then be the mother and father of Cahokia. And meanwhile you and Sintikala will live a long and happy life together, and you will always fly. Even when you are on the ground."

Marcellinus raised his eyebrows. "Now you write poetry?"

"Where you two are concerned, somebody has to." Enopay checked to make sure Sintikala could not overhear him but switched to Latin anyway as he continued. "Marcellinus and Sintikala are perfect together. It is beautiful to see. And the rest of us had to wait *so long* for the two of you to realize it, because you are both so amazingly stubborn."

"I wanted it sooner," Marcellinus said. "We did lose a lot of time."

"Oh, you are still young," Enopay said.

Marcellinus cocked an eye at him. "You say so?"

"Fifty-one winters is not old. You still have much time. Look at Howahkan. Nahimana. Matoshka. More ancient than the hills and still hobbling around annoying people."

"May all the gods hear your wisdom," Marcellinus said.

Enopay looked at him very seriously. "I am not as young as you think I am, Eyanosa. And you are not as old as you think you are."

Marcellinus nodded. "And what of Enopay the Bold? I think he will do many, many things."

"Will he?"

"At harvest, Enopay counts grain. In war, he counts soldiers. In peace, he counts the days and nights and watches where the sun sets, for he is something of a shaman, but without believing the wild ideas that shamans believe. Tell me, Enopay, is today really midsummer?"

For the first time, Enopay looked impressed. "I did not know you had seen me doing that. Yes, Youtin counts true. The sun stands still on the horizon when it sets and will go no farther north. It is midsummer." He looked smug. "Yet for years we have not had a Midwinter Feast on the real midwinter day, because when it is so cold, Youtin stays abed too long in the mornings, and when he rises, he shivers so much that he cannot keep good count."

"And perhaps, in addition to studying the heavens, Enopay will write down the first history of Cahokia and the mound-builders, or a geography of Hesperia on a series of scrolls for the libraries of Roma and Alexandria."

"That sounds like a great deal of finger-talk."

"And he will go to Roma to see all of its wonders. Perhaps even as an ambassador for Hesperia."

Enopay looked at him very seriously. "Perhaps I will. I want to see everything, Gaius Marcellinus. I want to see the whole world."

It was rare that Enopay called him anything other than Eyanosa. For a moment, Marcellinus felt oddly sad. Despite his earlier joke, Enopay *was* growing up.

Enopay was watching him. "It is wrong that I should feel such a thing?"

"No. Never."

Enopay looked sad, too. "But when I go to Roma, you will not come with me?"

Marcellinus considered it again. "I do not know. In truth, perhaps that depends on Roma as much as on me."

For now, Marcellinus appeared to be safe. But an Imperator could always be deposed, or die at dinner in his palace choking on a stuffed dormouse, or simply change his mind. Who could say?

The Senate might demand Hesperian gold. Or its army might once again attempt to acquire Cahokian wings and liquid fire to wage war in Europa or Asia. Who could predict Roma's future policy toward the huge and mostly "unexploited" continent of Nova Hesperia? Their peace and freedom might prove to be short-lived.

But if Aelfric were here, the Briton would tell Marcellinus not to fret over a future he could not control. After all, Roma still had the other sons of Chinggis Khan to deal with. Hadrianus might have his hands full for many years to come.

Enopay was trying to read his eyes. "Of course. Roma is capricious. But you do not rule it out?"

Even if he could be sure of his reception, to go to Roma, Marcellinus would need to leave Sintikala and Kimimela behind and be away from Cahokia for two years or more. He could not imagine being willing to make such a sacrifice.

But many things about his current situation would have been impossible to predict twelve winters ago, or five, or three. "No, I do not rule it out."

Sintikala and Sooleawa hugged, and the young Hidatsa woman skipped back to Isleifur Bjarnason. Sintikala turned to survey them, then winked at Enopay and said: "You are too serious, Wanageeska. As always."

Marcellinus laughed aloud. "You say so? *Sintikala* says such a thing?"

"I say it." She met his eye with a fierce and smoldering gaze. "But for you, I am Sisika."

Mortified, Enopay looked around him. "Perhaps I should go."

"You should not." Sintikala put her hand on Enopay's arm, shook her head, smiled. "The Wanageeska and I will behave."

"You will stay, and we will eat together," Marcellinus said. "No, wait: you will go and rescue Tahtay from the Tadodaho and invite him and Taianita to join us, and then you will encourage Kimimela to return here, too, with her very unattractive new friend of the Blackfoot if she must, and *then* you will stay."

"Will I?" Enopay glanced at them both, still nervous.

"Yes, you will," Sintikala said. "We have spoken."

ACKNOWLEDGMENTS

As my Hesperian journey draws to a close I find I'm still thanking many of the same people I was thanking at the outset. There's a good reason for that. I've had a terrific team around me all the way.

Stupendous thanks are due to my agent extraordinaire, Caitlin Blasdell; my awesome and perceptive editor, Mike Braff; my dedicated and tireless publicist, Alexandra Coumbis; and everyone else at Liza Dawson Associates and Penguin Random House/Del Rey for their imagination and energy. The last few years have been hard work, but they've also been immense fun, and the above-named industry professionals have brought a lot of that fun. It's been a pleasure.

Gratitude, respect, and wine and water in perpetuity go to my intrepid beta readers Karen Smale, Chris Cevasco, Peter Charron, and Fiona Lehn, who truly went the distance. I salute them for their valiant service.

I'd also like to sincerely thank everyone who offered me support and friendship during the writing and, aye, promotion of these books—old friends and new; fellow writers, readers, and non-readers alike. I won't attempt to name you all—that way lies madness—but please know that I'm both cheered and humbled.

Thanks as ever to my parents, Peter and Jill Smale, who started the ball rolling by stoking my interest in the world around me. And love and gratitude to my very patient spouse, Karen, who has helped to keep my life running smoothly in the present day while I've been off adventuring in my alternate thirteenth century. Time to take some real vacations again, I think.

APPENDIXES

APPENDIX I

DRAMATIS PERSONAE

ROMANS

Hadrianus III—Imperator

Soldiers of the Legio XXXIII Hesperia

Gaius Publius Marcellinus—Praetor
Lucius Domitius Corbulo—First Tribune,
tribune of the Second and Third Cohorts
Aelfric—Tribune of the Fourth and Fifth
Cohorts (Briton)
Marcus Tullius—Tribune of the Sixth Cohort
Gnaeus Fabius—Tribune of the Seventh and
Eighth Cohorts
Leogild—Quartermaster (Visigoth)
Pollius Scapax—First Centurion
Thorkell Sigurdsson—Scout (Norse)
Isleifur Bjarnason—Scout (Norse)

Soldiers of the Legio III Parthica

Quintus Decinius Sabinus—Praetor
Antonius Caster—First Tribune, tribune of the
Second and Third Cohorts
Sextus Bassus—Decurion

Soldiers of the Legio XXVII Augusta Martia Victrix

Lucius Flavius Agrippa—Praetor
Mettius Fronto—First Tribune, tribune of the Second and Third Cohorts

Soldiers of the Legio VI Ferrata

Calidius Verus—Praetor
Aurelius Dizala—First Tribune, tribune of the Second and Third Cohorts (Thracian)
Statius Paulinus—Tribune of the Fourth and Fifth Cohorts
Flavius Urbius—Tribune of the Sixth and Seventh Cohorts
Vibius Caecina—Tribune of the Eighth and Ninth Cohorts
Manius Ifer—Centurion, then tribune of the Tenth Cohort
Appius Gallus—First Centurion
Titus Otho—Ship's master, *Providentia*
Aulus—Adjutant
Furnius—Adjutant
Sollonius—Adjutant
Einar Stenberg—Scout (Norse)

Other Romans

Julia—Ex-wife of Marcellinus
Vestilia—Daughter of Marcellinus

CAHOKIANS

Ranking Cahokians: Rulers, Clan Chiefs, Elders, Shamans

Great Sun Man/Mapiya—War chief, paramount chief of Cahokia
Sintikala/Sisika—Chief of the Hawk clan

Demothi—Second in command of the Hawk clan
Ojinjintka—Chief of the Thunderbird clan
Chenoa—Chief of the Thunderbird clan
Anapetu—Chief of the Raven clan
Pahin—Chief of the Raven clan
Wahchintonka—Leader of the Wolf Warriors
Matoshka—Cahokian elder, Bear clan
Howahkan—Cahokian elder
Kanuna—Cahokian elder, grandfather to Enopay
Ogleesha—Cahokian elder
Youtin—Elder shaman
Kiche—Young shaman, acolyte to Youtin
Huyana—First wife of Great Sun Man
Nipekala—Third wife of Great Sun Man (Blackfoot)
Ituha—Paramount chief of Cahokia, historical uniter of Cahokia
Avenaka—Wolf Warrior lieutenant, war chief, brother to Huyana

Warriors of the First Cahokian Cohort

Akecheta—Centurion
Mahkah—Young warrior, then leader of the Second Cahokian Cohort
Hanska—Veteran warrior, then leader of the Third Cahokian Cohort
Takoda—Veteran warrior, son of Nahimana, husband of Kangee, adjutant, Bear clan
Napayshni—Veteran warrior, adjutant
Mikasi—Veteran warrior, husband of Hanska (Omaha, adopted as Cahokian)
Yahto—Warrior

Other Cahokian Citizens

Tahtay/Mingan—Young man, son of Great
Sun Man, war chief (also Blackfoot)
Kimimela—Young woman, daughter of
Sintikala
Enopay—Young man, grandson of Kanuna,
adjutant
Dustu—Young man, confidant of Tahtay
Hurit—Young woman, Raven clan (Algon-
Quian, adopted as Cahokian)
Luyu—Young woman, Wakinyan clan
Nahimana—Older woman, mother of Takoda,
Bear clan
Chumanee—Young woman, healer
Kangee—Wife of Takoda, Turtle clan
Ciqala—Son of Takoda and Kangee
Wachiwi—Young woman (Oneida, adopted as
Cahokian)
Leotie—Sister of Anapetu, Raven clan
Dowanhowee—Sister of Anapetu, Raven clan
Nashota—Daughter of Anapetu, Raven clan
Ohanzee—Warrior, Raven clan
Chogan—Young warrior, Raven clan
Kohana—Brother of Great Sun Man
Patachee—Mother of Great Sun Man
Wapi—Artisan

SHAPPA TA'ATANI

Son of the Sun—Paramount chief
Taianita—Word slave
Panther—Clan chief
Beaver—Clan chief
Snake—Clan chief
Turtle—Clan chief
Deer—Clan chief
Crow—Clan chief

OTHER HESPERIANS

Iniwa—War chief of Ocatan
Otetiani—The Tadodaho, Chief of the Onondaga
Cha'akmogwi—Chief of the Yupkoyvi
Chochokpi—Chief of the Yupkoyvi
Tlin-Kit—Chief of the Tlingit
Fuscus—Word slave (Powhatani)
Pezi—Word slave (Iroqua)
The Chitimachan—Word slave (Chitimachan)
Unega—Scout (Cherokee)
Sooleawa—Buffalo caller (Hidatsa)
Coosan—Centurion (Ocatani)
Sinopa—Warrior (Blackfoot)

MONGOLS

Chinggis Khan—Great Khan of the Mongols
Jochi—First son of Chinggis Khan
Chagatai—Second son of Chinggis Khan
Ogodei—Third son of Chinggis Khan
Tolui—Fourth son of Chinggis Khan
Subodei Badahur—General
Jebei Noyon, the Arrow—General
Liu Po-Lin—Adviser to Chinggis Khan (Jin)
Yesulun Khatun—Wife of Chagatai

APPENDIX II

THE CAHOKIAN YEAR

The approximate correspondence between the Julian calendar and the Cahokian moons and festivals is as follows:

Januarius	Snow Moon
Februarius	Hunger Moon
Martius	Crow Moon
Liberalia	Spring Planting Festival
Aprilis	Grass Moon
Maius	Planting Moon
Junius	Flower Moon
Vestalia	Midsummer Feast
Julius	Heat Moon
Augustus	Thunder Moon
September	Hunting Moon
Sol Sistere	Harvest Festival
October	Falling Leaf Moon
November	Beaver Moon
December	Long Night Moon
Bruma	Midwinter Feast

In Cahokia, the exact dates of spring, midsummer, harvest, and midwinter are determined by the position of the sun on the horizon at sunrise and sunset, as measured from the Circle of the Cedars.

To maintain the alignment of the lunar cycles with the annual solar cycle, a thirteenth month is added to the Cahokian calendar every three years. This is the Dancing Moon. As its name implies, the Dancing Moon can be inserted into the Cahokian calendar at the most convenient time, as chosen by the shamans.

Other ceremonies and celebrations occur during the Cahokian year but are scheduled when the signs, time, and weather are right, at times that may appear arbitrary to the uninitiated.

APPENDIX III

CAHOKIA AND THE MISSISSIPPIAN CULTURE

Many people are familiar with the Aztecs and the Maya and the other great civilizations of Mesoamerica. Far fewer seem to know of the thriving and extensive cultures of North America in the centuries before the arrival of European ships.

For more than five hundred years the Mississippian civilization dominated the river valleys of eastern North America, building thousands of towns and villages along the Mississippi, the Ohio, and many other rivers. Like the Adena and Hopewell cultures before them, they built mounds by the tens of thousands: conical mounds, ridge mounds, and the distinctive square-sided, flat-topped platform mounds. In all likelihood the founding events of Mississippian culture took place in Cahokia and then radiated out across the continent.

In its heyday Cahokia was a huge city covering more than five square miles, occupied by about 20,000 people and containing at least 120 mounds of packed earth and silty clay, many of them colossal. In the twelfth and early thirteenth centuries Cahokia was larger than London, and no city in northern America would be larger until the 1800s. Cahokia's skyline was dominated by the gigantic mound known today as Monks Mound, a thousand feet square at the base and a hundred feet high. Monks Mound had four terraces, and archaeological data reveal that it was topped with a large wooden structure 105 feet long and 48 feet wide. This great earthwork and longhouse overlooked a Grand Plaza nearly 50 acres in area, meticulously positioned and leveled with sandy loam fill a foot deep. Cahokia's central 205 acres were protected by a bastioned palisade two miles long and constructed of some 20,000 logs, enclosing the Great Mound and Great Plaza and eighteen other mounds. The downtown area was surrounded by perhaps a dozen residential neighborhoods, some of which had their own plazas. Cahokia was bounded several miles to the west by the Mississippi and to the east by river bluffs of limestone and sandstone and was surrounded by the floodplains of the American Bottom that allowed the cultivation of maize in vast fields to feed its population.

Much of Cahokia was built in a flurry of dedicated activity around 1050 A.D., but to this day nobody knows why or by whom. The city and its immense mounds are not claimed by any existing tribe or tradition, and no tales about the city's foundation or dissolution have been passed down through oral history. The Illini who lived in the area when white settlers arrived appeared to know little about the mounds and did not claim them or show much interest in them. However, archaeologists and ethnographers are reasonably confident that the ancient Cahokians were Siouan-speaking, and I have gone along with that assumption in the Clash of Eagles trilogy.

We can, however, be certain that the original residents of the Great City did not call it Cahokia. "Cahokia" is actually the name of an Algonquian-speaking tribe that probably did not come to the area until several hundred years after the fall of the city. Nor did the Iroquois call themselves by that name. "Iroquois" is probably a French transliteration of an insulting Huron word for the Haudenosaunee. However, in this case and some others I have used familiar terms to avoid needless obscurity. For the river names, I may be on firmer ground (so to speak). The Mississippi and Missouri rivers are named from the French renderings of the original Algonquian or Siouan words, and the Ohio River was indeed "Oyo" to the Iroquois. "Chesapeake" and "Appalachia" have their roots in Algonquian words.

Even for names that are unambiguously Native American, it is sometimes not clear when those names started to be used. The individual names of the Five Nations of the Iroquois might not have been in wide use before 1500 A.D., although the ancestral Iroquois certainly had a strong cultural tradition by the 1200s and were building longhouses long before that. I also may have anticipated the foundation of the Haudenosaunee League by a few hundred years. Other aspects of the longhouse culture, along with the clothing and weaponry styles, are taken from the historical and archaeological record. As far as the "hand-talk" is concerned, the Plains Sign Language did indeed become something of a lingua franca, though perhaps not as early or universally as I have postulated.

Otherwise, in writing the Clash of Eagles books I have tried my best to remain accurate to geographical and archaeological ground truth. The size and layout of Cahokia are accurate for the period to the extent that the geography of the city and its environs has often not so subtly driven the plot. Every mound featured in the book exists, and I placed the Big Warm House and the brickworks and steelworks in open areas where there were no known mounds or buildings. The Circle of the Cedars corresponds to a monumental circle of up to sixty tall cedar marker posts designed as an early calendar, based on seasonal celestial alignments. The established large-scale agriculture and fishing, available natural resources, food types and weaponry, pottery and basketry, and so forth, are as accurate as I could make them. Granaries, houses, hearths, storage pits, and so on, all match current archaeological findings. Chunkey was a real game. The clothing depicted is true to the times, including details of Great Sun Man's regalia and his copper ear spools of the Long-Nosed God; much of what later would become stereotypical Native American clothing, including large feather war bonnets and extensive bead-work, probably originated centuries after Cahokia.

We have much less detailed knowledge about the so-cial structure of ancient Cahokia, and extrapolation can be dangerous. Although Hernando de Soto found strongly hierarchical chiefdoms with a complex caste system in his 1539–1543 expedition to southeastern areas at the tail end of the Mississippian era, it does not follow that those social systems were universal. In fact, in Cahokia's case the evidence may point the other way—to a heterarchy of diverse organizations within the city. I have assumed a pragmatic, rather nonhierar-chical structure for Cahokia rather than the supersti-tious and ritual-bound structures that some postulate for such societies.

Clearly, I have given the Hesperians credit for a few additional technological achievements. Native flying machines are unsupported by the archaeological record, although because they are made of sticks, skins, and sinew and wrecked Catanwakuwa and Wakinyan are ceremonially dismantled and often burned, we might not find their remains even if they had existed. However, birds and flying were highly revered in the cultures of the Americas before the European invasion. Hawks, fal-cons, and thunderbirds were venerated and are central motifs observed throughout ancient American cultures. There is evidence for a falcon warrior ideology in Caho-kia and also strong suggestions that the birdman cult originated in Cahokia before spreading across the Mis-sissippian world. Feathered capes, birdmen, and falco-noid symbolism abounded. Bird eyes, wings, and tails are extremely common iconography on pots, chunkey stones, and other items. In many Native American tradi-tional stories, key figures are able to fly.

Catanwakuwa and Wakinyan may be a stretch, but oddly, I may be on slightly safer ground with the Sky Lanterns. Although this is speculative, it has been suggested that balloons might have been feasible for peoples at a Mississippian technology level. Julian Nott, a prominent figure in the modern ballooning movement, has pointed out that the people who created the Nazca lines in pre-Inca Peru had all the necessary technologies and materials to create balloons. To prove his point he has constructed and flown a hot air balloon with a bag consisting of six hundred pounds of cotton fabric made in the pre-Columbian style, launched and powered by burning logs, with a gondola constructed of wood and reeds. For the Cahokians, the cotton would have been the key. Cotton grows only weakly in Illinois north of the Ohio River and can be wiped out easily by frost, and so realistically, their cotton would have had to be imported from the south. But since the Cahokian trading network extended to the Gulf of Mexico, this would have been at least possible.

The Mourning War is an authentic idea, with many historical examples of long-standing feuds and territorial disputes between native peoples of North America. Although there is no direct evidence of such a large-scale and pervasive feud between the Mississippian and Haudenosaunee nations, there is archaeological support for an increase in the palisading of towns and villages from 1200 A.D. on in those cultures and also in Algonquian territory. Clearly, these peoples were not establishing such vigorous defenses just for fun. And although people nowadays tend to associate the practice of scalping with the colonial wars, it was in fact a form of violence frequently perpetrated long before the arrival of Europeans.

The Iroquois were noted for their competence in the lethal arts. However, there are no grounds for believing them responsible for the deaths of the Cahokian women buried in Mound 72 (the Mound of the Women), as Great Sun Man tells Marcellinus. In our world, those women probably perished as part of a homegrown ritualized killing. In reality the women might not even have been from Cahokia; their teeth and bones are more typical of people originating from the satellite towns and eating poorer diets.

Just in case there is any doubt, the People of the Hand include the ancestral Pueblo peoples at the tail end of the Great House culture centered in Chaco Canyon, and the People of the Sun are the postclassic Mayan culture.

Many of Cahokia's mounds still remain, and walking among them inspires awe. The Cahokia Mounds State Historic Site is just across the Mississippi from modern St. Louis, Missouri. It is well worth a visit and, failing that, can be investigated on the Web at www.cahokia mounds.org.

APPENDIX IV

THE DECLINE AND RISE
OF THE ROMAN IMPERIUM

In the Clash of Eagles series the classical Roman Empire does not fall on schedule, and in 1218 A.D. a Roman legion crosses the Atlantic to invade the newly discovered North American continent. There they face a mighty wilderness, confront the Iroquois and Mississippian cultures, and get much more than they bargained for.

Now and then I encounter polite incredulity at the notion that the Western Roman Empire could survive until the thirteenth century with recognizable classical legions, their soldiers armed with the familiar gladius, pugio, pilum, and all the rest. Some people assume that since the Roman Empire declined and fell in our universe, it *had* to fall. That the Imperium's collapse was almost preordained, a consequence of marauding tribes from without and moral decay and degenerate leadership from within.

I think this greatly overstates the case.

First, let's look at what really happened. Then I'll offer a straightforward way in which it might have turned out very differently.

In the third century A.D., everything went to hell for Rome. It's known as the Crisis of the Third Century, and for good reason. The crisis was foreshadowed by the atrocities and persecutions of the Emperor Caracalla (198–217 A.D.)—of whom more later—and the utter bizarreness of his successor, the flamboyant and decadent zealot Elagabalus (218–222 A.D.). The emperor who followed, Alexander Severus (222–235 A.D.), tried to bribe the Empire's enemies to go away rather than facing them in battle, alienating his legions, which eventually assassinated him. Certainly dodgy days for the Roman leadership.

This breakdown of Imperial power was followed by a half century in which twenty-six men ruled as emperor, many of them army generals who claimed the position by force. In the process of almost constant civil wars the frontiers were stripped of troops, allowing a broad range of incursions by foreign "barbarian" tribes plus a resurgence of attacks from the Sassanids to the east. Just to mess with the Empire further, the Plague of Cyprian (probably smallpox) hammered it from 250 to 270 A.D., further reducing military forces while helping to promote the spread of Christianity.

Although it took until 476 A.D. for the Western Roman Empire to founder completely, leaving Constantinople as the power center of a transformed Eastern Empire, the rot was clearly irreversible after the Crisis of the Third Century. Organizationally, the most ominous step was the precedent of dividing the Empire into parts. Once division of the Empire became acceptable (during and after Diocletian's reign, 284–305 A.D.), the demise of Rome was inevitable. No coming back from that.

But was all this predestined? Somehow programmed in? Could the Crisis of the Third Century have been averted?

Yes. Rome had introduced significant constitutional changes before, notably under Augustus (27 B.C.–14 A.D.). With sufficient will and strong leadership, such things were possible.

So let's go back to the beginning of the third century. Emperor Septimius Severus died in 211 A.D., leaving the Empire to be ruled jointly by his sons, Caracalla and

Geta. Caracalla was thoroughly unpleasant, and his murders, massacres, and persecutions make him a close runner-up to Caligula for paranoid brutality. Caracalla clearly had no intention of sharing the Empire with a brother he hated and murdered Geta within the year. Caracalla then strode off as sole ruler into his reign of terror.

By all accounts, Geta was a much calmer, more thoughtful, and more reasonable man than his brother (although maybe this is a low bar). And perhaps on one critical day in December 211 A.D., Geta could have been just a little luckier, surviving Caracalla's attempt on his life.

In the world of Clash of Eagles, this is exactly what happens. Geta escapes his grisly fate and flees Rome for Britain, where he is greatly respected by the legions. Factions align. Senators and armies choose sides. The Empire descends into a bloody ten-year civil war and almost collapses in the process. But ultimately Geta wins.

Geta and the Roman Senate have experienced a cataclysm they never want Rome to experience again. They have looked into the abyss of chaos and societal collapse and backed away. Thus, when Geta proposes civil reforms to limit his Imperial power and that of his successors, and plants the seeds for military reform to curtail Roman legions' bad habit of supporting their own candidates for the throne and acting as kingmakers, the Senate is right behind him. The Severan Dynasty solidifies the Empire. Classical Roman culture perseveres. And there is much rejoicing, Roman-style: feasts and gladiatorial games and such.

Nothing about this scenario is at odds with Roman psychology. From Julius Caesar onward, the Senate would have dearly loved to curb the powers of both its dictators and its generals. Emperors used the power of the legions not only to put themselves into the Imperial purple but also to maintain themselves there . . . and to win arguments with the Senate.

If legions are not distracted—and often destroyed—by

the Imperial struggles all through the third-century crisis, Rome's long-term future looks much brighter. A strong army can defend Rome's borders. Strong emperors can beat back the Parthian resurgence.

What about the "barbarians"? you say. Well, massive migrations of hostile tribes into the Empire had been halted in earlier centuries by the likes of Julius Caesar and Trajan (98–117 A.D.). Similar incursions could have been held at bay again by a succession of determined emperors and competent armies in later centuries. The surge of Goths into the Balkans in 376 A.D. could be terminated and future troubles deterred by means of ruthless massacres. For examples, see how Rome razed Carthage to end the Third Punic War in 146 B.C. and how Trajan smashed the hell out of Dacia in 101–106 A.D. If the Romans were anything, they were ruthlessly efficient in slaughtering their enemies. It wouldn't have been pretty. But it would have been effective.

In my scenario, Emperor Geta quite unknowingly puts in place the safeguards that prevent the crisis. His successors prove to be equally competent. The Empire continues to be ruled through strong central control. The military stays solid. The Rhine is never crossed by hostile tribes; Rome is never sacked by the Visigoths. The Empire is never split by power-sharing emperors, and Byzantium—Constantinople—never rises to become dominant. The Western Roman Empire lives on.

I think that does the trick. If you agree, feel free to stop here.

If not, let's dig deeper into the Official Causes of Rome's Decline and Fall.

Here we hit an interesting wall, and for me the most telling point: if even professional historians and other well-read experts can't agree on why Rome fell, the conclusion that its fall was inevitable is pretty hard to sustain.

For Edward Gibbon, "the decline of Rome was the natural and inevitable effect of immoderate greatness."

Meaning that the Empire was unsound to begin with because of lack of civic virtue, and its use of non-Roman mercenaries and the advent of Christianity ultimately caused its death knell. Vegetius, too, blamed military decline resulting from immoderate use of mercenaries. Many have proposed a slow decay of Roman institutions all through the centuries of the principate.

Prominent economists, however, blame unsound economic policies. Joseph Tainter, an anthropologist, blames social complexity and diminishing returns on investments. Military historian Adrian Goldsworthy points to the weakening effect of endless civil wars and the decline of central authority. Historian William McNeill blames disease, and geochemist Jerome Nriagu names lead poisoning.

There are, in fact, *more than two hundred* different theories for why Rome fell. This preponderance can perhaps be blamed on the lack of strong evidence—the death rates from the Cyprian plague are guesses, for example, and precious few economic documents survive from the Rome of the third to fifth centuries A.D.

But to simplify: a number of these causes look suspiciously like effects—the effects of a weak central authority, combined with an out-of-control military promoting its own favorites for emperor and weakening the borders in the process—and seem avoidable.

In my scenario, the much more moderate Geta has defeated his notoriously brutal brother Caracalla in a sustained civil war at the beginning of the third century A.D. and ushered in an alternative time line in which the Empire is not weakened by almost a century of turmoil. With the military reforms I've postulated, mercenaries are less necessary and can be kept under firmer control, and their leaders are less likely to rise up against Rome. The borders stay firm. The so-called barbarian tribes are forced back or eradicated.

The economy remains strong, bolstered by plunder. The religion of the Christ-Risen thrives, but church and state remain separated. People still die from plagues and contaminated water, but with a strong central authority paying attention and without the general devastation of almost constant civil war, many dire effects can be mitigated. Thus, the Roman Empire expands in a series of fits and starts through the rest of Europe and ultimately into Asia.

But does it live on unchanged? Does Roma still have recognizable legions in the thirteenth century?

Maybe so.

The Romans did adapt when they needed to. They adopted new ideas when they found them. But only if they saw an overwhelmingly good reason to do so.

And if they didn't, they stayed with the tried and true. In fact, the Roman army was extremely conservative. Weapons and tactics remained largely unchanged between the Marian reforms of 107 B.C. and the late third century A.D. The military formations used by Julius Caesar were still commonly used well into the third and even fourth centuries. As it turns out, most Roman military disasters were caused by the army's strategic and tactical inflexibility.

Beyond the tactics, the rituals of the military triumph remained unchanged throughout Roman history. Contemporary books discussing Roman army marching camps written three hundred years apart describe exactly the same layout, and this is backed up by archaeological evidence. Often even the individual signa—the symbols of various centuries and legions—persisted for centuries.

Weapons and armor barely changed either. The Roman pilum endured unaltered for six hundred years, and swords and daggers for almost as long. By the third century A.D. helmets were evolving to provide more protection, based on innovations copied from the barbarians. But it took a long time for those changes to manifest. Back in Urbs Roma, the same thing. Cowell's *Life in Ancient Rome* reports that the main elements in Roman clothing "remained practically unaltered throughout almost the entire thousand years of Rome's history." Rome was already well into its decline by the time major sartorial changes kicked in. Housing styles, likewise.

And why? Underlying it all, Roman society was based on a system of patronage, a vertical patron-client relationship that defined Rome from top to bottom and was strongly resistant to change: "the web of interlocking obligations was tightly woven and made change difficult" (Everitt, *The Rise of Rome*). Keeping their society stable was job one, and by and large the Romans did an outstanding job for centuries.

Unlike our own society, in ancient Roma change was not a given. It came slowly and at a cost.

Some of those slow changes are evident in the 33rd Hesperian Legion of Gaius Marcellinus. The legions are certainly recognizable but by no means identical to their third-century counterparts. By 1218 A.D. tribunes have more direct responsibility for specific cohorts than they did in ancient Rome, and auxiliary forces are an integral part of the legion rather than being treated as a separate unit. (Over the long haul, such assimilation would be essential for efficient command and control.) In the Clash of Eagles trilogy soldiers are allowed to marry while in the army and take furloughs between campaigns. Neither was permissible in ancient Rome, and both improve morale. Most crucially, promotion in the Roman army is now essentially merit-based. Although there's still a tendency for some tribunes to be political appointees, skilled and determined men such as Marcellinus and Aelfric can and do work their way up the ladder to prominent leadership positions. The shapes and functions of Roman weapons—gladius, spatha, pilum—have not changed, but in the thirteenth century they are made of steel rather than iron.

And so, in the Clash of Eagles series, the Empire marches on.

We see the world of Clash of Eagles from the close point of view of Gaius Marcellinus, who doesn't spend a whole lot of time pondering history. He has other things to worry about. But if these books were set in Europe or Asia rather than North America, a number of other differences in society and technology would be apparent. If I get the opportunity to write further in this universe, maybe we'll get to see more of the slow but steady changes time has wrought across the Roman world.

APPENDIX V

TRAVELS IN NOVA HESPERIA: GEOGRAPHIC NOTES

In *Eagle and Empire*, Gaius Marcellinus and his allies and enemies rove extensively across Nova Hesperia. This section is for readers who may want to follow these travels on a map of modern-day North America. However, if you're coming to this appendix before reading the book, you should note that it contains significant plot details and spoilers.

After conquering the western coast of Nova Hesperia, Chinggis Khan splits his army into several parts to subdue and explore the region and make plans for his eastward expansion into the continent. This division into several units was a common Mongol strategy. In addition to allowing the plunder of a greater expanse of territory, it helped ensure sufficient grazing for the horses. Grass was always a limited resource for a mounted force the size of the Khan's.

The army of Chagatai takes a northern route. With the help (willing or otherwise) of the Tlingit, the Haida, and the peoples of the inland plateau, his army follows the Columbia, Snake, and Clearwater rivers east and crosses the Continental Divide at what is now known as Lemhi Pass, on the border between Idaho and Montana. Lemhi Pass was a major route across the mountains for the Blackfoot and other tribes and is the pass that was traversed by Lewis and Clark in their westward exploration. Lewis described it as a "large and plain Indian road," but it would be no picnic for an army the size of Chagatai's. In *Eagle and Empire*, Chagatai drives the defeated Shoshoni ahead of him. It is they who hurry down the Missouri River into Blackfoot territory and ultimately provide Tahtay and the Cahokians with their first warning of the Mongols' advance.

Meanwhile, the army of Chinggis Khan crosses the Rockies much farther south in Colorado via the Monarch Pass route, and the forces under Subodei Badahur and Jebei Noyon travel far down the Pacific coast to the Oaxaca region of Mexico. There, with extensive help from the People of the Sun—otherwise known as the Maya of the Postclassic period—they arrange to portage the battle junks overland to the Gulf of Mexico. Once passage across the isthmus is assured, Subodei Badahur returns to the Khan's camp to brief him and get his orders for the eastward assault.

The expedition to the southwest led by Marcellinus and Sextus Bassus takes them three hundred miles up the Missouri River by quinquereme to where the Kansas River flows into it at the confluence where Kansas City, Missouri, is today. From there they travel eight hundred miles overland by way of the Native American route now known as the Santa Fe Trail through Kansas, Colorado, and New Mexico. The trail leaves the Missouri River and drops down to the Arkansas River (known as the Kicka River in *Eagle and Empire*). They follow the Arkansas River, and where the Santa Fe Trail splits, they take the so-called Mountain Route rather than the more hazardous Cimarron Crossing to Santa Fe. From there it's less than two hundred miles to Chaco Canyon.

The People of the Hand are of course the Ancestral Pueblo People, historically known as the Anasazi, although that word stems from a term of abuse in Navajo and is not now favored. Yupkoyvi is Chaco Canyon, and Pueblo Bonito is the Great House that Bassus's men attempt to defend. Marcellinus's expedition is arriving at the very tail end of the Chaco Culture, when many of the Great Houses were abandoned and occupation of the area was sparse, a mere shadow of its former glory. The Sentinel Rock, from which the alarm is belatedly given in the book, is known today as Fajada Butte. The town of Tyuonyi lies within Bandelier National Monument. The massive band of warriors of the Hand who later come to Cahokia to join the Hesperian League assembles from Tawtoyka—our Mesa Verde—and other extensive cliff dwellings that existed all across the Four Corners area that included parts of Utah, Arizona, New Mexico, and Colorado.

After the massacre at Yupkoyvi, Marcellinus and his meager group of survivors are taken on a forced march of some four hundred miles to a plains area in southern Colorado. The Mongol great camp where Marcellinus first has the pleasure of making Chinggis Khan's acquaintance is situated close to the Colorado–New Mexico border.

After tea and murder with the Khan, Marcellinus returns eastward down the (terribly named) Canadian River through New Mexico, the Texas Panhandle, and Oklahoma to the Arkansas (Kicka) River. The Arkansas flows into the Mississippi at Napoleon (now a ghost town) in Desha County, Arkansas. In the meantime, of course, Subodei Badahur has attacked the Legio VI Ferrata by sea and then devastated the Market of the Mud (in southern Louisiana, near New Orleans) before heading north up the Mississippi.

Once Marcellinus's party joins the fleet of Calidius Verus, they travel some 85 miles north up the Mississippi to Shappa Ta'atan, which is situated where Helena, Arkansas, is today. There they battle Badahur's river fleet. From Shappa Ta'atan back to Cahokia is about another 350 miles.

The Khan's army rides east toward Cahokia along the Platte River (called the Braided River in *Eagle and Empire*) and eventually meets up with the army of Chagatai to do battle with the Romans. Forward Camp, where the Romans prepare for the final confrontation, is in the rolling tallgrass prairies of eastern Nebraska at the confluence of the Platte and Wemissori rivers, not far from where Omaha is today.

APPENDIX VI

GLOSSARY OF MILITARY TERMS
FROM THE ROMAN IMPERIUM

A glossary of Roman terms, Latin translations, and military terminology appears below, along with a few Mongol terms.

Many aspects of Roman warfare have remained unchanged since classical times, but language evolves, and in a few cases the meanings of words have migrated from their original usage in the Republic and the early Empire.

Ala: Cavalry unit or "wing." An ala quingenaria consists of 512 troopers in sixteen turmae; an ala milliaria consists of 768 troopers in twenty-four turmae (plural: alae).

Animus: Martial spirit.

Aquila: The Eagle, the standard of a Roman legion; often golden or gilded and carried proudly into battle. The loss of an Eagle is one of the greatest shames that can befall a legion.

Aquilifer: Eagle bearer; the legionary tasked with carrying the legion's standard into battle (plural: aquiliferi).

Arban: Unit of ten warriors (Mongol).

Auxiliaries: Noncitizen troops in the Roman army, drawn from peoples in the provinces of the Imperium. Career soldiers trained to the same standards as legionaries, they can expect to receive citizenship at the end of their twenty-five-year service. Originally kept in their own separate units, auxiliary infantrymen have been integrated into the regular legionary cohorts.

Ballista: Siege engine; a tension- or spring-powered catapult that fires bolts, arrows, or other pointy missiles of wood and metal. Resembles a giant crossbow and often is mounted in a wooden frame or carried in a cart (plural: ballistae).

Barding: Armored protection for horses, constructed of hinged metal plate or scale, chain, leather, or cloth.

Caligae: Heavy-soled military marching boots with an open sandal-like design.

Cardo: Colloquial term for the wide main street oriented north-south in Roman cities, military fortresses, and marching camps (more formally known as the Via Praetoria for the southern part and the Via Decumana for the northern part).

Castra: Military marching camp; temporary accommodation for a legion, often rebuilt each night on the march.

Cataphractaria: Armored heavy cavalry, with both horse and rider protected by metal plate or scale armor. Riders generally are armed with a heavy spear similar to a lance (see also barding, chamfron, contus).

Centurion: Professional army officer in command of a century.

Century: Army company, ideally eighty to a hundred men.

Chamfron: Armored facial protection for horses, generally extending from the ears to the muzzle and constructed of metal plate or scale, or leather.

Close order: Infantry formation, with men massed at a separation often as small as eighteen inches, making a phalanx or another close formation difficult to penetrate or break up.

Cohors equitata: Mixed unit of cavalry and infantry that trains together, generally consisting of six centuries and four turmae, ten centuries and eight turmae, or some other combination with a similar ratio of foot soldiers to cavalrymen (plural: cohortes equitatae).

Cohort: Tactical unit of a Roman legion; each cohort consists of six centuries. Sometimes the First Cohort in a legion is double-strength.

Contubernium: Squad of eight legionaries who serve together, bunk together in a single tent (in a castra) or building (in a fortress barracks), and often are disciplined together for infractions (plural: contubernia).

Contus: Heavy wooden cavalry lance, typically around twelve feet in length, wielded two-handed or couched under the arm (plural: conti).

Cornicen: Junior Roman officer who signals orders to centuries and legions with a trumpet or cornu.

Cornu: Horn used to communicate signals and instructions to troops, carried and blown by a cornicen. A brass instrument around ten feet long, curved into a G shape, and looped around the head (plural: cornua).

Corvus: Literally, "crow"; a wide gangplank or rotating bridge that anchors a Roman warship to the bank with a heavy metal spike or can be embedded into the deck of an enemy vessel so that it can be boarded.

Cuneus: Literally, "wedge" or "pig's head"; dense military formation used to smash through an enemy's battle line or break through a gap.

Cymba: Boat.

Damnatio Memoriae: A drastic punishment, the ultimate condemnation for a legion or individual who brings discredit to Roma. The name of the legion or individual would be erased from the historical record, expunged from lists and monuments as if it had never existed.

Decurion: Professional army officer in command of a turma of cavalrymen. Roughly equivalent in rank to a centurion.

Dignitas: Dignity.

Drekar: Dragon ship, Viking longship (Norse).

Duplicarius: Decurion's deputy, second in command of a turma.

Forum: Public square or plaza, often a marketplace.

Gladius: Roman sword (plural: gladii).

Greek fire: Liquid incendiary, probably based on naphtha and/or sulfur, although the recipe was lost in Europa and is a closely guarded secret in Nova Hesperia.

Harpax: Harpoon, naval grapnel fired by a ballista, that allows an enemy vessel to be secured and winched alongside for boarding.

Hasta: Heavy thrusting spear used by infantry. Generally around six feet long (plural: hastae).

Imago: Image, copy, ancestral likeness. The image of the current Imperator displayed on a standard or banner.

Imperator: Emperor; Roman commander in chief.

Imperium: Empire; executive power, the sovereignty of the state.

Jaghun: Unit of one hundred warriors, or ten arbans (Mongol).

Knarr: Cargo ship; high-sided and broader, deeper, and not as long as a longship (Norse).

Lancea: Short javelin (plural: lanceae).

Lares: Roman household gods, domestic deities, guardians of the hearth.

Legate: Senior commander of a legion, more completely known as legatus legionis. By the thirteenth century, "legate" and "Praetor" are synonymous.

Legion: Army unit of several thousand men consisting of ten cohorts, each of six centuries.

Legionary: Professional soldier in the Roman army. A Roman citizen, highly trained, who serves for twenty-five years.

Medicus: Military doctor, field surgeon, or orderly (plural: medici).

Mingghan: Unit of one thousand warriors, or ten jaghuns (Mongol).

Navis: Ship.

Onager: Siege engine; torsion-powered, single-armed catapult that launches rocks or other nonpointy missiles. Literally translates to "wild ass" because of its bucking motion when fired. Often mounted in a square wooden frame.

Open order: Infantry formation, with soldiers in battle lines separated by up to six feet and often staggered, providing room to maneuver, shoot arrows, throw pila or swing gladii, and switch or change ranks.

Optio: Centurion's deputy, second in command of the century (plural: optiones).

Orbis: Literally, "circle"; a defensive military formation in the shape of a circle or square, adopted when under attack from a numerically superior force.

Patrician: Aristocratic, upper-class, or ruling-class Roman citizen.

Phalanx: Mass infantry formation, generally rectangular and in very close order. A solid block of soldiers.

Phalera: Military decoration awarded for distinguished conduct, usually a sculpted disk of gold, silver, or bronze. Worn by an individual legionary or cavalryman or paraded by a military unit on the staff of the unit's standards (plural: phalerae).

Pilum: Roman heavy spear or javelin (plural: pila).

Porta Praetoria: South gate of a legionary fortress or castra, leading onto the Via Praetoria (or Cardo).

Praetor: Roman general, commander of a legion or of an entire army. In the Republic and early Empire the term also was used for some senior magistrates and consuls; the latter usage has died out by the time of Hadrianus III, and only legionary commanders are referred to as Praetors.

Praetorian: A special force of elite troops who served as the Imperator's personal guard and often trained with him or were trained by him. May also serve as shock troops.

Praetorium: Praetor's tent within a castra or residence within a legionary fortress, situated at the center of the encampment.

Primus pilus: See senior centurion.

Principia: Legionary headquarters building, situated at or near the center of a legionary fortress.

Pugio: Dagger carried by legionaries; Roman stabbing weapon.

Quinquereme: Heavy Roman warship with five banks of oarsmen on three levels, one above the other, in a two-two-one pattern.

Roma: The city of Roma, capital of the Roman Imperium, although often used as shorthand to mean the Imperium as a whole.

Sagum: Military cloak made of a rectangular piece of heavy wool and fastened with a clasp at the shoulder.

Scorpio: Torsion crossbow that fires metal bolts; a small Roman artillery piece built on the same principles as a ballista but designed to be used by a single legionary.

Scutum: Roman legionary shield (plural: scuta).

Senior centurion: Also known as the primus pilus. The most experienced and highly valued centurion in the legion, he commands the first century within the First Cohort.

Signifer: Standard-bearer; the legionary tasked with carrying a signum for a century (plural: signiferi).

Signum: A century's standard, usually consisting of a number of metal disks and other insignia mounted on a pole (plural: signa).

Spatha: Roman long sword, often used by cavalry (plural: spathae).

Testudo: Literally, "tortoise"; Roman infantry formation in which soldiers in close order protect themselves by holding shields over their heads and around them, enclosing them within a protective roof and wall of metal.

Trebuchet: Siege weapon designed to fling large nonpointy projectiles using a lever arm; the Mongol trebuchets are traction trebuchets, powered by large teams of soldiers pulling ropes in unison, rather than counterweight trebuchets that take advantage of gravity.

Tribune: Roman officer, midway in rank between the legion commander and his centurions. Originally a more generalized military staff officer; by 1218 A.D. the tribunes have administrative and operational responsibilities for specific cohorts within their legions.

Triplex acies: Three-line battle formation.

Trireme: Heavy Roman warship with three banks of oarsmen, one above the other.

Tumen: Unit of ten thousand warriors, or ten mingghans (Mongol).

Turma: Squadron of cavalry, subunit of an ala. One turma consists of thirty troopers and two officers (a decurion and a duplicarius) (plural: turmae).

Urbs: City.

Vexillation: Large detachment of legionaries that form a temporary task force with a specific strategic purpose.

Virtus: Valor.

APPENDIX VII

FURTHER READING

In addition to the books listed in the Further Reading sections of *Clash of Eagles* and *Eagle in Exile*, I found the following useful in researching and writing *Eagle and Empire*.

Kenneth M. Ames and Herbert D. G. Maschner, *Peoples of the Northwest Coast: Their Archeology and Prehistory*, 2000.

Anthony Aveni, *Empires of Time: Calendars, Clocks, and Culture*, 2002.

Duncan B. Campbell and Brian Delf, *Roman Auxiliary Forts 27 BC–AD 378*, 2009.

Lawrence W. Cheek, *A.D. 1250: Ancient Peoples of the Southwest*, 1994.

Craig Childs, *House of Rain: Tracking a Vanished Civilization Across the American Southwest*, 2008.

Clayton Chun, *US Army in the Plains Indian Wars 1865–1891*, 2013.

Ross Cowan, *Roman Guardsmen 62 BC–AD 324*, 2014.

Ross Cowan and Sean O'Brogain, *Roman Legionary AD 284–337: The Age of Diocletian and Constantine the Great*, 2015.

Thomas J. Craughwell, *The Rise and Fall of the Second Largest Empire in History: How Genghis Khan's Mongols Almost Conquered the World*, 2010.

Raffaele D'Amato and Graham Sumner, *Imperial Roman Naval Forces 31 BC–AD 500*, 2009.

Louis A. DiMarco, *War Horse: A History of the Military Horse and Rider*, 2012.

Daniela Dueck, *Geography in Classical Antiquity*, 2012.

Elizabeth A. Fenn, *Encounters at the Heart of the World: A History of the Mandan People*, 2015.

Nic Fields and Adam Hook, *Roman Auxiliary Cavalryman: AD 14–193*, 2006.

Nic Fields and Donato Spedaliere, *Rome's Northern Frontier AD 70–235: Beyond Hadrian's Wall*, 2003.

Horace Greeley, *An Overland Journey from New York to San Francisco in the Summer of 1859*, 1860.

Valerie Hansen, *The Silk Road: A New History*, 2012.

Michael Johnson and Jonathan Smith, *American Indian Tribes of the Southwest*, 2013.

John Keegan, *A History of Warfare*, 1994.

D. Lindholm, D. Nicolle, and A. McBride, *Medieval Scandinavian Armies (1), 1100–1300*, 2003.

Randolph Barnes Marcy, *The Prairie Traveler: A Handbook for Overland Expeditions*, 1859.

Randolph B. Marcy and George B. McClellan, *Exploration of the Red River of Louisiana in the Year 1852*, 1854.

Timothy May, *The Mongol Art of War*, 2007.

Sean McLachlan, *Medieval Handgonnes: The First Black Powder Infantry Weapons*, 2010.

Frank McLynn, *Genghis Khan: His Conquests, His Empire, His Legacy*, 2015.

David Nicolle and Adam Hook, *European Medieval Tactics (1): The Fall and Rise of Cavalry 450–1260*, 2011.

David Nicolle and Adam Hook, *European Medieval Tactics (2): The Revival of Infantry 1260–1500*, 2012.

David Nicolle and Victor Korolkov, *Kalka River 1223: Genghiz Khan's Mongols Invade Russia*, 2001.

David Nicolle and Angus McBride, *Attila and the Nomad Hordes*, 1990.

David Nicolle and Angus McBride, *Armies of Medieval Russia 750–1250*, 1999.

Lincoln Paine, *The Sea and Civilization: A Maritime History of the World*, 2015.

Timothy R. Pauketat and Susan M. Alt, *Medieval Mississippians: The Cahokian World*, 2015.

Timothy R. Pauketat and Diana DiPaolo Loren, *North American Archaeology*, 2005.

C. J. Peers, *Soldiers of the Dragon: Chinese Armies 1500 BC–AD 1840*, 2006.

Stephen Plog, *Ancient Peoples of the American Southwest*, 1997.

Marco Polo, *The Travels,* edited R. E. Latham, 1958.

Charles M. Robinson, *The Plains Wars 1757–1900*, 2003.

Gordon L. Rottman and Peter Dennis, *World War II Glider Assault Tactics*, 2014.

Paula L. Sabloff, *Modern Mongolia: Reclaiming Genghis Khan*, 2001.

Sarangerel, *Riding Windhorses: A Journey into the Heart of Mongolian Shamanism*, 2000.

Si Sheppard and Christa Hook, *Actium 31 B.C.: Downfall of Antony and Cleopatra*, 2009.

Stephen Turnbull, *Genghis Khan and the Mongol Conquests 1190–1400*, 2003.

Stephen Turnbull and Wayne Reynolds, *Siege Weapons of the Far East (1)*, 2001.

Stephen Turnbull and Wayne Reynolds, *Siege Weapons of the Far East (2)*, 2002.

Stephen Turnbull and Wayne Reynolds, *Fighting Ships of the Far East (1): China and Southeast Asia 202 BC–AD 1419*, 2002.

Stephen Turnbull and Wayne Reynolds, *Fighting Ships of the Far East (2): Japan and Korea, AD 612–1639*, 2003.

Stephen Turnbull and Wayne Reynolds, *Mongol Warrior 1200–1350*, 2003.

Jack Weatherford, *Genghis Khan and the Making of the Modern World*, 2004.

Jack Weatherford, *The Secret History of the Mongol Queens*, 2010.